"With precision, detail, and narrative excitement"
(*Booklist*), award-winning and bestselling novelists
W. Michael and Kathleen O'Neal Gear "boldly portray the
stark atrocities" (*Library Journal*) of the European invaders
in the battle for early America . . . as seen through the eyes
of a courageous Native American couple.

Praise for *Coming of the Storm*

"Smooth, brisk-paced. . . . Rich historical details and keen
characterizations . . . offset by the graphic depictions of
battlefield violence."

—*Publishers Weekly*

"Irresistibly intriguing . . . brings the past vividly to life."

—*Booklist*

Praise for *Fire the Sky*

"Powerful . . . historical accuracy and deliberate parallels
with present-day events lend additional drama to scenes
of domesticity, politics, and battle."

—*Publishers Weekly* (starred review)

"Fascinating historical, anthropological, and cultural information. . . . The adept Gears . . . leave readers eagerly
anticipating the next episode."

—*Booklist*

More praise for the Gears

"Draws you into a magnificent, sweeping world . . . so real
you can almost breathe in the air of it. . . . A novel that
will stay with you for years."

—*New York Times* bestselling author Douglas Preston

"A lively tale of warring clans."

—*Kirkus Reviews*

A SEARING WIND

Book Three of
Contact: The Battle for America

W. MICHAEL GEAR AND
KATHLEEN O'NEAL GEAR

Pocket Books
New York London Toronto Sydney New Delhi

Pocket Books
A Division of Simon & Schuster, Inc.
1230 Avenue of the Americas
New York, NY 10020

This book is a work of fiction. Names, characters, places, and incidents either are products of the authors' imagination or are used fictitiously. Any resemblance to actual events or locales or persons, living or dead, is entirely coincidental.

First Pocket Books paperback edition October 2012

POCKET and colophon are registered trademarks of Simon & Schuster, Inc.

For information about special discounts for bulk purchases, please contact Simon & Schuster Special Sales at 1-866-506-1949 or business@simonandschuster.com.

The Simon & Schuster Speakers Bureau can bring authors to your live event. For more information or to book an event, contact the Simon & Schuster Speakers Bureau at 1-866-248-3049 or visit our website at www.simonspeakers.com.

Manufactured in the United States of America

10 9 8 7 6 5 4 3 2

ISBN 978-1-4391-5393-2
ISBN 978-1-4391-6708-3 (ebook)

To
Worthington's Red Canyon Jake,
a noble name for a noble sheltie.
Jake,
you are living proof that
dogs are remarkable persons.

ACKNOWLEDGMENTS

OUR EDITOR, JENNIFER HEDDLE, HAS BEEN A CONstant companion in Black Shell and Pearl Hand's struggle against the Kristianos. On behalf of ourselves and our characters, thank you, Jennifer, for all the hard work you've put into this series. We particularly appreciate your insightful comments and the thoughtful direction you've given us.

Our old friend, noted raconteur, and constantly evolving Renaissance man Dr. Howard Willson, once again, offered words of wisdom at just the right time. Howard, we'd have screwed up a really good hemopneumothorax without you. Next time, beer and dinner are on us.

HISTORICAL FOREWORD

HISTORIANS STILL WONDER WHY HERNANDO DE
Soto turned north after the battle of Mabila. Diego Maldonado's ships were anchored just to the south in either
Pensacola Bay or Mobile Bay. True, his men might have
mutinied, seized the vessels, and sailed away. But the majority of de Soto's supplies, his army's clothing, wheat for
the host, wine for communion, gunpowder, flags and banners, furniture, tents, tanned leather—in short, everything
of value for the maintenance of his army—had been consumed by the fires of Mabila.

Instead of heading south to resupply, de Soto ordered
his men north into the November cold. His army consisted of men—many of them wounded—who had only
the clothes on their backs, their weapons, and the iron
they'd salvaged from Mabila.

The mauling de Soto's troops had taken during the
fighting, coupled with the loss of supplies, was the turning
point. Perhaps, deep in his subconscious, de Soto actually
understood the situation. He would not be the last mega-
lomaniacal leader who insisted that his followers accompany him into disaster. On the other hand, de Soto had

always succeeded despite long odds. As he led his army into Mississippi on November 14, 1540, he had no idea that the proud Chicaza nation would be waiting for him. And had he been told, given his disdain for the native peoples, he would never have believed that they were every bit as politically adept, capable, and clever as he himself was.

As terrible as Mabila might have been, after Chicaza nothing would be the same. The destruction of Hernando de Soto's army would be only a matter of time.

Essence

Pain, terrible pain, squeezes tears from her clamped eyes. Unbearable heat sears her skin until it curls and bubbles. Smoke clogs her nostrils, carrying with it the stench of burning bodies.

Are the agonized screams real . . . or simply painful memories dredged from the past?

She keeps her eyes shut, terrified to open them lest, once again, she see human beings exploding, torchlike, into flames. She knows how their arms flail, heads back, hair bursting into halos of living fire. Mabila is burning around her. The sound of houses roaring in flames, the shrieks of men and women burning alive—the sizzling of human fat—are bad enough. She can't stomach the sight, the whirling . . . the billowing smoke . . .

Chaos. All is a maelstrom of fire, smoke, terror, and death.

Please, Breath Giver, make it stop!

"Elder?" a soft voice intrudes from another world.

The horror recedes, the smells fading from her nostrils, the sounds whimpering away into a familiar silence.

Mabila slips painfully into the past . . .

"Elder?" the voice asks again.

She wills herself to open her eyes, blinks, and finds herself lying flat on her back on the packed red clay of the plaza. Around her, people are hovering, staring down at her like curious vultures. They whisper to one another behind their hands. The worry in their wide eyes unnerves her.

"Elder?"

She places the voice; it belongs to the hopaye—the high priest of Chicaza. His face intrudes into her field of view and blocks the distant sky. He gives her a concerned smile and asks, "Are you all right?"

"Mabila," she says, voice hoarse.

"What about Mabila?"

"I was just there."

The hopaye nods, and the concern in his eyes shifts into curiosity. "The people say you were walking across the plaza when you collapsed. Your souls have been flying outside of your body, elder. I was called. Just in case . . ."

She waits, glancing past him to the baking summer sky—blue, with patches of fluffy white cloud. The sun is brutal; hard white light beats down. The sensation of heat, she realizes, is from the relentless sun. Not the fires of Mabila.

". . . In case I was dead." She says what he will not.

"You were in Mabila," he states, intent dark eyes on hers. A droplet of sweat trickles down the side of his face. There are beads of it in the pores on his nose. He smiles. "You are here now, with us. Mabila . . . that was years ago. When you were young."

"Yes." She is aware of the people crowding forward, confusing her memories with a Spirit Dream.

Fools.

"What about Mabila?" the hopaye asks.

"The essence," she whispers, hoping her voice will carry to the past. Black Shell needs to know this.

"What essence?" the hopaye asks.

She smiles, letting her souls float. Her memories are filled with the night she and Black Shell went back to Mabila. What was she thinking as they hobbled back to the shattered city?

Ah, yes.

Lost in the moonlight, so long ago . . .

To Black Shell she whispers, "The battlefield . . . this bloody and smoking earth . . . compresses everything into purity. Hatred, fear, compassion, exultation, rage, love, misery, euphoria . . . any human quality is experienced to its fullest. Words are poor things when trying to convey the triumph or tragedy, the glee or despair, or the fear, pain, or desolation of the souls. Those things must be lived in battle to be truly understood."

Limping ahead of her, Black Shell says nothing, his broad back swaying with each step as he avoids the rotting corpses—the sprawled dead of Mabila.

From a distant future, the hopaye's voice asks, "Do you understand, elder?"

Black Shell continues to limp away from her as if she's rooted. She watches in panic as he disappears through the shattered and splintered wooden gate. It gapes like a perversely broken mouth—a charred wound in Mabila's once-formidable defensive walls.

"Understand?" she asks absently. "Had you asked me the morning before the battle of Mabila, I would have told you I was prepared for the horror, the desperation, and the ensuing pain. I would have told you that the chance to kill Adelantado Hernando de Soto was worth the coming blood and misery. After all, we were fighting to save our world."

"Elder?" The hopaye's face swims into her vision, as if through clear water. "Let us help you up. We need to move you to the shade . . . get you to drink something."

Hands reach out. She feels her bony body raised; the dank odor of sweaty people who press too close replaces the stench of Mabila.

Absently, she says, "Black Shell? Oh, Black Shell, the question still lingers: How many lives is a world worth?"

"Elder?" the hopaye inquires.

"I have to tell him . . . Warn him . . ."

"Who?"

"Black Shell. He has to understand. Mabila was but a flickering spark. Ahead of him, at Chicaza, is the searing wind . . ."

ONE

ACROSS THE FLATS THE MOON-BATHED WALLS OF
Mabila stood silent and abandoned in the night. Were the
town occupied, it was only by the shadows of the dead.
Those wraiths who walk in silence, arms raised imploringly to the darkness above. In the soft light, accented by
white-rimmed clouds in the east, the town seemed eerily
peaceful. The bastions still towered, casting triangular
shadows onto the high palisade. Charred plaster added
false patterns of darkness to the town's fortifications.

Odd, isn't it? How moonlight, still air, and mass death
can create the eerie illusion of tranquility?

I grunted at the irony.

My wife, Pearl Hand, cast a worried look my way. "Are
you all right?"

I snorted and ignored the pain in my left thigh as I
limped across the trampled grass. The occasional corpses
we passed had already been rendered to bone by crows,
maggots, vultures, and the accursed Kristiano *puercos*. Rib
cages reflected as shell-white lattice. Partially fleshed

skulls seemed to stare at us through black-hollow pits, now empty of eyes. Sometimes the cold white light gleamed on a bow stave or the polished handle of a forgotten war club.

The dead lay everywhere.

Are they the lucky ones?

De Soto's Kristianos had killed them quickly, lancing many of them in the back, slicing others with sharp *hierro* swords. Most had bled out within a hundred heartbeats. Others, pierced through the guts, had died more slowly. Put in perspective, they'd watched their world die in mere moments.

As a survivor of Mabila, for the rest of my life I'd be a witness to the inevitable.

Who am I? My name is Black Shell, of the Chief Clan, of the Hickory Moiety of the Chicaza Nation. Once, not so many turnings of the moon past, I would have introduced myself as *akeohoosa,* an exile dead to my people. In the terrible aftermath of Mabila, concerns as petty as a man's origins seemed disgustingly vain.

I paused to ease my smarting leg and stared down at a sprawled corpse. Partially skeletonized, it lay on its back, one arm thrown wide; the forearm consisted of exposed bones, fingers missing. Chewed away no doubt.

"Why are you stopping?" Pearl Hand hissed from behind me.

I studied the nameless corpse and wondered who he'd been as a man. Not even a half moon past his heart had been beating, blood rushing in his veins. His souls had been full of plans, concerns, courage, and fear.

Cocking my head, I searched for any hint of spiritual essence that might cling to his greasy bones, dried gristle, rotting muscle, or leathery tatters of skin. Extending a hand, I tried to feel for the spirit's presence, as if it might have some temperature similar to dying embers.

"Who was he?" I wondered, thinking back to the

thousands of excited men who had streamed into Mabila before the battle. They'd come dressed in their best, bearing polished bows, quivers full of brightly feathered arrows, engraved war clubs, and decorated shields. Anticipation had sparkled in their eyes, their supple bodies bursting with life and vigor. They had literally danced as they trained. Their anxious smiles, the echoes of their rising and falling voices, remained so clearly within . . .

Dead.

All dead.

Looking closer, I could see between the scavenged ribs to the place where a Kristiano lance had been thrust through the man's back. Like so many he'd been run down from behind by a cabayero, skewered, and left bleeding and broken on the field before Mabila.

I straightened and turned my attention to the town's high walls; they rose tall, plastered, and true. Moonlight buffered the black soot, softened and smoothed the outlines. The smashed main gate gaped dark and foreboding, as spiritually empty as the eye sockets so hollow and black in the dead man's skull.

I took a deep breath, aware of the stench: rot and death carried on the cold night wind. "What is the price of a world?" I shot a glance at Pearl Hand.

Her eyes looked like glowing black stones in her perfect, triangular face. The moon accented her straight nose but turned her full lips into a black slash. Her hair might have been an extension of midnight where it was pulled back into a long braid. My gorgeous wife may have lived only twenty or so years, but she'd paid for her beauty; circumstances had turned her into a bound woman, one traded from chief to chief. Life had treated Pearl Hand poorly. She'd come to my bed older, wiser, and toughened. The hopeful illusions and romantic dreams a woman her age should have possessed had been rudely stamped out of her souls.

This night she wore a dark fabric blanket over a long hunting shirt that fell to her knees. Her feet were clad in moccasins tightly laced to her calves. She might have been but another shadow, one to be carefully massaged from the night around us.

"Whatever we have to pay, husband," she replied firmly. "It's the only world we have."

More than five thousand men . . . variously burned, cut, pierced, and butchered. Skipper, my dog. Blood Thorn, my friend. Tastanaki, Red Chief of the Coosa Nation. Tuskaloosa, the high minko, supreme chief of Atahachi. The thlakko Darting Snake, war chief of the Tuskaloosa Nation. And so many more . . .

"And for what?" I wondered as I glanced anxiously toward where the campfires of the Kristianos winked in the distance. Unable to travel—we'd counted more than two hundred of their men wounded—they'd made camp as far from Mabila as they could, and upwind from the thousands of burned and rotting corpses.

"Come on," Pearl Hand said, coaxing me. "We don't have all night. Morning's too close as it is."

I nodded, picked up my limping pace, and made for the gate as quickly as I could. She was right; we didn't want to be caught anywhere in Mabila's vicinity come morning.

As we neared the gate, we passed the place where my dog Skipper had been killed. He'd saved my life, appearing out of nowhere in the middle of the battle. He'd attacked Antonio's cabayo—the great, round-hoofed beast Kristianos rode to war—just as Antonio was about to split my skull with his *hierro* sword.

Pearl Hand, bless her, had retrieved Skipper's body while I lay half-fevered from my wounds. Together we had prepared him, painted his brown hair with colored clay, and laid both food and water in his grave. As we'd covered him in a low mound of soil, we'd prayed his life-soul toward the Spirit path that led west to the edge of the world.

There, come spring, he would make the leap over the abyss and through the Seeing Hand—the constellation that marked the opening to the Sky World. As valiant as he had been, I had no doubt that he'd be honored by the Sky Spirits and escorted to the Land of the Dead.

I hesitated as we passed the place where Antonio had nearly killed me. He'd cut a deep slice into my leg—hence the limp—and a lesser one still festered and burned in my left arm.

"What are you stopping for?" Pearl Hand asked, casting a nervous glance toward the distant Kristiano camps.

"I'm looking for my bow."

"I told you, I already looked."

I had a habit of losing my bow after battles. I'd had to go searching for it after the fight at Napetuca, too. That time I'd hidden it in willows as I ran for my life. This time I'd lost it while fleeing Antonio and his vile cabayo. I stepped over and kicked the animal's great skeleton, happy to have at least managed to kill it.

Cabayos are hornless creatures with round hooves and flowing hairy tails, and they run like the wind. Kristianos—called cabayeros—ride them to war. Mounted thus, cabayeros can smash the most disciplined formations of infantry. Had I not killed Antonio's cabayo that day, Antonio would have killed me. Fortunately I was able to drive a couple of arrows into the animal's chest.

That it was now nothing but bones was no surprise. The Kristianos had come the next day and stripped the cabayo's carcass of its meat. Kristianos will eat anything. Even their vile *puercos* after the beasts have feasted on human dead.

Nowhere could I see my bow, though several of my arrows lay trampled in the grass.

"Black Shell," Pearl Hand reminded me, "if we're going to do this thing, let's be about it. I'm worried enough as it is. Let alone coming here without the dogs."

She referred to the rest of my dog pack: Bark, Squirm, Blackie, Patches, and Gnaw. To a trader like me, dogs were as essential as legs. Big and strong, they carried the trade packs. Or at least they had before Mabila.

I winced as I hobbled through the town's splintered gate and stopped short to stare at the carnage. Everywhere were ruins—even the great trees, black-charred and dead.

I hadn't been on the plaza since the night Pearl Hand had tied a dead man's face over mine and led me—wobbling, bleeding, and hidden under scavenged Kristiano clothing—toward escape.

Perhaps I haven't mentioned that my wife is incredibly clever and innovative when it comes to keeping me alive. That she is half-Kristiano, and speaks their language, is another blessing. She's also beautiful and talented at the arts of love. No one has killed more Kristianos. The Apalachee call her *nicoquadca*—the highest ranking of their warriors.

I stared at the corpses littering the plaza. On either side, the charred wreckage of houses merged with the night. Misshapen lumps inside the blackened walls would have defied identification had I not known that they were the piled bodies of men—warriors trapped when the Kristianos fired the town. They'd burned alive by the thousands, hemmed by the town walls, unable to flee between the tightly packed houses that roared fire and belched smoke. Clumps of incinerated corpses could be seen beneath the collapsed ash of houses. Others were piled atop each other where they'd been trapped in narrow passages. Even now, weeks after the holocaust, the stench caused my stomach to tighten.

"Let's hurry," Pearl Hand suggested hoarsely. "I don't want to be here a moment longer than necessary."

I'm right there with you, wife.

Making a face, I limped forward, picking my way

around the sprawled bodies. The Kristiano dead were missing, collected by the survivors to be prayed over, their single souls sent to the boring afterlife they called *paraíso*. As Antonio had once explained it, there were no animals or plants, no hunting, no feasting, just singing in the company of other Kristianos.

And these people wanted us to convert to the worship of their god?

I hobbled around a burned pack, seeing, of all things, a pile of Kristiano boots. They'd obviously been picked through, but the scorched and curled leather couldn't be mistaken for anything else. Nor could the remains of one of their heavy cloth tents, gaping holes burned in the fabric.

Just beyond lay another charred bale of what had once been fabrics, the gay Kristiano colors now mostly ash. We passed some of their big jars, green things that had held oil. Borne on slaves' backs all the way from the gulf, they'd ended here, shattered and broken as their contents exploded and ignited.

To my right lay the incinerated remains of a Kristiano saddle that I'd seen stripped from the cabayos the morning of the Mabila battle.

Above us, atop a low mound, stood the wreckage of the Mabila minko's palace. I remembered how the fire had reached the round wooden barrels that held the black powder that fired Kristiano thunder sticks. With a mighty bang louder than a lightning strike, the whole palace had blown apart. High Minko Tuskaloosa's body had been tossed so far into the air he'd landed with a splat on the hard plaza, broken like a corn-husk doll.

I stepped around a litter of ruined Kristiano baggage and proceeded to the incinerated house that Pearl Hand and I had occupied before the battle. Since it faced the plaza, the Kristianos had set fire to it first. To my relief, only five charred corpses lay among the ashes. Partially consumed roof timbers remained where they'd fallen, like a black spiderweb.

"There." Pearl Hand pointed. "That's what's left of the packs."

I limped over, ash puffing around my feet. Grunting with pain, I knelt down and began sifting through the piled ash and charcoal. I found the remains of Blackie's pack. A fortune in heat-calcined shell disintegrated under my fingers. Nothing remained of Bark's pack; the buffalo wool, feathers, and medicinal plants it had contained were now ash. The wood carvings, greasepaints, bone awls, and other goods were gone. My *chunkey* lances, trader's staff, and alligator-hide quiver? Vanished.

I found my chunkey stone, squatted, and held it to my chest. I was about to leave when I started, then reached under the fallen remains of a bench.

Miraculously, part of Squirm's pack remained. The charred leather cracked as I peeled it back, revealing flats of copper. They had been worked into different shapes: split-cloud and turkey-tail hairpieces; turning-world gorgets; images of Eagle Man. These I handed to Pearl Hand, and, reaching into the recesses, my fingers encountered a smooth, cool surface.

"Found it," I whispered as I withdrew the sacred mace. It lay heavy and resilient in my hand. As long as my forearm, the thing was solid copper, the top ending in a flaring design that we called a "turkey tail." Even as I touched it, I could feel the tingle of ancient Power run through my muscles and bones.

Memory returned of the day the great Apalachee *hilishaya*—or high priest—walked up to our lean-to and handed it to me. Back-from-the-Dead had said, *"Out of all the Nations, Horned Serpent chose the worthiest man he could find."*

I felt the *sepaya*—the piece of Horned Serpent's horn that rode in its pouch on my chest—begin to warm. I'd broken the piece of brow tine from the Spirit Beast's head when he was devouring me in the Sky World . . .

But that's a story for another time.

I rose, winced at the pain in my leg, and cradled the heavy copper mace to my breast. A fortune in trade lay ruined at my feet. Around me, thousands of dead remained in twisted and macabre piles. Overhead, stars—like frost on the blackness—glittered and shone.

"Come," I whispered to Pearl Hand. "We've work to do."

TWO

OUR WORK WAS THE DESTRUCTION OF HERNANDO DE Soto's army. He called himself the *Adelantado,* and his ruler, *el rey* Carlos—who lived far across the sea—had supposedly "given" de Soto our world. I'm still a little fuzzy on this, but their high Spirit leader, head of the *católicos,* somehow deluded himself into believing that their god had created our world. And that silly notion—in their eyes—made it all right for their *el rey* Carlos to claim our Nations.

Which, of course, when you think about it, is foolishness. Everyone knows that Breath Giver created our world. It is common knowledge among all peoples that in the Beginning Times—just after the Creation—Crawfish dove to the depths and brought up mud to form the land. Spirit Vulture smoothed it with his wings, and the great serpents crawled down from the heights, drawing the water that would become our rivers behind them. Spirit Beasts ruled the three worlds of creation: the Sky World, the middle world, and the Underworld. And through them all Breath Giver wove the red and white Powers to keep everything in balance.

Having land, sky, and water, Breath Giver created the animals and plants, and finally human beings. Then came the heroes: First Woman, or "Old-Woman-Who-Never-Dies," gave birth to Corn Woman, who gave birth to the hero twins, Morning Star and the Wild One, or the Orphan. They in turn killed the monsters, like Cannibal Turkey, Stone Man, and the other predatory creatures, and made the middle world safe for humans.

We'd never heard of this *jesucristo-dios,* or Kristianos, or *católicos,* until they came to our world. Given the way de Soto and his Kristianos treated us, we wanted to hear nothing more. Myself, I have the scars on my neck where they clapped me into a *hierro* collar and tried to work me to death.

To the Kristianos we were less than animals—things to be captured, enslaved, raped, brutalized, then replaced as necessary. I would not rest until the last Kristiano was dead.

But when would that be?

I pondered the question as I cradled the recovered mace and limped along a winter path south of Mabila. Pearl Hand padded silently behind me; I could sense her worried gaze each time I tripped or stumbled from fatigue.

I hugged the copper mace to my breast, possessed as it was of a Spirit all its own. According to Back-from-the-Dead's story, it had come all the way from fabled Cahokia long, long ago. There, in dim antiquity, it had been crafted for the great lords, living gods who sat in splendorous high palaces atop incredible earthen mounds in a great walled city. From the heights they had sent out conquering armies, colonies, and traders. And in the end, they had come to rule the world.

Not only did copper have Spirit Power, but the mace

had been forged and blessed by the high priests of Cahokia. It had been wielded by countless great lords, passed down generation to generation, and finally carried hence, borne by great minkos and their heirs.

Until it had come to me.

Now the mace remained a potent symbol of the struggle to save our world and destroy the Monster.

I tripped and gasped as my leg jolted with pain.

Behind me, Pearl Hand asked, "How is your leg?"

"It hurts."

"You're limping more."

"I'm tired."

Voice flat, she said, "I know."

I continued on, hearing the scolding bark of a fox squirrel in the high branches as we passed too close to one of his nut caches. In the distance, turkeys were calling. A vole rustled among the leaves as it scurried away. Overhead the winter-bare branches made a lacework against the cloudy sky.

Exhaling, I watched my breath fog and fade. "After the battle I had a dream."

"You've told me."

"In it, I was at Split Sky City . . . the abandoned center of the Chicaza Nation. It's the place where my ancestors are buried. Horned Serpent came to me in the dream and told me that the battle of Mabila was the turning point."

"You've told me," she repeated. "All the Kristianos' supplies and belongings had been carried into the town. Like our trade, it's all gone to ashes. Their clothing, banners, saddles—even the gold cup their priest used, all destroyed."

"When we were in Mabila, I noticed that they'd picked up the metal, what they could find. We've scouted their camp. They are doing something with it, heating it and pounding it with hammers. I fear they are fashioning more armor."

"They are resourceful." Pearl Hand sounded pensive as she walked along behind me. "But we've hurt them, Black Shell. You've seen how they dress now, in clothing scavenged from Mabila's outlying villages. Possessions that used to take four or five hundred slaves to carry—tents, food, chairs, oil, leather, cloth . . . even the long-tailed golden crosses . . . it's all gone. Burned inside Mabila."

"They still have their weapons. And that accursed armor." During the battle at Mabila I'd seen Kristianos with forty arrows stuck in their armor. Shooting at them was the same as pitching cactus spines at a turtle.

"Black Shell, Mabila took something else from them. Where once they walked arrogantly, now they, too, limp. That armor that concerns you so is no longer shined. When they stare at the forest, it is with fear, knowing that they are no longer invincible."

"Tell that to the dead at Mabila." I winced. "Tell that to Blood Thorn." He'd been our friend and companion ever since the Uzachile lands. I'd come to think of him as a brother, but when the Kristianos had turned our trap at Mabila against us, he'd chosen to die rather than continue the fight. Blood Thorn's decision had torn a hole in my souls, leaving an empty place that would never be filled.

"I know," she whispered.

As we approached a tall canebrake, I could smell the dank odor of standing water. A trilling whistle intruded on the forest sounds.

The guard had spotted us.

"It is Black Shell of the Chicaza," I called.

"Welcome back," a voice replied in an Albaamaha accent. "We cast gaming pieces to divide your possessions last night. You know, just in case you never returned."

A young warrior appeared out of the jointed green cane, a smile on his face. "But here you are, so I guess the Kristianos didn't catch you, and that wonderful sword is still yours."

"Sorry to report that we eluded them again. Good to see you, Water Spider."

A cape made from woodpecker feathers hung from Water Spider's shoulders, protection against the chill. He wore knee-high moccasins, and a long apron woven from hemp hung down past his knees. Tattooed lines ran diagonally down his cheeks and accented two black streaks painted across his forehead. I could see the Long-Tailed Man talisman that hung from a cord around his neck. A hardwood bow was clutched in his right hand, a quiver of arrows visible on his back. He slouched insolently as we approached.

Water Spider was one of the lucky ones. He'd hidden beneath a pile of corpses outside Mabila and escaped during the night. Now, along with a handful of other survivors, he waited, hoping for a chance to kill a couple more Kristianos.

"As to our possessions, sorry," I muttered, still gloomy. "Better luck next time."

Then Water Spider's eyes fixed on the mace, and he gulped. "Is that what I think it is?"

"All we could salvage this trip."

"Along with some copper," Pearl Hand added, walking up beside me. "Any news?"

He nodded, reaching up to scratch where his hair had been pulled up into a tight bun atop his head and skewered with a turkey-bone pin. "A runner came in last night. The great ships are still at the bay down south in Ochuse. They've sent some scouts inland, probably looking for these Kristianos."

I glanced at Pearl Hand. She cocked her head, her gleaming black braid falling to the side. Expression thoughtful, she said, "In Apalachee last winter, the *Adelantado* was able to resupply. If he meets up with them again, everything we destroyed at Mabila will be replaced."

I considered that. "That may be the *Adelantado*'s only

hope. Marching south would take his army a minimum of ten days. And first they'd have to cross the river . . . then the swamps. Perfect country for ambushes."

"Pensacola warriors are watching the trails." Water Spider glanced up as a hawk sailed over. "If the Monster marches south, he'll have to fight the whole way." He gave us a slight grin. "The Pensacola are hoping for just that, figuring to grow rich on the spoils."

Pearl Hand resettled the sack containing the copper we'd salvaged. "From the looks of their camp, the Kristianos aren't going anywhere. Too many of them are still recovering from wounds."

"Even better," Water Spider said with a nod. "It will slow them down, spread them out. Make them easier to pick off."

"If they go south," I mused.

At the tone in my voice, Water Spider and Pearl Hand both shot me curious glances.

I shifted the weight off my aching leg. "It's just that heading south to resupply would make sense. That's what everyone is expecting. But since when has de Soto ever done what we expected him to do?"

Water Spider looked at me like I was an idiot. Pearl Hand, however, cast a thoughtful glance at the leaf-strewn ground.

"You've told me his men don't know how to live off the land." Water Spider spread his hands wide. "And if they've lost their supplies, what are they going to do? Head back toward the Coosa Nation? The Coosa warriors I've talked to tell me the only reason de Soto got out of Coosa without a fight was because he had their ruler, the Coosa High Sun, as a captive and hostage. If he goes back, they'll be after him like a swarm of mad wasps."

"He knows that." Pearl Hand shifted, her dark eyes half-lidded with thought.

An image of de Soto formed in the eye of my souls. I

could picture his droopy eyes, the long nose and thin mouth. I'd last seen him fighting his way out of the trap we'd set for him in Mabila. De Soto should have been panicked, desperate, with doom all around him. Thing was, he'd had a smile on his narrow, bearded face. Excitement had simmered behind his normally arrogant brown eyes, as though a fire of delight burned in his evil Kristiano soul.

Pearl Hand said softly, "But for someone failing to close the town gate in Mabila, he'd have died there and he knows it. We may only have killed forty or fifty of his *soldados*, but hundreds more were wounded. Not to mention the number of cabayos we killed."

"You misread him," I said just as softly. "Think from his perspective: High Minko Tuskaloosa led him into the perfect trap. We had him surrounded by five thousand warriors inside a fortified town. His men were caught relaxing, their guard down. By rights we should have killed him there, and he knows it."

"All the more reason for him to want to get out," Water Spider argued. "And fast."

I said, "The man I saw fight his way out of Mabila wasn't defeated. I'd have seen it in his face. He was already plotting a way to turn disaster into victory. Yes, he lost his supplies, and yes, we killed many and wounded hundreds, but he saved his army and turned our trap against us."

I glanced north up the trail toward Mabila and the Kristiano camp. "The man I saw that day, he doesn't think like we do. He doesn't see a calamity when he looks at the ruins of Mabila. He sees a victory."

"That's crazy," Water Spider mumbled.

"No." Pearl Hand sighed. "Black Shell is right. It's just that we've never fought an enemy like this one. Until we realize that, he's going to continue to beat us at every turn."

At the defeat in her words, depression bore down on me like a terrible weight.

Our hidden camp was on an old levee in the Albaamaha River back-swamp. The low sandy ridge was surrounded by canebrakes. Ponderous bald cypresses, yellow lotuses, water oaks, and tupelos filled the swamps. At night swarms of mosquitoes made hovering clouds above, held at bay only by smoky fires and the resin-laced grease we smeared on our bodies.

Through the thicket of bare branches we could see the river shining silver in the light as it wound its way west toward its confluence with the Tombigbee. From there it snaked its way south to the gulf. Around our camp, thick vines of grape and greenbrier, thorny walking stick, and honeysuckle wound up through the trees like a lattice.

What the camp lacked in amenities it made up for in security. No patrols of mounted cabayeros could find us, and even had they known our location, the big animals would have floundered in the swampy bottoms, sinking to their briskets.

By the time *soldados* worked out the trails, we would have been long gone, melted away among the thick boles of bald cypress.

A late-afternoon sun slanted out of the southeast by the time I led the way—limping painfully—into the little camp. The smoky air carried the smells of frying catfish and goose. My gut growled suggestively.

I nodded at the seven other occupants, three warriors and four women, refugees of the Kristiano occupation of their country. I barely noticed the new lean-to off to one side. Made of cane, it had been lashed up among the grapevines. Freshly peeled bark gleamed against the green stems. A heavy leather pack, large, travel scarred, and worn, was propped against one of the support poles.

The small shelter belonging to Pearl Hand and me sat

at the top of the levee. Shelter? It was barely more than a ramada covering a fire pit and rolled blankets. Atop our pitiful collection of belongings, the five dogs were sleeping contentedly. Only the occasional flick of an ear gave proof that they were alive.

A trader's dogs are his livelihood. More than just bearers of burdens, they are family. We choose large animals, strong of bone and body, capable of long hours on the trail. A trader's dog must be smart, companionable, and most of all, obedient. His ultimate responsibility is to guard as well as transport. Our dogs were more than just tools; we owed them our lives.

The Kristianos, too, had dogs. Theirs were rangy, tall things, bred for war. Kristianos used them to wreak havoc on an enemy during an attack, employed them to chase down fugitives, and worst of all, ordered them to maul helpless slaves to ensure obedience. As a slave wore out, the dogs were loosed, biting and snapping, to keep him on his feet. When that failed they tore out the person's throat, ripped open their bowels, and savaged the remains. Then the beasts ate the dead in front of the cowering slaves. Imagine trying to sleep, desperate to forget the horror, while several paces away, a war dog loudly gnaws on your beloved daughter's skull.

I hated the things, considered them but another Kristiano perversion of nature.

Kristiano dogs know how to kill; trader's dogs know something else: how to fight. One of my dogs would never start a fight with village dogs. But when the locals don't keep their mongrels off? Well, a trader's dog has to take care of himself. My dogs—especially Bark—had spent their lives doing exactly that.

At Napetuca, de Soto had loosed his war dogs on us. Pearl Hand, Blood Thorn, and I would have died right there but for my dogs. Again at Mabila, our dogs had taken on de Soto's and kept them at bay. When Antonio tried to ride me down from atop his great cabayo, Skipper saved my life at the cost of his own.

Just the thought of my debt to Skipper, and the love I had for all of my dogs, made me smile as I hobbled up to our ramada and whistled.

Bad mistake.

All five of them came at a charge. The impact of those frantic bodies toppled me onto my back, so fierce was their greeting.

Bark, his bony and scarred head bobbing, began baying his joy. Not the smartest of my dogs, he was big, black, thick bodied, and loyal to a fault, and if there was anything he loved more than fresh deer liver, it was a scrap. He was just plain lethal in a dogfight.

Gnaw was the largest, a broad-chested, muscular creature with a dainty white-tipped tail. The heavier the pack, the more he liked it. Of them all, he was the most aloof, almost standoffish. He'd been Blood Thorn's favorite, and since Mabila, Gnaw had spent his time looking back down the trail, as if waiting for his friend to appear. Sometimes his grief seemed worse than my own.

Squirm pounced on my chest, giving me that half smile dogs have, crinkling his nose to expose his canines. I'd traded for him when he was a puppy up in the Yuchi country. Squirm had long brown hair, a white blaze on his face, and a white bib. His specialty was "squirming" out of packs.

Blackie—well, the name says it. He and his litter-mate Patches were young, new, and still had just enough puppy in them to make them frisky and disobedient. Patches looked like he'd been put together with chunks of brown and white hide, and he had a wolfish and lean-looking face.

I eased myself into a seated position, snapped my fingers, and endured the ensuing trial of thrashing dog bodies. My healing leg only got stepped on four or five times.

"Enough," Pearl Hand ordered after Gnaw tromped on my leg a final time, bringing a wince to my over-licked face.

The dogs backed off, tails wagging, ears pricked, glancing back and forth between us.

"We'd better feed them," I said, pulling myself upright and grimacing as I straightened my leg.

"They've been fed," a gruff voice called from the side. "Though any trader worth the name would have seen to that a couple hands of time past."

I craned my neck to see a muscle-bound wedge of a man step out from under the recently constructed lean-to. "Two Packs?"

A gap-toothed grin split his familiar tattooed face. But a hardness lay behind his normally affable eyes. We'd last seen him at Coosa, leaving him on the canoe landing as de Soto's army marched into the capital. Two Packs was a bear of a man. Brawny, with legs like tree trunks, he'd gained his name for the size of the packs he carried in the trade. I'd traveled with him for years. Both Blackie and Patches came from his breeding pack.

He had his hair up in a bun, pinned with a polished chokecherry pin. A plain brown hunting shirt was belted at his waist, and a bear-hide cloak was pushed back over his shoulders. His craggy and rawboned face had been greased against the mosquitoes, effectively darkening his clan tattoos.

Pearl Hand shot him a curious look, then offered a hand to help me to my feet. Under her breath, she asked, "Think he brought a couple of women with him? Or is he just going to drool every time I walk by?"

Two Packs, you see, had a certain appetite for women. I couldn't be sure that his arrival wasn't motivated by the fact that Pearl Hand was my wife—and off-limits. A challenge for his more masculine appetites to overcome.

I stumped forward and clapped Two Packs in a solid hug. "By the Piasa's balls, how do you come to be here?"

His hug drove the breath out of my lungs. "It's where I need to be, Black Shell." He pushed me back to arm's length and looked me up and down. His gaze stopped at the scab peeling off my arm, and again where the slice in the top of my thigh was crusted and oozing between Pearl Hand's stitches. "Looks like you've had a close call. You're not taking care of yourself." Then he glanced toward Pearl Hand. "She still hasn't figured out that a real man would make her bed a warmer place?"

"No. And you'll stay out of her blankets. Otherwise she'll put a couple of holes in your hide and you'll never live long enough to heal."

He chuckled, but the old humor wasn't there. "She never really liked me."

"Maybe because you're not likeable?"

"If you were really my friend, you'd lie about the obvious and spare my tender feelings." He clapped me on the back and stepped forward, stopping before Pearl Hand. "With your permission, I'd like to share your fire and discuss some things."

I blinked in amazement. *Is this really Two Packs?* Normally he'd have offered her a cheap shell gorget for a turn in the blankets. You know, just to set her off.

"Of course," Pearl Hand replied, off balance. Then she shot me a worried glance. Oh yes, something was very wrong.

THREE

As Two Packs ambled off for his lean-to to get wood and some food for our meal, I frowned. "He's not his usual self."

"No." Pearl Hand used a twig to coax the coals together in our hearth. "And my advice would be to treat him carefully." She sent a thoughtful glance his way.

I frowned after my old friend.

We said little as he packed more than an armload of wood. While I tended the fire, Pearl Hand retrieved a wooden bowl she'd scavenged on an earlier trip back to Mabila.

Two Packs had obviously established a relationship with the other refugees since the women at the fires freely offered him bits of this and that. Not that it mattered; we were all in the same condition. Everything was communal.

"This ought to fill the old belly hole," Two Packs grunted as he returned with a slab of bark piled with steaming meat, fish, and cattail bread.

We made our food offerings to the fire and began to eat. Two Packs had seated himself across from us; he growled at the dogs when they crowded around. They probably thought the newcomer would fall easy victim to their soulful eyes, sad expressions, and pitiful looks.

"Flea-bitten mongrels," he muttered, avoiding our eyes as he waved the dogs away. "How're Blackie and Patches fitting in?"

"Very well," Pearl Hand answered. "They're from good stock."

The old Two Packs would have smiled at that. The one across from me just nodded and asked, "Skipper?"

"Saved my life at Mabila," I whispered. "His souls are traveling the Spirit Road west toward the Seeing Hand. He'll make the leap into the Sky World next spring. Fetch will be waiting for him on the other side."

I saw the slightest tightening of Two Packs's expression, but he only nodded again. "Blood Thorn?"

"Dead at Mabila."

He stopped chewing, shoulders sagging. "I am sorry to hear that. I liked him. What happened?"

I remembered the final look in Blood Thorn's eyes, his soot-streaked face lined with the jagged tracks of tears. "I think he finally ran out of hope. When you've been that beat up and betrayed, death starts to look pretty good."

Which, I fear, is what I am coming to believe.

We were silent for a time.

Finally Pearl Hand asked what I was unwilling to: "What led you to seek us out?"

"Coosa," he slowly replied, "has nothing left for me."

My impulse was to ask if his wife, Willow Root, had finally thrown him out for womanizing. The tone in his voice, however, led me to caution. Instead I asked, "Your family?"

He gave me a squinty, sidelong look. "The Kristianos have a word, 'tamemes.' You've heard it?"

"What they call the slaves who carry their burdens."
Pearl Hand supplied the definition.

"*Tamemes!*" Two Packs said it like a curse. "Willow Root's
clan was ordered to provide people, *tamemes,* to carry the
Kristiano packs. My boys, Red Tie and Black Rope, were
handpicked for the job by the Bear Clan mikko. What
could they do? It was an order."

I felt a chill run down my back—one colder than the
wind blowing down from the north. Red Tie and Black
Rope might have been Two Packs's sons, but they belonged to their mother's clan.

Again Pearl Hand asked what I could not. "What happened?"

"They were on the trail to Etowah, chained by the
neck, when Red Tie was insulted by a Kristiano guard.
Red Tie threw down the funny wooden thing he was carrying . . . some kind of Kristiano chair. Black Rope,
chained behind him, did the same with his load."

I winced.

"When the Kristianos came, my sons tried to fight
back." Two Packs swallowed hard. "When it was all over,
the monsters cut their heads off, leaving the bloody col-
lars to swing on the chain. Others were made to carry
their loads."

I closed my eyes, having seen it myself too many times.

"So, I am here," Two Packs answered, his eyes fixed on
some distance beyond his souls.

"What news of Coosa?" I hoped to change the subject.

Two Packs shrugged. "Chaos. The High Sun is de-
posed. Supposedly he's up in the hills, trying to organize a
force to retake the capital. Half the talwas have revolted,
different mikkos declaring their independence. Raiding
parties are roaming the country, towns have been burned.
The whole Nation is coming apart like a loosely woven
basket in a great wind."

Pearl Hand asked, "Who has claimed the high chair?"

Two Packs gave a vague shrug. "When I left there was no shortage of 'High Suns.' At least three factions of the ruling Wind Clan are fighting each other for control. The other clans are split, fighting each other depending on who owes what to whom. It's all madness."

"They might work it out," I said hopefully.

"And then there's the sickness," Two Packs said. "Something the healers can't cope with. A fever followed by a terrible coughing that ends up with people sweating the souls out of their bodies and drowning in their own phlegm. Charges of sorcery are flying back and forth . . . people killing each other because they think their neighbors are witching them, making them sick."

I glanced at Pearl Hand, sharing a look of understanding. "The Death?" I asked, referring to the illness that had devastated the Nation of Cofitachequi before our arrival there last summer.

She shrugged. "Or another of the Kristianos' diseases. Maybe the one that almost killed you at Uzita."

Two Packs slapped his thick leg. "You were right all along. Both of you. Where the Kristianos go, only death and misery follow." He looked back and forth at us. "I was there that night when you went before the High Sun. You told the Coosa what would happen. I remember how they mocked you, how they scorned your words." Two Packs paused. "I myself thought you were a little crazy."

"You can't comprehend the threat until you've been face-to-face with Kristianos," Pearl Hand said kindly.

"Yes, well, I've nothing left. They've taken everything . . . ruined my Nation . . . my home and family. Our world is dying. I want to help save what's left."

I looked at the big man, once the most vibrant person I knew. *Old friend,* I thought, *even our victories are defeats.*

As I slept that night, my dream soul wandered in search of terrifying nightmares—and found them.

In an instant I was back in Uzita, the town where the Kristianos had landed a year and a half before. I was chained by the neck, blood leaking down from cuts the *hierro* collar made in my skin. I bore a heavy wooden box, the chains clanking as I slogged my way down a muddy trail. Ahead of me, a captive struggled beneath an awkward bale of cloth, bloody sweat streaking his whip-lashed back.

To either side of the muddy trail lay beheaded corpses. Sometimes the bodies had been partially tossed onto the vegetation, other times they lay parallel to the trail. The heads ended up wherever the Kristiano guards had kicked them. Crabs feasted as they plucked bloody flesh with their pinchers. Flies swarmed above the maggot-ridden meat, barely disturbed by the clicking claws.

"Work!" Ortiz, the Kristiano slave boss, bellowed in Timucua. Whips cracked in return, and a man screamed.

I heard the war dog growling, saw it ghost in from the side. It came fast, slinking low to the ground. I shied away. As I skipped awkwardly to the side, the heavy wooden box put me off balance. Too slow. Fangs sank into my leg.

Then I was down, screaming. Dogs leaped in from all directions. The box crashed, wood splintering. I caught the faintest glimpse of Blood Thorn's decapitated head as it rolled from the broken box, then the dogs were on me.

I struggled to rise, trapped by the collar and the relentless length of chain. As dogs tore my flesh, I batted at them with futile hands. One was savaging my gut. Each time it yanked my skin, I was jerked rudely forward. I gasped in horror, eyes wide. Within moments, my belly would tear. Intestines would spew out like coils of eels.

I reached out, desperate for a stick, anything to defend myself. And there, on the muddy trail, Blood Thorn's severed head was staring back at me, grinning . . .

"Black Shell!"

My body was rocking as the dogs bit and jerked. I cried out, whimpering.

"Black Shell! Wake up!"

. . . I blinked awake to a cold night, a dark ramada obscuring the sky. When I flinched at the next shove, I realized it wasn't war dogs but Pearl Hand hammering on my chest.

"Wake up! Blood and pus, Black Shell! You're dreaming. Half the camp is awake."

I sucked full breaths of the chilly night air and sat up, the blanket falling away. "I was a slave in Uzita. The dogs were after me. Blood Thorn . . . his head . . ."

Pearl Hand sighed and pulled her long hair back with anxious fingers. "You're safe, Black Shell. Just a dream." She sounded weary.

"It was so real." I fell back into the bedding, still trying to catch my breath. "Ortiz was there."

I couldn't stop the sudden shiver. It ran through my bones and muscles, powered by terror.

I barely heard Pearl Hand saying, "Well, thank the winds it wasn't Antonio. Dream or not, he'd probably have killed you."

I reached down and felt the wound in my thigh. It was weeping pus again, hot to the touch and stinging. "If you'll recall, he almost got the job done at Mabila. Would have but for you and Skipper."

She lowered herself beside me, pulling the blanket up to her chin. I could sense her watching me in the darkness. "He didn't get away unscathed. Between your arrow slicing his cheek open and that sword cut across the nose, he's now the ugliest Kristiano in all the world."

"Had it not been for his accursed metal hat, I'd have left him with half a head."

She chuckled at that. I wasn't sure it was funny, but her laughter made me feel better.

"Black Shell?"

"Hmm?"

"Was Horned Serpent in your dream?"

"Not this time. A Spirit Dream is different. No, this was just terror. Sorry I woke you up."

She gave a frustrated snort. "I have my own terror dreams. Sometimes I'm captive in the old mico's palace in Telemico. Sometimes I'm walking among the dead at Napetuca. Lately it's Mabila, hearing the screams, smelling the smoke, and ducking from the flames." A pause. "You always wake me before the end comes."

I smiled in the night, reaching over to take her hand. "We help each other."

"You fill my heart."

"And you fill mine." I drew a breath. "But the dreams, they keep getting worse."

I felt her nod.

I shifted uncomfortably before I forced myself to say what I'd been afraid to earlier. "I think we need to hunt."

"How will shooting a couple of deer or turkeys banish bad dreams?"

"Turkeys? Deer? What are . . . Oh. You miss my point."

"Which is?"

"Maybe hiding out in the swamp is part of the problem. Maybe our souls are punishing us, hoping to drive us back into the fight. We're not supposed to be squatting on our butts, swatting mosquitoes."

Silence.

Then she said, "Your leg is barely healed. You can't run. Not like you did in Apalachee."

"No, but we can lay traps. They've had weeks since Mabila without a hand being raised against them."

She rose on one elbow to stare at me. "You said you saw Blood Thorn in the dream. Is that what this is all about? Going out to die like he did? Is that what's pushing you?"

I pursed my lips, hiding the fear that burned bright in

my gut. "No. Not like that. We both know we're not getting out of this alive. Someday soon one or both of us will stop a crossbow arrow, be gutted by a cabayero, or be cut down like a cornstalk."

"Pus and blood, must you *always* be so optimistic?"

"Pearl Hand, we should have died in Mabila."

"We would have if you hadn't let me dress you as a Kristiano."

"You *skinned* a dead man! Made me wear his face like a mask!"

"And for that brief moment, you were so handsome."

I ignored the teasing in her voice. "I was dripping blood, limping, dressed in sweat-stinking Kristiano clothes . . . peering out through a dead man's eye holes."

She gave me a playful jab in the ribs. "Maybe Antonio can skin his next victim and don the face. He'll never win a woman any other way, as gruesome as you left him."

I laughed softly. Pearl Hand had once again worked her magic. Then I turned serious. "I mean it, we need to go hunt them, learn what they are planning."

"And Two Packs?"

By the Piasa's balls, what would we do about Two Packs?

She said, "Black Shell, he's as dispirited as Blood Thorn was at the end. Maybe he thinks ending on a Kristiano lance won't be as painful as living with what he's lost."

Blood Thorn's death was hard enough. How would I feel if my good old friend Two Packs met the same end?

"He's got to find his own way," I decided. "If we don't take the initiative, we're going to end up as lost as he is."

I tried to sound bluff and self-assured. But deep down, I knew the source of the nightmares.

After Mabila—and the horrors I lived there—I am afraid.

FOUR

THE NEXT MORNING, UNDER THE SOLICITOUS glances of the other refugees, we packed what few belongings remained to us. I stared out at the river, watching the water suck and swirl as it created patterns on the surface. Our lives were like that, unorganized, churning this way and that.

Two Packs walked up, the heavy, use-scarred pack strapped to his shoulders. His wide mouth was pressed into a flat line. Something unfathomable lay behind his brooding eyes. He shifted, thrusting a moccasin-clad foot forward.

"What's the plan?" he asked as I rolled my blanket and bound it tight with cord.

"We're going to scout. Figure out what the Monster is planning next. After that we're going to lay traps along his way, see if we can pick off one or two." I gave him a knowing squint. "And we're going to hope you don't get us killed in the process."

Canting his head to the side, he said, "I don't follow that last."

"You ready to die?"

He avoided my eyes, his gaze on Pearl Hand as she slipped our few wooden bowls into her fabric sack. She'd braided her long hair, and her dress molded to every curve of her body. For once, Two Packs didn't seem to notice.

"I don't know," he finally admitted. "I'm . . . I'm all hollow inside."

"Better figure it out." I jerked the knots tight. The dogs were watching, prancing about unsurely. Wondering where their packs were, I suppose.

"Black Shell? How do you do it?"

"I hate. I remember each atrocity they've committed, and that drives me on. Will they kill me in the end? Of course. I'm a walking corpse following a trail to its end. Meanwhile, I'm doing everything in my ability to ensure that they're broken and destroyed before they finally kill me."

"And that's how you survive each day?"

I cringed at the pain in my thigh as I stood and swung the blanket up. He watched as I slipped my Kristiano sword through my rope belt. It was the only weapon we'd managed to bring out of Mabila that night. "I figure it's a sacred contest. How many of them can I kill before they finally get me?"

He grunted and gave me that old familiar grin. "For the first time since I heard my boys were dead, I think I can understand." He paused, a twinkle lighting his eyes. "Too bad these Kristianos don't have women with them."

"Oh, they've got two. Not that you'd be interested."

"When it comes to women, I'm always interested." He was trying so hard to sound like the old Two Packs.

I shot him a sidelong look. "Kristiano women are covered from head to foot in layers of clothing. Why? I am forced to conclude that they are so weasel-tooth ugly

34

that it's the only way their men can stand to look at them."

We took the back trails, winding through dense forest, searching out the most arduous route—places that a patrol of cabayeros would avoid. That they were about was no secret. When we crossed trails, it was to find the round-hoofed tracks and occasional piles of balled manure. The stuff had a signature acrid smell.

By nightfall we'd reached the thicket of honeysuckle and grape where Pearl Hand and I had hidden after our escape from Mabila.

The roll of clothing Pearl Hand had stripped from the dead *soldado* still hung in the branches where we'd left it. Just the sight of it brought back memories of my protests as she'd forced me to climb into it. Then, under the cover of darkness, and with the bearded Kristiano's skinned face tied over mine, she'd walked me right out of Mabila's shattered gates. Her command of *español,* coupled with my garb, had tricked the guard. The fool thought I was just another wounded Kristiano *soldado* being helped by his *indio* slave.

"So, this is our new home?" Two Packs asked after muscling his way in through the brush.

"Let's pray not," I replied. "But you'll have to keep your voice down. Talking like your normal self is going to bring half of the Monster's army down on top of us."

He cocked his head in that old familiar manner, asking, "So, what are we going to fight them with? Rocks?"

Pearl Hand cocked a suggestive eyebrow.

"You have an idea, wife?" I knew that look. It made my gut squirm.

She studied the clouds, half-screened by the thick brush. They were rolling down from the north. She sniffed the breeze. "I think I smell rain on the wind. It should be a wet, ugly, and miserable night."

"You'll conjure weapons from the storm?" Two Packs began to chuckle.

Pearl Hand gave him an offhanded shrug. "If we need weapons, I'd rather have the best than try to cobble something together out here in a downpour."

"Which means?" Two Packs seemed confused.

With every thread of my being, I kept my face straight. "Which means we're going to steal weapons from the Kristianos. Tonight. In the middle of the storm."

But inside, my heart was pounding. My mouth had gone dry.

Pearl Hand's mocking smile added to my dismay. "Sometimes, husband, you are so smart you amaze even me."

I don't hate it when Pearl Hand is right. That happens with such shocking regularity that I'm used to it. I just hate it when she's so *smugly* right.

We *were* in for an ugly and miserable night.

It began as a misty light drizzle that strengthened as the day faded into gloom. We observed the Kristianos from beneath a winter-brown screen of honeysuckle, downwind from the cabayo herd. Our field of view was excellent, the aforementioned animals having already grazed off what would have otherwise been a tall stand of grass.

The Kristiano camp sprawled just shy of the tree line to our north, perhaps six bow-shots distant. Just the glimpse of them as they clustered around their fires sent my heart racing. Behind the men, in what seemed the center of the camp, I could see a farmstead, the houses roofed with thatch. Over the distance we could hear talking, sharp barks of laughter, the occasional clang of metal, and the hollow chopping of an *hierro* ax as it split wood.

Breath Giver help me, I really *don't want to do this.* Images of Mabila, of Napetuca, of my captivity in Uzita, all flashed between my souls like sick lightning. Fear was carving a hollow place in my gut—no matter what I'd bravely said back in the riverside camp.

I faked courage as I pointed for Two Packs's benefit. "You'll notice how they've laid out their fires. It's a defensive formation providing a circle of light in the event of a night attack. The men walking along the perimeter with crossbows are the sentries."

"What about those houses in the center?"

Pearl Hand told him, "That's where de Soto, his subchiefs, and the critically wounded will be staying. When Black Shell and I go in, we're just going to see what we can pick up along the outlying camps."

Two Packs asked, "Wouldn't the best weapons be with the chiefs?"

"*All* of their weapons, even those carried by the *soldados*, are good." I kept the quiver out of my voice. "Our goal is to stay close to the edge of camp. If something goes wrong, we can flee into the darkness." *Please, Horned Serpent, may it be so.*

I swallowed down a dry throat.

When did I become such a coward?

"What about the cabayos?" Two Packs chewed his thumb, gaze on the grazing animals. "Won't they ride you down?"

I nodded back toward the rear of the honeysuckle where the dogs were obediently lying. "That's what the dogs are for. Here's the plan: If we're discovered, we'll run for the tree line. Once past the fires, it'll be too dark for them to see. They'll be fire-blinded until their eyes adjust."

Pearl Hand added, "It will take time to catch up the cabayos, mount them, and charge after us. If that happens, you order the dogs out. When the dogs are snapping and barking, the cabayeros will be confused. It'll buy us time to escape."

Two Packs gave me a sober look. "What about your leg? You're not exactly running as fast as a swamp rabbit when a bobcat comes calling."

"Believe me," I growled in a show of false courage, "my leg will be the least of my concerns."

Pearl Hand interjected, "Even with Black Shell limping, we can make it to the trees in less than a finger's time. Most of that way will be in darkness. I'm not worried about what happens after we get out. It's being surrounded in camp that makes my bladder tighten."

I nodded in fervent agreement, struggling to come to grips with the situation. I *needed* to do this. I *had* to do this. The disaster at Mabila had taken something out of me. Before the battle I had been cautious but dedicated. Now my most fervent desire was to turn and run. To surrender to the despair and slowly rot away from the inside out.

I reached down, fingering the sepaya. The bit of Horned Serpent's brow tine was warm to the touch, vibrating through its leather pouch.

Surely, I thought, *if Power was against this, the sepaya would be stone-cold.*

Or maybe . . . after Mabila . . . Power has given up?

Just the notion sent a tremor of fear through me.

Blood and pus, let's just get away from here. I closed my eyes, willing myself to utter that final statement of defeat. I took the breath . . .

"Let's get dressed," Pearl Hand declared firmly, wiggling backward under the stalks.

I hesitated, hating myself.

If she can do it . . .

Sick to my stomach, I pushed myself back with my elbows, wriggling like an awkward snake. You ever seen a snake crawl backward? No? There's a reason why.

Behind the screen of brush, the dogs waited, ears pricked, their coats matted and wet in the drizzle.

Pearl Hand helped me don the dead Kristiano's armor. Maybe she noticed my shaking, halfhearted movements. Maybe she didn't. It was dark and raining. Perhaps she just thought I was cold.

I admit that I ran the day I first heard Horned Serpent's voice. But over the years I'd laid cowardice to rest.

Until Mabila . . .

The batted coat with its metal plates was really too small, but as on that fateful night in Mabila, I squeezed into it. The old dried blood was smelly, and the odor of smoke clung to the fabric. A reminder of the circumstances in which I'd obtained it.

The metal helmet, however, had benefits. It shed water better than any bark rain hat I'd ever worn.

Full dark came with a vengeance. I had trouble seeing my hand before my face. Fine, I could look as scared as I wanted. When we pushed through the brush, the flickers of the Kristiano fires were plainly visible. Visions of death and terror tried to paralyze my muscles.

The dogs had been given orders to stay with Two Packs. They did so reluctantly; it helped that Blackie and Patches were used to taking orders from my old friend.

The moist air carried the armored vest's moldy odor to my nose. I was back in a dead man's clothing, which—as a good Chicaza—should have had my souls shrieking with dread. Chicaza don't like being close to the remains of those killed violently. It reeks of perverted red Power—the tainted kind that will sicken the souls.

But what did a man worry about sick souls when he was about to walk into a Kristiano camp?

"You two be careful," Two Packs ordered. "If I hear shouts or see cabayos running in the firelight, I'll send the dogs after you."

"Let's go." Pearl Hand reached out and took my hand as she started for the distant winking fires. At her insistent jerk, I stumbled along after her, wishing I could throw up.

After a couple of steps, she let go of my hand and we felt our way across the trampled field.

"Remember," she murmured, "I'll do the talking. If anyone asks you anything directly, just cough a lot while I answer."

"Oh, yes." Most of my *español* consisted of curses and promises of mayhem. Not the sort of thing to tell a suspicious guard.

Fool! You'll be so panicked the words will freeze in your throat.

Hard, cold rain began to fall in earnest. The loud pattering on the *hierro* helmet covered any sound of my limping feet as I reluctantly followed Pearl Hand toward the fires. I could see men hovering around them, throwing on additional logs, holding their hands out to the heat.

"Maybe Power favors us," Pearl Hand whispered as she caught me. I'd stepped into a hole. My fear-weak muscles barely held.

She added, "In this driving rain, we'll be in and out before they suspect."

We'd originally planned on hovering at the edge of the fires, watching until the Kristianos sought their blankets. Then, a hand of time later, we'd walk in. Assuming of course that they were all asleep.

"As hard as this rain is coming down, this might be the best chance we get," I muttered, wincing at the pain in my leg.

As if Horned Serpent himself had heard, we could see the silhouettes of the sentries as they backed in toward the fires.

Pearl Hand agreed. "All the better. Just keep your face averted so that no one gets a close look at you. If only I had a beard to paste to your chin, they'd never suspect."

I know I sounded hysterical when I said, "You could always kill another *soldado* and skin his head. You know, keep it in your pack for nights like this."

"I'll see to it. Good thinking."

She was joking. Wasn't she?

"There"—she pointed—"between those fires. The gap is a little wider."

I heard the tension in her voice. No one got close to Kristianos without being afraid. Then it hit me: If they caught me, I didn't need to worry about being made a slave. All I had to do was shout, *"Yo soy el Concho Negro!"* Antonio would run up and chop my head off with one swipe of his sword.

Pearl Hand, however, they'd strip naked, chain spread-eagle to the ground, and . . . well, you can guess what they'd use her for. The urge to vomit tickled the back of my throat.

"Don't look directly at the fires," she reminded as we walked into the light.

Her attention was on the crowds of men clustered around the fires as the rain beat down. They faced the flames, hands out, stepping as close as they could to keep dry and warm. Most wore their helmets and had blankets around their shoulders. Their clothing steamed on the fire side. When they got too hot, they'd turn, presenting their backsides.

I could hear the voices now, talking softly in *español*. Occasionally someone would laugh, but it was without the boisterous quality of happy men.

My throat was so tight I couldn't have pounded a swallow down it with a wooden pestle.

We were easily visible now, and I kept my head down, hiding as much of my face as I could behind the helmet rim. Pearl Hand, a bark hat over her head, walked with an unaccustomed stoop to her shoulders, the way a cowed woman would.

Between the streams of water running off the helmet, I shot terrified looks at the Kristianos. If they noticed us, it was only to dismiss us immediately.

Then I got a closer look. Most of them were wearing rags beneath their threadbare blankets. I could see rents in their sleeves . . . and more than a few wore moccasins. Moccasins?

I remembered the burned boots we'd seen the night we returned to Mabila. And the charred tent—but one of many carried into Mabila. Had *any* of the tents survived?

Looking around, I realized that the *soldados* were sleeping in crude shelters built of matting scrounged from outlying villages. Nowhere did I see a tent.

Shielding my eyes from the fire's glare, I identified the blankets they cowered under as being of local manufacture, and there were not many of those, either. The men crowding the fires were huddled against the cold rain with arms crossed tightly for warmth.

"I begin to understand," I said softly.

"What?"

"They lost so much in Mabila."

"Except their weapons," Pearl Hand retorted, pointing.

Ahead of us, next to one of the patched-up shelters, stood a rack of the long spear-axes. Taller than a man, spear-axes were topped with a lethal point, but one side ended in a sharp ax blade with a vicious, hooklike bottom. We'd seen the things used to great effect to reach out and slice a man's head off.

Keeping a careful eye on the men around the fires, we splashed our way around the shelter, searching in the reflected light.

"Careful," Pearl Hand warned me as a figure came plodding our way. "Just walk normally."

"I'd love to, but my leg hurts." Heart leaping in my breast, I limped along beside Pearl Hand. The man—wearing one of their round helmets—barely nodded as he approached. And, to my relief, I realized he was limping worse than I was.

"*Buenas noches,*" Pearl Hand said as he passed us.

"*¿Esta noche? ¿Qué está bien?*" he replied, stumping past.

"What did you say?" I asked when he'd passed beyond earshot.

"I told him 'good evening.'" She sniffed in irritation. "He said there was nothing good about it."

I took a deep breath to keep my heart from leaping out of my throat. "Breath and thorns, I thought we were dead."

"Not enough light." She gestured toward the fires. "Their bodies block most of the fires." A pause. "Ah, there!"

I followed her to one of the shelters. She bent, removing a pack from beneath the shelter. On the march, Kristianos carried their weapons by lashing them onto a pack. This one bore a crossbow with its quiver, a sword, and a knife. She grinned as she straightened and pulled out one of the short arrows, testing the *hierro* tip with her thumb.

"We don't want to take too much." I tried to keep the quaver out of my voice. "We'd look suspicious hauling half of their weapons away. So let's get out of here."

She fingered the crossbow's wet wood, then slipped the heavy pack over her shoulder. I was ready to run—as fast as I could with a hurt leg—but to my surprise, Pearl Hand was staring intently at the cluster of huts no more than a vigorous rock's throw distant.

I almost cried, "What are you thinking?"

"Shhh!" Then she headed straight for the center of camp.

Desperate, I looked back at the darkness beyond the

knots of men around the fires. *Safety. Right there. All we need to do is back away, and we're free.*

Pearl Hand, however, was walking purposefully toward the huts. For a moment, heart pounding, I couldn't make myself move. Then, my guts in a cold knot, I cursed under my breath and hurried after her.

Blood and muck, she's going to get us killed.

FIVE

AT NAPETUCA, WHEN THE FIGHT TURNED AGAINST us, Blood Thorn and I had fled to the safety of a lake. There, after two days treading water, I was dying from the cold. As my souls slipped away, I was dragged down to the Underworld by the Spirit Beast we call Piasa. Part panther, part snake, and part bird, the Piasa rules the Underworld. He frightens me. But not even Water Panther scared me as much as Horned Serpent had the time he seized me in his mouth and bore me to the Sky World. There, he ate me alive while I wailed in abject terror.

As I limped after Pearl Hand, I was almost as fear-numb as I'd been when Horned Serpent crushed my body and swallowed it. Almost.

Somehow I managed—breath shivering in my chest—to follow her into the very heart of the Kristiano camp.

Soft voices came from under the cobbled-together shelters where men shivered in misery. The damp air carried the scent of pus and unwashed bodies. These were the miserably wounded, hoping to convalesce, unable to stand or make their way to the fires. Instead they had to huddle beneath their leaking roofs, curled in soggy blankets, praying desperately to their *dios*.

I made a face as I passed one such. I knew that smell: The odor of a rotting limb tickled my gag reflex. Arrow wounds always infected. I hurried even faster after Pearl Hand.

We were nearly to the first hut, its wet sides gleaming in the firelight. Pearl Hand slowed, and I hobbled up, demanding, "Have you taken leave of your—"

She slashed her arm for silence, sparing me a quick look. Just that faint glimpse in the rain-muted firelight was enough. Fear shone from her eyes.

I cursed myself under my breath. Panic had overcome my wits. What if someone had heard us speaking in Mos'kogee?

Sobered, I followed as she crept close, balanced against the weight of the pack, and placed an ear against the clay wall. She listened for a moment, then straightened, lips by my ear. "The two Kristiano women and their servants."

As I'd told Two Packs, a couple of de Soto's nobles had brought their wives along. That fact had amazed me when I first saw them in Uzita. That they'd made it this far—dressing as they did and carrying their entire households with them—amazed me. Any woman with sense would have adopted our style of clothing instead of covering her entire body with a cocoon of fabric. How they stood the heat, dealt with ticks and chiggers, or even managed to walk was beyond me.

Pearl Hand was on the move. At the next hut, she leaned close, listening.

"Nothing," she whispered.

I stiffened as a dark form came splashing through the night, head down. From the dress, the walk, this was one of their slaves. Even in the darkness I could tell he was

Timucua, among the first captives who had adopted the Kristiano god and subjected themselves to the monsters. I turned, using the helmet to shadow my face.

The man barely spared us a glance, slogging barefoot through the cold mud.

At the next hut, Pearl Hand listened again, hesitated, and shook her head.

In the exact center of camp, where it was illuminated by a roaring fire, stood the largest of the structures. Once a multiroom farmstead, the building was walled with daub, roofed with thatch. Several of the cabayos stood tied to the ramada, heads down. Each had one of its rear feet lifted and cocked in a way I'd never seen before.

More to the point, two guards in full armor dripped water on either side of the doorway. Each held a spear-ax, and from the movements of their heads they were talking.

Pearl Hand grabbed my hand, leaned close, and whispered, "Stop walking like you're sneaking. Act normal."

Sure. When at any moment a voice was going to call out an alarm?

But I held her hand, bent my head toward hers, and let her lead me past the gap. We walked, illuminated by the fire, in plain sight. From the corner of my eye, I watched, waiting for the Kristiano cry of ¡alto!

Neither of the guards even looked our way as we slipped into the darkness behind the big house.

While my heart leaped around my chest like a frog, Pearl Hand dragged me under the eaves in back. There she yanked me down into the dark recess against the wall. I gasped as the action pulled painfully at my wound.

I could hear voices, loud and argumentative, from inside.

Pearl Hand eased out of her pack and leaned close, whispering, "If anyone comes by, kiss me hard, fondle my breasts."

"Huh?"

47

"Like a man would with a slave woman, fool," she growled in my ear. "Now be quiet while I listen."

So I huddled there, partially protected from the rain, thankful for Pearl Hand's warm body against mine. For a time I tried to understand the rapid-fire conversation within, picking a word or two of *español* from the mix. For the most part, it was just gibberish. What was plain, no matter what the language, was the heated nature of the exchange.

Voices began with *"Adelantado, por favor..."* But plead as they might, the end was always the same: a violently snapped order barked out in a manner that brooked no contradiction.

"What are they saying?" I finally whispered.

"Shhh!"

I'd begun to shiver, this time from the cold. While we were behind the drip line, the water cascading from the roof was splashing in pools, spattering us.

"¡Basta!" de Soto's voice roared from within. *"Es mi decisión. ¡Afuera!"*

Pearl Hand gave my hand a quick squeeze. When she rose, I couldn't get up. The cold, the stiffening of my wound, and the fact that my legs had gone to sleep left me feeling foolish and helpless. Pearl Hand pulled me up, held me until I could stand. I took a few tottering and tentative steps, and we started back the way we'd come.

"What did they say?"

"Later."

Somehow we lost our way among the pitiful shelters. I knew the direction we needed to go, but we were winding along, seeking the darkest route. The rain was getting lighter.

I heard voices and, looking back, could see Kristianos emerging from the farmhouse. De Soto's council was breaking up. These were the subchiefs, better dressed than the *soldados,* to be sure, but still shabby looking. Many had arms or legs bandaged. As they donned their helmets against the rain, they broke into small groups around the fire, arms waving, still arguing and shooting wary glances back at the doorway where de Soto remained.

I wanted to hurry, but Pearl Hand reached out to slow my frantic steps. "Careful," she whispered. "We're supposed to act like we belong here."

"I don't belong here any more than I belong in a Piasa's bowels."

Two men started in our direction, coming with purpose.

"We're spotted." My voice almost broke with panic.

Pearl Hand glanced back, gauging the approaching pair. "Shhh! Impossible. They're just coming this way. Walk normally."

I tried to. I really did. Then metal clinked just ahead. Slowing, I could barely make out the shadowy forms of slaves huddled among a collection of thick posts driven into the ground. The clink came again, and from experience and nightmares I knew the sound: chains.

In the gloom I made out perhaps thirty naked people. They'd done their best to press together for warmth—as much as the short chains would allow. Firelight reflected off their wet skin and gleamed on the *hierro* links. These in turn were fastened to the posts. Over the patter of rain on my helmet, I could hear the chattering of their teeth, the low moans of suffering.

Just to the left was a rudely domed hut, smaller, with a low roof. I wondered at how silent it was and why it would be adjacent to the chained slaves.

As cold as I was, I could imagine their misery. Was there any way to set them free? In the darkness, without tools, it would be impossible. *Yes, and even if you did, they'd immediately run. The whole camp would be alerted.*

I could hear the men behind us now. Pearl Hand shot a look over her shoulder and led me off between two of the sodden shelters. She crouched, slipping out of her pack, and pulled me down. Again my leg screamed its agony.

Together we eased under the edge of a mat overhang, merging with the shadows. I landed atop a chunky crossbow, its angles poking angrily into my flesh. A man's sleep-purled breath came from no more than an arm's length away. His sweat-sour Kristiano stink burned in my nose. In the darkness, I thought I could see his blanket-covered form. My fingers encountered a quiver full of crossbow arrows next to his blanket.

Splashing feet announced the arrival of the two, their conversation heated. They were obviously trying to keep it low, but the passion carried. I caught the words *"loco"* and *"imprudente."*

"¡Este es un decepción!" I knew that voice, remembered it from when we had taken the young Kristiano captive. *Antonio!*

Images of his cruel face flashed between my souls. He'd smiled as he rode me down outside Mabila, sword swinging. That same sword had slung crimson gore in Napetuca, and Antonio had laughed as he lopped off the arms and legs of captive warriors outside the Apalachee capital of Anhaica.

And tonight he will smile his last. I dragged the crossbow out from underneath me, starting to rise. I'd have at least a heartbeat or two before Antonio recognized the threat. By then I'd be beating him to death.

Pearl Hand's grip, strong as an eagle's, tightened around my arm. As I tried to pull away, she squeezed harder. In the darkness, I could barely make out the shaking of her head.

I started to whisper, "But it's—" only to have her place the fingers of her other hand over my lips.

Antonio's companion kept repeating, *"Desastre,"* over and over.

"*¡Silencio!*" Antonio hissed. "*¿Quieres matar? Sí, el Adelantado se oído . . . hay nunca pero muerto por usted! No se permite discordia.*"

"*Solamente quedamos desilusianado,*" the companion said sadly.

"*Cobarde,*" Antonio spat. Then he barked a short laugh. "*Necesitas una mujer. Con un pene duro, siempre hay esperanza.*"

"*Sí, feo. Otra vez te piensas con sus huevos.*"

I heard the slap of a hand on a shoulder, as if for reassurance, and the two splashed off.

Pearl Hand kept her talonlike grip on my arm, leaning forward to whisper, "Not now! Come. We've got to talk."

Easing from under the shelter, I raised my head, glancing around. Antonio and his companion skirted the chained slaves, calling out, "*¿Qué pasa, Marcos? ¿Tienes mujeres para dos hombres?*"

"*Sí, señores. Joven y linda, y con virginidad!*" a guard answered, rising from the door of the low, round-roofed hut. That shocked me. I hadn't even seen the man.

Biting against the pain, I clambered to my feet and shouldered the quiver. My hands held the reassuring weight of the crossbow. Pearl Hand rose, hard eyes on Antonio and his friend as they each bent to place indistinct objects in the shadows near the hut door.

Rain pattered on my helmet, but the drops were smaller. I glanced up. The sky might have been brighter. Or it might have been just my imagination.

Pearl Hand led the way; we skirted around the chained slaves. The great watch fires were still surrounded by men, but I could see that the flames had burned down considerably. The wet wood that had been added was puffing clouds of gaudy red smoke into the air.

"I could sneak up behind him," I said insistently, "just close enough to drive an arrow through his back."

"And wake the whole camp?"

"I *owe* him."

"We all do. Now is not the time. We need to get out of here."

"Pearl Hand, it's Antonio who—"

"And if you try to kill him, you'll kill *us* in the process! Don't be a fool!"

As she led me around the miserable, shivering slaves, I wasn't surprised to see a doorway in the low hut. The guard crouched to one side, a sodden blanket around his shoulders, helmeted head down to shed the rain. Just enough fire was burning inside to illuminate the interior. I stopped short, staring.

Inside, Antonio was on his knees, stripping off his batted armor shirt. Even as I watched, he began undoing his belt. In front of him sat a despondent woman, stark naked against the chill. Her hair hung in a filthy tangle over her shoulders. Expressionless, eyes vacant, she wearily dropped onto her back and spread her muscular brown legs to expose the black triangle of her pubic hair. She turned her head to the side as Antonio—pants knotted around his knees—threw himself onto her limp body.

I pulled an arrow out of the quiver. She was someone's daughter or wife. She'd been a young woman with a life and future, full of dreams and love. Once she'd laughed, smiled, and delighted herself with the little things in life: a pretty sunrise, the first spring flowers . . .

"Black Shell," Pearl Hand growled, "there will be a time. I promise."

"Yes, and it's now."

I took a step, only to have her pull me back. "Not now! I have things to tell you. *Important* things."

Indecision tore at me as I watched his skinny white butt jerking up and down. *It's not even ten paces. I can drive an arrow right through his spine.*

"Black Shell," Pearl Hand said insistently. *"Please?"*

I grudgingly started to turn away, but a gleam caught my eye: the objects Antonio had leaned against the hut wall. I studied the situation, considering where the guard crouched, the curvature of the wall. "I must do something before we leave. And no, I won't kill the wormy little Kristiano maggot."

"What?"

"Trust me." I slipped the weapons pack from my shoulder. "Stay here and don't move."

"Black Shell, so help me . . ." I could hear the terror behind her voice.

"Shhh! It will take but a moment."

I eased through the shadows, crept along the side of the low hut, and reached out, fingers trembling, to retrieve my prize. I backed away, feet sucking in the mud, and hurried to Pearl Hand.

My only regret was that Antonio would have no idea who was responsible.

Still, not until we'd reached the edge of camp and eased out into the night with my prize did I realize . . .

I wasn't scared any longer.

SIX

"WE'RE ACTING LIKE A BUNCH OF FLUSHED QUAIL. Why do we have to be in such a rush?" Two Packs groused as he slogged down the muddy trail ahead of me. Pearl Hand followed, the dogs winding in and out of our path as we slipped and scrambled.

This was the first time they'd ever taken the trail without packs. You'd have thought they were puppies again, running and coursing, tails slashing the dew-covered grass. They'd pounce, feet first, trying to catch voles or mice, or charge off after rabbits, flush bobwhite, mockingly growl as they pushed and shoved.

As I struggled under the weight of my own pack, battled for footing in the slick clay-black mud, and endured the pain of my wound, I vowed that first thing when we arrived wherever it was we were going, I'd look for leather and start building new packs for my frisky beasts.

As daylight grayed the east, I could see the spoils from our night's scout: two heavy weapons packs—in addition to Two Packs's battered trade pack—swinging from the man's wide shoulders.

Me, I hobbled along as best my wounded leg and fatigued body would allow. Granted, my load only consisted of blankets, a couple of sacks of provisions, the sacred mace, and, of course, my prize stolen from Antonio. But it had been a long day, followed by a longer, colder night. My reserves had been pushed about as far as they could go.

In answer to Two Packs's question I replied, "Pearl Hand says march? We march." My breath fogged before my face.

Behind me, she called, "They're going to be right behind us."

I muttered, "I wish you'd tell me—"

"Save your breath for travel, husband," she retorted. "Find us a place to lie low, then I'll tell you everything. Besides, I need to think about it, put everything in its place."

Two Packs tilted his wet head, shooting an evil squint at the low clouds visible through the dripping branches. They continued to scud down from the north trailing misty strings of rain.

"Where, exactly, are we headed?" he asked.

"Apafalaya," she answered. "It's the closest Nation to the west, isn't it?"

Made up of Albaamaha-speaking people, the Apafalaya Nation lay on the lower reaches of the Black Warrior River and consisted of a collection of towns, each with its own mikko—a relative of the High Mikko Apafalaya.

"Maybe you'd better not introduce yourself as a Chicaza for once." Two Packs half turned to give me a knowing look.

"Why not?" Pearl Hand asked.

Two Packs shrugged his massive shoulders. "I've traded there for years. Generations ago the Chicaza conquered the Albaamaha. That was back when the Sky Hand People—the ancestral Chicaza—lived at Split Sky City. Warfare with the Choctaw and the Natchez off to the west led the Chicaza to strengthen their western border along the Tombigbee River. Split Sky City became more of a ritual site than a capital. Holy ground, if you will. Some, like Tuskaloosa's ancestors, moved south, establishing their own Nation. The Albaamaha who remained in the Black Warrior valley allied with him. The Chicaza took a dim view of that but never got around to reasserting control. Most of their efforts have gone into fighting the Natchez, Quizquiz, and Choctaw. And they've paid for it. Chicaza is a smaller Nation now, toughened by war. They like to train their young men by raiding the Apafalaya before they send them off to fight the Natchez. The constant raids drive the Apafalaya into a frenzy. But knowing the Chicaza just use them to train young and inexperienced warriors? That makes those people foam at the mouth."

"Ah, the price of Chicaza arrogance." Pearl Hand's tone brought a flush to my neck. She so loved to goad me on occasion. "Is that who Black Shell was fighting that long-ago day when he ran away and got declared a coward?"

"It was the Natchez," I snapped, so fatigued I didn't bother to keep the acid from my voice.

"My, touchy today."

I took the bait, craning my head around to see her give me a wink. Bad move. I had just started to turn when I tripped over my feet and tumbled face-first into the mud. The sacred mace hit my back with the force of a swung mallet. Burdened by the pack of blankets, swords, Kristiano armor, and bowls, I didn't have the strength to get up.

"Black Shell?" Pearl Hand was crouching beside me, concern in her eyes.

"Sorry." I ground my teeth against the pain. "I guess all of my Chicaza arrogance has finally run out."

"Forgive me. Are you all right?"

"My leg hurts." I rolled over, checking the wound. Miraculously, it hadn't broken open again. The dogs were crowding around, getting in the way, sniffing, trying to figure out what I was doing down on their level. Gnaw struck his wet nose to mine, licking me across the lips.

Vile beast.

"Come on." Two Packs pushed the dogs aside with a foot, then leaned down, and despite the load he carried, lifted me to my feet. I wobbled, panting for air.

"It's the wound," I murmured. "It's as if I can't get my old strength back."

Two Packs gave me a mocking smile. "You're not the trader you used to be."

"Maybe I never was the trader I used to be. Thought of that, have you?"

He studied the mulberry and chestnut forest around us. Water had left dark streaks down the bark; thick vines hung like crooked gray rope. The forest was oddly quiet, the musty smell of wet leaves heavy in the cold air. "I know this trail. About a hand's time up yonder"—Two Packs pointed—"there's a cluster of farmsteads off to the north. We walk past on the main trail to where it starts up the slope. Our tracks will fade, and we can circle back through the forest. Any pursuing Kristianos will ride right on past."

"I can make it," I promised.

"Good. I really want to hear what you learned last night in the Kristiano camp." He glanced at Pearl Hand, clearly irritated by her continuing silence.

My concentration went into limping along the forest trail, trying not to fall over myself or any of the dogs, who occasionally, and negligently, wandered into my path.

The farmstead Two Packs referred to consisted of six,

two- or three-room houses a little way off the trail. The occupants had chosen this place because a stream ran out of the hills to the north, occasionally flooding the field-studded delta before it cut down into the black clay and meandered south.

We reached the place by midmorning. Like so many of the homes around Mabila—with its infestation of marauding Kristianos—the locals had fled. I stopped at the edge of the small clearing, seeing the houses neatly roofed in thatch, the clay walls painted white and red. The doors had been sealed, and no smoke rose from around the eaves.

The little settlement had all the fixings: three ramadas, several log pestles and mortars, screened latrines in the back, and a high granary standing on smoothed posts. A central fire pit was filled with wet charcoal; seats made of log had been placed around it, the wood polished smooth by human butts.

Small garden plots beside each house had furnished pumpkins, squash, beans, beeweed, and goosefoot to complement the cornfields along the floodplain. Persimmon, hickory, walnut, quapaw, and mulberry trees surrounded the margins, no doubt tended by the farmers.

I leaned against the largest house while Two Packs slung the load from his shoulders and untied the door fastenings.

I ducked inside, squinting about and finding a central puddle-clay hearth, neatly cleaned with a fire already laid. The side and back walls were fitted with high sleeping benches, while beneath them, sealed ceramic jars were canted on their rounded bottoms. Several wooden boxes, their tops engraved to depict ivory-billed woodpeckers, no doubt held personal items. On one sleeping bench a pile of toys rested: corn-husk dolls; a child's bow and practice arrows; a bola and its stones; and small, crudely made bowls and jars.

I looked no farther but made my way to the bed, hitched myself onto the frame, and gasped in relief.

"Dogs," Pearl Hand ordered, "out!"

I watched my beloved dogs, desperate to catch one last sniff, slowly funnel out into the morning. Bark remained in the doorway, his scarred head cocked, tail wagging as he watched us. Like the rest of us, he had to be hungry, wondering where the next meal would come from.

So was I.

Two Packs opened his pack, retrieving a fire bow. While he bent to the hearth, Pearl Hand began pulling jars from under the benches, opening the wooden lids, and inspecting the contents.

"Where do you think they went?" Pearl Hand asked.

"The whole countryside is turned upside down," Two Packs growled. "As I remember these people had kin up in Talicpacana town as well as in Mabila."

"Albaamaha?" I asked.

Two Packs nodded as the first fingers of smoke rose from his spinning dowel. "Pot people." He referred to the Albaamaha habit of burying their dead in large ceramic jars after the bones were cleaned in the charnel house. "Good people and hospitable. The matron, Tight Mat, she's a widow and a most handsome woman." He grinned. "She always took *special* care of me."

"Figures." I looked at Pearl Hand, who stood and exhibited a pot filled with milled corn.

She said, "I'll take a water jar down to the creek. We can make a gruel, add some of the walnuts and dried blueberries. Then there's cattail-root flower and some beeweed for taste."

"That's the most wonderful thing you've ever said to me."

She gave me a measuring glance, reading my fatigue. "If it is, your memory must be as worn out as the rest of you." Then she was out the door.

I never saw her return. Silly me, I'd fallen into a deep

sleep. Perhaps I dreamed. I don't know. But for the first time since Mabila, I didn't wake up screaming.

The fire in the puddle-clay hearth popped and spat bright yellow sparks toward the roof. Outside it was cold, windy, and wet. The storm couldn't make up its mind if it was raining or snowing. For us the snug house was a blessing with its cheery warm fire, dry beds, and solid roof overhead.

On the dirt floor, the dogs lay sprawled just back from the fire, lost in dreams. Two Packs, Pearl Hand, and I perched on the pole beds built into the walls. In the dancing firelight, Two Packs inspected the Kristiano sword I'd given him. Then he resumed his study of the crossbow, running fingers down the polished wood, checking the pull on the bowstring. It was a mark of the weapon's power that even Two Packs—the strongest man I knew—couldn't set it by hand.

Me, I admired the prize Antonio had left propped against the women's hut: the highly polished sword he'd used to kill so many of our people. The one that had sliced so deeply into my arm and leg. Now it was mine, and all I could dream about was how I'd use it to cut Antonio into little bloody chunks of meat.

"Things are changing." Pearl Hand leaned forward, arms propped on the bed frame, expression thoughtful. "The last time I overheard one of their councils, it was among the Uzachile. That time, each of de Soto's *capitanes* had a say. They argued among each other, de Soto listening, asking questions. This time when the *capitanes* tried to disagree, he snapped at them. He demands immediate and complete obedience."

The fire accented the hollows of Pearl Hand's cheeks, her straight nose and firm jaw. It seemed to sparkle and play in her large dark eyes and cast gold highlights on her rich black hair.

"They were talking about food. They are out. The question was whether the wounded were well enough to travel and which direction they should head." A pause. "They argued about how far the slaves could carry what few possessions they have left."

I said, "Those poor captive wretches we saw won't be able to go far. And after this storm? Half of them will be dead."

Pearl Hand nodded sadly. "The *Adelantado* is very aware of that. It's one of the reasons he picked Apafalaya as his next destination. He thinks that by professing peace, he'll be able to trick the mikko into providing *tamemes*, food, and clothing."

"And he'll probably get it," Two Packs added. "I know the mikko. After the disaster at Mabila, he'll be torn in half trying to decide if he should run, hide, waffle, or fight."

"De Soto ordered his men to be on the trail by midday today," Pearl Hand added.

"But his ships are south," Two Packs murmured softly. "Surely they'd have food."

Pearl Hand gave us both a knowing look. "Believe me, the *soldados* and *capitanes* know full well how low rations are getting. Winter is coming, and this storm just emphasizes the threat. Most want to go south, but de Soto reminded them of how scarce food was in the salt-scrublands south of Apalachee."

"What about the piles of baggage he lost at Mabila?" I asked. "Surely the ships brought enough supplies to refit his army. Clothing, boots, food, tents . . . everything that burned."

She cocked her head, giving me a baffled look. "One of the *capitanes* asked about the ships. A man named Maldonado is in command of them. De Soto angrily replied, 'We don't know where to look for Maldonado. He could be anywhere.'"

"I don't understand." I fingered my chin and resettled myself on the sleeping bench. "Any of the recent captives could have told him about the ships at Ochuse. Even to the point of giving him directions on where to find them. It's a major topic of conversation in every town and camp south of Mabila."

She shrugged, looking mystified. "Then for once it would seem that we know something the Kristianos don't."

"Do we? Or is he keeping it to himself for some reason?"

Two Packs looked confused. "Is he intent on his own destruction?"

Pearl Hand shook her head. "He didn't sound like it. He sounded so sure of himself, as if he were the holder of some great and absolute truth."

"Just wait," I countered. "As dispirited as his *soldados* are, they'll scramble off like children after sweet corn cakes the moment they hear those ships are waiting."

Pearl Hand's stare sharpened. "Do you think?"

"Think what?" My turn to be baffled.

A crooked smile bent her lips. "Do you think that's what he's doing? Hiding the fact from his men? Think about who he is, how he sees himself. You've said it yourself: He's arrogant unlike any man we've ever known. No matter what the setback, he's always found a way. Just like on the plaza at Mabila, or when White Rose surrendered Cofitachequi to him, or when he tired of fighting the Apalachee." She nodded thoughtfully. "He thinks he can save himself."

"How?" Two Packs demanded.

I sensed the truth of it. "Pearl Hand is right. He's always done the unexpected, and it's always paid off."

"Still . . . Black Shell makes a point," Pearl Hand told him. "The *soldados* and cabayeros are shaken, many of them wounded, without supplies. If they learned about the ships, they'd bolt for the coast."

"Where the Pensacola are waiting to wipe them out."
I tenderly prodded the scabbed wound on my thigh.
"His only chance is to keep them as far from the ships as
he can."

Pearl Hand chuckled to herself, eyes fixed on the fire.

"Want to share with the rest of us?" I asked.

An ironic smile on her lips, she said, "He's in a real
predicament. The only way he can replace what was
burned in Mabila is by meeting up with the ships down
south. But if he does, his men will revolt, demanding to
be taken back home."

The lines of concentration in her high forehead deepened. "You heard Antonio and his friend? That discussion they had?"

"My ability in that language is limited to hurling insults."

"Thank Breath Giver above you have me. Antonio and
his friend believe everything is lost. They as much as called
the *Adelantado* a fool. Both think it's a disaster—and that
they're being misled. Even better, Antonio said, *'No se permite
discordia.'* De Soto punishes dissent in the ranks. And Antonio and his friend weren't the only ones. No one in that
camp was happy."

I shot her an evil look. "You should have let me beat
him to death with that crossbow."

"Had I, you might not have had the chance to steal his
sword and armor." Her smile turned wry. "You remember
what Antonio's friend called him? I'll repeat it: *'feo.'* You
know what *feo* means?"

"Uh . . . no."

"It means 'ugly.' The wreck you made of Antonio's face
at Mabila is sticking with him."

I allowed myself the smallest of grins, reliving the moment. I'd already sliced his left cheek open with an arrow.
Then I'd whipped a sword cut across his face, the blade
stopped short by the margins of his *hierro* helmet. It had

opened a gaping split down to the cheekbones and left his nose hanging.

"And the rest? You know, after the part about his being ugly?"

Pearl Hand chuckled. "His boon companion has come to the conclusion that Antonio only thinks with his balls."

I remembered how he'd stared at Pearl Hand's body when we had him captive down in the peninsula. At the memory I reached over and patted my stolen prize.

Pearl Hand saw, arching an eyebrow. "Happy with that, aren't you?"

"I told you to trust me." Even as I said it, I pulled Antonio's sword from its scabbard and rapped the hilt on the hard curve of his once-impregnable *hierro* breastplate. "This is the second time we've stolen his armor."

"He's going to be furious," Pearl Hand said thoughtfully.

"Fuming and foaming at the mouth." I smiled agreement, studying the breastplate. "It's always been way too big for him."

"So, what's the plan?" Two Packs asked.

I studied the shining sword, firelight gleaming on the *hierro* blade. The hilt was a thing of beauty, a silver basket woven to protect the hand, the grip soft leather bound by threads of stringlike metal. Red and green polished stones, almost transparent, like the finest chert, had been set into the silver. They sparkled in the light.

I'd seen this same blade so fouled with blood at Napetuca that it slung thin streamers with every stroke Antonio made as he waded through victims. I touched the keen edge, painfully aware it had eaten deeply into my own thigh and arm. My wounds almost ached at its mere presence.

I mused, "De Soto is heading away from his supply, away from any chance to escape. You say the Apafalaya mikko is unreliable?"

Two Packs shrugged. "The answer to that floats like a leaf on the wind."

I tapped a thumbnail on Antonio's blade, hearing it ring musically. "If the Apafalaya mikko is going to fight, fine. If not, I say we race the Monster to Chicaza."

"And then?" Pearl Hand asked.

Tingles of fear—mixed with excitement—ran along my bones. "I figure out a way to convince my brother not to murder me. Then I work out how I can give Antonio his sword back." My jaws ground before I added, "Point first."

SEVEN

RESTED, WITH FULL BELLIES AND PACKS, WE STARTED across the wooded hills that lay between us and Apafalaya territory. The way led beneath spreading red and black oaks, immense hickories, and tall black gums. As if to break the monotony, the forest was sprinkled here and there with tall and majestic cedars. Periodic stands of pine were surrendering to maples and poplars—evidence of old burns.

The atrocious black clay soil, thankfully, had given way to loamy yellow dirt that provided solid footing. Occasionally, as we topped ridges, crumbling outcrops of sandstone lurked beneath the leaf mat.

Low gray clouds masked Mother Sun's path across the Sky World. Their bottoms were torn, as if snagged; dark masses trailed streamers of rain, sometimes severe, other times tapering to a misty and silent drizzle.

I was feeling better—but then I also had the *hierro* helmet, so my head was dry. Pearl Hand and Two Packs slogged miserably along, protected only by bark rain hats. The dogs padded happily over roots, rocks, leaves, and deadfall. When they got to feeling too wet, they'd walk up close beside me, stop short, and shake from nose to tail tip.

Maybe they liked my bellow of rage. More likely they knew I was wounded—certainly not moving fast enough to give them a healthy kick. Whatever their motives, they acted amused as they skipped gleefully away from my wrath.

Around us the forest was uncharacteristically quiet but for the heavy drops of water that dripped from naked branches. They hit the leaf mat with a mild slapping sound. When they burst on my *hierro* helmet, it was with a ringing noise.

No more than a hand's time on the trail, and we were cold, soaked, shivering, and thoroughly miserable. Our only solace was that the Kristianos—many severely wounded—had to be even more wretched.

You're headed home, Black Shell. And when you get there? What then?

I'd been branded a coward, declared dead to my family and clan. So great was my disgrace that I'd been exiled— all relations with home, hearth, and my people severed forever. The declaration of akeohoosa wasn't something my Chicaza made lightly.

Reconciliation could be had. It involved making an application to the high minko and the hopaye during the moon before the Green Corn Ceremony. What we called "the Busk." Gifts had to be sent, apologies tendered, and offerings made. Then, at the height of the ceremony, when the sacred fire was rekindled, signifying the rebirth of the world, the poor wretch might be forgiven, his reputation renewed.

At least, it could happen that way if the akeohoosa wasn't Chief Clan. If he wasn't the direct heir to the panther stool—the future high minko of the Chicaza Nation. If he wasn't someone like me.

Chief Clan was held to a higher standard.

No matter what the threat from de Soto, no one is going to be happy to see me.

I was feeling even more depressed when Gnaw trotted in from the side, stopped short, and shook from nose to tail. I roared as the cold spray soaked my clothing.

A couple of nights later we made camp in the ruins of Split Sky City. "Ruins" may be too strong a term. The place has become—and will forever remain—a city of the dead. Perched atop a high bluff overlooking a loop of the Black Warrior River, it was designed by my ancestors and built with the blood, sweat, and hard labor of the conquered Albaamaha.

My ancestors called themselves the Sky Hand, named for the constellation that marked the opening in the Sky World: the Seeing Hand. In mid-spring, right after sunset, the constellation lies on the western horizon. At that time the souls of the dead, after traveling to the edge of the earth, can leap across the narrow gap between worlds. Those found worthy pass through the Seeing Hand and continue their journey toward the Path of the Dead and the revered ancestors.

The unworthy tumble into the abyss.

My people lived at Split Sky City for generations. They created a great Nation that dominated both the Black Warrior River and the Tombigbee, off to the west. It is said that the Coosa, the Apalachee, and the Pensacola bowed at mention of the Sky Hand—and that tribute poured into Split Sky City from all corners of the world. That not since fabled Cahokia had a people gained such prestige.

And then, so the stories go, the great high minkos began to think of themselves as gods. Not just in Chicaza, but all over our world. In their arrogance, they challenged the Spirit Beasts, and perhaps even Breath Giver.

Whatever the cause, the Spirit Beasts refused to call the rains. The winds blew cold and bitter weather down from the north, frosting the few drought-shriveled crops left in the fields. Famine—as always—led to war. Red Power raged across the land.

Even before the terrible droughts, fires, and freezes, Split Sky City had become a sacred shrine for both the ancestral Chicaza and the Albaamaha. The greatest honor that could be paid to a recently deceased leader was to bury his remains in the mounds at Split Sky City.

After more than one hundred and fifty years of war, the great Nations were either broken and vanished or collapsed into the surviving Chicaza, Albaamaha, Coosa, Natchez, and others. They existed as mere shadows of their ancestral magnificence. That vanished greatness extended to Split Sky City, now a collection of grassy mounds, shrines, and haunting burials. Here, the ghosts of our ancestors walked on moonlit nights. Here was our most holy ground.

Approaching the city we crossed the long-abandoned farmland. The forest here was young, the trees no more than a hundred years old. The leaf mat beneath, however, still bore the stippled irregularities of fields. Low humps of earth marked where houses had stood. Occasional bits of broken pottery protruded from the blanket of leaves where squirrels and deer had disturbed the soil; the dirt was black from ash.

The trail wound through brushy forest margins, and when we stepped into the open we stopped short. Breath puffing in the cold air, I marveled at the great earthen mounds of Split Sky City. Nothing I'd seen in my travels could rival it, though I'd heard that Cahokia was larger.

In awe of the immensity, I shook my head, trying to imagine the city as it had been at its height. How many people? How many buildings? How tall had been the mighty temples atop those still-impressive earthen mounds?

Pearl Hand stepped out beside me, a look of disbelief on her face. Her lips parted, eyes widening. She stood speechless.

"Looks a little more overgrown," Two Packs blurted irreverently. He pointed to the fuzzy growth of poplars that had sprung up in the old stickball grounds. "Didn't the Albaamaha used to cut those out?"

I sighed, touching my forehead respectfully as I started forward past the shrines that marked the boundaries of the sacred city.

"They did. Maybe they've had more pressing problems dished out to them recently."

"Everything's falling apart," Two Packs muttered, shaking his head. "Maybe we're living the end of the world. Ever thought of that?"

"More often than you could know," I whispered, following the trail across grassy flats and past the Panther Clan mound. Atop its grass-covered heights, a small ramada stood, its roof in tatters. Pilgrims no doubt had built it for protection as they offered prayers to their ancestors, the pitiful construction a far cry from the great temple that had once dominated those heights.

As I entered the plaza, a shiver slipped down my spine. Images played at the edge of my vision, as if colorful, feather-bedecked players, ball sticks in hand, raced just beyond the limits of my vision. The distant whisper of wind in the winter-bare branches might have been the echo of watching crowds, cheering the long-dead players.

I shot a worried glance at the Chief Clan mound, its green top square and prominent against the stormy sky.

Are you up there, great-uncle? Even now do you see me pass below?

The eerie feeling of hidden eyes, watching, evaluating, made the hair at the nape of my neck lift.

Pearl Hand stared around, struggling to take in the

majesty of the place. Then she glanced at the darkening sky. "Night's coming. Where to?"

"The canoe landing." I pointed northwest toward the gap between the old tchkofa mound and the towering Chief Clan mound. The bulk of the Raccoon Clan mound marked the trailhead that led down the only easy slope to the river. "If there's any shelter, it will be there."

Even the dogs acted cowed as we walked across that silent and vacant land. I winced, sensing the dead as they reached out to finger the hem of my hunting shirt. Their whispers hid in the tall grass as they pointed at and hissed about my Kristiano helmet.

Another shiver played between my souls; I inexplicably reached around and brought the great copper mace from its carry sack. Holding it before me, I arched my back and limped forward.

Filling my lungs, I called out, "I am Black Shell, of the Chief Clan, of the Hickory Moiety. Let me pass in peace!"

Face straight, I ignored the curious looks Pearl Hand and Two Packs shot my way.

As if in reply to the mace's presence and my challenge, a warmth filled the sepaya where it bounced against my breast.

"Afraid the dead wouldn't recognize you?" Two Packs asked dryly as we passed beneath the tchkofa mound.

"In this hat?" I asked from the corner of my mouth. "My own mother wouldn't know me."

"Knowing what I do of your mother, you'd better keep that hat on when we get to Chicaza."

Joking broke the tension, but the Power of the place, the eyes of the dead staring so intently, pressed down from all sides.

Generations of feet had worn deep trails into the slope that descended to the canoe landing on the Black Warrior River. Just up from the high-water mark, pilgrims had constructed a small temple with clay walls and a split-cane roof. Around it, guardian posts in the shape of Panther, Snapping Turtle, Falcon, Raccoon, and Rattlesnake stood facing the cardinal directions. Stepping inside and squinting in the dim light I could see the image of Tailed Man rendered on the rear wall, indicating it was an Albaamaha shrine. A stack of dry wood had been placed below one of the benches surrounding the walls. Other boxes contained ritual materials—feathers, masks, capes, and wands. Those we didn't touch.

Two Packs busied himself with the fire while Pearl Hand and I scouted the riverbank for driftwood. As much rain as we'd had, nothing was dry, but with a hot enough fire, even the stuff we scrounged would burn. And we needed to leave as much wood drying out for future use as we'd found. To do so was just polite.

I stopped in my task and turned uneasy eyes on the river. Murky brown water lapped at the sandy shore; its surface roiled, sucked, and swirled, all patterned with the spreading rings of falling rain. After being wounded in Mabila, I'd hung between life and death. Fevered, I'd had a Spirit Dream, the images of it as perfectly preserved between my souls now as they'd been then. My feet had been planted right here, on this very spot. As I had looked up at Split Sky City, Horned Serpent had risen behind me, his majestic wings spread . . .

I glanced nervously over my shoulder. Nothing but evening-silvered water stretched smoothly across to the other bank.

"Want to tell me about it?" Pearl Hand asked.

"Everything it means to be Chicaza . . . it all comes back to here. To this place."

She shot a look across the river, then back to where a couple of canoes rested upside down on logs just off to our left. "Sure you don't want to cross? We've just enough daylight."

I indicated the darkening clouds. "It'll rain harder tonight. Maybe snow. And, dear wife, if I'm not safe surrounded by my ancestors, where on earth will I be?"

Swallowing hard I fingered the sepaya, aware that it had turned as cold as the damp air and every bit as uncaring.

Two Packs had no doubt kindled the fire by now. "We'll stay." My words sounded weak, even to me.

After we'd eaten, I sat on the back bench with the copper mace clutched in my hands.

I had always dreamed of returning to Chicaza. Exiles never truly forget. The memory was like a nagging splinter driven deep into my souls. The sort of irritating thing you pick at, dig for, but can never really pull out. Over time the festering seeps ever deeper, hardening. Though eventually scabbed, it forever remains an ache felt most poignantly in the lonely hours.

Some exiles dream of entering the plaza as long-lost kin, forgiven, even vindicated. Somehow people have discovered over time that they were wrong, that a terrible injustice was committed, and by families and clans they line up, smiles beaming, as if to express their heartfelt apology.

Another common fantasy is the victorious return at the head of a conquering war party. Having vanquished the home armies, the exile stalks into town elbow-to-elbow with his companions. Head high, he glares from side to side, enjoying the bent heads, the furtive looks from under lowered brows. The home folk chew their lips, dreading retribution for their injustice and wishing they'd never driven the victim away in the first place.

And then there was my obsessive little daydream. I saw myself entering Chicaza town, dressed in finery, shell necklaces dangling, a gleaming gorget at my throat and a copper breastplate shining on my chest. My face would be painted like a Cahokian lord's, bracelets clattering on my arms. With a knowing smile, I'd stand before my family, trade packs at my feet. While I regaled them with stories of the Timucua, the Caddo, and the Guale, I'd lay out strings of shell beads, shining pieces of copper, medicine herbs, Taino tobacco, and Calusa carvings.

When it was all done, they'd stare at such an accumulation of wealth as no Chicaza had seen since the high minkos had ruled at Split Sky City. But the dreams—like the very trade—had become ash.

Not that I was impoverished. The Kristiano armor and weapons alone were worth a fortune. It's just that I now looked exactly like what I was: a rag-clad survivor fleeing a terrible battle with what little plunder he could carry away.

Power help me, how do I go home now? What do I say? How do I enter Chicaza without looking like a failure?

Eyelids drooping, I watched the damp wood burn. It hissed, snakelike, on the coals. The sound, reminiscent of the Beginning Times, hinted of Power, magic, and wonder.

Intricate and sinuous, the smoke rose, looping around, spiraling in a clever dance. My souls grew light, wavering and airy. Light as the smoke itself, they followed the weaving patterns, turning and twirling.

I felt myself lifting, growing ever lighter and more feathery. Around and around, I danced with the smoke. *Becoming one with it, I allowed myself to drift up, pirouetting and curling . . .*

Beyond the door, rain began to patter on the packed sand. The sound mixed with the rising and falling hiss from the wood; the winding smoke was alive. Like thread it rose, only to slip sideways in the cool air.

My souls mingled with the twirls of smoke, borne aloft by the hissing fire.

Savor the sensation. Dance with the smoke. Dream, Black Shell. Dream.

EIGHT

My body floated, weightless, flipping this way and that, drifting out through the doorway and into the night.

Rocked by the warmth.

Borne upon the air like a prayer.

Dreaming...

As I floated with the smoke, the world seemed to glow, pulsing with an energy akin to that of a beating heart. The river, its surface patterned like a shining serpent's skin, slowly flowed past. And when I looked up from the canoe landing, past the temple, it was to see Split Sky City in all its glory. The metropolis was alive, thriving, and filled with throngs of colorfully dressed people. This was how the Chicaza heroes Old White, Green Snake, and Two Petals would have seen the place so many generations ago.

Atop the Raccoon Clan mound stood a massive building, its grass-thatch roof rising like an ax blade toward the oddly orange sky. People, wraithlike and oblivious, passed around me. Their voices—thousands of them—echoed and vibrated through my very being.

"All of the past to choose from, and you pick this?" an almost purring voice said from behind me.

I turned, startled—and froze in my tracks.

Piasa!

Instinctively I started to raise the copper mace, as if to strike the terrifying creature emerging from the river. Cold fear settled around my heart, and the voices, almost overwhelming but moments before, had gone still, the silence as heavy as frost on a winter meadow.

Piasa pinned me with glowing yellow eyes, the pupils black and bottomless. I watched in horror as the water panther rose, water slicking away so quickly the Spirit Beast appeared instantly dry. Its pink cougar's nose sniffed, whiskers quivering. Then the creature licked its lips, exposing long white canines and a cat's rasping tongue. It spread great wings that rose from its back and flicked the snake's tail that sprouted behind its hips.

On yellow-scaled feet, the toes tipped with eagle talons, it padded out onto the sand. In the head fur I could now see the three-forked-eye pattern that marked Piasa as master of the Underworld.

"What do you want?" My voice strangled in my throat.

Piasa's lionlike eyes fixed on me. "What I'll have in the end: you, Trader."

"We've bargained this before. The Power of trade holds. I said you could have my life. I have yet to hear your offer in return."

"I'm waiting." Piasa fixed on the copper mace held menacingly before me. Did the lips curl? Was that the barest essence of a smile? Did Piasa even have a sense

76

of humor? The creature reached out with a tentative foot, talons spread, as if it would snatch the mace. I pulled back, stepping away.

"It's not yours," I said with a growl. Well, at least as much as one dared growl at a Spirit Beast capable of disemboweling a person with a single lazy swipe of a taloned foot.

Piasa cocked its head, studying the mace. "Do you know where that came from?"

"Cahokia."

"Ah, yes, marvelous Cahokia." Its head extended, the flat pink nose sniffing. "The copper smells of the far north and of the trader who carried it to Cahokia. The scent of he who crafted it lingers, along with the echoes of each hammer blow used to forge the piece." The beast stepped even closer, its nostrils and whiskers quivering. "And the Cahokian lord who once wielded this mace from his splendid palace high atop the giant mound? He might have been the greatest of all of them. Master of most of the world. His scent? Well, the metal reeks of it." The large yellow eyes narrowed to slits. "And now it comes to you, Black Shell? You think to add your stench to such a piece? Do you think yourself equal of those incredible lords who came before?"

I swallowed hard. "My only purpose is the destruction of the Monster." My heart had begun to beat again. Just beat? Hardly. It pounded in my breast like a stone maul against a sodden log.

Nothing frightened me like Piasa.

Come on, Black Shell, you were eaten alive by Horned Serpent. You felt your body crushed as it was swallowed. What can Piasa do to compare with that?

I didn't want to find out. I took another wary step back, desperate to keep distance between us.

"Destroy the Monster?" Piasa's lips curled. "Didn't work out so well in Mabila."

"Kristianos are tough to kill. They fight better than we do, and with better weapons. That accursed armor alone—"

"It's always excuses with you. The glib tongue . . . the chatty misdirection."

I bottled the fear inside me, stepping forward. "I'm fighting for our world! *May the ancestors help me!* Why are you always against me?"

The creature's long fangs had a white glow in the dusky light. "Because I think you're a failure. You're anything but a hero. Your own people threw you out as a coward. And, of all men, Horned Serpent chose you? Has faith in you? Where are your victories? It's almost two winters now. And the Kristianos continue to pollute our soil with their filthy feet, violate our Power with their long-tailed cross." It spit its anger, the droplets like fire on my skin. "You will doom us all, Black Shell. I will curse your vanished souls for the time we've wasted."

"We're all afraid," I answered, remembering the long-ago words of Snapping Turtle when he explained Piasa's violent rage. "I can only die. But for you, facing an eternity of slow dissolution as your memory fades from the minds of men? The most terrible Spirit Beast of all, just evaporating into nothingness? No wonder you're afraid that—"

Quick as a lightning flash, the raptor-clawed foot fastened around my throat and crushed my windpipe. The bones in my neck grated and groaned. Pressure built inside my skull; my tongue jammed painfully against my teeth.

Those terrible yellow eyes were but a finger's width from mine, the black pupils expanding, swallowing my souls. As pain and terror grew, I felt myself falling into those endless inky depths. The creature's hot breath purled against my face. Stiff whiskers tickled my cheeks.

"Threaten me, will you? Challenge my courage?"

I could feel my body being shaken, but the sensation was remote, as if from a distance. My arms were flopping loosely. The mace spiraled away. The way my legs jerked this way and that they might have been made of rope. My frantic lungs heaved and sucked at my collapsed throat.

With a feline purr, Piasa said, "Time for you to die, putrid human."

The constriction around my throat tightened, flashes of sparkling light dancing at the edge of my narrowing vision. Blood pounded in my ears, my bones creaking under the pressure. Terror burst in my breast, hot and paralyzing.

From the side, a weary voice called, "Let him down. You're acting like a fool."

The pressure hesitated, and finally eased.

So quickly was I released that I slammed onto the ash-stained sand, coughing and gasping. Lifting my hands, I cradled my throat, sucking in great gulps of air. As the haze cleared from my vision, I fixed on Piasa, crouched as if to pounce, tail lashing in anger, wings wide and threatening. Those dreadful eyes remained fixed on mine, violence burning behind the eerie yellow.

"He *mocks* me!" Piasa thundered.

"One does not mock that which he truly comprehends," the soft voice replied. "And Black Shell possesses a level of understanding and sympathy that you, great Piasa, have not yet achieved, nor, I daresay, even allowed yourself to investigate."

The hateful yellow eyes narrowed. With a sinuous, almost reptilian grace, the cougar head turned and the glaring eyes focused on someone off to the side. Lungs still pumping, I blinked and followed Piasa's gaze. An old man stood at the edge of the water. I placed his age as at least sixty winters, his face lined and weathered to a dark brown. Long white hair was pulled up and pinned in a bun. His faded and worn buffalo-hide cape was missing patches of hair. Beneath it, a serviceable fabric hunting shirt was belted at the waist with a rope that supported some sort of pouch on his left hip. His right hand gripped a trader's staff, graced with white feathers. The left held an old-style monolithic hand ax—the sort mikkos once handed down as badges of office.

"Seeker," Piasa roared, "what can this *human* know that I do not?"

"The many faces of fear." The old man followed his statement with a knowing smile. "Black Shell, you see, has lived with fear all of his life. You, Piasa, as a Spirit Beast, now face it for the first time. A curious irony, don't you think? Here stands a human who hasn't even passed thirty winters, and he has an intimate understanding of fear and its nature. You, an immortal whose existence stretches back to the Beginning Times, find yourself confused, distraught, and unable to deal even with fear's minor effects. So, you see, he does not mock you. Why? Because he has an understanding—as you yourself do not—of how incapable you are of accepting, let alone controlling, fear." The old man's sympathetic eyes bored into Piasa's.

"Why do I listen to you?"

"Because, despite yourself, you learn. And because you have no other friend."

I stared in amazement. Piasa—lips now curled as if in disgust—shot me one last distasteful look. I swear, I was giving the terrible creature my complete and focused attention, but it was as if he vanished, the movement so fast it didn't even blur. Only the widening ring of water showed where Piasa had dived into the river.

"I'm not sure he'll ever manage." The old man cocked his head thoughtfully as he watched the widening rings. "Living beings are born to a wealth of emotions. They suckle fear, loneliness, helplessness, triumph, and tragedy. It becomes part of them."

"Piasa has his war with the Thunderers in the Sky World." I massaged my throat, thinking of the lightning bolts tossed down by the Winds—the monstrous ivory-billed woodpeckers—that hovered at the four corners of the world.

The old man smiled benevolently. "Do you think of it as warfare like people know it? No, Black Shell, consider it more like a game of stickball between matched teams. A scoring of points if you will. No matter the outcome, the Thunderers will never destroy the Underworld. Piasa and the tie snakes will never conquer the Sky World. They must forever remain exclusive to each other."

"Who are you?" I crawled forward and retrieved the copper mace.

"'May the ancestors help me'? I believe those were your words just before you enraged Piasa to the point of murder." The old man cocked his head, studying me through knowing brown eyes.

"You're an ancestor? From the Sky World? Come down to rescue me?"

"In order: yes, no, and no." He looked up at Split Sky City, now appearing as the forlorn and abandoned place I knew. The grassy mounds stood alone beneath the rain-thick sky. "Nothing is forever, Black Shell. Perhaps I should have taken the western road, made the leap through the Seeing Hand, and followed the Path of the Dead." He glanced back at the river. "But then, the Underworld is a place of immense beauty and magic. I've barely explored it."

81

"I ask again. Do you have a name?"

A fleeting smile bent his lips. "I've had many names, Hickory . . . Runner . . . among others. But in the end I was known as Old White, and sometimes as the Seeker."

I stumbled to my feet, gaping in disbelief. "You traveled with Green Snake and the legendary Contrary, Two Petals. It is said that you crossed the known world, coming home only to die. But then, just at the end, you traded Horned Serpent copper in return for the chance to send your souls to the Underworld."

"Something like that." He tilted his head to the rain, though the droplets never seemed to patter on his ancient skin. "Meanwhile, not even legends live forever. Not with Kristianos on the loose. My question is: Have you devised a way to enter Chicaza?"

"I assume the sepaya and the mace will suffice to at least gain us an audience with the high minko. After that, it's up to Power." I smiled uncomfortably. "And my brother's ultimate dedication to clan and family."

A wry smile bent the old man's lips. "Believe me, when it comes to family, not even appeals to Power, Eagle Man's justice, or the potential wrath of the Spirit Beasts can provide cover or safety. Like you, I have some experience with exile. My advice? There are other men of authority among the Chicaza. Respected and beloved elders who, like you, have felt the call of Power. I'd adopt an image of humility and piety. At least in the beginning. Me? I always kept self-righteous rage and indignation in reserve until after I had the situation under control."

"I think I understand."

"Win the respect of the respected, and everything else will come in due time." The Seeker arched a snowy eyebrow. "A good trader employs all of his assets to his greatest benefit. But don't take Chicaza honor lightly.

Oh, and watch out for your mother. She's . . . should we say, unforgiving?"

"I seem to recall that."

He gave me a fond smile. "Now, if you will excuse me, I must go attend to Piasa. He will need a steady voice to diffuse all that rage before he panics the fish, eels, and turtles. And Breath Giver help us if he bites a tie snake's head off before I can calm him. Such a thing would upset the water beasts to the point that they might call enough rain to flood the entire world."

"I traded Piasa my life, you know."

"It's the talk of the Underworld. Piasa doesn't know what to offer you in return. You have him in a regular stew. Even the Contrary is laughing." The old man turned, walking into the river. "So much trouble. Given what we've seen of Piasa's inability to cope with fear, we can only hope he never falls in love. Should that occur, his distress might melt the very rocks."

And with that, he disappeared under the roiling waters.

I blinked, Pearl Hand and Two Packs's faces swimming into focus. They both crowded in front of me, concerned eyes fixed on mine.

I started, rearing back, aware that I still sat on the temple bench. Beyond I could hear rain pattering on the canoe landing, and the very air seemed to whisper with the ghosts of Split Sky City. Glancing past Two Packs's shoulder, I could see the dogs sprawled on the floor, sound asleep, and no doubt thankful to be out of the cold winter rain.

"What happened to you?" Pearl Hand demanded.

"I was at the canoe landing . . . ," I said, off balance. "Talking with the Seeker."

"Who?" Two Packs's expression was dubious.

"An ancestor," I whispered, clearly seeing the old man

83

through the eye of my souls. "And before that, the Piasa . . ." I winced, reaching up to press at my throat.

"You made a horrible sound," Pearl Hand declared. "Startled us half out of our skins. You were sitting bolt upright, back arched, a terrible expression on your face. We rushed over, but you were stiff as an old oak branch. Your eyes had no focus. It was as if we weren't even here."

"I was on the landing." I pointed toward the rainy night beyond. "Piasa came. Tried to strangle me. Then Old White, the Seeker, called him off."

"Who is this Seeker?" Two Packs shot a nervous glance at the door. "Is he out there? Now? Even as we speak?"

"An ancestor. He too was Chief Clan," I whispered. "Long dead. Well, maybe dead. According to the stories, like me he was an exile. After roaming all over the world, he returned to Split Sky City with Green Snake. The Seeker had come home to die. But at the last minute—so the story goes—he bribed Horned Serpent to carry him down to the Underworld. With copper for payment, he stepped out of a canoe." I pointed toward the door. "There. Just beyond the shore. He was last seen being engulfed by Horned Serpent and carried down into the depths."

"You have colorful ancestors," Two Packs muttered.

I grunted uncomfortably. "Oh, yes. Murder, mayhem, and magic. Some legacy."

Pearl Hand took a deep breath and squeezed my hand. "You frightened me. One moment you were here, the next your souls had flown."

"I'm here," I whispered, disturbed by how clear the images were. "It was a Power dream."

Pearl Hand's skeptical eyebrow arched. "Don't you normally have those when you're dying?"

"Yes." I swallowed hard.

She shook her head, turning loose of my hand. "Sometimes, husband, you really worry me."

You're worried? You ought to live it from my side.

NINE

OUTSIDE APAFALAYA I FELT THE FULL IMPACT OF THE loss of my trade packs. Over the years I'd become affluent, possessing copper, buffalo wool, exotic medicinal plants, rare feathers, beautiful beaded necklaces, breastplates, blankets, fine dress, and paints. Now we only had seven pieces of heat-tarnished copper, whatever trade Two Packs carried, and what was on our backs. How, then, was I going to make a grand entrance into Apafalaya?

Was it even necessary to stop there? The Nation was composed of six towns stretched up and down the Black Warrior River bottom. The capital, Apafalaya town, lay a short distance upriver from Split Sky City.

Apafalaya consisted of perhaps five hundred souls clustered around a chief's mound on one end, a temple mound on the other, and a small plaza between the two. A World Tree pole crafted from red cedar dominated the plaza; its length was painted in red and white spirals. Two chunkey courts lay to either side, and an *akbatle* goal post sat atop a pole on the south.

Most of the people lived in surrounding farmsteads clustered along the low terrace just up from the back-swamps. Once or twice a year the river tended to overrun its banks, replenishing the sandy soil. The back-swamps are productive fisheries as well as rich in fowl and small game.

Whatever the benefits of attempting to rally the Apafalaya mikko to attack de Soto, the final reality was that the good mikko would never commit all of his resources to the fight. Perhaps it was the legacy of living just across the hills from the Chicaza. Generations of warfare had taught the Apafalaya that it was better to dodge and weave rather than stand and trade blows. Any real hope of breaking the monster's back lay with Chicaza.

But how was I going to convince my brother to commit Chicaza's military to the fight? And worse, how would I get him to do it on my terms? The Chicaza way was to march out in perfect formation, squadrons of warriors moving in unison. Wooden shields at the fore, ranks of war-club-wielding warriors provided mobile shelter for archers. They, in turn, rained war arrows down on the enemy from the safe comfort of the formation's center.

Each squadron's warriors came from one *iksa,* or clan. Membership in the elite squadron was an honor sought by every aspiring warrior within his iksa. The clans were hierarchically ranked in normal society, with Chief Clan at the top and Skunk Clan at the bottom. In combat, however, the squadrons were ranked by their bravery, obedience, and ruthless efficiency. If the Skunk Clan squadron stood when others didn't, or they broke the enemy lines and won the battle, they marched in the front of the formation and received honors and acclaim. Such competition for war honors, coupled with training and obedience, had given the Chicaza a military proficiency unequaled among the Nations.

Overall command of the squadrons was the duty of

the *tishu minko,* generally the highest-ranking minko of the Raccoon Clan—and normally the hallowed bearer of the war medicine box. The tishu minko's orders were relayed by the *hetissus,* or war seconds. This was accomplished through a series of whistles and gestures, and, if necessary, by runners. Orders were received and implemented by the squadron *abetuska,* or "warrior killer." This was a man elevated to the command of his clan squadron based on his competence and experience as a warrior and combat leader.

According to our legends this manner of making war had originated in fabled Cahokia and allowed the lords there to conquer most of the known world. The ancestral Sky Hand had used such methods to overcome the local Albaamaha and Koasati, and to found an empire. Strategies and tactics were studied, improved upon, and tested over the generations until my Chicaza had become the envy of Nations. True, someone like the Coosa might have been able to overwhelm us with sheer numbers, but even the poorest Chicaza squadron would claim five enemy dead to the Coosa's one.

The very success of Chicaza warfare now worked against me. I remembered my little brother, an awe-filled and gangly boy. Like me, he had spent his life absorbing stories of Chicaza superiority. Down at the root of his souls, he firmly believed, as I once had, that no enemy on earth could stand against Chicaza arms.

So, Black Shell, assuming your brother doesn't order you chased out of Chicaza at the first mention of your name, how are you going to convince him to fight this your way?

I made a face, glanced up at the gray and menacing sky, and felt entirely helpless as I remembered Old White's Spirit admonition of piety.

Pearl Hand's *hierro* knife shaved long and curling slivers from the ash-wood shaft I peeled. Part of my insecurity—

I had come to believe—had its roots in my lack of the things that made me . . . me. One of those was my trader's staff, my old one having burned with everything else back in Mabila.

As I sat hunched before the fire in our camp, I continued working on my new staff. I would engrave a spiral around its length and carve the top in the shape of a woodpecker's head to honor the Winds, who resided at the edges of the earth. Having seen the West Wind in my first Spirit Dream, I knew exactly what the giant birds looked like.

Finding white swan's feathers? That might be something of a trick in midwinter—and this far inland. Swans tended to winter along the coastal areas to the south. I could have scraped by with egret feathers, but swan was necessary to keep the Power right.

"We'll cross the Tombigbee tomorrow," Two Packs noted. "That puts us smack-dab in Chicaza territory. You can bet they'll have scouts out."

I nodded, raising the staff and inspecting it in the firelight. "I'm hoping for that."

"What are you thinking?" Pearl Hand asked where she crouched at the edge of the fire and used damp, sand-impregnated cloth to polish the blade of my old Kristiano sword.

Tomorrow I would hand it over to Two Packs. He didn't understand *hierro* or why it needed polishing in order to keep the odd brown scale from forming on its surface. He should have been able to figure it out; even sacred copper eventually discolored. Metals always have their own Power and need some kind of care. For a seasoned trader like Two Packs, it should have been second nature.

The problem of how to approach Chicaza had been devouring me for days. Thinking of piety, and of what few assets remained to me, I glanced at Two Packs. "Tomorrow, as soon as we cross the river, I need you to go ahead, old friend."

He shot me a look from behind narrowed eyes. "An envoy to your brother?"

"Precisely." I gestured to the sword Pearl Hand was polishing. "And I need you to present him with that. Tell my brother that I won it in an archery contest with a Timucua chief. I've carried it from Irriparacoxi to Apalachee. From the Hichiti lands to Cofitachequi. I used it in combat against the Kristianos at Mabila and bore it from the smoking ruins when Pearl Hand and I made our escape. It has served me honorably, and now I hope it may so serve him. A token of affection. But you must tell him it comes from Black Shell the trader. As I am akeohoosa, make no mention that he is my brother or that I am of the Chief Clan. Do you understand?"

"I do." Two Packs hunched forward and rolled his heavy shoulders as if to relieve them of a great weight. As I watched the swelling muscle tighten and flex, he said, "I'm to be the go-between."

"It might allow us to find some way to overcome certain . . ."

"Unpleasantries?" Two Packs clapped his hands with a pop. The dogs shot to their feet, growling and barking.

"Here!" I snapped. "It's just Two Packs. Lie down. And, pus and blood, stop that infernal barking!"

Bark, true to his namesake, was last to give up, baying anxiously, shooting Pearl Hand apologetic looks even as he refused to shut up, his tail wagging defiantly.

"Sorry." Two Packs grinned sheepishly. "Getting back to the subject, what do you want me to do? Petition the high minko to lift your banishment? I have trade in my packs. Nothing like what you lost at Mabila, but still the best I could bring from Coosa. It's yours to use as you wish."

"No. Keep your trade, old friend." I glanced at Pearl

Hand. She was watching me, understanding behind her large dark eyes. "As to forgiveness, it's too soon, if it's even possible at all." I clasped the sepaya, feeling its outline through the leather pouch. "Banishment was the price Horned Serpent demanded of me. I pay it willingly. Tell my brother that my only request is that he meet with me, listen to me. Make sure he knows that were it not for de Soto's presence, I would have continued to honor my people's decree of akeohoosa. Further, that once de Soto is destroyed, or has escaped, I shall be gone from their lands posthaste. Two Packs, you must impress on him that nothing I do or ask is for my own good. You can do that, can't you?"

"I can." Something in his voice hinted of unhappiness.

From the corner of my eye, I caught the tightening of Pearl Hand's lips and the hard glance she gave Two Packs.

"That's it?" Two Packs asked. "You just want to *talk*? And then you'll be gone?"

I gestured futilely. "By Piasa's hanging balls, if it means getting a fair hearing, I'll give up the honor of even setting a single polluting foot in their town plaza. The Kristianos are weaker than they've ever been. If the Chicaza can catch the Kristianos off guard, hit them by surprise when the time is right, they prevail and save our world."

"Just like that?" Two Packs demanded. "They can do what the Coosa, Apalachee, and Tuskaloosa couldn't?"

I met his skeptical eyes. "Perhaps. If Pearl Hand and I can gain enough of my brother's trust to explain how this thing can be done. And assuming he believes us in the end. Otherwise my brother's first instinct will be to march out and meet the monster head-on in an open plain where the Chicaza squadrons can maneuver, charge, flank, and—"

"Be crushed by the cabayeros and mixed weaponry," Pearl Hand interrupted, eyes half-closed as she visualized it. "And once the *Adelantado* has the Chicaza squadrons broken and scattered, the Kristianos will cut them down like stems of grass before a flint scythe."

"Exactly." I smacked a fist into my palm. "This goes to the very heart of being Chicaza. We have survived by military discipline, training, and excellence in arms. Chicaza believe—down to the marrow in their bones—that their squadrons can defeat any army that marches against them."

Two Packs sighed, resignation in his eyes. "I understand, old friend. No matter what, I shall be glib of tongue and as persuasive as ever."

"The high minko knows you, doesn't he?" Pearl Hand asked. "You've traded with him before?"

"Oh, yes," Two Packs answered. "I've always found him a shrewd and cunning adversary. He's a smart man, uneasily swayed or taken advantage of. A trait that seems to run in his family. And, like his 'thrown-away' brother here, a bit bullheaded at times . . . and as stubborn as a snapping turtle on a trotline."

None of which gave me any sense of reassurance.

The following day, after hiring a canoe to carry us across the Tombigbee, I watched Two Packs stride away up the forest trail. He carried his trader's staff before him, the Kristiano sword strapped to his side.

"We're betting almost everything on you, old friend," I whispered.

"*Almost* everything?" Pearl Hand asked.

"I have one other possibility," I answered, jabbing my new staff at the soil. "In the vision, Old White told me I needed to approach Chicaza with humility and piety."

"That's not you," she said dryly.

"Of course not. But I have a plan."

"Why doesn't that reassure me?"

"Because, my love, like usual, it's a long shot."

The weather finally cleared, sunlight bathing the forest around us. In the stark blue light, the gray-barked branches above made a weblike tangle against the sky. Slanting shadows cast by the low winter sun mottled the leaf mat as we followed one of the old trails northwest along the floodplain. For generations traders and war parties had made their way through the shadowed forest depths where we walked. I could imagine the scuffing sounds of their moccasins, the faded memories of clacking wood as war clubs and bows banged against shields and medicine boxes.

The air remained chill, our breath rising whitely to fade and vanish against the overarching background of ancient trees. Many of them were marked by slashes hacked into the bark by parties of warriors, the scabbed-over markings a monument to men years dead and raids long forgotten.

"Do you think Two Packs will succeed?" Pearl Hand asked.

"My brother knows him, has traded with him." I shrugged. "We will know soon enough."

She walked along in silence, Bark pacing beside her on the wide trail. Gnaw and Squirm padded just in front of me, noses twitching as they sampled the forest air. Blackie and Patches were behind, zigzagging, acting young, as was their right.

"It's just you and me again," I mused. "We haven't traveled thus since before Uzachile."

She flipped her gleaming black hair back before shooting me a ravishing smile. "Somehow that seems a lifetime ago. As if we were different people."

"Maybe we were." I reached for her hand. "We only had a few days of bliss after we escaped Irriparacoxi and before I was captured at Uzita. If I could have any wish, it would be to go back to those blessed days and live them forever. We would just wander, free of care, lazing in the sun and making tender love in the shade."

She closed her eyes, head back, as if savoring the images behind her eyelids. "I could go back," she whispered. "And I'd never want for anything again. Each moment spent enjoying your company and playing with the dogs would be lived with appreciation and joy. Who cares if we never saw another human again? Just you and me, morning mist rising from swamps, green forests, and sunshine."

I blew a frosty breath. "Remember how miserably hot it was? We could sure use some of that now."

"My feet have been so cold for so long they've lost feeling."

"Tonight," I said in promise, "we'll make a big fire to keep your feet warm. Then we'll snuggle under the blankets and I'm going to savor every inch of your body, over, and over, and over again."

At that she laughed, shook her hair back, and gave me a saucy wink. "We'll see."

"How's that?" Pus and blood, she wasn't going to play shy, was she?

"Since you've been wounded, on those few occasions I can coax you into it . . . Well, you don't seem to have the same old stamina."

"Tonight I'll have you begging for mercy."

"Husbands who brag had better be able to back up any hollow words with hard action." She was giving me that challenging look, the one where her dark eyes gleamed and her full lips curled in amusement.

"Think you've got more energy than me?"

"I *know* I do."

Then she changed the subject, catching me off guard. "Tell me about your brother, Black Shell. You grew up with him. What was he like as a boy? What kind of man do you think he became?"

"Most likely a good one." I thought back. "He was called Wind Rabbit, just two years behind me. What can I say? But for being Chief Clan, and being trained for the high chair, we were like most brothers. We squabbled over some things, backed each other over others. Little brothers always hate and worship their big brothers, often in the same breath. So it was with him. I was being groomed for leadership so I got the majority of the attention. Wind Rabbit always took second place. Thinking of that now, I wonder how it's influenced his leadership."

"How did he react when you were declared akeohoosa and cast out?"

I felt my guts tighten. "I'll never forget the look in his eyes. Disbelief, horror, and fear, all mixed together. He stood bravely beside Uncle, head high, mouth like a firm line. But in his eyes I saw something terrible."

"Terrible how?"

"That frantic desperation that glitters in the eyes when a person's world has just been destroyed. The slackening of the face . . . a person betrayed down to their souls and shaken to their bones."

"So . . . do you think Wind Rabbit believed you were a coward?"

"Of course." I gestured with my staff. "In the words of Uncle, Mother, and the rest, I was declared unworthy, unfit, and a failure. To a boy Wind Rabbit's age, it's tantamount to a declaration by Breath Giver himself. The judgment of the very gods." I shrugged. "The only good news is that according to Chicaza law, no one would have mentioned me again. I'm dead to them, just as if I'd been killed that day fighting the Natchez. My return? It's the same as a corpse come back from the dead."

"Not everyone wishes the dead to return."

I added thoughtfully, "When the dead come walking back, they often bring memories best left buried with them."

"Will your relatives see you that way?"

"It's been so many years . . ." I shrugged. "Banishment is a penalty my people take very seriously. When they hear

I'm back they might dispatch a war party to ensure my rapid departure. One way . . . or another."

"Whatever their response, we will deal with it," she replied. "We've dealt with war parties before. And, instead of worrying about the Chicaza, were I you, I'd be saving my energy for tonight."

"How's that?"

"Something about husbands who boast."

"Oh . . . right."

Of course it was empty bragging. Not only is Pearl Hand healthy and vigorous, she knows how to coax a man beyond even his wildest fantasies.

By the time she allowed me to drift off into exhausted sleep, my dreams were filled with Pearl Hand, and love, and the gift of sharing, instead of blood, death, and disaster at the hands of my relatives.

Family

"Elder? Are you warm enough?"

The question pierces her rambling thoughts with the stinging intensity of a thorn snapped from a smilax stalk. For a moment she struggles to place herself. Where? The images are sliding around in her souls, jumbled, mixing the past with the present.

Past and present, dream and reality, they are so hard to keep separate.

Then the familiar and simple furnishings in her house come into focus.

Yes, I am in Chicaza.

"Elder?" the patient voice intrudes again, and she blinks, seeing the Convert. His name has vanished somewhere in the conflicting haze of memory. She knows him only as "the Convert," one of the Adelantado's indios—an Ocute tameme who'd escaped the slave collar and chains by claiming the Kristiano god as his own. He'd been a boy then, too young to realize the ultimate price of the bargain he'd made.

"Are you warm enough?" He is peering at her with concern. "I could build up the fire for you."

She squints with her rheumy eyes, fills her lungs as much as she can, and puffs. Her breath doesn't fog before her.

"No, I have my blanket."

She watches him frown, step back from her bed, and take a hickory root from the pile by the door. This he tosses on the fire, crackling in its puddled-clay hearth. Sparks curl and rise only to wink out before they reach the smoke-blued haze drifting out the smoke hole and into the night.

"It's snowing outside," he tells her. "By morning water will be freezing in the pots."

She nods, giving him a toothless smile. Cocking her head, she can hear the winter silence outside. But for the popping of her fire, the stillness of the night is only broken by the faint bickering of the neighbors.

A brother and sister, they are fighting again. He is a concerned Chief Clan uncle, irritated by his sister's daughter. The girl is flirting with a boy from the Skunk Clan. He thinks the boy unworthy, and worse, untrustworthy when it comes to his niece's treasured virginity.

A bellow of rage is followed by the hollow "pop" of a clay pot smashed in anger. Then comes a shout of "Go away! Come back when you can keep a respectful tongue in your mouth!"

Silence descends on the night.

The Convert is titillated by the knowledge that prohibited sex may be involved. His toothless grin stretches the wrinkles on his old face and gives him a clownish look.

Not for the first time, she wonders, How did I—of all women—end up among the prudish Chicaza?

"Families," the Convert says. "You really have to love someone to fight that bitterly."

His words stir the memories in her souls the way a hickory stick does stew. Images rise and swirl, then surface, only to submerge again in the fog of memory.

In an instant, Black Shell's face appears as fresh as if it were but yesterday. The image is so clear that she can fix the place and time: on the trail, destined for Chicaza. The dogs are there, trotting ahead, tails wagging. Dogs never look to the future, content only in the needs of the day.

Black Shell's face, however, is pinched, worried, excited, and anxious all at the same time. Behind his almost fevered eyes, she can read his concern: After all those years as an exile, he is going home.

"You were such a fool," she whispers to him, almost surprised that he doesn't respond from so far in the distant past. "All those years you promised *yourself that you were no longer a true Chicaza. Because you loved your family with all your heart, the wound they inflicted cut through the center of your souls. With each step forward, you bled more and more. How much deeper could they cut? How much more could they make your wounded souls scream?"*

She grows aware of the Convert crouching by the fire, his hands out to its warmth. He is listening intently and in awe. By morning her words—always a source of wonder to the Chicaza—will be repeated in every household.

She ignores him. To Black Shell, she says, "A friend can only betray you. An enemy seeks nothing more than to destroy you. But to brutally murder a person's hope, love, and trust? That's an act only family can accomplish."

And in that instant, she is back on the trail, following Black Shell into Chicaza. Knowing all along that his family awaits just beyond those rolling, forested hills.

TEN

"WHAT IS THE PLAN AGAIN?" PEARL HAND ASKED AS we walked quietly down one of the forest paths that skirted the low hills east of the Tombigbee. To the right, Green Hickory Creek, a tributary of the Tombigbee, was thick with old oaks, shagbark hickories, occasional bald cypress, and gum trees. We waded across small streams, the crossings shaded by overhanging branches.

"I've been thinking about what Old White told me. In all of Chicaza, there is only one man more respected than the high minko."

"And who is this?"

"His full name was Abeminko Who Takes the Blood-Spotted Shield. He was born to the Raccoon Iksa, or clan. When I was a boy, he served as my uncle's tishu minko, the second in command and head of the Chicaza council. A little over a year before I was outcast, Spotted Shield led a full battle walk against the Quizquiz Nation." I pointed off to the northeast. "Unbeknownst to any of our people, the Quizquiz were hosting the Natchez, Casqui, and Pacaha Nations in a war council at their capital town, hoping they could join forces to attack Chicaza. Not only were the great minkos present in Quizquiz, but they'd all brought delegations of warriors and their stickball teams. The Nations were camped up and down the banks of the Father Water."

"Sounds like bad news." Pearl Hand bent down to help Gnaw remove a batch of cockleburs before they could embed in his fur.

"Spotted Shield's scouts had no more than reported the situation before the Chicaza force was discovered. They were more than halfway across the fields, headed for the capital, when a mass of warriors poured out of Quizquiz. Spotted Shield immediately ordered his hetti-sus to call the retreat. The abeminkos kept the squadrons in formation as they turned back for the forest.

"What began as a mobile retreat grew into a four-day battle as Spotted Shield fought his way back to the forest against overwhelming odds. To this day, no one has ever determined how many warriors the Quizquiz and their allies threw against Spotted Shield's squadrons. The surviving Chicaza described it as a 'frenzy' of massed men. There were so many attackers they tripped over each other, a tangled confusion of mixed formations. What they couldn't do through maneuver, they tried to accomplish by massed attacks meant to literally smother the struggling Chicaza squadrons."

Pearl Hand straightened, pitched the cockleburs to the side, and sucked her fingers. "Spotted Shield escaped?"

"Barely. Only his courage and brilliance on the battlefield, coupled with Chicaza skill and discipline, kept the raid from total disaster. As it was, he lost nearly a third of his warriors."

"And the Quizquiz and their allies?"

I looked up at the trees, the high branches gray against a glassy blue sky. "They lost about half of their forces, either killed outright or wounded so badly they couldn't continue the fight. Spotted Shield marched nearly a hundred captives back to Chicaza, his surviving warriors brandishing a couple hundred enemy scalps on cedar branches. Trophies they'd managed to take during the fighting."

Pearl Hand nodded as we continued on our way. "I take it the Quizquiz retaliated?"

"They tried to. Remember, they'd originally called the council in hopes that they could put together a military coalition strong enough to crush the Chicaza once and for all. To the Quizquiz it appeared that Breath Giver himself had offered us up on a platter. And right in their own cornfields!"

"Was the alliance ever formalized?"

I chuckled. "Oh, they chased after Spotted Shield, only to fall into ambush after ambush once he made it to the forest. As the survivors came staggering back to Quizquiz, first the Pacaha, then the Casqui packed up and straggled home. The Natchez? Well, without the Nations from the other side of the river, they were no better off than before."

"Then I take it Spotted Shield came home a hero?"

"A hero to everyone but himself. The tishu minko relinquished his position, surrendered his war honors, and buried his weapons in a hole before the Men's House. He cast off his fine robes, dumped his possessions in the center of the plaza, and walked away in rags."

"Why?" Pearl Hand ducked a branch.

"Spotted Shield was a humble and devout man." I ducked behind her, hearing the branch rasp as it slid over my pack. "He couldn't figure out how he could have walked into such a disaster without some kind of warning from the Spirit World. Up until the moment the scouts came running, panting, crying that Quizquiz was full of warriors, he had no idea that anything was wrong. None of the usual signs—an owl hooting in the day, a crow roosting in the trees, a warrior breaking one of the taboos, the war medicine being dropped—none of those things had happened. Even the priests who accompanied them and the young women who expected to sing for the warriors as they fought had conducted themselves in an exemplary manner."

Pearl Hand shot me one of those knowing looks. "Maybe Power wanted him to walk headlong into that mess?"

"You and I have the same reservations about Power." I shot a wary look at the surrounding forest, the back of my neck prickling. Bark stopped short, his back hair rising. Squirm's ears pricked, his nose quivering. Gnaw began a low growl, attention fixed on the maze of tree trunks to our right.

"Easy," I ordered. "Quiet."

The forest around us had gone deathly still.

I stepped forward, giving the dogs a "down" signal as I called out, "I am the trader known as Black Shell. With me is Pearl Hand of the Chicora. We approach under the Power of trade and bind ourselves to it."

Silence.

Pearl Hand shifted, allowing the crossbow strap to slide down her arm. I gave her the desist sign.

"We come in peace," I added. "It is our purpose to speak with the holy man known as Old Wood."

More silence.

I half kicked an old acorn. "The Chicaza I knew were smart enough to recognize that a woman, a man, and five dogs pose no threat to the people. Come out and show yourselves."

A faint shifting in the shadows, shades of brown seemed to slip, then faces formed against the background as if from the forest itself.

"Who did you say you were?" a young warrior asked as

he eased forward, a hardwood bow held crosswise at his waist, a nocked war arrow ready to draw.

I took his measure along with that of the two others who crept silently from concealment. None of the young men seemed to have passed twenty winters, but all were blooded warriors given the tattoos and the beaded fore-locks hanging down to their noses. Each wore a mottled brown hunting shirt and high moccasins. Each carried a bow backed by full quivers.

"I am known as Black Shell. I'm a trader. My wife, Pearl Hand, and I have come under the Power of trade and bind ourselves to it. We wish only to have counsel with Old Wood."

"Why would you bother him?" the first asked, hard black eyes taking in the Kristiano weapons, unsure of their design or purpose.

"You've heard of the Kristianos?" Pearl Hand asked, jutting her hip to brace the crossbow.

"Something, yes." The young warrior gave her a shy smile, as if he'd finally realized what a beautiful woman she was. Then, being Chicaza, he glanced away, careful lest he give offense for staring at another man's woman.

Ah, I was home.

"We need to speak to Old Wood," I said insistently. "We require the holy one's counsel. We would speak to him of the Kristianos and the threat they pose."

"And you know something of Kristianos?" the second asked, frowning.

"We come from Mabila," Pearl Hand replied. "That is why we need to see Old Wood." She shot me a glance to make sure she was correct.

At mention of Mabila, they straightened, interest piqued.

I stepped forward, looking him hard in the eyes. "That's right. Pearl Hand and I come from Mabila, bear-ing the lessons we learned there. I don't need the holy man known as Old Wood nearly as much as I need to hear wise counsel from the man who once called himself Abeminko Who Takes the Blood-Spotted Shield."

"Ah," Pearl Hand whispered in Timucua. "So, they are one and the same?"

"Indeed." I let my gaze bore into the young warrior's. In Chicaza dialect I added, "And now you will take us to Old Wood. We need to see him now."

He still hesitated, trying to figure out if we were some kind of threat. "I still don't—"

"Because, young fool," I declared hotly, "the Kristianos are coming to Chicaza. When they get here they will want to take the high minko and the beloved elders hostage. They are coming to confiscate your corn, to rape your sisters and mothers. Assuming you don't want to die like the thousands at Mabila, you will take us to Old Wood *now!*"

My use of the imperative tone, common among highborn Chicaza, did the trick. He swallowed hard, turned, and gestured to his companions. "Let's do it. If it's the wrong thing, Old Wood will tell us."

Turns out it was just as well that we'd run into the warriors. Chicaza is densely populated, the rich sandy loam in the bottomlands perfect for the cultivation of corn, beans, and squash. Clusters of small farmsteads—often three to six houses—their granaries, and their fields dot the land. So, too, do small and intermediate-size villages and towns. These report to town minkos, and they to the clan minkos in Chicaza town itself.

But for the guidance of the young warriors, we might have spent days asking for directions at the small towns, chasing out trails, and asking further directions at the next town.

Worse, Old Wood had chosen a remote, hard-to-find location for his hermetic retreat. The place was in the western uplands, flanked by thickly wooded ridges and nestled in the bottom of a narrow valley.

My body was tense, almost prickling from anxiety as we walked down the wooded slope and into a grassy clearing beside a small creek. Here a couple of cornfields had been hacked out of the walnut and gum trees. The fields lay just below an old terrace where a square-walled house stood. The walls were thickly plastered. A split-cane roof extended the drip line at least an arm's length from the walls. The dwelling stood beneath the protective branches of an ancient chestnut tree. In the rear, behind the latrine screen, a granary rose on four tall posts. Roofed with bark shingles and sporting woven willow-stem walls, I could see it was brimming with corn and squash.

The ramada with its pestle and mortar stood off to the right, a few dried leaves still clinging to the branches lashed to its sides—once protection from the slanting summer sun.

The three warriors escorting us slowed as we emerged from the forest trail. They cast uneasy glances at each other, and then at Pearl Hand and me, wondering, no doubt, if bringing us there had been smart.

I was wondering that myself. Here, after all, was one of the most intimidating men I'd known as a boy. Not only had he been a towering warrior, but by leaving his authority and influence behind and adopting a life of sacrifice and poverty, he'd become almost godlike to rank-and-file Chicaza.

"You all right?" Pearl Hand asked softly in Timucua.

"Just a little nervous," I answered, almost wincing when the three Chicaza shot us warning looks. They were gripping their bows so hard the knuckles were white beneath that smooth brown skin.

At that moment an old yellow dog, white in the muzzle and with graying eyes, limped out. He raised his blocky head, baying in a hoarse voice, his tail whipping in time with each "arrrooowww."

"Dogs," I ordered, brandishing my unfinished staff. "Down."

True to their training, they dropped onto their bellies, attention fixed on the old dog that waddled forward, panting. The beast's teeth, colored with age, had been worn down to the gums, the canines like flattened pegs.

"Elder?" one of the Chicaza called, cupping hands to his mouth. "Strangers come. They demanded to speak with you about the Kristianos."

What if he recognizes me? Tells me to leave before I pollute his doorway? I stopped short, waiting, grinding my teeth, prepared to turn and vanish into the forest.

Some hero I was, my heart pounding, a squeamish feeling in my guts. *Thank Breath Giver, he's not home.*

I drew a breath to state as much when a voice from the forest called, "Who comes, Wildcat? What do they wish with me?"

The young man called Wildcat stepped forward and touched his forehead respectfully. "They say they come from Mabila, beloved elder, and wish to talk to you about the Kristianos. They invoke the Power of trade and say they bind themselves under it."

"Who says these things?" The man who emerged from behind a thick tangle of raspberry and grape bushes wore only a patched and frayed brown hunting shirt that fell to his knees; long black hair threaded with white tumbled in silky waves over his shoulders and down past his waist. Plain buckskin moccasins clad his feet, and a rope served for his belt.

No matter how poor his dress, his face left no doubt that he came from nobility, tattooed as it was with the forked eye and the dark band of the Raccoon Clan. The slant-lined cheek tattoos proclaimed him an abeminko, or "chief-killer," referring to a personal victory he had over a Yuchi *bale gabidane*—as they call their chiefs—up on the Tenasee River. Old Wood, I realized, had been able to shed everything but his skin—and it would mark him forever, no matter how hard he tried to forget.

He remained as impressive as I remembered him—and just as scary now as he'd been when I was a boy. When his penetrating gaze met mine, I felt my souls chill. Time stopped. He'd pinned me the way a child with a long thorn might skewer a beetle.

Pearl Hand, sensing my turmoil, stepped forward, calling, "Hopaye, we come under the Power of trade and bind ourselves to it. We wish only to discuss the arrival of the Kristianos in Chicaza land and the implications it has for your people."

"I am no hopaye." He cocked his head, hard dark eyes cataloging us from head to foot. For long moments his attention fixed on Pearl Hand's crossbow, then he frowned at my sword and the pack of armor I carried. "Wouldn't your purposes be better served by speaking with the priests and chiefs at Chicaza town?"

Pearl Hand shot me a questioning glance; her expression hardened as I remained rooted. While my heart thumped in my chest, panic settled down around my liver.

He asked Pearl Hand, "Woman, how are you called?"

"I am Pearl Hand of the Chicora. Among the Apalachee I am known as nicoquadca. Most recently I served as war adviser to High Minko Tuskaloosa and his thlakko, Darting Snake. After Mabila, I have come here, relentless in my desire to destroy the Kristianos and the pollution they have brought to our world."

He tilted his head slightly to indicate me. "And your companion? Do you speak for him, too?"

Gods, Black Shell! Say something! I fought down the panic, making the "enough" hand sign and ending it with a jerk. A sudden welling anger turned the tide of fear that had been drowning my souls. "I am known as Black Shell," I began stiffly. "I serve the Power of trade . . . and Horned Serpent. I carry his sepaya. For the last two years I have fought the monster de Soto and his army. Now they are coming here, to Chicaza."

He gave me the sort of scrutiny a cautious bird of prey would give a snake. A quiver at the corner of his mouth tightened his lips. And meant what? Humor? Disgust? Or was it just a nervous tic?

"Again," he asked softly, "why do you come to me instead of the high minko?"

I shook myself, rolling my shoulders to ease the tension. "Because, of all the Chicaza, you, elder, might have the capacity to understand what we tell you."

"Ah, a capacity for understanding? That is what you seek?"

"We seek the destruction of the Kristianos."

His eyes had taken on an odd sheen. "And you claim to have fought these Kristianos?"

"Our battle began when I was captured in the Uzita lands."

"I have never heard of Uzita."

"A people who live far down the peninsula. After my rescue we chased the Kristianos to Uzachile, fought against them with the Apalachee, and raced them to Cofitachequi. We beat them to Coosa, and finally sought to trap them at Mabila."

His eyes went again to the sword I had taken from Antonio. "I heard that Mabila was a disaster. That Tuskaloosa's trap was turned backward upon itself. How did you make your escape?"

Something in the look he was giving me made me hesitate. I blurted out, "Pearl Hand dressed me in a dead Kristiano's clothing." I couldn't tell him the rest. He was, after all, a Chicaza holy man. Confessing to wearing a dead man's face would have been akin to an admission of witchery. "Disguised, we walked out the main gate at night. Pearl Hand spoke to the guard in *español*—that's their language. With the armor, the clothing, limping as I was, they thought I was one of theirs."

Old Wood turned to the escorting warriors who'd stepped off to the side, listening in awe. He gave the hand sign for "go," saying only, "Thank you for bringing the traders here. Meanwhile, I would ask you to take word of their arrival to the high minko. Please say nothing of their presence to anyone else."

"Yes, beloved elder!" Heads bobbed as the young men, wide-eyed, backed away and touched their foreheads respectfully. Then they turned and vanished into the forest. They'd barely passed out of sight before I could hear excited whispering that slowly faded into the forest silence.

Old Wood stepped forward, hands clasped behind his back. "Pearl Hand has told me she is Chicora. Why, Black Shell, do you not identify yourself as Chicaza? You speak as one of us. Or was your mother a foreign woman? Perhaps a slave? One who removed you from us at a young age and took you home to her clan and people?"

I winced and lied, "She . . . was Coosa, elder."

The quiver began to play at the corner of his mouth again, and I felt miserable. Pearl Hand's sidelong gaze was taking my measure. I wanted to squirm right out of my skin.

I wasn't ready for it when he calmly stated, "They said you were a coward, Black Shell. Is that why you can't face me?"

Anger mixed with the confusion fermenting in my gut. "No. It's . . . it's . . . I don't *know*! After everything that's happened, the captivity, the gratuitous death, the misery and suffering, the hatred and desperation . . ." I laughed, the sound of it maniacal, even to my ears. "I was *devoured* alive by Horned Serpent! I carry the sepaya." I lifted the hide bag that contained it. "I've even outwitted Piasa in the Underworld. One would think that approaching you would be the least of my worries."

A thin smile bent his lips for the first time. "No enemy is as formidable as the one you keep in your heart. No foes can wound a man as deeply as the ones whom he loves. That places you at a grave disadvantage."

I nodded, feeling like a man suddenly stripped naked, exposed from all directions.

Old Wood stepped even closer, alert eyes taking in the Kristiano armor, the way I stood on my wounded leg, and the healing scar on my arm. "But that doesn't answer the question. Why did you come to me?"

"Old White sent me."

"Old White? From the legends?"

"He came to me in a vision outside Split Sky City. He told me that my way home was through humility and piety. You, revered elder, are the most pious man I know in all the world."

"You've been gone for what, over ten years? How do you know what I've become?"

I looked him hard in the eyes. "Even as a boy, I thought you were the greatest of us. If, after having all these years to work at it, you haven't become even greater, then my faith was foolishly placed."

A sadness entered his expression. "I did not come out here seeking greatness, Black Shell."

"And I did not become Horned Serpent's chosen because I wished adulation and renown."

"I removed myself from people and the distractions of politics and petty rivalries in order to be one with Power, to understand who and what I am."

"Have you found answers?"

"Only more questions. Such as the one I just asked you."

"Our world is in danger, respected elder. The Kristianos keep coming. They will destroy Chicaza and everything we hold dear. I need the high minko, the council, and the clans to understand the threat. I fear that instead of worrying about the Kristianos, they are going to focus on me, on what happened years ago. You might persuade our people that I come seeking no advantage. I am akeo-hoosa. When de Soto leaves, so will I. Finally, there's this: If we try to fight the Kristianos in our traditional way, they will destroy us."

He cocked his head, glanced at Pearl Hand and then the dogs who waited so obediently. "I think perhaps we should discuss this over food. You both look tired, and I would share a meal just for the opportunity to look at the curious weapons you carry."

ELEVEN

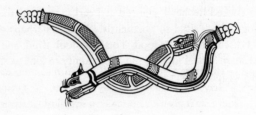

LIKE EVERYTHING ELSE ABOUT OLD WOOD, HIS
house was simple: four walls, a roof, a central hearth, and
a single pole bed in the back covered with worn but serviceable bedding. Pearl Hand and I were perched on the
edge of it. His few possessions consisted of undecorated
brownware bowls, jars, and cups. Even his old dog, called
Knuckles, looked serviced and worn. Supper consisted of
a corn, squash, and venison stew without seasoning of any
kind. The only drink was water.

After the meal Old Wood sat on the packed-clay floor,
no matting or hides to cushion his ascetic butt. In the
firelight he studied Antonio's metal breastplate and
sword. The Kristiano clothing I'd used so successfully to
walk among the enemy was carefully folded where he'd
placed it after a thorough inspection.

Pearl Hand had demonstrated the crossbow earlier,
and I'd sheared off a couple of saplings to impress upon
him how a single stroke of a Kristiano's sword could sever
a man's head from his body.

I watched the interplay of emotions on his face as he listened to our story. Unlike most of the war leaders we'd dealt with over the years, he didn't interrupt or scoff, but let us tell it in our own words. Or at least he let me tell it in my own words. Each time Pearl Hand interjected something, a look of irritation crossed his face. I'd told her about Chicaza men, and she knew their reputation, but it was eating at her.

"Had the Albaamaha not failed to close the main gate at Mabila, we would have killed de Soto," I concluded. "Battles often hinge on the smallest of things. In this case, that open gate allowed him and his *capitanes* to fight their way out of the trap. Our forces still had him surrounded and would have managed to finally kill him." I paused. "Then, elder—as it always happens—a squad of cabayeros appeared. Once they came charging down, all was lost."

Old Wood nodded, a grim expression on his face. "You are telling me that a band of fifty men could fight their way out of a trap where they were surrounded by thousands?"

I leveled a finger at him. "You fought your way out of Quizquiz. Had you possessed Kristiano armor, their marvelous weapons, and cabayos, you'd have won the field and taken the city. In the process you'd have easily destroyed the Natchez, Pacaha, and Casqui armies to the last man." I shrugged. "All but for the few who escaped by running like terrified rabbits at the first opportunity."

"These cabayos . . . tell me about them again." He studiously ignored Pearl Hand.

"They are animals, grazers, larger than elk, with rounded hooves. All in all, they're easier to kill than a buffalo, but the Kristianos cover them with armor to protect them from our arrows. The only way to bring them down is up close where you can pick your shot and drive an arrow through cracks in the armor."

He thoughtfully tossed another stick into the fire, then

resumed his study of Antonio's *hierro* chest piece. Periodically he'd tap it, listening to the musical ringing. "And they ride these animals in formations? Massed, so that they can spear those who flee before them?"

"The Kristianos form both cabayos and *soldados* into squadrons. Like our own military, their commander, de Soto, orders their movement and maneuvers. What the cabayos give them is unbelievable speed, mobility, and invincible mass. Imagine, if you can, a hundred warriors mounted on bison. Then imagine they can organize their maneuvers the way a tishu minko does warriors. What chance would even the best battle-hardened squadron have of stopping a massed charge when the bison smashed full-tilt into the shield line?"

He thought for a moment, then asked, "Cabayos actually do this? Surrender their spirits to human domination to the point that they will fight for their masters?"

"They do."

"What sort of souls do cabayos have?"

"I don't know. Nor do I want to. None of my meetings with cabayos have been pleasant, let alone conducive to either long life or continued health."

He studied me, avoiding so much as a glance at Pearl Hand. In Chicaza society women had their own place and Power. The province of war wasn't one of them. From the corner of my eye I could see Pearl Hand's jaw muscles tensing.

Finally he asked, "Black Shell, from the time you were a boy you were trained to command, to understand the art of war. You've seen the Kristianos destroy every force thrown against them. But how good were the Uzachile, the Apalachee, and the others?"

I smiled grimly. "The Uzachile were competent, elder. And the Apalachee, they know how to fight Kristianos. Matched squadron for squadron, Chicaza are better warriors. But never speak disparagingly of Apalachee military ability. In the end, they would have beaten de Soto. Not through a massed assault, but through endless ambush and harassment. The Monster understood his peril . . . and left." I rubbed my nose. "Cofitachequi, before the plague, could have easily destroyed de Soto's starving army as it staggered, hungry and disorganized, out of the pine barrens. The Coosa had the manpower and numbers, but they were defeated by their own parasitic politics before a single warrior even took the field."

I raised my hand, thumb and forefinger almost touching. "At Mabila, High Minko Tuskaloosa came this close. But for the open gate, and but for the unfortunate arrival of the cabayeros, de Soto would have been killed and his army fleeing through the swamps for Ochuse with the Pensacola hot on their tails."

"But you think de Soto is coming here?"

I nodded. "He's in Apafalaya as we speak. The mikko there will do anything he can to rid himself of de Soto. Which means he's going to send the Monster here, to Chicaza, even if he has to carry the murderous filth on his own shoulders to do it."

"You don't think he'll stay in Apafalaya?"

"No. The Apafalaya know enough to have hidden their corn supplies, and probably their women and children as well."

After thinking for a moment, Old Wood glanced absently at Pearl Hand. "Chicaza will not stand for the molestation of our women."

"I am well aware of that."

Pearl Hand chuckled slightly. I shot her a warning glance.

Old Wood found no amusement in the notion that a woman would laugh about such a serious subject.

I jerked a thumb toward Pearl Hand. "She's killed more of them than I have. The Apalachee made her a nicoquadca."

"Biting my tongue for the next couple of moons"—Pearl Hand narrowed a squinting eye—"and 'acting appropriately' is going to be one of the hardest things I've ever done, elder."

He gave her the sort of smile reserved for inquisitive children. "We Chicaza believe that Breath Giver decreed separate ways and Power for men and women."

"It's a miracle that you can manage to reproduce," Pearl Hand replied through her own sweet and inoffensive smile. "That coupling business can get so spiritually messy."

"Wife," I warned as Old Wood's expression tightened.

Ignoring her, he spoke softly. "If I am to help you, I would know how you ended up as an exile, Black Shell. It was said that you turned and ran in the middle of a battle with the Natchez."

I was so desperate to change the subject I didn't even hesitate. "I *was* scared to death. I was staggered by a blow to the head. Horned Serpent whispered in my ear, '*Run!*' And run I did. To this day, I can't tell you if I was a coward or not."

Pearl Hand snorted, then added, "Horned Serpent told you that had you stayed and fought, you would have died."

I kept my attention trained on Old Wood. "Young men are required to face death, and even to give their lives in the supreme sacrifice. Those who die well are received by their ancestors. But I heard the call so clearly: *Run!* And I *saw* Horned Serpent that day. It wasn't until I journeyed to the Spirit World that I learned I was his chosen."

"You have *been* to the Spirit World?" Old Wood was watching me skeptically now.

And here, I understood, was where we would either win or lose Chicaza. I carefully shook the sepaya into my palm, offering the bit of horn. His wide eyes fixed on the translucent red brow tine as I said, "My dealings with the West Wind, with Piasa, and with Old-Woman-Who-Never-Dies are my own business. Suffice it to say that Horned Serpent took me—and after my return from the Sky World, nothing has ever been the same again."

He reached out, then drew his fingers back as the sepaya pulsed. He swallowed hard and nodded, even if he was having trouble believing what was coming out of my mouth. "Your claims border on the fantastic."

I replaced the sepaya and gave a slight shrug.

Pearl Hand, through gritted teeth, said, "If the Chicaza choose not to believe us, we will go on. Who is farther west? The Natchez, the Quizquiz?"

Old Wood fixed his eyes on the wall behind her head, as if speaking past her. "Past the buffer zone to the northwest, along the great river, are the Quizquiz. Across the river from them are the Casqui, relatives of the Kaskinampo. To the west and south are the Natchez."

Pearl Hand snapped, "Then we shall go there and see if we can gain allies to destroy whatever Black Shell's fool brother doesn't tackle."

"My fool brother?" I shot Pearl Hand a look of disbelief. By the Piasa's dangling balls, I was trying to win Old Wood over to our side!

She was glaring as she said, "He'll be a fool if he doesn't listen to you, Black Shell. Blood and pus, *who cares* if you were an outcast? You and I are the only people in our world who know how to destroy the *Adelantado*. Your brother can accept our help, or he can face de Soto on his own. If he chooses the latter, he—and your Chicaza—will pay for their error in blood."

I was gasping for air, trying to think of a way to save the situation, when Pearl Hand turned to Old Wood, adding, "Elder, I can play the political game with the best of them if I have to. You were with us until you started thinking about Black Shell's exile and the reasons for it.

Has he been to the Spirit World? Yes. He carries the sepaya to prove it."

She dropped to her knees, eyes level with his. "So, you're asking, why did Horned Serpent choose a disgraced coward? A lowly trader? A man exiled from his holy Chicaza iksa, without home and people?"

Old Wood hesitated, shocked by the invasion of his ever-so-Chicaza male person by a strange and belligerent female.

Pearl Hand jabbed a finger at his chest, making him flinch. "Because he's Chief Clan, born to leadership, trained, and then molded by additional years of travel and education. He knows the Nations, the trails, the warp and weft of politics. And he knows—as you so well pointed out—the art of war."

She stood, giving me a cold look. "My apologies, husband. You're being blinded by your stubborn loyalty to Chicaza. In your heart, you're crying, desperate for it to be the Chicaza who finally bring the *Adelantado* down. But Power doesn't care if it's the Chicaza, or the Quizquiz, or the Natchez who finally destroy him."

She strode purposefully toward the door, stopping only long enough to glance back. "Remember the larger issues at hand. Don't get sucked into some hole of remorse where all you do is peel scabs off old wounds."

Then she was gone.

Old Wood, his lips quivering with rage, ground out his words. "If that is the sort of woman you *chose* to marry, I'd say you have managed to punish yourself in a manner more terrible than anything your uncle might have designed. But one thing's for sure: Living with her proves you are no coward."

Then, with a disgusted flip of his wrist, he indicated I should leave.

The following morning, just before daybreak, I tended the fire. We were cooking the last of our dwindling stores:

a bit of cornmeal, some dried meat, acorns, and dried mulberries. Frost lay heavily on the trampled grass, and the dogs were huddled in round balls, noses buried in their tails as they watched me poke the fire with a long stick.

Like me, they were wondering just what they were going to eat. Fact was, today I would have to spend hunting, maybe fishing, whatever it took to fill five empty dog bellies.

I cast a scathing glance at Pearl Hand. We hadn't spoken, nor even touched, sleeping back-to-back under the blankets. I remained irritated with her. We had *needed* Old Wood's goodwill. Now I had to wonder if it was even worth approaching my brother and the Chicaza council or if I should simply send a message to Two Packs, telling him we were headed on to the Natchez.

Besides, it wasn't as if I hadn't warned her about the Chicaza and their curious ways. As a people, we funneled all of our energies into ritual purity and martial superiority. And she was partially right when she'd uttered that snide comment about sex being a spiritually messy business for us. Our hopayes—the priests—spent a great deal of time trying to balance the need for male spiritual purity against the perpetual need to populate the next generation with warriors and clan matrons.

At that moment, Old Wood emerged from his doorway, naked, his clothing hanging neatly over his right arm. He didn't even glance our way but walked barefoot across the frost and down to the creek. Raising his arms high, he faced the east, praying to the first pinkish glow on the horizon. Then he waded into the water and began his daily bath.

Pearl Hand, lips pursed, watched as Old Wood carefully lathered and soaped his long hair, then rinsed it out. She sighed. "I'm sorry." A pause. "I shouldn't have let him get the best of me like that. It's just that he was so . . ."

"Condescending?" I asked mildly.

"Blunt?" she countered.

"Thick-headed?"

"Loggish?"

". . . Loggish?" That stumped me.

She gave an airy gesture, her attention on shredding the last of our jerked venison and dropping it in the stew pot. "Well, his name is Old Wood, isn't it? Can't get much more pithy than that."

And we were laughing, the old familiar dancing glances passing between us.

"What can I say? He's just Chicaza."

She pulled her hair back then laced her arms around her knees, crouched against the morning chill. Two frown lines etched her brow. "What really set me off was the way he went after you. You should have seen the look on your face. Like you'd just been kicked in the gut. You've always maintained that you dislike your people, made fun of them, but that's only a mask you've adopted. Down in the narrow places between your souls, you still bleed from the wound they gave you."

"I got over it years ago."

"Lie to yourself." Her voice tightened. "But don't lie to me."

I growled defensively and irritably, and prodded the coals up around the bottom of our little brownware pot. Coals were great things—you could push them around, pile them up, and move them at will. Unlike Pearl Hand. The only person who had ever pushed her around was the Cofitachequi mico—and the old woman had ended up ruined while Pearl Hand walked away with a few bruises and stiff joints.

There was a lesson in that, if only I was smart enough to learn from it. But then, for a man who prided himself on being smart . . . well, as Pearl Hand noted, I lied to myself a lot.

"Very good," I muttered, jabbing resentfully at the un-offending coals. "We'll start for the Natchez as soon as we find the dogs a solid meal."

I watched her skeptical eyebrow arch—the one she always raised when she wasn't sure I was doing the right thing.

I stood, walking out to meet Old Wood as he strode up from the creek. During my discussion with Pearl Hand, he'd slicked the water from his skin, wrung out his long hair, and dressed in the faded brown hunting shirt. Against the chill he'd added a turkey-feather cape upon which his long wet locks rested.

"Elder," I greeted him. "Good morning."

"And may Breath Giver and the ancestors bless you, Black Shell."

I gestured toward the north, where the majority of the Chicaza towns lay. "I was wondering if I could manage to get a message to Chicaza town?"

"You would send word to your brother?" he asked mildly, the faintest of curiosity behind his soft brown eyes.

"No. To a trader, a man named Two Packs. He's currently at the high minko's, telling anyone who will listen about how the Kristianos treated Coosa and how they can best be dealt with."

"And what would you tell him?"

"That Pearl Hand and I will meet him among the Natchez."

He gave me a cool inspection. "Why the Natchez?"

"He and I both traded there in the past. We are known to the Great Serpent, as they call their high minko. We may be able to motivate the Great Serpent to ambush the trails west of here, to catch the Kristianos as they march out of Chicaza. They will be weaker than ever, strung out on the trails, nursing wounds from their battles here."

He gave me the look a commander gives his second. "Why do you think there will be fighting here?"

"Because, as we both proved last night, the Chicaza are a proud and unbending people. The one thing de Soto demands is that people prostrate themselves before him. To make a Chicaza bend is to insult him. The *soldados* will want women for their beds. Slaves will do at first, but some Chicaza wife or niece will eventually be carried off, stripped, tied to the ground, and a line of men will use her as meanly as they can. As sure as Mother Sun rises"—I pointed at the horizon, now eerily crimson—"there will be bloodshed."

"You are sure you wish to go to the Natchez?"

"Or the Quizquiz. De Soto will learn that they are the largest, most influential Nations in the vicinity. He will not want to head north to the Kaskinampo. They won't have the food stocks he needs. Natchez, Quizquiz, it makes no difference."

He studied the frosty grass at his feet, scuffing it with a wet toe. Perhaps living as a barefooted ascetic had made him impervious to any feeling, physical or personal? "This is your woman speaking?"

I bristled. "Elder, she has killed more Kristianos than any man alive. The greatest mikkos in our world receive her with honor and refer to her as 'war chief.' That she was willing to endure a certain amount of disrespect among the Chicaza does her more honor than the Chicaza. But she's right: It's the destruction of the Kristianos that truly matters. She was also right when she observed that as long as I'm here, the focus is going to be on me, on what I did—and what I might want to gain—instead of on killing the *Adelantado* and his army."

With a ghost of a smile he asked, "Still picking scabs off old wounds?"

"Perhaps." I paused, head cocked, an eye narrowed. "I had a vision at Split Sky City. Old White, the Chicaza hero, came to me. He told me to approach Chicaza with humility and piety. This morning, I discover that piety fits me as poorly as Kristiano armor. As soon as I can find enough food to fill my dogs' bellies, we'll be taking the main trail west into the forest. I'm not feeling any too humble."

"And certainly not pious." He spread his arms to the morning sun as the first light peeked through the fuzzy treetops. "You are familiar with my story?"

"I was a boy when you made your retreat from Quizquiz. I remember the day you walked away, leaving everything, even your name, behind you."

He cast a sidelong glance Pearl Hand's way. "I was dismayed because Power had given me no warning of the disaster that awaited me."

"It was only a disaster in your eyes, elder."

"I lost nearly a third of my men."

"A lesser man would have lost them all and himself in the process."

"I appreciate the kindness behind your words, but in those days I was blinded by pride and arrogance. When Power sent me no warning, it was to teach me humility and forbearance. Yet, when I awakened this morning, it was with the terrible realization that nothing has changed. All these years of seeking, of study and discipline, and I find myself as flawed and prideful in my poverty as I ever was as a mighty tishu minko. My error is so great that even though Power has sent you here, I not only ignore the warnings but scorn the messengers."

For the first time since arriving, I could feel the sepaya begin to warm against my skin. He must have felt it for he glanced reverently at the leather pouch.

"Pearl Hand cannot change her ways, elder. She is a blooded war leader and every inch a noble. As much as I appreciate your understanding, perhaps among the Natchez—"

"I will make my own peace with your wife. Assuming you take no offense at my attempts to win her friendship."

"Elder, Pearl Hand defends her honor with that long *hierro* knife hanging from her belt. Power brought us together because we've been hammered, stomped, and dragged through the bitterest challenges life could offer. Pearl Hand walks her own path. That she chooses to walk it with me? I find that fact singularly miraculous."

"So . . . what do I do?"

"Walk up to her, bow politely, and offer an apology for being everything the Chicaza expect of a man. Then take a seat at our fire, and treat her as a blooded warrior while we share our meager meal with you."

"That," he said wistfully, "may prove to be a challenge. She's . . . she's a *woman*!"

"Oh, come. A man smart enough to save an entire army can figure out how to eat breakfast with a capable woman."

"You and Power expect so much of a man."

"Yes. A pity, isn't it?"

TWELVE

OLD WOOD GAVE IT HIS BEST. I THOUGHT HE WAS doomed from the start. Seated by our fire, you would have thought he was constructed out of the same old wood he'd taken his name from. Sun-dried rawhide would have been more flexible. His muscles knotted like stone balls; his jaw seemed to be clamped like a shell cutter's vise. And the poor man had no idea what to do with his eyes. Thank Power he'd given the dogs a basket of dried fish. They gave him something to look at as he managed to stare at everything but Pearl Hand.

What can I say? He was battling against an entire lifetime.

Pearl Hand watched him with cautious amusement, her moves graceful and reserved as she served up his portion of the breakfast stew.

"With Two Packs in Chicaza town, the high minko should at least be apprised of the threat." I lifted my cup to my lips, sipping the hot stew. As chilly as the morning was, it felt good. "The first thing de Soto will attempt is to take the high minko hostage. Once he has him, he's going to feel invincible."

Pearl Hand glanced over to where Bark growled at Gnaw. "But can the high minko grasp the depths of Kristiano treachery? That they will approach under the white Power of peace? Maybe even send the White Arrow? Does he understand that as soon as he is within their ranks they will take him prisoner, chain him by the neck, and use him against his own people?" She shot a look at the fidgeting Old Wood. "Like all the others, your high minko's simply going to accept that Kristianos play by our rules of civilized behavior."

"How can they not? To defy the laws of Power is to deny the very foundations of creation," Old Wood said, even more unsettled.

"They abuse Power any way they wish as long as it serves their purposes." Pearl Hand raised her hand. "And it has come as a shock to everyone that Power doesn't strike them down. It can't."

I saw disbelief in his eyes and added, "When I was in the Spirit World, Old-Woman-Who-Never-Dies told me that this war will be decided by men. For some reason, the Power of the Kristiano *jesucristo* and Breath Giver are balanced, like our notion of red and white Powers. Neither can ultimately triumph over the other."

"You have proof of this?" Old Wood looked distressed. It wasn't just his notions about women that were being shaken today.

I pressed my palms together, choosing my words carefully. "During the fighting in Apalachee I carried my sepaya for the great holy man Back-from-the-Dead the day he battled the Kristiano priests before the walls of Anhaica. Back-from-the-Dead and the priest faced each other, each calling down their Powers. Nothing happened—as if the entire world was frozen—until they were interrupted by the screams of a dying woman. After that, it was a matter of arms."

"Oh, sure." Pearl Hand snorted. "As I remember it, you were running for your life, dragging that fool hili-shaya along behind you. I can still see your path down the creek, marked by fluttering cardinal feathers torn from the man's cloak." She gave me a fake smile. "And who was it that sneaked up to your rescue as the *soldados* were about to skewer your heart with crossbow arrows?"

"You, my love." I used a cloying voice, dripping with irony. I glanced sidelong at Old Wood. "She never allows me to forget the days when she kills more of the Kristiano vermin than I do."

"Or the times I pull your stringy buttocks out of whatever fire you've managed to kindle around you," she added tartly.

"Uh . . . That, too."

I thought I detected the first cracking of Old Wood's reserve. Then the smile died on his lips. "Last night you insisted that if we marched out in traditional squadrons, we'd be crushed. What do you recommend we do?"

"Chicaza town is fortified?" I asked.

He shook his head. "Anyone who invades Chicaza has to pass a gauntlet of scouts, and behind them are the out-lying farmsteads. When an enemy is approaching, we'd rather face him with a mobile force on ground of our choosing."

"Which would be disastrous against Kristiano cabaye-ros and armored *soldados*." Pearl Hand glanced at the ring of dogs as they licked the grass for the last bits of fish. Old Knuckles sat off to the side, watching with unsure eyes.

"Ambush the trails?" I suggested. "Make them fight their way in. See if we can hit them while they're strung out in the trees."

She shook her head. "At Apalachee we had thick brush, wild patches of second-growth forest, and swamps. Here the forests are open beneath the high canopy—perfect for cabayeros. We don't have mountain passes for choke points like we had outside Cofitachequi, and they're coming with full bellies after emptying Apafalaya's granaries."

"You're right," I agreed. "And they've had their noses bloodied at Mabila. Many are still feeling their wounds, wary of how close they came to dying. Individuals won't be straggling or straying from the protection of the main group."

Old Wood had listened thoughtfully. Now he asked, "What about small parties who attack and fall back as bait to lure the pursuers into an ambush?"

"We've used the tactic successfully in the past," I told him. "On those occasions we had time enough to construct traps for the cabayos—pits, deadfalls, sharpened stakes, trip lines, those sorts of things. There must be a way to safely evacuate from the ambush when things go wrong. And, elder, they *will* go wrong. The Kristianos have taught us that bitter lesson over and over."

"The problem with ambushes"—Pearl Hand raised a finger for emphasis—"is that they must be intricately planned. We won't know the *Adelantado*'s route until he comes. Before that, we'd have to have warriors assembled, escape routes established, and traps built."

Old Wood mildly said, "Why not just place our men in hiding, bait the enemy into the kill zone, and shoot them down?"

I reached over and tapped the armored breastplate. "Because they are like turtles, elder. Our arrows just bounce off them . . . or stick. At Mabila, I saw Kristianos that looked like porcupines, and but for the restriction of movement, they fought on with grim determination."

"To kill them," Pearl Hand added, "takes a shot to the face that penetrates the brain or cuts through the spine or blood vessels of the neck. Other than that, you must shoot under the armpit when a *soldado* lifts his sword, or shoot through his foot or lower leg, hoping to slow him down enough that you can pick your shot for a fatal wound."

I watched Squirm roll onto his back and wriggle, all four feet pawing the air. "In the early days, Kristianos were easy to ambush. Unfortunately, the Apalachee taught them a great deal about ambushes—and how to avoid them. We might get lucky once or twice in the beginning, but my guess is that they'll remember very quickly."

"And we can't forget the cabayeros." Pearl Hand made a "pay attention" gesture. "When the ambush is finally overrun—and it will be—your escaping warriors have to be able to vanish into the underbrush. They cannot escape across open fields or through old-growth forest. Cabayeros consider it the height of sport to run down fleeing warriors one by one, or en masse."

"Chicaza are fleet runners," Old Wood reminded her.

"Elder, I have *never* seen a human come close to matching a cabayo's speed, let alone outrun one. You *must* take our word on this."

He gave me a scowl. "You make them sound invincible."

"Good," Pearl Hand snapped. "As soon as you lace that notion into your thinking, you'll have a whisker's chance of surviving your first combat with Kristianos. Not winning, mind you, just surviving."

He finally gifted her with a bitter look. "So, the only way to beat them is not to fight them?"

I responded mildly. "The only way to beat them is to fight them when they are not expecting it."

"That was tried at Mabila." Old Wood lifted an eyebrow. "How many thousands died?"

I lowered my eyes, saying nothing.

Pearl Hand spread her arms. "There are no easy answers. We might just surrender and allow the Kristianos to kill our world and destroy everything we believe in. Or we could remove ourselves from their path, hope that they go on to bother someone else, but that in the end is also surrender. Or you can choose as Black Shell and I have, to fight them—no matter the cost in blood and misery—until they are finally destroyed." She raised a hand to still his protest. "If you choose to fight them, elder, you must grant them their military superiority and figure out a way to attack them when their guard is down. Under all that armor, they are just men."

At that moment the dogs perked, growling, eyes and ears alert as they turned toward one of the trails. Knuckles tilted his head back, howling, "Arrroooowwww!"

We could hear the patter of approaching feet. Old Wood stood, straightening his hunting shirt. A young warrior, his bow in hand, wooden shield on his arm, trotted into the clearing. Spying us, he approached, chest heaving from his exertion, sweat steaming in the cold air.

"Elder?" He dropped to one knee, touching his forehead in respect. "High Minko Chicaza requests that you accompany me to Chicaza town immediately. He has need of your counsel. Invaders come from the east—an entire army. The Kristianos that we have heard so much of are coming here."

The messenger glanced sidelong at Pearl Hand and me. "He has also asked that the strange traders from the east follow. He was aware of their arrival before your message and is anxious that they have not bothered you, beloved elder."

Even as he spoke, eight young men burst from the forest, an empty litter chair on their shoulders. My brother wanted Old Wood to ride in luxury.

Old Wood looked at me, a flatness behind his eyes. "It would appear, Black Shell, that you have your wish. I will take you to your brother and ask that he listen to your words." He hesitated. "Though I have no idea if I'm doing you any favors in the process."

I am going home! The words spun around my souls the way a worm creates a cocoon. Once again I amazed myself with the way giddy anticipation could jet through my veins in such close association with abject terror. Almost twelve long years had passed since I fled Chicaza. Even after all that time declarations of condemnation and loathing still rang in my ears: "Coward!" "Banishment!" "Disgrace!" But most of all, "Akeohoosa!"

I hobbled along after Old Wood's litter, my pack of Kristiano armor bouncing on my back, Antonio's sword swinging from my hip. And, in its sack on my back, the copper mace bumped reassuringly against my spine.

Is going home a mistake?

I couldn't help but remember the stunned hopelessness that had cored out my very guts as I fled Chicaza. Eventually I would have died of despair or starvation had I clung to the outskirts of Chicaza territory. A lesser man might have been taken as a slave by another people, perhaps to be executed on the square, or if lucky and brave, adopted into some foreign clan.

Instead, hungry and frightened, I'd stumbled onto a party of traders: Coosa men and their dogs. They'd been headed for the Natchez, hoping to travel on to the Caddo. That night they fed me, told story upon story of the trail, of the places they had been and the people they had met.

I found a single, thin thread from which to cling.

So—having fashioned my first trader's staff—I began with nothing but the Power of trade. I told stories of the Chicaza rulers in return for food and shelter. On occasion I was given some little trinket, perhaps a bit of shell or a pouch of tobacco. From those humble beginnings, I began to build my trade stock. I met men like Two Packs and traveled with them, and learned. Having been trained as a noble, I knew how the rulers thought and behaved and felt at ease in their company.

I found my way. I saved myself.

Now I wondered if there was any way to save Chicaza, and why I cared so much.

They called me a liar! Said I invoked the name of Horned Serpent to save myself . . . that not only was I a coward but also that Spirit Power would punish me for disrespect.

Mother would be there, older, gruffer, her hard eyes boring into mine. Would she even bother to speak to me? Or would she treat me as if I didn't exist?

My gut began to churn.

"Husband?" Pearl Hand asked as we stopped at a creek crossing below yet another of the countless farmsteads. People were watching from the yards before their houses. I waited as the litter bearers lowered Old Wood, and one by one, in order of rank, they bent to drink.

"Yes?" I turned my attention to the dogs, ordering them back so they didn't foul the water.

She stepped close, concern in her dark eyes. "You all right?"

I chuckled. "Honestly, wife, I don't know. All those years I imagined the way I would finally return to Chicaza, it wasn't like this." I gestured to the warriors as they helped Old Wood reseat himself in the chair. "Following along behind a beloved elder like an afterthought."

"And how did you see it?"

"I was going to make a grand entry . . . the way we did at Cofitachequi. I'd be painted. Shell and copper necklaces would drape my neck. A polished copper chest piece would rest over my heart. My turkey-tail headpiece—polished to mirror brightness—would ride atop my head, and I'd be wearing the finest of linen aprons. Around my shoulders would be a spoonbill-feather cape, and swan-feather sprays would adorn my arms."

"Wanted to really rub their noses in it, huh?"

"You might say I've had the acid bitterness of an unripe acorn stewing in my heart."

The warriors neatly swung Old Wood up on their shoulders, not even glancing back to see if we'd taken our time to drink. What did they care? We were just strangers—an inconvenience to rapid travel.

I laid my pack to the side, dropped onto my knees, and sucked up the cool water. When I stood, Old Wood was turned in his litter, waiting, his hand out to keep the bearers in place. They kept shooting occasional glances back, irritated at the delay.

As I reslung my pack I called, "Afraid you'll lose us, elder?"

He flashed a smile. "I'm not worried about you, Black Shell. It's Knuckles who concerns me. He's almost older than I am. Keep an eye on him, will you? If he starts to falter, I may have to put him in the litter and run along behind with you."

I chuckled at the kindness of his lie; then I motioned for the dogs to drink. They piled into the creek, lapping at the water, wading around. Knuckles was doing fine. He panted a little more and walked a bit stiffly, but at the pace we were keeping, he'd make it.

"Wouldn't the high minko take it poorly if the litter arrived bearing Old Wood's dog?" Pearl Hand asked. "Wouldn't that be considered some sort of insult?"

"Oh, yes. If the miscreant were anyone but Old Wood. Having the reputation of being the greatest warrior and holy man in our time buys him a heap more behavioral leeway than being a clanless trader."

"I'll keep that in mind."

"We'll live longer that way."

"Let's see if I have it. When your brother sends a litter for me, I ride up top? Bark runs along behind? We all stay healthy?"

"You're quick."

"Faster than a Coosa war arrow . . . and just as pointed."

We resumed our journey, and as we made our way through villages, I was constantly reprimanding the dogs, keeping them in line. People crowded the trail to see Old Wood pass. They called their greetings, touching their foreheads in respect.

Then we'd be through the collection of cane-roofed dwellings, alternately crossing winter-fallow fields thick with standing dead corn and then woods consisting of walnuts, hickory, gum, ash, and maple. Occasionally we'd pass travelers headed the other way. Politely they'd step off the trail, touching their foreheads as Old Wood passed. I'd forgotten how populous Chicaza was.

In late afternoon we crested yet another of the timbered ridges and dropped down onto the flats. The trail here was like a deep rut worn into the forest floor. Even roots had been chopped off to make the passage quicker.

Breaking out of the trees I could see Chicaza town, smoke rising lazily in the gray and misty midday light. The town had been built in a delta between two creeks—one on the east, the other on the west—that ran south toward the Tombigbee River. While the loamy soil had been cleared for agriculture, occasional hickory, oak, and mulberry trees rose above the fields. The latter were yellow and stubbly from still-standing cornstalks. Once past the fields, the land gave way to old-growth timber and low rolling hills on the east, north, and west. Floodplain and back-swamp forest rose like a fuzzy gray wall to the south.

My heart began to pound as I remembered the town the way it had been. Grand, magnificent, the virtual center of the world. Could this be the same place?

Each of the two hundred or so buildings was topped by a steeply pitched thatch roof, the effect reminding me of a series of square-bitted hatchets chopping at the sky.

Here and there tall granaries rested atop support posts; ladders hung down from the cane doors. The World Tree pole, painted in red and white spirals, dominated the skyline, easily twice the height of the high minko's palace. The latter stood on the northern side of the square plaza, its high roof crowned by two eagle statues. Clan totems had been carved atop other tall poles, and from the distance I could see effigies of Panther, Raccoon, Deer, Crawfish, and Skunk. Each of the iksas had a clan house facing the plaza according to the status accorded to it. The Deer and Skunk Clans marked the plaza's southern boundary.

People scurried back and forth between the surrounding dwellings, leaving no doubt that more than the usual business was afoot.

It struck me then: *What a shabby little town!*

Anhaica, Telemico, Coosa, Hiawassee, Atahachi, and even Mabila—with its splendid walls and great shade trees—belittled this haphazard collection of dwellings. The notion stunned me. As a boy, I'd believed Chicaza to be the greatest Nation of all, and during my years as a trader, I'd never been back to draw a comparison.

At that moment a group of boys, ranging from eight to perhaps ten, rounded one of the outlying houses. Naked and barefoot in the cold, they ran, bows in their hands, quivers bouncing on their slender backs. In the rear, trotting hard on their heels, the trainer followed, a willow switch in his hand. I could hear the rising melody as the old, familiar war song carried on the winter afternoon.

> May the red Power bless me,
> And forever our enemies fall.
> May their blood turn to water, and their courage flee,
> When our tishu minko issues the war call.
> Power grant me courage and strength of arm
> As I lay low our enemies and keep Chicaza from harm.

For just an instant, I might have been a child again, running naked in the freezing air. Here was the heart of Chicaza. My people no longer built great cities, temples, and walls. Instead we suckled terrible young warriors, steeped them in the traditions and skills of war, and drilled discipline and glory into their bones.

As one of the boys began to lag, the trainer leaped forward, slashing the willow switch across the boy's vulnerable buttocks. Sting as the whip might, the humiliation of such a blow carried an even greater weight. The lad shot forward, taking the lead from his fellows.

I flinched at the very memory.

I'm home.

THIRTEEN

THE SEPAYA ON MY CHEST FELT WARM WHEN WE FI-
nally made our way across the plaza and stopped just
short of the *tchkofa*—the grandest structure in all Chicaza.
Supported by a log framework, the tchkofa dome was
covered with a thick layer of earth. The Chicaza council,
composed of iksa minkos, met inside, away from the eyes
of the people. Under the shelter of that smoky roof, pol-
icy was made, grievances were addressed, and the politics
of my warrior people were conducted.

Pearl Hand and I laid our goods beneath a ramada to
the right of the tchkofa doorway. After the litter chair was
lowered, Old Wood was ceremonially lifted to his feet by
burly warriors. He glanced at us, asking, "You will be all
right here until I call for you?"

"Of course, elder. And we'll see to Knuckles."

The plaza was filled with people, their attention
fixed on Old Wood. They whispered excitedly, eyes
gleaming.

I motioned for the dogs to guard our belongings and

hitched my belt around my waist, setting Antonio's sword within easy reach.

Our entrance into Chicaza had been anticlimactic. All eyes had been on Old Wood. People had bowed. Some had dropped reverently to their knees. All touched their foreheads in solemn respect.

The glances the Chicaza spared for us were mildly curious, and then intrigued as they spotted the Kristiano equipment. A couple of people pointed, wondering what the stuff was, having never seen its like before.

Since we were accompanying the beloved elder on what was obviously a solemn and official mission, no one considered it prudent to call out to us. They just naturally figured we were some kind of servants.

I'd spent a lifetime announcing my presence, calling out to all who would listen that I, a noted trader, had just entered their town. I expected to be the center of attention. Black Shell, the tainted exile, had returned to Chicaza—and his arrival didn't even merit a yawn.

The sensation of being ignored was just plain eerie. It further served to stagger my already unbalanced souls. Gnaw looked up at me with his soulful brown eyes, his expression asking, "So . . . what's next?" His white-tipped tail slapped the dusty ground in emphasis.

The dogs might have been watching us. Everyone else's attention was on the tchkofa, where the high minko, the tishu minko, and the Chicaza council would be meeting. That's where the real excitement lay.

"You have a plan?" Pearl Hand asked, straightening, her eyes taking in the crowd that jostled around us. They were dressed in fabric or leather hunting shirts, many with blankets around their shoulders. Tall moccasins protected their feet from the cold, and many wore warm capes crafted from bear or buffalo hide. Every male in sight over the age of puberty carried weapons. They peered intently, seeking a better view of Old Wood where he stood beside the guardian posts and waited to be escorted into the tchkofa.

"Find Two Packs," I said, anxious to hear what he'd learned about Chicaza's disposition toward the Kristianos. Meanwhile, heart thumping, I searched the crowd for familiar faces. Was someone going to point, shouting, "Look! It's the akeohoosa Black Shell! Pelt him with excrement!"

Twelve years was a long time. Could that old man talking to Old Wood be Goose? The hunter who once offered each of his first-season deer to Uncle? I couldn't be sure.

Then I saw my cousin, tall, straight, his face tattooed in lines. When I'd known him as a boy his name had been Makes Grass, my *pok nakni,* one of Uncle's grandchildren descended from his second wife, a Raccoon Clan woman. Makes Grass had grown into a tough-looking warrior and carried a hardwood bow, a quiver of war arrows, and a heavy wooden shield on his left arm. Three honorary miniature white arrows were stuck through his hair bun, evidence of the highest distinction in battle. He glanced my direction; I froze, only to have his gaze pass over me as if I were smoke.

"Nervous?" Pearl Hand asked, having seen me flinch.

"I was literally chased from Chicaza by people throwing trash, feces, sticks, and stones. If they'd caught me, they'd have doused me with ashes, urinated on me, and beaten me half to death." I looked glumly at the crowd. "Shouldn't my reappearance bring at least a little disapproval?"

"Don't tempt fate," she growled.

"I feel like a mixture of fire and ice: excited, anxious, frightened, and very nervous. I was swallowed alive by Horned Serpent in the Sky World. I've fought and killed Kristianos and stood face-to-face with the *Adelantado* himself. I've argued with, and cowed, the greatest minkos in our world. I survived Kristiano captivity, Napetuca, and Mabila. Why does being here upset me so?"

She shot me that thin-lidded look. "Because, my dear lover, you are living your own personal dilemma. There are two Chicaza peoples existing inside you: the ones you hate and mock because of the injustice they meted out, and the ones you love for their courage and bravery. You delight in ridiculing your Chicaza heritage and take pride in the ways you've raised yourself above their pettiness. Then, in the next instant—as at Cofitachequi and Coosa—you are passing yourself off as a Chicaza minko, and proud to be one." She laid a comforting hand on my shoulder. "Now that you are face-to-face with your people, you must decide who and what they really are."

. . . And what role I am going to adopt here.

She smiled as she saw the question register behind my eyes.

Think, Black Shell. These are your people. You know them. How do you play this?

Not as a Chicaza, that was for sure. No matter who I was to the rest of the world, I'd been declared akeohoosa. And Pearl Hand had been right that night at Old Wood's: The last thing I needed was to have everyone's attention centered on me when de Soto and his murderous filth were rolling down on Chicaza.

Act like an akeohoosa, and you'll be treated like one.

That was a fact.

I watched as Old Wood was ceremoniously led into the tchkofa. At the door, the tishu minko, a man I recognized as Red Cougar Mankiller, of the Raccoon Clan, raised his staff of office and shouted, "Now comes the beloved elder Old Wood, of the Raccoon Clan, of Hickory Moiety!"

From inside came the calls of approbation and greeting. Assuming the council was already in session, there would be the ritual interruption as Old Wood—one of the most prominent Chicaza—was seated. My guess was that my brother wouldn't have started such a serious debate without him. That meant it would take another two fingers of time at least before the council finished the invocations, smoked the sacred pipe, said the prayers, shared the black drink, and actually began discussing the Kristiano problem.

"We've got to be nobles," I whispered. "But how?" Blackie yawned and scratched, obviously missing the import of our dilemma.

I looked around, cursing the Kristianos for burning all of our possessions back at Mabila. "We really need to find Two Packs."

Pearl Hand's shoulders twitched as she shrugged. "Dogs, stay." She looked at me. "Do we need to carry the Kristiano armor with us?"

I glanced at the crowd, then shook my head. "This is Chicaza." Then I gestured to one of the older boys. Not quite a man, he was still at the stage where he was all eyes, skinny arms and legs, and mussed-up hair. He had a quick smile, twigs in his locks as if he'd been wrestling in the leaves, and a Panther Clan blanket wrapped around his shoulders.

"These things arrived with the beloved elder Old Wood and are gifts to be presented to the high minko. Please explain that to anyone who might show an interest in them. These dogs are here to guard them." I pointed at the old dog, who'd immediately flopped onto the ground, panting. "And that is Knuckles, the elder's animal. Inform his relatives in the Raccoon Clan that Old Wood holds them responsible for the dog's care."

"Yes . . . of course." He was obviously struggling with who I was and where to place me within the rank and relations of his Chicaza world.

Ordering the dogs to stay and guard, I took Pearl Hand's hand and we set off, heading first for the palace.

Along the way I told passersby, "I am looking for the trader Two Packs."

The third person we encountered smiled and pointed. "Ah, he's residing in Minko Flying Squirrel's house. Just there, east side of the plaza and down three houses."

"Everyone knows everything," I sighed.

We walked wide around the chunkey court, and I couldn't help but cast an evaluative glance at it. The clay was raked and level, obviously well cared for. My estimation of my brother's administrative competence rose.

At Minko Flying Squirrel's I stopped. The house was in the traditional trench-wall style, rectangular, with a soaring thatch roof. The high ridgepole was topped by a weathered carving of Panther. Additional images of panthers were painted on the white walls. The tall clan totem—sporting a clawing cougar—towered above the plaza. A pestle and mortar stood out front by the mat-walled summer house, the latter being little more than a lavishly appointed ramada.

"Two Packs?" I called in Coosa-accented Mos'kogee. "You in there?"

"Just a moment," he bellowed back.

I glanced at Pearl Hand; her eyebrow was curved in a questioning arch.

We waited just long enough to begin wondering why we were waiting so long when he opened the wooden-slat door. Naked but for a breechcloth donned so quickly it sat crooked on his hips, he grinned and waved us in.

Ducking inside the spacious structure, we found a typical Chicaza minko's dwelling: the fire in the center of the room; high pole beds along each wall; pottery, boxes, and fabric bags stored below the beds along with interspersed personal items. A small shrine covered in cougar hide stood just behind the puddle-clay hearth. Excellently rendered wood carvings of cougars stood in each corner of the room. The floors were covered with neatly swept cattail and cane matting.

Then the woman grabbed my attention. Dressed in a simple pullover, she was fussing with the bed to our right. As I watched her smooth the rumpled blankets, I noticed that her long hair was down and disheveled. She straightened, shooting me a knowing look, a slight smile on her attractive face. Then she arched her back—an act that emphasized her full breasts—and cocked her hip. With a flash of her eyes, she tossed her hair back in a sensual motion before combing it out with her fingers.

She gave Two Packs a saucy wink, pulled her dress straight, and neatly caught the shell pendant he tossed her. Walking to the door, she frowned slightly and turned. Her inquisitive gaze fixed on me for a moment; then she gave me a ravishing smile. With a slight nod of recognition, she ducked out. My last glimpse was of her swishing hips as she tucked a blanket around her shoulders and sauntered away.

"I hope that's not someone's wife," I groaned.

"Paid woman," Two Packs said with a yawn as he slipped on his coat. "Name's Wild Rose. She's Koasati, taken in a raid as a young girl and gifted by her captor to the Deer Clan. The way Wild Rose tells her complicated story, as she grew into adulthood, the woman who owned her was Deer Clan. The Deer Clan woman had a husband—a Crawfish Clan man—who began to find Wild Rose interesting. Promised to buy her from Deer Clan and have her adopted by someone in Panther Clan so that he could marry her properly as a second wife."

"Let me guess. I'll bet the Crawfish Clan man didn't talk this all out with his wife first, ask her if she wanted to have her ex-slave as a second wife?"

Two Packs shot Pearl Hand and me a healthy, if gap-toothed, grin. "Nope. In the ensuing squabble, divorce, and recriminations, it went all the way up to the high minko for judgment. Since Wild Rose had acted honorably, and the Crawfish fellow had made the promises, and the Deer Clan woman divorced him, Wild Rose came out with a settlement that she used to buy her freedom from Deer Clan, who didn't really want a troublemaker like her anymore. She ended up as a paid woman, making a tidy living, thank you."

"Thought you Chicaza took a dim view of recreational shaft-and-sheathing," Pearl Hand snorted, giving me the eye.

"Paid women are different," I muttered. "Two Packs, we need to look presentable. All we've got are our trail clothes and some pieces of copper. We need face paint, something, anything, to make us look like we're nobility worth listening to."

He gave me the kind of grin the old Two Packs would have—the kind that made his rawboned face look blocky. "I thought you might. It's nothing fancy like the outfit you wore in Coosa, but you can probably get by."

He bent to where his packs were stashed under the pole bed and tossed first me, then Pearl Hand, a roll of clothing.

I shook mine out to find a crimson-dyed cloth shirt. The material was obviously of Kristiano manufacture, the cut reminiscent of Coosa design, loose in the shoulders, hanging to the knees, and needing a belt at the waist. I looked over at Pearl Hand, who held up a black fabric dress. She paused, admiring beadwork across the bodice that depicted Morning Star, his eagle-winged arms outspread.

"This is Kristiano cloth. Where did you get these?" I asked, stunned.

"At Coosa. In the beginning the Kristianos were free with their gifts. The cloth was given to the nobles, many of whom owed me." He stared woodenly at the clothing. "My wife cut and sewed both of those in the days before my boys were ordered away. When I left, I rolled them up, thinking they might come in handy for the trade."

I shucked off my travel clothing and pulled the light material over my head. Then I watched as Pearl Hand removed her brown, travel-smudged dress and slipped the black fabric over her muscular body. In an instant she was transformed into a stunning dark shadow. The white shell beads glimmered in the firelight as if the eagle-man design were alive.

"How do I look?" she asked.

"I'd marry you in a minute," Two Packs growled, wiping his mouth as if he were drooling.

"What's the matter?" I asked. "Wild Rose not worth the price of a shell pendant?"

Two Packs gave me his wolfish look. "Oh, she's as good as any. It's just been a while since I've had the urge."

"Glad to see you're coming around," Pearl Hand told him dryly. "What about the political situation here? What is the word on the Kristianos? Will the Chicaza fight?"

Two Packs spread his arms wide. "Since I've been here, I've heard all kinds of conflicting notions. Apparently a group of Chicaza fought at Mabila. None of them came home. Not a single one. And worse, there's been no word of what went wrong there. The priests are worried that the Power was wrong, others think their warriors were defeated because they didn't take the war medicine box with them. Others think the Kristianos might be made into allies. And then I've heard some, like the Panther Clan minko, here, who want to march out, defeat the Kristianos, enslave the survivors, and capture all spoils."

"The usual," Pearl Hand said with a sigh.

Two Packs made a face. "I've told them all I know. The high minko and the council listened as I related what happened at Coosa and what you told me about Cofitachequi and Apalachee. They grilled me about Kristiano warfare but didn't seem to believe me when I said they couldn't win."

"Figures," I muttered.

Two Packs placed a thick hand on my shoulder. "I told them that you two were coming, that you could answer their questions. I didn't exactly tell them who you are, just that you were both war chiefs who'd fought the Kristianos in the past. And won."

I glanced at Pearl Hand, noting the wry twist of her lips. "Before we go, we need paints. Old Wood will call for us when the time is right. But when we enter the tchkofa, we have to look and act the part."

"What about me?" Two Packs asked.

"Just be yourself. You know better than any of us what happened at Coosa. If nothing else, my brother has to understand that he cannot place himself at risk. If they take him, like they took the Coosa High Sun, Chicaza is lost."

"And the paints?" Pearl Hand reminded us. "We may not have a lot of time."

Two Packs grinned. "Wild Rose. She's got paints, jewelry, even clothing and adornments to spare." Then he added, "For a price."

FOURTEEN

WE SAT UNDER THE RAMADA, WAITING, WATCHING, and listening as rumors slipped through the crowd like mullets in sea grass. Their attention was split, half of it centered on the tchkofa. The other half was focused on Pearl Hand, me, and Two Packs, dressed as we were, our pile of Kristiano armor beside us, the dogs sitting patiently in a protective ring around us.

I had unpacked my copper mace and now cradled it in my hands. When the people saw it, they'd literally gasped, pointing, whispering among themselves. We had metamorphosed from faceless servants into nobles.

Two Packs, forever sniffing out opportunities for self-aggrandizement and self-promotion, walked along the periphery, his face painted in blue and yellow, explaining to people that we were foreign nobility come to address the council about the Kristianos.

Myself, I was nervous and fidgety. Any moment now I'd be face-to-face with my brother, my mother, my sisters. And then what? My reception could be anything from being tossed disgracefully out on my ear to a welcome-home hug.

Okay, probably no welcome-home hug.

The important thing was that they listen to me, and if not me, to Pearl Hand. Which, in either case, would be a stretch for them. We've established their views on akeohoosas like me. And though the Chicaza occasionally fielded women warriors, they were considered *berdache:* women's bodies containing male souls. Such women generally took other women for wives and kept their own households. Pearl Hand had as little chance of holding their attention as a bit of milkweed down.

As I considered these things, I tried not to mess with my face paint. Wild Rose—as Two Packs had promised—did not disappoint. Her house was a tidy three-room affair at the edge of the Wildcat Clan grounds. I had remarked on the berry bushes that grew around the yard and next to her summer house.

"So her clients can come and go in anonymity," Two Packs replied. "She also has another door out the back."

"Ah," Pearl Hand sighed, "Chicaza morality. The tighter a people tries to lace themselves into a coat, the more they long to wiggle out of it when no one is looking."

Wild Rose had greeted us at her door, her knowing gaze lingering on me. She'd taken in my blood-red shirt before fingering the textile. Then she'd slowly and thoroughly inspected Pearl Hand in her form-fitting black dress.

"You could be real competition," she'd said at last.

"You honor me," Pearl Hand replied easily. "But I like keeping the vows that bind me to my husband."

At which point Wild Rose turned her attention back to me. "So, Black Shell, the akeohoosa, has returned to his people. Why haven't they started pelting you with trash?"

"With the exception of Old Wood, no one knows who I am. You, however, seem to have recognized me right off."

She gave me a clever smile. "You were a dream of mine when I was a little girl. The day they chased you away broke my heart."

"I don't remember you."

"You wouldn't. I was a Koasati slave back then." She glanced at Two Packs. "What service might I provide?"

It was Pearl Hand who said, "In a couple of fingers of time we must address the Chicaza council. We have the dress but lack ornamentation and paints."

"And what's in it for me?"

Pearl Hand smiled. "A copper piece manufactured in distant Cofitachequi. Once it was the property of the high mico there. You'll find it slightly discolored from the fires at Mabila, but well worth the use of your paints and a generous selection of your jewelry."

Wild Rose remained silent, her gaze locked with Pearl Hand's. "Very well. If your word is good."

"I make the offer under the Power of trade," Pearl Hand replied. "And as a woman who, like you, has lived by her wits."

A ghost of a smile crossed Wild Rose's lips as she gave me a sidelong glance. "It appears, Black Shell, that in contrast to your brother, you've married well." She had then stepped aside, gesturing grandly. "Make yourselves at home. Let us see what we can do about making your appearance worthy of the glorious Chicaza council."

She'd been as good as her word. I caught myself just in time as I reached up to dab at my face paint. Wild Rose herself, accompanied by Pearl Hand's suggestions, had painted my face. A black forked-eye design outlined in white had been placed on a split background—red on my forehead and cheeks, blue accented by black lightning bolts on my chin.

Pearl Hand had chosen red for the right side of her face and black for the left, indicative respectively of warfare and death. The blue band of her native Chicora nobility was painted from ear to ear across her eyes and the bridge of her nose.

All of our peoples believe that colors have intrinsic Power. Think of how bright and vibrant the color of fresh blood is, literally alive with Power. Yet, when it dies, it slowly turns to black as the Power fades. When we don the paint, we accept and integrate the Power it reflects. With our reliance on red and black—the colors of strife and combat—we were making a political statement that no Chicaza could fail to recognize.

Around us, people continued to stare.

I continued to fret.

So, Black Shell, when you finally walk in there, just how are you going to introduce yourself? "Greetings! The banished coward is home!"

Even as I grappled with the problem, the *ayopachi*, the orator, appeared in the tchkofa doorway, calling, "The beloved elder Old Wood requests that the traders be brought before the council."

I felt my heart drop like a heavy, cold stone into the hollow of my gut.

Time.

And I had no idea what I would say.

Shoulder to shoulder and seated by clan, people packed the tchkofa. Anybody with even a modicum of status had managed to squeeze into the round, earth-covered room with its heavy log ceiling. My heart was pounding, a fluttering in my guts, as the ayopachi cleared the way for us.

People crowded so close to the aisle that the Kristiano armor thumped shoulders, elbows, or heads that jostled too close. Curses erupted in the wake of our passage. I swallowed hard when we stopped in the small open area before the sacred fire. One of the four logs popped, sparks rising toward the open smoke hole above.

The tchkofa was divided into sections, each of the

iksas having its piece of floor. The Chief Clan's area was in the rear. The high minko stood beside the panther chair in advance of a knot of people. In the place of honor to the high minko's left stood Old Wood. An impassive expression masked his thoughts. Beside him would be the tishu minko, Red Cougar Mankiller, and several of the hopayes, or high priests. The older man to the high minko's left I recognized as Flying Squirrel Mankiller, the Panther Clan minko at whose house Two Packs was staying. Behind and between the two was my cousin Makes Grass, though I was sure he had a man's name by now.

On the point of trembling, I met the high minko's gaze across the hot fire. For the first time in twelve years, I stared into my brother's eyes. In my mind he'd remained frozen in time, forever the horrified little boy who'd watched my disgrace with wide, disbelieving eyes. That long-ago day, hot tears spawned by fear and betrayal had marked his round, brown cheeks. His quivering chin and clenched fists signaled the depth of his distress.

Before me stood a handsome man, tall, with broad shoulders. A bear-hide cape was draped back over his shoulders, revealing a deep chest and rippled belly. A white apron hung down to his knees, an eagle embroidered upon it with black thread. He cradled Uncle's copper-headed ceremonial ax, its handle carved in the shape of intertwined red and white serpents. Uncle's words haunted my memory. *"This will be yours one day, Black Shell."*

The ax had become my brother's burden to bear.

At least ten strings of shell-beaded necklaces hung at his throat. Atop his head, a polished copper hairpiece in the shape of a falcon gleamed in the firelight. His face was painted, half red, half white, indicating he brought no preconceived desires for either peace or war to this council.

Like a blow to the gut, it hit me: But for the call of Power it would have been me perched there on the three-legged stool with its thick covering of panther hides.

He frowned slightly, trying to peer through my paint, distracted by the vibrant red Coosa shirt and the pack of Kristiano armor. Then he turned his attention to Pearl Hand and the Kristiano dress that conformed to each of her sensual curves. I saw the slightest quiver of his hard lips, then he fixed, puzzled, on the crossbow she held across her flat belly.

I could read the question in his eyes: Who'd put such a small bow on a handle? Was it some curiously designed toy? From his experience such an arrangement would only be good for rabbits and squirrels.

Brother, you've a hard education ahead of you.

When I saw my mother it felt like a fist had closed on my throat. She stood in the *ishki minko*'s place, behind my brother's right shoulder. A red myrtle-fiber dress clung to her still-slim body and she'd draped her neck with shell and copper beads. Breath froze in my lungs as she turned her attention on me. Her hard features, the set jaw and high cheeks, remained unforgiving. Age, however, had etched her mouth and chin with the finest of lines. She looked even more implacable. Her eyes might have been obsidian pebbles: cold, hard, polished, and unforgiving.

I had to order myself to breathe again.

My two younger sisters waited immediately behind Mother. My memories of both consisted of mixed images of giggling, silly little girls. They had grown into attractive young women, and both were obviously pregnant. Behind them stood several of my male cousins and their mothers, each positioned according to their lineage's rank.

To my brother's right was the Old Camp Moiety, composed of the Deer Clan, Hawk Clan, Crawfish Clan, and finally the Skunk Clan in the south beside the Fish Clan.

My brother's gaze returned to me and fixed on the Cahokian mace. His eyes widened. Following his gaze, people around the great hall began to shift and whisper. Those not rude enough to point indicated the mace with their chins or a tilt of the head. Mother, too, now stared with a calculating curiosity. Then her eyes narrowed, wary lines deepening around her mouth as she tried to assess our importance.

The sepaya warmed against my chest. A slow smile curled my lips, my anxiety fading. *Mother, you and the family are in for a most upsetting evening.*

The ayopachi straightened, head back, asking the ritual question: "Who comes before the high minko and his Chicaza council?"

I took a half step forward, the polished copper mace cradled in my hand. Nerving myself I mustered enough of the canny old trader inside to proclaim, "I am Black Shell Mankiller, known among Nations as Ahltakla, 'the Orphan,' the chosen of Horned Serpent. I have fought the Kristianos all the way from the Uzita lands in the far south. After the battle of Napetuca I was borne to the Sky World by Horned Serpent and devoured. Among the Apalachee I carried the fight to the invaders for an entire winter and raced their squadrons to Cofitachequi. I counseled the Coosa High Sun and plotted the *Adelantado*'s destruction at High Minko Tuskaloosa's side. And now, from the smoke and carnage of Mabila, I come here, offering my services to the greatest warriors of our world."

I paused. "Provided they are wise enough to hear the words of one who has fought the enemy for so long and learned their ways."

At that, I looked straight at Pearl Hand. As I'd hoped, everyone's gaze followed mine.

"I am Pearl Hand Chief-Killer," she stated with authority, "of the Chief Clan, of the Chicora people. I come to Chicaza having killed more Kristianos than any person now living. I have spied on the Kristiano councils, speak their tongue, and know the deceptions that coil in their treacherous hearts. I fought at Napetuca, was declared nicoquadca by the Apalachee and thlakko by the Tuskaloosa. I will share my knowledge and advice with the Chicaza, provided they will hear my counsel."

Unease ran through the room, people awed that a woman would speak with such authority. Mother leaned forward, whispering into my brother's ear, her glinting eyes on Pearl Hand. But my brother ignored her to the point she poked him in the side, whispering even more intently. Instead of replying he stared at me with stunned recognition. A tingle ran through me as I narrowed an eye and inclined my head slightly.

Here I am, brother. Returned from the dead and claiming to be the chosen of Power. So, what are you going to do about me?

I guess the poor man had a right to look astounded. Mother poked him harder, trying to get his attention, the frown lines growing angry in her forehead.

"Ishto Minko"—I used the Chicaza term of address—"Abeminko Pearl Hand and I offer our services freely. We are charged with the destruction of the *Adelantado* de Soto and his army. For this task, Power chose us, and we are dedicated to its completion. We come under the Power of trade and bind ourselves by it. However, if you and your council decide you have no use for our services, we will be obliged to continue on."

I could almost read his souls, twisted with curiosity and disbelief. My appearance, let alone my claims, smacked of the incredible. Could he take the word of a branded coward and liar? He kept studying the copper mace, an emblem of supreme authority and status. His curiosity grew as he turned his attention to the exotic Kristiano armor.

154

Mother—never one slow about her wits—was now staring at me. Her eyes widened with shock; her hand started to rise, then stopped short. In an instant, rabid loathing filled her expression, her eyes darkening, her jaws grinding. When her fist knotted, the tendons stood from the back of her hand.

My two sisters now gaped in dismay and amazement. They glanced at each other, mouthing the question.

Mother pressed against the high minko, whispering frantically into my brother's ear. He raised a hand, signaling for her to desist. When she didn't he slashed it angrily.

Come on, brother. Are you your own man or Mother's puppet?

A bead of tense sweat trickled down my side as I held my brother's hard stare, daring him.

Then he stepped forward, head cocked. "You make remarkable claims . . . *Orphan*."

I touched my forehead in respect. "I've had a remarkable life, High Minko. Our purpose here is simple: Do you wish our help and counsel against the Kristianos? If you do, we will share our hard-won knowledge without expectation of reward. If you do not, we shall immediately take our leave of Chicaza."

"You sent me the strange metal sword," he stated, glancing at Two Packs. The burly trader nodded from his place in the rear.

"You may keep that as our gift in return for the opportunity to address this council. Do *not* let the Kristianos see it, or even know that you possess such a thing. They will demand it back and show no polite manners in the taking of it."

"We have ways of dealing with bad manners," Tishu Minko Red Cougar muttered. I saw one of my sisters nod in grim agreement. Her eyes, however, were as hard and bitter as Mother's.

Pearl Hand propped the crossbow butt on her jutting hip. "The Kristianos will take what they wish, Tishu Minko. Either through treachery and hostages or by force of arms. If you deploy your squadrons to stop them, the cabayeros will blast through them like a great wind through a field of grass. Your vaunted Chicaza warriors will fall like frail stems against their mighty gale. *Hierro*-clad *soldados* will slice through anyone left standing the way an obsidian knife cuts hot fat."

She turned, taking in the entire tchkofa. "I say this meaning no disrespect to the Chicaza or their courage." She tapped Antonio's breastplate where it hung on my back; the *hierro* rang musically. "What you must understand is that the invaders are better armored, armed with more dangerous weapons, and they have the cabayos—giant war beasts that carry cabayeros like the wind. The Kristianos are an army the likes of which you have never fought, an army beyond your comprehension."

She circled slowly, addressing each of the clans, one by one. "I know because I fought beside Chicaza warriors at Mabila. Many of your finest marched under the White Arrow to join Tuskaloosa. I helped to train them. And I watched them die, valiant and courageous to the last man."

She had them hooked, passion in her voice, fire in her eyes. "The plan was perfect. Brave Tuskaloosa lured the monster de Soto, his Kristiano chiefs, and their terrible cabayos inside the walls of Mabila. We *had* them! More than five thousand of us surrounded fewer than a hundred Kristianos. But when the trap was sprung, they fought their way back through the gate. And even then, out on the plain, we finally would have killed them."

The silence was so intense that I flinched when a log popped in the fire.

Pearl Hand's voice lowered. "But before we could do so, the dreaded cabayeros came. They emerged from the Piachi trail, and like a storm they blew down upon us. Those of us who had fought them before knew enough to run." She raised a clenched fist. "But most didn't listen. They had never seen cabayeros before. Perhaps they didn't understand the threat—no matter how many times Black Shell and I tried to hammer it into their heads and souls. Or perhaps it was the novelty of seeing men riding such strange and terrifying war beasts that overcame their sense."

She shook her raised fist. "All but the Chicaza! They alone followed the order to withdraw. They covered the retreat of those who ran. And but for them, many more would have died on the field." She smiled fleetingly. "The cabayeros blasted through them, the beasts tumbling men like kicked pots, riders lancing them as if skewering fish in a shallow pond."

She lifted her head, chin forward. "Many Chicaza managed to make it back within the walls. Many helped to free the slaves we rescued from the Kristianos. And finally, the last of the Chicaza died battling man-to-man with the *soldados* who breached Mabila's walls. Even at the last, when the Kristianos managed to fire the town, none of the few surviving Chicaza admitted defeat. To the last, they fought."

She paused. "I came here for them. To tell you how your warriors died. I came to tell you to honor them, and cherish them, and to make offerings for their souls. It matters not that they died in distant Mabila. You have Horned Serpent's word that their souls are already on their way to the Seeing Eye and the Sky World, where they will be greeted by the ancestors."

She took a breath, looking at me. "I have said my piece, Orphan. If they have no further use for us, we can leave now."

I nodded, knowing full well that Pearl Hand, at least, had just won over most of the council.

I turned, inclining my head toward my brother. "High Minko, in the name of Horned Serpent, we have spoken."

Mother smiled, a victorious glint in her eyes. She filled her lungs, raising a hand. Whatever it was, it would be bad.

But it was Old Wood who stepped forward, asking, "If I may, High Minko?"

"You may speak, beloved elder."

I watched Mother give the elder a sly sidelong glance, but she stepped back.

Old Wood gave Pearl Hand and me a thoughtful inspection. Then he turned to the council. "I was surprised when these people appeared at my house. I came to realize that Power sent them to me. No matter who this man might have been"—he pointed at me—"he is a smart and pious individual. I have questioned them both on spiritual and military matters. Black Shell—who calls himself the Orphan—wears a sepaya."

The hopayes perked up at that. Whispers ran through the crowd. My brother's frown deepened. Mother's eyes narrowed craftily.

Old Wood added, "How he obtained it, I have no idea. But the fact that he wears it and does not boastfully flaunt its Power tells me a great deal about his character."

The hopayes were whispering back and forth.

Old Wood turned to the high minko. "My opinion, High Minko, is that whoever the Orphan might have been, he is someone different today. An exile possessed of a sepaya and a Cahokian mace? A woman honored by so many peoples as a war chief? Their presence here reeks of Power and should not be summarily dismissed."

He touched his forehead respectfully and resumed his place, hands folded before him. His thoughtful gaze had fixed on the fire before him, frown lines adding to the seriousness of his expression.

Mother couldn't stop herself. "Beloved elder, you actually *believe* these lies?"

"They do not lie, Ishki Minko." Old Wood humbly kept his gaze on the fire. "I believe they are the chosen of Horned Serpent. And with that, I have spoken."

I stood erect, the copper mace shining in the firelight. Through narrowed eyes, I watched as my brother's fingers tapped absently on the handle of his ax, a swirl of conflicting emotions behind his eyes.

When Mother shook her head and took another breath, he gave her another "desist" wave and glared angrily at her, asking, "Tishu Minko?"

Red Cougar stepped forward, gesturing helplessness. "While I would be most interested in learning what they know of the Kristianos, if this man is who I think he is . . . Well, I defer to you and your iksa obligations."

Meaning I'd been declared akeohoosa by Chief Clan, so they could bloody well make the decision if we stayed or went.

By now the great room was awash with whispers, jostling people, and shuffling feet. Through the growing hubbub I heard the name "Black Shell" and "He's back!" whispered from lip to lip.

I watched my brother's eyes as he glanced from minko to minko where they sat at the heads of their clans. Calmly he called for their votes. One by one they abstained, leaving it up to him. Mother had been conversing with my sisters in low tones; now she stepped up, again whispering in my brother's ear. All the while, he kept his eyes fixed on me, a familiar irritation behind them.

I held my breath, curiously calm as my fate was being decided.

At last he spoke. "Given who this man once was, the Chief Clan will need time to make its decision. Ayopachi, please escort them from the council."

"Yes, High Minko."

And just like that we were ushered out of the tchkofa and into the welcome chill of the cold gray evening. People boiled out behind us, pointing, whispering, gawking for all they were worth.

"That went well," Pearl Hand said with her usual caustic humor. "Think they'll come to a decision before supper? Or should we consider an invitation to a feast to be a long shot and go find our own?"

FIFTEEN

MY TRUE IDENTITY SPREAD THROUGH CHICAZA town like the fires had swept Mabila. Silly me, I should have understood the implications. As we waited, boys carried firewood into the tchkofa. I rubbed Gnaw's ears and noted the comings and goings of runners as they bore messages to and fro. Night began to fall.

People watched us as we watched them; Pearl Hand used her *hierro* knife to turn large sticks into small slivers. I pulled a tick off Squirm's haunch. In the growing chill, we sat snuggled under our blankets.

Still, no word came as to our status.

When Wild Rose appeared out of the gloom, Two Packs stood and greeted her. "Good evening. Worried about your jewelry?"

She gifted him with a seductive smile, then tilted her head as she turned to me. "Word is out, Black Shell. Or should I call you Orphan? Clever, that. But everyone knows who you are. Have you thought about a place to stay tonight?"

I stood. "Two Packs is at Minko Flying Squirrel's. Maybe the good minko would allow us—"

A mocking smile played at her lips. "And to think you were going to be high minko once upon a time. Is that all you know of your people and their ways? No clan will offer lodging until Chief Clan has lifted your akeohoosa status. Or had you forgotten the Chicaza concept of honor?"

"I've spent the last twelve years struggling to *forget* the Chicaza concept of honor."

"Pack your things." She made a circular motion with her fingers. "I will put you up." A pause. "For a small bit of additional trade."

"And food for my dogs?"

She gave them a sidelong look. "Pus and blood, they're the size of small deer. Feeding them for more than a couple of days might drive me to ruin."

"It'll take more than a dog pack to drive you to ruin," Two Packs told her bluffly. Then he clapped me on the shoulder. "Go with her. In the long run, it might be the wisest move." He winked at me. "Wild Rose knows everything about Chicaza and its politics."

"What if the High Minko summons us?" I asked.

Wild Rose snorted in a most unfeminine manner. "Have you forgotten the weasels' lair of Chief Clan politics? If your brother doesn't consult every lineage head, every venerable elder, every influential cousin, and smooth any feathers he's ruffled lately, someone will go out of their way to politically embarrass him, speak poison, or otherwise chop him off at the knees."

It was so great to be home.

As we packed up, I noticed that two young warriors— both tattooed with Chief Clan markings—followed along at a distance. My brother keeping track of me?

Then again, it might have been Mother's doing. She wasn't one to let any potential advantage go to waste.

Two Packs told us good night and headed to the Panther Clan minko's palace for food and what was sure to be a night of motivated gossip.

Wild Rose led us to her back door, the one screened by the maze-work of berry bushes and vines. "The front room is for business," she explained. "You will be comfortable here. Wood is stacked by the door along with kindling to make a fire. The latrine is behind the matting out back."

And then she was gone.

I made the dogs lie in a line just inside the door and took one of our ceramic cups to steal hot embers from the fire in the front room. By the time I'd made my way back through Wild Rose's house, Pearl Hand had a fire laid.

As the flames crackled up, she seated herself on one of the pole beds built into the wall and arched her skeptical eyebrow. "What do you think?"

I chuckled ironically. "I have no idea. Did you see the consternation on their faces when they realized who I was?"

Pearl Hand unpinned her hair, letting it tumble down over her shoulders. "Something tells me your old clan is going to be a hotbed of discussion tonight. You shocked them—and calling yourself an orphan? Masterful. Nothing you did or said implies any kind of threat or demand."

"That doesn't mean we're going to succeed." I dropped down in front of the fire and put my arm around Gnaw's furry neck. He tried to lick me in the mouth.

Worthless mongrel.

Maybe it was my growling gut, but some premonition hinted that our sojourn in Chicaza wasn't going to end well. "My suspicion is that we should consider ourselves lucky if we're on the trail for Quizquiz tomorrow morning."

A voice beyond the door called, "Hello? It is Black Marten. I come bearing dog food."

I rose, opening the wooden door on its leather hinges. A chunky young man, broad through the shoulders, wearing a bear-hide cape, stood there. A heavy fabric sack was slung over his back. He had a pleasant face, mostly made up of cheekbones so prominent they gave his head a diamond shape. His hair was in a warrior's bun and pinned with a turkey-bone skewer. The parts of his face that weren't cheekbones consisted of a smile, two twinkling brown eyes, and a nose so flat it barely deserved mention.

"Beloved elder Old Wood sent me with a deer half. He said you needed dog food. My brother, he's a pretty good hunter but not such a good provider, you know? He hung this a couple of weeks back and never got around to retrieving it. Mostly it's jerky now."

"In here," I said with a grin.

He dropped the sack just inside, the dogs immediately sniffing, noses quivering and wiggling as they anxiously inspected the soiled old bag. Blackie started to oozle forward, inching along on his belly. Knuckles looked worried, probably afraid his age worked against him getting his share.

"What do I owe you?" I asked.

He gestured it away. "Nothing. I do this for the elder, and it's just worth it to see you up close. You're really akeohoosa? The same Black Shell who was going to be high minko?"

"Among other things," I replied dryly.

"Talk is all over town about you."

Pearl Hand asked, "And what do they say about us, Black Marten? Is it good or bad? Should we just pack up and leave, or are the Chicaza interested in what's going to happen when the Kristianos finally arrive?"

"It is known that beloved elder Old Wood spoke in your favor. Everyone, except maybe those in Chief Clan, is dying to find out what's going to happen." He shot a glance at the piled armor and walked over, head craned. "This is the fabled Kristiano armor?"

Pearl Hand gestured. "Take a close look. For the most part a Kristiano *soldado* who wears this cannot be killed. It stops our arrows cold as if they were shot into a boulder."

"Through Spirit Power?" he asked.

"It's just metal. Similar to copper but harder, thinner, and much stronger."

"Touching it won't witch me? Harm my souls?"

"No," I told him. "It's been purified."

"How?" he asked, still unsure.

"By Horned Serpent, blood, and water," I answered with the first thing to pop out of my mouth.

For the next finger of time, Black Marten studied the Kristiano armor, asking question after question. Finally he shook his head. "It is said that you watched our warriors die at Mabila. When they did not return, the rumors were rampant that they had been polluted by the enemy, that they had been witched, that they had offended the red Power in some way . . . broken a taboo."

Pearl Hand told him, "We were out-fought that day."

With a sloe-eyed, sidelong glance, he said, "Power always decides who wins."

"Not with Kristianos," I half growled. "Here is the lesson you must learn: Think of a battle. On one side are ten heavily armored veteran Chicaza warriors. All are from the same iksa squadron and have fought together for years. Arrayed against them are one hundred youths, clad only in hunting shirts, poorly armed with practice arrows, and as yet uninitiated into the Men's House. Who would win?"

"The ten warriors."

"Exactly. The Chicaza are the finest warriors in *our* world. The Kristianos come from a *different* world. They have better armor, better weapons, war beasts beyond our comprehension, and the skill to use them all in combination."

He paused. "Can we even hope to win?"

"We can." Pearl Hand pointed to her head, squinting as if thinking hard. "But it must be done through cunning, discipline, and restraint. They must be lulled into dropping their guard and coaxed into a place where they cannot use the terrible war beasts against us. Having killed as many Kristianos as I have, I can tell you this: Once out of their armor, they die like any other man."

He nodded, sighed, a perplexed look on his face. "I need to get back. I will consider the things you have told me."

After I closed the door, I said, "Well, that's one. We have . . . let's see . . . only the rest of the Nation to convince."

She gave me that droll expression I found so dear. "That's one more than we had on our side but a half a hand past."

A nervous throat was cleared outside the door. Someone hesitating to announce his presence? Black Marten, no doubt. Wishing not to be rude.

I called, "Did you forget something?"

Only when I opened it did I see my brother standing in the dark, a gleaming and thick-furred winter bear hide over his shoulders; the thing's legs—feet sporting claws—hung down past his waist. He still wore the copper headpiece, his white apron almost dazzling in the firelight. The look on his face was anything but friendly.

SIXTEEN

"COME IN, HIGH MINKO." I STEPPED BACK FROM THE door.

Surreptitiously he glanced back at the darkness and signaled two warriors with a flick of the finger. He ducked in and closed the door behind him. Then he gave me the sourest scowl. "Of all the places you could stay, you picked *here*? She's a *paid* woman. How much lower could you fall?"

"It warms my heart to see you too, old friend. Once I knew you as Wind Rabbit. You have taken a man's name by now . . . or do you wish me to refer to you as high minko?"

"Is that sarcasm I hear in your voice?"

"No." I smiled wistfully. "I'm just on uncertain ground here, unsure of how to behave. But for the Monster bearing down on Chicaza, I would never have set foot in this land again."

"That's why you have come? Because of the Kristianos?" I heard a softening of his voice.

I nodded. Pearl Hand had risen to her feet, hip cocked

defiantly, arms folded beneath her breasts. She was measuring my brother, toe to headdress, with a gaze as sharp as obsidian.

He bestowed on her the slightest nod, sighed, and glanced at the dogs; they waited obediently for the deer carcass to be removed from its sack. Their gaze shifted between me and the sack. Squirm had drool leaking from his jaws. The beloved elder's dog, Knuckles, just looked sad.

"I heard that you'd become a trader." Then he bent down, petting the dogs one by one. They weren't impressed, high minko or not; their rapt attention remained fixed on the deer sack.

That he'd greeted the dogs at all touched something deep down between my souls. "Meet my family. That's Bark whose ears you're scratching. The fresh scars are from killing Kristiano war dogs at Mabila. The big gray one is Gnaw. Now you're petting Squirm. He got the name because given enough time, he'll wiggle out of any pack. Blackie and Patches are the young ones. We got them in Coosa, bred by the trader who's here, Two Packs. And that old one, Knuckles, belongs to Old Wood. We're just keeping him safe."

My brother shook his head, a humorless chuckle deep in his throat. Then he stepped over, inspected the Kristiano armor, and seated himself on the edge of the bed beside it. For a long moment he studied me with weary eyes. "You broke my heart when you left, Black Shell. Or . . . do I call you Orphan?"

"Black Shell is fine when we're alone. The Uzachile named me the Orphan, *peliqua* in their tongue. I did not want to give offense to anyone in the council by using my own name." I paused. "You never answered. What is your man's name?"

"He Who Takes the Choctaw Hair Mankiller."

"It must have been a noteworthy fight and a grand naming ceremony."

"What really happened to you that day?" he asked softly, eyes reflecting the past.

I knew exactly what he meant. "We came out of the trees, caught the Natchez war party by complete surprise. They did all right . . . formed up despite the confusion. I was scared to death, but I charged forward, my shield before me. I don't even think I landed a blow before something bounced off my head. The next thing, I was on the ground . . . on my hands and knees. I remember throwing up. Then I looked up into the sun, and there, blinding, glorious, his wings spread like wavering fiery rainbows, was Horned Serpent."

I swallowed hard. "He told me, *'Run!'* I heard it as plainly as I hear you now. Saw him as clearly. And run I did." I met his challenging stare. "I told Uncle and Mother the truth, brother. I was Chief Clan, in line for the panther chair. My sense of honor beat with each pulse of my heart. I did not lie."

"They said you did."

"They didn't see what I saw." I reached up, absently clutching the sepaya through the blood-red Kristiano shirt I still wore. "As I found out later, Horned Serpent knew exactly what he was doing."

"And that was?"

"Preparing me."

He continued to watch me through skeptical eyes. I couldn't blame him. As high minko, and politics being what they are, he was lied to constantly, and by just about everyone seeking advantage or favor. And I'd once been branded the biggest liar of all.

He said, "The fact that Old Wood speaks for you carries a great deal of weight. Why did you go to him first?"

"Something Old White told me at Split Sky City. He came to me in a vision." He didn't need to hear about my problems with Piasa.

"Old White? The great legendary hero of the Chicaza people came to you, an akeohoosa?"

Pearl Hand's eyes had narrowed to slits, and her jaw was clenched. Her right hand gripped her knife handle so tightly the knuckles were white.

My brother shot her a sidelong warning glance.

I saw where this was going. "Forget it, High Minko. We will be on the trail to the Natchez come first light. But I owe you this: *Do not attack the Kristianos head-on.* Heed me on this."

I waved down his protest before he could utter it, adding, "The tishu minko will insist. So will the iksas. The squadrons have always prevailed; it's a belief as deep as our souls. But if you let them march out in formation, the cabayeros will cut through the formations like hungry trout through schools of minnows. The vaunted Chicaza discipline will shatter into chaos and confusion. Then, just as the abetuskas begin to re-form the ranks, the cabayeros will crash through them again, and again, and again. Behind them the *soldados* will approach like a wall of impenetrable *hierro*"—I reached over and tapped the metal breastplate—"and murder the survivors like a flock of disoriented bobwhites caught in a net."

He didn't believe a word I said.

Pearl Hand placed a hand on my shoulder. "Black Shell, it's just like Coosa. You can't save a people who won't listen . . . won't believe."

I exhaled wearily. "Yes. I know."

"All right!" Choctaw Hair gestured his irritation. "I believe you! I know you, Black Shell. Or I did. What do you want us to do? *Surrender?*"

"Pus and blood, no! I want you to destroy the filthy invaders. Of all people, the Chicaza can do this! But it's got to be done carefully, judiciously, and cautiously."

"How then?"

"Guile, gamesmanship, and political skill. The only way

to beat them is to get them out of their armor, scattered, disorganized, and half-asleep. At the same time you and the rest of the minkos have to avoid becoming their prisoners and hostages. Chicaza honor will be your greatest strength, and the weakness that could kill you and your people."

"Honor? A weakness? How?"

"Because the Chicaza live by honor, and the enemy will use it against you like a poison. Kristianos lie, they cheat, they steal, and they breathe treachery with the very air. Slave or minko's wife, if she's captured she'll be chained to the ground and raped by tens of unwashed men. They insult our gods and spirits and profane the dead. Your food becomes theirs. You must surrender your palaces, the tchkofa, and the temples . . . all of Chicaza town. Hand it over to them."

The look he gave me normally would have been reserved for the insane. I spread my arms wide. "Hard to swallow that? Here's what you'll have to endure if you expect them to honor the laws of hospitality: After raping your wives and sisters, they will sleep in your beds. Wandering in and out of the temples and Men's House, they'll finger the sacred medicine boxes, removing pearls, copper, or anything that excites them. They will expect honored Chicaza warriors to carry their burdens like slaves, and if the warriors resist, they will be chained by the neck with *hierro*." I lifted the necklaces, exposing the scars on my neck. His eyes widened.

"If the chained Chicaza refuse to work, they will be whipped. If they try to fight back, the Kristiano war dogs will be loosened upon them. The foul beasts are trained to tear a person's guts open." I pointed to the area just above my hip bone. "Here. Then they hook the intestines and pull them out through the wound as the man screams. Once the victim is finally dead, his head will be cut from the body to free the collar and the corpse thrown to the side. There, untended, unmourned, the hideous *puercos* will be allowed to devour the dead."

"What is a *puerco*?"

"Imagine a beast with a flat nose, small eyes, and floppy triangular ears, round of body and covered by sparse bristly hair. The tail ends in a curl. They grunt, bob when they run, and rut in the ground."

"These Kristianos use them in war?"

"No, food. After the beasts eat the dead, the Kristianos eat them."

"Black Shell, is this a way of ingesting the souls of their victims?"

"High Minko, they think our souls are unclean until we accept their *dioscrísto* god. After that the Kristiano soul—they claim there is only one—goes to a place called *paraíso*. It is barren, sterile, without animals or plants, or even dogs. There they sing and smile in the company of all the other murdering Kristianos. Why anyone would want to go to such a place is beyond me."

For long moments, brow pinched in thought, he sat, eyes distant. Finally he asked, "Why do they come here?"

"Looking for gold," I answered.

He gave me a quizzical look.

"It's a metal. Comes in little yellow specks that can be occasionally found in the streams in the eastern mountains."

"If it's in the mountains, why do they come looking for it here?"

I shifted my weight, giving him a sympathetic look. "Because the man who leads them, the *Adelantado*, this Hernando de Soto, has convinced himself that somewhere in our world is a Nation filled with vast stores of gold. And once convinced, he is not the sort of man who will allow himself to fail." I smiled wearily. "Even if it means the total destruction of himself, his army, and all the Nations in our world."

"He sounds insane."

"Worse. He learned that the Coosa people believed their high mikko, the High Sun, to be god. Since de Soto took him prisoner and 'married' his niece, he too began calling himself a god."

"Why does Power endure his insults? Why don't the Spirit Beasts strike him down? Why doesn't red Power sicken his souls? Or is he some sort of terrible witch, using Power in perverted ways?"

I shook my head, tired of answering the same old questions. "When I was in the Spirit World, Old-Woman-Who-Never-Dies told me that his Power and ours balance. Like the red and white Powers, neither can destroy the other. She told me that men must decide this through war and conquest. Even the Piasa is terrified."

The stunned expression on his face melted into disbelief. Bloody dripping pus, I'd gone too far. Desperately I added, "All you need to know is that when the *Adelantado* comes here, you will have only one way of destroying him."

"And what is that?" he asked somewhat sharply.

"By evacuating Chicaza town, removing all the sacred objects—anything you don't want polluted by their presence. Women, children, and elders need to be relocated into hills at least a hard day's run from here. Somewhere beyond the cabayeros' slave-hunting sweeps. Forest trails must be ambushed by warriors using thickets where they can launch arrows and then fade away. Traps must be constructed: deadfalls, sharpened stakes, pits, anything that will disable a cabayo. The important thing is to kill the cabayo first. His rider, once set afoot, is easy prey."

I had his full attention as I continued. "Doing these things may not be as easy as it was in the past. At Mabila we almost destroyed them. Many of them were wounded and are still healing. They will not be as arrogant now."

Pearl Hand interjected, "De Soto will. Where a sane

commander would consider his escape at Mabila a miracle, the *Adelantado* considers it proof of his invincibility."

"That will depend upon what is happening in Apafalaya," I countered. "If the Albaamaha are fighting him every step of the way, bleeding him, the Kristianos—"

"Apafalaya folded before the invader like a pigeon's wing," my brother said. "The Apafalaya minko massed his forces on the banks of the Black Warrior River, figuring to destroy the enemy as it sought to cross. The Kristianos, we hear, secretly built a giant raft upriver and ferried a small party of their warriors and war animals across. Upon learning of this the Albaamaha fled. As we speak the Kristianos are leaving Apafalaya town behind. We will know their direction within the next two days as our scouts monitor their march."

"They always have a way." Pearl Hand gave me her bitter smile. "The *Adelantado* wins again. By now the slaves will have told Ortiz that de Soto's victory at Mabila has broken the spirit of the surrounding Nations."

My brother gave her the distasteful look Chicaza reserved for women who spoke about things that were not their business, and added, "The spirit of the Chicaza is *never* broken."

Pearl Hand met his gaze, held it, and said flatly, "Then you had better preoccupy yourself with how to use that spirit of yours, because when we sneaked into their camp at Mabila, I heard the *Adelantado* himself set Chicaza as a goal. They believe you have enough food stored here to keep them through the winter."

"You *heard* them?" My brother's voice dripped skepticism.

"¿Hablas usted español, cacique?"

At Choctaw Hair's blank look I translated, "Do you speak the Kristiano tongue, High Minko?"

He sighed, rubbing his hands together, a trait I remembered from when he was a worried boy. "How come you, Black Shell, of all people on earth, know these things?"

"Because I was chosen. Everything from my birth, my education and training, my banishment, and the years I spent traveling among Nations was planned. Right down to the desire that led me south to find Pearl Hand and Kristiano captivity. It was all orchestrated by Horned Serpent. For this I was born, and for this I will die."

"And if I choose not to believe you?"

"We will continue west to either the Natchez or the Quizquiz."

"They are your enemies!" he cried.

"High Minko"—I stiffened—"I am *the Orphan*, the Ahltakla, the chosen of Horned Serpent. My enemies are the Kristianos, and the Kristianos only. We came here to aid the Chicaza, to make them understand that everything that they believe will give them victory over the Kristianos will instead lead to disaster. If you choose to dismiss the lessons Pearl Hand and I have learned at the expense of so much blood and death, you may. Under the Power of trade, we will continue in search of a Nation and minko smart enough to listen."

He narrowed his eyes, lips thinning with anger as they had when he was a boy. I was pretty sure no one had spoken to him in that tone of voice since he'd ascended the panther chair. Under my hard gaze he slowly composed himself. Then a smile began to form. "You always left me dazzled and intimidated by your greatness, intikba. When you left, I staggered and stumbled in an attempt to take your place. After all those years, as I finally begin to live up to the expectations Mother and Uncle had for me, you return, and leave me again standing in your shadow."

Intikba. In violation of clan law, he'd called me his big brother. I smiled, offering him my hand, pulling him to his feet and clasping him to my breast in a fierce hug. "No, nakfic, you and the Chicaza are the lucky ones. What I was chosen for? It comes at a terrible price. One that has and will continue to cost me everything I hold dear."

He pushed back, as if to stare down into my very souls. "You . . . and Horned Serpent . . . you really think there is a way to destroy such an enemy?"

"I do. But, High Minko, understand this: Trapping and killing Kristianos is a terrifying and deadly business. Nothing is ever sure. Attempting to manipulate and finally destroy them will be the most dangerous thing the Chicaza have ever attempted. Our discarded and rotting corpses may end up feeding maggots and *puercos*."

I watched his expression harden as that sank in. "I believe you. And having learned what I came here to find out, I now have to go. If I can convince the others, will you come to a meeting at the Men's House to explain what you have told me?"

I pointed at Pearl Hand. "She would not be allowed inside. The tchkofa would be a better location."

"But she's a . . . Yes, I see. Always trouble, aren't you?" He opened the door, glanced at his warriors. Guards, no doubt, to ensure no one saw the high minko slipping from Wild Rose's back door. They nodded, and he disappeared into the darkness.

Pearl Hand wasn't amused by his last words. " 'A woman'? Isn't that what he was about to say?"

Lost in thought, I lifted the bottom of the dogs' sack, spilling the deer carcass on the floor. I cut a roast out for Knuckles. At my signal, the dogs tore into it.

SEVENTEEN

AFTER THE HIGH MINKO'S VISIT PEARL HAND AND I talked late into the night. Okay, we argued until we finally fell asleep. She wasn't impressed with my brother. I insisted that he'd eventually come around. After all, I had. I dreamed the argument over and over, all night long. Generally it ended with Pearl Hand—goaded to the point of insane rage—slitting my brother's throat with her sharp *hierro* knife.

How could you help but love the woman?

I still recall the profusion of blood and the incredible vividness of its color. I was awash in the image when I was awakened rudely before dawn by Gnaw sticking his cold wet nose in my ear.

Despicable beast.

I walked the dogs, shivering in the cold drizzle, and managed to take my morning bath in the creek. Chilled to the bone I returned to find Pearl Hand bent over the fire. Shoulder to shoulder, we crouched, mixing up corn-cake batter, rolling it into balls, and baking them in the coals.

"Sorry," she said. "He just enraged me."

"My being here compounds his problems."

Her dark eyes bored into mine. "It's because he thinks you're a liar. That's what really sets my wood afire."

I found persimmons and dried berries, adding them to a pot of water and boiling it down to make syrup. One by one we dipped the hotcakes into the sweet sticky juice and enjoyed our breakfast.

"Hello?" Wild Rose called at the room hanging. "You up? And is that food I smell?"

"Come and join us," Pearl Hand replied.

Wild Rose pushed the hanging aside, entering our small room. She wore a simple shift woven from soft flax thread. Hanging to midthigh, it revealed muscular legs beneath smooth brown skin. The way she'd belted her narrow waist emphasized her full breasts, a remarkably flat belly, and provocative hips. Glossy black hair tumbled around her shoulders, swaying as she seated herself.

Fully aware that she oozed sexuality, Wild Rose smiled, helped herself to a hotcake, and dipped it in the syrup. Erotic delight expressed itself in her closed eyes, the way she chewed, and the happy sounds in her throat. Eyes still closed, she licked her full lips with a slow deliberation.

Before Wild Rose opened her eyes, Pearl Hand—lips quirked—used her fingers to sign, "You're drooling. Want me to leave?"

I gave her my most threatening and menacing look, adding a brief shake of the head. For which I received an amused wink and shadowy smile.

I hate it when she has fun at my expense.

"You've made quite a splash," Wild Rose informed us after she finally swallowed and opened her eyes. "It's the talk of every household. You even managed to lure the high minko to my back door! A shocking bit of gossip should it ever get out."

"You seem to know a great deal," I mentioned casually as I checked to make sure Pearl Hand was behaving.

Wild Rose gave me her "you're an idiot" look and in a dry voice said, "What do you think I get paid for? Sure, I've got a sheath that can squeeze a man's hakchin until he's whimpering with delight. But mostly they come here to talk, to relax, to be the person they can be in no other place. Men tell me everything . . . things they wouldn't tell their best friends." She glanced at Pearl Hand. "Ask her. She knows."

Pearl Hand shrugged noncommittally.

Wild Rose explained, "It's in the way she moves, how she dresses, the looks she gives other men. Relax, Black Shell, you've married a real woman. One who knows how to take life by both hands and wrestle it into submission. Think of your poor brother. Three wives now. All simpering adornments and breeding stock. Not a brain in any of their heads. He doesn't make love with them the way you do with her." She jerked a thumb at Pearl Hand. "The high minko's only a breeder fulfilling his duty to the iksas. This one you've married? You couldn't find more woman than her."

Pearl Hand shrugged again, the tension leaving her shoulders. "When your life depends on it, you learn to see the little things . . . how a man holds his head, where his eyes focus—or don't. The dangerous ones look at you differently. They have a set of the lips, something predatory leaking out of their souls."

Wild Rose gave her another thoughtful glance. "I'd love to hear your story."

"Perhaps later," Pearl Hand told her. "But for the moment you know who we are and why we're here. In your opinion, what are our chances?"

Wild Rose dipped another corn cake. "That depends on what the high minko told you last night. If he suggested you be elsewhere, that's where I'd be."

"He understood the nature of the threat," I answered. "He said there were clan politics to attend to."

Her look turned quizzical. "You must have told a persuasive story, Black Shell. The high minko doesn't have a reputation for confrontation, especially when it comes to Chief Clan politics."

"I see."

Pearl Hand's eyebrow arched.

I explained, "You remember the cesspool of Coosa politics? Chicaza's the same, only smaller."

She nodded. "Each lineage elder in the Chief Clan imagines himself on the panther stool?"

"You've got it." And the different matrons envisioned their sons eventually assuming the mantle of leadership, and while they'd unite behind my brother against the other clans, they'd gleefully cut his throat if it meant the advancement of their own kin. And, of course, within each lineage, cousins waged a battle with each other for authority, prestige, and status.

"Who are the players?" I asked. "I'm twelve years out of date."

Wild Rose chewed, swallowed, and smacked her lips in satisfaction. "You remember Dogwood Mankiller? He and your uncle got crosswise after you left. Dogwood, his brother Takes Hair, and Dogwood's sister's son, Falls Twice, will do anything within their means to thwart your family."

"What about Matron Painted Clay? She and my mother never got along."

"Things change. Painted Clay's sons, Medicine Killer and Blood Elk, supported your brother."

I remembered Medicine Killer as a brash young warrior. He'd earned his name by charging through a line of Choctaw warriors, dodging the blows and arrows, until he reached the Choctaw tishu minko. The man had turned to flee, and Medicine Killer's war club split the war medicine box he carried in half, dumping its contents on the ground. The horrified Choctaw had turned and run for all they were worth.

To the western Mos'kogean peoples, the war medicine was one of our most important religious possessions. On the outside, it looked like a magnificently carved, engraved, and inlaid wooden box. Leather arm straps were laced through slots in the sides and allowed it to be worn like a backpack. Inside were kept talismans of Power. Things like sepayas, scalps, sacred crystals, dried falcons, eagle skulls, copper effigies, and other items that concentrated Spirit Power. When Medicine Killer smashed the box, he essentially smashed the soul of Choctaw warfare.

Wild Rose sighed. "Good old Medicine Killer. I miss him. Used to be he was a wild time, insatiable. The man has a hakchin as thick and hard as a . . . Well, never mind. He's a family man now, dedicated to raising his nieces and nephews."

"So, he'll argue for peace with the Kristianos?" Pearl Hand prompted.

"Medicine Killer?" Wild Rose shrugged. "There's no telling with him. One day he's a white chief, dedicated to peace and tranquility. The next he's as red and chaotic as menstrual blood . . . ready to bash heads."

I asked, "Is Fine Red Woman still alive?" Acknowledged head of her own lineage, she'd been my family's occasional ally or opponent, depending on the situation.

"Oh, yes. Ancient as an oak, going blind, but still sharp as a chert flake. You'd have known her grandsons. Nowadays they are known as Buffalo Back Mankiller and Copper Sky. If Buffalo Back turns against you, Blood Elk will become your advocate. Or the other way around. It doesn't matter what the merits might be."

"And Copper Sky?"

"Since you left he became a hopaye. His souls are more suited to the pursuit of Power than war. If he looks like he's napping, he is. He has trouble sleeping at night. Wakes up whenever, and so energetic you'd think he was ready to run a race. Almost can't contain himself."

I wondered how she'd know that. Hopayes generally didn't dally with women—even their wives—in an attempt to keep their Spirit Power unpolluted by chaotic female influences.

"What of Posi Fire Cloud?" I asked, remembering the volatile and cunning woman who had forever battled with my mother over clan politics. Jabs, digs, attacks, vitriol, backstabbing, and figurative throat-cutting had consumed their lives since they'd been children. Who knew when it started or why, but more than once their shenanigans had almost split the Nation in two. Exactly such a division had led to the split between the Tuskaloosa and Chicaza in the days following the abandonment of Split Sky City. If our peoples had a single failing, it was factional politics.

By the Piasa's balls, Breath Giver, don't we ever get a break?

"Old Posi Fire Cloud?" Wild Rose gave me a veiled, thoughtful look. "I was saving her for last. When you left Fire Cloud used your disgrace to her fullest advantage. Over the years she's thrown that in your mother's face at every opportunity until even people in her own lineage have asked her to stop."

"And now I'm back." I remembered the hard look in Mother's eyes as she kept trying to whisper into my brother's ear back in the tchkofa.

Wild Rose smiled. "I've got to hand it to you, Black Shell. No matter how your return works out, it will be a most entertaining time."

"What about my sisters?"

"The oldest girl took the name of Clear Water after her first seclusion in the Women's House. She immediately married Tishu Minko Red Cougar as a second wife. He's bred two daughters out of her, and she's carrying a third child due in spring. Myself, I don't know what to think of her. She's as tough as your mother, but with a romantic streak. She may be Red Cougar's second wife, but the gossip is that they dote on each other. It is said that she lets her feelings for him get in the way of her clan responsibilities, but she's young. Give her a few years and she'll be as heartless as the ishki minko."

That didn't surprise me. "And my youngest sister?"

"She took the name Silent Spring after she was declared a woman. She's married to the Alibamo town mikko, Fire Tail Mankiller. If they'd had Albaamaha mikkos like that in the olden days, the Sky Hand never would have conquered the Black Warrior Valley. Silent Spring is the man's first wife, and she's borne two bandy little sons of his seed. She too is carrying, but not due until around summer solstice."

"Mother must be so happy."

"Breath Giver knows, as fertile as they seem, your lineage appears to have a solid lock on leadership for the foreseeable future." She hesitated, studying me. "And both of the girls appear ready, willing, and able to step into your mother's moccasins should the need arise. Neither of them, I'm told, is happy about your arrival here."

Pearl Hand had been giving me that old familiar knowing look. "So, lover, after hearing this, maybe heading on to the Natchez or Quizquiz might not be such a bad idea?"

I gave her a strained smile. "Why, Pearl Hand, it's just family. You know how they are."

"Maybe I'll sleep somewhere else. Any night now one of your loving kin is going to sneak in and cut your throat."

EIGHTEEN

WE'D BARELY FINISHED EATING WHEN A RUNNER came for me. The young man, Green Stick, was Chief Clan. I could tell that by the cut of his hair. Not quite old enough to be a warrior, he was assigned to run errands, fetch things, and assist his elders. He looked both uncomfortable and entirely fascinated and awestruck to be scratching at Wild Rose's forbidden back door. He'd be telling his incredulous friends all about it by nightfall.

Like so many people who place great emphasis on connubial virtue—and violently discourage and punish adultery—the Chicaza allow a huge amount of wiggle room for a class of "paid women." Wild Rose, and the five or six others who plied her trade, were widely respected, often acted as consorts, and had no inhibitions when it came to social relations with men. They talked politics, war, and gossip, offered marital advice, or gave their opinion on anything a man might want to indulge in.

Young Green Stick, therefore, was all eyes as he

stepped into Wild Rose's back room. Remembering what it was like to be that young and inexperienced, I imagine he expected to see men and women bumping bellies on every sleeping bench.

"What can I do for you?" I asked with a restrained smile.

"I am to escort you to the Men's House . . . uh . . ." He realized he didn't how to properly address me.

"I'm known here as Ahltakla, the Orphan."

"As you will, Ahltakla. I am directed to escort you to the Men's House to discuss the coming of the Kristianos."

Pearl Hand looked up from where she was combing through Bark's hairy coat in search of ticks as I said, "Let's go, wife."

Green Stick gulped like a landed fish, clearly distressed by this. "But it's the *Men's* House!"

"Pearl Hand's a war chief, boy. There may be a handful of Chicaza who've taken more ishkobo than she has. But she's carved those scalps off of Kristiano skulls." I gave him an evil squint. "Now, give us a moment to prepare ourselves."

Green Stick swallowed hard and jerked a nod. If his eyes got any bigger, his head was going to pop.

Wouldn't it be nice if I could intimidate the rest of them as easily?

With Two Packs's gift of the brilliantly colorful and incredibly exotic Kristiano-cloth garments we had the choice of wearing the height of formal dress or wearing our travel clothing like forest vagabonds—and no in-between. I decided on the latter, but to add some dignity to our appearances we sneaked some more of Wild Rose's face paints and draped ourselves with her jewelry.

Pearl Hand twisted her long hair into a tight bun and pinned it in place with my copper turkey-tail headpiece. Then she strapped the *hierro* carapace around her chest and carried her crossbow, a full quiver of arrows over her shoulder. I hung Antonio's sword at my side and placed the dead man's *hierro* helmet on my head, wishing I'd taken the time to polish it to a high luster. Finally I picked up my heavy copper mace. Thus decked out, we emerged into the cold air and were shocked to find sleet balls pattering down from the leaden sky.

The walk to the Men's House drew stares from the few people who were out in the growing storm. The weather fit my mood: gray, unsettled, and threatening. When we set foot in the Men's House, it was going to generate a tempest.

Green Stick had begun to shiver, though whether from the temperature or the fact he was escorting a woman to the Men's House, I couldn't say. Nevertheless, he kept his head up and his back straight as he plodded through the wreaths of falling sleet.

At the door stood two warriors wrapped in bear-hide blankets, bark rain hats sheltering their heads. They stared warily as we approached through the swirling sleet.

Stepping up onto the low mound, I stalked forward, greeting them with, "Ahltakla, the Orphan, and Pearl Hand, war chief of the Chicora people, have been summoned by the Chicaza. At your request, we are here."

The warriors gaped first at my Kristiano hat, perhaps hearing the musical sound the pattering sleet balls made on the metal. Then they turned disbelieving eyes on Pearl Hand. I found their expressions amusing. A woman expected admission to the most sanctified and concentrated bastion of purified male Power in all of Chicaza?

"Are we or are we not requested?" I asked, adding to their fluster. Green Stick was trying unsuccessfully to blend into the plaster wall, his eyes gone big again.

The one on the right managed to find his voice. "Women are not allowed. Any Chicaza, even you, knows that."

"I am *not* Chicaza. Even *you* know that. We were called here to discuss how the Chicaza can kill Kristianos. War

Chief Pearl Hand serves the red Power of war. Or do you think she's dressed for mat weaving?"

"She can wait outside."

"When the Chicaza finally wish to discuss war, and how to kill Kristianos, we will be available." I turned, stepping down onto the level ground. Pearl Hand gave the warriors a curt nod and shifted the crossbow to display its polished wood. Then we started back the way we'd come.

"So," she asked, "what did we just accomplish?"

"Authority," I told her. "We've just done a very *un*-Chicaza thing. No sane man would bring a woman to profane sacred male space. Therefore, I am something different. And you, attempting to enter the Men's House for a war council, armed to the teeth and wearing armor, set yourself apart from any woman the Chicaza know."

"And how long do you think it's going to take for them to come around? The Kristianos are on the march, maybe no more than a couple of days away."

I shot her a knowing glance from the corner of my eye. Sleet was sticking in the angle where her headpiece was pinned. "They know. Meanwhile, stories are circulating about us. Remember Black Marten? He's been telling everyone that we know how to kill Kristianos. So has my brother."

"And Old Wood?" she asked.

"He is the proverbial worm eating its way through the acorn of Chicaza suspicion. By now the tishu minko must be clicking his teeth to know what we know and putting pressure on the Chief Clan to bring this thing to some sort of conclusion. In Panther Clan, Minko Flying Squirrel has been listening to Two Packs, hearing stories of Kristiano treachery at Coosa, and wondering if that's Chicaza's future."

"Then," she wondered, "who'd be against hearing us speak?"

"Best guess? My mother."

"Your *mother*?"

"You heard Wild Rose. Old Posi Fire Cloud beat Mother over the head with my disgrace. Mother's a proud woman and the most prominent and influential in Chicaza to boot. Put yourself in her place: Your son—the boy everyone expects to be the next high minko—turns out to be a coward in combat and a liar. One who blasphemously claimed sacred Power told him to run. The only worse scandal would have been if I'd been caught driving my peg into my sister's sheath. In Mother's eyes, it would have been better if I'd sneaked in during the night and cut her and Uncle's throats."

"Husband, by the time this is over, you may wish you had."

"Ahltakla! Wait!" The cry came from behind.

We turned as one of the bear-robe-clad guards scampered across the whitening ground.

"They ask that you return," he said insistently, arms out. "The woman comes dressed as a warrior, yes? Then they will hear her, even if it means they must purify the building after her departure."

I glanced at Pearl Hand, wondering if she could see the kink in my lips. It came from hiding a smile. "Then we should not keep the Chicaza waiting."

Sometimes small victories are so precious.

This time when we approached the door, Green Stick was long gone. As we stepped up to the threshold, the intricately carved wooden door was thrown back, and both guards preceded us inside.

I ducked through and into a spacious, high-ceilinged room. As an uninitiated boy, I'd never been allowed inside. That would have come after my first successful experience in combat. We all know how *that* turned out.

The mats covering the floors had been woven into complicated geometric designs. A crackling fire warmed the center of the room, and the walls were decorated with all manner of trophies: war clubs, bows, shields, leather helmets, painted human skulls, arm bones, leg bones, scalp locks, and the like. Intricately carved wooden statuary depicting Ivory-Billed Woodpecker, Falcon, Eagle, Snapping Turtle, and Rattlesnake—all totems of war—stood around the walls. Between them ran split-wood plank benches cleverly mortised into the sculpture sides. Beneath the benches lay wooden boxes, ceramic vessels, piles of cloth, and feathered ornaments to be worn at ceremonial events.

In the rear of the room, behind the fire, stood a clay altar, upon which rested a tripod. The sacred war medicine box should have been perched upon it. My guess was that due to Pearl Hand's impending arrival, it had been removed. And, looking around the walls, I noticed other gaps, the underlying plaster reflecting the objects' dimensions where no soot had settled.

Ah, yes. They'd taken down the sacred masks of Morning Star, the Wild One, Bird Man, and the Falcon Dancer lest they be offended by Pearl Hand's presence.

I turned my attention to the men who watched us with undisguised emotion. Some stood with clenched fists, grinding their teeth as they perched on the balls of their feet. A few looked apoplectic enough to bite a hickory stick in two. Others appeared half-scared at the possibility of ritual pollution. They peered owlishly at Pearl Hand and seemed to have nervous fingers. Still others watched us with amusement, as if they couldn't believe the absurdity of what was happening.

"Greetings, warriors," I called, stopping and drawing myself up. "I am the Orphan, the chosen of Horned Serpent. I have come at your bidding, of my own free will, and without expectation of reward." I gave them a grim smile. "Actually I'd very much appreciate the opportunity to kill a couple more Kristianos."

The warriors shifted uncomfortably. I saw Old Wood in the rear. His brown lips bent into an ambiguous smile.

"Your turn," I whispered to Pearl Hand in Timucua.

She raised her crossbow, rapping it against the *hierro* breastplate; the metal rang. "I am Pearl Hand, of the Chicora. Among the Timucua peoples I am known as paracusi. I have stood in council with the Kristiano invader and looked into his eyes. I have heard his lies and understand his treachery. The Apalachee call me nico-quadca. I have given war counsel to the Cofitachequi high mico and advised the Coosa High Sun. Among the Tuskaloosa I was given the rank of thlakko, or war chief. I have walked among the enemy, hearing their cries and plans. Now I will advise the Chicaza if they have the wisdom to listen."

My brother stood just behind the fire; Tishu Minko Red Cougar rocked back and forth, as if ready for a fight. I studied my sister's husband. He was tall, muscular, with a well-featured face and mobile lips. Several threads of gray sprinkled his black hair. He looked like a tishu minko ought to: tough, lean, and dangerous.

One by one I picked out once-familiar faces from among the members of the Chief Clan behind them. Yes, there was Dogwood. Both Takes Hair and Falls Twice looked as if they were longing for the chance to beat me to death. Remembering what Wild Rose said about Buffalo Back I glanced at him, then his rival, Blood Elk. Neither one seemed happy to see us. Which didn't help me to figure out which one would be on my side.

"We make you welcome," a voice called from the side, and I saw a man of perhaps thirty-five winters step forward. He wore a clean brown hunting shirt, belted at the waist. In his right hand he held a gourd rattle. In his left were two painted, hollow medicine tubes, the kind priests use to blow sacred words into liquids like black drink or stewed rattlesnake master.

He'd changed over the years, but I recognized Copper Sky. At the time of my banishment, he'd been a struggling warrior who just couldn't quite manage to advance. Looking at him now, he still didn't cultivate the image I'd come to expect from a hopaye. The look wasn't in his eyes . . . that reflection of the reverent and holy. Despite his age, to me he just looked young and inexperienced. Given a choice, I'd have taken Old Wood as high hopaye any day.

"Good Hopaye, we are pleased to be here. How may we be of service to the Chicaza?"

"We seek counsel, Orphan."

In the back row, next to Medicine Killer, stood Black Marten; the man's eyes were thoughtful in his wide-cheeked face.

My brother raised his hands, lifting Uncle's old copper-bitted battle-ax. "We have asked you here to tell us what to expect from the Kristianos."

"How soon before they arrive, High Minko?" I asked.

"We've sent a squadron of the Panther iksa to challenge their crossing of the Tombigbee River. Should the Kristianos force the crossing, our squadron will kill as many as they can until the enemy establishes itself on the near bank. After that they are to retreat unless the Kristianos are so badly mauled as to be vulnerable."

"Kristianos badly mauled?" Pearl Hand murmured indulgently. "I don't think so."

I bit off a smile, stating, "After they cross and brush the Panther squadron aside, how long before they arrive here?"

The tishu minko answered, "Three days at the earliest, four if they maintain their current rate of march and the storm doesn't worsen."

Pearl Hand's lips curled into a bitter smile before she said, "Too late to ambush the trails."

I added, "They'd fight their way through no matter what."

"Evacuation," she stated simply, then cast skeptical eyes on the Chicaza. "But that will depend on if these people have the discipline."

"*Discipline?*" the tishu minko asked. "Woman, these are *Chicaza* warriors!"

Pearl Hand stepped forward, cocking her head as if she were inspecting some unusual curiosity as she met the man's gaze. "And your enemy, Tishu Minko, are Kristianos. A people more deadly than any you've ever fought. Defeating them is about when you fight, if you fight, and most of all, *how* you fight. All of these things have to be decided beforehand, and with great judiciousness. Once planned, the greatest care must be taken in the implementation and execution of the attack."

He was glaring at her, lips pressed into a thin line.

I smacked my mace into my left hand. "We will tell you the same thing we told the Coosa High Sun: If you would save Chicaza and its people, you have three days to evacuate Chicaza town. You must remove everything you hold sacred, including the graves of the dead. Anything, or anyone, who remains behind becomes the property of the Kristianos. Next, you must make a choice about how you want this to end. One way is that you burn Chicaza town on the way out, including any food stores you can't remove. If you do that, the enemy will continue on, headed west. Or they might loop back to Apafalaya. Our guess is that the *Adelantado* will continue west."

"The other choice"—Pearl Hand picked up the narration—"is that you decide to destroy them here. In that case, you must leave the granaries full, accepting that, like a plague of worms, they're going to eat it. The advantage to this is that Chicaza town isn't fortified. Handled correctly, over time they will become careless, lazy. If they have no trouble from the Chicaza, and if you can keep your women and children beyond their reach, they will drop their guard."

"Why are the women and children so important to them?" Falls Twice asked.

"They are only interested in older children who can work," I replied. "The lowest ranked among them, the *soldados* and herders, have no women. Figure four hundred men with empty beds and aching loins. When they arrive, they will expect to put Chicaza women in their blankets."

"And if they capture them," Pearl Hand told them bluntly, "you will be honor-bound to avenge the rape of your female relatives. Any, and I repeat, *any* attack on an individual Kristiano will result in full retaliation by the entire Kristiano army."

"Full retaliation?" my brother asked. "It is a matter of clan justice and personal honor to revenge rape or insult. The iksas will demand it."

I lifted my mace for attention. "You will all grow weary of hearing me say this, but Kristianos do not honor or respect our ways. We share *nothing* in common with them. Even their notions of the Spirit World are incomprehensible. They do not believe in our rules or common courtesies. They *use* the White Arrow only as a means to lull suspicions before they take high minkos and entire Nations hostage."

Minko Flying Squirrel nodded. "That is what Two Packs tells me. They entered Coosa under the White Arrow, and promptly enslaved its leaders and occupied the palaces and fortifications."

Pearl Hand added, "They did the same at Cofitachequi. And also among the Cherokee."

I raised my voice. "If they tell you they come under the White Arrow, it is a lie. If they profess friendship, it is to gain an advantage. When they claim they will meet you unarmed, it is with a sword hidden behind their backs. They keep only one kind of promise."

"What is that?" Buffalo Back asked.

"When they swear they will murder you for refusing

them, they mean it. If they promise to burn your families alive should you disobey their commands, they are telling the truth. They keep any promise that involves pain, blood, death, or dismemberment."

That elicited a solemn and reserved look.

"Why not march out and meet them as they emerge from the forest?" the tishu minko asked.

It was Old Wood who said, "Because of the war beasts, these cabayos the Orphan tells of, and because of the armor." He stepped forward, walking up to Pearl Hand. I admired the beautiful war club he held so reverently. The handle was carved, smoothed, and polished in the shape of a swan's head and neck. The wood looked old, stained almost black. Set at the top, as if it were a stubby wing, was a ground-stone ax head made of translucent red chert.

Old Wood cocked his head as he stopped, glancing suggestively at Pearl Hand's metal breastplate. "May I strike you, War Chief?"

Pearl Hand granted him a grim smile. "I've never given any man that permission before, but yes, beloved elder. And you need not hold back. I will be perfectly safe."

I hadn't even taken breath to object when Old Wood pivoted, slamming his stone-headed club into the center of Pearl Hand's chest. The force of it staggered her, the *clang* loud in the room. Fragments of shattered chert exploded and pattered around the room, causing warriors to duck and scramble. Pearl Hand barely caught herself, a stunned look on her face.

Just as quickly, she stepped forward, the crossbow dropping in her left hand as she clawed her *hierro* knife free. As the point touched the old man's chest, she froze, her hot glare on the stunned men. "And now, were I a Kristiano, the beloved elder would be dead. Not from a sword or distant crossbow arrow. Not from a spear-ax or thunder stick, but a simple knife." In the sudden shocked silence, she demanded, *"Do you begin to understand?"*

I saw the tishu minko's eyes blazing as he reached for his war club. My brother had taken a half step forward, hand out as if to reach for Old Wood. He had a look of abject terror on his face.

Pearl Hand removed her knife, slipped it into its sheath, and touched her forehead respectfully as she bowed to Old Wood. "Thank you, venerable elder. I hope I didn't startle you."

"Unfortunately, you did, noble War Chief." He gave her a relieved smile, then turned his attention to the gaping Chicaza. "If this one had been any ordinary woman, I would have knocked her off her feet." He gave Pearl Hand a sly sidelong glance as he poked a finger into the shallow dimple his ax had left in the metal. Fingering the bright silver scar at the bottom, he said, "After today I will never again forget that you are a war chief, Minko Pearl Hand."

He looked around the room. "The rest of you might want to rethink your prejudices the way I have rethought mine." He dismissively tossed the shattered club to the side. It bounced off the matting and slid to a stop at the foot of the falcon statue—as though the sole subject of the bird's shell-and-copper stare.

I watched as he walked to the door and waited while the warriors unlatched it. Then he vanished into the swirling white outside.

In Timucua, I asked, "Are you all right?"

Pearl Hand gave me a thin look. "I'll have beautiful bruises where the edges of this thing bit me. But if that's what it takes to be minko in this country, it's worth it."

NINETEEN

HANDS OF TIME LATER WE WERE STILL SEATED around the Men's House fire. The debate had flared hotly, ebbed, and flared again, but the majority of the Chicaza iksas wanted to fight. The Kristianos had killed their kin at Mabila. Such actions could not be left unavenged.

I mulled that over as I watched the pieces of Kristiano armor and weapons being passed from hand to hand.

As in the tchkofa, the iksas each had their own space within the Men's House. Our spot, as visitors, placed us in front of the door. Cold air blew in around the gaps to freeze our backsides. My stomach was communicating—by means of loud gurgles—that it was definitely unhappy with its current similarity to an empty sack. It wished to be filled—preferably with something hot, dripping fat, and tasting like roast venison or goose, or maybe baked turkey, or corn bread, or goosefoot-flour patties, or . . .

"We should burn the town after we evacuate," Blood Elk insisted stubbornly. "If Minko Pearl Hand is correct, the Kristianos won't even stop here. They'll be half-starved by the time they reach Alibamo town. If that is burned, too, they will enter the forest in dire straits. We can ambush them time after time, whittling away at them until there is nothing left."

"And the Quizquiz will take credit for finishing them," Buffalo Killer growled back. "For all we know, the Quizquiz, upon hearing about our war, will foolishly come to the Kristianos' aid. No, I say we leave Chicaza town full of food. Let the Kristianos believe themselves safe. When their guard falls, we move in and kill them to the last man. That way we get all the armor, the weapons, the incredible beads and other things."

Medicine Killer sat cross-legged on the other side of the fire, the Kristiano breastplate in his massive hands. Ever since Pearl Hand had removed it and passed it around, warrior after warrior had fingered it, tapped it, hefted its weight, and inspected the mark left by Old Wood's war club.

The bloody rag that wrapped Falls Twice's left hand had finally stanched the bleeding. I'd warned them all that Antonio's sword was sharp before I passed it around the room. Falls Twice either hadn't been paying attention or didn't believe *hierro* could cut like obsidian. They now understood when I told them how a single swing of a sword had severed Tastanaki's arm at Mabila.

Pearl Hand raised her hands for attention.

"Yes, Minko Pearl Hand?" my brother called, recognizing her.

"In the end it comes down to this: You can fight a running battle with the Kristianos as Blood Elk suggests. Doing so, you can pick your ground as the Apalachee did. Attacking their moving columns you will inflict occasional casualties but no great victories. You will also ensure that they leave Chicaza quickly. If you weaken them enough, perhaps the Natchez or Quizquiz can finish them."

I continued. "The other option is to give them Chicaza town and enough food to see them through the winter. If you take the time to study them, learn their weaknesses, and avoid premature violence, you might be able to sneak in some night a couple of moons from now and crush them once and for all."

"If we accomplish that objective, their weapons and spoils become ours," Dogwood Mankiller noted softly. "Some of the invaders would be captured along with their women. Perhaps we might even take some of the war beasts alive, learn to use them in battle as the Kristianos do."

"Perhaps," I agreed, wondering if Spirit Power would allow us to ally with such soulless beasts as I believed cabayos to be. "No matter which course you choose, you must prepare yourselves. The enemy is capable and deadly. Victory will come at a terrible cost. Many of our people will die."

Hopaye Copper Sky shrugged his shoulders. "It is the way of war, Orphan. The red Power demands a sacrifice of blood. If our warriors die honorably, they will be received with great fanfare as they follow the Path of the Dead across the Sky World to the land of the ancestors."

Pearl Hand gave each man a thoughtful inspection to add emphasis to her words. "Let's say you choose to let them winter here. Assume that you manage to keep your warriors from trying to exact revenge each time a Kristiano insults them. Through sacrifice and forbearance you manage to assure the monster that he is in no danger. The Kristianos become lazy, dismissive, and careless. Finally, you decide to strike. Even if it seems to be a complete surprise and all odds favor us, these are Kristianos. They will have a trick, some way of turning your advantage against you at the last moment."

"They always do," I agreed.

"Bah!" Flying Squirrel cried. "You'd have us believe

these Kristianos breathe fire, leap battle lines like magic, and will land in our rear in the blink of an eye! These are children's stories to frighten us."

"By the Piasa's bloody balls, you'd *better* be frightened," I bellowed back. "Because you have never faced such disciplined and terrible warriors. They *always* manage to do the impossible!"

Pearl Hand gestured for calm as the others roared derisively. "Quiet. Please. Hear me. I've already seen Chicaza warriors killed to the last man by Kristianos. We told you earlier tonight how they turned our trap at Mabila against us. Even after all the time Black Shell and I have fought them, they still shock us with their inventiveness and fury."

"And you need to seriously consider something," I added into the sudden silence. "You are Chicaza. You dare not lose."

"Now you're talking like a Chicaza, Orphan," the tishu minko agreed, a grim smile on his lips.

"No, I'm talking as someone who has viewed the Chicaza heart from afar."

"I don't understand," my brother—who'd listened silently for most of the evening—spoke.

"Widen your vision, High Minko. Whatever you decide tonight, your entire world depends upon it. I don't just mean the suffering, humiliation, and bloody death of thousands of Chicaza. I'm not just talking about a military defeat the likes of which the Choctaw or Natchez might deal."

"What then?" My brother studied me intently.

"What happens to the Nation if you and the other minkos are taken captive? What if the mighty iksas march out in their squadrons, only to be crushed like dry leaves under the Kristiano boot? The bodies of the dead—in the thousands—will be left to rot on the field, as happened at Napetuca and Mabila. What if the surviving warriors are made to carry Kristiano baggage, chained at the neck, while their naked wives, sisters, and daughters are staked spread-eagle to the ground and raped by man after man?"

I'd shocked them to their roots.

I continued softly. "What impact will that have on any surviving Chicaza? I could ask: Will you still even *be* Chicaza? I'm talking about down in that sacred place inside that believes Chicaza are specially chosen by Power.

"Or will that fiery spirit be forever broken like an old pot? Cracked . . . and shattered?"

They stared at me, horror in their eyes.

"If that comes to pass"—Pearl Hand lifted her chin and slitted her eyes—"then by the time the Kristianos finally leave, there will be no Chicaza Nation. The Spirit that makes you great will lie like cold, wet ashes in your chests."

I said humbly, "Lose this thing . . . and you lose everything."

With a gravity I'd never seen before, my brother nodded. For long moments he traded glances with the tishu minko, then with Flying Squirrel. He got a nod from Minko Wide Net of the Deer Clan, and another from Minko Cut Hand of the Crawfish Clan. Then he took the measure of other Chief Clan lineages. Most made hand signs in support.

He turned back to us, his expression that of a man condemned to the square. "It is the order of the high minko and the Chief Clan, with the concurrence of the iksas, that we will evacuate Chicaza town and leave the food as a trap for the Kristianos."

Leaning his head back, eyes closed, he prayed, "Breath Giver, help us to have the courage and dedication to destroy the invaders."

Because if you don't get it right, brother . . .

I couldn't finish the thought.

Pearl Hand, having strapped Antonio's armor to her chest, led the way out into the frosty night. A light snow had fallen and now crusted the ground, reflecting what little illumination penetrated the thick clouds.

I looked back through the door, seeing my brother, head bent, locked in deep discussions with the minkos. "Poor man."

"Better him than you," Pearl Hand muttered. "My gut is an empty hole. Come on, we need to put something in it, and by the Tie Snake's rattles, we've got to feed the dogs and take them for a walk."

"Ahltakla?" a voice called from the snowy gloom.

"Yes?" I turned, seeing a cautious young man, his head draped with a thick fabric blanket that left his features in shadow. He looked miserably cold, and I could make out bare knees above his moccasins.

"Now that the war council is over, I am tasked with escorting you to the palace."

"I'm hungry, and my dogs need to be cared for."

"Your dogs have been taken care of. The Coosa trader saw to it just after dusk. My orders are to bring you."

I glanced at Pearl Hand, who said, "Husband, I'm tired, hungry, and in no mood for socializing unless it involves a deep-pit-roasted venison haunch, warm raspberry tea, and steaming freshly baked bread."

I growled my irritation and gave her the "accompany me" sign. She mulled it over for a couple of heartbeats and grunted acquiescence. The smile that bent her full lips, however, promised trouble for whoever had delayed her meal.

We followed our guide across the snowy plaza, past the red and white World Tree post, and around the chunkey courts. This pleased me. The underlying clay might have been wet and walking across it would have left irregularities in the surface.

Obsessive chunkey players hate people who do that.

Our guide said nothing as he climbed onto the veranda before the palace. He unhooked the latch and lifted the plank door to the side, and Pearl Hand and I boldly strode in.

The warmth hit me like a delightful wave. A great fire—the four logs laid out in the cardinal directions—burned brightly. Guardian posts rose at either side of the door, the heads perfectly carved renditions of eagles; their eyes of polished copper appeared animated. Wings taken from real eagles had been extended to their full length, dried, and cunningly affixed to the posts, adding to the lifelike effect.

The floor matting was woven as a single continuous piece and done in geometric patterns. Thick hides of deer, elk, buffalo, bear, and beaver covered the benches attached to the walls. Beneath them I could see the usual wooden boxes, folded blankets, ceramic jars and pots, fabric bags, and other belongings. Wooden carvings of Eagle Man, Morning Star, the Orphan, the Winds—represented by ivory-billed woodpeckers—and Deer Man hung from the walls. Bows, shields, war clubs, occasional human arm and leg bones, and, of course, trophy skulls were lashed to the wall matting between the larger carvings. Here and there human scalps dangled, the long dry hair waving in the slight draft.

The high minko's three-legged chair stood empty behind the fire. One of the chair's poles was red cedar, representing the Sky World. The second was bald cypress, which grew from water and symbolized the Underworld. The third, hickory, denoted our middle world. Panther hide covered the seat.

The room's sole occupant was seated to the right of the fire. My empty gut twisted as I met Mother's gaze. She sat upon a cushion made of a buffalo robe doubled over on itself. Her legs, knees together, were appropriately folded beneath her. Despite my growing panic, I marched straight for her, head high, the sacred mace carried before me. Adding a bit of swing to my hips made Antonio's sword sway jauntily at my side.

Her fierce gaze never wavered as I stopped before her and cradled the mace like a baby. "You asked for us, Ishki Minko Cane Mat Woman?" I used the honorific.

She continued to study me, no expression on her chiseled face. Up close, I saw she'd aged well, her hair remaining black but for a couple of silver strands only detectable upon close inspection. She'd piled it high on her head and pinned it with a stunningly large whelk-shell columella. Patterns of fine lines radiated from the corners of her eyes; her nose remained straight and prominent. From the line of her jaw I could tell she'd lost her back teeth. The resulting jut of her chin created interesting patterns in the wrinkles around her mouth. Mother's cheekbones, however, remained smooth and youthful, the fire behind her eyes blazing and immortal.

A beautifully tanned deer-hide dress, literally covered with chevron-patterned quillwork dyed in red, yellow, blue, and white, was belted at her still-slim waist and emphasized the woman's perfect hips and slender legs.

"What did they decide?" she asked sharply.

"Chicaza town will be abandoned, the granaries left intact as a means of inducing the Kristianos to stay. The high minko, the iksa minkos, and the council will study the enemy, seek to quell his suspicions, and when the time is right attempt to destroy him."

She seemed to already know this, for no change of expression so much as flickered behind her baleful eyes. Then she turned her attention to Pearl Hand. That my wife wore Kristiano armor, carried a crossbow and quiver of arrows, and glared back like an enraged panther seemed unimportant. Rather Cane Mat Woman studied her attentively, finally locking eyes with Pearl Hand. For long moments the silence stretched.

I could feel the tension building, tight and straining, as the two indomitable women took each other's measure.

Softly, Mother said, "She seems worthy of a better man than you."

As if she'd anticipated this, Pearl Hand fired back, "In all of my life, beloved matron, I've only *chosen* one man. The others were merely whimpering boys in comparison."

"It's apparent, then, that you've been exposed to a poor selection of men." Mother's expression and tone remained aloof. "Perhaps you should look around Chicaza. Even our untried youths will be an improvement."

"You take risks, old woman," Pearl Hand growled through clenched teeth.

"And if *he* is your choice, it seems you'll take anything."

I fought the urge to wince as Pearl Hand's eyelids lowered, her expression straining like a cougar on the verge of leaping. "Easy," I said in Timucua. "She's baiting you, testing you."

"Talk like a human being," Mother snapped, shifting her glare my way. "And yes, woman, I take risks all the time. They pay off with such regularity it bores me."

"Why are we here?" I asked, slicing down to the bone.

"Because obviously you've fooled your brother. He always worshipped you. Apparently you can float back into his life like a moldy leaf, and he's right back in your palm."

"You're not worth my time tonight," I muttered, a dull rage burning in my much-too-empty gut.

I turned and had taken two steps when she called out, "Why are you here, coward? Do you really think you can have your banishment lifted? That if you persuade us to fight your battle for you, you'll be asked to come home?"

I stopped short, shoulders dropping as I sighed. Marching back, I dropped to one knee so I could stare at her eyeball to eyeball. "Old woman, I am the chosen of Horned Serpent. My purpose, my *sole* purpose, is the destruction of the *Adelantado* and his murdering army. If the earth opened up tomorrow, and Piasa and Horned Serpent dragged every last Kristiano down and buried them alive, I wouldn't remain in Chicaza a moment longer than it took me to pack and head back east."

I let the truth of that fill my souls.

"The chosen of Horned Serpent?" She chuckled dryly, a bitter set to her lips. "You are my lying and cowardly son. And that's who you will always be, you piece of akeohoosa filth. After what you did to me, what you cost my brother and our clan, I prayed that I'd never hear your name again. Let alone have you polluting my palace."

"*You* were the one who invited us here. Perhaps I should be away lest I stay here too long and cause you to burn the place down in order to purify it of my taint." I snapped my fingers. "Oh, wait. Can't do that. We need it for the Kristianos. But that's all right, matron Cane Mat Woman, because when it's all over—win or lose—my pollution is nothing compared to what the Kristianos bring."

Her jaw muscles were flickering, a searing rage behind her eyes. I saw again the old pulsing vein that stood out on her temple when she was infuriated. A slight tic that I'd never seen before jumped in her cheek.

"Get out." She barely breathed the words.

I rose, straightened, and walked with all the dignity I could.

Outside the door, the cold felt wonderful. I stopped, gasping for breath, my muscles bunched like knotted rope. Breathing deeply, I tried to still the pounding of my heart.

"Charming woman, your mother." Pearl Hand stopped beside me, raising her face to the falling flakes. "Who do you think will kill her first? Me? Or de Soto?"

"If I hadn't heard the war council decide to trap de Soto . . ."

"Yes, yes." Pearl Hand placed a reassuring hand on my

shoulder. "Come on. If I don't eat something soon I'm going to go back in there and rip that woman's heart out for supper."

"I think you'd find it hard chewing."

"You're right. Bad idea. For days I'd be irritated at having to stop and pick the gristle out of my teeth."

TWENTY

WE'D BARELY MADE IT BACK TO WILD ROSE'S BEFORE
word came. Black Marten told the story, a stricken look
on his face. The Panther Clan squadron that had tried
to slow de Soto's crossing at the Tombigbee River was in
full retreat. They'd made a show of force, parading along
the riverbank, shouting threats, rattling their bows on
their hardwood shields, and launching an occasional
arrow.

Unbeknownst to them, the Kristianos had sent a small
detachment of cabayeros upriver. There they'd built large
rafts and crossed the cabayeros as they had at Apafalaya.
The Panther Clan squadron had barely escaped behind
fortifications. Several warriors had been ridden down and
lanced before the retreat was complete.

The effect had been sobering, and as the rest of the
Kristiano force began to cross, the squadron had melted
away into the forest.

"They didn't panic," Black Marten told us, his expression strained. "The squadron leader found himself

flanked, and they'd never fought men who rode beasts before. The warriors who were killed were among the fastest runners in the squadron, but they could not escape. And here's the amazing thing: The Panther iksa warriors rained arrows on the invader. They saw their shafts bounce off! Heard the war points striking like hailstones on rocks. And . . . *nothing*! Not a single Kristiano was even wounded!"

Pearl Hand's gaze narrowed. "And nothing lies between the *Adelantado* and Chicaza town but forest, scattered farmsteads, and a couple of villages."

The evacuation of Chicaza town began that very night. By morning men, women, and children were packing, the entire town turned upside down. The clan chiefs, coordinating with both the high minko and the tishu minko, orchestrated the operation. Each iksa was responsible for its own packing, and each had a separate destination among the outlying towns and villages once they left Chicaza town. The idea was that the people would be spread throughout the countryside, beyond the reach of the Kristianos, and in low enough concentrations so as not to stretch the local food supplies.

"Sure," Wild Rose had growled angrily as she packed her wealth. "Uproot my trade, turn my business upside down."

Pearl Hand had given the woman an amused look. "And since when did it become difficult to conduct your 'trade'? Seems to me all you need is a couple of blankets: one to keep your backside off the frozen ground, and the other to cover his."

Wild Rose had given her a flat look in return. "Blankets will do, but I'll miss the comfort." She looked back at her snug house. "Will I really have to burn it when this is all over with?"

"They leave disease behind them," I replied.

"It's a new house, no more than three years old."

"Kristianos bring misery to everything they touch," Pearl Hand murmured.

A pale sun illuminated the southeastern horizon as I led the way south, just one of many on the trail. At a high point, Pearl Hand and I drew the dogs to the side, watching the procession of men, women, and children filing out of Chicaza toward the various forest trails.

The sight reminded me of lines of ants, all struggling beneath heavy burdens. The figures were dark against the snow, breath rising and puffing from their mouths. Blanket-wrapped, their feet bound in cloth, they struggled onward, plodding wearily, almost desperately, across the frost.

In the crystalline cold, the only thing I could hear was the soft rasping of their clothing, the barely audible panting of breath. Beyond that there was no talk, no laughing or angry shouts. Nothing.

And then it came to me.

These are people in shock.

Yesterday morning at this time they had been waking, tending morning cook fires, half of them lounging in warm beds. Those who thought about more than the normal concerns of their daily lives might have been curious about the council session to be held in the tchkofa. They might have wondered about the stories told of the Kristianos. And half of them would have yawned, rolled over, and gone back to sleep.

In an instant, as if their world were a ceramic pot, they'd been turned upside down and shaken out into the snow and an uncertain future. Now they plodded out of Chicaza town, bearing their worldly baggage on their backs.

Some had pack dogs, others had only themselves. Minkos, of course, rode on litters, their slaves bent under their possessions. Ahead of them lay the frozen dark forest and—given their burdens—a hard day's walk to the next shelter. From there they would be ordered on again, until finally the minkos had their people beyond the range of slave-hunting cabayero sweeps.

"Your thoughts?" Pearl Hand asked as she stopped beside me and watched the slowly crawling line of people cross the snowy cornfields.

"Sadness," I replied. "Sure, we've seen this before. Felt it even. Remember the evacuation of Telemico in Cofitachequi?" I shook my head. "But this time it's more poignant. It's the middle of winter. It's going to be miserable for a lot of people, especially the children."

"Not nearly as miserable as wearing a Kristiano collar and sleeping naked in the snow. And those poor women may end up shivering, but it's only from the weather. Me, I'll shiver from the cold any old day rather than be quaking from the anticipation of having an unwashed Kristiano rip my clothes off, throw me on the ground, and grope me as he drives his peg between my legs."

"You'd find a way to cut his throat later."

She nodded, eyes narrowed as she watched the refugees. "Of course. But I've had the world smack me down hard, survived the humiliation and degradation. Learned how to turn it into a weapon. These Chicaza women? They've been protected all their lives . . . had it beaten into their heads and souls that if their precious sheaths are violated, they're somehow dirtied and polluted." She gave me a knowing look. "It would break most of them, wound their souls to the point they'd rather die than look their relatives in the eyes again."

I thought about how my sisters had been raised. Now they were young matrons, with children of their own. I could guess how they'd react to endless rape by a bunch of sweat-reeking Kristianos.

"Come on. Let's get to Black Acorn town. We need to find a place to stash our belongings. After that my brother and the tishu minko are going to want us close." I smacked my thigh, calling, "Come on, dogs."

"Black Shell," she called after me as I started down the trail, "you know what the chances are of pulling this off, don't you?"

I pinched my lips, chewing on them with nervous teeth. We'd been cautiously optimistic before the battle at Napetuca. Desperation and frustration had accompanied every small victory in Apalachee. We'd watched our hopes crushed at Cofitachequi. Coosa had been a lost cause from the beginning. And just when we'd been ready to give up, Tuskaloosa's faith had given us hope. Only to have it scorched to ash at Mabila.

"Horned Serpent still believes in us," I whispered fervently. "And the Chicaza have listened."

"So far."

"Yes. So far. My brother is a smart man. So is the tishu minko and Old Wood. They will demand obedience from the iksas, and they will study the Kristianos before they make the mistakes of Mabila."

At her continued silence, I slowed, looking back. Pearl Hand's face was a study of conflicting thoughts. The dogs piled up at my heels, looking at me with curious eyes.

"What?" I asked.

She hesitated, then finally said, "Black Shell, don't take this wrong, but you are partially blinded when it comes to your brother."

"Blinded how?"

"You still love him. It colors your opinion of him."

"And how is that?"

"Granted, most of the minkos like him, but they don't really respect him. Your brother doesn't have your strength of character. At his core he's unsure of himself. And leering over his shoulder like some perverted perching vulture is your mother. She worries me."

"She'd worry a rock," I growled.

"Promise me something."

"Of course."

"Whatever you do, husband, don't trust any of them. Not even for a moment."

"You forget, they made me akeohoosa."

"And every time you start thinking of them as family, you rotted well better keep reminding yourself of that. Because mark my words, when they finally try to manipulate you, they're going to use your love against you."

"I have no love for them."

"Sure." She paused, a hard squint in her eyes. "Of course you don't."

Three days later, clinging to the high branches of a giant black oak, we watched the first Kristiano cabayeros as they filed out of the eastern woods, splashed across Deer Creek, and fanned out through the cornfields leading to Chicaza town. Once assured that no ambush awaited them in the standing dead corn, they began reaching down from their saddles, plucking dried ears from the brittle stalks.

"You'd think they were hungry," Pearl Hand offered sourly.

I glanced at the Chicaza hidden in the trees around us, taking in their reaction. Various minkos were clinging to the branches like peculiar fruit. For the moment they just stared in wonder.

After the vanguard, de Soto and his *capitanes* and nobles rode out, their eyes on Chicaza town no more than ten bow-shots before them.

I pointed. "The tall one with polished armor and the remarkably purple shirt, that's de Soto. Behind him, thick through the shoulders, on the white cabayo, that's Ortiz, the translator. The others clustered around him are the nobles. The closer they ride to de Soto, the higher their rank."

"And there's Antonio." Pearl Hand pointed. "At the rear and left. Maybe he's not as important as his father was."

I glared across the distance, wishing that like the hero Morning Star, I could shoot an arrow halfway across the world. Had I been able to, the little pustule-sucking maggot would have died right there.

"What are they doing?" one of the minkos asked.

Calling orders and waving, the *Adelantado* sent cabayeros in a wide sweep around the town. Slightly ahead of them ran the war dogs, coursing back and forth, sniffing for fresh sign.

"Checking for an ambush," Pearl Hand replied. "Watch this. See how fast the cabayos move? And they're only at a trot. Not only that, but from the saddle, the riders can see over the corn. Unlike fleeing from pursuing warriors on foot, you can't hide, can't dodge. The long lances they carry have *hierro* points. When they ride a warrior down, the lance doesn't stick in the victim's body but slides right out again for immediate reuse."

"And pay attention to the war dogs," I told them. "They are trained to hunt our people. Depending upon the command, they will simply grab a fleeing man or woman and hold them. Or, if told, will rip a human being apart."

As a man who loved his dogs, I really *hated* the Kristiano war dogs.

Once the cabayeros determined the perimeter was safe, the riders cautiously rode in among the buildings. I heard the lilting note of a Kristiano horn signaling the all-clear.

"So that's the enemy?" my brother said thoughtfully. He clung to a fork in the branches just above me.

"That's the enemy."

"Men riding animals; I'd have never believed it." The tishu minko shook his head where he propped himself between the branches to my left. Red Cougar had a strained look on his tattooed face, his lips pressed thinly. "How do the souls of the beasts and men accept the relationship? There has to be Power in it."

"Magical," Medicine Killer whispered. "Like some sort of Spirit Beasts come to life."

"And even more deadly," Pearl Hand growled. "As you'll find out if they ever catch you in the open."

Across the distance I heard faint shouts as the cabayeros dismounted and started searching the clan houses, Men's House, and tchkofa.

"Look, there's more," one of the minkos called.

The bulk of the cabayeros emerged from the forest trail, crossed the creek, and followed the *Adelantado* and his party into Chicaza town. Unerringly they made for the palace. Over the distance I watched de Soto dismount as his scouts continued their search of the buildings. Shouts of delight could be heard as they climbed the ladders to find full granaries.

Then the forest began to disgorge the long line of *soldados*, the clanking of their weapons and armor carrying in the cold winter air. Among them were chained columns of slaves. They plodded wearily along, backs bent under baskets or lashed-up packs. One group carried pieces of the heavy metal thing they used to Spirit-temper the *hierro*. I remembered how I myself once had labored under the weight of the thing.

If there was any good news, it was that they carried a pittance compared to the past. The fabric-covered chairs, the unwieldy tents, the round wooden kegs of thunderstick powder, the heavy square bales of cloth, countless jars of oil and drink, and so many other things were gone. Destroyed at Mabila.

"Black Shell?" Pearl Hand called. "Look at them. But for the armor, you'd think they were *indios* like the rest of us."

"They're sure dressed like we are," I replied. "Remember how they marched into Ahocalaquen? The line of them seemed to stretch on forever. Remember the fanfare, the great banners, the shining armor and colorful clothing? Remember how it seemed there was no end to them? Look. In just this short time the last of the *soldados* has cleared the forest."

She frowned across the distance. "I don't think there's more than a hundred cabayos left to them. And the Kristianos only number seven hundred or so? Have we killed so many?"

I tried to make a count as the slave women and converted *indios* emerged from the forest. These carried metal pots, cookware, and bundles of personal belongings. The packs were so much smaller than they'd been when the Kristianos marched out of Cofitachequi.

My brother gave a skeptical grunt and pointed. "What are those things?"

"*Puercos,*" I growled. I made a face as the bouncing and trotting herd poured out of the forest and into the fields. The boys around them used long poles to jab at them and keep them moving. The standing corn was almost more than the *puercos* could bear as they crashed into the stalks to topple the plants. Then, grabbing dried ears, they ripped them loose, chewing as they made their ear-flopping escape from the herd boys.

In the town, Kristianos were calling orders to the arriving troops. Others were riding through the fields, estimating the amount of standing corn. Even as I watched, I could see the scouts reporting. De Soto was nodding, gesturing this way and that, as if apportioning the buildings to different nobles.

The sepaya warmed on my breast.

"All right, brother," I said, "they've taken Chicaza town and swallowed the bait. They're going to stay."

"Then we've a couple of moons to figure out how to kill them."

Unfazed, Pearl Hand muttered, "Assuming you're smart enough."

He shot her the kind of wary glance a smart and prudent man would.

But smart enough? That was always the rub, wasn't it?

TWENTY-ONE

LOCATED IN THE FLAT DELTA BETWEEN THE CREEKS, and with forest close on the north, east, and west, Chicaza town was easy to sneak up to, especially in the gloom after sunset.

"You're sure you want to do this?" Pearl Hand asked as she laid her hand on Bark's thick and scarred head.

"Oh yes," I answered, the nut of a plan having planted itself in my head. "Winning this depends on wearing them down, confusing them over the long term."

"And not dying in the process."

"How could I have been so silly as to forget that?"

"Just concentrating on the important things, my love. Wouldn't want them to slip by the wayside."

"Of course. Important point."

We eased between the thick trunks of trees, and I could feel my heart begin to pound. I hated the tingling of fear that ran down my spine on frigid mouse feet. My mouth had already gone dry. Sneaking up on Kristianos had that effect.

Bark gave a soft growl, and I gestured at him to stop, sit, and lie down.

Why did I bring Bark? He's the dumbest of the lot.

He was also unstoppable in a fight. And if the Kristianos turned their enthusiastic war dogs loose to hunt us, Bark would ensure a rapid rearrangement of their priorities. Still, I should have brought Gnaw along. He not only obeyed, but he didn't get carried away with himself. Bark, as his name suggested, would on occasion plop onto his rear, raise his head, and bellow until the world stopped.

A situation sure to bring cabayeros charging down on top of us.

I fingered the war bow I'd been given. It was originally taken from the far-off Tula people who lived at the edge of the western prairies; I think my brother gave it to me in a fit of ill humor. Made of Osage orangewood, it took all of my strength to draw an arrow and hold it long enough to aim. But when I released, it drove a hardwood arrow halfway through a shagbark hickory trunk.

Drawing that bow had brought home the fact that I was still recovering from the wounds I'd received at Mabila. Maybe I'd even have had trouble drawing my old Caddo bow. The one that had disappeared outside Mabila where I'd fought Antonio.

"So, what's the plan?" Pearl Hand asked.

"You saw what they did today."

"They rode around on the cabayos and tore down most of the surrounding farmsteads. Then they roped up the wood and matting and dragged it back to Chicaza."

"Normally, no more than four hundred people live in Chicaza town. It's mostly a place where the iksas come together for meetings . . . a collection of clan houses, charnel houses, granaries, and storehouses. The Kristianos don't have enough housing for their men, slaves, and women. Half of the *soldados* are sleeping on the frozen ground in those miserable mat shelters of theirs. So for the next couple of moons, they're going to be stripping the country for building materials. Next they'll be sending out woodcutting parties."

"Just like they did in Apalachee," she finished, a knowing look on her face.

"And we'll be waiting for them. But in the meantime, unlike Anhaica, there are no defensive walls around Chicaza. We can sneak close at night, and, well . . . raise a little havoc."

"And what do you hope to accomplish? An armed pursuit?" She was looking around the darkening forest floor. "Got a notion of where to turn and ambush? I don't see any place in here where the cabayeros can't circle around and lance us from behind."

"Nothing so dramatic." I patted the bow. "I'm just thinking of slipping into range and launching arrows into the outlying camps. Maybe three or four shots. Then we ghost away in the darkness."

"And hope you hit someone?"

"That'd be nice. But if you were a Kristiano, how well would you sleep after a couple of random arrows fell from the night sky?"

She chuckled. "And if this were to happen with some regularity?"

"It will wear on them like sand between the teeth."

So we did it. We slipped to the edge of camp just as the *soldados* were climbing into their blankets, their forms barely illuminated by the low fires.

I shot three times, arching the arrows into the sky. At the sound of dismayed cries, we turned and ran. Well, all but Bark. He stopped short, tail whipping, as he bellowed one long defiant staccato string of "arf's."

The following night some of the Crawfish Clan warriors sneaked close and shot into the outlying camps while calling out Chicaza insults. It became a nightly ritual. Then, come morning, cabayeros, lances in hand, would scour the woods, looking for us, anxious to pay us back for the heightened alarms.

By then we were up in the hills, waiting in the brush, where we could ambush them and flee.

Through it all, my brother, the tishu minko, and the squadron leaders watched, listened, and learned.

Two days later, the first of the messengers arrived. The man, an *indio* captive, came trotting out from Chicaza town with a large white-painted arrow held before him. Our scouts watched the man as he came plodding down the main trail. The fellow was from Apafalaya, an Albaamaha speaker, which was a close dialect to Chicaza Mos'kogee.

Even as he was brought before my brother and his council in the Black Oak town tchkofa, the man made no effort to hide his fear. And little wonder; the last Apafalaya emissary de Soto had sent had been killed at the Tombigbee River fight.

At the council were my brother, Tishu Minko Red Cougar, Minko Cut Hand of the Crawfish Clan, and Minko Alibamo—my youngest sister's husband and leader of an allied population of Albaamaha who lived a couple of days' journey to the northwest.

The emissary, his white arrow clutched as if it were sacred wood, entered, dropped to his knees, and touched his forehead to the floor in obeisance.

"Speak," my brother said softly.

Without the slightest raising of his head, the man said, "I am sent by the *Adelantado, el gobernador de* La Florida, *en el nombre del rey Carlos cinco,* who asks that you stop your harassment of Chicaza town and the Kristianos. The *Adelantado* wishes only peace and harmony with the Chicaza people. He asks that you come in peace to have counsel with him and his *capitanes.* If you will do so, he guarantees your safety and will reward you and the Chicaza people with fine gifts from his homeland."

"I see," my brother said, and shot me a questioning glance, indicating the White Arrow with a gesture of his fingers.

"It means nothing," I told him. "The Kristianos consider symbols sacred to us—like the White Arrow—to be inherently evil. Tied to a bad god they call *el diablo*. What they see is a pointed stick with feathers and a little white paint. Their word of safe passage is no more than the sound of air expelled from their lungs. To them, a word can be taken back as easily as drawing breath."

"That's incomprehensible," Minko Cut Hand exclaimed. "Words carry the colors and weight of the soul, especially when uttered in the presence of the White Arrow. Don't these Kristianos fear the reprisals of Power?"

"No," Pearl Hand told him in a sharp tone. "They call their god the one and only *true* god."

"That's foolishness," Fire Tail, the Alibamo mikko, growled. "We all know that Breath Giver made the world. And even while you Chicaza believe you were created from clay inside a distant western mountain, and we Albaamaha believe we climbed up through the roots of the World Tree to this world, we still respect the Spirit Power and the laws and rules of behavior Breath Giver instilled in each of our peoples."

"Kristianos dismiss such notions as nonsense," I said simply.

"Then they are witches," Cut Hand said in a hesitant voice.

I raised my hands to emphasize my point. "Listen to me. Their spirit Power is no stronger than ours. I was there holding the sepaya when Back-from-the-Dead battled with the Kristiano priest. They faced each other, each calling on his Power. Back-from-the-Dead held the great Cahokian mace and drew from the sepaya. I could feel its heat. The Kristiano held his long-tailed cross, called upon *jesucristo,* and made crisscross signs with his right hand . . . and nothing happened."

My brother glanced down at the groveling Apafalaya messenger, then at me. "What do you mean, nothing happened?"

"Just what I said, High Minko. For some time the two priests threw their curses at each other. I swear, I *felt* the Power in the air, but neither was superior to the other. Had the women they were burning to death not screamed and broken the spell, we might still be standing there, locked in a perpetual stalemate."

"Have you discussed this with Copper Sky and the other hopayes?"

"It hasn't come up." I didn't want to tell him what I thought of Copper Sky or the other hopayes.

My brother apparently read my reluctant dissembling; a frown deepened in his forehead.

Pay attention here. You see, I'd been in the presence of *powerful* medicine men, shamans, and priests. Like the day I'd first walked into Back-from-the-Dead's presence. Those with real Power give a person an eerie feeling that raises the hairs on the back of one's neck—like you know there is lightning bottled up in a long-necked jar.

Around Old Wood, I got the feeling that I was in the presence of a venerable and respect-worthy individual. Copper Sky? He left me feeling nothing. But for conscious effort, I'd forget he was even present in a room. On the other hand, I had heard that he was a master of Power plants, that he knew the medicines and could correctly diagnose witchcraft, curses, and spells. His emetics could purge a person within a finger's time, and he was known for healing every kind of illness, from soul loss to battle wounds.

Just don't ask him to send his souls to the Spirit World to fight evil spirits.

"Messenger," my brother said gently, "please take the White Arrow back to the *Adelantado* and tell him he is an invader in our lands. Explain to him that we cannot accept his offer of the White Arrow until he indicates to us that he understands and honors the Power behind it.

"Further, if he means to broker a peace between us, he will stop his cabayeros from riding sweeps through our country. I just heard this morning that two of my people have been ridden down by his beasts and taken captive. If he releases them unharmed, it will be a first sign that we *might* eventually trust him to keep his word."

The Apafalaya man literally crawled backward on his hands and knees until he was outside the tchkofa door. Then he rose, nodded to the guarding warriors, and started back toward Chicaza town and his terrible captor.

"Think he'll run?" Pearl Hand asked.

"Not while he carries the White Arrow," my brother replied wearily. "What does it mean when the captive messenger considers his duty sacred and inviolable, and his Kristiano master doesn't? How did the world get turned so upside down?"

The messengers kept coming. De Soto meanwhile extended his cabayero sweeps, occasionally catching unlucky stragglers and the foolhardy when they happened to stray too far from cover. The best count we had of the Chicaza captives was between twelve and fifteen. Not bad after two full weeks of occupation.

Pearl Hand and I, having fought a winter war against Kristianos before, exiled ourselves to the forest. There, with a couple of Chief Clan warriors—cousins of mine appointed by the high minko—we plotted ambushes and built cabayo traps.

White Necklace Mankiller had passed nearly thirty

summers, was tall, and—though he didn't look it given his stringy muscles—was strong as a bull buffalo. In his medicine pouch, White Necklace kept four of the little white honor arrows bestowed by the Men's House for valor in combat. A nasty pink scar ran along his cheek, and his right collarbone had been broken so many times it looked like a knotted rope. Like the rest of him, his face was long and thin, with hollows under his cheekbones and a firm jaw.

Split Shield Mankiller was my mother's sister's daughter's son. Technically he was in line for the high minko's chair should my brother die and my two sisters lose all their male heirs. Given that Silent Spring had already borne boys, and that both of my sisters were pregnant again, his chances were dwindling.

Split Shield, too, carried several of the honorary white arrows. A little shorter than me, he was perfectly proportioned, broad chested, with a narrow waist and muscular legs. Pearl Hand told me he was a handsome man. The sort Wild Rose would consider a keeper.

They were both spies.

My brother wouldn't have been my mother's son otherwise.

Pearl Hand and I couldn't have cared less. Our job was killing Kristianos.

The problem was, this wasn't Apalachee. Nor were these Kristianos the same arrogant and self-confident plundering raiders we'd fought around Anhaica.

Crouching with Squirm and Blackie, I watched from a tangle of grape and raspberry as the latest Kristiano patrol worked its way down the deeply rutted forest trail. A dull silver sun was shining in the eastern sky. The high canopy of maple, oak, and gum trees cast dappled patterns on the Kristiano armor, on the rough clothing and tailored hides they wore. Their shields, however, were polished *hierro* riveted to a thick wooden frame. I remembered how, when they'd first landed at Uzita, the shields had been painted in various designs. The paint had long ago worn off, and our local replacement colors seemed unable to duplicate the vibrant reds, yellows, greens, and purples.

Gone, too, were the bright and marvelous cloth shirts, the thick canvaslike pants, and the shining high boots. Instead these riders wore clothing made out of native blankets, mulberry cloth, or tanned deer or elk hide beneath their armored breastplates. Where the *hierro* had once been polished and smooth, it now had a gray appearance; when the light hit right, dimples and ripples could be seen in that once-perfect surface. Each marked the impact of an arrow or war club. The same could be seen in their *hierro* helmets.

The five riders picked their way carefully down the trail, eyes flicking this way and that, wary as hunted red wolves. They held their lances at the ready, and two rode with crossbows slung over their shoulders.

The cabayos, too, seemed wary. I could see it in the way they picked their path so carefully, their rounded hooves occasionally cracking on a rock or root. The funny pinlike ears kept swiveling this way and that, the beasts looking at every stump and shadow as they approached.

I breathed softly, feeling the breeze on my face, and thanked Breath Giver that the cabayos couldn't wind me or the dogs. At least not until they passed my hiding place in the brush. Then, hopefully, as they caught my scent, they'd be far enough into the trap that my appearance above and behind them would drive them into the killing zone where we'd hidden pointed stakes, dug pitfalls, and placed down timbers.

If everything worked perfectly, we might get one, or maybe two. If it worked at all, the Kristianos would enjoy a little excitement and ride out of the trap with our arrows stuck in their armor. If it worked poorly, we'd be lucky to get away with our lives.

Blackie was quivering, ears pricked, his tail rigid. Squirm's entire body tensed, a low growl buried in his throat. I gestured for silence and resettled my Tula-made bow. A heavy war arrow lay nocked in the braided gut string.

Just a little farther, come on.

I really wanted to see what this bow could do against *hierro* plate.

Just as my hopes were rising and my heart began to beat with the joy of the hunt, the first rider pulled up. He looked at the brush thicket that closed down on either side of the creek crossing. Then he lifted his hand and pushed back the visor on his helmet. I was so close I could hear it screech.

"Alto, amigos. No me gusta este. Pienso que está un emboscada."

"Claro," the one behind called, pulling his cabayo up and scanning the brush that hid Pearl Hand and the others.

I froze, one hand on Blackie's back, my head slightly lowered, as his gaze probed my location. *By the Piasa's balls, surely he can't see us.*

"Mira, es mejor en este dirección." The first rider pointed, wheeled his mount, and trotted off between the tree trunks searching for another way to cross the creek.

"Blood and pus!" I growled under my breath, unwilling to move, hoping desperately that they'd return.

They wouldn't. No more than three bow-shots upstream the banks were low enough that the cabayos could cross without too much difficulty.

Even as I listened, I could hear the creak of saddles, the rattle of equipment, and the faint hollow thumping of hooves as the patrol made the crossing.

I waited long enough to be sure they weren't coming back around behind us and stood. The dogs immediately

ran for the trail, sniffing zigzag patterns where the cabayos had stood. Head back, I stared up at the morning
sky, visible through the maze of interwoven branches,
grapevines, and greenbrier above.

Angrily I pitched an acorn into the distance and
walked down the trail.

Pearl Hand, her crossbow cocked, rose from one side
of the pitfall. White Necklace rose from the other.

"I don't know what went wrong. The leader just
stopped, stared at the brush, and said something about
not liking it."

"*Emboscada.* I heard," Pearl Hand said, pulling the crossbow arrow out of its channel and easing the bowstring
back to rest.

"What's that mean?"

"That's the word for 'ambush.'"

"How?" I demanded, then looked at White Necklace. "You checked my position. What could he have
seen?"

"Nothing," White Necklace said insistently. He'd
gotten his name by killing a Casqui warrior who'd
wrapped his neck with shell beads. "Did the wind
change?"

"No," I growled. "The cabayos didn't even spot me.
The cabayero just seemed to *know*."

Pearl Hand exhaled wearily. "You should be proud,
husband."

"Proud? They just backed *out* of my trap and went
around!"

"Because we've taught them," she told me, arching her
eyebrow. "Any time there's close cover, they'll pay."

"And that's supposed to make me happy? We're here
to kill Kristianos."

She gave me a winning smile. "We've bled them too
often, killed the stupid ones. The problem now is how do
we kill the smart ones?"

I made a face. "If Antonio had been here, we'd have had our chance."

Split Shield appeared from the brush across the creek. "What happened?"

"They went around." Pearl Hand grounded her crossbow.

"They spotted us?" he asked.

I shook my head. "If they'd seen me, they'd have loosed a couple of arrows my way and charged the brush. By the Piasa's swinging balls, it's as if they can *smell* a trap now."

"Like I said," Pearl Hand told me, "it should make you proud."

I was still growling to myself when Black Marten came trotting down the trail, his shield on his arm, a strung bow in his right hand.

"What happened?" He, too, was clearly disgusted by the Kristianos' newly developed "good sense."

"We're going to have to think up something different," I told him.

"Ahltakla?" He met my eyes. "While I was watching the escape route, one of the high minko's runners arrived."

"What?" I cried. "He knows better than to send anyone out here. What if the Kristianos had been fleeing back down that trail?"

Black Marten shrugged. "The runner would have had to hide."

"What did he want?" Pearl Hand asked.

"We've caught someone. He speaks no language we can understand. His face is tattooed in starburst patterns, and he wears one of the Kristiano long-tail crosses on his chest. The high minko would like to have your advice on what to do with him."

"One of the slaves?" Pearl Hand wondered.

"Let's go see." I glanced back at our trap, irritated by

the labor we'd put into it, only to have the filthy Kristianos ride around it. "Because as it now stands these accursed Kristianos refuse to cooperate with our best efforts to kill them."

"Turns out they're just rudely inconsiderate," Pearl Hand agreed.

TWENTY-TWO

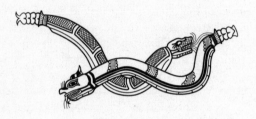

MY BROTHER HAD SENT HIS KRISTIANO PRISONER TO High Corn town, a hard day's run to the south. Why so far away? To keep the prisoner beyond the normal daily range of the cabayero sweeps.

Chicaza political organization differed from the talwa system the eastern Mos'kogee peoples used. Instead, towns were established and governed by various iksas. High Corn town—a collection of nearly a hundred houses—had been established by Hawk Clan, of the Old Camp Moiety.

High Corn town occupied a gravel-topped terrace above the flood stage and overlooking cornfields along a creek filled with bald cypress and tupelo. Off to the west, beyond the fields, rose low hills timbered with old-growth forest.

In the beginning, the rich floodplain along Blue Mussel Creek had produced excellent corn, hence the town name. Over the years—as so often happened—the corn crops withered as the soil played out. Talk was that High

Corn town would be relocated in the next couple of years onto an old, long-abandoned site that the Hawk iksa had occupied in my great-grandfather's time.

We arrived late that evening, escorted by my brother's runner, the indefatigable Green Stick. According to the story he related, the Kristiano prisoner had taken leave of his party and squatted behind a bush to relieve himself. Even as he grunted and strained, two young warriors stepped out of their hiding place behind him. On silent feet they had crept up and, with one carefully placed blow of a war club, knocked him senseless.

We entered the plaza, seeing the earth-covered tchkofa on one end. A World Tree pole rose in the north center, and a palace—home of the local Hawk Clan minko—stood just behind it.

A crowd had gathered to the right of the turtle-shaped tchkofa, and it was there that Green Stick led us. Passing through the press, Green Stick called, "Make way for the Ahltakla and his party. Make way in the name of the high minko. We have business here."

People backed away as Pearl Hand and I walked forward. I could hear whispers on every lip, could see the awed expressions in the fading light. News of my return, my brother's acquiescence to my presence, and—without a doubt—my mother's disgust had been carried from one end of the Nation to the other. People, no matter what their iksa, relished any juicy gossip about Chief Clan and its internal frictions, squabbling, and backstabbing politics.

The last of the crowd parted, revealing a wooden square. The name is descriptive. Two upright logs were planted in the ground. A crosspiece was laid over the top and another along the bottom to form an open square— just the right size to hang a human being inside if his hands were tied to each upper corner and his feet to the bottom ones.

As per custom, the captive had been stripped naked before being tied. Of medium height, he was well muscled, his face, breasts, arms, and upper thighs tattooed with Timucua designs that came from down in the peninsula where de Soto had originally landed.

The man's head hung in defeat, blood-matted hair falling over his face. Like all men in a square, he labored for breath, ribs rising and falling. Then he shivered, puffing out a frosty exhalation.

In Timucua, I asked, "How are you called?"

He started at the familiar words, lifting his head, trying to shake the hair out of his eyes. Hoarsely, he said, "I was known as Stalks the Mist, an iniha sworn to the council of the great chief Holata Irriparacoxi."

When he flipped the last of his dangling locks away, recognition filled his eyes. "Black Shell."

"Greetings, Ears." I glanced around at the crowd, then cocked my head as I inspected the bindings at his wrists and ankles. "Looks like your fortunes have fallen."

We'd called him "Ears" for his necklace of pierced human ears cut from victims as battle trophies. After casting his lot with the Kristianos at Uzachile, he'd given up the necklace for one of the long-tailed crosses.

His expression fell as he said, "Jesus has abandoned me because of my *pecados*."

"I don't know that word."

He smiled wearily. "The great Kristiano god can forgive the evil we do. These evil actions, they are called *pecados*. I was forgiven for a time. The Kristiano priest told me so. Then everything changed at Mabila."

"I've wondered about that. I saw you squatting below the Mabila minko's veranda just after the Kristianos entered the plaza. I thought that after I drove an arrow through de Soto's eye and shot my second through Ortiz's heart, I was going to put my third arrow here." I pressed the pad of my finger against the bridge of his nose. He flinched at my touch, eyes crossing as he tried to follow my finger.

He vented a bitter laugh. "That was when I committed my greatest *pecado*. I thought all was lost when the fighting started. Being *indio* myself, I tore off the *santa cruz*, ripped the clothing from a dying warrior, and disguised myself as one of you. I ran, picked up weapons, but to my horror, the *Adelantado* fought his way out the gate."

I nodded, remembering the confusion.

Ears chuckled grimly. "Once I was outside, I saw the cabayeros enter the field and ran toward them. I stripped off the warrior's clothing as I ran. As Don Vasco Gonzales charged to lance me, I fell to my knees and crossed myself in the manner of the Kristianos, and cried, '*Ayudame! Soy Kristiano!*' At the last minute, Vasco pulled up his lance and spared me."

He swallowed hard, suffering through another bout of shivering that left him incapable of speech. Recovering enough, he added, "Vasco might have spared me, but *dios* did not. When I ripped *la vera cruz* from my breast and cast it aside, I offended *jesucristo*. I am *perdido*. Lost."

"That the Kristiano called Vasco spared you, and *dios* did not, fills my souls with delight," I told him coldly. "You and I have unfinished things between us."

He nodded, sagging in the square. "Napetuca."

"Napetuca," I agreed. "Among other things."

"Make way!" an older man called from behind me. I turned, seeing that he carried the painted and feathered wand of office appropriate for an ayopachi. "The high minko comes to see the prisoner."

The crowd parted to allow my brother to walk forward. He wore his bear-hide cloak with its dangling clawed feet; a long war shirt was belted at his waist and hung down to his knees. His calves were covered with knee-high moccasins. A falcon headdress, made of a skinned bird, the wings spread wide, was pinned to his hair bun.

"So," he asked, "Ahltakla, do you know what people this man comes from? Is he a Kristiano?"

"No, High Minko. He's a freed slave we call Ears. His people are some of the southern Timucua. I had dealings with his chief, a man named Irriparacoxi. I wagered all of my trade against the Kristiano sword you now own. He would have had Ears here kill us, but we left in the night. Later, the good Irriparacoxi gave this man to de Soto." I paused. "He probably considered it good riddance."

"He has a real name?"

"Among the Timucua he was called Stalks the Mist." I told my brother about the necklace of dried human ears and how he'd finally given them up to satisfy his new Kristiano master.

Meanwhile, Ears finally noticed Pearl Hand, saying, "So, you remain with this piece of filth? I had always prayed that I would be the man to finally cut your throat after Don Antonio did his best to rape you to death."

Pearl Hand arched a skeptical eyebrow. "Is that how he thinks he's going to kill me?"

"That is *el feo*'s brag to the others." Ears did his best to shrug. "Me, I'd use my shaft like a lance to gut you."

Pearl Hand gave him the same slim smile of disgust I'd seen on her face when she was pinching lice between her fingernails. "Neither you nor Antonio would survive the attempt."

"From the looks of things, I will never have the chance to see if your boast is true." He wet his lips, rolling his head on his neck as if to ease the muscles. "But the *Adelantado* is out there, and Antonio will find out soon enough that you're still alive. When he does he will offer these stinking Chicaza enough wealth that they will gladly turn you over."

I'd been translating the conversation to my brother and watching his expression harden at mention of the supposed manner of Pearl Hand's death. Chicaza are such prudes that even the mention of rape offends their prickly sense of honor.

In a flat voice, my brother said, "Tell him that all the copper, shell, and exotic trade in the world will not tempt the Chicaza to surrender you to the Monster."

After I translated, Ears said with a sneer, "Then the Chicaza are as stupid as you and your slut wife."

As Pearl Hand translated my brother's expression hardened.

I asked, "So, Ears, de Soto thinks Concho Negro is dead?"

"It is believed that you died at Mabila. A couple of days after the battle, Antonio found your bow lying where you dropped it outside the walls. He figured that you'd have come back to collect it had you survived. He treasures your bow. A symbol of his victory over you that day."

Some victory. I would have killed him but for his armor. He'd have killed me but for Pearl Hand's last-minute arrival. I'd scarred his face horribly, and he'd come within a gopher's whisker of crippling me. He'd lost a ca-bayo, I'd lost a favorite dog. Victory? I'd call it a poorly fought draw for both of us.

And now I find out the *hoobuk waksee* has my favorite bow?

I glanced at Pearl Hand. "They think we're dead."

"Why is that important?" my brother asked.

"The *Adelantado* knows we're inciting resistance against him. Among the Hichiti Nations, as well as at Cofi-tachequi and Coosa, they offered a high minko's ransom in trade to anyone who would betray us to them."

My brother arched a suggestive eyebrow. "Maybe I won't tell Mother. As much as she hates you, I could see her inviting the invader down for mint tea to discuss your price."

"Well, if she ever finds out, remind her to play coy and take her time. The idea of being sold out for a couple pieces of corroded *hierro* really worries me. I should be worth at least a dozen of their fancy copper pots, five or ten of those marvelous mirrors, a couple of casks of their remarkable colored beads, and at least six bolts of that stunning cloth."

Pearl Hand muttered, "The cloth was burned at Mabila. I'd hold out for *hierro* axes, myself."

A flicker of a smile played at my brother's lips. "What of this man?" He indicated Ears, who was now shivering violently. It would grow colder as darkness descended.

I pursed my lips, frowning. "He was a two-footed maggot when I first met him at Irriparacoxi's. After the Kristianos got him, he converted to their god and abandoned his ancestors. At Napetuca he betrayed Paracusi Rattlesnake and the Uzachile Nation, then, later, he participated in the mass murder of hundreds of captives."

Ears, his teeth chattering, asked, "Black Shell? What are you saying?"

"We're discussing your future, you foul piece of shit."

"Soy detastable," he whispered, head falling. *"Tengo muchos pecados."*

"What did he say?" I asked Pearl Hand.

"He says he agrees with everything you were saying about him."

I nodded and turned to my brother. "He's lived all his life in warm country. If you want him dead by morning, leave him out here. If whoever captured him wants to prolong it, they'll need to toss a blanket over him and feed him."

I started to walk away when my brother asked, "Doesn't he know things? About the invader? About what de Soto is planning?"

I hesitated, glancing back at my brother. He'd cocked his head questioningly. Ears hung, dejected and shivering, his teeth chattering in the sudden silence.

"Unfortunately, he might have a use. So, yes. I'd keep

him alive for the time being." I paused, then added, "As to what de Soto is planning? I can tell you: He's hoping to get his hands on you and the rest of the nobles to ensure that the attacks stop. He wants enough food to feed his army through the winter. He wants Chicaza blankets, capes, hunting shirts, leggings, and winter moccasins because his *soldados* are freezing. He wants as many of our women as he can lay his hands on so that his *soldados* can sleep warmly, or just pump their loins when the urge suits them. Additionally he wants enough Chicaza prisoners to carry what remains of his supplies—and what he hopes to steal from Chicaza—on to the next Nation. And when he gets there, it will all start over again."

My brother nodded, glancing uncertainly at Ears.

"That's all there is, little brother." I pointed at the captive. "Just be sure that when you're finally done using him, you cut him into small pieces. I'd toss his right foot and a couple of pieces of his left leg into the creek to be carried to the sea. Leave his left foot and some other pieces of his right leg in the trees for the birds to scatter hither and yon. Detail warriors to bury some bits of him here and there around Chicaza. Oh, and give his hands to the village dogs to pull apart and chew up."

"Black Shell?" Pearl Hand asked cautiously.

"We *don't* want to leave any chance that his souls might make it to his people's afterlife. His ancestors were probably honorable men and women."

"What of his head?" my brother asked.

"When the time comes, we'll have a trusted warrior sneak close to Chicaza town and toss it in among the *puercos*."

Pearl Hand had translated this to Ears, and once again he glared at me. "You still don't get it, do you? The *Adelantado* has beaten you at every turn! Even at Mabila. You trapped him, but his god and his Power carried him to victory! I am here because for that one moment, my faith in his Power wavered. And for that moment, his god cursed me."

"His god is no greater than ours," I growled. "At Anhaica I watched the monster's priests call down curses from their god. The Apalachee hilishaya held them at bay and then escaped. Our Power and theirs balance."

Ears spat, the effort puny given his thirst. "Think what you will. Who knows the ways of Power? But I can tell you this, Black Shell: Even if the Power is balanced like you claim, the *Adelantado* is smarter than you are. No man alive has more courage. His heart is fierce and burns with a controlled fire that will leave your lifeless corpse scorched and dead in the end. Nothing—not you, not the Chicaza, not any Nation in our world—has a chance of defeating him!"

"You'd think he was a god," I said bitterly.

"Only a god could have come this far against so much," Ears hissed back.

Gut churning in disgust, I stalked away. I heard my brother order, "Ensure that he stays alive. Someone cut him down, but keep a close eye on him. *Make sure* he does not escape."

As I pushed through the crowd, memories of Ears at Napetuca wound like tie snakes through the eye of my souls: the cold lake water; Blood Thorn, teeth chattering, his war paint running in streaks as he paddled up to his chin. Ears calling out threats from the shore. Bragging of how he'd betrayed us to de Soto.

Then I remembered walking through the piles of dead and rotting warriors on the grassy plain, searching desperately for Pearl Hand's body.

I relived the day when, high in the old pine, I watched the Uzachile's desperate uprising inside the walls of Napetuca. They'd grabbed whatever they could, mostly pieces of burning firewood, and attacked the Kristianos. We'd watched with a grim mixture of horror and wonder as the brave Uzachile fought like mad badgers until they were cut down to the last man, their bodies piled in the plaza.

But de Soto hadn't been finished. He'd ordered his Timucua converts to kill all the chained Uzachile slaves. And Ears—freshly elevated after his betrayal of our ambush—had led the execution party.

So much misery.

Barely aware of my brother's feet whispering on the frozen ground behind me, I walked out past the last of the houses and stared up at the dark skies.

The soft impact of snowflakes tickled my cheeks and nose. The memory of Ears's chattering teeth clicked somewhere inside me.

"Black Shell?" The high minko came to stand beside me. "Are you all right?"

"No." A sensation of disgust tickled the bottom of my throat. "And I don't think I ever will be again."

"He will never leave here. I give you my word."

"Thank you, brother. I just need a moment to think. Meanwhile, you've got Pearl Hand to translate."

I heard his quiet retreat, my head still tilted to the sky.

"Was he right?" I questioned the night. "Is the Monster really smarter than we are? Stronger? More cunning?"

And what if he is, Black Shell? Then what?

TWENTY-THREE

As Pearl Hand, the dogs, and I headed north the following morning, snow continued to fall, making our journey back to Black Oak town that much more miserable.

My souls were as gloomy as the weather. As if sensing my despair, Gnaw and Squirm kept shooting me worried glances, their tails wagging hopefully. When that didn't coax a smile from my thin lips, they tried rubbing against my knees.

At their whining insistence, I relented enough to reach down and rough up their ears when they pressed close. Both dogs skipped away, tails wagging. Squirm made an "arroooow" sound as he yawned in triumph.

Dogs, I believe, were created by Breath Giver as monitors of our souls. I'd met many humans clueless to a person's needs, but never a dog.

Tonight you shall have a quarter of venison if I have to give away my last piece of copper.

We passed parties of warriors, occasional refugees, and messengers hurrying past. Everyone was full of news.

The Kristianos had torn down all the farmsteads and villages that lay within a half day's run of Chicaza town. The wood, matting, and thatch had been hauled back and the Kristianos were frantically building additional housing for the suffering *soldados* who camped in the frozen mud.

Additionally they had large, heavily guarded wood parties working in the hills, cutting, limbing, and hauling timber back to Chicaza. So far they had not started construction of a palisade but were making some kind of curious penlike structure of posts and cross-poles.

Pearl Hand and I remembered the odd piles of scrap wood they had erected around Anhaica. Those piles hadn't made any sense either—until the Kristianos used them to burn living human beings. From the descriptions, this was something different. But what?

"I don't like it," I told Pearl Hand. "Anything they build has to be for some foul and perverted purpose."

She gave me a sidelong assessment. "You've been sour and surly ever since last night. Ears is getting nothing more than he deserves."

"It's just not how I imagined it would be. I saw myself killing him in battle, running him down, unleashing my anger, and destroying him."

"Ah," she said in that knowing voice.

"What do you mean, 'Ah'?"

"You're feeling robbed. That's the heart of it, isn't it?"

"I'm not following you."

"Sure you are. It's one thing for you, the chosen, the Orphan, to destroy the monsters. Instead you learn that two young warriors manage to bag Ears while he's out shitting behind a bush. How inglorious.

"Then, to make matters worse, you find him tied to a square in abject misery. He's not *your* prisoner. No, he even belongs to a different iksa. Someone else gets the joy of making him suffer. These people don't even have the foggiest understanding of the depth of Ears's evil. All you can do to assuage the injustice of it all is to ask that when we're finally done with him, he be carved up into pieces and scattered to protect the peace and quiet of his distant Timucua ancestors."

"Perhaps."

She threw her arms up. "That's all you've got to say?"

I finally chuckled. "Very well. Yes! I wanted him! For all the things he did to us, to Blood Thorn, and to all the other poor wretches he murdered and tormented. I *earned* the right to kill him. Then Power just up and gives him to two *strangers!* And worse, they don't even have to *work* to get him! He just walks in front of them, lifts his flap, squats, and *snap!* They have him. By the Piasa's swollen balls, how *unjust* is that?"

"Unacceptable."

"Absolutely."

"Now get over it."

"I don't want to get over it."

"Really?"

"It feels too good to be mad at everything." I hauled back and kicked an acorn as hard as I could. I watched it go bouncing over the leaf mat to ricochet off a chestnut bole. "What would really help is if I could kill some Kristianos. But the pus-licking cabayeros won't ride into our traps anymore. It's disgusting. Everything is disgusting."

"So, what are you going to do about it?"

"I don't know. That's what's so frustrating." Finally I sighed. "What if Ears is really right? What if they are smarter than we are?"

"Do you believe that?"

"I really don't know anymore."

Black Oak town had been transformed since the evacuation of Chicaza town. Now the place resembled an armed camp. Warriors lounged in the small plaza, their bows and war clubs propped suggestively. Full quivers of arrows were strapped to their backs. Shields decorated with Power designs and denoting the various iksas leaned against house walls, the tchkofa, and anyplace else.

Between Black Oak and Chicaza town lay several lines of scouts to keep an eye out for wandering cabayero patrols. Should one head this direction, war chiefs were ready with established routes of escape. Squadrons had been assigned responsibility for different patches of brush, cabayo traps, and other defensive positions. Most wished the Kristianos would come and chafed under the enforced restraint.

I chafed with them, wanting nothing more than to rush out and shoot a Kristiano full of arrows. Which meant what? That I wasn't any smarter than the rest of the warriors?

Ears's scornful statement about de Soto's superiority burned in my souls like poison ivy under a breechcloth.

The Chicaza didn't just roll over. Warriors considered it a high honor and the best of luck to be chosen for the nightly infiltration past the Kristiano patrols to shout, shoot arrows, and otherwise harass the invader's sleep. As many as four or five of these false attacks were initiated each night. The hope was that weary Kristianos eventually would become careless ones.

Wild Rose had established herself in a house belonging to an elderly woman of the Wildcat Clan. Like her old house in Chicaza, this one, too, had three rooms. Wild Rose ran her business—booming now—out of the front room. The fact that she had a constant line of men slipping in and out fascinated me. Prior to initiating war or a raid, the warriors were ritually and spiritually cleansed by fasting, praying, taking sweat baths, partaking of black drink, and smoking. After that, intricate rituals were observed on the war trail, all the way down to how a warrior could sit or sleep.

One of the biggest taboos was contact with a woman. Chicaza considered sex to be the ultimate pollution of male Power. A warrior wouldn't lie with a woman until he'd been spiritually purified of the red Power of war. The four-day ritual included more fasting, sweating, praying, smoking, drinking, and vomiting.

But the Kristiano war proved different. Everyone had undergone the ritual preparation for war, painted themselves up, and marched out . . . only to sit down and wait for the leadership to order an attack. This wasn't like the war trail against a distant enemy where discipline was easily enforced, a line of march was maintained, and progress was measured by the day. Instead the Chicaza loitered in frustration. How long did a warrior need to maintain purity if he wasn't going to fight for a moon or two?

And bit by bit Wild Rose's business had blossomed.

She used the middle room for her personal area, and we were rented the back room—a square space previously used for little more than storage. With the dogs, Two Packs, and our bedding, we just about filled it.

Still, it beat sleeping out in the snow.

I'd been wandering around the town, talking to warriors, listening to them grumble about the orders they'd been given. No matter what the Panther Clan warriors who'd fought at the river said, the majority of the Chicaza still held it in their hearts that if they could just march out in formation, they'd crush the Kristianos.

I no longer tried to dissuade them. I'd been a trader long enough to know when an argument simply could not be won. In this case, though the Chicaza chafed under their renowned discipline, it was saving their lives.

I was halfway back to the house when Two Packs came striding across the plaza, his cape flapping around his wide shoulders, a pinched look on his blocky face.

"There you are."

"What's happening?" I asked.

"You're wanted. We've just received word. Tishu Minko Red Cougar has been captured along with one of his squadron leaders. He and an abetuska were scouting a party of Kristiano woodcutters when a group of cabayeros came up behind them. The word is the tishu minko put up a good fight, slightly wounded one of the cabayos, but was knocked down and tied up."

I closed my eyes, taking a deep breath to still the sense of anger and futility in my breast. "How long ago was this?"

"Yesterday evening at dusk. Warriors followed along behind in the hopes of freeing him. The cabayos moved too fast for them to catch up and try an attack. At least one scout has been able to get a glimpse of him. He's still alive. Somehow the monsters have figured out that he's important. De Soto is paying particular attention to him."

I chewed my cheek as I listened, imagining just how it was playing out. The tishu minko was being fed, entertained, and coddled—anything to demonstrate the Kristianos' peaceful intentions and emphasize their natural superiority to their erstwhile and hopefully gullible captive.

"Let's see." I stared up at the gray winter sky overhead. "The next emissary will be trotting out of Chicaza tomorrow morning, bearing a message from the tishu minko to my brother, telling him all is well and that the Kristianos come in peace. The fight at the river crossing was all a misunderstanding. If the minko will just surrender himself and his council, everyone will profit."

"That's how it usually works."

"It does."

Two Packs shot me a sidelong look and lowered his voice. "There's another reason I came in search of you. A woman is waiting in your room. Pearl Hand is keeping her company."

"A woman? I'm surprised you didn't insist on keeping her company while you sent Pearl Hand after me."

"Not a chance." Two Packs tried to keep his face expressionless. He'd been a trader for longer than I had and was generally pretty good at it. This time . . . not so good.

I grunted as a means of saying I was on my way. He gave me a gap-toothed "good luck" grin as we parted and slapped me on the back.

I stopped long enough to pet the dogs where they lay in the afternoon light—what there was of it given the cloud cover. I was growing tired of cold gray, rain, and snow.

Then I unlatched the plank door and stepped inside. It took a moment for my eyes to adjust.

"Hello, Black Shell," a woman said as she stood, hands properly clasped before her. She gave a slight, acknowledging nod of the head.

Blinking in the gloom, I asked, "Do I know you?"

"These days I am known as Clear Water."

Ah, my sister had come. Either Mother had talked her into assassinating me or her husband's capture had tilted her over the edge of indiscretion. "These days people call me Ahltakla. Mother might be upset if she learned you called me Black Shell."

Pearl Hand stood from where she'd been kneeling by the fire. In Cherokee she asked, "Would you like me to leave?"

"No. Stay. If she believes me to be akeohoosa, it would be like being alone with a strange man. And in Wild Rose's unsavory quarters to boot. If she wants help getting her husband back, you'll want to hear it."

"What are you saying?" Clear Water demanded in frustration. From the tone of voice, she was used to getting her way.

"Matron, we were discussing the purpose of your visit here and how to proceed."

Clear Water clenched her fists, her delicate face drawn. She'd grown into a beautiful young woman, the swell of her pregnancy visible beneath the bobcat-fur cloak that hung from her shoulders. The hem of a myrtle-fiber dress extended below the cloak, and warm knee-high moccasins clad her feet. She'd pulled her long hair up and pinned it with a whelk-shell columella.

"I didn't know where else to go."

I said, "Don't worry about him. For the moment he's being treated extraordinarily well. The Monster is feeding him, regaling him with stories, and doing his best to impress the tishu minko with how peaceful and kind he is."

Clear Water stepped closer. My eyes had adjusted to the gloom. I could see the pinched worry that lined her forehead, the tension behind her large eyes. "You're not lying to me?"

I experienced a spear of anger. "I *do not* lie! No matter what Mother and Uncle might say to the contrary. De Soto is acting as he always does, trying to subvert the leadership with false promises of peace and friendship. He doesn't take chiefs captive and chain them until he can get the entire leadership wrapped in his web."

She seemed desperate to believe me. I gave her a knowing smile. "You really love him?"

She flushed, glancing away, giving a slight nod of the head. "If he wasn't tishu minko, Mother would tell me I was a fool." She paused. "I'm only second wife."

"I'm told that, second wife or not, he returns your affection. I'm happy for you. Life is too short, too harsh, and too brutal. When you find joy with another human being, relish and revel in it."

"Mother would call you a fool and a romantic."

"I would expect no less from a Chicaza matron who has lived the entire span of her life within the ever-so-liberating walls of her palace. Mother never loved anyone but her brother. The only passion that ever touched her heart was derived from political one-upmanship . . . a hollow and fleeting satisfaction at best. She will die bitter and angry, no matter how long she lives or how many her triumphs might be."

Clear Water bowed her head. "You sound bitter and angry yourself."

"Only when it comes to her . . . and the Kristianos."

"Then why are you here?"

"Because I hate the *Adelantado* more than I despise Mother. Because to save our world, the Monster must be stopped. The high minko, Old Wood, and your husband listened to reason. After the terrible loss of Chicaza warriors at Mabila, and given the reports of the Panther squadron at the river, they are willing to attempt the unimaginable."

"The unimaginable?"

"The complete destruction of the Kristianos." I shrugged. "Chicaza can do it. But only if we have the discipline and military talent to mislead the invader, to manipulate him into a vulnerable position. And, even if we manage to lull their suspicions, strike them when they are most vulnerable, nothing is certain."

She was giving me a shrewd appraisal, thinking the entire time. However delicate and feminine this one might have looked, she was no piece of brainless female fluff. "My husband believes you, has faith in you. When he told me, it came as a complete shock. I tried to dissuade him, but whatever happened in the Men's House that day convinced him."

"You tried to dissuade him?"

"Black Shell, my memory of you isn't flattering. The important thing is that Red Cougar smiled indulgently, waved aside my objections, and asked me to trust his intuition. I did. Now he is captive."

"And you're scared to death of what they'll do to him."

She was made of stern stuff. Her expression barely hinted at the panic inside. She was thinking of the square, her husband stripped naked in the cold as laughing Kristianos thrust burning torches between his legs to literally cook the man's genitals.

Pearl Hand added from the side, "He's too valuable for the moment. Alive and well treated, he'll be used as bait to lure the high minko into de Soto's trap."

"Is there a way to rescue my husband?"

I shook my head. "He'll be very well guarded. Ransom is out of the question. We have nothing the Kristianos want that doesn't entail our complete surrender. The only prisoner we have that might be worthy of exchange is Ears, and my guess is that de Soto won't think a Timucua convert is nearly as valuable as a Chicaza tishu minko." I shifted uneasily. "The *Adelantado* is going to want the high minko himself in trade along with some guarantee that we'll let his army get some sleep at night."

"And women," Pearl Hand reminded me. "He always wants women."

"Yes. But given what was destroyed at Mabila, and as miserable as this weather has been, he might settle for blankets instead."

"He's de Soto," Pearl Hand countered. "He's going to want those blankets *and* women to keep them warm for his men."

My sister frowned. "You mean he's going to want Chicaza women? I'd heard that women already accompany his army."

Pearl Hand told her, "Those belong to the nobles and high-ranking cabayeros. The common *soldados* don't have enough status to merit their own. They used to have slave women to serve them, but most of them starved to death or froze."

"And if they demand them here"—Clear Water's eyes narrowed—"it would be considered the worst of insults."

"That's where this gets very tricky," I replied. "High Minko Choctaw Hair is going to have to balance on a

tightly stretched rope to keep any negotiations from disintegrating into a premature attack. On the one hand he
must keep the Kristianos satisfied that they are safe,
maintain his freedom, placate and control the iksas, and
ensure that the Kristianos receive just enough of what
they ask to keep them from ever-widening sweeps in
search of captives.

"On the other, he's got to keep the squadrons assembled and ready to attack at a moment's notice. There can
be no hesitation, and there will be no second chance."

"A difficult task," Pearl Hand agreed, "and one that
will take all of your brother's skill, finesse, and discipline."

Clear Water's lips pursed as she thought about it. "My
brother is a good man. Solid and dependable." She shot
me an evaluative look. "But he's not Uncle, if you know
what I mean. When Uncle was high minko, his word was
law. My brother has . . . let us say, a different tempera-
ment. He depends on my husband, on Medicine Killer
and Blood Elk, along with Flying Squirrel, Minko Fire
Tail, and Minko Cut Hand, among others. He ensures he
has their support before he makes a decision, and they
ensure that it is obeyed."

"You're saying what?" Pearl Hand demanded. "That
he's weak?"

Clear Water's expression hardened, irritated that this
foreign woman would dare question her brother's fitness.
"Not weak. My brother would rather build consensus
than impose his will, knowing that if he consistently did
so, opposition and resistance would result."

"He doesn't like confrontation," I said mildly. "Great
leaders never do."

At the same time I made a "desist" gesture with my
fingers that I hoped only Pearl Hand could see. This was,
after all, my family. We fought among ourselves like a
pack of famished weasels, clawing and ripping for each
other's jugular—but let an outsider even hint at some-

thing remotely unflattering, and those same claws and fangs united into a formidable defense.

I continued. "The problem is that as wise as the council might be, the high minko can't take them with him when he goes to meet the *Adelantado*. Somehow de Soto has to be convinced that the Chicaza are different than, say, the Coosa or Tuskaloosa."

"Different how?" Pearl Hand asked.

"We tell de Soto that the high minko's rule is not absolute. That even if he ordered the iksas to surrender, they would continue to do as their own minkos and councils decided."

"What?" Clear Water looked shocked. "That's not true."

"No," I said, seeing it begin to unfold between my souls. "But who's going to tell the *Adelantado* any different? Ortiz relies on a string of different translators to convey his meaning. They are helped along by sign language, which covers the basics, but the intricacies? That's a different story."

Clear Water gave Pearl Hand a cool look. "Your wife could circumvent the translators."

"Pearl Hand doesn't go near them," I snapped. "They know her. The moment she let slip that she spoke their tongue, Antonio would insist on seeing her."

"I'll keep my breasts covered," Pearl Hand said dryly. "He'll never recognize me."

"It's an old joke," I told my sister. "Apparently before we captured him down in the peninsula he'd never seen a woman."

"He did offer to make me his first wife," Pearl Hand reminded me in an emotionless voice. To Clear Water, she said, "That was before Black Shell drove an arrow into his arm, killed his father, carved up his pretty face, and left him scarred. These days the Kristianos call him *feo*, which means 'ugly.'"

My sister studied me from the corner of her eye. "You have truly become a warrior?"

I sniffed at the incredulous look in her eyes and drew a breath to make a caustic reply; Pearl Hand beat me to it, her voice dripping sarcasm. "Become a warrior? Woman, he has lectured war chiefs and minkos on how to kill Kristianos. No other man alive in our world has killed as many Kristianos. When you speak to him, show some respect."

My sister ground her teeth under the rebuke, but something had changed, quickening in her gaze as she studied me.

"Whatever you're thinking," I told her, "don't try it. These are Kristianos, a people unlike any you've ever dealt with before. They have no honor, no respect for either your social position or that you're Chief Clan. If you fall into their clutches, they'll strip you naked and you'll be serving men by nightfall. Pregnant or not, all they care about is that you're pretty and have a warm sheath."

Pearl Hand gave my sister a veiled look. "The last woman who tried to manipulate them—heir to the high chair at Cofitachequi—ended up as a captive and destroyed her Nation in the process."

I added, "Her little sister warms a Kristiano bed to this day, spreading her legs on demand to one of the unwashed vermin."

An irritated smile bent Clear Water's lips. "Yes, yes. I understand. And no, I'll never allow myself to get close to them. Wouldn't want to, given how alien they are."

"Then what are you thinking?"

"Isn't that obvious? I'm considering how best to get my husband back."

"It will take guile, courage, and patience. The *Adelantado* will deal with you believing he is in the position of strength. If the Monster so much as suspects treachery, he will take your messenger captive. If he decides to emphasize his anger he will cut off your messenger's arms, legs, penis, and testicles and leave the poor wretch where your warriors can find him. Whoever goes in there will have to find just the right balance between arrogance and humility. He'll have to have an uncanny sense of when to push and when to dissemble. You need someone not only smart but also expendable."

The way she studied me, head tilted, eyes narrowed, and lips pursed, left me uneasy. Clearly my sister had grown into a very clever and thoughtful woman.

"I think I have just such a person in mind." She finally flicked a hand in a dismissive manner. "If you'll excuse me, I must go find the high minko. My brother and I have things to discuss."

And with that she slipped through the door and was gone.

"What was that about?" I wondered.

Pearl Hand had that intuitive look as she focused on the door. "Given what I suspect about your sister . . . nothing good."

TWENTY-FOUR

My wife is a smart and perceptive woman. The following morning, I, Pearl Hand, and Two Packs were summoned to the tchkofa by a somber-looking ayopachi bearing his brightly painted staff of office.

It had snowed again that night, the ground covered by a thin white blanket. Our breaths puffed in the cold air, and I couldn't help but think about the poor captives in de Soto's camp. Reports from the scouts indicated that they were huddled together for warmth under whatever rags the already threadbare Kristianos had discarded as useless. After Anhaica a sane commander would have realized that feeding and sheltering his captives would extend their usefulness, but then I'd never been sure that de Soto was sane.

At the tchkofa I was surprised to see a large crowd of warriors gathered outside, breath puffing as they tucked furry capes tight or clutched thick blankets about themselves. Shields were stacked against the building wall, their weapons hanging from their backs and war clubs tied to their belts. They watched our approach with obvious interest.

"What do you think?" Two Packs asked. "Are we in trouble for something?"

"We've done nothing wrong," I countered. "I'd say this is just another planning session."

"They don't usually insist that Two Packs attend a planning session," Pearl Hand noted. "And look at the excitement in the warriors' eyes. Something's happened."

"I'll bet that de Soto's messenger has arrived to announce that he'll trade the tishu minko for the high minko," I muttered in realization. "My brother's going to want a solution to the problem."

We stepped through the large door and into the warm interior; the ayopachi cried, "High Minko, Matron Cane Mat, minkos, and beloved elders, I announce the arrival of the Ahltakla, Minko Pearl Hand, and the trader Two Packs. Summoned, they are now present."

"Under the white Power, let them enter in peace," my brother replied, rising from the panther-hide stool behind the fire. With his palace in Chicaza town occupied by de Soto, the stool was carried wherever he went.

We marched down a narrow aisle with people crowded to either side. They were seated according to iksa rank, legs crossed, blankets over their shoulders. All eyes were fixed upon us. Glancing around I realized that most of the leadership of Chicaza was present.

My brother was watching me with half-lidded eyes, a wary tension in his expression. To my surprise and displeasure, Mother was standing just behind him, poison in her hard black stare. Clear Water lurked at her right elbow, and Silent Spring crowded close behind. At my brother's right stood Old Wood, his gaze thoughtful. Medicine Killer, Takes Hair, Blood Elk, Copper Sky, and the rest of Chief Clan's influential leaders crowded behind. Raccoon Clan filled the ranks to the left, followed by Panther Clan's prominent men, and so on around the room.

I stopped short before the fire, dropped to one knee, and touched my forehead respectfully, the mace cradled against my chest.

"Greetings, High Minko. How may we be of service?"

"We ask you to share our solemn hospitality." My brother shot a glance at the ayopachi and ritually clapped his hands four times. "Prepare the pipe."

I watched as the hopaye turned to the inlaid box by my brother's feet and reverently opened it. From inside he retrieved the sacred pipe: a large piece of greenstone carved into the shape of a crouching eagle, the bowl in the center of its back. Next he brought forth the long stem, which, as was traditional, had been carved to represent a colorful serpent. Eagle, being a symbol of the Sky World, and Serpent, emblematic of the Lower World, were joined together in our world. The symbology compounded the Power from each of the three worlds of creation.

Tobacco was shaken from a beaded pouch, prayed over by the hopaye, and carefully tamped into the bowl with a long wooden dowel.

As the hopaye retreated, the high minko himself stepped forward, lit a stick from the fire, and crouched to puff the pipe alight. Exhaling blue smoke toward the smoke hole above, he prayed, "Hear us, Breath Giver. Hear us, Powers of the Sky World. Hear us, noble ancestors. Grant us the wisdom, courage, and opportunity to strike the invader. Grant cunning and valor to those we ask to risk everything in your name. Bless us in our quest to destroy this malignant enemy who has come among us."

Bearing the pipe, he walked up to me, offering the stem.

I pulled on the sweet tobacco, filled my lungs, and exhaled as I prayed, "Horned Serpent, hear my prayer. As you instructed, so I have come. Combined with the Powers of the Sky World, joined with the Powers of our world, and united with the Powers of the Underworld, grant us the opportunity to finally put an end to the Monster's threat."

Next he offered the pipe to Pearl Hand. She took the stem, inhaled, and blew the smoke toward the shaft of daylight shining through the opening overhead. "Breath Giver, I only ask for de Soto's beating heart. Let me hold it in my hand as it beats its last."

Two Packs took the stem, puffed, and exhaled, praying, "Give me vengeance on the men who killed my sons."

My brother handed the pipe back to the hopaye, clapped his hands another four times, and stepped back as a large steaming shell cup was brought forward. Crafted from half of a large whelk, the cup was filled to the brim with hot black drink.

I shot a questioning look at my brother, a growing unease in my belly. I could sense Pearl Hand's rising anxiety, see the tightening of her eyes. Why the formality? This was the sort of ceremony used in a consecration or in the brokering of some great political alliance.

My brother remained aloof, no expression on his face. Behind him, Mother looked angry enough to bite a hickory stick in two. Clear Water, back straight, chin up, watched with a satisfaction gleaming in her eyes that sent tickles of worry through my gut.

What are they up to?

I took the shell cup when the hopaye offered it and, as was expected, drained the whole thing. The liquid was almost scalding. My tongue would feel like fuzz the next day and the roof of my mouth would blister.

With a clap of his hands, my brother ordered the cup refilled, and Pearl Hand drank the shell dry, all the while glaring distrustfully at my brother.

Two Packs, apparently missing the import, took the cup when it was refilled and swilled the hot holly tea down as if he were half-dead of thirst. Upon finishing, he smiled and managed a polite belch.

My brother clapped his hands again. "Arise, Orphan. You are aware of the tishu minko's capture by the invader?"

"Yes, High Minko. Has the *Adelantado* sent a messenger in the tishu minko's name requesting a meeting?"

"He has."

"And does the invader claim that his intentions are peaceful, that his firmest wish is that the Kristianos and Chicaza become great friends? Does he claim that the tishu minko remains but a cherished guest? And that the only reason the tishu minko is not freed is because de Soto values his company?"

"How did you know?" my brother asked.

"We have heard these words before," Pearl Hand told him bluntly. "He used the same ploy to keep the chiefs captive at Napetuca. Next he will say that his fight with Panther Clan at the river was a misunderstanding. Does he ask that you, High Minko, come to him accompanied by all of your clan leaders and war chiefs? Ah, I see by your expression that is indeed the case. And does he offer amazing gifts and a willingness to become your brother?"

"He does."

Pearl Hand gave him a grim smile. "Nothing changes, High Minko. A weasel remains a weasel no matter how vehemently he protests that he is really a mouse."

My brother fixed his gaze on mine, a calculating glint in his eyes. "Then how should I go to him?"

"You should not!" I cried. "Haven't you heard a word we've said? He's holding the tishu minko as bait to lure you in. By the Piasa's balls, High Minko, if he gets his hands on you Chicaza is lost."

"Minko Tuskaloosa met de Soto." My brother arched a

questioning eyebrow. "You yourself told me the story. Tuskaloosa led him all the way down the Coosa River and trapped him in Mabila."

"Where—if you will recall—Tuskaloosa was killed. Blown into the sky and sent tumbling to earth when his palace exploded." I challenged him sharply. "He died, and his Nation died with him. That worked out well, didn't it?"

"But the situation isn't exactly the same here. Tuskaloosa was seeking to lead the Kristianos into a trap. We have already managed to place the enemy where we want him. We just need to buy time until the invader relaxes, lowers his guard. Then, when the time is right, we strike. To do that, we need someone inside their camp."

"And if you make a single mistake," I countered, "de Soto will clap a chain around your neck, threaten to burn alive those Chicaza he's already taken captive, and order you to call the rest of our people into captivity. Chicaza will not be served if its high minko takes such risks and ends up as a prisoner."

My brother gestured around the tchkofa. "Then what do I do? Simply let Tishu Minko Red Cougar endure his captivity? Perhaps I should send Old Wood, one of our most precious beloved elders? Or maybe Minko Flying Squirrel? And when he goes, I have to hope that he can outsmart the enemy, obtain Red Cougar's freedom, and evaluate the Kristiano defenses?"

"That's ludicrous," Pearl Hand growled in Timucua. Two Packs, knowing the language, gave her an unhappy scowl.

That's when Clear Water stepped forward, voice ringing out, "So, Orphan, according to you we need to have someone capable of understanding how the invader thinks and behaves, correct?"

"That would seem advantageous," I agreed.

"And it would help if the person the high minko sent

understood something about how the Kristianos organized their camp, how they managed their defenses." She cocked her head, frowning as if searching for the right words. "We need a person who knows how they conduct combat. Someone who would know when they would be vulnerable."

"Are you thinking of converting one of the Kristianos to our cause?" I asked mildly. "Otherwise I'm not sure where you're going to find such a person. Certainly not among the Chicaza iksas, for as talented as our people are, none have had the opportunity to study the Kristianos to a sufficient degree to have any hope of success."

Mother was giving me a baleful glare, her jaw clenched so tightly the lines pinched around her mouth. Whatever was happening here, she was heartily opposed.

My sister arched a high brow. "Mockery serves no purpose here, Orphan. The Kristianos are parasitic vermin, ignorant of even the simplest courtesies we reserve for our vilest enemies. Conversion, even if it were possible, is out of the question."

"I say send a volunteer or a slave," Mother growled just loudly enough to be heard.

"Send a slave?" Clear Water asked. "We've already discussed this. He would have no ability to pass himself off as a Chicaza noble. He might agree to any ridiculous thing. The Kristianos would see right through him if they had any sense at all."

I added, "You are correct, Matron Clear Water. Your enemy has held enough minkos and holatas as hostages to know how they act. And in a place called Tapolaholata down in the peninsula, a man tried to pass himself off as a chief in an attempt to free hostages. When de Soto discovered he'd been tricked he left a line of corpses behind him. The deceiver's decapitated head was stuffed down into his pelvis so his dead eyes stared out the bloody hole where his anus had been."

My sister's expression hardened. "And do you think de Soto would commit such an atrocity if the high minko were to displease him?"

"Without the slightest hesitation," Pearl Hand said coldly, her posture stiff, wary.

Clear Water snapped, "In that case we would not want to expose the high minko to such a fate. Agreed?"

I crossed my arms. "Absolutely."

My brother kept pursing his lips, shifting from foot to foot. Mother looked as if she were about to burst, her jaw clamped, the veins in the sides of her head standing out. The tic in her cheek was jumping around like a panicked mouse.

Clear Water touched her chin, as if musing. "We need someone who knows the enemy, can act like a high minko, and cannot only spy on the Kristianos but also comprehend what he is seeing. That would include a familiarity with Kristiano warfare."

"Good luck," Two Packs muttered under his breath.

Clear Water pounced. "But, good trader, you told us what happened at Coosa. The Orphan faced down the Coosa High Sun in his own palace. You told us how noble Black Shell's bearing was, how he practically cowed the leadership of Coosa with his presence and personal Power."

"It wasn't exactly like that," I began. "But for the high priest's words—"

"Did you or did you not portray yourself as a Chicaza lord?" Clear Water demanded, her voice imperious in the suddenly quiet room.

"Oh, no." Pearl Hand reached out, grabbing my elbow and squeezing. "This isn't happening."

I drew myself to full height, the mace before me. "I'm fighting to *destroy* the Monster. I fight with what I have at the moment. If it means deceiving the Coosa as a means to gain an audience, I'll do it. My *only* concern is the destruction of the Kristianos." I stiffened. "And I make no apology."

I realized that all eyes were on me, heads nodding, and Clear Water was smiling as if she'd just achieved some incredible victory.

"Black Shell," Pearl Hand whispered insistently, "don't do this!"

Do this? Do what? "Wife, they've got to understand that whomever they choose, the chances are good that he's *not* coming back!"

Mother, glaring daggers, said, "This is a mistake."

My brother gave her a sidelong glance filled with sadness and clearly announced, "We must use the tools Power provides us."

I gaped. *What? Pus and blood, how did he expect us to . . . ?*

"He's an accursed liar," Mother hissed. "A *disgrace* upon this clan and a *blot* upon my family."

As the meaning of their conversation began to sink into my thick skull, Clear Water wheeled on Mother. "And if he survives this, it will be proof that he was telling the truth. If he lives, you and Uncle will have been proven wrong. Power will have declared that even back then, he was Horned Serpent's chosen."

Surely they can't mean . . . ?

Clear Water turned her attention to the packed tchkofa as she shouted, "Power has given us a hero in our time of need. Horned Serpent has sent us the Orphan, Minko Pearl Hand, and the trader Two Packs. They will walk defiantly into the invader's camp. *The Orphan will mislead the Monster, learn his plans, and tell the Chicaza when it is time to strike!*"

A loud cheer went up, chiefs and warriors leaping to their feet, stamping, clapping, whistling. Beside me, Pearl Hand was cursing vehemently.

In the bedlam, I just stared, my heart beating with fear and disbelief. On my chest, the sepaya seemed to burn with an internal fire, the ancient copper mace warm and tingling to the touch.

"Thunder and smoke, Black Shell," Pearl Hand cried through the din, "tell them no!"

Around me, the crowd began to chant, *"Black Shell! Black Shell! Black Shell!"*

Courting Terror

In the beginning, his image consists of nothing more than filaments of smoke that drift in the noxious black shadows of her dreams.

Over the years she has skilled herself in the recognition of his evil infiltration. This time she fails to interpret the drifting patterns of hazy smoke as they curl in the air around her. Cautiously they weave into a fabric.

She remains unaware, her defenses somnolent as figments of better dreams fade into the growing gloom.

Not until the black clots of smoke begin to thicken and solidify does she comprehend her danger—and by then it is too late. Precious moments will be lost before she realizes he has thoroughly breached her defenses.

By the time the cold, hard recognition sinks in, he has already begun to solidify. The image of his long face sharpens. Deep lines run from the corners of his protruding and hooked nose down to frame his pursed mouth. Black and full, the beard does little to disguise his hollow cheeks, though it seems to augment his pointed chin.

Last to set are the hard brown eyes, flat and expressionless as they drill through her defenses and into her vulnerable heart. As she opens her mouth to scream, his weight drives her backward and down. His hard flesh crushes her against unforgiving earth. As the clothing is torn from her, it burns across her skin. His cold length presses against her naked and defenseless body.

Even as she draws breath to scream, Hernando de Soto's face fills her vision. Her souls rip and tear as they are spooled into the depths of his brown gaze. Then his mouth fastens on hers, sucking and devouring, his tongue spearing past her lips. Each of her screams is born in silence as he greedily inhales them from her lungs.

Trapped with her back against hard stone, she struggles futilely as his knee is jammed between her thighs. She endures the pain of torn muscles as her legs are forced apart. His hands encompass her breasts, fingers digging painfully as he seeks to rip them from her rib cage.

De Soto's sucking brown eyes enlarge until they fill her vision and she gazes into the stark reality of his soul. In that instant she realizes her body is merely a convenience.

She recoils as his erect shaft probes her. In a moment he will arch his back and drive the fiery spear deep inside . . .

She awakens with a gasp, her heart hammering crazily, blood racing in her ears. Her vision is blurred from the terrified shivers wracking her old body, and she draws in great gulps of the cold air, seeking to dampen the hot and feverish horror that burns inside her. Knotting her fists, she beats at the blankets covering her body, only to sag in weary realization that the unoffending cloth is just that.

Dream. Just a horrible dream.

With the realization comes wondrous relief.

She lies back, panting from exhaustion as the fear-sweat cools on her body. Above her the familiar poles and thatch composing her shadowy roof fill her with comfort. She is home, in Chicaza. Most of a lifetime has passed since she last looked into the Adelantado's eyes.

He terrifies me, even after all these years.

She swallows down a dry throat, grateful that the twisted knot in her guts has eased. Once again, she surrenders to violent shivering, then rubs her ancient face with a withered, dry hand.

"Black Shell, oh, dear Black Shell, how did we ever delude ourselves into thinking we could fool him?" She turns her head to the side, jamming a fist into her mouth in an attempt to stem the whimper.

TWENTY-FIVE

"Of all the idiotic, irresponsible, *stupid* things!" Pearl Hand wheeled like an angry cougar, half-crouched as if to spring, but she only shook her finger in my face. Her eyes glittered with anger and fear. "Pus and blood, Black Shell! Why? Are you that tired of life?"

She'd waited to unleash her wrath until we'd made it to the confines of Wild Rose's little room. Hands raised in placation, I said, "It may be the chance we need—"

"They *played* you! Just like I said they would. That silly bitch of a sister of yours and that brother you so dote on maneuvered you like a fish in a weir, and when they had you where they wanted, dropped a bit of bait. You . . . you snapped it up! Knowing full well it was a trap!"

She stormed back and forth. Well, as much as she could storm in the confines of Wild Rose's little back room. Having only three paces in either direction seemed to bottle her rage even more. The dogs—proving their superior good sense—had slithered under the beds, making themselves incredibly small and inconspicuous. Gnaw had his big head thrust under a burden basket, as if *that* would protect him; the rest of the pack were shivering violently.

I wished I could wiggle under the bed with them and shiver, too.

"Gods!" Pearl Hand shook knotted fists before her, mouth working, hair whirling behind as she twisted away. "What makes you think Antonio isn't going to recognize you? He *knows* you!"

"He thinks I'm dead."

"He *thinks*? That's what you're pinning your life to? What Antonio *thinks*? Did you come back to Chicaza and lose any sense you ever had?"

I winced. "It won't be that bad. Remember? We stood face-to-face with de Soto in that village at Uriutina. Why is this any different?"

"Uriutina?" she thundered, thrusting her face into mine. "You mean the time when Ears figured out we were planning to kill de Soto? Then told him? And now you ask if this time will be any different? Is your brain so small it's forgotten how that turned out? Does the *massacre* of Napetuca *freshen* your recollection?"

I felt that characteristic warm sweat break out on my face—the kind stimulated by humiliation and rebuke. The sort of discomfort that's preceded by stinging red ears and distinct intestinal upset.

"I'll tell them no," I said meekly. "Tell them . . . I've changed my mind."

She shook her head, jaw muscles working under her smooth cheeks. "You really *have* lost all of your wits. What, by the Piasa's foul breath, has happened to you?"

"I said I'd tell them—"

"They *already* think you're a coward—that you ran to save your skin when you were a boy." I stared down the slim finger she leveled at my nose and found two hot black eyes burning behind it. "Black Shell, if you back out now, it will be a repudiation of Horned Serpent! You might as well declare yourself a fraud before the whole world! The Chicaza will despise you. Everything we've gained here will be thrown away. Our best hope is to sneak away in the middle of the night, run like red wolves for the Natchez, and hope that word of what happened here never reaches that far."

"Is that what you want?"

"What I *want*?" She glared frustrated anger at me. "What I *want* is de Soto dead and you alive! Is that so difficult for you to understand?"

"But if I can lure de Soto into believing he's safe here—"

"You'll be *in his camp!*" She was back to hammering air with futile fists. "The instant Antonio sees you, he's going to grab the first weapon he finds, shouting, '*Concho Negro!*' and you're dead!" She uttered a tortured cry I'd never heard before. "And *worse*, you've dragged me and Two Packs into it, too! Your bloody Chicaza think we're the answer to their prayers? That somehow the *three of us* are going to ensure that everything works out?"

"Keep your voice down. Half the town can hear you."

"I don't give a packrat's left testicle if de Soto himself hears! I'm about ready to run down your cunning little sister, and when I do . . . by Breath Giver, she'll never plot another twisted little scheme!"

"Pearl Hand, I—"

"Get out!" She pointed at the door. "Just . . . leave!"

"But I—"

"Go, Black Shell. Leave me alone. I've got to think."

"I didn't have any—"

"If you want your balls left hanging intact, you'll be out of here *now!*"

I nodded, ears burning as hot as the sepaya. Calling the dogs, I unlatched the door. They beat me out into the cold night, tails between their legs, heads down, streaking into the darkness and glorious escape.

Pus and blood! Maybe it would be better if I just walked into the Adelantado's camp and let him kill me outright.

"She's scared," Two Packs assured me as we huddled before the fire in the Panther Clan house. Around us, people slept on the pole beds that lined the building's walls. My relieved dogs lay in a clump just inside the door. I hoped I didn't look as sad and pitiful as they did.

From Two Packs's solicitous and sympathetic eyes, any such hope on my part was pure illusion.

I sighed and tossed another piece of wood into the fire, watching as flames slowly flickered around the sides. "The last time I even came close to making her this mad was in Apalachee. I'd gone off to help Back-from-the-Dead fight a Spirit battle with the Kristiano priest."

"I heard that didn't turn out so well." Two Packs gave me a knowing glance from the corner of his eye. He was sitting with his muscular arms wrapped around his knees.

"But for the timely arrival of Pearl Hand, a couple of Kristianos would have driven crossbow arrows right through my heart. They had me and the hilishaya dead to rights. After she got me out of that mess, you should have heard the tongue-lashing she gave me." I rubbed my face. "But it wasn't anything like this."

"Like I said," Two Packs grunted, "she's scared."

"Since when did you learn so much about women? I thought all you were interested in was how to get them on their backs."

A bit of a smile flickered around his lips. "I like women."

"I noticed."

"No. I truly *like* them. I enjoy spending time with them, talking, being in their company. Here's the thing: Long ago I began to take them seriously. Coosa, Yuchi, Apalachee—it doesn't matter what the Nation, men take their women for granted. Especially their wives." He gestured to make his point. "We think of them as different, separate and distinct. Even lying with them, we expect that it's up to them to make the experience pleasurable. They're taught that by their grandmothers and aunts. Serve the men. And they do.

"My secret? I've made a study of all the ways to make a woman literally vibrate with delight when we're coupling. Then, when I finally wear them out, I hold them, listen to them, and cherish them." He grinned. "Funny thing, they *always* relish having me come back."

"Pearl Hand and I have found that magic."

"I know." He gave me a halfhearted wave. "And once I understood that, I stopped trying to seduce her."

"She thought you were a leering pest."

"How complimentary!" He made a "pay attention" gesture. "She loves you with all of her heart. That's why she's so panicked. She's terrified of what de Soto is going to do to you."

"He's going to kill us eventually. Pearl Hand and I both know that."

"She's made her peace with your dying in battle. But the idea of you ending up as a captive? That, my friend, is a whole different animal. It will take her a while to skin that one."

I rested my chin on my knee, watching the flames. "My sister did have me pretty well boxed in at that council. It was as if she knew what I'd do."

"She's smart, that one," he agreed. "And worse, she's really in love with the tishu minko. That being the case, she's as dangerous as Pearl Hand."

"If I hadn't seen it, I'd have never believed it. Clear Water even trampled her way right over Mother's objections. You don't know my mother—or how significant it is that Clear Water defied her."

"Now, your mother, there's a woman who's never known love."

I shot him a glance. "And just how do you think my siblings and I got here?"

"I said love. I'm sure the process of breeding was endured with as much courage and stoicism as she employed to tackle every other responsibility dropped on her shoulders." He gestured with a callused finger. "It all goes back to the underlying notion that women serve men. Your mother served her clan, ensured the success of her lineage, and all the while her souls dried up, twisted, and shriveled."

Growing up it never had crossed my mind that a mother could be different. Even later, after I'd been exiled and watched other women with their children, it hadn't soaked in how special my rearing had been. With Mother, everything was a rule, an example, a lesson for leadership.

"The miracle"—Two Packs interrupted my thoughts—"is that you, your brother, and Clear Water have turned out so differently."

"How's that?"

"Your mother is narrowly and completely focused on herself, her clan, and the immediate politics of the situation. She's been so tightly laced into her responsibilities she never took time for herself. If you suggested the notion, she'd take it as a sign of weakness. But you, Black Shell, have time for Pearl Hand and love her with all your heart. Your brother? He loves his people and would do anything for them. His very compassion is his greatest potential flaw. Clear Water, like you, is in love—terrible passionate love. As to Silent Spring? I haven't seen enough of her."

"Maybe we got it from our father. He was a Raccoon Clan man, the tishu minko back before Old Wood. I never knew my father well. He was killed before Silent Spring was born."

"And your uncle?"

"He was a tyrant like Mother. Maybe more so." I smiled at the thought of the stern old high minko. The memory of his expression the day I'd been exiled from Chicaza sent a spear of pain into my heart.

After a period of silence, Two Packs asked, "So, are you really going to pass yourself off as the Chicaza high minko and seek to fool the Kristiano monster?"

I nodded. "But no matter what my sister is plotting, you stay out of it."

He shook his head. "I'm going with you."

"It's too dangerous. They'll take one look at you and their thoughts are going to be filled with how good you'd look in the slave line."

"Not if I'm your personal servant. You told me how that Cofitachequi princess got to keep her servants."

I gave him a dry look. "You? My personal servant? Tell me your souls have gone flying somewhere and taken your wits along with them."

"What high minko wouldn't have a servant?" He was rubbing his chin thoughtfully. "And I can help keep Pearl Hand from drawing too much attention."

"She's not going, either."

"Oh, stop it." He looked irritated. "You're just fooling yourself if you think we're not all in this together. Think clearly. The three of us, we're expendable."

I sighed. "If anything happens to you—"

"It's already happened, old friend . . . on the day the Kristianos murdered my boys."

"I don't want your death haunting me the way Blood Thorn's does."

Two Packs placed a hand on my shoulder, squeezing. "Like me, he did what he had to. That's all any of us have: honor and duty."

I took a deep breath. "But Pearl Hand isn't going. I insist. Rot and pus, she's mad enough she might just agree with me."

"Her? Stay behind? Gods, you're a deluded fool. Meanwhile, I've got an idea about how to keep her safe."

I arched a suggestive eyebrow. "Send her on to the Natchez?"

"Now you're talking foolishness. No, let me think on this a bit. Maybe talk to Wild Rose."

"If Antonio gets as much as a look at her—"

"Leave it to me." He frowned. "How soon are you planning on going to Chicaza town?"

"Tomorrow morning. I want to sneak close with the scouts, see what the town looks like. If I have to make a run for it . . ." But that was just fooling myself. If things turned ugly, I was already caught.

The nightmare of the *hierro* collar eating into my neck sent a shiver down my spine. The last time they'd caught me I would have died but for Pearl Hand.

And if they caught her this time? Just the thought of the things she would endure before she managed to get herself killed sickened me.

And they will all be my fault!

TWENTY-SIX

WE HAD LIVED IN A SIMILAR CIRCUMSTANCE DURING the fighting around Apalachee. There, too, we had operated out of a small camp hidden in a thicket. But back then Blood Thorn and the Orphans had been with us. Skipper had been alive, and even though the fighting was deadly, we'd all hoped that we could eventually wear down de Soto's resistance and drive him from the land.

Could that really have only been a year ago?

I took a deep breath as I surveyed distant Chicaza town, flanked by its two streams, the woods close behind it. The problem was going to be the approaches. Even if I could convince de Soto to let me pass back and forth at will—which was a long shot—when the time came to attack, how were the Chicaza going to concentrate their forces without discovery?

The forests around Chicaza town gave some cover, but it was open beneath the mature trees. Perfect ground for cabayeros to ride down Chicaza warriors. While a man might hide behind a tree trunk, the Kristianos had practiced circling their cabayos at a fast trot. Inevitably they'd pick a man off with one of their long lances.

I heard the rasping of clothing against bark as my brother climbed up to my high vantage point. He tested each branch as he climbed, eventually finding a perch just below mine.

"What do you see?" he asked.

"A problem," I replied. "Assuming this pigeon-brained scheme works and I don't get clapped into a collar and chewed apart by Kristiano war dogs, how do you and the tishu minko assemble the squadrons for an attack without the whole town knowing?"

He glanced out at the fields. "When we relocated the capital after Uncle's death, we chose this location because it's open out in front and the creeks provide an obstacle to attack from the sides. We could place squadrons around the town and cover any approach. Up until now our greatest defense was the Chicaza squadron. Who in their right mind would attack us?"

I chewed on my thumb as I squinted across the distance. "Well, making an approach is going to be a problem when the time comes. That's perfect ground out there for Kristiano cabayeros." I paused. "You do believe me about this, don't you?"

"Yes, brother," he said solemnly. "If nothing else, you've convinced us, no matter what our hearts insist. We won't try an open, massed attack. I give you my word." He glanced out at the town. "Meanwhile, Old Wood—excuse me, Abeminko Who Takes the Blood-Spotted Shield . . . Gods, it's hard to refer to the beloved elder that way. He's assumed his old name and the rank of tishu minko until we can get Red Cougar back."

That surprised me. "He's a good man, brother. If he thinks the Power is right, trust his instincts. Especially if this goes badly and they take me and Pearl Hand prisoner."

"You've given thought as to how you want to go in?"

"Riding in your litter. I'll need a small escort, enough to look believable. I'll need to take gifts. We've already sent the traditional four deer—and de Soto figured out the meaning behind that clear down in the peninsula. But these are Kristianos. They always want food."

"I'm ahead of you. Word is that Skunk Clan had a rabbit drive out west. I ordered them to bring the entire catch. But a couple hundred rabbits won't feed that bunch."

"I don't want them fat, just placated. And they're wearing rags so any capes, blankets, or warm clothing that can be spared would help. Not too much. We want them grateful but not warm and comfortable."

"I understand." He paused. "Mikko Alibamo and his brother Mikko Lashki wish to accompany you."

"Why do the Albaamaha want to risk themselves?"

"For the honor. Fire Tail, mikko of Alibamo town, is married to Silent Spring. He's your alok, your brother-in-law."

For a moment, I couldn't find the words. "Brother-in-law? He's forgotten I'm akeohoosa?"

The high minko gave me a slow smile. "What you are doing . . . every Chicaza with a beating heart is ready to volunteer to accompany you. Do you understand? You, Pearl Hand, and Two Packs are heroes."

I swallowed hard, my heart pounding. As a distraction, I pointed to the fringe of the forest in the south. "I want the squadrons assembled there. As many warriors as the iksas can commit. They're to be as far away as possible, so fill the ranks with women, old people, the young, anyone you can dress like a warrior. Have them put on a good show, singing, shouting threats, waving weapons. De Soto has to believe that any treachery will have immediate consequences."

"You'll have it." He narrowed an eye. "What if something goes wrong?"

"Then you need to get those squadrons back into the trees. Evacuate the women and children while the abetuskas withdraw the squadrons in an attempt to lure the cabayeros into the traps we've built. Remember: Shoot the cabayos first. When you get the riders on foot they're easier to kill. After that your war is going to degenerate into the grueling task of killing them by ones and twos, wearing them down. Mobility is your tactic, ambush is your friend."

"Yes. I have heard. We understand. But as to the cabayo traps, the Kristianos know where most of them are."

"In the heat of pursuit, maybe they'll forget." I was forever an optimist.

He glanced up at me, eyes pensive. "How are you feeling? About tomorrow, I mean."

"Scared down to my bones."

"Scared? Power chose you, Black Shell, out of all the men in our world. I would think that like the heroes from the Beginning Times you would be fearless and bold."

I chuckled at his naivety. "I'll gladly face Cannibal Turkey, Stone Man, or any of the Spirit Beasts from the Beginning Times. As it is, Piasa wants to rip my heart out, and I've faced him down enough times. But Kristianos? The very thought of going among them fills my souls with terror."

"But you go?"

"I go."

He bent his head. "When sister came to me with the idea, I thought it was a perfect solution. You and Pearl Hand know the enemy, can weasel out their intentions. Only now do I begin to understand what this will cost you, the risk you are accepting." He hesitated. "Perhaps the interest of the people would be better served by your continued counsel rather than putting you at peril. It would be at my order. No one would doubt your courage."

"Why are you saying this?"

He looked away. "When I was a boy, I lost my brother. Suddenly, I have him back. And he is every bit the man I dreamed he should be. As quickly as this"—he snapped his fingers—"he could be taken away from me again."

I had my way out. No loss of face, no recriminations. I have to admit, I really considered it.

"Thank you, nakfic."

"Good. I'll go down and tell everyone we're going back to Black Oak town. They can begin—"

"I meant thank you for the opportunity." I shook my head. "After Mabila, I was shaken, unsure and afraid. Pearl Hand and I sneaked into their camp one night. I stole that armor from Antonio, and in the process, I got my courage back."

He listened quietly.

"The battle with fear," I told him softly, "is constantly fought. If I take this way out now, what if I take it again, later? What if it becomes a habit?"

"There is a balance between mindlessly accepting risk and good sense."

"True. But Mother and Uncle declared me a coward and a liar—outside of incest, the two most heinous crimes a Chicaza can be accused of. If we were in Coosa or Cofitachequi—anywhere but Chicaza—I might actually bow to the good sense you're offering." I smiled down at him, heart sinking. "But I'm in Chicaza. Mother is just over the hills to the south, still believing me to be a coward."

He nodded. "I understand."

"How's Pearl Hand? Still irritable?"

He arched uneasy brows. "Irritable? Just being in her presence makes me nervous. She's been sharpening that *hierro* blade of hers, glaring arrows at anyone who dares to disturb her. Even blooded warriors tiptoe around her and speak most respectfully. She practically oozes the promise of mayhem and violence."

"She's scared."

"Scared? It's more like she's spoiling for a chance to rip a man's guts out."

"Excuse me. I misspoke. She's wavering on the verge of blind panic."

"If you say so."

"I do." I willed myself to say the next. "Brother, if this goes badly, I want your word on something."

"Of course."

"If I don't make it, and Pearl Hand somehow does, I want you to make a place for her. She's not like any woman you've ever known. If she survives capture it will be because she's endured and overcome, killed, and escaped. But she will do so at a terrible cost. She'll be injured, down deep in her souls. Do you understand?"

He met my eyes, nodding, jaw firm. "She will have an honored position among us. We will treat her as if she descended on a beam of light from Mother Sun. I will ensure that she's given a place in the Men's House, that she's provided a dwelling and revered like a beloved tishu minko."

"Thank you," I said hoarsely. "And there's one more thing: If I'm made a slave and chained in a collar, I want you to promise that no matter what, you'll kill me and the rest of the captives. Do you understand?"

He nodded absently.

"Nakfic, until you've been chained, made to suffer like they are suffering, you'll never understand that a quick death is a wondrous mercy."

He swallowed hard. "I understand, tikba."

As I was carried out from the assembled Chicaza squadrons, I was overcome by an eerie mixture of emotions.

My heart began to swell in my chest as I looked down at the men carrying my litter on their shoulders: two Albaamaha mikkos, Alibamo and Lashki, both relatives by marriage; two Chicaza minkos, Flying Squirrel and Cut Hand, both clan leaders and proud men; and finally Medicine Killer and Takes Hair, both celebrated for courage and skill in battle.

The sense of destiny and uncertainty lay heavily upon my souls. At the same time, I was being borne toward the thing that most terrified me: Kristiano captivity. I was about to face the Monster, look him in the eye, and attempt to outwit him.

I was scared half to death.

To hide my identity, my face was painted, half red, half white. Black forked-eye designs had been drawn around my eyes, my chin covered in black. De Soto would expect such a design. By now he and his men knew that white denoted peace, red war, and black death. It signified that I was willing to accept any of the three; the choice between peace, war, and death was de Soto's to make. In addition, the paint had been laid on thickly, obscuring my facial features.

Pray that he really believes me dead.

Even if he recognized me, would he believe an itinerant trader would be set atop a strange Nation's throne as a gaudily dressed high minko?

I carried the sacred copper mace; my shoulders were wrapped in a stunning cougar-hide cape. A brilliant white hunting shirt, its front embroidered with a clawing eagle, was belted at my waist with a crimson rope. From it hung a long-tailed apron that ended in a point between my knees. Beaver-hide moccasins rose up above my knees, the tops turned down to expose the silky fur. My hair was pulled tight into a bun, greased, and pinned with a polished and gleaming split-cloud copper headpiece. Endless strands of shell-bead necklaces hung at my throat.

I must have looked magnificent.

If he suspects who I am, even for an instant, he'll order me taken, beaten, and made a slave.

And Pearl Hand? Despite my vow to the contrary, she'd refused to be left behind.

I glanced down to where she walked side by side with Two Packs. I'd been stumped when I first saw her. Under Two Packs's ministrations, Pearl Hand's hair had been grayed with ashes. Her face was painted black on the right, white on the left, the division perfectly straight. She wore an old, thickly woven pullover dress that obscured her figure; a buffalo-hide robe wrapped her shoulders. Around her neck hung a necklace made of human jawbones sawed in half at the chin and joined with finger bones. A beautiful blood-red pack rested on her shoulders, the image of a skull embroidered on the rear. In her hands was a long staff festooned with swan, eagle, and vulture feathers, indicative of the three bird kingdoms: the grazer, the predator, and the eater of the dead.

"Who's this?" I'd asked. Only her smile, crooked and mocking, along with that familiar arch of the brow, had given her away. I just stared, stunned at the sight of her. She looked twenty years older than she was—and not the least bit attractive.

Two Packs had grinned, gesturing grandly. "High Minko, meet Death Speaker, your new medicine woman and sorcerer."

"How do I look? Inviting?" She'd given a provocative flip of her hip.

"'Death Speaker'?"

"Sounds ominous and not very feminine, don't you think?" Pearl Hand fluttered her feathered stick. "Kristianos already think we have relations with their *diablo* Spirit. Not even the limpest hoobuk wakse among them would want to lie with a woman tainted by death and witchery."

Two Packs had added, "And it gives the two of you an excuse to keep close. Kristianos are ignorant of Chicaza ways. As far as they know, no Chicaza high minko would ever dare to meet with a visiting chief unless his sorcerer was at his side."

"And your purpose in accompanying us?" I'd asked.

Two Packs had dropped to one knee, touching his forehead in respect. "I am your translator, High Minko. It would not be prudent for you or Pearl Hand to appear to know too many languages. The Kristianos have slaves from all over. Who knows what I can learn from them."

"I just wish I had my *hierro* knife," Pearl Hand had muttered, slipping a long bone stiletto from her sleeve, then reinserting it. "I don't feel nearly as safe with only this."

"Perhaps I can trade for another for you," I'd told her with a smile. Now, however, I wished I had even the false courage I'd had back in camp.

I felt the litter sway as I was carried out past the Chief Clan squadron, my small escort of warriors leading the way. As we moved out into the weather-beaten winter grass, a great cheer went up from the Chicaza squadrons. I looked to either side, seeing them stretching all the way across the meadow and fronting the tree line. How many people? Perhaps four or five thousand? All carried weapons of some sort, even if the children were only armed with sticks. From a distance it would look impressive.

Then I turned my gaze toward Chicaza town, perhaps ten bow-shots to the north. My heart began to pound as a Kristiano horn rang out with its unique, clear tone. Cabayeros began to pour out of the town, wheeling around, forming up in ranks to either side.

"Horned Serpent help us if this goes wrong." As high minko, I carried no weapon other than the copper mace. And the Monster would want to capture or kill me first thing.

I'd never been the primary target in a fight before. The feeling wasn't pleasant.

Behind me the rest of my little procession fell into ranks. Black Marten and his warriors carried perhaps a hundred and fifty rabbits that had been commandeered. Others bore folded stacks of blankets, winter capes, and assorted articles of clothing.

Everyone looked nervous and excited. And but for Pearl Hand, Two Packs, and me, none of them knew just how terrified they should be.

Horned Serpent, grant me courage.

I struggled to gird myself with the thought. On my chest, the sepaya began to warm and pulse with each beat of my heart. My mouth had gone dry, my guts twisting with fear.

Again the trumpets sounded, and the *soldados* began to tramp out, clanking their shields as they formed up in a solid line behind the cabayeros.

Crossing that beaten field partially grazed by cabayos, dimpled with their piles of dung, could have taken no more than a finger's time. To me, my heart bursting with terror, it seemed half of a lifetime. I started when someone behind me gave the signal and flute music—the traditional signal of peaceful intentions—carried on the suddenly still air.

In Timucua, I called down, "So, wife, are you ready to run?"

"Like a panicked rabbit. I still haven't forgiven you for agreeing to this madness." She shot me a sidelong glance from her black-and-white face. "Fortunately for you, I doubt we're going to live long enough for you to endure even the smallest measure of my wrath."

"Your optimism bursts my heart with joyous song."

"I hope it's more melodic than that ragged ill-timed flute music. Didn't any of you Chicaza ever study how to *play* an instrument? Or does this have some military purpose?" She narrowed an evil eye. "Like driving an enemy to surrender just to stop the pain?"

Two Packs, fluent in Timucua, burst into nervous chuckles.

I remembered why I loved the woman so desperately. "Listening to this?" I asked. "I'd surrender to stop it, wouldn't you?"

She jabbed her feathered staff toward the Kristianos. "Unless it drives them into the kind of insane madness that precipitates a charge."

"Wife, you've always got your new bone stiletto."

"Blood and pus, you're right. And if I have to hear any more of these wheezing flutes, I'm going to kill someone. Anyone."

I actually smiled. Pearl Hand's irreverence in the face of death always reassured me.

"Here they come," I warned.

Within moments, we would know if we were going to live, die, or precipitate the destruction of the Chicaza world.

TWENTY-SEVEN

MY OLD CAPTOR AND TORMENTOR ORTIZ AND HIS group of slave-translators led the way. De Soto and his nobles followed behind in an armored knot. While de Soto's party stopped a stone's throw beyond the cabayero line, Ortiz's party walked out farther. Behind them stood one of the priests, with a wooden cross, delicately carved, on a tall pole. I hadn't seen their golden one since we'd taken it at Mabila. Who knows where it vanished to?

I gripped the copper mace, forcing myself to sit erect, head high, the litter swaying as we approached. If my heart beat any harder it was going to crack my breastbone.

Courage, Black Shell. If they so much as sense your fear, you'll be made a captive and all will be lost.

"Stop here," I ordered. "Let me down."

My chair was lowered and I rose to my feet, walking forward. "Two Packs, tell them who I am."

The burly trader stepped up, calling out, "The Chicaza minko, son of Cane Mat Woman, of the Chief Clan, of the Hickory Moiety, of the Chicaza people, bids greetings to the Kristianos. You are in Chicaza land, occupying our capital. The high minko asks why you are here and what your purpose is. He asks why you have taken the tishu minko captive and why you have invaded his lands as enemies."

I watched an Albaamaha translate to a Tuskaloosa, who translated to a Coosa, who in turn translated to a Cofitachequi, who, in addition to signing, spoke in broken *español* to Ortiz. Ortiz answered, speaking slowly in *español* and rudely signing. The reply came down the line of translators to the Albaamaha. "We come in peace. Sent by the white Power. Your tishu minko attacked us unjustly, but he is unharmed. A guest."

I fought the urge to smile. Each of the different translators had subtly changed the message, though I hadn't been able to understand Ortiz's complete response. I dared not look at Pearl Hand for her take on this.

"Tell the Kristiano that my tishu minko was run down on purpose and made prisoner. Witnesses saw this. You have asked for this council and therefore are the parties asking for peace. You say the tishu minko attacked you unjustly? Such statements are not the acts of men who wish peace. When will the tishu minko be freed?"

I paid better attention this time. What got to Ortiz was, "He is unhappy that we captured his noble and wants him turned loose now."

Ortiz explained something in great detail that was translated down the line. What had been said was boiled down to: "Your noble is a valued and well-treated guest. He is happy with us and we wish you to be happy with us, too. Are you here in peace?"

I gave the Albaamaha a narrow glare, considering. Then I shot a hard look at Ortiz. Just the sight of his bearded face sent a chill through my stomach. The image flashed in the eye of my souls: *"Work!"* he'd bellowed, his face in a snarl. I almost shivered at the memory of the chain, the feel of the collar cutting into my neck. In that moment, desperate fear ran through me. As quickly, it passed, leaving me shaken and unsure.

Courage, Black Shell. I reached up, reassured at the feel of the sepaya.

"Two Packs?" I called.

"High Minko?" He stepped up.

"Ask which languages these slaves speak. I am talking to too many people."

While Two Packs questioned them, I fought to keep from cringing, all the while battling my memory of Ortiz, his dogs and whips—the terrible desolation of being chained to the palisade at Uzita. Again I saw the rotting corpses of the dead. Beheaded after the war dogs tore them to pieces, they'd been left to bloat, stink, and writhe with maggots at the side of the trail.

"High Minko," Two Packs told me, "this last one is from Cofitachequi. I can speak with him."

"Good. Get rid of these others." I waved the translators away. Ortiz kept shouting questions the entire time. Mostly, I only understood *"¿Qué pasa aquí?"* The rest was a rattle of chattering *español*.

"That one!" Two Packs pointed and spoke in the drawling dialect of Cofitachequi. "The high minko will speak with that one. Tell your master we do not need these others."

"Is this wise?" Pearl Hand whispered, bending close to my ear.

"I don't know. But cutting out these others makes our meaning more clear. Less chance for a misunderstanding." I was keeping an eye on de Soto's party. They stood in a defensive formation a bow-shot to the rear. I could tell that the *Adelantado* was growing impatient. He was smacking a fist into his gloved left hand, shifting from foot to foot. The cabayeros waited on either side of him, the winter breeze teasing the manes and tails of their mounts. Long lances rested butt-down in the stirrups.

I glared hatred at that long line, aware that if they attacked, we were all going to die. There, finally, on the fifth cabayo to de Soto's right, I saw Antonio, his face marked by two long red scars. Afraid he'd sense my stare and recognize me, I glanced away, heart thumping.

Ortiz asked the Cofitachequi how Two Packs spoke his language.

"I am a trader from Coosa," Two Packs answered. "I speak many languages."

Ortiz nodded, giving a dismissive wave of the hand. All right, so far, so good.

"*¿Quieres usted estar en paz?*" Ortiz stepped forward, glaring into my eyes.

The Cofitachequi translated, "Do you want peace?" Two Packs followed suit.

"Hohmi," I replied in Chicaza.

Two Packs translated, and the Cofitachequi said, "*¡Sí!*"

At that, Ortiz turned, lifting an arm, and de Soto and his party walked forward. A drum began beating in the background and I watched as the Kristianos matched their steps to the rhythm. The ragged cabayeros tensed, tightening their grip on the lances.

Ah, yes, they know that if treachery is planned, this is the moment we will unleash it. Just knowing proved that Mabila and Napetuca had been worth something.

De Soto, in full armor, walked forward with each step clanking metallically. Behind him came two *soldados* leading cabayos. Mounts in case we tried to kill him.

He stopped before me.

My stomach tightened, a quake running down my spine. I was face-to-face with the Monster.

You are an abomination.

I stared into that long visage with its half-lidded and arrogant brown eyes. Gray hair—something I hadn't noticed at Mabila—had invaded his beard. The lines around his oddly protruding nose were even deeper, his mouth hard.

A tremor of fear and revulsion poured through me as I looked into those heartless eyes. In that instant I glimpsed the blackness within, the pulsing evil, like a coiled midnight worm writhing around his souls.

Then I caught the reflection of my image in his large black pupils—and the swelling sensation of pollution seemed to wash over me. The urge to cringe, back away, and run in panic for the distant forest sent a shiver through my bones.

And the reflection that caused it? In his gleaming eyes I'd seen myself as nothing more than an insect, a creature with no more meaning than a wasp that had to be treated with just enough respect that it could be lured into a place where it might be swatted and forgotten.

Careful, Black Shell. Courage. You face a sucking and heartless evil. Think!

I'd forgotten how tall he was, and though his men wore rags, he was richly dressed in a remarkable purple coat, the armored breastplate beneath it polished to a reflective silver.

We stood there, eyes locked, communicating our dislike with an eloquence words could never match.

"*¿Tienes un nombre?*" he asked.

"What is your name?" Two Packs translated.

"Ishto Minko Chicaza," I replied, forcing arrogance into my unnerved souls. "And you are *Adelantado* de Soto. Two Packs, tell him we know his name and that he is an invader. Tell him that we learned much of him from the Apalachee, with whom we trade."

I listened to the translation, watching de Soto's eyes harden at the mention of the Apalachee. He turned, speaking softly with Ortiz. The latter shrugged, saying something back. I struggled to keep from breaking out in a cold sweat. I was gambling with the future of every man, woman, and child in Chicaza.

De Soto spoke, the words imperious, his gaze daring me, seeking to intimidate.

I caught most of the meaning as Ortiz spoke to the Cofitachequi translator, who then told Two Packs, "The *Adelantado*—born of the sacred sun—has been lowered to earth by his god and the holy trinity. He is a messenger of God's will, sacred in his being, and comes to bring a new Power to this world. He comes in peace, and as proof of his words, wishes you to note the color of his skin: white—the color of God's peace and tranquility."

This was a new twist. De Soto was claiming to be born of the sun? Divine? In the beginning he'd just murdered and enslaved because he was invincible.

I made a dismissive gesture. "Do not try to impress me. Why are you here?"

De Soto lifted his chin, slitted gaze fixed on me. "I am sent by the great divine being."

"Breath Giver has nothing to do with you, piece of filth," I growled.

"Careful," Pearl Hand said. "Or have you changed the plan? If you've decided to try to kill him here, I'd like a little warning first."

Two Packs listened to the stammering Cofitachequi, saying, "De Soto wants to know what you're discussing."

Pearl Hand said, "Tell him we're trying to understand his single soul and why his god chose him to try to conquer our world."

The *Adelantado* seemed to have recovered his temper. The story came slowly. "God chose me because I have never been defeated. You would know what sort of man I am? At the age of sixteen I burned a Panamanian *cacique* alive to get his gold. I fought my way through Panama, Nicaragua, and Peru. When the situation was lost, I charged into the fray, my sword swinging. Just as at

Mabila. Every time . . . like that. I prevailed because God protects those who *dare*!

"Friends and allies betrayed me. They envied me, and they tried every means to take what was mine. My enemies sought to destroy me in *España,* lying even to *el rey,* the king. But I outsmarted them and grew rich and more powerful than any of them."

He gave his speech with a flat-eyed, half-lidded look, continuing as the Cofitachequi translated. "I became the greatest of them. The richest and most influential. I was made governor of Cuba and given this land of La Florida to conquer, because no one else was worthy. And no one, especially a bunch of *primitivo, diablo*-worshipping *indios,* will keep me from completing God's work. I will prevail if I have to burn every *indio* in this land."

He gave me a mocking smile. "So, do you wish to burn . . . or have peace?"

Staring into his dismissive eyes, hearing his lies about godhood, goaded my smoldering anger. *Come on, Black Shell. You're a trader and expert at negotiation.* I needed to push him just far enough, make him just wary enough. The breeze that had been blowing from behind eddied, and I caught a concentrated smell of something acrid and vile. Then, just as quickly, it was gone.

"Tell him," I announced before he could say more, "that I have come to meet him in hopes that we can find a way to avoid the kind of war he fought with the Apalachee, but if such war is his wish, we will accommodate him.

"Further, I have issued orders that if I am taken hostage, as Mikko Cafakke was, my squadrons will retreat and harass his men day and night. We promise to fight his Kristianos as the Apalachee did."

De Soto heard this, his expression hardening, eyes flat with promise. "*¿Quieres una guerra, indio? Si quieres, tenemos todo que puedes aguantar.*"

"He says that if you want a war, he'll give you all you can stand." Two Packs had stiffened, his face like stone as he continued the charade of translating from the Cofitachequi.

Ortiz turned to de Soto, talking softly, hands gesturing, arguing for something I hoped Pearl Hand could understand.

"Death Speaker?" I whispered, seeing the Albaamaha translator was out of hearing. "Are we about to die?"

"You balance on the edge," she whispered harshly. "The Monster considers taking us hostage to ensure Chicaza obedience. The slave master argues for peace."

Two Packs muttered, "Maybe we should just back away? Call it off?"

"Easy," I cautioned him. "One thing at a time, old friend." My gut twisting, terrified of making a mistake, I pointed to the red side of my face. "*Adelantado,* if you choose war, your army is behind you, mine is behind me. If you utter the word, we shall fall upon each other. You will kill me and the peace party who have come to you under the white Power. My successor will then do everything under the red Power of war to defeat you and your army the way the Apalachee did."

I pointed at the gift bearers. "On the other hand, behind me are emissaries bearing food, blankets, and some clothing, which, after Mabila, your men could use. These are offered in peace." I pointed to the white side of my face. "I see no presents among the men behind you. No gifts for the Chicaza or their high minko. Does this indicate your preference is for war?"

Heart pounding, I watched de Soto as the words were translated. His only reaction was the faint thinning of his lips. Locking eyes with mine, he spoke, and while I caught occasional words, the gist of it was this: "You must forgive my lack of gifts. If you have heard of Mabila, you know that despite my desire for peace, our offers have often met with treachery. If you will accompany me back to the town, I will feast you and present you with many fine things, including *hierro,* a metal you have never seen before."

I clasped the mace before me, saying, "I will make a counteroffer, *Adelantado.*" I turned, ordering the porters, "Bring forth the gifts and clothing. Lay the things here, to the side, so the *Adelantado* may see."

As the warriors began bringing the plunder forward, I turned to de Soto. "These things I offer in exchange for Tishu Minko Red Cougar. Your messenger informed us that you enjoyed his company." I smiled grimly. "As fine as his company must be for you, I miss him even more. He is family, married to my sister."

"And if I send him back?" De Soto's deadly stare sent shivers down my back.

"These gifts are but a sample of what we can provide. There is more where this comes from, including venison, turkey, fish, pigeons, and other meats. We have warm clothing, including blankets. You have the Chicaza town granaries with their corn, beans, and squash, but we can send nuts, breads, and meat."

Ortiz said something, then de Soto told me, "Perhaps you will stay with me until these things are delivered?"

I narrowed an eye, adding coolly, "This is not Coosa, *Adelantado.* I have given my orders. If you do not allow me to return, the iksas will be at war with you, and your army will have no rest."

The breeze wavered, and that curious stench drifted to my nose again. Not like rotten garbage, but what could it be?

Ortiz and de Soto bent their heads together and whispered. Then the *Adelantado* gave me his unnerving insect stare, his thin-lipped smile mocking. "Your people will not barter for you if you are prisoner? Yet you come for your mikko?"

"He is a relative," I said with a shrug. "I have an obligation to him. Unfortunately for you, I do not have enough brothers and sisters to have marriage obligations to every person in the entire Chicaza Nation."

Ortiz chattered away in de Soto's ear. As he did, the *Adelantado* kept trying to read the path of my souls. I glared back, wishing I could reach out and choke the life out of him. He glanced behind me at the distant ranks of Chicaza, as if evaluating the threat they posed.

"This is it," Pearl Hand said warily in Timucua. "If you strike de Soto hard enough in the head with the mace and jump on him, I might be able to drive this bone stiletto into his throat. Two Packs? Can you keep Ortiz off until we kill the Monster?"

"Oh, yes," Two Packs growled.

De Soto flicked his hard gaze at Pearl Hand as she spoke, then back to me as he said, "I will take your gifts today. And if there is no attack tonight, no arrows dropping from the dark sky, and if you come tomorrow as you did today, I will return your chief to you. It will be a test."

"If you return our tishu minko and take no others captive in the meantime, I will return here tomorrow with additional gifts. We will slowly and cautiously determine whether there is to be peace or war."

With that I backed away and touched my chin—though it sickened my gut to give him any sign of respect. As regally as possible, I seated myself in the chair.

"Take me back," I told the porters. "We have done all we can today."

Only when they had lifted me onto their shoulders and we turned, heading back, did I ask, "Pearl Hand, what's he doing?"

Half-afraid she'd say he was waving his cabayeros after us, I heard her respond, "He's headed back into town. The cabayeros are following him."

The shakes caught me by surprise, beginning in my chest, moving out my arms and legs.

I wanted to throw up. But as demeaning as such a display would have been for Black Shell the trader, it would have been downright humiliating for a high minko.

And there were my bearers to consider. Coward though I might be, I couldn't spew onto such brave men. I just couldn't.

TWENTY-EIGHT

THOUGH A FREEZING RAIN FELL, A BONFIRE BURNED brightly in the center of our hidden camp deep in the thickets along Deer Creek. Around us Chicaza minkos, abetuskas, and blooded warriors huddled under blankets, their breath glowing ghostly in the firelight.

My brother sat to my right, Pearl Hand and Two Packs to the left. Mikko Alibamo and Mikko Lashki, along with Minkos Cut Hand and Flying Squirrel, crouched in places of honor beside him. Medicine Killer and Takes Hair—who had also borne the litter—were seated immediately behind the high minko.

Old Wood—or Blood-Spotted Shield, as he again was known—stood across from us, his lined features accented by the flickering yellow light.

I chose my words as carefully as I could. "We barely avoided disaster today. De Soto and I are like two spiders who meet by chance on the trail. We are circling each other, front legs raised, fangs bared, each trying to out-bluff the other."

Pearl Hand said, "Ortiz kept telling him not to be in a hurry, that they have time to negotiate. He repeatedly told de Soto that if peace could be obtained, it would reduce tensions among the *soldados*. Most of all, Ortiz wants to avoid another winter war like they had with the Apalachee. He thinks the men will revolt. De Soto told him that he'd hang the first mutineer by the neck. And keep hanging his men for disobedience until only the brave were left alive."

My brother thoughtfully mused, "Is that something we could use against them?"

"Not reliably," I replied. "We heard this clear back at Uriutina and hoped to exploit it after we killed de Soto at Napetuca."

"But that didn't work out so well?" Blood-Spotted Shield asked.

Pearl Hand said, "It's never worked out. If the Kristianos ever would have revolted, it would have been after Mabila when they had hope of finding the rescue ships at Ochuse. Instead they follow de Soto as if he were a Spirit leader."

I jerked a thumb in the direction of Chicaza town. "Spirit leader? You heard that fecal spew this morning? He now claims he's descended from Mother Sun, sent here by god. He's using our belief in Power—and his sickly skin color—against us. The bad news is that in most Nations people may well believe it. After all, he comes riding strange beasts, wearing that accursed armor, and seems invincible in battle just like the stories of the Beginning Times."

Pearl Hand propped her chin on her hand as she stared thoughtfully at the fire. "I wonder what his 'Rey Carlos' and that 'Papa' Antonio told us about would think if they heard de Soto claiming to be a god?"

"I think the Monster's desperate. The more he learns of our beliefs, the more he's going to use them as a weapon against us." I looked at them one by one. "De Soto's claim to be divine, born of the sun, and lowered to earth by Breath Giver is only as dangerous as our willingness to believe it."

Pearl Hand leveled a finger. "But we were there. We know that he came from the sea. That he unloaded his army from great boats. Think back, Black Shell. Remember how dazzled you were the first time you saw them? His claim of godhood is an easy lie for the average minko to swallow." She paused. "Made more so by our belief that anyone who would blaspheme so would be struck dead on the spot. Yet he lives."

I nodded, remembering my first sight of the Kristianos. I had indeed thought them magical.

"Did you hear anything else during their discussion?" my brother asked Pearl Hand.

"De Soto did say one thing that was telling. One time, he looked directly at Black Shell and said, 'This one is smart as well as arrogant. We would do well to keep an eye on him.'"

"But they didn't mention plans to take me hostage?" I desperately wanted to know the answer to that.

Pearl Hand shot me a knowing glance. "Your comment that you'd ordered the Chicaza to fight like the Apalachee if you were taken hostage had a real impact. It was after that that Ortiz really began to counsel restraint."

I said softly, "We must be very, very careful."

"What next?" Choctaw Hair asked.

"That is your decision, High Minko. I am only an actor playing a part."

He smiled slightly, his hollow stare on the fire. "Perhaps we are all playing parts. What do the rest of you think?"

Mikko Alibamo spread his hands. "Until I was out there, feeling naked and defenseless, I didn't understand the threat posed by the cabayeros. I imagined myself having to fight them, seeing how rapidly they moved . . . the advantage of height they have from the beasts they ride. I'm thinking of how to defend my town if they head that way."

"You don't want to fight them in the open," Mikko Lashki agreed. Then he made a face. "But they are so ugly! And what a horrible joke Breath Giver has played on them, making their hair grow on their faces! It must have been some sort of curse."

"I must admit," Minko Cut Hand said with a shy smile, "being that close to them was unnerving. They are so . . . *alien*. I begin to understand just how different they are. This de Soto didn't even have the decency to ask who we were. But I'd give all my nieces in marriage to a Natchez farmer for a chance to get my hands on that purple coat and silver armor."

"That's the dilemma," I interjected. "They have fantastic wealth, even now, after so much was burned. And at the same time, nothing I've ever seen in this or the Spirit World frightens me like they do."

"If you were scared, you didn't show it." Two Packs reached out and slapped my back. "Me, it was all I could do to keep my voice from quivering."

"I'm just glad that the minkos who carried me out there and back are men of honor," I told him. "Otherwise they'd be telling you all how I shook, going and coming."

"They just seemed like men," Medicine Killer said cautiously. "Ugly, it's true. And dressed like no men I've ever seen, but still men."

"And that's what they are," Pearl Hand declared hotly. "Rich? Yes. Dangerous? Absolutely. Treacherous? Beyond any doubt. But once they relax, climb down from their cabayos, and take off that armor, we can kill them all."

I nodded in agreement. "The scary part is getting to that point without de Soto discovering the ruse. Did you see Antonio?"

"Off to the right on a cabayo." Pearl Hand rubbed her jaw. "He didn't seem to suspect a thing. He just fingered his lance and licked his lips, as if waiting for the order to charge."

"I sure made him ugly, didn't I?"

"You did."

My brother asked, "How much of a threat is he?"

"If he recognizes me or Pearl Hand, we'll be immediately captured and either mutilated or burned alive."

"De Soto only knows us by reputation," Pearl Hand said pointedly. "He put a price on our heads long ago. When we are in the presence of Kristianos, no one must use our real names."

My brother nodded. "You all understand that?"

Around the fire, heads bobbed.

He asked, "Will de Soto free Red Cougar Mankiller tomorrow?"

I took a deep breath. "If he doesn't, we may have to rethink our next moves. Should it come to that, I don't envy you, High Minko. The decisions . . . well, they may come at a terrible personal cost."

He met my hard stare. "Meaning if he ends up chained to the slaves, a collar around his neck . . ."

"The greatest mercy will be to sneak close at night and kill him."

"Let us pray that you, Black Shell, are clever enough to ensure that won't happen."

"We will see." I massaged my tired face. "What have you heard about the gifts for tomorrow?"

"They're on the way." He glanced up at the gray-tinged night. "But with this mist falling and freezing, the trails are a slick mess. They may not be here until too late."

"We can wait," I told him. "Neither de Soto nor the tishu minko is going anywhere."

Takes Hair groused, "What galls me is leaving them in peace this night. With weather like this, we could have crept right in among them and shot arrows into their very beds."

My brother gave him a sympathetic smile. "We're keeping our word, brave warrior. And if they don't keep theirs on the morrow, we'll be right back to sneaking in, shooting, shouting, and ensuring they don't sleep more than a wink."

As for myself? Standing face-to-face with de Soto had frightened me down to the bones. And now all these people expected me to outwit the Monster? De Soto's droopy-lidded, soulless eyes were going to be filling my nightmares.

Additional rabbits, a couple of deer, and roasting dogs arrived the following morning as we were being dressed and having our faces painted. Every time Pearl Hand and I had to go face de Soto, we'd have to be made up. All it would take would be one mistake in front of Antonio, and we'd be lost.

Not even the chance for peace with the Chicaza would outweigh de Soto's rage with Pearl Hand and me. From the days in the peninsula and all through the Nations to the east, we'd thwarted him too many times.

Even as paint was applied to my face, tension began to twist my gut into a knot.

"What do you think?" I asked Pearl Hand, glancing sidelong to see her beautiful features being covered with black, the white side already finished. "Do we get the tishu minko back today?"

"Depends," she answered, trying not to move her jaw as gleaming black was smoothed on her cheek. "How well did we fool the Monster yesterday? And what counsel did his nobles give him last night?"

"Maybe they were too busy sleeping?"

"If that's so, they might want to sleep again tonight, and we'll get the tishu minko back." They finished with her face and she turned, saying in Timucua, "You'll be your sister's favorite brother."

"You really don't like her, do you?"

Pearl Hand glanced down at her hands, finding them dusted with a coating of the ash that had been massaged into her hair. "I know what your family did to you. It may take me a while to find redeeming traits among them."

"They only acted as they were told."

"Your sister still put you and me at risk. It was, after all, her idea to substitute you for the high minko."

As they finished with my face, I cocked my head. "You've come to know my brother. Can you imagine him facing de Soto? Knowing where he can push? What he can successfully get away with?"

"No," she admitted before giving me the eye. "Are you sure *you* know what you can threaten? What *you* can get away with?"

"We're alive so far."

"Oh, yes . . . after one whole meeting. We've still today to survive."

"And all the days after that," I agreed, my smile full of false bravado. "But what if I'd told you last summer that we'd be eyeball-to-eyeball with the Monster, attempting to trick him into lowering his guard so we could sneak in and cut his throat?"

"I'd have said you were a maniac."

"Yes, yes, but outside of the obvious, what would you have said?"

"That I'm honored to be the woman who shares your life."

"I see." I tried to keep from going maudlin. "I'm still trying to live long enough to endure your wrath for agreeing to this charade."

"De Soto will have plenty of opportunities to kill you before that happens, so don't resign yourself too soon. On the other hand, the notion of getting so close to him is starting to have a certain appeal." She slipped the long bone stiletto into her sleeve. "If he'd just take that breast-plate off I might be able to drive my blade right through his evil heart."

"When the time is right, woman."

"I suppose." She gave me a sad look. "Fear and tension just bring out the murderer inside me."

"Ah, the joys of love." I stood. "You ready?"

"After you, High Minko." She stepped close, adding, "Calling yourself that, here, in Chicaza, it really does bring you a certain amount of delight, doesn't it?"

"Oh, yes."

"Well, how about if we survive today, you and I sneak off to our bed a little early? Once past the fear and tension, another part of my souls is going to want to exercise itself."

"And that is?"

"Well . . . relief and survival just bring out the wanton seductress in me."

"I thought I was going to live only long enough to endure terrible retribution for getting us into this mess?"

"And just how do you think I plan to obtain my retribution?"

I gave her a loving pat on the shoulder. "Come on. You've given me a reason to live that I didn't have just a few moments ago."

TWENTY-NINE

WE PLAYED THE SAME GAME AS THE DAY BEFORE, though my litter bearers traveled a great deal more slowly given the icy grass. Even so, on more than one occasion, they came within a whisker's breadth of dropping me.

Again the Chicaza—under orders from the High Minko—paraded out in squadron formation as a show of strength. Again the Kristiano cabayeros barreled out in response, but this time they came in two racing lines that charged each other, spun, and whirled in a complex maneuver of flying beasts, glinting *hierro*, and shouting men. Then the whole came together, wheeled at the edge of Deer Creek, and in a thundering wave, cut across in front of the town.

"Feeling reassured, are you?" I called down to my bearers.

"Blood and pus," Alibamo muttered. "They move like the very wind!"

"And are as irresistible as a river in flood," Pearl Hand growled back. "Do you begin to understand?"

"Oh, yes," Minko Flying Squirrel said fervently. "They'd crash right through a squadron like a rolling boulder, wouldn't they?"

I added, "The only thing that slows them down is footing as the cabayos trample warriors beneath their hooves."

"This is meant to scare us?" Mikko Lashki asked.

"It's working," Cut Hand said soberly. "Black Shell? Pearl Hand? May Breath Giver bless you both forever for talking us out of attacking them head-on."

Pearl Hand answered, "May Breath Giver bless you for having the brains to listen. After all the times we've tried to describe Kristiano military superiority, who'd have thought it would be the proud Chicaza who finally had the sense to listen?"

"Maybe it's because we don't like losing," Flying Squirrel riposted. "And when Old Wood shattered that war ax on your armor in the Men's House, Minko Pearl Hand, it made an impression."

"Better start calling her Death Speaker," I warned him as Cut Hand slipped and almost fell on the ice-covered grass. I grabbed the chair sides—as if something so futile would have saved me.

The cabayeros having formed their line, the *soldados* now marched out, trotting in time to drums and horns, their armor clanking to the beat. As they lined up, one by one, they crashed their shields together, as if to display the solidity of their defense.

The horns blared again; de Soto and Ortiz marched out in advance of the Kristiano formation.

Fire Tail slipped and barely caught himself.

"By the Piasa's balls, don't drop me now! We'd look like fools."

"Yes, High Minko," Medicine Killer growled. "But as much as you ate for breakfast, we may have to hope Horned Serpent flies down and grabs you away at the last moment. We're doing all we can do under the extra load."

I laughed with the rest of them, oddly reassured by their teasing in the face of danger.

The *Adelantado* was once again wearing his purple coat, silver helmet, and polished *hierro* breastplate. His ornate sword hung from his belt. Two cabayos and a war lance were being held behind him, and a group of his nobles surrounded Tishu Minko Red Cougar. My brother-in-law stood with his feet braced, no expression on his face until his eyes fixed on me. I could see his surprise as he figured out who I was.

I made the hand signs for "patience" as I was lowered to the ground. Rising, I clutched my copper mace and marched up to de Soto. Pearl Hand and Two Packs followed closely behind.

Instead of the usual protocol and rituals, I asked bluntly, "Sleep well last night, *Adelantado*?"

The smile he gave me as this was translated wasn't exactly a thing of beauty. Neither was his eerie death-sucking stare. The Monster, it seemed, had even less of a sense of humor than the Piasa.

"You have kept your word, High Minko," Ortiz began.

"As a symbol of our word," I added, "the Chicaza offer the Kristianos these additional gifts." I raised my mace, signaling Black Marten and his warriors to bring the most recently scavenged goods forward.

After they were deposited and the warriors had retired, de Soto gave a nod of his head. *Soldados* clattered forward from their formation, retrieving the things we'd brought and packing them back into Chicaza town.

As soon as this was done, de Soto called, *"Trae él."*

Red Cougar was led forward, face stiff, a slight limp in his left leg. Having been run down by a cabayo myself, I was surprised he was doing this well.

"Greetings, alok." I used the Chicaza term for "sister's husband" and embraced him. "Clear Water sends her fondest wishes for your safe return. So does my brother. Breath Giver willing—if we survive—we'll talk later."

Red Cougar played his part, and as I released him, he gave me a confused nod and continued past to the waiting warriors.

One small victory!

De Soto and Ortiz had watched the entire exchange. Now Ortiz asked, "As a measure of our building trust, we would invite you to come and share a feast with us." He glanced behind me. "We assume that those who accompany you are nobles."

I gestured with the mace. "The woman is known among the Chicaza as Death Speaker. Her souls are filled with Power, *Adelantado*. She communes with the dead, hears their voices, and heeds their warnings. All of her life, she has trained herself in the arts of terrible magic and curses. Among her other talents is the ability to call a man's soul out of his body." I adopted a pained look. "There is a terrible fire where she sends the man's soul. Does that make sense to you?"

I listened as this was translated, seeing a slight quiver of Pearl Hand's lips as the words *"una bruja"* were whispered to de Soto. He involuntarily stepped back, his right hand making that odd crisscross pattern of touching the chin and navel, then each breast.

I then said, "In addition to her ability to kill through a curse, I bring her with me because she can detect lies."

"¡Padre!" de Soto called after this was translated, and the brown-robed priest came forward, his wooden cross in hand. *"Esta mujer es una bruja y está en connivencia con el diablo. Te necesitas vigilancia con ella."*

The priest began mumbling, crisscrossing himself, and dipping his long-tailed cross in Pearl Hand's direction. She maintained a dignified posture, head up.

"Mikko Alibamo," I called, and Fire Tail stepped forward and began introducing himself. Two Packs translated as the mikko extolled his family, clan, and people. He was followed by Mikko Lashki, and then by the others. In all, it took quite a while before introductions were finished.

De Soto was bored. He kept shifting, studying me through those empty brown eyes, his mouth pursing, which caused his beard to twitch. On occasion I caught faint whiffs of that strange acrid stink I'd smelled the day before.

I made myself glare back, all the while cringing inside. Yes, cringing. Try being the object of intense scrutiny by such a loathsome, heartless, and evil being and see how you feel.

"*Basta,*" he called, then added something else to Ortiz. They discussed for a while. Then the invitation was made: "We would invite the ishto minko and his nobles to a feast as a sign of friendship. We do this as a gesture of our growing goodwill toward the Chicaza. Further, we would learn more about your country and people. And we would have you learn more about us and the mission our god has sent us upon."

In Timucuan dialect, and affecting nonchalance, I asked, "Wife? Is this a trap?"

"Not yet," she replied. "They're actually encouraged by the prospect of peace. De Soto, however, doesn't trust you."

I wanted nothing more than to turn around, take our tishu minko, and run like panicked deer for the safety of the distant Chicaza squadrons. "Pus and blood! I don't believe I'm doing this. Very well. Two Packs, tell him that we're delighted by his offer."

I watched de Soto's face as the acceptance was translated, then listened as he and Ortiz discussed it.

"Trap?" I asked again, knowing I'd have but an instant to grab de Soto so Pearl Hand could stab him in the throat.

"Ortiz keeps saying, 'See what happens.' The Monster calls it 'a test of intentions,' whatever that means." Pearl Hand shot me a level look, her eyes flashing distrust.

My souls, already tied in knots, cramped with dread.

Orders were shouted in *español* and the *soldados* stepped smartly back, opening a gap through which we could pass. I locked step with de Soto, head erect, my heart so high in my throat I thought it would choke me.

To look back would have reeked of the cowardice that coursed through my veins like iced fear. But then, I didn't have to. I could hear the *soldados* closing in behind us.

Tell me I haven't just made the worst mistake of my whole life!

THIRTY

As I marched into Chicaza town, the eerie Kristiano horns blew, their milky notes sending a spear of fear down my spine. The *soldados,* upon a signal, clapped their weapons against their shields and marched in perfect lines to create a corridor down which we walked.

De Soto and I went first, followed by my nobles. Behind came de Soto's entourage of *capitanes.* Once they would have been dressed in a splendor of Kristiano fabrics. Now they wore a collection of stolen garments including women's dresses, rudely tailored blanket-coats, and hunting shirts. One burly and bearded ruffian wore a young girl's "virgin skirt" like a shawl over his shoulders. He had no idea why my warriors were pointing and snickering in disbelief. Another had two blankets tied around him like some sort of oddly made sack. Many, to my astonishment, had bound their feet in rags.

But then I got a good look at the *soldados;* more than half of them were barefoot on the nearly frozen ground. Ragged they might have been, but they had my little party surrounded—and there was nothing shabby about their *hierro* swords, the ready crossbows, or the couple of thunder-stick shooters surrounded by spear-ax men. We were encircled by a barrier of sharp *hierro*.

My mouth had gone dry, my throat tight as a clenched fist. I struggled to keep my expression blank while my heart hammered in my chest. Beside me, de Soto walked with a languid pace, his eyes drifting from man to man as we passed, as if taking note of his *soldados'* performance.

I almost stumbled at sight of the slaves, huddled against the cold, shivering, with chains running from collar to collar. They pressed against each other in the frozen mud, skin streaked and smudged with filth, rags wrapped around their crotches, hair like tacky black straw. When they shot furtive glances our way, it was with empty eyes, devoid of hope.

I barely caught myself as I reached for my neck, the gesture instinctive as I remembered the collar that had once rested there. I dared not let the Kristianos see the scars.

And there before us was the odd construction the Kristianos had made of posts and poles. The purpose of it came instantly clear: The thing was an enclosure for *puercos*! Hundreds of the beasts were penned inside, grunting, sprawled in the mud, their flat noses wiggling. The odor made my nose tingle, but it wasn't the stench I'd smelled periodically while talking to de Soto.

I couldn't stop the expression of revulsion and distaste but got control of myself before de Soto glanced my way.

There were plenty of women, almost all of them *indíos* dressed in patched and sun-faded dresses of colored cloth. Several of them had young children attached. They watched our arrival with somber brown eyes. The majority of these, I knew, belonged to various cabayeros and nobles. I caught a glimpse of the lady Garden. She'd been White Rose's younger sister and heiress to the high chair at Cofitachequi. Once she'd worn only the finest fabrics; now her dress consisted of a shabby, sun-bleached hemp smock with tattered edges. The baggy rag did nothing to hide her very pregnant belly. Across the distance she had little chance of recognizing me.

When we reached the tchkofa, we stopped, and the minkos with me muttered angrily at the vandalized guardian posts, the eagle wings now ripped away and the wood scarred. De Soto's two cabayos were then tied to them.

Giving us a sidelong glance, the *Adelantado* clapped his hands. His *capitanes* began chuckling to themselves, and I heard the words, *"¡Mira! ¡Los indios estarán asustado!"*

Immediately the cabayeros charged around the clan houses and into the plaza. In two lines they raced in a great circle around the long-tailed cross de Soto had planted where the World Tree had once stood. Their hooves pounded the soil, the thunder of their passing sending a quake of terror into my souls.

At a horn call, the cabayos wheeled, breaking right and left, circling, and flying at each other. Deftly they swerved at the last moment, the riders reaching out to clang their shields as they skillfully avoided collision. Immediately the two groups separated, each curving around the plaza like a perfectly synchronized flock of birds. Again they raced at each other, a bellowed order called at the last minute.

I watched in awe as they lined up and separated, a beast-sized gap between each of the riders. Instead of a wreck, the lines threaded through each other. The sight was miraculous, a thing of beauty to behold. A single misplaced animal would have brought disaster and collision, but their timing was perfect.

The two columns came together at the far end of the plaza, massed, and came charging toward us at a flying gallop, the lances dropping, points glinting in the light.

"Hold your places," I ordered softly. "This is a test of our courage."

Nevertheless, I winced as the ground shook beneath my feet, the roar of their approach ever louder, the beasts growing larger as their hooves flashed and clods of dirt flew.

My own panic grew until I remembered who stood beside me, a gloating smile on his face as he watched our reactions. Worse, the foul cabayos were ruining the chunkey courses, their once-smooth surfaces already a pock-marked travesty.

Pus-licking maggot! You think this will cow us? Anger washed through me.

I stepped over to Fire Tail, pointing at the approaching animals. "Do you see the place where the base of the cabayo's neck meets the shoulders, just above the straps? That's where you put your arrows."

To Flying Squirrel, I shouted over the building din, "When they get close, you need to leap to the opposite side of where they hold the lance. Before they can shift it over the cabayo's head, you can shoot an arrow into the beast's chest and roll away."

De Soto looked puzzled, his head cocked, confused by my reaction.

By then the charge was almost upon us.

"Watch this!" I bellowed, forcing anticipation onto my face.

At the last minute, the riders pulled back on the straps, setting their feet in the stirrups and lifting their lances. I watched the panting cabayos rear back, hooves plowing as the beasts slid to a stop.

"Excellent!" I cried, clapping my hands. I turned to the Chicaza chiefs. "There, did you see? They have just given us a lesson in how to kill them." I prayed that the terror in my heart could be misinterpreted as excitement.

De Soto seemed to buy it, the lines in his face deepening as he muttered something to Ortiz, who asked Two Packs, via the Cofitachequi, "What is he saying?"

I turned to de Soto, asking, "Can they do that again?"

"Of course," came the reply.

De Soto clapped his hands, shouting, "*¡Otra vez!*" and the cabayeros wheeled into two squadrons, cantering away along the edges of the plaza.

I turned to my chiefs. "The first time you were no doubt surprised. This time, think about how you would defend against them. Where would you put your arrow? How would you escape at the last minute? Pay attention to which hand holds the control straps. That hand does not hold a weapon, so you have a slight advantage on that side of the cabayo."

Ortiz was pestering the Cofitachequi, who was pestering Two Packs for a translation.

When the gist of what I was doing was translated, I watched de Soto's face redden with anger. "*¡Bastante!*" he bellowed. A horn blared a staccato of notes and the cabayeros pulled their mounts up, clustering in groups, no doubt awaiting further orders.

I glanced from minko to minko. "Do you begin to understand now?"

"How *do* we stop them?" Cut Hand asked.

"Can a single arrow bring a cabayo down?" Takes Hair wondered.

"What if you duck to the off side, shoot, and another cabayero is riding down on top of you?"

"Then you die," I answered, aware that de Soto stood seething in rage, his jaw clenched as tightly as his fists. "But if you learn nothing else—"

"Food is ready!" the Cofitachequi cried, adding "Impa. Impa." The Chicaza word for "food." Where he learned it, I have no idea, but it got the point across. De

Soto was marching in, stiff backed, cursing under his breath.

We could still die here, I reminded myself, unsure if I'd just scored a victory or a death sentence.

As we filed into the tchkofa, each of us fought the urge to touch the guardian posts, unwilling to get that close to the cabayos.

The wood was scarred, the ground around the posts hammered hard and flat with cabayo tracks; a half circle of droppings covered the earth about a cabayo's length away. I glanced back at the track-dimpled surface of the chunkey courts.

Filthy weasels.

The tchkofa had been the center of Chicaza social life; now it was jumbled with packs that had been shoved under the pole beds along the walls. A Kristiano cross hung in the rear, and the fire was a great roaring thing in the center of the room. Not only that, it smelled . . . just plain rank!

And on mats to the side, to my horror, lay two of the accursed war dogs. They were alert, heads up, ears pricked, watching us with complete and total concentration. Knowing dogs as I did, I could tell from the tension in their muscles that they waited for the command to leap.

"I'll remember you both," I told them under my breath, trusting dog ears to hear me. "One of you is for Bark, the other for Gnaw. You may be good at maiming and killing men, but let's see how you do against trade dogs."

The dogs fixed their gaze on me, perhaps hearing the threat more than they understood the words. A queasy sensation stirred my insides.

De Soto, still fuming, indicated where we should sit in the rear, and to my immediate annoyance, Kristianos walked back and forth between us and the fire—a behavior considered most rude. Among many Nations, walking between the minko and the fire was an offense worthy of death.

Many of his high-ranking Kristianos had filed in, including, to my amazement, both of the Kristiano women. Pale, their hair styled in piles of high ringlets and held in place with combs, they watched me through jaded eyes that might have been seeing just another curiosity. The younger of the two was pregnant, her fine-fabric dress spilling about her protruding belly like a pattern of waves around the bow of a canoe. She wore several strings of beads over the embroidered chest of her dress.

Having never seen them so close, I took a moment to stare. Outside of de Soto and his immediate *capitanes,* the women were the finest dressed of all the Kristianos. I could have made a fortune trading that fabric.

"*Mis capitanes,*" de Soto said, making introductions. "Luis de Moscoso y Alvarado."

I touched my chin as the man bowed. Yes, I remembered him from before. He seemed to have de Soto's respect. He was muscular, his armor polished, his hair curly. I wondered if he knew that the brown fabric he wore like a tunic was an Apafalaya maternity dress?

"Baltasar de Gallegos," de Soto said as a square-jawed man snapped his heels together and jerked a short nod of the head. He had a small mouth, light brown eyes, and an arrogant look.

"Nuño de Tovar," de Soto announced, "*capitán de los cabayeros.*"

I touched my chin, remembering him from sometime in the past. The way I recalled it, I was aiming an arrow at his face; he'd ducked at the last instant so it shattered on his helmet. His odd green eyes held no recognition.

"Juan de Guzman," de Soto said with pride.

This one was a *soldado,* bulky, his batted armor stained and stitched. When I looked into his black eyes, it was to see a man who, like de Soto, considered me nothing more than an insect.

There were more Kristianos filing in as the introductions were made.

When the long line had passed, de Soto extended an arm, saying, *"Sienta."* Then he seated himself beside me and turned his unnerving eyes my way.

My skin began to crawl. *Steady, Black Shell. Steady. You're sitting elbow-to-elbow with the most loathsome man alive. By the Piasa's balls, keep your wits!*

So close to the Monster, my nose wrinkled as I got a full whiff of that vile and noxious stench. How do I describe it? Like rotted corn mash? Spoiled onions? Suffice it to say that it almost burned the back of my nose. And then de Soto lifted his arms, clapping his hands, and the stench got worse.

Blood and pus! It's them! I was catching the combined body odors of tens of men who never washed but lived in the same clothing day after day. By the Piasa's balls, how did they stand each other?

I made a face, swallowing against the sudden urge to vomit. *Would it kill them to show even a little consideration and take a bath every now and then?*

"I have a question." The Cofitachequi translated de Soto's sibilant words to Two Packs, who said, "When the cabayeros were riding for your amusement, you were discussing them with your minkos instead of enjoying the entertainment."

Barely winning the fight with my gag reflex over de Soto's smell, I gave Two Packs a smile. "The game begins, old friend. Translate well."

"You'll know if I don't," he replied dryly, and glanced at Pearl Hand. "Death Speaker" had been sitting quietly behind me, her legs primly under her. To my knowledge, no expression had crossed her face, but she was hearing everything. Smelling it, too.

I turned to de Soto, struggling to keep my nose from

crinkling. "We were discussing the best way to kill your caballos. These are interesting and new animals, and the advantage they provide you, great *Adelantado,* is most impressive. Thank you for the display; we have learned a great deal from it."

"What did you learn, precisely?"

I smiled, calmly looking the Monster in the eyes. "We will not deploy our squadrons in the open."

"You surprise me." He yawned in feigned indifference, and I was able to see brown and rotted teeth. "Most *indios* tell us at great length how they are the finest warriors in La Florida."

"They are not Chicaza."

"Now you sound like an *indio.*"

I gestured around. "Do you see any great mounds, opulent palaces, or mighty temples here, *Adelantado?*"

"Compared to Coosa or Cofitachequi, no."

"All peoples have a special calling." I stared down at the intricately woven mat that we sat on, thinking about the labor that had gone into its manufacture. The Kristianos, however, would only see it as a utilitarian floor covering. "The Hichiti are renowned weavers, the Cofitachequi are builders, the Coosa revel in complexity. The Natchez devote themselves to the mystical with an even greater fervor than the rest of us."

"And the Chicaza?" he asked abruptly.

I gave him a bland look, hoping to disguise my hatred. I could have told him that we practiced bathing instead of wearing our own filth. Instead I said, "We dedicate ourselves to war."

He smiled, not even amused.

"You do not understand, *Adelantado.* Compared to Coosa or Tuskaloosa, or even Apalachee, you do not see great cities. Here, in our capital, you find no more than two hundred buildings, mostly clan meeting houses and granaries. But you do not see palisades."

"Why is that?" He was humoring me.

"Because Chicaza don't need them. You no doubt remember that all of Apafalaya was fortified, as was Tuskaloosa. When you proceed west on your journey, you will find Natchez, Quizquiz, Casqui, and Pacaha fortified. Yet our land here is productive—as the granaries you've captured testify. Our people live scattered about in farmsteads. Easy prey for any raiding party. You are a smart man, *Adelantado*. Does this strike you as different from what you've seen in the east?"

Now I had his attention, a quickening of his interest. "Perhaps it does."

I gave him a ghost of a smile. "As Chicaza we cherish maneuver and discipline. We train our young men from the time they are boys to be warriors. Maybe one out of ten dies before he can become a man. Another three out of ten are killed in their first three years as warriors. Advancement is by merit. Ingenuity is cherished, no matter what clan or lineage a young man might be born to."

He was listening intently as this was being translated, Ortiz gesturing with his hands. I shot a glance at the Kristiano women, wondering how, given the stench, they could stand to lie with their men at night. Maybe they were born without a sense of smell? Or they stank just as bad? Or maybe they just got used to it over time?

Concentrate, Black Shell. Your problem is de Soto, not if they have to hold their noses to mate.

"After the river battle with Panther Clan," I told him, "our people retreated, understanding that they were facing something new, something different. We have been studying you since, considering different tactics."

"Why are you telling me this?"

"Because you asked, *Adelantado*. You wondered why we

were talking excitedly during the cabayo charge. Did you see us afraid? Did you see us cringe back at the end?"

"No." His answer was clipped.

I studied him, wishing I could read his black-hollow eyes, peer into that dead-fish Kristiano soul. Blood and pus, was I making my point? Surely to have come this far, he had to be clever enough, cunning enough, to pretend to be manipulated when it worked in his favor.

"What point are you trying to make?" he asked.

I peered into his brown depths, trying to pierce his incomprehensible and alien soul. "You are a ruthless man, *Adelantado*. But you are also a practical one. If you and I go to war, our armies will maul each other."

I pointed at Two Packs. "This trader tells me that Coosa—which embraced you with open arms—is broken and destroyed behind you. Apalachee, however, remains whole and potent. If we cannot have peace, I will fight you using their tactics."

His smile hardened.

"*Adelantado*, can you afford another Mabila?"

The look he gave me chilled me down to my bones, his lips pinching, the beard quivering with rage.

Careful, Black Shell.

Pearl Hand had reached into her sleeve where the stiletto lay.

It took all of my courage to stare back, knowing the violence in de Soto's heart, remembering the way he'd fought his way out the gate at Mabila. How long we locked gazes, I cannot say. But when he finally nodded, I slowly became aware that the room was deathly silent but for the crackling fire.

"Very well, *indío*. I think you and I understand each other. We shall have peace provided there are no more attacks on my men."

"Chicaza discipline will ensure that my order is followed. Any Chicaza who disobeys does so on his own, and I will not hold you responsible for retaliation. However, if *any* Chicaza men or women are taken captive it will signal the end to peace."

"Ah, about women." He gave me a knowing smile. "I would have it known among your people that young women who lie with my men will be amply rewarded." He reached into a pocket and then extended his hand. The palm was filled with the marvelous chevron-patterned, multicolored beads I'd once salivated over.

I stiffened, eyes half-lidded. "We are not Coosa or Choctaw. We protect our women and their honor. They are not for hire. You understand what would happen if a warrior's daughter, sister, or wife was taken and abused?"

He gestured around the room where nearly a hundred Kristianos had now seated themselves. They were watching us like half-starved wolves. I caught a glimpse of Antonio in the rear of the Fish Clan section. That I had not seen him enter worried me. De Soto said, "We are an army of mostly men. The *capitanes* don't like sharing their wives. And men, you know . . . we have needs that cannot always be denied."

"*Adelantado,* I cannot change the ways of my people. We guard and honor the chastity of our women. I assume that you can control the passions of your men, as I can mine. If you are unable to enforce discipline in your ranks, let me know now."

He glared at me, eyes baleful, teeth grinding. I could see the rage building. Through gritted teeth he hissed, "*No hay mujeres para joder, no hay paz. ¡Si queremos una zorra, cogemos la!*"

Festering pus, Black Shell, you've pushed him too far!

Subtly, I shifted my grip on the mace. Since he still wore the helmet, I'd have to hammer him across the face. Someone had hit him in the face at Napetuca; it hadn't worked there, either.

But if Pearl Hand could grab him from behind, drive her stiletto into his throat . . .

I shot her a glance in an attempt to communicate my desperation.

Moscoso and Gallegos, sitting on the other side of the *Adelantado,* now leaned toward him, arguing vehemently. I swallowed hard. Everything hung by a strand. A wrong word, a misinterpreted gesture . . . and it was time to die.

Ortiz leaned forward, hands gesturing, as he pleaded in concert with the *capitanes.*

I waited, lips pursed, heart pounding like a pestle.

De Soto jerked a nod, biting off angry words. Ortiz repeated, "Your women will be safe." De Soto added another couple of additional sentences that Ortiz apparently didn't wish to repeat.

I got the gist, seeing the smoldering violence in the *Adelantado*'s expression. The empty blackness behind his eyes had been replaced by a seething rage that promised me retribution and hurt. But was it because he couldn't rape Chicaza women or because I'd implied he couldn't control his men?

By the Píasa's balls, that was a close one. My heart slowly resumed its normal beat.

Food came, carried in by slave women, and the Kristiano stench that clogged the air was ameliorated by the scent of roasting meat. We were fed liberally. I glanced at Pearl Hand as the wooden plates were laid before us. She gave me a knowing arch of the eyebrow and a slight smile.

I filled myself with corn, stewed rabbit, baked squash, and the most delightfully cooked venison I'd ever eaten. To my right, Two Packs, Alibamo, Lashki, Cut Hand, and the others stuffed themselves with the sweetly seasoned meat.

"How is this cooked?" I asked Ortiz. "Is this some special Kristiano spice? Something we could trade for? I've never had venison like this."

Ortiz didn't even translate the question. He just chuckled, chewing, and muttered an answer that left me near heaving.

"Es puerco."

THIRTY-ONE

I'm a trader. It comes with a trader's life that he must eat any number of unusual foods, many of which are considered polluted or taboo by his native people's standards. That I did not vomit the contents of my overfull stomach was a testament to my ability to swallow just about anything and keep it down.

The effect on my souls, however, was so staggering that I almost forgot that I was sitting beside the most hated and despicable abomination of a man my world had ever known. I'd even forgotten that I'd managed to wheedle a promise of peace out of the Monster.

I remained so distraught that I couldn't comprehend what a remarkable miracle it was to be able to take my leave, walk bodily out of Chicaza town, and settle myself on the litter for the ride back to the forest and the Chicaza lines.

Especially after the mayhem he'd promised with that one terrible glare.

Instead, all I could think about was that those foul *puercos* ate rotting corpses, and I'd just eaten a *puerco*!

My real dismay came from the grudging admission that I *liked* the taste of *puerco*.

But wasn't that the whole terrible contradiction of the Kristianos? Temptation and death, all mixed together.

I'd been so preoccupied I was barely aware of the excited chatter among my bearers.

"Did you see all the colors of their eyes?" Alibamo was saying. "Black, dark brown, light brown, green, even sky blue!"

"And their hair!" Takes Hair cried. "I'd love to have ishkobo from each one of them."

I made a face, one hand to my belly. "You have my blessing in your quest. Carving the scalp off of a single one is honor enough. But to get one of each color? You'd better hurry, they didn't have many red ones to start with, and I only saw two left."

"The smell of them . . ." Alibamo made a face. "It was all I could do to keep from gagging. Do they never wash? Or do they actually wish to stink like that?"

"Seek to reek?" laughed Takes Hair. "The good news is that they're easy to hunt in the dark. Just get downwind and follow your nose."

"The cabayo charge was impressive," Flying Squirrel added. "But for Black Shell's warning, I'd have run."

"Wait until you experience it for real," Pearl Hand muttered darkly. "Until you do, you'll never believe that all the terror in the world can be squeezed into your souls."

I shot her a look where she paced beside us, the setting sun shooting threads of silver through her ash-grayed hair. The half light left the black side of her face in shadow. "All right, wife. Let's hear it. What did they say that we could not understand?"

"A great many things. The most important for us is that de Soto has ordered that no Chicaza are to be run down and captured. That buys us time. Meanwhile, Moscoso, Ortiz, and Gallegos argue for peace. That little argument they had over taking women? That was a close one, husband. Don't scare me like that again, please. The *capitanes* barely talked de Soto out of cutting your throat. They managed to insist that given a choice the *soldados* would prefer a winter of peace over a warm bed."

"I thought for a moment I'd pushed too far."

She smiled, cracking her face paint. "You did. I was ready to leap on his back when he gave the order to kill us. I thought maybe I could drive this silly bone stiletto into his throat before I was cut in two." She paused. "The implication that he couldn't control his own men really stung him."

I sighed with relief. "Well, like you said, we bought time."

"More than that," she answered. "While they still think we're filthy *indios* condemned to their *infierno*, and tools of *el diablo*, they're impressed that we're not impressed."

"Explain that."

Everyone was listening intently as Pearl Hand said, "They were all talking about it. When de Soto ordered that cabayo charge at Coosa, the High Sun was plainly afraid. When the charge was ordered for Tuskaloosa, he feigned boredom—obviously a front and sham. As a result, de Soto never really trusted him."

"That might be, but Tuskaloosa still lured him into Mabila."

She dismissed it with a shrug. "Today, however, they expected anything but an analytic discussion during the charge. It's caused them to rethink, to be wary. They know they can defeat us in a stand-up fight. What worries them is that we won't give them the opportunity."

"That's a fact," Tishu Minko Red Cougar agreed from where he followed behind Two Packs.

Pearl Hand glanced across the grass toward the waiting squadrons. "They think they have enough food in the captured granaries to feed them until the weather breaks. But just barely. They want the Chicaza to provide additional food, a surplus, for when they head west in spring. And when that day comes, they are going to want *tamemes* to carry it."

"I don't know that word," Cut Hand said as he shifted the litter pole.

"It means 'slave,'" Two Packs told him bitterly. "Once the warriors are volunteered, they're chained by the neck like those poor wretches you saw. When they refuse, those accursed dogs are turned on them, or a whip is used." He raised a clenched fist. "Which is how my boys died."

"No Chicaza will ever stand for such a thing," Medicine Killer growled.

I narrowed my eyes. "We are in a grand game, my chiefs. If I am smart enough and careful enough, I can get the *Adelantado* to lower his guard at the last minute."

"You didn't inspire confidence today, husband."

I winced. "You should have lived it in my skin. I was trying to figure out how to kill the skoobale with my mace."

She snorted derisively. "Call him skoobale if you want. But there must be something that stiffens his penis. I learned today that he has a wife in someplace called Cuba. No less than five women now serve his bed, one being the lady Yellow Stem, once the Coosa High Sun's niece."

"And you learned this how?"

"Moscoso was wondering if you had a niece that de Soto could add to his collection."

"When the high minko hears this, it will enrage him," Takes Hair cried.

"For the coming moons, we must endure the insults, subdue our pride, and control our emotions. The high minko understands this. Do you?"

"And what?" Medicine Killer asked. "Act like Choctaw?"

"No, great warrior. Keep your anger inside, let it abide. I promise you that the day will come when we can retaliate. Meanwhile your hearts must be like granaries, a place to store your rage until you need it."

"Discipline," Alibamo said.

"Discipline," Flying Squirrel agreed.

"Brains before honor." I glared around at them. "Repeat that."

"Brains before honor," came the mumbled replies.

"Did you see all that *hierro*?" Takes Hair waxed enthusiastic. "We'd be the richest people in the world if we could capture all that."

"Me," Medicine Killer added, "I want one of the yellow-haired Kristianos for a slave. I'd keep him around just to grow his hair. Sun Hair, that's what I'd call him. I could trade cuttings of yellow hair like that for all kinds of wealth."

"They're not beaten yet," I reminded them. "And I don't want to discourage you, but every time we've had de Soto's fate sealed in a pottery jar, he's always broken his way out of the bottom and come close to cutting our throats with the sherds."

"Meaning?" Takes Hair asked.

"Meaning if we can kill him, it's going to come at a terrible price in lives and suffering. So, if you plan on obtaining that yellow-haired slave, you'd best pray that just this once, everything goes the way we want it to."

"And the odds of that?" Pearl Hand wondered.

"About as good as getting the geese to migrate north in winter."

She began smiling, then broke into chuckles.

"What?"

"Oh, I don't know. If I'd asked you yesterday, you'd have said the sun would have to rise in the west before you'd eat *puerco*!"

• • •

For two days we waited. The high minko withdrew the squadrons, dispersing them to clan villages and towns within a couple of days' run. Feeding that many people so far from food stores was quickly becoming a trial. And, best of all, we'd bought time. Orders had gone out from all the clan minkos that the Kristianos were not to be threatened, attacked, or otherwise harassed.

"So, what do we do?" my brother asked over the tchkofa fire the night we returned to Black Oak town. "Just let them rest in peace?"

I glanced suggestively at Pearl Hand. She shook her head, saying, "High Minko, do you have warriors you can trust to keep their heads?"

"I do."

"Have them appear just at dark, show themselves, and then in the middle of the night, slip close to Chicaza town. If they leave signs, an arrow here, a track in the mud there, the Kristianos will know they've been close."

I nodded, appreciating the way her head worked. "Just the knowledge that we've been close will keep them on edge. It's tough to get a night's sleep if you know a warrior's been prowling around."

"But it has to be carefully balanced," Pearl Hand warned the high minko. "Any threat must be only implied. If one of the warriors loses his head, goes too far, everything could collapse in flames."

"I understand." He peered intently at the fire. "You did a good job in there, brother. The minkos speak of you with the greatest regard."

I reached out, placing a hand on his shoulder. "It is only because they have a wise and thoughtful high minko to guide them. If the Cofitachequi, Coosa, or Hichiti Nation had been so ably led, the Monster never would have made it this far."

He nodded his appreciation, his smile thin and strained. "If we manage to achieve a victory. If we actually destroy them . . . have you given any thought to what you would do?"

I glanced at Pearl Hand. "For a long time now, it has been our assumption that the Monster's destruction would come at the cost of our lives. And, well, I have a debt to the Piasa."

He lifted an eyebrow. "We don't have a lot of water around here."

"That means little; I watched a tie snake leap out of a spring during a Spirit Dream. And there was one night down in the Uzachile lands that Piasa came in a downpour and stood outside our tent."

"What?" Pearl Hand cried. "You never told me that!"

"That was before I understood." I shrugged. "But I do now. I've seen him too many other places, including that night on the Split Sky City landing."

My brother said nothing, a thousand questions behind his soft brown eyes.

"Next time a Spirit Beast is prowling around in the night"—Pearl Hand jabbed a finger into my chest—"you rotted well wake me up."

I gave her a mollified and submissive nod of the head.

"And if you survive?" my brother asked softly. "What then? Back to trading?"

The discussion left me feeling uncomfortable. "Even the notion raises hopes that are better left deeply buried."

"There are some who think you might assume the panther chair here." He said it offhandedly, his gaze averted.

Ah, there it was.

Pearl Hand was shaking her head, muttering soundlessly to herself. I could see the distaste in her expression.

I laughed, actually amused. "Brother, you are high minko. Now, forever, and even after your souls travel the

Path of the Dead to the ancestors. And that, as they say, is the packrat's tail. The end of the story. The final word."

"I could never have accomplished the things you have, Black Shell. All of Chicaza is talking of your leadership, how you faced the invader, and how you made the Monster back down."

"Back down? Excuse me? These witnesses were present at events I never saw?" I threw up my arms. "Brother . . . *High Minko*, several times in the past days, I've literally been holding on by my fingernails. By some miracle, we have a temporary peace negotiated with that abomination of a human being. This peace of ours is supported by the thinnest of threads. Anyone who tells you differently is either a mindless idiot or an ignorant fool."

"Even my sisters, women who once despised you and refused to say your name, now sing your praises."

"And Mother?"

A look of despair filled his face. "Very well, there is at least one Chicaza who won't vote to place you in the panther chair."

"Brother, you are high minko." I clapped him on the shoulder. "I was chosen for another destiny."

He cocked his head questioningly. "And what if *I* asked you to take the panther chair?"

I glanced at Pearl Hand, who'd been quietly watching the fire, her triangular face somber. I wasn't sure how her thoughts were lining up, but I could guess.

"Brother, if you ask me, I will be honored and humbled. But the answer is no. Chicaza has the most qualified high minko it could possibly have. And until the day Pearl Hand and I leave, we are honored to serve you."

I stood, reached down, and tugged Pearl Hand to her feet.

We left him, his eyes fixed on the fire, and walked outside.

"That was a kind thing to tell him," she noted, gripping my hand in hers.

"It was the truth."

"So . . . what if we do survive?"

"I can't think about that. Neither can you. We only have the present. Just you and me and the accursed Kristianos."

She nodded, looking up at the star-frosted sky, exhaling in a pale fog. "We were close enough that with the right weapons, we could have killed him."

"I know. First, we didn't have the right weapons. Second, he was wearing that accursed armor."

She glanced at me, eyes like dark holes in her face. "And what if the opportunity arises? If we have the right weapons, and if he's not protected?"

I grimaced as I stared up at the night sky, missing the sight of Horned Serpent's constellation in the south. This was winter; he was safely bedded down in his lair in the Underworld.

"That's a gamble," I said. "We kill him, the monster is dead. We die on the spot, and warfare breaks out immediately with the Chicaza. That being the case, what happens? Do the Kristianos fold and mutiny? Or does Moscoso or Gallegos take control?"

"I watched them. The men respect them almost as much as they do de Soto. I heard Moscoso that night in camp outside Mabila. He's a competent leader. If we kill de Soto, my guess is that Moscoso steps right in behind him."

"We don't know enough about him," I added. "Obviously the Kristianos would take their rage out on the Chicaza, or try to. I think the high minko and tishu minko would act with discretion and fight a running battle through the forest. But after that?"

"I don't know." Pearl Hand tilted her head back, thick hair spilling over her shoulders as she scanned the night sky. "Either they'd head south for the coast, or perhaps they'd stay right here and attempt to carve out a Nation for themselves. Chicaza has good land, more resources than its people can eat."

"Or they might return to Tuskaloosa or Coosa? Maybe even Cofitachequi? Someplace close to the sea where their ships could land?"

She studied me. "Is that what we want? To take that chance? Or do we want to destroy them completely?"

I sighed. "I vote for destruction."

She squeezed my hand. "Me too. But that means we can't kill de Soto until the very end. Even if he's vulnerable and at our mercy, we have to let him live."

"The very notion wounds my souls."

"Mine as well. It won't be the first such wounds we've borne."

"No. And having you beside me? I can bear anything."

"Come," she whispered. "After making such a depressing decision, I need you to take me to our bed and cheer me up. Besides, if you don't use it, you might become a skoobale yourself."

"Not a chance."

Nevertheless, as we walked through the cold night toward Wild Rose's, I remembered de Soto's face as he raged about raping Chicaza women.

Yes, maggot, you will live for now.

But "now" wouldn't last forever.

THIRTY-TWO

Two days later, at our request, Ears was led into the tchkofa. I noticed immediately how he walked, each short step carefully placed, loosely taken, his body swaying.

I grimaced, knowing exactly what I was seeing. *Make sure he doesn't escape?* They'd obeyed the high minko's orders by cutting the thick tendon above the heel. I'd been terrified that the old Cofitachequi mico was going to do the same thing to Pearl Hand during her captivity.

Irritated by my sudden sense of compassion, I had to remind myself that this was Ears, who'd vowed to rape Pearl Hand to death and who had once served both Antonio and his late father. Ears had joyfully sought to destroy me clear back at Irriparacoxi's town. He'd perpetrated the massacre at Napetuca when he betrayed the Uzachile to de Soto.

The Chicaza were watching Ears with reservation, wondering no doubt why I'd called him.

Around me, seated according to iksa, were the minkos,

hettisus, and squadron abetuskas. My brother sat to my left, Tishu Minko Red Cougar beside him. So, too, was the tishu minko's kinsman Old Wood, back to his priest name with the return of Red Cougar.

"Place him just across the fire from us," I ordered. "I want to see his face."

Ears was led, a rope around his neck, to the spot reserved for speakers, his features illuminated by the dancing light.

He glanced around, picked me out immediately, and smiled bitterly. "Hello, Trader. If there is a stench in the air, I need only to locate you to determine the source of it."

He spoke in Timucua, and I gestured for Two Packs to translate. He was relishing his role. Traders rarely got to participate in the midst of a foreign Nation's political machinations.

"We brought you here for a purpose, slave," I told him coldly. "How you answer, what you tell us, will determine how you live the rest of your life."

"I am dead, Trader. *Jesucristo* condemned me back at Mabila when I tore his cross from my chest."

"He is but one god, and a Kristiano one at that. The fate of your souls is your own concern. What we can offer is a better existence in this life and even a say in how long you live it. A full belly, warmth and shelter, and limited drudgery? Do these things appeal to you? Perhaps even the chance to earn your freedom?"

"Why would you offer such?" His gaze had narrowed, expecting a trap.

"I ask myself the same question. I don't like anything about you. Your souls are warped and bent, and a darkness lies between them. Something festers inside that makes you a polluted human being." I paused, letting Two Packs translate the Timucua, then continued. "It turns out, however, that you have something to trade. You traveled with the Kristianos for nearly two years. You converted to their beliefs, served as one of their translators, and got to learn their ways."

His bitter smile curled his lips. "I even betrayed you and the Uzachile at Napetuca. I think that was my proudest moment, watching you shiver out in that lake, your jaws chattering so loudly it slurred your words." He cocked his head. "I always wondered, how did you survive that?"

"Spirit Power. The same Power you betrayed for the Kristiano god. And yes, I swore I'd kill you for what you did at Napetuca. The murder of the defenseless Uzachile at your hands was the worst. And had Blood Thorn survived, I'd have let him kill you in a square."

Ears gave me a slit-eyed stare. "You are all fools. You've grabbed hold of the Kristianos. And like the boys who grabbed the bobcat by its ears, there is now no way to turn it loose."

"As they also appear to have grabbed us. We are both circling, baiting our traps. Hoping the other steps first into the snare." I made a dismissive gesture. "What we Chicaza need to know is how the leadership works. If de Soto were to be killed, would Moscoso assume the leadership?"

His mocking smile conjured flickers of rage inside me. He glanced at Pearl Hand. "Come share my bed, camp bitch, and I'll tell this limp penis of a man everything he wants to know."

"Sorry," she told him with a bored expression. "I'd bed a corpse before I'd allow you into my blankets. Would you rather have your remaining days be pleasant or miserable?"

He grunted, heedless that the Chicaza had stiffened over his insult to Pearl Hand. "All right. Yes. They'll follow Moscoso. The *soldados* call him *el segundo*. You know what that means?" Before we could reply, he blurted,

"The second. Moscoso has always backed the *Adelantado* even when the others would have revolted. Third in command is Gallegos. In many ways Gallegos is the more competent when it comes to getting things done."

"And if de Soto is dead? Moscoso would continue looking for gold?"

"They are coming to believe that there is no gold here. Some still have faith. Others are more interested in staying alive long enough to establish a Kristiano Nation. They want *indio* slaves to farm for them and make them rich. Most, however, want to return to Mexico, Panama, or España. They just want to go home."

"Would they want to stay in Chicaza?" Pearl Hand asked. "Or would they go back to Mabila, Coosa, or one of the other Nations they've visited?"

"Mabila?" He nearly spat with disgust. "They consider it a place of demonic death. Of all the places, they liked Coosa the best. We all became nobles there. The rulers were easy to control, the land fat. But I heard them often say that it was too far from the sea."

"Would Moscoso and Gallegos fight over control of the army?" I asked.

Ears shook his head. "You're still living in Napetuca, Trader. Killing de Soto then would have split the Kristianos in all directions. Now they have a bond. If that gate had been closed at Mabila, and you'd killed the *capitanes* before the rest of the army arrived, the survivors would have fled south to Ochuse and the ships. That was your last chance."

"The loss of their supplies, clothing, all the trade . . . that shook them, didn't it?"

Ears nodded. "So did the number of dead and wounded. They think it was a miracle—the will of *dios*—that they survived." He twisted his face into a knowing leer. "That and the *indio* stupidity of packing thousands into a burnable town surrounded by walls."

I bit down on the hot rage his words kindled.

Careful. You need his advice. Even if it comes with a thick dose of arrogance.

"Where is de Soto going? If he's no longer searching for gold, what does he hope to find?"

"Some great Nation off to the west. Something bigger and richer than Coosa that he can conquer and become like a god."

After this was translated, I glanced around the room, asking, "Has anyone here ever heard of such a place?"

Heads shook.

I asked Ears, "If the Kristianos were to suffer another defeat like Mabila—"

"Defeat?" Ears cried. "They killed *five thousand* and escaped your trap, fool! To the Kristianos, Mabila is a victory! Proof of their god's love and support."

"All right, if they were to be summarily beaten, most of them killed, their cabayos dead or maimed, what would they do?"

He snorted at the ridiculous notion of it. "*Assuming* you could do this, they'd beat a fast retreat toward some Nation they call Mexico. It lies somewhere off to the southwest of here."

When this was translated, I glanced around, seeing heads shaking.

"The Chicaza know of no such place."

Ears shrugged. "Then once again, perhaps the Kristianos are smarter than you are. They've been there, and they know it's close, perhaps a couple of months' travel."

"Smarter?" I couldn't help but ask. "This is *our* land, and we've never heard of it."

He just gave me a half-lidded stare. "Of course they're smarter. They've got you just where they want you. Your high minko is still free, but if they are acting according to plan, they've already invited him to a feast. They've pledged friendship, and next thing you know, they'll send a cabayo for him to ride to meetings with the *Adelantado*. Then, when the time is right, they'll seize your nobles and Chicaza will do their bidding."

Oh, sure, me on a cabayo? "Take him away," I muttered.

As his rope was tugged, Ears called, "Did I earn my freedom, Trader? Or was that just a lie?"

"Feed him," I ordered. "Keep him warm and sheltered. We may have need for him again."

We watched as he was led, wobbly step after wobbly step, from the room.

"What do you think?" I asked Pearl Hand.

"It sounds like the Kristianos will be tougher than a stone nut to crack."

"What did you just learn from the slave?" my brother asked. "Even though Two Packs did his best to translate, much of it made no sense to us."

"If we learned anything," I sighed, "it's that our task is just as difficult as we thought it was. We're going to have to—"

A young warrior burst into the tchkofa. Trotting to the fire, he dropped to one knee, touching his forehead respectfully.

"High Minko!" he cried. "The Kristianos are coming on cabayos! They send a messenger! They wish Minko Black Shell to attend them! And not only that, *they send a cabayo for him to ride upon!*"

"A cabayo?" the high minko noted with surprise. "And what did the slave just say?"

My gut had already turned queasy.

"Don't remind me," I muttered.

THIRTY-THREE

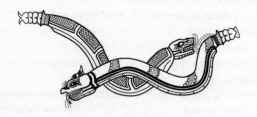

RIDE UPON A CABAYO? I'D BEEN ON ONE BEFORE, mostly unconscious, tied across its back quarters, my head hanging down, swaying with each step, and my skull cracked with pain. That once had been more than enough. Now they wanted me to trust my life and souls to one of those polluted and evil creatures?

Rocks would sprout wings first. This time I was putting my foot down!

Having reassured myself thus, I followed the exodus from the tchkofa and into the Black Oak town plaza. A crowd was gathered, standing far back. Cries of amazement ran from lip to lip. Their eyes were big as spindle whorls as they stared at the three cabayos that plodded into the plaza. Two bore riders: Ortiz and the one called Nuño de Tovar, the captain of the cabayeros.

The Cofitachequi translator ran behind, panting hard, calling, "The *Adelantado* seeks counsel with the Ishto Minko Chicaza! In a token of his respect, he has sent a cabayo to carry the high minko to Chicaza town!"

When this was translated, whistles of approbation, clapping hands, and stamping feet followed. Those eyes not on the cabayos and the Kristiano riders turned to me in worshipful anticipation.

I winced, experiencing a sensation like a great weight falling through my gut. *Oh, sure, putting my foot down.* I glanced at Pearl Hand. "What if I don't want to?"

The look she gave me through flat black eyes expressed no pity. "You're the one who wanted to be high minko."

"Rocks, it seems, are sprouting wings," I muttered in a pitiful voice.

I turned to Two Packs. "You'd better wander out there and stall them while Pearl Hand and I are painted."

"And if the *high minko's*"—Pearl Hand emphasized the words—"courage dribbles away like an old man's urine, I'll let you know the moment he slips out the back way and disappears into the forest."

"Hush, foul woman."

Her lips quirked as she asked me, "You're really going to do this? Ride one of those vile things?"

I gestured at the building crowd. "Look at them! Tell me there's a way out of this."

"Nope." She took in the crowd. They were shooting me speculative glances, talking, pointing at the cabayos waiting by the center pole. "Ah, the sacrifices of leadership."

I growled. "You and Two Packs have to *walk* the whole way."

"But at least our souls will be intact when we get there. And we won't end up broken and dying when the cabayo unleashes all of its disgust at having a filthy *indio* on its back." She shot me a sly smile. "You've been thinking about how you feel about cabayos? How do you think the cabayo feels about having to carry you?" My look must have been horrified, because she began to snicker and finally burst into giggles.

341

"You just wait . . . *Death Speaker*. After the thing eats my souls and kills me, *you'll have to ride it back!*"

I kept wishing that painting my face would take all day. Normally it's a boring process, about as exciting as watching a beech tree grow. And when done correctly, the person being painted is not allowed to move. That day it seemed like slip, slap, and I was ready.

I slowly dressed in my borrowed high minko's finery. All the while my gut tickled anxiously like a colony of ants was crawling around inside.

Two Packs, face grim, handed me my mace. "Good luck, High Minko."

"Bring your bow and arrows. If the thing tosses me off and kicks me to death, kill it."

He nodded, reading the worry behind my eyes. Blood and pus, nothing about cabayos was good. Outside Anhaica I'd watched one somersault into a creek and crush its rider to death. Fleeing from Uzita I'd been hammered flat and unconscious by a cabayo. I still remembered how sick I'd been, the beast's stench filling my nostrils as it carried me into captivity.

"Nothing good ever comes of cabayos," I muttered as I walked out and the crowd parted.

My brother, looking remarkably un-minko-like in the brown shirt he'd donned, glanced first at me, then the waiting cabayeros. The wide open space around them showed the Chicaza's inherent good sense to stay clear of both beasts and Kristiano riders.

Choctaw Hair said, "I'm sending Pearl Hand on the litter. But, Black Shell, is this a good idea?"

"Piasa spit! No! I don't like sharing the same world with the foul things, let alone climbing atop one."

He gave me a disgusted look. "I *meant* going to see the Monster without the squadrons assembled should things go wrong?"

I took a deep breath and tried to exhale my tension. It didn't work. Maybe I needed bigger lungs.

"We can't keep calling up the squadrons each time the pus-licking *Adelantado* wants to talk. The warriors would be run ragged; discipline would be stretched for no reason. No, I'll go." I thumped a fist against his shoulder. "But if we're not back tonight, you go to war. No negotiations. No concessions for our safety. We've discussed the tactics you'll need. The minkos who accompanied me last time have seen the cabayeros; they understand the threat. Just fight smart, brother."

"Brains before honor?"

"Now you're learning." I looked out at the waiting cabayos and the two riders. Pearl Hand appeared at my shoulder, her hair full of ashes, her face split in black and white. The litter was waiting at the edge of the crowd. Two Packs, a bow hanging from one shoulder, a quiver over his back, stood with his hands clasped before him. I could see the tension in his eyes.

Under my breath, I muttered, "Come on, Black Shell, you've been eaten by your Spirit Helper, how could a cabayo be worse than that?"

Rot and stink take me, I was about to find out.

Somehow I walked out past the last of the crowd, hearing the plaza go silent. The malignant beast they'd brought was a mouse-brown color, its back dipping down behind the shoulders and rising up to the bony and rounded rump. The thing had its head down, the pin ears flattened. Its large eyes were half-lidded, as if it were on the verge of dozing.

"*¿Listo?*" Ortiz asked, his Cofitachequi translator asking, "Ready?"

I almost forgot to wait for Two Packs's translation. I gave a jerk of my head, aware that the Chicaza, still timid, were nonetheless edging closer, wonder and awe in their expressions.

343

"These men will lift you onto the cabayo," Two Packs translated as several of the converted *indios* stepped up, their eyes wary.

Atop the other cabayos, Ortiz and Nuño were grinning, fists on the saddles of their beasts. They split their time between shooting anxious looks at the crowd and then amused ones at me.

Piss and blood! They know I'm terrified! And that just spurred a burning anger inside me. *All right, if this thing tries to kill me, neither of these fools is leaving the plaza alive.*

My last words would be, "Kill them all!" And the Chicaza would comply.

Ready to die, I steeled myself, fear tingling in my gut, arms, and legs. I took a breath. "You may place me upon the beast," I ordered, anger and desperation lending my voice an air of authority.

"*En este lado,*" Nuño said, pointing, and the slaves carried me to the cabayo's left side . . . and lifted.

My skin crawling, I managed to scramble onto the beast, alternately amazed at the warm, short-haired firmness of its wide back and the height from which I stared down at the crowd. The sensation of my legs around the great beast's barrel chest was remarkable. Amazed, I looked down the long neck, past the back of its head and pin ears.

A cheer went up from the crowd, and I sat . . . petrified.

"Grasp the neck hair," Two Packs, his voice strained, translated. "That's it. Hold tight."

As if I'd hold any other way?

"Do not kick the cabayo," I was told. "Be still. As long as Nuño holds the lead rope, it will follow him. Relax. Allow yourself to move with the cabayo. It will not hurt you."

Sure. And nasty old Piasa was chock-full of white Power. I knew a lie when I heard it.

344

I froze solid as an oak when Nuño's cabayo took a step. My beast shifted, sending a quake through me. Then it took another step and began to move. My heart hammered at the sensation of movement, at how I seemed to float along effortlessly. Below me, the crowd watched, rapt with amazement.

All of my attention was fixed on not falling off as the animal strode after its mates. The head rose and fell with each step, the hooves clopping on the packed clay of the chunkey court. It was a measure of my distress that I had more pressing concerns than the damage it was doing to the groomed clay.

Glancing behind I saw Pearl Hand's litter lifted onto warriors' shoulders; they trotted after us.

A great *"Hau! Hau!"* shout went up from the Chicaza, as if in celebration of some remarkable victory.

Accompanied by a stream of Chicaza we clopped out of Black Oak town and onto the trail. There, just behind the trees, a line of cabayeros waited, lances resting in their stirrups.

My blood ran cold. But then, the *Adelantado* wouldn't have sent Nuño and Ortiz by themselves. Had we attacked them, the reserve would have come on the gallop. The prospect of riding back to Chicaza town surrounded by cabayeros only added to my fear and distrust. And there, near the middle, Antonio sat atop a mount, his scarred face peeking out from beneath a battered helmet. He'd found another *hierro* breastplate somewhere, and this one fit him no better than the last one.

To my relief the cabayeros lined out, leading the way, leaving us in the rear.

"How are you doing?" Two Packs translated Ortiz's question.

"Tell him I will cut the liver and intestines out of his living body and feed them to the blue jays for subjecting me to this."

Two Packs told the Cofitachequi trader, "The ishto minko thanks the *Adelantado* for the remarkable honor you have bestowed upon him, and he only hopes he can return the favor."

I gave Two Packs my most loathing and baleful look.

He grinned back at me like some three-fingered idiot.

"Concentrate on moving with the animal," came the next instructions. "You are riding like a wooden statue. Loosen up and sway at the hips or you'll be falling off."

As it was I had to shift constantly to keep even with the animal's midline. Nevertheless, hating to take any advice from Ortiz, I bit my lip and did my best to comply.

By the time we'd entered the forest trail, I was beginning to catch on. Loosening my hips and swaying in time made all the difference. When we crossed a downed log, I tensed, amazed that the beast simply stepped over the obstacle without so much as a tremor or bump.

My next surprise came when, starting up the ridge slope, the creature began breaking wind, each eruption timed to the taking of a step. I just shook my head. You'd think a cabayo similar to a big pack dog. Of course the dogs always waited until we were in camp, everyone crowded around the fire enjoying the evening, before they lay down, lifted their tails, and perfumed the air with the annoying scent of digested rabbit, deer, or turkey.

Perhaps a hand of time later, I'd grown comfortable enough that I began to appreciate the novelty of the experience. I was amazed at the advantage I had looking down, out, and around. Not only that, but even at our plodding pace, the party following came on at a trot, their lungs heaving. Pearl Hand's carriers had sweat shining on their faces despite the cool temperatures.

"Do I dare speak with you?" I asked the cabayo.

One of the spear-point ears swiveled back at me.

"I am a Chicaza," I whispered, unsure if I dared mention my name. Did cabayos commune somehow with their masters? Or perhaps among themselves? Did they know that since coming to our world, I'd killed so many of them?

The ear swung forward, the head continuing to bob as it followed Nuño's cabayo.

Nothing in my entire life compares to that cabayo trip to Chicaza town. The experience is right up there with canoeing down rapids. Think of it as the sense of exhilaration that comes with the knowledge that you are doing what you would have considered impossible: riding a beast from another world, your head a body length above the world you once knew. My perspective had been irrevocably altered.

The arrival at Chicaza town was almost a disappointment—though my hips and knee joints had discovered a disadvantage to cabayo travel: They were aching from the unusual angle required to straddle the immense chest.

Dropping to the ground in the Chicaza town plaza, I winced as I took tentative steps. The Kristianos laughed, making fun of me. It reminded me of how I'd been treated at Uzita when they took me captive. I bit my lip, keeping my expression neutral.

A Kristiano stepped up from the side, taking the animal's lead rope from Nuño. And in that instant, the magic vanished. From no more than an arm's length, I looked into Antonio's hate-filled eyes.

I struggled to keep from signaling recognition; at the same time I was repelled by the still-healing wounds marring his visage. The scab had fallen from the long furrow my arrow had cut into his thinly bearded cheek, leaving a long welt of puffy pink scar tissue running clear back to his ear. Someone had sewn his cleft nose back together. My sword had cut clear down to the cheekbones before being stopped by the sides of his *hierro* helmet. Despite the stitches, Antonio's nose was slightly mismatched, the healing cleft red and angry.

Apparently he misread my reaction, perhaps thinking I was startled by his appearance. For instead of recognition, loathing twisted his mouth, and he ground his jaws, eyes narrowing. Then he spun away, stomping off; my cabayo followed, its hips canting with each step.

Perhaps ten paces away, Antonio stopped and turned, a question in his eyes as he shot me a glance.

Don't look at him, fool! You're supposed to be a high minko; act like one.

Smart me, I didn't reach up and finger my thick face paint, which would have given him a clue. Concho Negro was supposed to be dead. Back turned to Antonio, I stepped to where Two Packs stood, knees braced, catching his wind. "Tired?"

"That's a long run," he wheezed.

"You're not the trader you used to be."

He grinned at me. "Maybe I never was."

I chuckled and watched Pearl Hand rise when her litter was lowered. Shooting a sidelong glance at Antonio, I caught him barely giving Pearl Hand so much as a second glance. Our disguises seemed to have passed the test.

Blood and piss, must we always live on the ragged edge?

I took a deep breath, heart slowing. "All right, let's see what the Monster wants this time."

When I glanced back, Antonio was leading the cabayo off, head down. He didn't look back the way he would have had he suspected me.

I have to hand it to de Soto. He'd learned our ways well. A pipe was offered, as was black drink—though we drank it out of a metal Kristiano cup.

I tried to read the Monster's expression while this was going on. He just watched me through those flat and soulless eyes, as if he were attempting to comprehend some novel form of carrion fly.

When we were seated and food had been provided, he finally had Ortiz state, "There have been *indios* around our camps. They come in the night, sneaking around."

I nodded as I listened, asking, "Have there been any attacks?"

"No, but they worry my *soldados*."

I pressed my palms together as if considering and finally replied. "*Adelantado,* you are sure that there have been no attacks?"

"Not yet."

"Then my orders have been obeyed. As to the close presence of my people, it is their land. You are occupying property belonging to the iksas. You cannot blame them for being curious about who you are, what you are doing to their clan houses and dwellings."

"Their presence is a provocation."

I shook my head. "We are at peace. As to the fact that they come in the night? Of course. They still don't trust you not to take them captive. Meanwhile, you must understand that as long as we are at peace, I cannot order the minkos to keep their people away." I pointed to the left of where we sat. "That space right there belongs to the Raccoon Clan. And next to it, there, past that support post, that is the property of the Panther Clan. It is the same outside, around the plaza. I saw your *capitán* Moscoso step out of a house belonging to Panther Clan."

"But you are ishto minko!"

I cocked my head. "Perhaps you do not understand the iksas and how they function in our world. In the Beginning Times, when Breath Giver formed the first men of clay inside the sacred mountain far to the west—"

He cut me off with a slash of the hand as this was being translated. I waited for Two Packs to translate his outburst. "The *Adelantado* doesn't care about your silly stories. He wants the Chicaza to stop sneaking around his men in the night."

I gave de Soto a smile, nodding slightly and chuckling. "We are at peace, are we not? Is my face paint not completely white? Did I not come with only my translator,

349

Death Speaker, and a small escort? Does the *Adelantado* see the squadrons in their formations, ready for war? No, he sees only his friend and brother, sitting here as a man of peace sits."

"The *Adelantado* is pleased with your trust, but he demands that Chicaza do not sneak around his *soldados* and harass their sleep. It must be stopped."

"Tell the *Adelantado* that trust must run both ways. His *soldados* occupy houses and land provided by the iksas for the Kristianos' use. Each of the iksas has agreed to the peace, and if there is ever an attack, or a theft, or any violation of the peace, you must let me know immediately. The culprits will be appropriately punished."

He watched me through narrowing eyes, his expression pinched. I got the feeling he didn't like being lectured. A prickling of unease—like when one finds oneself face-to-face with an angry cougar—tickled my spine.

I added, "I would ask, *Adelantado*, what compensation has been offered to the iksas for the use of their property? You said that the Kristianos would offer presents, remarkably wealth, in return for our overtures. Meanwhile the Chicaza have provided food, blankets, and clothing for your shivering *soldados*. What have the Chicaza received in return?"

He took a deep breath as this was translated, nodding. "Very well, Ishto Minko. Upon your return, I shall send needles and beads, mirrors the like of which you've never seen. Wealth beyond your comprehension. In return, you will stop the *indios* from sneaking close in the night."

"The Chicaza accept your presents with delight." I inclined my head. "You, however, must understand that we have never seen your likes before. I cannot banish my people's curiosity with an order." I paused, just long enough, then continued before he could speak. "But what I can do is send those who are not afraid by ones and twos, to visit during the day. That way they can see who and what you are. It will reassure your *soldados* that so long as peace exists, Chicaza are not a threat."

"And the night visits will cease?"

I nodded. "I believe so, but I cannot promise. Like I said, the land belongs to the different iksas. I can only speak for Chief Clan"—I gestured at the floor—"this place where we now sit."

Expressionless, he fixed his stare on mine, and I realized again how dangerous he was, how alien a world he came from.

I struggled to keep my face impassive. *Yes, Monster, we play the game well. You will give on this, not knowing my ultimate goal but relying on your superior arms.*

Finally he spoke. "We will welcome small parties of Chicaza who come to visit and trade. Our priests are anxious to tell them about the true god and *jesucristo*. Those who come bearing gifts of food and clothing will be repaid with *hierro* needles, stunning beads, and the blessing of *dios*."

"*Adelantado*, we are in accord. Let us smoke, partake of black drink, and celebrate our continued peace and friendship."

He was right where I wanted him.

The question was: Did he have me exactly where he wanted me?

THIRTY-FOUR

I STARED UP AT BLACK OAK TOWN'S SMOKE-CHOKED tchkofa roof. The blue-gray haze drifted up through the square hole and rose toward the star-filled winter sky. Around Pearl Hand and me, the minkos, Tishu Minko Red Cougar, several hetissus—the tishu minko's message carriers—and the various squadron abetuskas were seated according to clan and squadron rank. They listened, arms clasping their knees, nodding on occasion, grunting dissatisfaction at other times.

My brother, Choctaw Hair, his expression somber, sat to my right. Pearl Hand looked pensive, her triangular jaw set; she sat to my left. The fire in the central hearth reflected in her large dark eyes.

Four logs were laid out in the cardinal directions. I watched as a young man pushed them together and added a couple of branches to freshen the blaze.

As the flames speared up, I said, "We need to be very careful with these visits. Choose only those warriors you know you can trust to keep their heads. I would prefer that the iksas send their abetuskas to start with."

"Why?" Red Cougar asked. He sat in the front of the Raccoon Clan contingent. He'd been quiet since his release, thoughtful, and introspective.

"Because when the time comes for the attack, each squadron is going to have to maneuver around the new dwellings the Kristianos are building. They'll have to negotiate the *puerco* pen and attack different objectives." I made an interlocking gesture with my fingers. "The Kristianos have changed the entire layout. Old passages are plugged. Additions have been built onto clan houses. Storehouses have been cleaned out and turned into dwellings. Where before you could have charged ten abreast, now you'll have to squeeze through in single file. In places, even the roofs are now overlapping."

"It isn't all haphazard," Pearl Hand added. "I overheard Moscoso and Gallegos discussing it. The buildings were placed so close together precisely to break up an attack by squadrons. They *want* our warriors bottled between the buildings."

"Why?" Flying Squirrel asked.

I gave him a knowing look. "Because five *soldados*, their shields overlapping, can defend a narrow gap between the buildings against hundreds of warriors. Behind them will be crossbowmen and perhaps thunder-stick shooters."

"We still don't understand these thunder sticks," Old Wood called from the rear of the tchkofa.

"They don't use them much anymore," I answered. "Probably because the black medicine-sand they pour down the tubes blew up at Mabila."

"You can find black sand lots of places," one of the abetuskas reminded me.

"It takes a special kind, blessed by some kind of Power

I don't understand," I answered. "I've looked at it, tasted it. It's not like regular sand but stinks of sulfur."

"Where do they get it?" another wondered.

I waved them all down. "We're getting away from the point. When you go to Chicaza town, you're going with the purpose of learning where each of the Kristianos lives. Especially the *capitanes* and nobles. Pay attention to the changes they've made. Don't just gawk at their strangeness, but think about how you'd attack. Think about how you'll maneuver in the dark. Memorize the route you'd take to get into town and how to escape out the other side if your squadron is shattered and disorganized. In short, my brave Chicaza: *think!*"

My brother added, "You must show discipline the entire time you are there. If you are insulted, you must not retaliate. Do you understand? This is a battle walk, and every bit as much discipline is required as would be in Natchez or Choctaw country."

Pearl Hand added, "When you are chosen to go to Chicaza town, go with the knowledge that clan totems have been abused. The World Tree has been cut down in the plaza and replaced with a tall long-tailed cross. Guardian posts have been defaced, the charnel houses burned."

Angry growls burst out around the assembly.

"Stop it!" I ordered. "Of course you are incensed. When you go and see for yourselves, bite your tongues, still your protests, and wait for your time. It will come. Your mission remains twofold: You are scouting the enemy, learning his disposition and ways, and you are allaying his fears. When you are in Chicaza town, you will smile, nod, and touch your chins. You will offer them food or clothing, and you will trade. As you do, learn where they stack their weapons, where they pile their armor, and how they come and go. Memorize the ground you will be fighting on."

Around the room, heads nodded.

My brother added, "Do you understand why you must be friendly, even if they are pissing on your clan house walls? Do you understand why you must swallow your pride for the time being and act as subservient as an Apalfalaya farmer?"

"Brains before honor!" Pearl Hand barked crisply.

Again heads nodded.

I summed it all up. "If you do this, manage to mislead the enemy, we will have a chance to kill them all. But if any of you can't hold your temper, if any of you accepts a fight, or steals, or in any way provokes the Kristianos, you personally will be responsible for our ultimate defeat and the deaths of your families."

I paused, my gaze going from man to man. "Do all of you understand the gravity of what we're about?"

"Yes, Ahltakla!" came their bellowed reply.

Under my breath, I whispered, "May Horned Serpent grant us the strength and cunning."

"Ittihallali," my brother responded fervently. *May it be so!*

In the following six days I went two times to Chicaza town, once on my own to monitor the first Chicaza who went to trade and scout the Kristianos. My hope was that my presence would ensure good behavior. Tishu Minko Red Cougar picked his men well; they acted with reserve but couldn't hide the wonder in their eyes as they inspected the cabayos up close, gasped at the glass beads and *hierro* awls and chisels they were given. Hardjawed, they said nothing about their clan houses, stripped of the guardian posts and the totem images that had once blessed them. The Kristianos treated their visitors to food and sent the Chicaza packing in good spirits—completely unaware that what had posed as Chicaza curiosity had been a complete reconnaissance by abetuskas.

Or so I hoped.

For the second time, de Soto sent a cabayo for me. While my trepidation about mounting the beast had diminished, no shortage of fears cascaded through my souls: *A Chicaza has killed a Kristiano outside de Soto's front door; he has discovered our plan; he's going to demand our women now; Antonio figured out I'm Concho Negro . . .* Or any number of other disasters.

As I rode back, my face thickly painted in white and blue, Pearl Hand followed again on the litter, and poor Two Packs trotted along beside. I took a small number of blooded warriors, bearing packs of meat, as an escort; their orders were to run like the wind and scatter at the first sign of trouble. Someone needed to get word back to the high minko if war came sooner than expected.

The ride was cold. A hard wind came blowing down from the north and made a tearing sound as it whipped the branches back and forth. The trees groaned with each new gust. And twigs clattered down around us along with other bits of detritus.

At Chicaza town, we were escorted to the tchkofa. My heart pounding, I touched my chin as Ortiz stepped out, his bearded face and brown eyes impassive.

"Greetings, Ishto Minko," was translated by Two Packs. Pearl Hand stood behind me, her face as impassive as usual. She kept her arms crossed, and I knew that her right hand grasped the stiletto up her left sleeve.

"Greetings, Ortiz. I was asked to visit you. I hope there is no problem?"

He gave me a faint, almost mocking smile. "The *Adelantado* has questions." He extended an arm, gesturing for me to enter.

I glimpsed his expression as Pearl Hand passed. Ortiz couldn't hide his dismay, and I fought a grin as he cringed back, fearing to be too close to such an evil-polluted witch.

As gloomy as it was outside, the interior of the tchkofa

reminded me of a cave. The slant of midday light through the smoke hole illuminated the northern floor, where de Soto sat in conference with his *capitanes*. Moscoso, Gallegos, Nuño, and the rest were gathered around in a ring. As I approached I saw that they'd ripped up the matting to expose dirt. What looked to be a map had been scratched into the clay.

When I stopped before them, the combined stench of their unwashed bodies rose. I tried not to breathe through my nose or make a face.

De Soto looked up, speaking. Two Packs translated, "Good day, High Minko. We thank you for coming on such short notice and hope it was not an inconvenience."

I touched my chin and experienced the same twinge of revulsion the gesture always cost me. I hoped the smile I forced didn't reflect either my fear or my disgust. "With two dangerous armies in close proximity, and with peace so newly made between us, a prudent leader is always wary and alert, *Adelantado*. Is there a problem?"

We traded gazes, the soulless brown eyes offering nothing, his lips barely twitching behind his mustache. I noticed a smudge of charcoal on the side of his protruding nose. The Monster inside was coiled but restrained today. Finally, breaking the impasse, he offered a faint smile.

Oh, yes, we both know that we're playing for time. Neither one of us is fooling the other.

The *capitanes*, too, seemed to feel it. They glanced back and forth between de Soto and me, eyes reserved, expressions thoughtful. The exchange affirmed what I already knew: They despised me and the Chicaza, having already discounted any threat we might be to them.

Good. Continue to think that.

De Soto gestured at the map they'd drawn on the floor. "*Cacique*, we are considering what we know of your country. Coming from a distant land, we are ignorant of so many things. We would consider it a kindness if you would tell us about the Nations surrounding the Chicaza."

I nodded, aware of someone entering from outside. As they made a space for me, I knelt, catching a glimpse of the newcomer: Antonio!

I paid him not the least bit of attention, battling to keep my expression calm as I studied the map. Pearl Hand and Two Packs crowded in behind me, both staring down.

Moscoso pointed with a long *hierro* knife as he spoke, the Cofitachequi translating to Two Packs, who translated to me. "This is Apafalaya and its river. Here we have your Chicaza. Just east here, this is the river where we fought your squadron. We call it the Chicaza River."

I nodded. "What do you wish to know?"

"What peoples are in these areas to the south, west, and north?"

I pointed to the north. "There, perhaps ten days' travel through hills and forests, you will find the great bend of the Tenasee River. That is the land of the western Yuchi Nation. They are currently allied with the Kaskinampo to their north."

I pointed to the northwest of the dot they'd made to indicate Chicaza town. "You have met Fire Tail, the Alibamo mikko. His town is there. Beyond it to the west-northwest and ten days' journey through barren forest, you will find the Quizquiz Nation, composed of five or six large towns on this side of the Father Water."

"What is that?"

"A great river so huge it is impossible to swim." I pointed to the south of Quizquiz. "Dominating the bluffs to the south you will find the Quigualtam alliance of the Natchez Nation. The Natchez are a prosperous and numerous people, their bottomland rich with wild foods and the uplands filled with fertile soils. We have a great deal of respect for the Natchez."

"And down here?" Moscoso pointed with his knife to the area southwest of Chicaza town.

"That is the Kallolosa Nation. It's a collection of Choctaw towns governed by High Minko Kallolosa. His name means 'Hard Black' because the ancestor who first took the name and founded the Nation donned the color of death before every war."

"How far?" de Soto asked.

"Perhaps five days through rolling wooded country, most of it old growth and passable by cabayos."

"You are at war with them?" Gallegos asked.

"Off and on. Chicaza and Choctaw are descended from the same people. We share many beliefs."

"Five days?" de Soto asked thoughtfully as he stared at the map, his chin resting on his hand. "Moscoso?" he asked, and there followed a rapid-fire exchange of *español*.

I'd been so engrossed, I'd forgotten that Antonio was standing in the rear, watching with a collection of *soldados* and cabayeros.

A decision made, de Soto raised his eyes to mine. "I would like to send a party to Caluza." He couldn't quite manage the correct pronunciation of Kallolosa. "High Minko, would you be willing to lead me and a squadron of my cabayos there?"

I considered it for a moment. He might be halving his forces? And he wanted me along? I inclined my head, saying, "I thank you for the kind offer, but I should remain in Chicaza to ensure that none of my people get into trouble with yours. Our peace is still too fragile. A simple misunderstanding that might be smoothed over by my presence might grow out of control."

He gave me that half-lidded and emotionless look that was anything but benevolent. De Soto, I was coming to understand, was at his most dangerous when he gave you that empty-eyed look.

"I understand. Could you, however, provide guides and interpreters for the journey? Trusted men who would allow us to approach the Caluza in peace and without misunderstanding?"

I gave him a compliant smile. "Such persons can be had. I, and they, will expect compensation for such services."

De Soto's smile thinned. "What did you have in mind?"

I glanced at Moscoso. "The blade, what do you call it? *Hierro?* It is a fine piece."

As this was translated, I watched Moscoso's expression tighten. He shook his head, hand protectively clasping the leather hilt. In the end he relented when de Soto matter-of-factly added something else. I caught the word *"matarlo."* It meant "kill him."

Moscoso gave de Soto a weary nod. The way he smiled at me as he handed over the blade did nothing to hide his complete hatred.

I admired the knife in the slanted light and said, *"Adelantado,* how soon do you want your guides and interpreters? I shall send four deer to High Minko Kallolosa first thing tomorrow under the White Arrow and inform him of your imminent arrival."

It was only later, when we were on the trail home, that I motioned Pearl Hand's litter up even with my plodding cabayo. "What did they say?"

She gave me a ravishing smile. "They are looking for land to build into a Nation. Gold was only mentioned once. Instead, their conversations were centered on finding a fertile farmland with access to the sea. They do not believe the Father Water is as large as you say it is but wonder if their large boats might float up it. Their new goal is to visit as many places as they can, learn the land

and peoples, then they will pick one to finally conquer to build their Kristiano Nation."

"I see."

She gave me a penetrating look. "They are more dangerous now. When they find the right place, they *will* stay."

"How? Had they not left Apalachee, we'd have beaten them eventually. De Soto knows that."

She nodded. "He has another reason for visiting all the peoples he can: He's looking for allies. He and Gallegos discussed this briefly, but I got the gist of it. De Soto believes that he can use *indío* Nations against each other. Moscoso asked him if he planned to use *indíos* to fight other *indíos* as he did when he defeated a great Nation called the Inca, in a land called Peru. De Soto said that same strategy would work here, too."

"If we have a fault, it's that we'd rather fight among ourselves than against him." I groused in irritation. "And Moscoso's hesitation about gifting me with your new knife?"

"Mine?"

"To replace that bone stiletto."

She gave me a thin smile, amplified by her black and white "Death Speaker" face paint. "De Soto told him not to worry, that eventually the *capitán* would get it back . . . from off your body when de Soto finally kills you."

She caught the knife when I tossed it over to her.

"There." I growled. "As long as you stay alive, I guess old Moscoso is going to be disappointed."

She fingered the long gleaming blade, tested the balance in her hand. The piece was beautiful, long and sharp on both edges, a much better blade than the one she'd taken off the guard she'd killed back in Uzita town. Flowery hand guards made an S shape and the handle was soft leather. A round knob topped the handle and was made of some yellowish metal. I assume it wasn't gold or Moscoso wouldn't have allowed de Soto to talk him out of it.

Lifting the blade before her, dark eyes thoughtful, Pearl Hand softly murmured, "You never know. I might just give this back to him one day. And in a most unpleasant way."

THIRTY-FIVE

MOSCOSO DIDN'T HAVE TIME TO FRET OVER HIS MISS-ing knife. Two days later my brother the high minko, Pearl Hand, Tishu Minko Red Cougar, and I watched Capitán Moscoso and forty cabayeros, guided by an escort of ten Chicaza warriors, take the southeastern trail toward Kallolosa.

"Despite the high minko's warning, I hope the Choctaw are ready for this," Red Cougar said under his breath. "Not that I have much love for the Choctaw, but even the Kallolosa deserve better than what they're about to get."

"Being run down by a cabayo and made captive changes your perspective, doesn't it?" I gave him a side-long glance and enjoyed the distasteful expression with which he watched the departing Kristianos.

He told us, "I remember the impact . . . my body fly-ing. Next thing I knew I was in Chicaza town with a *hierro* chain around my neck. Before I even could get my souls back, that Apafalaya slave was asking me who I was, where I came from."

I shared a grim smile with him. "I had to starve and work for them for a quarter moon before Pearl Hand got me out. You were lucky, Tishu Minko."

He nodded. "My honor and my life are yours, alok."

The last of the cabayeros vanished into the forest, and we turned, heading back to Black Oak town. As soon as the Kristianos were out of sight, work parties back in the forest behind town began chopping. They were using new Kristiano axes made of *hierro*. Not only did the things cut like a rabid beaver, but the novelty of them led to plenty of volunteers to work on the cabayo traps being laid out back in the trees.

After all, de Soto knew exactly where we were. He could destroy Black Oak town on a whim, and there was nothing we could do to stop him. The only recourse we had was to evacuate the town. Flee to the forest, and hopefully lead the pursuing cabayeros into the traps. If successful, we'd kill a couple of the cabayos and maybe their riders, meanwhile buying time for other Chicaza to make their escape.

"I have an idea," my brother said thoughtfully as he walked, hands clasped behind him, head down. The winter sunlight played on his bear-hide cloak and winked in his copper ear spools. "We've already dismissed the notion of attacking them while Moscoso's cabayeros are gone."

Pearl Hand snorted derisively. "The remaining seventy or so cabayeros would be more than a match for your squadrons. If you could get through them, the *soldados* could hold Chicaza town even without the help of the cabayeros."

"I understand, Minko Pearl Hand." He slowed, giving us a sidelong glance. "But what if we could halve their forces? Lure a large part of their army away? Keep them on the trail for perhaps a half moon? In that time one of the two forces might let their guard down."

Red Cougar grunted to himself, then added, "I've been to Chicaza town a couple of times since the peace. Our people have done their job well. I see Kristianos relaxing. Maybe too much so since they no longer seem to be worrying about the tracks we leave around their houses at night."

"De Soto isn't relaxing," Pearl Hand told us. "The *Adelantado* may say all the right things, offer gifts, and act grateful for the things we do, but I can't help wondering who is fooling whom. Curse the man for a seer, but he knows we are playing him."

"He knows," I agreed, voice flat.

"Explain?" my brother prompted as we stopped before the Chief Clan house.

"Like Pearl Hand says, it's in his eyes, the set of his mouth, the faint amusement he hides behind that beard. Brother, I've been a trader for years. I've been bargaining, reading people's faces, judging the depths of their wants and desires. A good trader develops a sense of when a deal is turning sour, or when he can ask for just a little more. It's part of the Power of trade. My intuition tells me that de Soto is playing with us the way a boy teases a snapping turtle in a wooden cage. Miscalculate and you can lose a couple of fingers; in the end, however, it is inevitable: The turtle's going to be dropped in the stew pot."

My brother nodded and kicked at one of the balls of cabayo manure left by the departing riders. Once the very sight of it had triggered panic deep in my souls. Now I thought of it as a nuisance. Worse, for some perverted reason I couldn't get my head around, Bark *ate* the stuff. Good thing he'd become Pearl Hand's dog.

"What would be tempting enough to induce them to split their forces?" Red Cougar asked.

"A chance to go make war on someone," Pearl Hand told him. "It would have to be someplace he hasn't been, and in a different direction than he's heading. Just like with the Choctaw down south, we need someplace that increases his knowledge of the land and peoples."

"You are sure?" the high minko asked.

Pearl Hand's eyes narrowed in thought. "Everything changed after Mabila. His men have come to the conclusion that they are not going to be rich from gold and jewels as happened in this far-off Peru. Now the Monster tells them that they are going to own land. Much land. And *indios* are going to be the slaves to farm it ... to build them great houses and become their property. I have heard the *soldados* discussing how they will all become *hidalgos*."

"Become ... what?" I asked.

"*Hidalgos.* Like minkos. De Soto is promising them that they will be lords."

"Does he think Chicaza will be the center of his new Nation?" the high minko asked.

Her gaze narrowed. "Not for the moment. Having knowledge of what is behind them in the east, most are intensely curious about unknown lands in the west. They speculate that somewhere out there may be another Mexico. A place of stone cities, gold, and glory. But if there is not, an empire of giant farms will satisfy them."

"I'm thinking about this idea of splitting their forces," I said. "And I think, yes, de Soto will volunteer part of his army for a raid on a recalcitrant town. He'll do it because it will take him someplace new, keep his *soldados* occupied, and give him the chance to show us how invincible Kristianos are. A way to intimidate us, keep us in our place, if you will."

Pearl Hand was giving me her skeptical look, one eyebrow arched. "He already suspects your motives."

"Of course. But if you and I go with him, he'll expect that I'm doing the same thing Tuskaloosa did: luring him into a trap."

Red Cougar cried, "That's exactly what you're doing! Why does this not reassure me?"

"Because Pearl Hand and I are a distraction. The real target is Chicaza town and the *soldados* he leaves behind, the ones who will be delighted to have him gone. The lazy ones who let their guard down. If the Chicaza squadrons are kept ready, and the right storm, or moonless night, or thick fog rolls in, and the Kristianos are asleep at their posts—"

Red Cougar clapped his hands. "We rush the town and destroy them." He hesitated. "But what about you? Eventually the Monster is going to discover the truth. And he'll still have half of his army . . . with you and a couple of Chicaza squadrons at his mercy."

"Pearl Hand and I expect to die." I raised my hands helplessly. "Who knows? Perhaps Power will find a way to save us as it did at Napetuca and Mabila."

"The hard part, brother, is that you'll have to crush his force at Chicaza town and then march like mad to meet de Soto as he returns. You dare not attack him in open country. If you can't ambush him in rough terrain, filled with brush and downed timber, withdraw. Your other choice is to attack in a swampy backwater where the cabayos can't maneuver."

"Even then it will be bloody," Pearl Hand told them, a chill in her voice. "Very, very bloody."

I took a breath, adding, "Kristianos never die easily."

Red Cougar, always practical, asked, "And if de Soto makes it back before we can set an ambush?"

"Scatter the people throughout the wilderness areas. Have them hide in the deepest thickets. De Soto and the surviving Kristianos are going to be enraged. Every town will be burned; any Chicaza they encounter will be enslaved. Your only hope is to sneak close at night and shoot arrows into their camp. Then, when they finally march, ambush their route. Use the forest against them. Deadfalls, pits, set fire to the meadows—anything to harass and delay them."

"First and foremost," Pearl Hand said insistently, "kill the cabayos. Once the cabayeros are on foot, we are evenly matched. True, they are protected by armor, but we are fleet of foot, darting and mobile. Stand back and shower the Kristianos with arrows; eventually you will win."

My brother took a moment to study Black Oak town, taking in the houses with wreaths of blue rising from the smoke holes. A soft staccato of *thump-thumps* could be heard as women milled corn in log mortars. Dogs lazed in the sun, and two old men were flaking out arrow points beneath the nearest ramada. They were telling stories, grinning toothlessly, and happy. A group of young boys were being instructed in the fine art of chunkey over by the World Tree.

I knew what Choctaw Hair was seeing, thinking: All of this would be destroyed if we made a single mistake.

I made my point perfectly clear. "The trick is to fight smart."

"Brains before honor." He smiled wistfully, a sadness in his eyes.

"And," Pearl Hand repeated, "expect it to be bloody."

From the time we thought up the plan to the day that I rode out of Chicaza town at the head of more than two hundred warriors took no more than ten days. To my complete surprise, de Soto took the bait after hardly any consultation with his *capitanes*.

My pitch had been: "*Adelantado*, one of my minkos has decided to use your arrival as the opportunity to declare his independence. He refuses to send tribute, believing that I will not spare warriors to march on his towns. Perhaps you would care to accompany me with a party of your cabayeros and *soldados*? Consider it an opportunity to demonstrate our current alliance." I'd smiled. "Of course, any captives that you might take—including the women— would be yours to keep."

"Where is this unruly chief?" His half-lidded eyes had met mine, the brown gaze reflecting no passion or curiosity. I could not but wonder if he and I had *any* similarity of emotion, feeling, or compassion.

"A series of small towns and villages south-southeast of here on what you call the Chicaza River. The people are Albaamaha but until now have subjected themselves to the Chicaza Nation. Their capital is Sakchomasha town. Translated, it means 'Where the water moccasin strikes.'"

"How far?"

"Five days by hard march cross-country. Seven if we follow the easier trail south along the river."

Sakchomasha—which the Kristianos, forever unable to pronounce our words, called "Sacchuma"—was home to Mikko Lashka. Lashka's Albaamaha already had plans to relocate the town in the fall. The aging buildings and half-rotten fortifications could be easily sacrificed. The fields were playing out after nearly twenty years of continuous cultivation. Situated as it was on the lower Tombigbee River, the location was far enough away that de Soto would have no idea what was happening back in Chicaza town.

We met de Soto's force outside of Chicaza town: thirty cabayeros and perhaps another eighty *soldados* followed by fifty converted *indios* of various nationalities, and the assorted camp tenders and slave women.

Pearl Hand and I each rode on a litter, borne side by side in advance of our force. Our faces were painted in red and black, the colors of war. Marching in their ranks, two squadrons of Chicaza tramped behind us. The warriors carried wooden and wicker shields, their shoulders plumed in feather sprays from woodpeckers or raptors, each depending upon his personal Power. Most wore a leather helmet—protection against blows from war clubs—and a chest protector. Their forearms were encased in heavy leather arm guards.

Each squadron was preceded by a standard bearer who carried a long pole upon which perched the clan totem. Immediately behind Pearl Hand and me marched the Wildcat Clan, their totem being a clawing bobcat. Behind them came the Hawk Clan, a great red-tailed hawk, its wings spread, talons grasping, atop their pole.

Two steps behind the totem bearer came the hetissu who would carry orders from me or Pearl Hand to the abetuskas. The latter marched in the first rank of warriors, his head adorned with his clan totem.

I made the motion and our scouts trotted out ahead, leading the way. What would have taken no more than three easy days by following the main trail we would cover in five by a snaking pattern of alternate routes. This deception would be a tricky business. The terrain had to be hard on the cabayos without appearing to be excessively so or de Soto—who'd been misled by every *indio* he'd met in our world—would recognize the sham immediately. The Kristianos, of course, would mark their trail so they could find their way back to Chicaza in case we abandoned them or they killed us.

Even as we were leaving Chicaza, runners were on the way to Sakchomasha to order the evacuation of the town. Lashki's Albaamaha needed to make it look like a rushed, last-instant affair with spilled baskets, hastily broken pots, and the fires still warm.

We would let the Kristianos loot the town and burn it. Mission accomplished, we'd start back to Chicaza town, following the arduous route back through the forest. If the Kristianos made a mistake, lowered their guard, or grew careless, my two squadrons—composed of roughly two hundred warriors—would seize the opportunity to attack.

What de Soto didn't know—and the fact on which Pearl Hand and I pinned our hopes of success—was that four additional squadrons of Chicaza warriors were marching a parallel course to ours. Their scouts were watching every step we took, relaying messages back to the abetuskas. At my signal, they'd deploy, ready to strike de Soto's rear like a great hammer.

"We are committed," Pearl Hand called from her litter. I could see the worry in her eyes, in the tense set of her shoulders.

I glanced back just before we entered the trees. De Soto and Ortiz rode at the head of the cabayeros, lances held high. The weak sun glinted off their tarnished armor. Behind came the *soldados,* tramping along, helmets bobbing, shields and packs over their backs, spear-axes like a prickly forest. The converted slaves behind them bore food and whatever supplies had been determined necessary.

Behind us, Chicaza town lay beneath a blue veil of wood smoke. Collections of *soldados* and cabayeros stood at the town's edge watching the departure of their friends. I could barely make out their distant waves of farewell. Even as I watched, they began to trickle back into the town. My fervent hope was that the next time I saw the place, it would be a blackened ruin, strewn with their bodies.

I chewed my lip as the trees obscured the view. From here on out, everything depended on good sense, skill, and no small measure of luck.

"Do you think we'll have a chance?" Pearl Hand called to me.

I shook my head, remembering the look in de Soto's eyes. "He knows it's a trap."

"Then why is he playing along?"

"Because the *Adelantado* expects us to make the mistake. He's betting we'll give him the opportunity to kill us or take us prisoner. If we have any advantage here, it's because he thinks he's the target."

She gave me that slit-eyed knowing look. "Then let us pray the men he left back there in Chicaza town think the same thing. They always get lazy when the *Adelantado* isn't around."

"It's a slim hope to gamble so much on."

Her expression pinched. "We're also betting on your high minko brother and Red Cougar."

"How's that?"

"We're taking on faith that they have the sense to know when, or even if, an attack on Chicaza town is feasible."

I barely nodded as the forest closed around us.

THIRTY-SIX

I THOUGHT THE MARCH TO SAKCHOMASHA WAS A masterpiece. Our scouts, understanding the importance of their work, led us through tough country and did it with a brilliance that I fondly admired. As rough as the going was, they always managed to skirt impassable swamp, the worst of the blow-down, and the thickest of the brush. The route they created even appeared to me to be the best path through swampy bottoms, up and down timbered ridges, across blow-downs, and over creeks.

Not only that, at sunrise and sunset, when our direction was most apparent, they kept us heading south-southwest. I could determine nothing that would have tipped de Soto off about our deception.

Each night we camped apart, my squadrons separated from the Kristianos by several bow-shots. The going was hard enough that warriors and Kristianos pretty much ate, collapsed, and slept.

Each night I stalked out far enough from camp to see that the cabayos stood with hanging heads—and that was after their riders had spent the day dismounting and walking the beasts through the boggy bottoms, around stacks of deadfall, or up the steep slopes.

On the fifth night—not much to my surprise—de Soto summoned me to his camp. As Ortiz waited impatiently with his Cofitachequi translator, Pearl Hand and I painted our faces. Two Packs crossed his thick arms, tapped his toe, and looked nervously at Ortiz.

De Soto's Cofitachequi translator didn't look happy; the man's eyes kept shifting to the brooding forest surrounding us. I understood his worry—and de Soto's, too.

You couldn't pick a better place for ambush.

The scouts had encamped us atop a densely forested ridge capped by a tangle of second-growth timber. Some time past—perhaps thirty or forty summers ago—a great storm had toppled the old mature forest. Perhaps a tornado? Some hurricane that blew up from the gulf? Who knew, but if I extended my arms I still couldn't measure the diameter of the decomposing tree trunks that littered the ground even after years of rot.

The current canopy hung low, vines twining up into the gum, maple, cedar, and oak that had sprung up when the forest floor had been suddenly opened to sunshine. Looking between the stems, trunks, and vines, a person couldn't see more than a pebble's toss in any direction.

An entire army could be hidden no more than half a bow-shot away.

The place had no graze for cabayos, just a thick and moldy leaf mat broken by a crisscross of rot-soft, damp, moss-covered logs. While I wasn't sure if the heartless Kristianos cared if their cabayos ate, I suspected they were really worried about the dense thicket in which we camped—and the disposition, let alone the numbers, of us *indios sucios* who might be creeping up on them.

If I'd been de Soto, I would have called for me, too.

Even as Two Packs, Pearl Hand, I, and a couple of runners approached their camp I could tell that the Kristianos were in no kind of jovial mood. The men looked muddy, worn, and fatigued. On the other hand, alert guards had been placed around the perimeter, and the fires were laid out in defensive circles. Despite their fatigue, the Kristianos were busy hacking at trees and brush as they fortified their position.

Ortiz led us through the camps. Kristianos paused in their labor to give us hard looks; they fingered their axes suggestively as we passed. I told Pearl Hand, "I'm not seeing any vulnerabilities here, are you?"

She responded, "The *Adelantado* is keeping his guard up. They're holding the cabayos in the center of camp, knowing they can't use them in this kind of cover."

De Soto's sole surviving tent stood just in front of where the cabayos milled behind a circular enclosure of rope. Made of their wonderful canvas, it appeared to be sewn together from unburned pieces salvaged from Mabila.

Ortiz stopped before the awning and announced that he'd brought the *"Chicaza cacique y la bruja."*

Within moments, de Soto and Nuño stepped out. The Monster wore his armor, his open-faced helmet clamped on his head. Canvas pants covered his legs, and everything was smudged, streaked, and filthy from days of travel through forest and swamp. Mud even caked the tall black boots that rose to the man's knee.

For a long moment, de Soto pinned me with a look that reeked of absolute loathing. Smoldering anger reflected in the hard set of his mouth and deepened the lines around his protruding nose. Whatever warped excuse of a soul burned inside him was coiled and ready to strike.

Careful, Black Shell.

Though I didn't need a translation of his barked demand of "When will we arrive at Sacchuma?" I waited until it was translated.

Instead of answering, I bent down and clawed back the thick leaf mat. Two Packs, catching my meaning, helped until we'd exposed bare earth. With a punky stick I drew a line. "Here is what you call Chicaza River." I made a hole on the west bank. "This is Sakchomasha." To the west of Sakchomasha I drew a half circle and poked a dot in its middle. "We are here, atop this ridge, hidden in the forest."

Rising, I slapped the dirt and leaves from my hands and gave de Soto a hard look. "Or would you have preferred to camp down in the open where the Albaamaha would undoubtedly discover us, run to their leaders, and alert them to our imminent arrival?"

De Soto glared at the map, then me, and then the map again. He stepped past me. My nose crinkled at the stench of his unwashed body, now worse than ever. He cocked his head, looking at the maze of trees in which we'd camped. Extending an arm, he gestured around at the growing gloom. His voice a threatening hiss, he said, "An army of Chicaza could be creeping up on us as we speak. You might have led us into a trap. If that is the case . . ."

"I might have," I replied easily as I looked out at the maze of vegetation. "If I were an Albaamaha seeking to kill Kristianos, I would choose just such a place. Fortunately we are surrounded by Chicaza scouts who will ensure that no one sneaks up on us in the night."

Even as that was being translated, I added, "You do not understand our ways, *Adelantado*. We are on a battle walk, allies on the way to attack Sakchomasha." I didn't lie when I told him, "We take battle walks very seriously. Nor do we underestimate our enemies, no matter who they might be."

He muttered under his breath as this, too, was translated, the deadly flatness cooling behind his pupils. His words came slowly, precisely.

Ortiz said, "The *Adelantado* wonders if, given the truth

of your words, you would be his guest this night. Since, if your words are true, there is no danger of an attack on your own forces, either."

Under his predatory look, I turned to Pearl Hand, asking, "What do you think?"

She glanced at de Soto, who stiffened slightly, distaste expressed by his thinning lips. Perhaps as much as I hated his deadly stare, he equally disliked being studied by a witch?

Her eyebrow arched. "We must be very careful."

Understating the obvious, are we, wife?

Aloud I said, "Death Speaker and I will accept the *Adelantado*'s hospitality. As long as he understands that tomorrow morning, before dawn, we are moving down, off this ridge, to attack Sakchomasha town before they can discover us. Like the *Adelantado*, I have no desire to fight Albaamaha in this place."

Again, as this was being translated, I added, "And I hope the *Adelantado* understands that if Death Speaker and I do not return to my squadrons in the morning, they will misinterpret your 'hospitality.'" I gestured again at the gloomy forest depths surrounding us. "Not the best of places for misunderstandings."

I watched de Soto grind his teeth, the muscles in his jaws hollowing his thin, already hatchetlike cheeks. The promise—lying like fire behind his narrowed eyes—was one of terrible retribution. But was he angry with me for standing up to him, or at himself for allowing a filthy *indio cacique* so much leeway?

My guts squirmed at the implications.

"We understand each other," Ortiz told his translator, who told Two Packs. I waited, acting my part, and touched my chin.

From the corner of my mouth, I murmured, "Wife, if you hear the first hint of treason in their talks, let me know."

"Oh, yes. But if they catch me by surprise, you'll know something's wrong when I drive my knife into the closest man's chest."

"Let's hope it doesn't come to that. I'll stay close to the Monster, just in case."

I studied de Soto's armored body. This time I had one of the *hierro* axes they'd traded to us. On the all-too-probable chance that this turned sour, I'd get a single chance to drive my ax into his face.

"I'll kill Ortiz," Two Packs told me at the same time he gave the man his best smile.

Turning to one of the runners, I said, "Inform the abetuskas that we're spending the night here. Keep everyone on alert, scouts in the trees, and the moment we're taken or killed, they are to attack. If we are not allowed to leave by morning, the squadrons are to fade into the timber, re-form, and call for reinforcements. Just remember: brains before honor."

"Yes, Ishto Minko." The man touched his forehead and trotted away. He might have been winding his way through denned rattlesnakes the way he skirted the Kristiano camps.

I thought it an apt comparison as we were seated for a supper consisting of boiled corn and some kind of dried meat that I suspected was *puerco*. Mint tea became dessert.

Through it all, de Soto and I eyed each other, passing glances back and forth that no amount of dissembling discussion could discount. The hatred between us was like a thing alive, pulsing and violent. Mine because of the misery and anguish he'd unleashed from the moment he set foot on our land. And his because . . .

"Why does he hate me so?" I asked out of the corner of my mouth. "Because he smells like rancid oil soaked in cloth while I bathe every day? Or is it something else?"

Pearl Hand gave a sharp, evil-sounding laugh, the kind filled with bitter understanding. "He hates you because you're meaningless in his world, Black Shell. To him you are nothing more than a pesky mosquito, a simple bug. But for the moment, he must elevate you, play to the illusion that you're important. It doesn't matter that dealing with you is part of the game, a matter of convenience to keep the Chicaza peaceful. What angers him is that he has to do it at all."

"That smacks of soul sickness."

"How would you feel if you had to treat a leech as an equal? Or give sham respect to an intestinal worm? Invite such a thing to share your meal, when all you want to do is step on it?"

"Even leeches and worms have their place."

"In your world, yes." Pearl Hand shot me a warning look. "What you don't understand, probably will never understand, is that it's all about *him*. The Monster doesn't see this world; he *owns* it. And if he doesn't it's only because he hasn't *taken* it yet. Nothing else matters. Only his ambition, his strength, and his constant need for gratification."

A chill ran through me as I shot a sidelong glance at de Soto. "What you're saying is that he's an abomination. A creature driven only by malicious desires and appetites."

"We have a term for such perverted beings," she reminded me.

Witch! I swallowed hard, my appetite fading.

Finally, as one of the slave women cleared away the wooden dishes, I forced myself to address de Soto. "*Adelantado?* What does our world have that your home . . . this Cuba, of which you talk . . . and Peru, do not?"

He studied me thoughtfully, made a dismissive gesture with his hand, and said, "What can it hurt to tell you? In España, where I was born, it is a poor land, of dry soils and little rain. In the new world, those who will seize opportunity will found dynasties. God rewards those who fight for him." He glanced at the priest, who crouched at a distant fire, and added, "I am his warrior, his right arm and sharp sword. He has brought me here, to fight in his name. I will not rest until this entire demonic world is *catolico*."

"Your god has appeared to you? Told you this?"

When this was translated, he gave me an indulgent smile. "I know this by the grace *dios* has given me. He has heard my prayers and seen my devotion. From the moment I dedicated myself to his service, he has given me victory over my enemies. Seen me through every trial."

"So, you are the chosen?"

He gave me a thin smile, eyelids lowered with satisfaction. *"Sí."*

Under her breath, Pearl Hand murmured, "If that's true we are all better off dying than allowing his god so much as a foothold in our world."

"¿Qué?" de Soto asked, a distasteful look on his long face.

I said, "Death Speaker was remarking on why your god chose you, *Adelantado*. Among our peoples, the nature of the messenger is part of the message itself." *So what kind of god puts an abomination like you at the head of a terrible army?*

He turned his languid eyes on mine. "Enemies and demons are everywhere. Some even here, at our fire tonight, *cacique*. Whatever it takes to defeat them, I will do. Praise be to God."

I steepled my fingers. "And what happens if your god loses? Will he abandon you? Or let you find another Power to serve? Perhaps this *diablo*?"

It was an easy question, a simple question. The sort any hopaye or hilishaya would have asked. After all, the Spirit world was a place of ebbing and flowing Power. If service in the name of white Power didn't work out, a person tried the red. If the Powers of the Sky World proved ineffective, one could tap those of the Underworld. If calling on animal Powers wasn't getting the job done, we'd seek something in the plant world. Everything was balance. Nothing was absolute.

"*¡Sacrilegio!*" He leaped to his feet. In the camps surrounding us, men straightened, making the crisscross over their breasts.

Had I somehow touched a nerve? I raised my hands in a deprecating gesture, touching my chin in an effort to ameliorate the damage before Pearl Hand decided she had to knife the nearest Kristiano out of desperation.

I was starting to feel sorry for Kristianos. Even a little bit for de Soto. The Monster thought he'd been chosen by his angry, desperate god to convert us. Surely he understood how ridiculous his quest was. Outside of military prowess and fancy trade goods, who in his right mind would subject themselves to his bitter and selfish deity?

No wonder de Soto was such a twisted and soul-sick monster.

"Perhaps something was improperly translated," I said easily, aware that a rabid gleam had grown behind de Soto's normally flat brown eyes. His hand was gripping his sword, the blade half-drawn from the scabbard.

The Cofitachequi was anxiously translating Two Packs's words into broken Kristiano. I thought he was stumbling over the words, repeating himself, and licking his lips too much.

De Soto cursed under his droopy mustache, slammed his sword back into the scabbard, and said, "*Indio,* you do not call upon *el diablo*! Never! Not in my presence. There is only the one god, the true god! Anything else is *blasfemia*! And I *won't* hear it!"

"My apology." I made the "it is finished" hand sign. Deciding to stay away from the incomprehensible Kristiano religion, I added, "Your god is your own."

That burning glow behind his eyes seemed to increase as he added something under his breath and ground his jaws.

"Remember," Pearl Hand cautioned me, her dark eyes on de Soto, who for once glared back at her, "it's all about him, his wants and wishes, his satisfaction and gratification. Nothing else really matters. Not his god. Not his king. Not even his men, or even, in the end, his life."

"*¿Qué es la problema?*" de Soto asked.

"Pus and blood," Pearl Hand whispered, "he's as incomprehensible as his god."

De Soto, however, had fixed his eerie witch-possessed eyes on me. He spoke for a moment, voice filled with terrible promise. Then, making an odd sniff as if he'd scented something unpleasant—maybe his own body odor?—he strode into his tent.

Ortiz gave us a curt nod, rose, and followed.

"What was that last?" I asked softly.

Pearl Hand told me, "He said 'You, *cacique,* and your Chicaza can either stand against me or surrender to me. One way you live, your soul saved by the true god. The other, you are dead and your soul is condemned to an endless fire."

I tossed a glance over my shoulder at the tent, a terrible fear stirring in my guts. His final words echoed between my souls, burned there by the man's hate, anger, and black loathing for me and everything in my world.

Pearl Hand whispered, "He is waiting to kill you, Black Shell. Not because you stand in his way, but simply because he has been forced to notice you. Just like our world. He wishes to conquer you . . . simply because you are here."

In a hollow voice, I whispered back, "I know."

THIRTY-SEVEN

WE FOLLOWED A GAME TRAIL OUT OF THE TREES AND into a series of fallow corn-and-bean fields. With the winter-gray forest behind us, the river to our right, Sakchomasha town lay directly ahead. A thin haze of blue smoke rose from the steeply pitched roofs and seemed to glow in the slanted morning light. Fingers of mist danced on the river's flat surface, silvered in the dawn. But for birdcalls, the morning was silent.

"Hetissus!" I called as my Chicaza emerged from the forest trail. "Order the abetuskas to form their squadrons."

"Form squadrons," they called, repeating the command.

I watched in pride as my Chicaza created two hollow boxes four ranks deep on a side, the archers in the middle as they nocked their arrows.

"One left and one right," I ordered. And the hetissus bellowed their commands. Without hesitation, the squadrons separated, leaving a space for the Kristianos to emerge into the frost-whitened field. And in that moment, it hit me: I was ordering Chicaza squadrons around just like a real high minko. For this Uncle had trained me. The sensation was awe inspiring.

The cabayeros filed out accompanied by a thumping of hooves, the cracking of timber, and the clank of metal. The animals huffed and whickered amid the clatter as they lined up in response to rolling *español* orders bellowed by Nuño de Tovar.

De Soto emerged in their rear as the cabayeros filed into lines in front of my squadrons. Through the gap now came the *soldados*, tramping in time to a drum, their shields clanking, wood knocking.

In the distance, I could see no change in Sakchomasha, but a faint cry carried across the distance. A flock of birds erupted from behind the town's palisade.

De Soto wheeled his cabayo around, shouting something.

Ortiz addressed the Cofitachequi, who asked Two Packs, "What next?"

"Advance," I replied, gesturing with my arm in a way that couldn't possibly be misinterpreted by anyone.

A trumpet blared and the cabayeros started off at a trot. Next a skirmish line of *soldados* clumped forward across the stubble fields and standing dead corn. I followed, the squadrons bringing up the rear.

The trumpet blared again and the cabayeros went pounding off, the ground shaking under their feet. The sound reminded me of a slow fading thunder. I took a moment to study the reaction of my squadrons. Oh, yes, they were impressed with the speed and fury, even as it receded.

As we proceeded across the fields, the cabayeros split in two, racing around the town walls, discovering what I knew they would: Sakchomasha was empty.

By the time we arrived, cabayeros had dismounted and

attacked the wooden gates with their *hierro* axes. The cord bindings for the door panels were no match for the keen-bitted tools. It took less time for the Kristianos to dismember the gates than it would have taken to muscle them open. A point not lost on the watching Chicaza.

I stopped the squadrons in the open before the gate and called orders to surround the town. At least I'd make it look like we were cutting off anyone's escape. Which we would have, had anyone been silly enough to disobey Mikko Laski's order to evacuate.

I returned to my hetissus and ordered, "Have the squadrons search the surrounding woods. Ensure that anyone they find turns and runs like a rabbit for the swamps and thick forest. I wouldn't want any of the curious to be captured. Tell them that we can't save them from slavery should that happen."

"Yes, Ishto Minko!"

The abetuskas broke the squadrons into companies that left at a trot for the trees. In the town I could hear wood breaking, the occasional pot being smashed. The ruination was accompanied by shouts of frustration alternating with those of delight as the Kristianos went searching for loot.

We waited perhaps a hand of time before Ortiz and the Cofitachequi translator came striding out. The bearded Kristiano gave me a grand beckoning wave, and I started forward with Two Packs and Pearl Hand behind me.

"The town is empty," Ortiz growled to the translators. "The *Adelantado* is concerned."

I studied Ortiz for a moment, then glanced around at the town and then the river where it roiled and sucked below the terrace to the east. Morning sunlight had turned its surface into burnished copper. Fingers of mist still lifted from the water.

"It would seem that Albaamaha scouts discovered our

advance. That we did not catch them by surprise is a disappointment. The town is the *Adelantado*'s to do with as he wishes."

Ortiz gave me the sort of flat stare that said, "You're a liar." Aloud he said, "Come. You can provide your 'gift' to the *Adelantado* in person."

We followed Ortiz through the gate, past ransacked houses with gaping doors. Images of Tailed Man had been torn from walls. Broken pottery, spilled corn, and overturned boxes emptied of their contents littered the ground.

In the plaza, de Soto wheeled his gray *cabayo*, trampling the chunkey court and leaving tracks on the stickball field as he shouted orders and pointed this way and that with his sword. Nuño de Tovar kept pace, often sidestepping on his *cabayo*, the beast's long tail sweeping as it pranced and clopped.

Again I admired the grace with which the Kristianos rode; their actions were one with the animal's. Given my few anxious and awkward travels atop one of the beasts, it all hinted of magic.

Ortiz stopped us at the edge of the plaza while riders and *soldados* appeared from between the buildings and shouted reports to de Soto.

Finally the *Adelantado* noticed us. His expression went grim as he directed his *cabayo* our way. Pulling up just ahead of us, his sword pointed like a sliver of ice at my chest. He addressed me in a rattling of *español*.

I could hear the anger in his voice.

What the Cofitachequi told me was, "The *Adelantado* has found no one in the town. Not even a sick old man or a blind woman. He thinks that you have misled him, brought him here, and warned these people to flee."

I tilted my head, looking up into his hot gaze as the *cabayo* clopped ever closer to me. "In the first place, the Albaamaha knew that if they did not send their tribute,

Chicaza might march against them. In the second, though we came as rapidly as we could, your Kristianos are slow and make a great deal of noise in the forest. And third, perhaps Sakchomasha had a spy, someone who sent a fast runner to warn them that I was marching with Kristianos." I gave him a grim smile. "And, knowing your reputation as fighters, perhaps they chose to run instead of face you."

His cabayo was crowding me, sidestepping, chewing at the *hierro* mouthpiece that de Soto kept sawing back and forth. Me, I didn't like being that close to such a big animal. If de Soto kicked it, the beast would flatten me. The smell of cabayo filled my nose, and I had to dodge my head to avoid its long muzzle. But I refused to give ground. The cabayo didn't seem to like it any more than I did.

"The *Adelantado* wonders if perhaps you have drawn him out here with the express purpose of separating him from his forces in order to ambush him in the forest. Perhaps in alliance with the very Albaamaha who live here."

As this was translated, de Soto and I glared at each other, the loathing and hatred barely contained. That I didn't give before his cabayo added to his anger.

I gritted my teeth, saying, "Tell the *Adelantado* that if he had any hesitation about splitting his forces, he could have brought them all *with him*! As to working with the Albaamaha"—I gestured vigorously, which made the cabayo shy back—"I *give* him Sakchomasha town to do with as he pleases. *Burn it* for all that I care."

And with that I pivoted on my heel and stalked away. The heat of de Soto's stare burned into the back of my neck. I listened, ears prickling, for the sudden hammering of hooves, the grunt of cabayo breath as the beast lunged for my back, but only de Soto's cursing could be heard.

Close, Black Shell.

The problem was, one of these times, one of us was going to push too far. It was now as inevitable as mosquitoes down on the coast.

"You almost got us killed just now," Pearl Hand said softly. "What you didn't hear was de Soto telling Ortiz how he ought to gut you on the spot. He said he has put up with your insolence long enough."

"Then why didn't he?"

"Ortiz counseled against it, reminding de Soto that he's separated from the rest of his army by rough country. Ortiz thinks that killing us would mean a running fight with the squadrons all the way back to Chicaza town." She gave me a sidelong glance. "De Soto's response was that he's going to wait for our ambush on the way home. That's when he's going to kill you."

I shook my head as we passed the last structure before reaching the gate. "I'll never attack Kristianos when they are expecting it."

Even as I said that, I glanced in the doorway of the women's house we were passing. Antonio emerged, a pile of fine flax-thread menstrual blankets in his arms. I could have told him they were tainted with the red chaos of female monthly bleeding. I could have explained that any contact with such taboo and polluted fabrics would sicken his soul, weaken his heart, and cause him to be shunned as unclean by male companions. Assuming, that is, that the pollution didn't kill him outright within the next moon.

Instead, he and I just locked eyes, and I saw him frown. His ruined face tensed, as though he were struggling with recognition. Then I saw him glance at Pearl Hand, puzzlement in his pursed lips.

Battling to keep my expression calm and tearing my gaze away, I tried to act as if he were just another Kristiano.

Had he recognized me? And if he realized that Pearl Hand and I weren't among the dead at Mabila, would his suspicions matter to de Soto—a man who already loathed and detested the game we were playing?

The fact is, I told myself, *we're all plunging headlong into a tornado of violence and death.*

THIRTY-EIGHT

DE SOTO BURNED SAKCHOMASHA TO THE GROUND. IF he expected some kind of outrage on our part, or if he sought to measure the extent of our hostility as he leveled the town, the results must have disappointed him. Since the town had been slated for abandonment, my Chicaza barely gave the flames a second thought.

As I turned my eyes back to the northwest and Chicaza town, I wondered what was happening there. My Kristianos weren't making mistakes. What about the ones in Chicaza town? Had they let their guard down? Even as I stared longingly across the distance, was Chicaza town burning? Were the disorganized Kristianos fleeing into the forests, or even better, lying dead and mutilated on the field of battle, the few survivors taken as captives?

Or did my brother and Red Cougar misread the signs, attack in vain, and suffer a horrible defeat?

The latter notion plagued me. After all, Kristianos always seemed to come through.

The march back to Chicaza town was a strained affair,

our scouts leading the way back along the same tortuous route. But we marched well in advance of the Kristianos this time, and each night the camps were located even farther apart.

Our scouts, sneaking close under cover of darkness, reported that de Soto kept his men on the alert, roving guards maintaining bright fires, their weapons close at hand.

The tension between the two groups was palpable; no illusions were left to either side.

On the third night, well after dark, a runner arrived from my brother.

"The high minko reports that the Kristianos in Chicaza town have maintained their discipline, Black Shell. Not only that, but the weather has been so pleasant, the nights clear and warm, that any attempt at infiltrating would have proven fruitless and dangerous."

I sighed, leaned back, and let the low fire warm my cold hands. "Once again, what we hoped the Kristianos would do and what they have done are two different things."

Pearl Hand gave me a wistful smile. "At least your brother disappointed me."

"Disappointed you?"

"I expected him to make some sort of suicidal attack in spite of your instructions. I'm delighted that he failed to live up to my expectations once again."

"I see . . . I think." A man is always happy when one of his relatives finally excels in his wife's eyes.

Pearl Hand continued. "Which leaves us with the problem of de Soto. He's still just as strong as he was and showing no sign of capitulation. If anything, he's more wary now than before we left for Sakchomasha."

I grunted my irritation. "If this trip has done anything, it's been to remove any doubt from either of us about the true nature of things. De Soto and I, we are like a raccoon and a water moccasin trapped in a storage pit."

"Explain that."

"He's the water moccasin and I'm the raccoon. He can strike at any time and kill me. But if he does, he knows he'll get scratched and bitten, perhaps fatally in the process. Meanwhile, I know that if I can just keep from getting bitten, eventually I can leap, bite him in the neck, and devour him."

"An apt description," she agreed, tilting her head back. I used the moment to admire the smooth hollows of her cheeks, the line of her jaw, and the way firelight reflected from the contours of her throat.

If only she and I could leave, wander away, spend the rest of our lives in some secluded—

Forcing myself back to reality, I studied the weary messenger, his clothing travel stained, twigs and debris in his hair. "Get some food and rest. You'll need to be out of here before first light. Tell my brother that de Soto, too, has been on his guard the entire time. Inform him that our relationship with the Kristianos is growing ever more dangerous. Tell my brother to keep a lid on our people. The slightest provocation will be like triggering a deadfall trap. We just don't know how heavily the weight will fall."

"Yes, Orphan."

I watched him touch his forehead and walk to one of the camps where he had relatives. Then I turned my attention back to the way the firelight flirted with Pearl Hand's beauty.

She gave me that knowing sloe-eyed look. "Thinking about things?"

"Always. This time I'm thinking about how, a short time from now, when we're under the blankets, I'm going to run my hands down your smooth throat, over your shoulders, and across your naked chest. I'm going to trace patterns around every dip and rise of your body. And all the while I'm going to—"

"Orphan?" Black Marten called as he trotted up to our

fire. He'd drawn the task of runner for the abetuska in charge of the guards. "I've just had a report. A Kristiano is sneaking around out in the trees just back from our fire line."

"Just one?" I asked.

"Just one." Black Marten dropped to a knee, head cocked. "He's just lurking out there, skulking in the shadows, peering at the fires. He'll sneak close to one, watch for a bit, and then back away. He'll circle and sneak close again. It's . . . Well, it's like he's looking for someone."

"Who?" Pearl Hand asked.

Black Marten shrugged. "We don't have a single Kristiano in camp. We've taken no one prisoner on this raid. It doesn't make sense."

"Any way you can recognize him come daylight?" I asked. "Does he wear a particular kind of helmet? Or maybe something about his clothing?"

Black Marten shot me a grin. "Better than that. Big Bat got a look at him in the firelight. You can't miss him: young, with an ugly scar running across his left cheek. And an even worse one crossways across his nose."

"Antonio," Pearl Hand whispered.

I nodded, erotic thoughts about my wife dissipating like mist on a hot day. "That glimpse of us in Sakchomasha was just enough to make him wonder. It's eating at him so much he's willing to dare the night and the Chicaza. That's something to think about."

Black Marten asked, "As dark as it is, and as poor as he is at sneaking around, it shouldn't be too much trouble to shoot a couple of arrows into him."

I considered it, meeting Pearl Hand's knowing gaze, her brow lifted suggestively.

Then Pearl Hand asked, "Black Marten, are the Kristianos sleeping in their armor again?"

"Just like last night, Minko Pearl Hand. They're ready to fight at a moment's notice."

"So," I mused, "if we don't get Antonio with the first

shot, he'll squeal like a dying *puerco*. That will bring the Kristianos to full alert. Come morning, when they figure out he's missing, there will be questions we can't answer."

Pearl Hand sighed, "And we'll go to war right here in the middle of the forest."

"He's always been an irritation and a nuisance. Not to mention cruel and vindictive."

"So, what do we do?" Black Marten asked.

I gave him a thoughtful look. "For now, just get rid of him. Scare him. Hunt him all the way back to his camp. You know, let him catch faint glimpses of warriors closing in on him. Make sure he gets back to his camp alive, but make sure he knows that Chicaza control the night as well as the forest."

Black Marten gave us both an amused smile. "Should be fun."

Pearl Hand added, "You be rotted careful, and don't take your little game too far."

"Yes, Minko." He touched his forehead and was gone.

I said with a sigh, "Antonio's going to figure it out."

She absently fingered the laces on her cloak. "Most likely. But we may be killing each other long before he can manage to get a good look at us without our face paint."

"I can't forget how he cut off Apalachee legs and arms, leaving those poor captives maimed for life."

"He's a monster," she whispered. "An abomination serving at the behest of an even greater one."

I remembered the expression on de Soto's face as he rampaged around on his cabayo in Sakchomasha. Nothing could stop him now. In his twisted Kristiano soul, he was already clapping me into a collar and snapping his whip on Chicaza captives.

But we've got other plans for you, Adelantado.

The afternoon we marched into Black Oak town was cool, dry, with a slanting winter sun shining down on the hillside settlement and the forest of black oak, ash, walnut, and gum trees that surrounded the collection of houses.

Pearl Hand and I, atop our litters, were deposited before the tchkofa, runners having long since alerted my brother and his council to our approach.

We were ritually greeted, the hopayes calling benedictions. The warriors retreated to their cleansing in the Men's House, though not to the grueling four-day affair with its purging, singing, and fasting. No fighting had taken place, no ghosts needed pacifying, and the ugly red chaos of war hadn't been unleashed.

Pearl Hand and I took time enough to greet the dogs and endure the happy mauling of tongues, tails, licks, and wrestling. We barked and howled together, yipping and playing. Bark finally plopped on his butt, lifted his scarred nose, and made a helpless "arrrroooooo" howl that had half the town looking our way.

Squirm made his snarly-face smile, slinking happily around the perimeter, tail whipping like a flail. Blackie and Patches tumbled all over each other in the effort to press close for pets. Gnaw, he just leaped onto my chest, trying to tumble me to his level, where he'd have licked me to death.

"It's all right," I told them. "You didn't miss anything, and the fight is still to come."

"You're all getting fat," Pearl Hand chided, dropping down to lace her arm around Bark's thick neck. "These Chicaza are treating you too well."

"Ahltakla? Minko Pearl Hand?" the ayopachi called. "The high minko requests your presence."

The dogs trailing along, we were escorted to the tchkofa. Just inside the door, I made them lie down and stay where they could see us. Then Pearl Hand and I approached the fire.

To my annoyance, Mother was there, seated upon a

folded bison hide, a hawk-wing fan in one hand. Were I pressed, I couldn't have said whether her look communicated more loathing than the parting glance de Soto had given me. They were that close.

We were greeted respectfully with the pipe and black drink, and after all the rituals had been dutifully attended to, my brother asked, "Did any good come out of this?"

Avoiding so much as a glance at Mother, I seated myself to his right and helped Pearl Hand as she settled onto the mat beside me. Then I looked around, finding Red Cougar and my sister Clear Water. Off to the left sat the clan minkos—in short, most of the Chicaza leadership, maybe thirty people in all.

"We know that neither side is going to let its guard down." I raised my hands, making the sign for "that's how it is."

"We have an impasse. We threaten them as much as they threaten us. We don't want to attack their small but terrible army head-on. They don't want to fight a grueling war of attrition against our greater numbers and evasive tactics."

"So, what do we do?" Clear Water's lips formed into a pout.

Red Cougar gave her an indulgent smile. "Brains before honor. We wait for the right time, and we'll continue watching, learning."

"While we wait, they've been building," Flying Squirrel interjected. "Since you left, they've stuffed five new buildings in between the clan houses. They roofed them with thatch stolen from farmsteads. With nothing else to do, they build and build. You'd think they were beavers. Chicaza town is turning into a packed maze."

"A maze, yes," Fire Tail agreed, "and a defensive one at that. There's no way we can run a squadron into Chicaza town and keep any kind of cohesion. They've laid out the dwellings so that the doors are faced inward, allowing them to emerge and split up to either side. A few men can hold the gaps between the houses against many."

"We could chop through the house walls," Cut Hand said. "But, even with the *hierro* axes, it will take time. If we manage to take one house, they'll just fall back to the next. The way they've packed those buildings in, we can't mass our archers and rain arrows onto them."

"Limited routes of attack," I said thoughtfully, picturing our warriors trying to tackle armored Kristianos among packed houses. Once again, the Kristianos were playing to the benefits of that marvelous armor. In essence, the buildings acted as a way to extend their line of battle.

Pearl Hand said, "Our challenge is finding a way to turn their advantage against them."

"The way they always do to us," I reminded everyone. "The difference is that de Soto—brilliant and self-gratifying witch that he is—always seems to figure out our weaknesses. Surely what he can do in an instant, we can figure out over the course of days."

Mother gave a loud sniff of disdain. The entire time, her narrowed gaze remained fixed on me. If she thought that glare was going to bother me, she was right. My skin was crawling.

"You'd think we could," Red Cougar agreed. "Meanwhile, we may be running into another problem."

"And that is?" my brother asked.

"*Puercos,*" Red Cougar grunted. "Occasionally our people have been given gifts of *puerco* meat. It's become a mark of status and influence to serve it at a feast. Demand for the meat is running through the people like a fever. Several of our young men—in defiance of orders—have managed to sneak in, climb over the fence, and make off with the little squirming ones. On several occasions, the Kristianos have come close to catching them."

"What happened to the highly vaunted Chicaza discipline?" Pearl Hand asked.

Mother growled something incomprehensible beneath her breath.

Lashki made a face. "When it comes to *puerco,* Chicaza discipline is as ephemeral as Albaamaha obedience. But the problem isn't completely our fault. When our people have tried to trade, offering as much as a deer carcass for a *puerco,* the Kristianos turn them down. They always say the *puercos* belong to the *Adelantado,* and they can't trade them away. So people go back with even more deer, blankets, breads, what have you. Sometimes the value offered is enough to buy half a town. No matter what is offered the Kristianos refuse to trade! It's rude."

"So the young boys sneak in at night and take for free what the Kristianos deny them," I replied wearily.

"That is the case." My brother rubbed his face. "And eventually it is going to lead to tragedy when one of them is caught by the Kristianos."

Pearl Hand asked, "Do they know that by risking themselves they could be mutilated or burned alive . . . perhaps enslaved?"

"They are *Chicaza!*" Mother hissed, as if that were all the justification needed. "Unlike banished cowards, they have courage."

I bit my tongue.

It was Pearl Hand who slitted a threatening eye and in thinly veiled Timucua said, "Old woman, you are poison eating at the health of your people. One more wrong word about my husband, and you and I will tangle."

"Say that in my tongue," Mother said balefully. "And if it means what I think it does, I'll have your guts pulled from your body, you foreign bitch."

"Stop it," I snapped. "Both of you."

But Pearl Hand and Mother were glaring at each other like angry panthers.

It was my brother who said, "Mother, desist. The Kristianos are enemy enough. We do not need to be making more from among our friends."

I took a deep breath.

Pearl Hand clamped her jaws in fury, the look she gave Mother promising mayhem and violence.

"I'm happy to oblige," Mother said, eyes enlarged and dangerous.

But whether she acknowledged my brother's request or Pearl Hand's challenge, I couldn't tell.

THIRTY-NINE

TWO DAYS LATER I WAS RIPPING MEAT FROM A GOOSE carcass and tossing it to the dogs, making sure that each got his just due. The young man called Green Stick—attended by a growing crowd—came wobbling and staggering into Black Oak town. I tossed the bones where the dogs couldn't get to them and licked the grease from my fingers.

As he came closer, I could barely recognize the young man who had escorted us to the Men's House back in Chicaza town. He staggered along naked, partially supported by several of his relatives. The expression on the young man's face told of both horror and excruciating pain. What particularly caught my attention as the crowd parted were the blood-brown stubs where his wrists would have been.

Rushing out with the rest, I gaped as he was led toward the Chief Clan house across from the tchkofa. I saw Mother on the veranda and blinked to be sure I wasn't dreaming. Yes, she was speaking with Ears, talking earnestly, her hands forming signs I was too distant to make out.

How did Ears—of all people—come to Mother's attention?

The approaching crowd caught her by surprise. She looked up, saw them coming, and quickly waved Ears away. The Timucua slave left, hobbling slowly on his maimed ankles, as Mother walked out to meet Green Stick and the crowd.

"What is it?" Pearl Hand asked, emerging from Wild Rose's back door, the dogs clustering around her as they alternately watched the confusion at the clan house and shot longing glances at the goose skeleton where I'd pitched it atop the ramada.

I took a deep breath, shivered, and swallowed my distaste. "Green Stick. Remember him?"

"One of your kinsmen." She gave me a sidelong glance. "He was just escorted into town . . . missing his hands. We've seen this before."

"Outside Anhaica?"

"The very same."

"The Kristianos chopped them off?"

"And used hot metal to sear the stubs as a means of stopping the bleeding." I rubbed the back of my neck, feeling sick. "And Green Stick, no doubt, has been sent with a message."

"But we haven't been causing the Kristianos any trouble." She frowned and crossed her arms. "Outside Anhaica, each mutilation was accompanied by the demand that we stop fighting."

Black Marten broke through the crowd and came charging toward us at a pounding run. His face was grim as he caught my eye, gesturing and calling, "Orphan! Come quick. The high minko wishes your counsel."

"Come on, wife," I said miserably. "Let's go hear what terrible thing is bearing down upon us now." I looked at the dogs, waggling a finger at them. "And don't you go tearing down the ramada to get at those bones. We've enough trouble as it is."

The clan house was packed, literally shoulder to shoulder, with Chief Clan kin. Black Marten had to bellow, "Make way! By order of the high minko, make way for the Orphan and Minko Pearl Hand!"

A shuffling commenced that ended in Choctaw Hair standing and waving as he shouted, "All of you, out! Go! Yes, this is clan business, but I will decide who deals with it. And how it is dealt with. Now, the rest of you, wait outside. I want only immediate family in here. Black Shell, Pearl Hand, you stay."

We tried to ease to the side as stunned and irritable people pushed past, clogging the door.

When the room was cleared, my brother, Mother, and Clear Water remained with Aunt Red Branch, Green Stick's mother and my first cousin. Red Branch knelt over her son, running frantic fingers over his hair. Green Stick lay on the floor before the fire, his back on the matting. Someone had draped a blanket over his naked and cold body. He held his arms up, the severed stumps pointed at the roof. Both hands had been taken above the wrists; when the hot *hierro* had been applied, the cooked flesh had pulled back until the two ivory-colored forearm bones protruded a knuckle's length from the browned and seared meat.

Green Stick was trembling, his jaw working, eyes feverish with pain and horror. "Water. Please, something to drink," he whispered hoarsely, as if his throat were raw.

Clear Water immediately found a long-necked brownware jar, which she placed to his lips. Red Branch lifted the youth's head as he drank greedily.

My brother studied the wounds, his expression pinched; then he glanced up at me. "You've seen this before?"

I nodded, aware that Mother was alternately shooting disdainful looks at the boy and then me. Before I could reply, she said, "Tell the strangers to leave, Choctaw Hair. They are not kin. Not even Chicaza. I am the ishka minko and will not have them interfering in *our* business!"

My brother's lips quirked before he turned and said, "Stop it, Mother. Black Shell is here by *my* order. Since his return you have done nothing but spit poison while the rest of us are struggling to stay alive. Even if he was a coward back then, even if you and Uncle were right, this man belongs to Power. He has come in our time of need. I, and the council, will listen to him." He clenched a fist before Mother's nose. "And you will cease spewing your poison, or I will have warriors carry you bodily to some remote location in the forest down south where you will be restrained."

She gave him a fierce glare, then shot a cunning look my way. "Of course, High Minko." But I saw no retreat in her obsidian-hard eyes.

My brother turned to me. "What does this mean?" He indicated Green Stick.

I bent down beside Red Branch, Pearl Hand across from me. "What is the message the *Adelantado* sends?"

Green Stick swallowed hard, face working. The pain burning up his arms had to be overwhelming. "He said that there will be no more stealing. Any who try to take a *puerco*, or any other Kristiano things, will be treated like this." He raised his stumps as if to gesture, and tears crept from beneath his lashes.

Not unkindly, Choctaw Hair said, "You know that I gave the order to leave the *puercos* alone. Why did you—"

Mother interrupted, "The stinking Kristianos are living in our town. They are *polluting* our temples, *disfiguring* our clan totems! They have taken what is ours and made it theirs. And what do we get in return? A few beads? Some metal tools? What if Green Stick did try to take a *puerco?* What is that compared to what we've supplied the intruders with this last winter? Nothing, I tell you. Absolutely nothing!" She worked her overshot jaw, daring Choctaw Hair or Clear Water to disagree.

My brother replied, "Mother, the idea was not to provoke them. The plan was to get them to lower their guard, to grow lazy. To lull them into a belief that they had little to fear from us."

"Bah!" she growled, waving a limp hand my way. "The akeohoosa talked you into that so he could get to ride around on one of their cabayos. You think I don't know what this is all about? Can't you see, my son? He's *made himself* high minko! Turned you into a laughingstock!"

I closed my eyes, rubbing the bridge of my nose. Across from me, Pearl Hand had tensed. I knew that crouched pose, what the hand on her knife meant. Tired to the core, I gave her the sign to back down. Pearl Hand just rolled her eyes in response.

"It was me!" Green Stick cried, a miserable expression on his face. "I wasn't smart enough, matron. My Power was wrong . . . and it abandoned us. The others . . ." He clamped his eyes shut.

"What others?" Choctaw Hair and I asked at the same time.

Mother barked, "Youths always travel in packs. It matters not. Green Stick, I want you to be quiet and rest. Your Power is fine. You're home, back with your family. Red Branch, get him on his feet. I'll have a litter provided. You need to move him south, someplace where if fighting breaks out, he won't be in danger."

"Wait a moment," Clear Water said sharply as she bent over Green Stick. "There were more of you? Who? And where are they?"

Green Stick swallowed hard, struggling to see where Mother sat, his pained face betraying indecision.

But about what?

"Tell your cousin," Red Branch told him. "What others? Who went with you?"

Mother said sharply and insistently, "Stop plaguing the boy! Can't you see what's been done to him? He's got enough on his souls without us picking at him. Let him alone. Red Branch, get the boy out of here. My own litter will carry him south to—"

Clear Water spun on her heels. "Mother? What have you done?"

I blinked, seeing the realization dawning in my brother's eyes. He sighed, rubbed his face, and asked, "Green Stick, who went with you? Where are they? Your high minko demands that you answer."

Green Stick, looking sick, gave Mother a pleading glance, then hesitated before he said, "White Fawn and Blue Stork. They . . . They won't be coming back. The Kristianos ordered them shot with their own bows and arrows. Some of the slaves . . . It was quickly done. Then the bodies were roped to the *puerco* pens. A warning to anyone else who might try to steal one."

Like my brother and sister, I was watching Mother's face, seeing that slight flicker of irritation and fear. Then her jaw shot out, and her gaze turned cold as she ignored our inspection.

Choctaw Hair laid a reassuring hand on Green Stick's forehead, saying, "What did the matron ask you to do?"

"Bring her a *puerco*," Green Stick said without hesitation, as if it were the most normal thing. "She'd never tasted any. And, after all, like she said, she's the matron. She deserved it."

In the eye of my souls, I saw how the whole thing had unfolded—Mother, the youths, and the terrible result. Of course they never hesitated. Who'd dare to turn down the Chief Clan matron?

I rose, sick to my stomach, and walked out into the day. People clustered, waiting, looking expectantly at me.

Behind me, Pearl Hand stepped out and laid a hand on my shoulder.

"Come on," she whispered. "Let's go take the dogs into the woods. Anything to get away from here for a while."

"What word?" Black Marten asked as he searched my eyes.

"High Minko Choctaw Hair will explain everything," I said woodenly. "He's still learning the details."

"Are we attacking the Kristianos?" one of my distant cousins asked. "For what they did to Green Stick, we must have revenge!"

Assertive grumblings ran through the crowd.

I said nothing as I pushed through the crowd and headed for Wild Rose's. Pearl Hand's reassuring presence behind me was my only solace.

But I noticed Ears where he stood, shadowed in a doorway, watching us pass.

FORTY

WE'D STOPPED FOR THE NIGHT IN A COPSE OF LONG-needled pitch pines. Our bedding lay on the thick mat of needles, the scent of the trees in competition with our hickory-wood fire. The night was chilly, a thick layer of clouds rolling across the Sky World, masking the light of Father Moon and the frosty stars above.

Around the fire the dogs were flopped, most curled into balls, their noses buried in their tails. Gnaw's white-tipped tail marked his location where he lay behind me. Squirm had his head on my blanket, firelight gleaming on his blazed face. Patches and Blackie huddled together off to the side, as if taking comfort in closeness.

None of the dogs seemed to share my pessimism about the future. How many days did we have left now? And when it finally came, what would this next battle cost us? If we lost, if Pearl Hand and I were killed, who would care for the surviving dogs?

"Your thoughts?" Pearl Hand asked. She sat across the fire from me, her hair in a tight braid that hung down her back. A bear-hide cape was snugged around her broad shoulders. Her breath frosted in the cold night air. Bark's scarred head lay in her lap like a blocky lump. She continued to pet his thick neck fur.

I studied her triangular face in the firelight, delighting in the way the yellow flickers caressed her smooth skin and cast shadows around her high cheekbones and soft dark eyes.

"My thoughts are nothing nice, wife. I'm saddened and sorrowful." And how had Ears ended up in the palace? Mother couldn't speak so much as a word of Timucua.

Pearl Hand's slim fingers traced the swell of Bark's cheek. Each time she did the fringe on her shirt made his ear twitch with a tickle.

"Saddened?"

I tossed a stick into the fire, watching the sparks dance and rise from the coals. "We always defeat ourselves," I said dully. "Here, at Chicaza, we've got one very slim chance of destroying the Monster. But only if we do everything perfectly. There can be no mistakes, not a single miscalculation. The entire Chicaza leadership knows this. Even sworn enemies like Blood Elk and Buffalo Back Mankiller understand and accept the responsibilities enough to delay their personal quarrels.

"In defiance of every custom and belief, the proud Chicaza have allowed me to impersonate a high minko. My brother, the noble descendant of a line of high minkos going back to Split Sky City, has swallowed his pride and position for the good of the people. All for the desperate chance to destroy de Soto.

"Even the Albaamaha allies—a people perpetually skeptical about us—have sacrificed and gone to the extreme to see this thing through."

Her smile was fleeting. "You should be proud. Not even Tuskaloosa could have pulled this off without a breakdown in obedience. Your Chicaza haven't loosed a single arrow since the peace was declared."

I grunted, gazed on the dogs where they sprawled in the firelight, happy to be camped out again.

"I'd be incredibly proud. But right when the tension is tightening like pulled rope, Mother—knowing the stakes—sends three boys off to steal her *puerco*."

Pearl Hand's expression remained fixed.

I clenched a fist, inspecting the tendons and knuckles in the firelight. "She did it because she could. An exercise of authority. Why? Because I was leading a Chicaza war party. Because her high minko of a son couldn't discover a weakness that would allow him to sanely attack the Kristianos. She did it because things weren't being run the way she thought they should be. Maybe it was a petty response to the fact that even her daughters had deserted her for my side."

"You're sure you're the cause?" Pearl Hand's eyebrow rose into an eloquent curve. "That's a bit arrogant on your part, don't you think?"

"She's Uncle's sister," I muttered. "Were Uncle still alive—no matter what sensible advice had come to him—he'd have marched the squadrons out to drive the Kristianos from Chicaza territory. Period. One great battle to settle the entire matter."

"And your Chicaza would have been destroyed."

"Broken, scattered, and crushed," I asserted. "But Mother doesn't see it that way. She can't. The world that still exists in her souls doesn't account for Kristianos. And it never will. Instead, to salve her frustrations, she sends those boys out to die and be mutilated."

"Black Shell—"

"No! I'm mad as a slapped water moccasin. Every time we have a chance to fight the Monster, we're undercut. It's always some personal ambition that leads to our failure. In Cofitachequi it was White Rose. In Coosa it was the mikkos and their political machinations. At Mabila it was the warriors who neglected to close the gate so they could get into the fight sooner. Here it's going to be an old woman poisoned mindless by hatred for her son."

Pearl Hand studied Bark's scarred face, her fingers smoothing the fur on his neck. The big dog sighed, his sides working in a huff. "She'll bear the responsibility for the rest of her life. That might be punishment enough."

"Her? Never. She's already convinced herself that it was a simple request. Were you to ask her, she'd give you that defiant glare and tell you it was the boys' fault for being stupid. How else could they have allowed themselves to get caught on such an easy errand?

"But Green Stick?" I raised my hands in despair. "He's forever maimed. Why? So Mother could taste *puerco*? So she could prove her status? Pus and blood, if she'd just waited until the conditions were right and we killed the Kristianos, she could have had a herd of the putrid things!"

Blackie and Patches lifted their heads to give me worried stares. Squirm and Gnaw were so used to my outbursts that the only reaction I got was that jaw-smacking swallow dogs make when they're slightly disturbed.

I gave her a glum look. "Makes you wonder why Power doesn't just turn the Spirit Beasts loose to wipe us all out. The world would be a better place."

She gave me her deadpan look. "Power has no choice but to bet on us because if we lose, the Kristianos win."

I took a deep breath of the cool, pine-scented air. "Yes, I know."

We watched the fire for a while. I was on the point of suggesting that we undress and crawl under the bedding. I wanted, *needed*, to bury myself in Pearl Hand's marvelous body. I was desperate for the sensation of her flesh warming to mine. For that magical moment when our bodies merged into one.

But the dogs leaped up, growling, and a voice that I

placed as Dogwood Mankiller's called from the darkness, "There you are! The high minko sent me to find you! It's the Kristianos. Some of them raided Black Oak town this afternoon. They rode in on cabayos and just took things. They struck several women who protested. It means war!"

My thoughts churned and raged inside me. The sense of looming disaster—black and depressed as the night—weighed like stone in my souls. The rare chance to hold and make love to my wife had vanished in a frustrated moment. Ugly anger burned inside me. Adding to the effect, I felt completely and totally exhausted: physically, emotionally, and mentally.

Oh, yes, I was ready for war.

When we reached Black Oak town, it was to find the place in a slow boil. The town itself was dark, guards posted around the perimeter, though we had explained insistently and often that Kristianos did not venture out at night.

We made our way to the tchkofa, where warriors crowded around the doorway, many of them wrapped in blankets as they tried to catch what sleep they could.

Immediately we were rushed inside.

Every one of the minkos, including my brother, had painted his face red. Anger shone from their eyes.

"What's happened?" I demanded warily.

"Four of them," my brother told me. "They came in the early afternoon. What were we to think of it? Kristianos often ride around the area, scouting, keeping track of us. Or we thought perhaps they were coming to trade. The four Kristianos tied off their cabayos, walked around. But no one was here to translate. Two Packs was gone with the rest of us to scout Chicaza town. Some of the warriors and their wives tried to help the Kristianos, offering them things for trade."

Mother turned her cold eyes on me, saying, "I saw it. They just took the things the Crawfish Clan women offered. They gave nothing in return. And they are rich! One of their *hierro* knives, anything would have been appreciated. They just started to walk off. That's when Old Woman Crow grabbed her blanket and tried to jerk it back."

"It turned into a scuffle," Minko Cut Hand told me. "One of the Kristianos backhanded Old Woman Crow. Knocked her off her feet and split her lip. Some of her friends tried to interfere and were slapped around. One, Flaxen White, was kicked. Her son grabbed up his war club and would have attacked the Kristianos, but Blue Jay Mankiller held him back, reminding him that any attack would be in disobedience of the high minko's orders."

My brother gave a nod of appreciation and added, "So the Chicaza held back, and so emboldened, the Kristianos—laughing and making fun of us—loaded their cabayos with what they could carry and rode off."

Minko Cut Hand, stung by the treatment of his Crawfish clansmen, squared his shoulders. "First we endured the mutilation of Green Stick. Though he is not of my clan, he is Chicaza. Now they have done this. The time has come, High Minko, to make an end of this."

Old Wood was sitting in the rear of the Raccoon Clan area and calmly stated, "We have been watching the Kristianos, studying them. I see a pattern developing: They are becoming more arrogant. Our relations with them are deteriorating. The tension among our people is building; the warriors chafe more and more. During the time the *Adelantado* was gone to Sakchomasha, I went several times to Chicaza town, hoping to discern the moment when we might sneak in and destroy them. I was struck by two things: First, despite taking them a gift of food, nothing was given to me in return. Second, they barely tolerated my presence."

"Which means?" Red Cougar asked his kinsman.

"It means that they consider our offerings of food and clothing as their just due. Call it tribute if you will. But where they once showed us respect, they now openly display how much they despise us." Old Wood touched his forehead deferentially and concluded, "We have bought all the time we can. The sooner we strike, the better now. Any delay will only add to their wariness and make them more alert. Or worse, if they come back and seize our goods again, someone will kill one of them. After that we will no longer control the time and place for our attack, but will have it thrust upon us at a moment's notice."

My brother nodded, sighing. He glanced at us. "Black Shell? Minko Pearl Hand? Your thoughts?"

"Beloved elder Old Wood is right," I said. "If we hesitate, one of our people or one of theirs will strike the spark that burns out of control. Our 'peace' is becoming more of an illusion by the day."

Pearl Hand flipped her long hair over her shoulder, nodding agreement, and asked, "How long would it take to assemble the squadrons? And once assembled, can you keep them hidden?"

"I can. In anticipation, we've moved food stores into some of the timbered areas close by."

I flexed my hands in anticipation. "That leaves the time for the attack."

Red Cougar said, "Kristianos never leave camp at night. As soon as we can move the squadrons close, I'd say hit them at first light as soon as we can see to fight."

Dogwood Mankiller raised his hand for recognition. At the high minko's nod, he said, "The day was warm today, and windy from the south. We've had a week of this, but we are coming up on spring equinox. I can almost feel it in my bones. Tomorrow is going to be even hotter, the winds stopping. At this time of year, you all know what unreasonably still, hot air; bright sunlight; and a blue, cloudless sky mean?"

"Big spring storm coming down from the north," Old Wood said, nodding. "Depending on when the winds stop, I'd say two days from now at the earliest."

My brother shot a glance at Red Cougar. "Tishu Minko, send the runners. Have the squadrons in place by tomorrow night."

"You can do that?" I asked. "That quickly?"

"Ahltakla, they've been waiting in hopes of a strike since you took de Soto to Sakchomasha. The abetuskas can have them in position within a half day." He glanced at me, a pained smile on his lips. "Upon hearing of Green Stick's fate, I thought having them on alert might be a good idea."

"High Minko," I murmured, "you are a wise man."

He gave me a wounded look, one that touched my soul. "And I have a mission for you, brother. Tomorrow, I need you and Minko Pearl Hand to go to the *Adelantado*. I need you to complain about what these four Kristianos have done, demand that he turn the culprits over to us so that we may mutilate them the way Green Stick was mutilated. Tell him he has four days to surrender them to us. Do you understand?"

Pus and blood! I swallowed down a fear-tight throat as I answered, "You're hoping to allay any fear of an attack on de Soto's part for at least the next four days."

"And tell him that until the raiders are punished, some of our people might be tempted to retaliate against his cabayeros should they be caught riding around."

My brother was smarter than I thought. Fear wiggling like a worm in my gut, I told him, "You want us to give him an incentive to keep his snooping riders close to home where they can't stumble onto an assembled squadron."

Choctaw Hair's pained eyes remained on mine. "I'm

adding to the effect by sending you in tomorrow with a couple of squadrons to back you up."

"Not necessary," I said, trying not to sound condemned. "Unless he's throwing up defensive works around the town, he's not ready to initiate hostilities."

"Yet," Pearl Hand muttered under her breath. From the corner of my eye I could see she was rod-stiff, as frightened as I.

Mother was glaring at me, her eyes burning like hot coals.

My brother didn't budge. "The squadrons are not negotiable. I want you to get his full attention, Black Shell. And on your return, I want him to see you order those squadrons to disperse. Not march off in formation, but break up and scatter back toward Black Oak town, as if disbanding after a threat."

"I understand." My appreciation for my brother's cunning increased. The unsettling sense of darkness and futility slowly ate up the last of my courage and hope. I couldn't help but ask, "What happens if he simply gives me that flat-eyed, arrogant stare and says, 'My men do as they wish, dirty *indio*,' and he takes me captive?"

Mother cackled. "Then maybe you'll have finally found a way to serve your people, you bit of walking filth."

I managed to place a restraining hand on Pearl Hand's arm as she started forward. My brother's pained expression pinched even more. The others lowered their eyes, a token of embarrassment.

"Come," I told Pearl Hand. "We've preparations to make. And we'd better get some rest."

"Oh, yes," Mother chortled. "Sleep well, coward. Tomorrow night, Breath Giver willing, you'll be sleeping in a collar, accompanied by the clinking of one of their chains!"

FORTY-ONE

THAT NEXT MORNING DAWNED JUST AS DOGWOOD Mankiller had insisted it would: warm, clear, and still. As the sun rose above the trees, I could see the tips of their branches, thick with buds, some preparing to flower. Here and there, visible on the slopes, spears of pine and cedar could be seen as dark-green lances hidden within the gray thicket of trees.

A line of geese honked their way north, and the first sprigs of grass were visible beneath the mat of flattened brown grasses at the edge of Chicaza town's cornfields. A colorful flock of parakeets fluttered through a green-budded chestnut that overhung Deer Creek. I could smell the earth, the musty scent of dry vegetation and rich soil.

On either side, at the edge of the trees, my two squadrons from the Sakchomasha raid were forming up according to the shouted orders of the abetuskas.

Even as they did a trumpet note called out from Chicaza town, and I could see the distant guards pointing, some running full tilt back into the clustered buildings.

The *Adelantado,* it would seem, had been made aware of our presence.

"Ready?" I asked Pearl Hand as I climbed into the provided litter. She'd angrily refused my impassioned plea to remain behind for the dogs' sake, saying, "I'm not letting you die alone in there, Black Shell."

She gave me a wooden look, the effect accented by the ashes in her hair and the face paint: right side black, left side white, the demarcation between them a perfectly straight line down her nose. "It's as good a day to die as any. My *hierro* knife? Your Kristiano ax? I'll remember to go for the throat; you remember to strike for the face."

I'd been expecting something a bit more sentimental.

"Of course," I murmured, and gave the signal to be raised.

Two Packs started out ahead of us with two standard-bearers to either side, falcon war images atop their poles.

I fought the urge to poke at my own face paint, red on the right, white on the left, indicative of a choice to be made for war or peace. De Soto would at least understand the gravity of our mission before he ordered me seized and burned to death as a lesson to the Chicaza.

The dry grass rustled underfoot as I was borne forth, ten porters behind me bearing sacks of cattail-root bread, dried venison, and other foodstuffs. But only ten, which any good chief from my world would understand was a neutral gesture—one politely offered from a position of strength. Twenty sacks would have signified my great goodwill. One bag would have indicated nothing more than the miserly offer of a very angry chief. No food? That would have signified we were having a talk under truce while in a state of war.

Theoretically de Soto would understand this as completely as he did the face paint.

We crossed the corn-and-bean fields, trampling

brown and ropy squash vines, and as we approached the town, de Soto's *soldados* tramped out, Ortiz at their head.

The trumpet blared again as I ordered my bearers to a stop. I kept my gaze fixed on Ortiz, noting his black beard, streaked here and there with white. His round-cheeked face, puggish nose, and thick brow were lined. A wary curiosity lay behind his brown eyes. He'd donned a *hierro* breastplate, an Albaamaha flax-weave shirt poking out from beneath. War moccasins were on his feet and rose over worn and dirty canvas trousers.

"Good day, High Minko." He was taking in my face paint, looking back to see the ten bearers and their small-ish sacks. "Your visit is unexpected. May I be of service?"

"I have business with the *Adelantado*. Some of my young men were executed, another maimed, for trying to steal Kristiano *puercos*. Since this was done in defiance of my orders, I have no complaint. The *Adelantado* saved me the effort of punishing them myself."

Two Packs translated this. The Cofitachequi turned it into *español*.

I continued. "Then, yesterday, four cabayeros rode into Black Oak town and stole from several old women of the Crawfish Clan. They abused them, struck them, and took their possessions by force. But for the discretion of several warriors, the Kristianos would have been attacked and killed. I am here to determine if the *Adelantado* approved of this raid and theft, or if, as happened to me, his order was disobeyed. If the latter, I have come to demand the thieves be turned over to me."

Ortiz heard this, his eyes turning thoughtful as he studied me. I watched a faint smile curl the thick mustache that covered his upper lip. He turned, calling something to one of his men.

The fellow cried, "*¡Sí, Capitán!*" and spun on his heel. He was gone like a loosed arrow, running back among the new dwellings crowded between the clan houses. I stared at the cluster of buildings, most so close the roofs were touching. Any direct assault would entail breaking the formations into small parties that would have to filter through the narrow passages between the buildings. The gaps could be held by a small number of *soldados*. All they had to do was step back and a line of cabayeros could sally forth from any location. Chicaza warriors would have no warning before the cabayeros charged into their midst. With the open plaza behind the buildings, de Soto's reserves could be directed to any threatened area. Once again he was relying on his armor and mobility.

I glanced again at the thick thatch roofs where they basked gray and dry in the hot sunshine. It brought a shiver to me as I remembered Mabila.

I swallowed hard and turned my attention back to Ortiz, who was talking with one of the *soldados*. Pearl Hand was listening intently to what they were saying.

A trumpet blared from behind the wall of houses and the *Adelantado* appeared in the gap between the buildings. Behind him came Moscoso, Nuño de Tovar, and yes, lurking in the rear, Antonio scurried along behind. There was no mistaking that ruined face or the suspicion even the scars couldn't mask as he shielded his eyes from the sun and studied me.

De Soto walked out imperiously, asking, "*¿Qué pasa aquí, Ortiz?*"

I could tell that he was mad, his face cold, pinched, and livid. Anger had him nearly vibrating, his back rigid, his hands clenched into fists. The striking purple coat was thrown back, exposing his polished *hierro* carapace. The man's ornate sword clattered at his side. He gave me a look hot enough to singe hair.

Antonio was squinting, stepping out to the side to get a better view. I forced myself to ignore him, but my heart began to pound. The little maggot was going to scream, "*¡Es el concho negro!*" any moment.

I couldn't follow the conversation as Ortiz rattled on in *español*. A sidelong glance at Pearl Hand, however, told me that she was having no such problem. Something being said had her eyes gleaming hawkishly as she watched the Kristiano leaders.

De Soto turned, meeting my eyes and asking, *"¿Es la verdad? ¿Quieres clemencia por los ladrones?"*

Ortiz spoke at some length to the Cofitachequi, who nodded, then addressed Two Packs, saying, "The *Adelantado* has already apprehended the thieves. They made the mistake of bragging upon their return. They acted in violation of the *Adelantado*'s orders, and he is attending to their punishment. As a chief, you must understand that disobedience cannot be tolerated. Two of the culprits will be executed for initiating the plan. The two who accompanied them will be whipped in public as an example to anyone who might consider such disobedience in the future. Is this satisfactory?"

I waited until Two Packs finished his repetition in Chicaza and answered. "How will I know the guilty ones will be punished?"

When Ortiz heard the translation, he gave me a cold smile. "The *Adelantado* sees your squadron formations back in the trees. He sees your face paint and the anger in your eyes. As a result, he understands the gravity of the situation. But more than that, he demands obedience from his men. The four who stole from your people did more than disobey, they showed a lack of respect for their *Adelantado*. Defiance is a crime of even greater consequences than petty theft in violation of our peace."

I shot de Soto a look, meeting his seething anger with my own. I nodded, saying, "His punishment of the raiders will suit the Chicaza for the moment. But in four days I will come again, and when I do, I demand to see the bodies of the two dead Kristianos." I smiled. "At that time, I will come with a great many sacks of food, and we shall have a feast to celebrate obedience and discipline among the ranks. Such a feast, among the Chicaza, is a way of smoothing over disagreements like theft, be it of *puercos* or blankets."

I paused. "Meanwhile, you should know that many of my people are upset by the raid and abuse of our old women. I would ask the *Adelantado* to keep his riders close for the next couple of days. Neither he nor I wish any misunderstandings about why cabayeros are riding around the countryside."

Ortiz heard all this and turned to de Soto, saying, "*Adelantado, el cacique piensa que el castigo es mas severo y duro para Osorio, Reynoso, Ríbera, y Fuentes. Él suplica que te perdonas los hombres que están involucrado en esta fechoría. Él piensa que sería major sí puedes perdonar los hombres en este caso.*"

De Soto's anger faded into skepticism as Ortiz spoke. He studied me, looking slightly perplexed; then he turned his attention on Ortiz. The man looked distinctly uncomfortable. And well he should. It had to be hard telling de Soto that I'd be back in four days to feast over the bodies of his executed *soldados*.

The *Adelantado,* however, nodded, slowly turning to his *capitanes*. They all discussed for a while, ignoring me. Then, gaze hardening again, de Soto tilted his head my direction and said something else. Moscoso and Nuño looked unhappy. Antonio was creeping slowly to the side, all of his attention on me and Pearl Hand.

Ortiz faced me, looking slightly ashen now that he was out of de Soto's view. He said something to the Cofitachequi, who in turn told Two Packs, "The Kristianos are preparing to leave Chicaza. The *Adelantado* would like the high minko to provide two hundred *tamemes* to transport various packs and foodstuffs to the land known as Quizquiz."

"Easy, old friend," I whispered as Two Packs's back knotted with rage. The word *"tameme"* might have been a

421

whip laid across his flesh. "Remember that you are Two Packs, the wiliest trader in the world. Keep your expression neutral and turn around and deliver the message to me."

Two Packs did, his face stony, his eyes slitted. But he bit off the words when he told me they wanted *tamemes.*

I then cocked my head, glaring into de Soto's chestnut-colored eyes. Four days? Within four days— weather permitting—no Kristiano would be carrying anything again. Not even the blood in his veins.

"Inform the *Adelantado* that I will discuss this with my council."

"You can't!" Two Packs's face went red with anger.

Pearl Hand sharply ordered, "Two Packs, just tell them."

"Tell them." I ground my jaws. "Four days. We'll feast, and he'll get his accursed *tamemes.*"

Two Packs wheeled back to face the Cofitachequi, and I finally redirected my attention to de Soto. He'd watched the entire interplay, that soul-dead flatness cooling behind his eyes. His lips, visible behind the mustache, had a mocking curl, as if he knew full well that it had been an affront to demand Chicaza burden bearers.

Two Packs, through clenched jaws, replied.

De Soto said something, gaze locked with mine in a battle of wills.

Ortiz in turn told the Cofitachequi, who said, "If the Chicaza are too proud, surely you can find two hundred Albaamaha to carry our baggage. Perhaps the ones from Sacchuma?"

The burn was in my belly, lighting a fire through my chest. By the Piasa's balls, I wasn't really a Chicaza noble, not after all the years I'd been an exile. But you couldn't have told that to my souls that day.

I've been your slave, you pustulous monster, and now you're asking me to order innocent human beings into your chains?

De Soto, Moscoso, Nuño, and Ortiz were now locked in some sort of serious discussion. Each was offering an opinion, gesturing with his hands. From the tone I could tell that they were unsure about something. I shot a side-long glance at Antonio. When my eyes met his, something clicked; it was the final confirmation of his suspicion.

"Husband?" Pearl Hand said softly, tension in her voice. "The Monster and his seconds are discussing ways of taking us captive to ensure that porters are provided."

Blood froze in my veins. "If they try it, there's not much we can do up here in these litters." So, did I order myself lowered? And then what? Try to kill de Soto with my heavy copper mace and *hierro* ax? Turn and run? Wave the squadrons forward in an attack that would leave hundreds dead? Allow Antonio—who was now creeping closer, step by step—to attack us? The way he held his head like a hunting robin emphasized the odd delight in his eyes

Horned Serpent! Give me a sign!

Then Antonio giggled with glee. *"¿Adelantado? ¿Por favor? ¿Conoces usted quien es el indio?"*

De Soto and the others paused in their discussion. *"¿Perdona me, Antonio?"*

Antonio pointed at me, my fear rising like a flood. *"Adelantado, mira. Es el concho negro. ¿Te recuerdas? ¡Él vive! ¡Y está aquí! ¡Como un cacique!"* And to my amazement, he laughed.

De Soto, the subject of our capture delayed, stepped close, giving me a thorough scrutiny. Despite the panic inside, I glared back with a narrow-eyed stare.

Waving at me, de Soto said, *"Ortiz, preguntalo. ¿Quién es?"*

I could feel sweat beading under my armpits, my heart hammering. The sepaya was quivering like a frightened fawn against my chest.

"Husband?" Pearl Hand asked softly as Antonio stepped around, his incredulous stare fixed on her.

"Easy," I said through gritted teeth. "One wrong move and we're dead."

"What's happening?" Two Packs asked, his shoulders knotted into bulging muscle. His thick fingers were grasping air, as if in preparation to crush flesh.

By then the Cofitachequi had translated Ortiz's question. "High Minko, the *Adelantado* wishes to hear your name."

As Two Packs was repeating the inquiry, I blurted, "Two Packs, ask the Kristianos why this ugly man is staring and pointing at us. Tell the *Adelantado* that such behavior is disrespectful. If this man is not dismissed, I will climb down from here and discipline him myself!"

Two Packs stepped in front of Antonio, glaring into his excited eyes as he spoke. The Cofitachequi, starting to panic, kept stumbling over the words, stammering.

Antonio immediately realized his danger and scurried back. Two Packs could have picked up the little weasel and snapped him in half without even grunting from the effort.

Meanwhile the Cofitachequi was saying, "The cabayero thinks the high minko might be a trader named Black Shell. And the witch woman might be his wife, Pearl Hand. Old enemies of the Kristianos."

Two Packs—still glaring threats at Antonio—repeated it.

Making myself ignore Antonio, I fixed my gaze on de Soto. He stood watching all this with thoughtful detachment. With his left hand, he fingered his beard as if in indecision. His right was propped on the ornate silver basket of his sword handle.

Forcing bravado to cover terror, I said stiffly, "Tell the *Adelantado* that I am the high minko of Chicaza and will be treated as such. That his cabayero thinks I am a lowly trader, without title or honors, is an affront and an insult. The choice is now the *Adelantado*'s: Either we leave now and return in four days to see his dead thieves, feast, and provide *tamemes,* or if he wishes to consider me some rootless trader, I will stand in my litter and give the signal for war." I paused, still ignoring Antonio. "Choose. Peace or war?"

Two Packs shot me a look of strained horror, swallowed hard, and gave my terms to the Cofitachequi. I watched de Soto's expression as the demands were made.

For long seconds he might have been a lizard on a log for all the reaction he displayed. We just stared at each other, he with that characteristic emptiness, I giving him a glare that I hoped communicated heat instead of the frantic panic that froze my souls.

Antonio just stood rooted, muttering, *"Viven. Impossible,"* over and over.

De Soto shot him an irritated look; shook his head, as if to rid it of impossible thoughts; and said, *"Hay paz. Estamos acabados aquí."* With a final arrogant sniffing sound through his beak of a nose, he turned and started back through the gap between the buildings.

Moscoso and Nuño glanced incredulously back and forth between Antonio and de Soto. Then they turned their stunned looks on me and Pearl Hand, as if trying to believe what they heard.

Antonio gaped in disbelief, then pointed at us, saying, *"En el último, me tendré sus sangres. Lo prometo."*

"¡Antonio!" de Soto bellowed. *"¡Afuera! ¡Ahora! ¡No me haces mas problemas!"*

Antonio jerked as if slapped, took two steps in retreat, then gave us a grin that twisted his brutally scarred face.

"Lo prometo," he cried, shaking a fist as he went. Then he disappeared through the gap.

Ortiz, the *capitanes,* and the *soldados* watched us with wary eyes. Ortiz growled something to the Cofitachequi, who told us, "The *Adelantado* apologizes for the cabayero. If you will bring *tamemes* in four days, we will feast, and there

425

will be many fine gifts for the ishto minko Chicaza. The bodies of the dead thieves will then become yours to dispose of as you wish. Yet another gift from the *Adelantado*."

I just stared at the roofs arching over the gap, watching heat waves rising off them to shimmer against the flower-blue sky. Exhaustion replaced terror as my heart rate slowed. The day had indeed grown hot. I was sweating—from both the heat and the panic that was slowly ebbing away.

I *hated* Kristianos. Gaze fixed on the heat waves, I felt the sepaya warm on my breastbone.

"Take me back," I said unsteadily.

Pearl Hand shot me a glance rife with relief as the litters were turned around. As we marched away, she said, "It's hard to believe, but Antonio just saved our lives. Until the little maggot accused us of being Black Shell and Pearl Hand, they were arguing how best to take us captive in order to ensure the delivery of the *tamemes*. De Soto was on the verge of ordering it. We were that close."

"We have to destroy them," I said through a dry throat. "Quickly. We have no choice now."

FORTY-TWO

PEARL HAND AND I SAT NEXT TO MY BROTHER IN the Black Oak town tchkofa, a low fire snapping and crackling. The blaze barely lit the interior, but anything larger would have been oppressive in the already warm confines of the great lodge. As it was the minkos seated around us watched and listened intently, firelight flickering on their somber faces.

I remained distracted, my thoughts flying around like bats. Most overwhelming was that we'd survived. We'd been a gnat's hair away from ending up as de Soto's prisoners.

And then, just as we'd been carried into Black Oak town, I'd seen that miserable slave, Ears, stepping out of Wild Rose's front door. You couldn't miss him, not with that wobbling walk caused by cut tendons. At the sight of Pearl Hand and me, he'd sneaked off around the corner. Where had he come up with enough trade to partake of Wild Rose's charms? That she'd even allow him in her bed disturbed me.

I tried to concentrate on what Pearl Hand was saying.

"...Are you listening? Ortiz lied! He told de Soto that you wanted him to forgive the raiders. The ones de Soto was going to execute for disobedience. Ortiz said you were pleading for leniency!"

"What?" I cried, shooting a worried look at my brother. Behind him, Clear Water was watching thoughtfully.

Mother, in the dark recesses behind them, snickered, "That's Black Shell for you. Always the traitor, isn't he?"

"I never said any such thing!" I growled.

Pearl Hand glared in Mother's direction, refusing to take the bait. "At the same time, Ortiz was lying to us. Playing Black Shell and de Soto against each other. Why? It only makes sense if Ortiz is friends with the raiders and was trying to save their lives. It also gives us an idea of Ortiz's cunning and courage. The gamble could cost him his life should he be found out."

"And he will," I promised.

Pearl Hand waved me down. "Ortiz expected that we'd be taken hostage. Once that was done de Soto would never discover the fraud."

"I'm just surprised that de Soto was really going to kill two of his men and punish two others." I fingered the copper mace in my lap. "After all, it was only some old *indio* women they stole from."

Pearl Hand gave me that knowing look. "Ortiz didn't lie when he said that disobedience to the *Adelantado* was the real offense. But Ortiz never told de Soto a single word you said about feasting or demanding to see their bodies four days from now. He knew that the request for *tamemes* would make your demands irrelevant."

"It doesn't matter." I shot my brother a look. "There's no time left. De Soto is packing, preparing to leave. We have three options. One, we attack now, in force. Two, we withdraw and harass his line of march. Or, three . . . we send Chicaza people to become his *tameme* slaves."

"If the Monster wants *tamemes*, let his dead souls search for them in the Underworld," Two Packs growled. "I'll break his head before I see any of our people chained in his collar."

My brother watched Two Packs's display with faint amusement. Generally strangers didn't voice their opinions in a Chicaza council session unless asked. Raising a hand to still any further outburst from Two Packs, he said, "We will attack, of course. Better to hit them hard, by surprise, in hopes of dealing them a staggering blow."

"How's the weather?" I asked.

Red Cougar, sitting just to the left of the high minko, lifted his head, his gaze on the fading evening light visible through the smoke hole. "I think we've got another day before the storm. We'll know it's coming when the wind turns from the north."

"Wind is perfect for masking any sound of approaching warriors," Fire Tail noted from his place across the fire. "But long-range archery suffers as the arrows are blown off course."

My brother gave him a reassuring smile. "What do you care? You won't even be there."

I glanced at Fire Tail. "You're going to miss the fight?"

He gave me a pensive look. "If all goes well, I hope so. The high minko and I have come up with an alternate plan. My warriors are building a wall across the Tallahatchie ford on the Quizquiz trail. A fortification, if you will. Should a party of Kristianos manage to fight their way out of Chicaza town, we'll be sitting right astraddle of their escape route. It falls to me and my Alibamo to ensure that none survive."

Pearl Hand reminded him, "Don't forget Mabila's gates. With their *hierro* axes, they chopped right through in a matter of heartbeats."

"Which is why we're building three parallel walls across the trail," Fire Tail told her. "When they breach the first wall, we fall back to the second. To attack us, they must negotiate the narrow space between the first and second wall. With no place to go, trapped in those narrow confines, we can shoot down upon them. Then, when they breach the second wall, we fall back to the third, and once again they are contained between the second and third walls. And, should they manage some miracle—"

"They will," I muttered.

"—and breach the third wall, we have escape routes planned into thick forest where we can ambush any pursuers. The cabayos won't be able to follow."

"May Breath Giver walk with you," I prayed.

Fire Tail winked at Choctaw Hair. "High Minko, just be sure you kill them all in Chicaza town. If it falls to the Alibamo to finish the job, you know we'll be insufferable. Probably become as arrogant as you Chicaza."

It was a mark of the times that this brought laughter from all quarters.

Two Packs raised his thick hands, the gesture almost imploring. "Whatever happens, after today, there's no turning back. My sense is that de Soto thinks he narrowly averted a misstep. More than anything he wants those *tamemes*. Anyone who goes back to Chicaza town will not be allowed to leave."

"No, they won't," Pearl Hand asserted. "De Soto and the *capitanes* were discussing the best excuse that would entice us to enter Chicaza town. De Soto's plan was to invite us to watch the raiders being pardoned. Then he'd simply order the *soldados* to surround us. A messenger would be sent to the squadrons saying that we were staying as guests until the *tamemes* arrived."

"Who disagreed?" I asked.

"For obvious reasons, Ortiz," she told me. "He didn't want you questioning why the raiders were being released. Instead Ortiz thought a feast of *puerco* would provide every bit as powerful a lure. After all—or so Ortiz claims—what *índio* can turn down *puerco*?"

"This one," I growled, thumping my breast.

Pearl Hand continued. "Because our arrival was unexpected, de Soto didn't have time to set a trap for us. He was trying to innovate as he went along. Ortiz told him outright that if they just grabbed us where we stood, the watching squadrons would witness the treachery, and the Chicaza would go to war."

"No *tamemes* that way," Two Packs said sourly.

"As it was"—Pearl Hand fingered her ash-stained hair—"our fate was hanging in the balance. Moscoso argued for inviting us to a feast, offering to personally command the troops who captured us." She tapped the knife on her belt. "He said he'd waited too long to reclaim his property. Nuño insisted that we be invited in to receive gifts of *hierro* and beads. That Antonio interrupted when he did, the way he did, allowed Black Shell to act indignant. The absurdity of Antonio's claim, coupled with Black Shell's threat to call the squadrons in, changed de Soto's mind. He wants *tamemes*, not war."

I sighed, smiling sheepishly. "I have to admit, that's about as scared as I've been in a long while. I—"

"I'll bet," Mother hissed. "The miracle is that you didn't piss your breechcloth and dribble it all over the litter carriers."

Pearl Hand leaned forward, Moscoso's knife magically in her hand. "Old woman, one of these days your tongue will only be the beginning of your troubles."

I managed to get a restraining hand on her shoulder, feeling the muscles, hard as river cobbles, under my grip.

"Enough!" Choctaw Hair roared, wheeling around to glare at Mother where she chuckled coldly in the shadows. "Ishki Minko, still your tongue! I won't have this." He turned back to Pearl Hand. "And no more from you, either. Matters between Black Shell and the matron are Chief Clan concerns."

Mother's spiteful voice rose in a wail. "He's not Chief Clan. He's akeohoosa!"

"Mother!" Clear Water rasped passionately. "You've taken this too far. Leave. Now. That, or so help me, I'll drag you out of here by the hair. If I do, Painted Clay and Fine Red Woman will find a way to remind you of it for the rest of your life!"

My sister, I decided, would make a wonderful matron.

Mother growled to herself, crossing her arms.

"Go!" Choctaw Hair pointed. "Now."

For a moment, Mother hesitated, then, stiffly, she rose to her feet, straightened her doe-hide dress, and said, "Something tells me that by tomorrow morning, the coward and his friends will have a fuller understanding of Chicaza honor." Without a look to either side, she walked primly from the tchkofa.

I narrowed my eyes, wondering what new insult she might be planning.

"I am sorry," my brother said wearily. "Some things . . ."

"Just are," I finished for him.

"Forgive me, High Minko . . . and you, too, Clear Water." Pearl Hand touched her forehead, the blade hissing back in the scabbard. "My husband's honor is my own."

I fought a smile. Pearl Hand knew her Chicaza. Nothing appealed to a Chicaza like defending another person's honor.

Red Cougar cleared his throat. "Family politics out of the way, I think we have an attack to plan."

I clapped my hands. "I think we do. And while I was sitting out there baking in the hot sun, I noticed something about the changes they've made to Chicaza town."

My brother, desperate for a change of topic, arched an inquisitive eyebrow. "And what would that be?"

One by one, I met the eyes of the surrounding minkos. "Think about how the town is laid out in a large, hollow square. Most of the largest clan houses and the tchkofa are on the north. The cabayos are generally herded in the meadowlands south of town and bounded by the two creeks. In addition, they've fenced most of the southern side of town to create the *puerco* pen. It's a good fence for keeping *puercos* in and people out. Not an easy barrier for anyone to cross. So we want to come in from the north. With the wind behind us."

"Attack at first light?" Old Wood asked where he sat behind Red Cougar.

I shook my head. "In the middle of the night if we can. As the storm blows in and the sky is the blackest."

"How will we see who is friend and who is enemy?" Blood Elk asked, baffled. "It will be chaos in the dark."

I gestured for attention. "A small group of warriors can infiltrate and set fires to light the way for the rest of us. The Kristianos have never been attacked in the middle of the night. If we can achieve complete surprise, they won't even have time to put on their armor. And even if they do, most of the cabayos will be far away, grazing south of town."

"*If* we can obtain surprise," Pearl Hand said thoughtfully, her brow furrowed with thought.

I glanced around at the others. "The key is to get the squadrons in close before they are discovered. For that we need darkness to hide the movement and the storm to cover the sound of so many warriors marching."

"And after we get into position?" Red Cougar asked.

"The only thing missing is light to see by. As dry as Chicaza town is, I know how we can obtain it."

Just this once, I hoped that the storm-calling serpents of the Underworld would be in alignment with the great Spirit Woodpecker who drove the winds down from the north.

Pearl Hand and I, exhausted, picked our way across the night-black plaza. It might have been a summer evening, as warm as it was. Overhead, the frosting of stars brightened into the Path of the Dead—the fork in the sky road marked by Eagle Man's gleaming star. At this time of night, the Seeing Hand had already dropped below the horizon. But I imagined the thousands of dead making their way to the western edge of the world, waiting at the cliff for the constellation to perfectly align. The just and worthy would make the leap, and then they would continue on their way to the Path of the Dead. The unworthy? Well, their footing would slip at the last minute, or if they leaped far enough, the hand would slap them down into the abyss between the sky and earth. No one knew how far a person fell or what they finally landed on. If anything. Not even the greatest priests—soul-fliers, like Back-from-the-Dead— had ever risked their souls to find out.

Whatever was down there must not have been good.

"It's a solid plan," Pearl Hand said thoughtfully, her souls still fixed on the attack. "Better than the one we had at Mabila."

"That's not exactly reassuring . . . if you'll remember how that worked out."

"Worried about my sneaking you out of the ruins of Chicaza town with a dead man's face tied over yours?"

"Something like that." I paused, stepped in front of her, and took both of her hands. Clasping them, I stared down into her starlit face. "We're going into battle again. Not just a raid, but a massed fight like at Mabila or Napetuca. The odds of one or both of us—"

"I know." She said it so simply.

"I just want you to know how much I—"

As she firmly repeated, "I know," and squeezed my hands, I could see her white teeth flash.

For a long moment we stared at each other, souls speaking what words could not.

"Come," she said softly. "Let's go see if Wild Rose has fed and walked the dogs. Then I want to wrap myself around you. I want to cling to your naked body and feel every part of you that's not inside me pressed against my skin. I want to play you like a flute and heal the wounds and fears with your music. I need you to make my souls drift into ecstasy and to tingle and pulse in waves of joy."

"Oh, yes. I promise."

"Good," she whispered, a grateful tone in her voice. "Because I think before this is over, we're going to wish we'd had more joy to shield us from the horror and pain."

I nodded, fearing that even the slightest statement of affirmation might influence the future.

At Wild Rose's, the back door was open to the night, and I tripped over something soft and heavy lying in the threshold. Catching myself, I leaned down, feeling a dog's cold body. Then came whining from inside.

"What is it?" Pearl Hand asked.

"Something's wrong. We need light." My heart had risen to my throat. A terrible fear—like a bitter wind—blew through my souls.

I made my way through the small back room, kicking our stew pot. It rolled with an empty ceramic ringing sound and thunked into one of the bedposts.

Pulling the door hanging back, I felt my way through Wild Rose's dark sleeping room before barging into her main room, heedless if she had a client.

This, too, was dark, and I crinkled my nose at the acidic smell of vomit. I fumbled around, finding kindling where she kept it near the door. Then, at her puddled-clay hearth, I used the twigs to fish around for coals. The red embers glowed like evil eyes of chaos. Blowing on the coals, I touched the dry sticks and wraps of kindling grass. As they flickered to life, I stared around, seeing Wild Rose propped on her bed, a blanket around her shoulders.

"Help . . . me," she whispered hoarsely. "Sick . . . So sick . . ."

Holding my burning twigs up like a torch, I stepped over, asking, "What's wrong?"

"Gut's . . . burning. Muscles . . . twisting like knotted ropes." Tears were leaking down her cheeks; I watched in horror as she broke into violent shivering. Then she jerked forward, stomach pumping as she tried to throw up. A hideous greenish goo mixed with clotted blood dribbled past her lips.

"Poison," she whispered. "Got to be . . ."

I backed up, staring around, and grabbed for more of the kindling to keep my tiny torch burning.

"I'll get help," I promised.

"Black Shell?" Pearl Hand's demanding voice came from the back, thick with panic. *"Where in pus and blood are you?"*

In that moment, Wild Rose's body convulsed, bucking and kicking. At the same time, her empty stomach kept pumping, and her eyes bulged as if to pop from their sockets. Sweat was beading, trickling from her shivering skin.

Horrified, I lit my kindling torch and stumbled back the way I'd come. In our tiny back room I lifted the feeble and flickering light. Pearl Hand crouched on the floor, her arms around Bark's neck. The dog was obviously sick, trembling, drool leaking past his jaws, his eyes unfocused. Under one of the pole beds, Blackie lay on his side, breathing hard, his tongue lolling. He, too, was convulsing, gasping for breath. Gnaw erupted in gagging spasms, dry-heaving, his whole body quaking uncontrollably.

In the doorway, it was Squirm that I'd tripped over. Loathsome white foam—clotted with drops of blood—

covered his muzzle, his wide eyes sightless in the flickering of my torch.

Desperately I thrust the torch into Pearl Hand's grip, crying, "Make a fire! I have to get the hopaye! Now!"

Then I leaped out the door, sprinting for all I was worth for the Raccoon Clan house and Old Wood.

FORTY-THREE

MY HEART HAMMERED LIKE A PESTLE MADE OF ICE. A dull refusal to believe what I was witnessing clung to my soul like cobwebs.

This could not be happening.

I worked on the fire in Wild Rose's front room as Old Wood and Copper Sky inspected the woman's body. By the time I'd returned, dragging a complaining Old Wood behind me, she'd collapsed to the floor. Her thrashing had grown so violent that she'd actually torn the cane matting, her fingers bloody where she'd ripped the nails off.

"What did you eat?" Old Wood demanded.

"Stew . . . ," she whispered. "Black Shell's . . . stew."

Old Wood looked down at me where I blew the fire to life; I gestured bewilderment. "We have no stew. We've been gone. Out in the forest last night until Dogwood Mankiller came for us. Then we had breakfast at the high minko's this morning. We ate in the tchkofa tonight when food was brought during the planning for the attack on Chicaza town."

"Gift . . . from . . . ," Wild Rose barely managed to say, then her body twitched, convulsed . . . and she died.

Copper Sky was inspecting the pools of vomit that stained the matting, finding chunks of undigested meat, bits of root that looked like chewed cattail, sunflower seeds, and other unappetizing pieces. Then, with his thumb and forefinger, he picked up a bit of fibrous material, raised it to his nose, and sniffed.

"Is that what I think?" Old Wood asked.

"Smells like water hemlock."

Old Wood leaned close and sniffed. Then he backed carefully away, saying, "Wash your hands, Copper Sky. Go now. Down to the creek. Wash them, and wash them, and wash them again. Use sand to scrub the tips of your fingers. Take no chances."

The hopaye gave Old Wood a grim nod, glanced uneasily at Wild Rose's sprawled body where it lay atop the torn matting, and hurried out the door.

I blinked, fighting nausea myself. "Who'd do this?"

Old Wood pursed his lips. "Let's go look in your room. You say the dogs are sick?"

"And Squirm's dead," I murmured woodenly. The horror was still too numbing. The pain would come later, along with the grief and the rage.

I led the way into our little back room and found Pearl Hand on the floor amid the sick dogs. She crawled to them, one after another, petting them, reassuring them. All but Squirm. He still lay half out of the door, his head pulled back at an awkward angle. The hideous white foam gleamed in the firelight, his sightless and dry eyes staring. I could see where his outstretched legs had clawed at the floor matting and scratched clay daub from the house walls.

Old Wood glanced down at Pearl Hand, and he reached down with a finger to dry one of the tears that streaked her cheeks. His smile communicated more than just reassurance but sympathy as well. Thank the Spirits that Knuckles hadn't been here.

Then he picked up the stew bowl I'd kicked. In the firelight, I realized it wasn't ours but a perfectly made, globe-shaped vessel with a short straight neck that ended in an out-turned rim.

"That's not ours," I murmured.

"The design is Chief Clan's," Old Wood told me, then he carefully lifted the bowl, sniffing at the rim. Instantly he jerked back, eyes narrowing as he studied the bowl.

"It's been licked clean," he added. "By the dogs, no doubt. After Wild Rose ate her fill."

I felt suddenly faint. "She often came and ate from our larder or shared our meals. We considered it nothing more than just compensation for the help she's given us."

Pearl Hand heard the past tense. "Wild Rose is poisoned, too?" She swallowed hard. "Dead?"

"Water hemlock," I told her. "The stuff is so dangerous I wouldn't even carry it for trade."

At that moment Two Packs appeared from out of the night, calling, "Still up? If you're as exhausted as I—" He stopped short, on the verge of stepping over Squirm's corpse, his eyes fixed on Pearl Hand's tear-streaked face where she cradled Patches's head in her lap. Then he glanced down at Squirm. As the truth sank in, he lowered his foot, head cocking in disbelief.

"Water hemlock." I felt numb. "Wild Rose said it was a gift for me. She's . . . She's . . ."

Two Packs sank down in the doorway, his hand dropping to pet Squirm's cold, hard flank. "Water hemlock? Someone wanted to make sure, didn't they?"

He closed his eyes, rubbing his thick, angular face with one hand as he petted Squirm's corpse with the other.

"Yes," I said absently, my souls racing. "It seems that

they did. And my guess is that, but for the planning session in the tchkofa tonight, they would have succeeded."

Then I stood, remembering. I took a step, slipped Pearl Hand's old *hierro* knife into my waistband, and pushed past Two Packs. "Excuse me. There's something I need to see to."

The sepaya was burning where it hung against my chest.

I'd never felt so peculiar, as though I were a remote spectator. One disassociated from his body and watching from afar. I remained aware of the blood in my veins, the air that filled my anger-fevered lungs with each breath. But the effect was as if a different person lived inside my bones and I only sensed these things secondhand.

For that time, that night, the remote part of myself, the removed observer, watched me walk through the plaza and across the stickball field with its newly sprouted grass. Everything had a dreamlike quality: the night, the stars, the warm air, the smell of wood smoke, and the musk of the latrines.

I stopped for a moment before the Chief Clan house, the seething inside me building into a fiery rage that burned away any inhibition. Step by careful step, I eased onto the veranda and peered around. Pots and jars, a couple of baskets, and some folded matting could be distinguished in the dark.

The door had been latched, but I slipped my *hierro* knife through the gap between the planks and the frame. The leather thong severed neatly. Bearing the weight of the door, I eased it open and set it silently on the mat flooring.

After the dark veranda, the room seemed well lit. A dying fire flickered in the central hearth. I peered around

441

at the sleeping figures beneath robes and blankets. Which would it be?

Ah, yes. First pole bed to my right. The shabby old cord blanket indicated a slave. From the way the feet tipped up so loosely, they had to have been lamed. That was him.

I'll say this for him, he slept deeply for a man who'd just killed a woman and a dog. Were it me, I'd have been tossing and turning, wondering what such actions portended for my souls, for my chances of ever making that leap through the Seeing Hand and into the Sky World.

But then, given the way I felt—the coldness, the emptiness and rage that pulsed between my souls—maybe that's just where I was headed myself.

He didn't feel my weight as I settled on the bench beside him. The tip of the *hierro* blade, however, brought him wide awake, and I clapped a hand on his mouth as I pressed the point under the angle of his jaw.

In Timucua, I said, "All it takes is a little more pressure. But then, you traveled with the Kristianos; you know how remarkably sharp their blades are. If you cry out, scream a warning, I'll slice through every vein and artery in your neck." I pressed the slightest bit harder. "Am I understood?"

I could feel his hard swallow through the blade, and he barely nodded, afraid of the damage the keen tip might do.

"Was the hemlock your idea?"

Ears tensed with panic, and I could feel his racing pulse all the way down the knife blade. I removed my hand from his mouth and dropped it to his throat just below the knife.

"Hers . . . It was hers."

"She doesn't speak your language. How did she manage to recruit you?"

"Traded with my captors." He gulped a breath. "Sign language is sign language. Here or in the peninsula."

"But she'd found a willing ally, hadn't she?"

"Why aren't you dead?" he asked after a pause.

"Pearl Hand and I ate in the tchkofa tonight. Wild Rose and my dogs, however, they enjoyed your stew."

He groaned and went limp under my grip. Probably a ploy to get me to relax. Then he'd make his move. This was Ears after all.

"I thought you wanted to rape Pearl Hand to death. That was always your end goal, wasn't it?"

He snorted. "Another way, a less fulfilling way, was presented to me. That you still live is the final proof that because of my foolishness at Mabila, God has deserted me. *Jesucristo* is punishing me. You are just the final disappointment. Go on, finish it."

"You really hate me, don't you?"

"You and that camp bitch Pearl Hand." He grinned up at me. "But as much as I hate you, I couldn't believe that someone actually hated you even more."

"Perhaps you should think of it as one of life's small miracles."

And at that, I stood, tightening my grip on his throat. Consider it a tribute to my rage that I lifted him bodily from the bed by his throat. One-handed. Then we went staggering across the matting, Ears kicking and thrashing, unable to find footing given his maimed ankles.

"*Mother!*" I bellowed as I passed the winking fire. "Wake up, you miserable old hag!"

Forms stirred on the pole beds, most of them jerking up, blinking.

I knew where she slept: the place of honor in the back, opposite the door and closest to the fire. She jerked awake, sitting up, pulling a brightly dyed blanket up around her. Her hair was down, disheveled; her eyes fixed on mine, going wide with disbelief. I was but vaguely aware of people sitting up, throwing off blankets in the background.

"You!" she cried. Her mouth dropped open as she realized who I was hauling along with me. Then she fixed on the knife that I kept pressed to Ears's neck.

I stopped before her. "Shall I tell you what I just told him? Or do you want to get the report from Old Wood? He and Copper Sky figured out that it was water hemlock. Wild Rose spewed bits of it all over her floor before she died."

I gave her a madman's smile. "Mother, you *worthless* old wreck of a woman, you *poisoned* my dogs! Squirm. He's been with me for years. Saved my life a couple of times. He's lying dead in the doorway. I don't think Patches is going to make it, either. Don't know how many of the others will live."

"I am *not* your mother. You have *no family!*"

I bent down, pulling Ears with me, hardly aware of the blood trickling out of his neck and down the knife's blood groove. The handle was growing slippery.

"Squirm *is* family, you *filthy swamp bitch!*" I roared, the rage burning hot and free. "So are the rest of them. My dogs! My wife! Worth more to me than all of Chicaza is to you, you empty, worm-eaten husk!"

Hot tears of rage broke free and traced down my cheeks. Existence became the pounding of my heart, the roar of blood in my ears, the spasming of muscles gone mad. An exodus of servants was bottled at the door behind me. I ignored the chaos.

Mother watched me with wide, terrified eyes, her hands rising, palms out, as if to fend me off. "Black Shell, you don't want to do this." But her voice sounded weak.

"What were your words tonight? 'Something tells me that by tomorrow morning, the coward and his friends will have a fuller understanding of Chicaza honor.' Wasn't that it? Wasn't that why you were so pus-licking smug when you walked out of the tchkofa? Because you'd already sent your foreign slave with the poisoned stew! What you didn't plan on was that Pearl Hand and I would eat in the tchkofa. You didn't figure on Wild Rose eating our food or the dogs finishing it, did you?"

At that moment, Ears thought he had his opportunity. He jammed himself against me, seeking to break my hold on his throat. But for the fact that his feet flopped like mullets in air, he might have done it.

With a howl, I whirled around, my fingers slipping on his bloody neck. We crashed to the floor, Ears scampering to get away. I launched myself onto his back, flattening him against the matting.

In Timucua, I hissed through gritted teeth. "Remember the innocents at Napetuca?"

He froze, panting through his crushed throat.

"This is for Water Frond; for Blood Thorn, who loved her; and for all the rest of the innocents you murdered!"

And with that, I cut his throat.

Rising, I watched him die; his breath rasped in and out of the slashed windpipe. Each panicked exhalation through the pumping arteries blew crimson spray across the floor. Then, dripping with his blood, I turned to Mother.

"No!" she screamed at the red chaos in my eyes, in the way my expression twisted with uncontrolled rage. *This is murder!*

"And what was it when you sent us *poisoned stew?*" I thundered back, and took a step.

"Justice," she squeaked, as if her throat were closing down. "Justice for what you did to me . . . to the high minko."

Looming over her, I really began to shake, the anger rising like a swollen flood. I ground my jaws, teeth straining. I seemed to be looking into Squirm's dead eyes, seeing his death struggles, the thick foam curdling on his jaws, reliving his final agony in my imagination.

Mother saw it coming and cringed. The image seemed to play somewhere far away, at a distance only visible to my screaming souls.

I grabbed her with one hand. She clawed and scratched, kicking out with her feet. Her eyes went wide as I lifted the knife. A droplet of Ears's blood plopped onto her cheek.

This ends now.

FORTY-FOUR

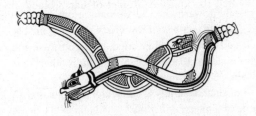

STARING INTO MOTHER'S EYES, I COULD TELL SHE UN-
derstood: Nothing was going to save her now. I pulled the
knife back, ready to drive it into her accursed guts.

But my trembling hand wasn't moving. It seemed frozen, as if trapped.

Black Shell?

The words existed separate from this world. Indepen-
dent.

Black Shell! No!

The words popped out of nothingness.

I was being dragged backward, the spell breaking.
Mother's image was falling away from me, retreating, our
eyes still locked in a terrible struggle.

I blinked, realized I was panting and out of breath as if
I'd run a long distance. I felt the knife peeled from my
cramping hand.

"Black Shell? What is *wrong* with you?"

I recognized the words as coming from a human voice.
And my brother's face intruded between Mother and me.

"Black Shell!" Clear Water was crying frantically as she pulled futilely at my shoulders. I could feel her pregnant belly pressing awkwardly against me. "Stop it! You're crazy! Insane!"

"She killed them," I whispered, the grief suddenly unbottled. "Squirm . . . Wild Rose . . . maybe others. It ends here!"

And with a violent shake, I threw them off. I made two steps toward the old woman before Choctaw Hair and Clear Water seized my wrists, dragging me back.

"*Think!*" Choctaw Hair cried, his face thrust into mine. "This is *murder,* Black Shell. She's your mother!"

"She doesn't think so."

"But the *rest of us do!*" Clear Water cried insistently. "The whole of Chicaza will. *I will!*"

I fixed on my sister's face, seeing the pleading behind her large brown eyes as she said, "She took you away from us once, Black Shell. In Breath Giver's name, don't let her take you from us again!"

My brother tightened his grip on my wrists. "If you kill her, she wins. You'll die in shame, tikba. Killing your mother is a crime so unthinkable we don't even have a punishment for it. And to do it now? Just before we attack the Kristianos?"

It would horrify the warriors. An ill omen. They'd believe themselves polluted and the whole of Chicaza unclean.

I blinked, looking back and forth between him and Clear Water. My shaking grew worse, and twisting away, I bent double and threw up. Then again. And again. Through it all, Clear Water kept a soothing hand on the back of my neck, Choctaw Hair supporting my arm.

Finally I straightened, wiping my mouth, and cast an enraged glare at Mother. She sat shock-still, her red, black, and yellow blanket pulled up to her chest; the veins in her neck were pulsing with each beat of her heart.

I heard pounding steps and turned just in time to see

Pearl Hand barrel into the room, hair flying, jaw set. She was panting hard, fire in her eyes as she slid to a stop. Her gaze went to Ears—now bled out in a pool of foaming crimson. Then she glimpsed my brother and sister, still clinging desperately to my arms, and finally saw Mother, whose jaw was now quivering.

"By the Piasa's balls," Pearl Hand gasped. "You stopped him in time."

"Barely," Choctaw Hair managed to say.

"The rest of the dogs?" I asked, panic rising.

"Patches is dead for sure." Pearl Hand's eyes narrowed to slits as she glared at Mother. "Two Packs stayed with them. Old Wood is trying to slide a cane tube down their throats so he can force water into their stomachs. An attempt to wash them out. It may be enough to save some of them, at least."

I closed my eyes, swaying on my feet. "Brother," I whispered, "get that foul old woman out of here. Away. As far away as you can. She's evil . . . bent and twisted."

"I am only protecting this family's *honor!*" Mother proclaimed hotly. "Look at him! He's made his return! It's not enough that he destroyed my brother! Now he's worked his way into your lives. Next, he's going to find some way to remove me, murder me, ensure that I lose what little authority and honor are left to me!"

"Honor?" Choctaw Hair whirled and bent down to stare into her defiant eyes. "You tried to *poison* your son! When that knowledge becomes public, you'll have protected your family all right. You'll have *destroyed* us!"

I watched Clear Water's expression pinch as the ramifications became clear. She placed a hand to her protruding belly, as if to protect the child who would be born under this stigma. "Blessed Spirits," she whispered. "When this gets out, the council might even demand a new high minko, someone from one of the other Chief Clan lineages."

"It can't get out." Pearl Hand propped hard hands on her hips, and her lips pinched. She kicked Ears's limp body where it lay on the bloody floor, spattered with my vomit. "We've got a war to fight, and we can't win if the Chicaza think Power's abandoned them."

"But the dishonor of attempted murder . . . And within a family. Our . . . family . . ." Choctaw Hair's words died, his tattooed face pained.

"What dishonor?" Pearl Hand asked reasonably, raising her hands. "This enemy slave"—she kicked Ears again—"from a people so distant you don't even speak their language, murdered a paid woman and killed a couple of dogs." She pointed at Mother. "And what if the noble ishki minko were to leave on a pilgrimage to pray and fast at some shrine deep in the forest? You know, as a means of spiritual cleansing? Call it self-exile, atonement because she'd just purchased the treacherous slave without knowing the depths of his hatred. That seems to keep the red and white pretty well balanced, don't you think?"

"Never!" Mother spat.

"Her litter will be out of here by morning's first light," Choctaw Hair said flatly. He rubbed the back of his neck as he stared glumly at Ears's corpse. "And I want this piece of filth strung up in a square. He may only be a corpse, but he's to be abused by everyone in retribution for Wild Rose's murder."

Clear Water's brow lined in a frown. "Wait. Black Shell, how did you know it was him?"

"I saw him step out of Wild Rose's as we were being carried back from the meeting with de Soto," I told her. "Perhaps others know that he was there."

"Then Wild Rose's murder might be portrayed as the act of a disappointed client?" Choctaw Hair mused, desperate for any option that protected our family's honor.

Feeling hollow and beaten, I said, "No. Treat Wild Rose's memory with respect, brother. Paid woman or not, she had more honor and integrity than a great many Chicaza."

At that I stumbled over to one of the beds, lowered myself, and hung my head. Pearl Hand settled beside me, her arm snaking around my shoulder in shared grief.

"You should sleep here," Clear Water said as she knelt before us and took my hands in her own. Sympathy filled her large dark eyes, her expression earnest.

"My dogs need me," I said dully. "They are family, too."

I didn't see Mother leave. Or the manner of her removal from Black Oak town. However Choctaw Hair and Clear Water did it, they managed the affair without incident or commotion.

The Chicaza ishki minko was simply gone, undertaking a pilgrimage to pray for success against the Kristianos.

And that was it.

Though of course there were whisperings. Too many people had seen her display in the tchkofa. That High Minko Choctaw Hair had managed the situation so skillfully brought him accolades.

A few found it remarkable that the matron's newest slave had also turned out to be a poisoner. The fact that his victim was the paid woman who rented rooms to Pearl Hand and me also garnered suspicion.

Fortunately Ears's body was hanging in a square where anyone passing by could heap indignity upon it. And a story was circulating among the other Chief Clan lineages that Ears knew Pearl Hand and me from previous battles with the Kristianos. It was said that he'd misled the ishki minko as a way to get close to me and Pearl Hand.

Which, for most people, was satisfactory. Especially since to press the matter would have reflected poorly upon them. It would have implied that they were gossips—which of course they were—and that the Chief Clan somehow had acted dishonorably.

Perhaps it was guilt. Or maybe my brother actually understood how deeply Pearl Hand and I were wounded and grieving. He ordered Wild Rose's body to be taken to the Chief Clan charnel house, where it was to be treated with honor.

He also ordered twenty kinsmen to assist me the following morning. They bore the litters, the two in the lead bearing the corpses of Squirm and Patches. Pearl Hand and I had tended their bodies; we'd washed them, then painted both dogs in red, white, and black patterns. I would forever remember the feeling of the sticky paint as I slicked it onto their soft fur. Offerings of food and water had appeared at our doorway and were now borne by the accompanying warriors.

Behind them, on separate litters, rode Gnaw and Blackie, still too sick to walk. Bark, for some reason, seemed to come out of it fine. He walked, unsteadily, on his own. Old Wood hadn't even needed to force a cane down his throat to flush his stomach.

Pearl Hand kept pace beside me as we climbed through the boles of oak, white ash, walnut, hickory, occasional cedar, and mulberry and onto the ridge behind Black Oak town. There an opening had been created some years ago by a lightning strike. On that high point I ordered the half-rotted logs to be dragged away and the soil cleared. With Two Packs's help we laid out the tomb. While my kinsmen sang the death songs, my wife and I gently lowered the two dogs into place, their white-painted muzzles pointed to the west and the Spirit road they'd have to travel to the edge of the world.

I personally said the prayers and placed beside them the offerings of food, a jar of water for each dog, and a couple of sticks—the sort both enjoyed chewing into splinters by the fire at night.

"Dearest old friends," I began softly. "You have shared fires and food, carried our burdens, and earned honor.

Squirm, you helped break the *Adelantado*'s attack at Napetuca. You saved not only us but also countless others. Both of you fought the war dogs at Mabila. Patches, you were younger, but I remember how you attacked the cabayos, how you outran the cabayero who tried to lance you that day. Fetch and Skipper are waiting at the end of the journey. Your leaving tears a hole in our lives. A huge . . . gaping . . ." I fought for breath.

I glanced at my three remaining dogs, all of whom sat, tongues lolling in the hot air, watching with worried brown eyes.

Turning my face to the sun, I cried, "Spirits, hear me! Honor the souls of these two courageous dogs. Guide them in safety to the afterlife. They are brave and noble souls . . . my friends."

Then I stepped back and emptied the first basket of earth over the log crypt. The twenty young men attacked the soil with digging sticks and began loading more baskets.

By midday, I stopped, wiping the sweat from my face. Pearl Hand had taken a break to water the dogs from a jar someone had been thoughtful enough to bring. Smarter than the rest of us, the dogs had long ago retreated to the shade of an overhanging elm, letting us do our work.

By late afternoon we had raised a conical earthen mound over the tomb. As tall as I was, the burial mound had sloped sides that wouldn't slump after a heavy rain.

I crouched; patted the cool, damp earth; and said, "Go in peace, old friends."

Then I stood, looked around the meadow with its newly dug barrow pit, and said to the sweaty workers, "Let's get Blackie and Gnaw loaded. It's time we get back."

Pearl Hand gave me a nod. "I think I can feel it."

"What's that?" Two Packs asked as he drank the last of the water and laid the empty jar atop Squirm's litter.

"The storm's coming," Pearl Hand said, lifting a hand to the clinging air. "Can't you feel it? The tension in the stillness?"

He shaded his eyes with the flat of his hand and looked north. "Nothing but clear sky as far as I can see."

My attention on the new mound, I said, "Isn't that where the mightiest of storms are brewed?"

FORTY-FIVE

FOR THE FIRST TIME IN MY LIFE, I DIDN'T HAVE TO walk to war. Looking back, that singular fact amuses me. I was the Orphan, after all. The long-lost, unofficially reinstated brother to the high minko. Pearl Hand was Minko Pearl Hand, the remarkable woman warrior who had been sent to the Chicaza by Power. We had risen so far above the lowly rank of a trader and a bound woman that we were carried to the forest behind Chicaza town on litters.

Two Packs, poor guy, had to walk. So, too, did the dogs. For whatever reason, they seemed to be bouncing back, though they greedily lapped up all the water they could hold at each creek crossing. Even as we proceeded, however, I saw them looking back, venting the occasional whine.

My thoughts, too, remained on the lonely mound in its high clearing; the words filtered through my souls: *Patches and Squirm aren't coming. We're all that's left.*

By late afternoon the winding trail we followed along

the ridgetop deposited us a couple of hands' travel north of Chicaza town. Here the leaf-strewn forest floor was teeming with warriors. Following the time-honored rituals of the "battle walk" they crouched or stood, and when they squatted or sat, it was on a piece of bark or cloth—anything to keep their butts from contacting Mother Earth. None of them would think of so much as leaning against a tree. No fires had been kindled by the hetissus, lest the Kristianos detect the smoke.

Even as we arrived at the Chief Clan squadron, the warriors were carefully painting themselves in patterns of red and black. Feather plumes were diligently preened by being drawn through callused fingers before they were fixed to shoulders or tightly wound hair buns.

I could hear the gentle rising and falling of war songs as the men wrapped three lengths of rope around their forearms. These served several purposes: First, they cushioned the forearms against blows from clubs, or hopefully, in this case, sword cuts. Second, they added to the warrior's fierce appearance. And third, there was one rope to lead home a captured *puerco,* another for the cabayo each warrior hoped to catch, and finally, the third rope was dedicated to the neck of any surviving Kristiano a warrior might take captive.

Pearl Hand and I thought the ropes represented . . . shall we say, unreasonable optimism?

On the other hand, if they helped to motivate my bloodthirsty Chicaza, so be it.

As the litters were lowered, I stepped out and clasped Two Packs to me, slapping him on the back. "Are you sure you want to do this?"

"They killed my boys."

"You're a trader, not a warrior. You haven't been trained."

He gave me his gap-toothed smile. "All I need is to get into that town. If nothing else, I can pick them up bodily and smash them on the ground."

"Try that, and they'll gut you on the way up," Pearl Hand advised him. "It's hard to toss a man while your intestines are spilling down around your knees."

He gave her a sober look. "I'll keep that in mind."

I punched his arm. "Throw rocks instead. They'll just clang off the armor, but you'll distract them enough that real warriors can kill them."

Two Packs drilled me with his gaze. "I'm under no illusions, old friend. I've got to do this."

I patted his elk-thick shoulder. "I understand."

By tomorrow morning, am I going to be mourning over your corpse, too, old friend? My guts seemed to drain out of me at the thought.

The assembly point was in old-growth forest a moderate distance up the ridge from Chicaza town. Far enough away that the Kristianos wouldn't hear us or discover us by chance, but close enough that the massed warriors could descend the ridge within a hand's time.

My brother was immaculately dressed, his face painted a blood red; the black forked-eye tattoos had been darkened with charcoal greasepaint. A black oval, too, had been drawn around his mouth. He looked remarkably fierce, the whites of his eyes accenting the effect every time he glanced to the side.

To his right the sacred and intricately carved war medicine box stood on its tripod. When the attack came it would ride on my brother's shoulders, bearing the concentrated Power of the Chicaza Nation into the fight.

Around High Minko Choctaw Hair were clustered the tishu minko and hopaye Copper Sky, and several of the hopaye's priests and sorcerers. Old Wood stood in the rear, but from the violent red paint on his face and the wooden shield with little crimson circles spattered all over it, he left no doubt that he had resumed the name of "Abeminko Who Takes the Blood-Spattered Shield." Good. We'd need his military prowess.

The other clan minkos and their seconds were shoulder to shoulder, staring down at where a map had been drawn in the stained yellow soil.

"The important thing is that the squadrons wait here, just outside the line of buildings, until the signal is given." Choctaw Hair glanced around at the gaudily painted faces of his chiefs and smiled, which made the black oval bend. "You'll know the signal. You won't be able to miss it."

"And what will that be, High Minko?" Flying Squirrel asked.

"The sound of combat, old friend. Or, if the Kristianos are particularly stupid, groggy, and slothful, it will be their screams as the infiltrators begin killing them."

All around, heads nodded.

"But," my brother said insistently, "you are not to order your squadrons in until you hear the fight start."

"Why not?" Cut Hand asked. "The greater the force we have inside, the better our chances."

"And how are you going to see to aim your arrows?" Red Cougar asked reasonably. "The infiltrators will start the fires. But until you have light to see, you'll be just as likely to shoot a kinsman as a Kristiano."

The high minko looked at Pearl Hand and me. "How long does it take them to strap on that armor?"

"Half-asleep, inside a dark house, and half-panicked? Perhaps a hundred heartbeats?" Pearl Hand shrugged. "If the infiltrators aren't immediately discovered, we should be all over them before they're ready. It all depends on the element of surprise."

I warned them, "If, for some reason, they've anticipated the attack, they'll be sleeping in their armor. If the infiltrators find them armed and ready, pressing the attack will lead to disaster."

Wide Net asked, "What about the cabayos? Can they ride them in the dark?"

"With the cabayos pastured in the meadow south of

town, the Kristianos won't even have a chance to call for them," Pearl Hand declared.

I saw uneasy glances among some of the minkos. "What?"

"They've moved the cabayos into the town." My brother read Pearl Hand's tightening expression. "Is that a problem?"

I took a deep breath, worry building. "They did this at Napetuca. The cabayos were in the town, already saddled and hidden behind the palisade. The *soldados* were hiding in their tents, fully armored, ready for war." I glanced around, meeting their eyes. "You have all heard how that worked out." I made an unpleasant face. "And there are no lakes for us to hide in outside of Chicaza town."

"We'll be attacking in the middle of the night," my brother countered. "If they know we're coming, the infiltrators will find out immediately as they try to sneak past the sentries."

Red Cougar added, "And even if the Kristianos charge out to fight us, what will they find as they stumble around in the dark? Nothing but flitting shadows as we melt back into the trees."

I glanced at Pearl Hand. She cocked her head slightly, her eyebrow arching.

"What?" my brother asked.

"The cabayos." I gestured impotently. "Why did they bring them into the town on this of all nights? Because they knew we were coming?"

Red Cougar gave me a blank look and shrugged. "They've been bringing them in ever since your last visit with the *Adelantado*. We haven't changed any of our behaviors. Select warriors are still chosen to sneak in and leave tracks in the mud where they can be found the following morning. We've done nothing that might tip them off that tonight's the night."

I glanced up at the muggy sky beyond the budding branches overhead. Where was our storm?

Old Wood—I mean Blood-Spotted Shield—said, "The cabayos are a risk we must take. We will get this one chance to surprise them. If they are indeed ready for us, it will be apparent long before the squadrons are in danger." He looked around. "You all understand what would happen if you threw your squadrons against prepared Kristianos. If they advance in strength from the town, you will order an immediate withdrawal." He smiled craftily. "There will be plenty of time to punish them as they march off toward Alibamo town, and Minko Alibamo's surprise there."

Chuckles sputtered and died.

"We attack tonight," my brother ordered. "If this opportunity isn't right, Power will grant us others."

Heads nodded.

He gave them all a sober look. "But if they come at you with massed cabayeros, scatter into the darkness. Save your warriors to fight them another day." He paused. "What is our strategy?"

"Brains before honor," came the chimed reply.

I glanced up. A crystal-blue late-afternoon sky was visible above the budding branches overhead. "Where is our storm?"

It was Blood-Spotted Shield who said, "Coming, noble Orphan. Can't you feel it? The thickness in the air, the stillness? Your storm approaches. Tonight, there will be blood."

"You don't need to do this." The red and black face paint lent emphasis to my brother's serious stare.

"Of course I do."

We stood beneath the high branches of a mulberry little more than an acorn's toss from where the squadron waited. Choctaw Hair watched as I belted Antonio's sword to my waist and slid it out of the scabbard to check the keen edge.

Pearl Hand had already collected her crossbow and her quiver of arrows. She'd vanished to somewhere else when I wasn't looking. I'd left the shield and *hierro* helmet behind. Going into battle I didn't want to look too much like a Kristiano.

I shot Choctaw Hair a sidelong glance, feeling the sepaya warm on my breast, and continued inspecting the war arrows that I dropped, one by one, into the quiver I'd borrowed.

I told him, "Horned Serpent chose me long ago. If there is a chance of destroying the monster, I must be there."

"So be there!" he cried. "But enter Chicaza town at my side. Take the fight to them with me."

"Protected in the center of a Chicaza squadron?" I turned, clapping a hand on his shoulder. "You *need* Pearl Hand and me to go in with the infiltration. If there's a trap waiting, we'll discover it. Pearl Hand will hear them talking about it. We'll see the signs."

"And if you're captured? Enslaved?"

"Then you will sneak in some night when we're on the trail and shoot Pearl Hand and me full of arrows. I will *not* die a lingering death in a collar." I paused to emphasize my point. "You've promised."

He refused to meet my eyes, clearly worried.

I gave him a reassuring smile, saying, "Nakfic, you must trust me on this. Horned Serpent chose me to fight this way."

"I'd rather have a brother than a hero," he muttered. Then, as if realizing what a sensitive subject that was, asked, "You know how to work the fire rope?"

After I dropped the last of the keen-tipped war arrows into the quiver, I picked up the length of rope, perhaps as wide as my little finger and as long as I was

461

tall. It felt tacky, and lifting it to my nose I smelled pine pitch.

"When I reach something burnable, I open the little clay pot and dump the coals on the wood, thatch, or whatever. Once I blow it into life I put the end of the rope in the flames until it catches fire. From there I run to the next place and set it afire. If the flame starts to go out, I whip the rope around my head a couple of times until it bursts into flame again." I gave him a disgusted look. "Of course I know how a fire rope works. The first time I used one of these it was to start fires in dry brush on a deer drive. I was maybe six."

"Now you're much older but no smarter."

"Why do you say that?"

"Because you refuse to go into Chicaza town with a squadron around you."

"Only now you're worried about my safety?" I leveled a finger at him. "You were the one who sent me to visit de Soto that last time . . . expecting us to be caught."

He lowered his head, shifting uneasily. "This time is different, Black Shell. I can feel it. And after what Mother did . . . What Clear Water said about family . . ."

Family? I glanced down where Bark, Gnaw, and Blackie were happily chewing what remained of a deer carcass. They were crunching enthusiastically on the bones, unaware of what was coming. How many more of my beloved dogs would I lose this night?

Off to the side I could see Two Packs where he crouched with a couple Chicaza warriors and inspected a large war club. How many more friends . . .

No, Black Shell, to go there is to fall into darkness.

"We are all expendable," I told my brother. "What is any single individual's life worth when the future of our world hangs in the balance?"

The shadow of a smile died on his lips as he looked off through the trees. Scattered among the boles, at least a hundred of his warriors were visible in the growing gloom. They were checking their weapons yet again, thinking of the coming fight, if not discussing it with their fellows. For the moment, they were calling on red Power, asking it to bless them. Some worried about their courage, others about how to fight this odd new enemy. In their imaginations, the arrogant and dumb ones were killing Kristianos by the fives and tens, and already leading their *puerco,* cabayo, and Kristiano captives home in triumph.

I wished them luck.

Then I looked up at the too-warm twilight sky, a trickle of sweat running down from my armpit. "Where's our weather?"

"Coming." Choctaw Hair leaned his head back, following my gaze through the maze of branches to the faint tracery of high, feathery clouds rushing south. "Can't you feel it? The heavy anticipation? It's as if the North Wind is spreading her giant wings and cupping the sky. We're at that last instant, just before she claps her wings together and the world recoils under the gale she unleashes."

"Let us hope," I answered, and reached for the little brownware pot. It hung from a hemp rope, the bottom lined with sand. Stepping over to the single fire kindled for the purpose, I used twigs to reach down and snare a glowing hickory coal. This I dropped into the small pot. Then I added chunks of dry walnut wood. They'd act as fuel for the glowing coal, smoldering until needed. "I'm ready."

"May the red Power fill you," Choctaw Hair said reverently. "To have known you as a man, tikba, has brought me honor and privilege."

"You too, High Minko."

I watched him turn and start back through the Chief Clan squadron toward where the war medicine waited on its tripod. As he passed each warrior, he had a word for him, a gesture, some recognition.

"He did all right," Pearl Hand said, making me jump as she appeared at my shoulder.

"Where have you been?"

She arched her eyebrow suggestively. "Maybe I had to pee. Maybe I didn't want to upset all the concentrated male Power here—let alone the war medicine—by exposing my polluted woman's butt to the ever-so-sacred Chicaza gaze. Never mind leaving a puddle of woman piss for them to step in and imperil their most pure male souls on the verge of battle."

"Uh . . . I see."

"You Chicaza are really going to have to broaden your perspectives about women and war if you're ever going to make anything of yourselves." She checked the latch on her crossbow, then propped the weapon on a canted hip. She gave me a saucy look, trying to mask the tension in her supple body.

"I'll be sure to mention that if we live through the night."

She winked at me and tossed her braid back over her shoulder. "I see you've got your face painted solid black. That for a reason?"

I thought of Wild Rose, Squirm, and Patches. "Death has been on my mind today. It will be dark tonight. Maybe I want to merge with the shadows."

"Got your fire pot? Arrows?"

"Of course."

She took a deep breath, glanced up at the darkening sky. "Let's go."

"Dogs. Come." I slapped my leg.

My pack—all three that remained—stood; Bark and Gnaw carried their chewed leg bones with them. Blackie kept looking back, as if knowing that Patches should be following. The longing in his soft brown gaze pulled at my heart.

Yes, I miss them, too, my friend.

Dry leaves crunching underfoot, we worked our way down the slope, past the vanguard of the Deer Clan squadron. As the most highly decorated, they would have the front, even before the Chief and Hawk Clan formations.

Somewhere, hidden in the forest to the west of Chicaza town, were the Raccoon and Crawfish squadrons. On the ridge over to the east the Panther, Wildcat, and Fish clans were forming up.

"How many warriors?" I wondered.

"Three or four thousand," Pearl Hand told me as she lowered herself over a knotted root that coursed along the slope. I stepped down after her, feeling the thick leaf mat underfoot give slightly. The dogs bounded down with no problem, leaves crackling under their paws.

"Good odds in our favor."

"We said that in Mabila."

"This time we can get away when it goes bad. We should have fought the battle of Mabila at night."

She gave me a chastising look from beneath a lowered brow. "You're sounding grim. Something I should know about?"

"A feeling of premonition. Gloom. I'm tired, wife. Depressed. What kind of world are we trying to save? We're fighting for whom? Remember how the Cofitachequi were betrayed by one of their own? Or the Coosa, whose politics defeated them even before the first Kristiano set foot in their capital? Men like Ears? You know, he's not the only scheming, selfish, angry—"

"It's your mother, isn't it?" She shifted the crossbow as she slipped through a collection of grape and greenbrier vines.

"She's just another in a long line. If we win this thing, we're winning it for the likes of them. So they can continue to spin their poison and pollute the world with their—"

"Paracusi Rattlesnake; Tastanaki; Tuskaloosa; Thlakko Darting Snake; Cafakke; Blood Thorn; your brother, Choctaw Hair; Two Packs . . ." She furrowed her brow. "Want me to continue? Or shall I remind you that our world is composed of a balance, red and white Power, order and chaos, constantly vying for influence?

"And as bad as Ears or your mother might be, you would prefer to surrender our world to the likes of de Soto? Sacrifice the memories of Blood Thorn and Tuskaloosa to an abomination? Come on, Black Shell, you *know* the Monster for what he is. You've looked into his eyes, seen his malignant Kristiano soul. You'd actually allow yourself to live in *his* world?"

I gave her a menacing look.

She ignored me, saying, "Horned Serpent has believed in you from the beginning. He told you the truth: The battle wouldn't be easy. Nothing was promised but a hard fight. Yet you would betray him and allow the Kristiano gods to win? And what challenge do they offer a person? Just believe in *dios-jesucristo*. Accept them as your gods and your *single* soul goes to *paraíso*, where it spends forever mingling with a bunch of rancid-smelling Kristianos?" She shifted her crossbow, asking, "Doing what? Just sitting there? They never tell you what they do in *paraíso*."

I growled under my breath. "Antonio said they sing and are joyous."

"How long can you just sing and be joyous? A year? Maybe ten? After a lifetime of it, and with eternity looming, how long could your soul stand that?"

I waved her down. "It's not that. It's . . . Well . . ." I surrendered and told her the truth. "My problem is that people I love keep dying."

"To be born is to die. It's unpleasant. But that's how Breath Giver made the world. Good times and bad. The struggle to achieve balance . . . it's something to *do*. Don't you understand? The Kristiano gods offer . . . what? Eternity in a place filled with only Kristianos? Black Shell, you don't even speak their language!" She shook her head in disgust. "Given a choice, I'll even take the Piasa over that."

I chuckled, feeling the sepaya warming on my chest. We clambered over a giant rotting log, its surface covered with green moss. My sword clanked, and I winced, grabbing the hilt to still it. From here I could see the trail leading down the slope. There, just beyond the gloom of the dusk-heavy forest, a graying indicated the edge of the trees.

"Quiet from here on out," I whispered. "Dogs, come, heel."

I reached out, laying a hand on Pearl Hand's smooth shoulder. "Tomorrow, I promise, no matter what happens you and I are sneaking away. I want to hold you, run my fingers through your hair. I want to lie with you and look into your eyes. You know that, don't you?"

I could barely see her answering smile in the growing darkness. "Forever, my love."

"Be careful tonight."

"You too."

I grabbed her close, hugging her strong and athletic body against mine. For long moments we pressed together—well, as well as we could with bows, quivers, and awkward crossbows in our hands. When we broke apart, it was like tearing something open in my souls.

Tell me this isn't the last time I'm going to hold her.

With the rustle of the dry leaves as our only sound, we eased down to the edge of the trees where two Chicaza warriors crouched behind thick myrtle trunks.

"What do you see?" I whispered, waving the dogs down behind me.

"Nothing unusual, Orphan. The same number of guards as last night."

"And the cabayos?" Pearl Hand asked under her breath.

"Inside the town."

"What have you heard? Orders shouted? A lot of metal clinking?"

The scout shrugged. "Metal? On occasion. Sometimes there is laughter, other times singing. Wait. There. See? That's the cabayero who rides past every so often. He crisscrosses, back and forth. But there is only one on this side of town. It will be easy to ghost past him."

"What about the cabayo?" Pearl Hand asked. "What if it smells or hears you?"

The scout's teeth flashed in the darkness. "Minko Pearl Hand, we've been sneaking in and out for weeks now. In the beginning, the cabayos always alerted the riders to our presence. Now, well, they just consider us part of the night."

I bit back laughter. The cabayos had grown used to us? For once we'd managed to outsmart the *Adelantado*'s great advantage.

Behind us, the first of the squadrons would be filtering its way down the slope, warriors feeling their way over roots and around trees.

I looked up at the sky, the first stars twinkling in the deepening blue-black. Not just twinkling but almost blinking. I'd seen that before. And stilling my souls, I felt it—the heavy tension in the air.

"Storm's coming," I whispered.

Pearl Hand nodded. "Let's unleash the thunder."

FORTY-SIX

THE STORM BROKE AT ABOUT MIDNIGHT. AND IT DID so with a vengeance. Out of the north, a low moan began imperceptibly and grew. The stillness stirred, a breeze tickling the backs of our necks. In the darkness beyond, I heard the lone Kristiano guard speak to his cabayo, as if to reassure it. I knew what the beast was smelling: thousands of *indio* bodies assembling just back from the tree line.

What began as a breeze puffed, eddied, and strengthened. I could hear the escalating roar as it tore through the distant trees. The clattering of branches flailing against each other was drowned by a rushing hiss and moan as the first major gust blew past.

"Let's go," the scout whispered. "The cabayero should be at the far end of his sweep."

"Dogs, heel," I commanded, then Pearl Hand and I rose, following the trail out into the darkness.

"Careful," the guard warned. "There's a ditch. Yes. Right here. Feel with your feet."

The last thing I wanted to do was fall with my sword

and bow clattering, even if the wind did cover any sound. Another gust batted me forward, trying to rip the quiver from my back, blowing strands of loose hair around my face.

I envied the dogs. With their better night vision and sharper noses, they probably thought this was easy.

Moments later, one of the houses loomed before us, a lighter shade of darkness. We crept under the overhanging roof, the wind whistling in the thatch over our heads.

I pulled an arrow from the quiver and nocked it in the bowstring, ready to draw.

"Let's just hope it's not a trap," the scout murmured.

"If anyone calls out," Pearl Hand said, "let me answer. If it's a single guard, maybe we can get close enough to kill him. If it's more, I might be able to confuse them long enough for us to escape."

"This way," I whispered, making my way along the clay-daubed wall and into the black gap between it and its neighbor—a new construction put up by the Kristianos. They'd left the walls unplastered, the freshly cut logs exposed to the elements.

My throat went dry as I led the way into the narrow black passage, feeling with my feet. The place smelled of urine. But then Kristianos were lazy that way. Instead of walking back to the latrine, they peed anywhere.

Reaching down, I ran my fingers over a dog's fur—Gnaw by the size of him—and shoved him forward, figuring he'd go wide around any obstruction. In a crouch, my hand on his tail, we proceeded, and sure enough a stack of baskets was in the way. At that moment a fierce gust of wind picked them up and sent them tumbling off into the darkness.

Moments later, I stopped at the corner of the house. Another loomed before us. The night was so black I could see nothing but the dimmest of shapes. From the wooden house on my left came a curse, and I froze. Pearl Hand cocked her head, listening, then leaned her lips next to my ear. "He's just cursing the storm."

"Where to?" I asked.

"Where else?" she answered, and I felt more than saw her point in the direction of the tchkofa. She wanted de Soto. Right in the middle of Chicaza town. About as far from an escape as we could get.

I froze when something moved off to the right. Metal clinked, and a familiar snuffling sounded.

Cabayo!

My heart in my throat, I watched the accursed thing sidestep, the metal clinking.

What? They chained the cabayo? To what? And why?

I tapped the scout on the shoulder and pointed him off to the west, away from the animal. *Power keep you safe, young warrior.*

I could just make out the beast watching us, its ears forward, head up and alert. I heard the faint whickering.

Bark growled in return, and I thumped him on the top of the head. If anyone ruined this, it would be him, barking his fool head off at just the wrong time.

"Come on."

Pearl Hand ghosted behind me, the dogs sniffing around, as we threaded our way through the maze of buildings. The new wooden ones the Kristianos had thrown up were easy to see. The slight glow of the night fires within illuminated gaps in the walls.

My thought was that unlike the clay-walled Chicaza houses, the Kristiano ones would burn clear to the ground like torches.

Finally passing the Raccoon Clan house, we headed out into the plaza. Cabayos—numbering in the tens— were bunched up around the goalpost at the far end of the stickball field. Not that I could really see, but none seemed to be saddled.

"Pus and blood," I whispered in stunned revelation. "We've caught them by complete surprise!"

"So it would seem," Pearl Hand agreed, looking around, her cocked crossbow braced on her hip. "By Piasa's balls, Black Shell, if we can get the squadrons in, we might do this mad thing."

Creeping forward, the Tula bow before me, I experienced a rush of exhilaration. *Please, Breath Giver, get the squadrons past that line of houses!*

If we could flood this place with warriors . . .

I shot a glance over my shoulder. Through a gap I could see a yellow flicker atop one of the dwellings behind the Raccoon Clan house. Our scout about his work? Driven by the wind, the flicker elongated into a line of flame that ran up the thatch. Four or five structures to the east, another flicker of light began to dance its way up a thatch roof. The scouts were definitely about their work.

"It's started," Pearl Hand said as a gust of wind pelted us with dust and little stinging bits of debris. I thought of all the places Kristianos urinated and crapped; then I wondered what was being blown against our bodies and into our hair . . .

"Kristianos are vile. Let's go kill some." I kept remembering the heat waves shimmering above the hot thatch that last day I'd been here. "As dry as that thatch is, the whole town will be lit up like daylight within a hand's time."

Pearl Hand started forward. "We don't want to be caught in the open when that happens."

"Hurry!" I started for the tchkofa at a trot, hearing the first whicker of alarm from a cabayo tethered back among the houses behind us.

An answering call came from the massed cabayos in the stickball ground. In the growing light I could see that they were contained by some sort of rope corral.

In every direction, flickers of light whirled crazily as

472

Chicaza scouts whipped their fire ropes over their heads to keep the pitch burning. I could see them reaching up with twists of burning grass, torching roof thatch.

The first roofs lit were burning brightly now, dots of fire all along the back row of the northernmost buildings. Each gust of wind whipped sparks into the air. Impossibly, the Kristianos still hadn't caught on. Of course, the fire burned *up* the roofs, and the wind was deadening the sound. It wouldn't take long before the flames began to burn *through*.

Meanwhile, I could imagine the squadrons. At the first sight of the flames, they'd started marching out of the trees.

Chicaza town was surrounded on the north, east, and west—the south mostly walled by the accursed *puerco* pen and its squealing mass of despicable creatures.

We had them!

At that moment, a cabayero came pounding through a gap on the eastern end of town, racing his animal for the tchkofa. Even as I watched, he was staring in disbelief at the irregular pattern of burning roofs.

"*¡Fuego!*" the cabayero screamed. "*¡Hay fuego en el pueblo!*"

The wind seemed to rip his words away.

Pearl Hand and I stared forward as the man slid his cabayo to a stop before the tchkofa, no more than two bow-shots away. The rider vaulted from the saddle and bolted through the tchkofa door. His beast trotted off a couple of steps, the control straps dragging. The cabayo looked first at the collection of its mates tied off in front of the tchkofa and then at the flames that twinkled and leaped from nearly every roof along the northern row.

"The Monster's alerted now," Pearl Hand said, shielding her face from another burst of wind, dust, bits of cabayo dung, and who knew what other debris. "We need to be outside his door when he emerges."

Hurrying after her, I finally smelled smoke.

Even over the wind, I heard the cursing. Saw de Soto and his subordinates as they charged out of the tchkofa. De Soto was already dressed in armor. His head was bare, the wind whipping his hair and beard this way and that. In that instant, I watched the incredulous look that filled his thin face, saw his mouth drop into a disbelieving O as he took in the burning buildings. For just that moment, he stood, stunned, then wheeled on his heel. Bellowing orders, he went for his cabayo.

I nocked an arrow as I ran.

The first cries of surprise and terror erupted from the dwellings, clan houses, and temples. Men burst from the doorways, many of them naked. Each spun around, looking up at his roof, arms wide, head back, crying his disbelief.

The northern half of Chicaza town glowed in the light of an irregular row of bonfires as the roofs caught, were fanned by the wind, and exploded into flames.

A man burst from the doorway of a burning house ahead and to our left. He stared at us, illuminated as we were in the gaudy firelight. "*¡Indios!*"

Pearl Hand slid to a stop, lifted her crossbow, aimed. I heard the *thick-twang* as she shot; the arrow caught the man with a snap, square in the breastbone. He staggered, eyes popping wide. After taking a couple of steps to the side, his knees gave, and he collapsed face-first into the dirt. Blood bubbled from the gaping wound in his back where the arrow had gone clear through. He kept kicking and clawing at the earth, his fingers tearing apart a pile of cabayo dung.

Shouts and cries came from all sides. Kristianos kept emerging from their burning houses, milling about, waving their arms. Everywhere I looked I saw what I'd never thought I'd see, what I'd come to believe impossible: Kristianos in confusion, chaos, and in some cases, hysteria.

I spun on my heel, drew, and drove a war arrow through a half-dressed man who charged toward us. He twirled at the impact, long black hair flying, and landed on his side. Half of my shaft protruded from his back. Gurgling and coughing, he thrashed, trying to reach around for the bloody arrow.

I winced. He'd been an *indio*, one of us. Perhaps a convert, perhaps just a man struggling to survive.

Doesn't matter. He's with them.

While the storm howled down upon us, the bellowing of combatants mingled with those who shrieked in panic and terror. I caught a glimpse of a Chicaza warrior leaping among a scrambling group of Kristianos. The attacker's war club was whistling and singing as the Kristianos ducked and scattered before him. One of them stumbled, fell, and the warrior's blow caught the man square on the top of the head.

De Soto! Get de Soto! The impossibility of what I was witnessing had distracted me. I turned, nocking another arrow, and started for the tchkofa.

In the gaudy light of the growing fires I saw de Soto—still too far away for a good shot—vault onto his cabayo. Wheeling the mount around, he reached down, taking a proffered lance from his servant. Then he kicked the beast in the sides and charged off into the smoke and flames.

"Blood and pus!" I roared. "He's getting away!"

I had made no more than three steps in pursuit when the *Adelantado's* war dogs, somehow left behind, fixed on me. Perhaps they remembered—or maybe they just went for the first *indio* they saw.

Like streaks, bellies low, ears back, they shot toward me, each stride elongating their slim bodies. I pulled up, drew my arrow, and released . . . only to see the shaft miss by a hair's breadth. I was frantically reaching for another arrow when the closest leaped.

Flinging an arm out to fend off the beast, I backpedaled and lost my balance. As I hit the ground, I scrambled, trying to collect myself. The thudding sound of impact, the huff of violently expelled breath, and a piercing yip added to my fear. The war dog was rolling, its four feet windmilling. Gnaw—apparently staggered by the impact—righted himself and leaped. Blackie beat him to the fight, sinking his teeth in the war dog's shoulder.

De Soto's other dog was sliding, clawing at the ground in an effort to turn, when Bark launched himself at the hapless beast.

Panicked as I was, I had no trouble scrambling to my feet. By that time, Gnaw and Blackie were in hot pursuit of the first fleeing dog. Bark, however, wasn't about to let his victim go. Heedless of the viciously snapping war dog, he had the creature by the front leg, shaking it so hard the squealing hound couldn't get its footing.

Once Bark had his quarry crippled, it was only a matter of time.

"Black Shell!"

I turned, squinting into the debris-laced wind. Pearl Hand bent over her crossbow, her foot in the loop as she struggled to cock it. She was glancing frantically at a group of Kristianos who'd spilled out of the burning Raccoon Clan house. Even as I looked, one was pointing at Pearl Hand, shouting, and waving his companions our way.

And Pearl Hand—setting the string and lifting the crossbow—only had one shot.

FORTY-SEVEN

THE LEAD KRISTIANO SAW ME AN INSTANT BEFORE I released. He ducked sideways, the arrow cutting a groove across the top of his shoulder. As he recovered his balance, I was drawing from my quiver.

Pearl Hand's crossbow made its singing *twang*. The Kristiano behind my adversary jerked at the impact, screamed, and stopped short. Two of his companions rushed forward to support him.

My target took one last look as I nocked my arrow, wheeled on his heel, and ran for all he was worth. Before I was sure of my shot he vanished after his friends into a gaudy orange plume of smoke that came billowing like a thing alive from between the houses.

An arrow nocked and ready, I covered Pearl Hand as she struggled to reset her crossbow.

Another tremendous gust rocked us, and I took stock of the situation. My eyes were burning, a cough tickling at the base of my throat. Blinking, I peered into the whipping smoke, turning my head aside as a gust of wind blew bits of ash, smoke, and grit at me. By the Piasa's balls, when was this wind going to lessen?

And so *much* smoke? Where had it come from? Above us the sky was filled with it, and more amazing it pulsed with an eerie yellow-orange glow that lit the whole of Chicaza town. The entire northern side of Chicaza town had become a wall of flame, the buildings fronting the plaza outlined in the odd red-orange light.

Before the tchkofa the huge long-tailed Kristiano cross loomed like a black wraith, its silhouette an ominous presence against the weird illumination that glowed in the sky.

I could see the cabayos, panicked, tossing their heads, pulling at the chains or ropes that bound them to guardian posts, ramadas, or logs. Through it all, men ran, naked or half-dressed, arms waving, hair streaming.

When was this wind going to let up? Sparks were twirling past like twisting formations of mad fireflies.

Amid the shouts and cries, I could hear the screams of cabayos, the crackling roar of the great fires.

Blood and pus, don't think of Mabíla.

I shook myself to shed the images that came bubbling up from hideous memory.

"Black Shell?" Pearl Hand asked, blinking at the smoke. "What are we doing?"

I gaped as one of the wooden Kristiano buildings in the back began to burn like a great pyre as its thatch roof collapsed. It settled in: *The wind isn't going to let up! This is just the beginning. And the coming storm is going to be a monster.*

"We're getting out of here!" I cried as a blast of wind sailed a section of burning mat past my head. I could have reached out and grabbed it.

Another wall of wind-driven smoke rolled over us, and I reached out, taking Pearl Hand's arm. The heat was tremendous, stifling, and we couldn't breathe. Panic surged. *Gods, not again. Not Mabíla.*

Run!

But which way?

Holding Pearl Hand's arm, I scuttled forward, head down, hoping I could find a way to clearer air.

I could hear cabayos over the fire's roar; the high-pitched screams they make when they burn to death is singularly horrifying.

An instant later, one exploded out of the smoke, its mane and tail on fire. The beast's eyes were wide with terror, its mouth open to expose white teeth, the nostrils distended. Hooves hammering the hard earth, the flaming apparition hurled past, sending us sprawling. Then it vanished into the maelstrom.

For the moment, we huddled on the ground, sucking air as an eddy brought relief from the smoke, soot, and sparks.

"Didn't think it would work this well," Pearl Hand managed to say through gritted teeth.

I struggled to my feet as a Kristiano, naked, bearded, and panicked, stumbled into view. Tears were running down his sooty face, and he coughed, snot flying from his nose.

At sight of us, he started forward. Then recognition flashed, and he turned, screaming, and sprinted off into the smoke.

"This way!" We had to head into the smoke, try to find a place where the wind was blowing fresh air between the building gaps. And hope the gale didn't blow a burning roof off a building and right onto us.

Come on, Horned Serpent, give us a break from this accursed wind!

I bellowed as a burning ember spiraled down from the sky and landed in the hollow above my collarbone. Flicking it away, I choked on smoke. Coughing, my eyes streamed tears.

Again I was living the nightmare of Mabila.

FORTY-EIGHT

THE IMAGES REMAIN SINGED INTO MY SOULS: BURN-
ing cabayos, suffocating smoke, bits of fire cavorting
through the haze and twirling in the air like things alive.
Until you experience it, you would not believe the sound:
the roaring torrent of flame, popping timbers, and sucking draft. Through it all wound the howl of the wind, occasionally whistling as it eddied around surviving walls.
But the worst, audible through the wailing storm, was the
eerie squealing of terrified *puercos*: a thread of warbling
sound that shivered my bones. It mixed with the shrieks
of panicked cabayos and the torn screams of men burning
alive.

And the stench.

The acrid billows of blowing smoke might have been
suffocating, but when a person could finally take a breath,
it carried the scent of burning hair, the tang of seared
flesh and fat, cooking human and animal meat.

Never letting my grip on Pearl Hand's arm slip, I
dragged her this way and that, trying to find relief from

the hot smoke that seared our throats, burned our lungs, and stung our eyes.

We fumbled our way through the inferno, wracked by bouts of lung-shredding coughing.

I saw a naked Kristiano emerge from the smoke, his hair melted to a shiny mass atop his head, eyes blind and streaming, hands extended before him as he felt his way forward . . . toward what? The man's skin was cherry red, rising in blisters. The breath wheezing in and out of his lungs made an odd squeaking and gurgling sound like I'd never heard.

Tottering from foot to foot, face expressionless and empty, mouth agape, he passed us. What had been a full beard was now but white ash on his cheeks and chin, the skin cooked where tatters of charred clothing fluttered from his body. He vanished into another billowing orange wall of smoky oblivion.

Leaning against each other, Pearl Hand and I lurched into clear air, sinking to our knees, coughing. What had once been a storehouse stood before us, the roof crackling and leaping with fire.

Blinking my eyes clear, I recognized one of the Kristiano women—the pregnant one. She wore a flimsy white fabric dress that did nothing to mask her condition. At that moment she was arguing with a bearded man who stood with his back to us. A sword hung on his hip, and had he turned, Pearl Hand and I were so incapacitated he could have killed us both as we crouched and coughed our throats raw.

Sucking for air, I watched the Kristiano woman pull loose from her husband. He turned to pluck at a chain that restrained his panicked cabayo. The beast had been fastened to a Deer Clan guardian post. Each time the man almost got the chain loose the cabayo would thrash and jerk it tight again.

Vivid orange and yellow light seemed to pulse as

smoke plumes scuttled above our heads. The woman shot a look at the doorway, wheeled, and ducked back into the burning house.

I was getting my breath back when the panicked cabayo kicked, just missing the frantic Kristiano's head. He fell back onto his rear, arms propping him up as he shouted curses at the terrified animal. Looking to his pregnant wife, he found her gone.

"*¡Francisca!*" He bellowed, "*¿Dondé estás?*"

"*¡Las perlas!*" Her voice barely carried from the door. "*¡Necesito mis perlas!*"

That's when the storm belted another powerful gust down upon us. Squinting against the dust, I watched the roof tremble and shake. Burned out around the poles, large chunks of thatch collapsed into the room below.

The woman's eerie and agonized shriek was drowned by the renewed roar of the inferno.

"*¡Francisca!*" The man threw himself at the doorway, only to be met by an eruption of fire, sparks, and gushing smoke. He tried to shield his face with his arms, ducking back.

"*¡Francisca! ¡Dios mio! ¿Francisca?*"

Pearl Hand was clawing at me, and I let her drag me to my feet. She'd watched the Kristiano's cabayo pull back in terror as the doorway spit fire and death. The animal jerked the guardian post from the ground as if it were a sapling. Then it was dragging the heavy post away.

Pearl Hand, head down and squinting, followed. I shifted, blinking at tears, and placed my hand on her shoulder, hoping she could see better than I. In my last glimpse of the Kristiano man, he was wilting before the flames that belched from the gaping door. The roar of the crackling fires drowned his desperate screams.

We emerged into fresh air, the marks where the cabayo had dragged the guardian post clearly visible in the lurid light.

The way led between two houses and into an open space before the Deer Clan charnel house. Miraculously the structure remained intact, although sparks were flitting and dancing like sick insects as they pattered onto the roof.

We sank to the ground again, coughing and gasping. After each episode, I spit black mucus. With a weary hand, I wiped at my nose and eyes. Feeling something burning at my hip, I glanced down and violently tore the little fire pot loose. Vision shimmering with tears, the notion of setting fires was the last thing on my mind. I gave it a powerful toss.

"How do you think the battle is going?" Pearl Hand asked between coughs.

I stared around at our little haven, the walls glowing around us. The door of the charnel house hung open like a black mouth. Blinking to finally clear my vision, I wiped my eyes clean of crusty goo. A flicker of dancing yellow atop the charnel house's thatch roof betrayed where my fire pot had landed.

"We're still alive," I managed to say hoarsely, and wearily staggered to my feet. "Kristianos are running in every direction."

"De Soto?"

"Charged off to the east. Haven't seen him." I blew black snot from my nose. "Hope he's dead."

"If there's justice in the world, he's—" Pearl Hand stopped at the same time I felt the trembling beneath my feet, heard the growing thunder.

Hooves! Hundreds of them!

I shot a look over my shoulder at the same time the first cabayo exploded through the gap between the houses. Behind it came a horde of the panicked beasts. The herd that had been picketed in the plaza had broken free of their rope corral.

I pushed Pearl Hand violently out of the way, falling

back and scrambling like a wounded weasel to get clear of the churning hooves. The image that stuck in my souls is of a blur of legs, the staccato sound of the hooves like violent hail.

Their labored breathing, their huffing, and the cracking of their hooves kept getting closer. Scrambling on all fours to get around the curve of a house wall, I escaped the surge of beasts without being trampled.

Only to have a section of burning cane mat fall on me from above. I beat the stuff behind me, screaming with fear. Free of it, I turned in panic. Fire filled the gap between the walls where but an instant before, I had been.

Trapped.

I had to get to Pearl Hand!

I ground my teeth at the thought of her hoof-crushed body, broken and bleeding as she lay dying in the shimmering orange firelight.

All I had to do was make my way around the house and back to the Deer Clan charnel house. She'd be there. Waiting.

And I'd find her healthy, scared, and relieved to have survived. She'd look at me with that wry arch of the brow and smile crookedly.

Braving a river of unbearable heat pouring out the doorway, I dove past. Heat radiating from the opening prickled my skin and burned like a roasting grill. Gasping in the hot air, I hurried past and cried relief as I encountered the churned earth left by the escaping cabayos.

Following the wall, I stared around, blinking. The roof of the charnel house was burning brightly now, crackling angrily as the fire spread.

Pearl Hand was nowhere to be seen.

I cupped my hands to call and turned when I caught movement to the left. "Thank the gods and . . ."

I blinked, staring as sparks and ash filtered down

through the firelight. The figure stepped out into the open, grinning.

"*Concho Negro!*"

I recognized him through the swirling smoke. Antonio! He came forward slowly, his sword extended and dripping with red.

Please, tell me that's not Pearl Hand's blood.

"*Esta vez, yo le mataré,*" he cried. *This time, I will kill you!* And he started forward.

FORTY-NINE

ANTONIO'S RUINED FACE LOOKED EVEN WORSE, THE scars having trapped soot. Tracks of tears had traced zig-zag patterns across the pink furrows. He wore only short pants that stopped above the knees; his skinny white chest looked odd in the orange glowing light. His feet were as bare as the day Pearl Hand and I had stripped him down in the peninsula. But the sword he held seemed perfectly serviceable.

I pulled my bow from my shoulder, stunned to discover that my quiver had vanished somewhere. But when? How?

Letting it drop, I grinned and reached for the sword.

Antonio stepped forward, his smile a nasty thing that exposed white teeth and crinkled his scars. At the sight of my blade, his eyes widened. *"¡Este es mi espada!"*

"En Mabíla," I told him in my bad *español*, *"yo robar lo."*

A section of burning cloth came twisting down from the heavens, and I ducked sideways.

Antonio lifted a shoulder, as if to shield himself from

the heat as he stepped too close to the burning house. The walls radiated like an oven.

His bare chest was smudged with soot, and bits of gray ash coated his shoulders and snarled his hair. He circled warily. Remembering how close I'd come to killing him last time, no doubt.

"This time we finish it," I murmured, moving slowly, feeling the searing heat from the house wall, aware of the growing roar from the charnel house roof. Before long it was going to make this place unbearable. I was really wishing I'd thrown that pot somewhere else.

Antonio rushed, and I used a warrior's parry to knock his blade aside. He was better than the last time we'd fought outside of Mabila. Yes, I'd wounded his right arm, forced him to fight with his left. He'd been so awkward that but for his armor I'd have killed him at Mabila. Since then, I realized, he'd been earnestly practicing while I'd been playing a high minko. The cool realization washed through me again.

He can kill you, Black Shell.

As if he read my thoughts, his mocking smile widened.

"¿*Feo?*" I asked. "That's what they call you now?"

At the word, he lunged at me—and I chopped at him with four rapid strokes, trying to accomplish with strength what I lacked in skill. Then I leaped back, wincing as the terrible heat from the burning house seared my back.

He started for me again, then jumped back with a cry as he stepped barefoot on a hot ember.

I saw my opportunity and charged, the *hierro* ringing as he and I traded blows, cutting and thrusting. His blade slipped inside my guard, and a terrible sting traced along my right ribs.

I dared not look down, but from the glee in his face, the anticipation in his eyes, he knew he had me.

Got to do this fast, Black Shell, before he recovers.

I feinted, skipped, and managed to cut his shoulder. Deftly he danced back, rapping my blade to the side as he did so.

A terrible gust drowned us with thick smoke, sparks and embers flickering past my burning and blinded eyes. I angrily slashed at the haze, squinting, trying to see.

When it cleared, he was blinking, tears leaking down his face. Slitting his eyes, he located me and closed. His sword's point flicked this way and that as he taunted, "*¿Estás listo por perdicion, indio sucio? Los demonios están esperando para usted.*"

I skipped aside as another gust of smoke and sparks eddied past, and charged him as he blinked at the sting of it.

The *hierro* blades rang, and I physically drove him backward. I'd spent my life carrying packs, canoeing trade up and down rivers. He'd spent his atop a *cabayo*. This was the way to beat him. I knocked his point away from my heart and rushed. If I could just get my fingers around—

I had him! I was glaring into Antonio's triumphant eyes even as I drove him physically back into the hot house wall. I felt the impact through his body as I slammed him into the searing clay.

I got a grip on his sword hand. My right arm across his chest, I pressed him against the burning wall. His face contorted as the clay burned his naked skin. A scream tore from his throat. I jammed my forearm under his jaw and crushed his windpipe.

Remembering the woman he'd raped that night outside Mabila, I drove my knee into his crotch. Each time my knee crushed his genitals, his body jerked. His expression twisted. Jets of pain glazed his eyes. The burning clay was cooking his naked back and thighs. Antonio's sword slipped away from his nerveless fingers. I shifted my grip, both hands clamping on his throat.

He tried to scream, bucking against me, clawing at my face. I watched his panic build as I pressed him into the roasting wall. Bits of burning thatch were falling around us, stinging my shoulders. I caught the stink of singeing hair—mine and Antonio's—mixed with the relentless smoke.

The back of my fingers felt on fire as I choked and cooked the life out of the maggoty weasel.

His chest heaved. Desperate lungs sucked futilely.

"For Fetch," I growled as I stared into his bulging brown eyes. "For the murdered innocents at Napetuca. Remember them? The ones who surrendered? The defenseless ones you hacked to death? And for the warriors you chopped into pieces and castrated at Anhaica. Remember how you severed their arms and legs, tying them off so they wouldn't bleed to death?" I glared into his wide, panicked eyes. Did I really hear his skin sizzling over the maelstrom? I reveled in the moment as his body ceased to spasm and quiver. A weary sense of relief came as his weight sagged, but I kept my grip, letting him roast on the hot wall. I turned my head away, ignoring the pain in my fingers.

I let him drop when I saw ash sticking to his wide and sightless eyes. Raising an arm against the terrible heat, I staggered back and dropped to my knees. Panting for air, I just stared at him, all the hatred and rage inside me draining away.

Wind gusts were playing with his ash-mottled hair, his eyes bugged, and his mouth was open where his tongue had been forced out between his teeth.

Wearily I grabbed him by a foot and dragged him out into the open. In our world, the evil are dismembered at death, and in extreme cases, their body parts are scattered. Oftentimes even hung in trees in order to prevent the evil from ever reassembling itself.

I could barely hold my sword as I raised it and

chopped at Antonio's neck. Two strokes later I'd severed his head. Then I hacked off his right hand. Fire and smoke swirled down around me, blinding my eyes, choking my lungs. My skin felt as if it were melting on my body. Any longer and I was going to cook with Antonio.

At least I had his head. Proof for Pearl Hand.

I stuffed Antonio's hand into his mouth. Grabbing his head by the hair, I staggered for the gap beside the charnel house wall. Arm up against the blasting heat, I ducked and ran blindly through the gap.

But for the wind, I'd have died in there, confused, panicked, with no sense of direction.

The memories of that desperate journey would stay with me: glassy images of flames leaping into the night; the contorted and blackened corpses of cabayos burned to death; a smoking pile of Kristiano saddles, the leather now charcoal; glowing red spear-ax heads lying amid the ashes of what had once been their long polelike handles; the burned-out metal frame of what had once been a Kristiano shield. I remember tripping and clambering over piles of dead Kristianos where they'd suffocated or cooked, trapped between burned-out buildings.

Staggering, lungs heaving and coughing, I emerged from the now-smoldering remains of the last houses. In clear, cold air, I dropped to my knees, tears of relief leaking from my stinging eyes. Blood from the cut along my ribs had heat-dried into a hard sheet that stiffened my side.

In the clearing between me and the forest, I could see dim forms moving in the reflected glow of the fire. A knot of fifteen or so Kristianos were running back and forth, shouting. Three of them held shields with which they tried to protect the rest. Even as I watched they retreated back toward the burning town.

Before them, the broken remains of a Chicaza squadron advanced behind a line of shields, but as the archers behind them shot arrows, the wind whisked them this way and that.

Immediately the tactical problem became clear. The Kristianos had only a few shields, a single spear-ax, and a collection of swords. To win, they needed to close with the Chicaza. But the closer they came, the less effect the gusting wind had on Chicaza archery. And for once, the Kristianos fought without the protection of their wonderful armor. In the end, it would only be a matter of time before the Chicaza destroyed them.

Pearl Hand? Where's Pearl Hand?

I struggled to my feet, bending and coughing. My side stung as if a hundred cactus thorns were embedded in it. Glancing down in the fire glow, I winced at the length of gaping skin. But for the clotted blood, I'd have been able to see my ribs.

My fighting was finished. I'd lost my quiver. No way I was charging around trying to kill Kristianos with my side hanging open.

Picking a section of open field, I staggered out, headed for the safety of the dark forest beyond. Antonio's head bobbed and jerked, his hair pulling at my blood-slick, burned, and blistered fingers.

"Pearl Hand? May Breath Giver guard you and keep you safe."

Me, I was starting to feel weak and dizzy.

Come on, Black Shell, you've got to get out of here.

But even as I made my weary way into the forest, I could hear voices. And they were calling in *español* . . .

FIFTY

MAKING MY ESCAPE THAT NIGHT WAS A TRIAL. THE forest around Chicaza town was crawling with little knots of Kristianos who huddled, terrified, at the fringe of the trees. Added to the mix, occasional panicked cabayos crashed this way and that, fleeing from any sound.

But I did catch glimpses of the battle on occasion. Across the flats I could see Chicaza town burning in the wind-whipped night. Laid out as a great square, it might have been a huge burning box, a wind-flattened inferno that shot eerie glowing smoke off to the south. The weird yellow-orange light illuminated the fields, the surrounding forests, and the confusion of silhouetted figures charging back and forth.

I could make out Chicaza squadrons, advancing, chasing a handful of Kristianos back toward the inferno. Whoever commanded them did so with great skill, because each time the Kristianos blew their horn and were reinforced by a small group of cabayeros, the squadrons retreated.

Then a distant trumpet would sound, and the cabayeros would race off to the north, where another batch of Kristianos were imperiled. As soon as the cabayeros left the squadrons would advance again, and the Kristianos would run for the safety of their burning town.

Through the chaos, a panicked herd of riderless cabayos raced back and forth, their heads low, tails out. Each time they charged past a Chicaza squadron, the formations would break, warriors scattering for fear of being attacked by cabayeros.

I staggered on, slipping through the dark, wincing as the pain in my side grew worse. Every burn on my body stung like a swarm of wasps had anchored themselves to my hide. The backs of my fingers ached where the clay wall had tried to turn them into toasted corn. I was panting, partly from the pain, partly from the night's exertions. Walking in a dark forest is hard enough when a person is healthy and rested.

Antonio's head—symbol of my victory—bounced and jerked with each step, as if to yank my arm from its socket. The hair I gripped cut into my fingers. The thing seemed to weigh more than a sack of rocks.

I kept tripping, stumbling, running into things. Did I dare make my way down to the open fields? As much as I'd be able to see better, so would any roving Kristianos; my thought was that after tonight, they'd be only too happy to avenge themselves on any hapless, wounded *indio* trader who happened to wander past.

Hurt as I was, I'd be no match for them.

While I still had Antonio's sword, I had no arrows for the Tula bow. If worse came to worst, I barely had enough strength to throw Antonio's head at them.

And then there was the thirst. It had been half a day since I'd drunk last. Then had come the exertion—not to mention the baking heat of the fire.

Come on, Black Shell. You can make it home. Just keep your wits about you.

I reached down and patted Antonio's expressionless face. Too bad I couldn't have chopped every bit of him into pieces. The hand still protruding from his mouth would commit no more evil in my world.

"So," I croaked, "the only one left is de Soto."

Taking one final glance back at the burning ruins of Chicaza town, I wondered just how long it would be before I stood over his lifeless body.

"Blessed Spirits, please tell me that killing Antonio hadn't come at the cost of Pearl Hand's life."

Where are you, wife?

I should have remembered the dreams. Just because my body was hurting, exhausted, and heedless didn't mean that my souls were. But all I had were fragments, flashes. Bits of images that whirled around like pictures drawn on fall leaves as they spiraled and fluttered from on high.

One such glimpse remained with clarity: Horned Serpent speaking to me, his great crystalline eyes like faceted quartz ablaze with sunlight. His rainbow scales reflected purple, crimson, yellow, and green. The great forked horns atop his head glistened, the deepest red I'd ever seen. I recalled the slightest bit of movement, as if he were spreading his wings . . .

And nothing else. Not a word of what we'd discussed. I couldn't tell where we'd been. The Sky World? Some forest? The Underworld? I know I was standing, feet on the ground, in front of him. All the other details had vanished into nothingness like the smoke from Chicaza town.

My dreams might have been a beautiful bowl, one decorated with remarkable and intricate designs. Until it was dropped, the sherds flying in all directions. In the aftermath I was trying to piece it all together. But so many of the sherds were missing. Something important had happened to my dream soul, some great understanding.

If only I could reconstruct the patterns that had once been incised upon the burnished clay of my memory.

That worry preoccupied me as I came awake. I blinked, trying to clear my rheumy eyes. When I sought to move my hands, I cried out at the stinging pain.

Burned. I knew that feeling. But how? Where?

I started to take a deep breath and bit off a cry, frantically gasping for shallow breaths instead. Pain lanced my side like lightning.

Breath and thorns, I hurt! And I'd have given anything for a simple drink of water.

Struggling to clear my vision, I tried to wipe at my eyes despite my stinging fingers, only to find them slathered with grease. Around me, the world seemed to be spinning, and I felt sick, as if I were falling and no direction was up.

Where am I? The question echoed between my souls.

Just then a cool nose bumped my face, followed in turn by a warm tongue. Through the blur covering my eyes I could see the gray outline of Gnaw's head. He snuffled at me, licked my face all over, and elicited my squeaky whimper of pain when he pushed too hard with his head.

"Down, old friend," I whispered. "Easy."

But where were Fetch, Skipper, Bark, and Squirm? I frowned, struggling to remember something important. They had to be somewhere close. They wouldn't go far without Gnaw.

Terrible thirst was driving me mad.

Must be water in the packs. I always kept a bladder of water in Fetch's pack. Never knew when the dogs might need a drink.

It felt so hot. Hot? Were we down in the peninsula? In the Timucua lands? There was some hot and dry country down there, especially south of Ocala town in the sand barrens.

But what would I be doing there?

Then I remembered: Stories . . . I'd heard stories . . .

Yes, of the bearded and pale sea peoples. All through the peninsula people told the most remarkable stories about the sea peoples. How they floated in wondrous wooden palaces with trees . . .

I hesitated as images of the floating palaces, lights glowing on their decks, formed down in the eye of my souls. As if I'd seen such things . . .

But where?

Gnaw was still standing there, his face close to mine. I could tell he was trying to communicate something important. In the dim gray light I could see the white tip of his tail through the blur as it wagged back and forth.

Cocking his head, he whimpered, pawed at me, and started away. After several paces, he stopped, glancing over his shoulder as if to see if I were following. The question filled his eyes, and he whined uncertainly.

"Go," I told him. "I can't follow right now."

Unaccountably I suffered a feeling of longing, as if watching his departure into the gray mist were of some major import.

But where was I?

Thirsty, so thirsty . . .

And tired . . . very . . . tired . . .

Reprieve

She is dozing, her body braced against the wall of her house. Her head is tipped back. Strings of her weedy gray hair barely cushion her scalp from the rough mud. The bright sun shines warm on her face. The direct light burns the world into a red haze on the backs of her eyelids.

Vaguely she's aware of a buzzing fly. Her souls, however, are sleep-numb and can't goad her into enough wakefulness to make her close her gaping mouth. More than once she's been rudely awakened when the beasts landed on her tongue. Then she snorts and chokes, trying to spit out the vile creatures. On those occasions, people generally avert their glances discreetly, covering their smiles.

Children are never so polite.

She hears the first of the cries. They are joyous, celebratory. Within moments the delighted screams intrude and bring her to wakefulness. She opens her eyes and shades them with a withered palm just in time to see Drawn Knee and Three Fingers appear around the curve of the tchkofa wall. They stride at the head of a joyous band of relatives.

She grins, finding herself delighted at the sight of the two warriors. Just days ago their canoe had been found capsized and downstream from where they'd been fishing in the Tallahatchie. Everyone had presumed them drowned and dead.

Now, looking little worse for wear, here they are, dirty, hungry looking, and travel worn.

At that moment, Bright Bead, Drawn Knee's wife, bursts from between the Panther Clan buildings and charges forward. As she runs, her breasts bouncing, she screeches with relief. The slim woman literally throws herself into her husband's arms.

She watches as the muscular man whirls his wife around, her feet flying off the ground and out.

People clap and cheer.

"Ah, yes. Enjoy him, dear girl." *She smiles fondly, resettling her old shoulders against the plaster of her house wall.*

Was I that foolish? *She thinks back to the moment after the battle of Chicaza when she first heard that Black Shell had been found in the forest, gravely wounded, and carried to Black Oak town.*

"I'd been worried to my bones. Searched all that night. Found Bark and Blackie. But not Black Shell. Remember the panic? How with each passing hand of time, my desperation grew?"

She nods to herself, reliving that terrible flight from Chicaza town, and her building terror.

"His side has been cut open, Minko Pearl Hand," *the Crawfish Clan warrior had told her.* "That's all I know. A group of our warriors carried him to the Chief Clan house. The hopaye has gone to see if there's anything he can do or whether he needs to prepare the body for the charnel house."

The fear had burst inside her like a dropped pot.

How I ran that day! *She grins toothlessly at the midday sun, hardly aware of the way her head is wobbling on her weak neck.*

And yes, I was as frantic as Bright Bead when I burst into the Chief Clan house. *Her heart had been pounding, sweat tracing streaks down the soot and filth coating her face and body. On legs trembling from exhaustion, she'd stumbled forward. Heart deadening in her breast, she'd fixed on Black Shell's slack face, his freshly washed body—and his sister hovering over him.*

When Clear Water had looked up, the way her eyes seemed to expand in her pale face and the pinched set of her lips elicited a desperate cry from Pearl Hand's panic-choked throat.

We always knew it would happen. *And in that instant, she'd known the worst . . . felt her guts sink, her knees give.*

"Black Shell?" she'd cried, stumbling forward, her crossbow clattering on the mat floor. Then she'd fallen to her knees, grabbing up his hand, staring at his slack face. The long wound had been carefully stitched. Threads clotted with dried blood puckered his pale skin. At the sight of the wound's length and location, her breath stopped short, the world wobbling around her.

Chicaza always wash the corpse before carrying it to the charnel house.

The grief exploded, cutting off her air, suffocating her with disbelief.

And then Clear Water said, "He's alive, Pearl Hand. Copper Sky has sewn up the wound. It is producing clear pus, but Black Shell will need some time to recover."

Alive? Alive! And she'd danced, ever so giddy—even hugged Clear Water, a woman she'd never entirely trusted. At her feet the dogs yipped and barked, tails wagging.

Oh, yes, I was foolishly delirious.

"And why not?" she whispers to herself as she watches the people crowd around Three Fingers and Drawn Knee. "We'd cheated death yet again."

Reprieve could be such an intoxicating brew. And when one has it, he should drink deeply of it . . . and revel in the delirium.

FIFTY-ONE

THIRST FORCED ME TO CRAWL BACK FROM OBLIVION. Until a person has really been thirsty, they'll never understand. We can do without food. After a couple of days, the craving eases. But the horror of thirst just gets worse and worse, culminating in acute suffering.

I awakened trying to swallow. Something a human can't do without moisture in his mouth. Instead, your tongue just lodges in the back of your throat and the swallow sticks there, painful and choking.

Trying to sit up, a stinging agony almost paralyzed my side. Which made me clutch my hands and cry out as I stretched the burned skin on my fingers.

Blinking my eyes open, I saw nothing but blur.

"Easy," a voice warned me. "You're safe."

"Water," I croaked.

"I need to lift your head a little." I knew that voice: Clear Water, my sister.

The first crazy thought to stumble into my souls was that I really hoped she'd live up to her name.

She said to someone, "Go inform them that Black Shell's awake."

I groaned as she helped me lift my head and shoulders and slipped a folded blanket beneath me. Then through my blurry vision, I watched as a clay cup was placed to my lips.

Bloody Piasa, yes! Cool water, a form of liquid magic, rolled across my tongue. As much as I craved more, she slowly but surely gave me little sips.

Then, with a damp rag, she sponged my eyes.

As my vision cleared, I recognized my surroundings: the Chief Clan house in Black Oak town. A fire crackled in the pit, and some of the slaves were employed in cooking. From the bit of cloud-gray sky visible through the smoke hole, it was daytime. And I could see misty rain as it fell through the square opening.

"What happened?" I asked. "Last I remember I was in the forest."

Clear Water let me drink again as she said, "A party of Wildcat Clan warriors found you exhausted and bleeding. They fixed a litter and carried you back here. Copper Sky cleaned the wound in your side and sewed it up."

The memories finally fixed themselves. All of the different pains I was suffering from made sense again. And I remembered the warriors and the agonizing journey I'd survived. They'd slung my body between them in a carry blanket.

Breath Giver bless each and every one of them.

Clear Water's eyebrow lifted. "You're a sight, Black Shell. Your shoulders are a mass of blisters, your eyelashes and eyebrows are gone, and portions of your hair are singed away. Copper Sky says that the backs of your fingers may scar, but the damage shouldn't be permanent."

She bent down and lifted Antonio's severed head, his fingers still protruding from the gaping mouth. Antonio's death-grayed eyes had sunk into the skull, the skin sickly pale. "The warriors who brought you in said you were adamant about clinging to this."

"The head belongs to a Kristiano named Antonio," I told her. "You might want to cleanse yourself after touching it. Both head and hand were fonts of evil before I chopped them off his accursed body."

She lowered the trophy to the floor. "Is that the hand that cut that gash in your side?"

"No, his other one. I didn't have time to hack it off. The fire was getting too intense."

Where's Pearl Hand?

I took a moment to sip more water, suddenly afraid to ask the question that formed on my tongue. I glanced instead at the door, feeling my heart begin to pound.

Fire. Smoke. Confusion. *What happened to Pearl Hand?*

Instead I asked, "De Soto?"

Clear Water shifted in an attempt to ease her pregnant belly. "Everything I've heard so far is confused. Outside you can hear all kinds of stories. One person will tell you that he's heard from the high minko himself that we're killing them all. The next person will insist that the Kristiano cabayeros escaped unscathed, that they broke up the squadrons during the fight. And if we're not careful, they'll be here within a hand's time."

"I was there," I told her. "I saw no more than a handful of mounted cabayeros. They were pressed hard to rescue bands of Kristianos under Chicaza attack. As to the rest, it was the terrified cabayos that escaped the inferno that were running back and forth through the formations."

Why isn't she mentioning Pearl Hand? Is it because she doesn't want to tell me?

Fear bloomed between my souls. Maybe no one had seen her. Maybe, like Antonio, the fire had left her a gruesomely burned and unrecognizable corpse. I'd seen enough of them at Mabila to imagine what my wife had become.

. . . And to die that way?

I clamped my jaws, glancing away.

As a result, I didn't see the shadow darken the doorway, but only looked when I heard the rapid footfalls on cane matting.

And she was there, long hair beaded with silver droplets of water. Her smile was worried but radiant. Raindrops glistened on her smooth cheeks and the straight bridge of her nose. As she settled on her knees before me, I just stared into her large dark eyes and let myself fall into those warm depths.

"Blessed gods," I whispered. "I was so worried about you."

She took me by the wrists, avoiding the burns on my hands. "I've been worried sick. Copper Sky said you'd be all right, but the warriors who brought you in said you were delirious. Perhaps due to a hit in the head, though Copper Sky could see no evidence of it."

"What about Two Packs?"

She gave me her amused smile. "He's fine. I only saw him long enough for him to complain that Kristianos can run like deer when they're scared. He never got close enough to smack one."

"And what of the battle?" I asked, anxious for the rest. "Did we destroy them?"

She gave me a halfhearted smile. "Unfortunately that remains to be seen. Your plan was perfect. How could anyone have expected the kind of winds we suffered? Chicaza town went up like a torch. It burned so fast and hot that the high minko couldn't get his formations in place before the town was consumed."

Her beautiful face went grim. "You remember the stampeding cabayos? The ones that would have trampled me to death if you hadn't shoved me out of the way?"

"What happened to you?"

"As they were thundering past, a gust of smoke blew through. Fire falling from the sky . . . it was terrible."

I remembered the chunk of burning debris that had nearly trapped me and nodded. Was that where I'd lost my quiver and arrows?

Pearl Hand continued. "When the air cleared, you were gone. I thought you might have escaped down the passage between the houses where I'd last seen you, but it was a roaring torrent of fire.

"My next-best guess was that for some reason you'd followed the cabayos. I hurried after you, following the cabayo tracks, knowing you had to be close."

"I was stuck behind the burning passage." I went on to explain what had happened . . . and how it had led to Antonio. After I finished, she reached down and pulled his severed hand from between his hardening lips.

"So, you got him at last." She turned the hand, inspecting the curled fingers. "Fetch and all the others will rest easier now." Her wry sidelong glance was measuring. "Not that he didn't manage to take a slice of you along the way."

"I'll heal. What about you?"

Pearl Hand narrowed an eye as she studied Antonio's head where it lay on its left side. She gently set his hand atop the right ear so the curled fingers cupped it. "That big herd of cabayos I was following may have been the key to the whole battle. They went charging out through a gap in the fires . . . and right into the middle of the Deer Clan squadron." Pearl Hand made an offhanded gesture. "What Minko Wide Net saw was a line of cabayos pouring out of the town and right at his center. He barely had time to order an immediate retreat when they smashed into his line. His entire squadron panicked and broke, fleeing back to the safety of the forest. And ran right into Choctaw Hair's formation.

"It was chaos. And those accursed cabayos didn't stop

there, but ran in circles around the burning town. And each time they came galloping out of the night, the Chicaza squadrons, thinking they were under attack, made an immediate retreat."

I blinked in frustration, remembering the glimpses I'd had.

Pearl Hand patted my shoulder, then glanced at Clear Water, who had reseated herself at the foot of my bed and was listening intently. "Meanwhile," Pearl Hand continued, "the Kristianos were caught by complete surprise. They fled, Black Shell. Ran like panicked quail. But for the confusion caused by the terrified cabayos, we'd have trapped them."

"De Soto?" I offered a quick and fervent prayer down in my souls.

"He lives. Remember when we saw him head east? He rode out to attack the Panther squadron. Flying Squirrel had his warriors in a line, driving the Kristianos back into the town. The *soldados* were in a panicked rout, only about half of them armed. Flying Squirrel had them trapped against the burning buildings. It would have been a massacre. Then de Soto rode down on him." She hunched her shoulders in futility.

"The oddest thing happened. De Soto lanced Flying Squirrel, but when he did, the *Adelantado*'s saddle fell right off the cabayo's back." She paused. "The Chicaza seized the opportunity . . . thought they had him. From all accounts it was a closely fought thing. The Panther squadron kept advancing, trying to kill de Soto. The violent wind threw the archery off so badly that a hit was mostly luck. The Kristianos huddled behind the few shields they had and sought to close with the squadron's front ranks. But the closer they got, the better the warriors could shoot in the high wind. In the end the Panther Clan would have surrounded the Kristianos and destroyed them . . . except someone got the saddle back on de Soto's horse. After that it was a stalemate, neither side having the advantage."

"I saw the same thing where I was making my escape."

Pearl Hand smoothed her wet hair with slim brown hands. I wished I could hold them, but it would have hurt too much.

"The same thing happened wherever the Kristianos were able to organize. The rest of them scattered into the forests along with occasional cabayos and slaves. Meanwhile, the town burned. And with it, everything but the few weapons the desperate Kristianos managed to grab on the way out."

"Who would have thought?" Chicaza stood in such stark contrast to Napetuca and Mabila. I'd come to believe the *Adelantado* was invincible.

"We broke them, Black Shell." She used a damp finger to wipe a strand of silky black hair back. "The high minko ordered the squadrons to retire when the fires burned down so much that combat maneuvering was pointless.

"I caught up with him a little before dawn. His plan was to attack again while the Kristianos were still reeling. Finish the job before they could get reorganized."

Pearl Hand paused and sighed. "With the squadrons in formation, your brother marched his forces straight for the smoking ruins of Chicaza town and the milling, stunned Kristianos."

"And?" My heart was pounding, desperate to hear the rest.

She tilted her head whimsically. "The heavens opened at the last minute. A downpour of rain and hail as if the skies had become a disgorging river. And it just went on and on. It was as close as I've ever come to marching underwater. You know what happens to twisted-gut bowstrings when they turn soggy? Even bindings on war clubs were coming loose. Rather than risk a fiasco, your brother called off the attack."

I nodded, trying to get my fuzz-filled thoughts to work. Questions kept forming beneath the surface, but I just couldn't get them to rise into any kind of coherence.

"Maybe our Power gave us the storm when we needed it, and his priests called the extra rain, negating our advantage?" It had all the characteristics of the kind of thing Power would do to interfere in human affairs. "Just once, couldn't we crush them completely?"

"We didn't do too badly," she replied. "In the initial attack we killed close to forty Kristianos. Additionally another forty or so of the slaves, *indio* servants, converts, and laborers died. If we are to believe the different counts made by the scouts, at least eighty cabayos are dead. Some burned to death, but most were shot by warriors. Even more were wounded during the attack. Scouts have observed the Kristianos caring for them."

She paused, her eyebrow lifted in amusement. "This part you are going to love. You know how they built the *puerco* pens on the south side of the town? And you recall how strong they made the fences? Tough enough that we couldn't pull them down and steal their prized food animals? With that terrible wind blowing the fire ahead of it, hundreds of *puercos* were cooked in their pens—literally roasted on their feet. So much fat cooked out of their bodies that it ran in a river down one of the drainages." She paused. "Only a hundred or so of the babies who could wiggle through little gaps managed to escape."

"We won?" I whispered inaudibly.

"Black Shell, our attack came so swiftly most of the Kristianos fled without their armor or weapons. The scouts can count the number of saddles that survived on one hand. Half the Kristianos are huddled naked by the dying fires in Chicaza town. Their blankets, their tools, what little clothing they had, most of the spear-axes and the few thunder sticks left? All burned. They are so desperate they are even trying to make control straps for their cabayos out of grapevines."

I smiled at that. Then I tried to shift—and wished immediately that I hadn't. Pus and blood, that hurt!

"The dogs?" I asked through an exhale.

She fixed me with a knowing look. "Bark and Blackie showed up after the fight. No one has seen Gnaw. I have gone twice, calling for him after dark. Black Shell, I think you should—"

"Gnaw came to me. Here." I felt my heart drop in my chest, a terrible aching hollow forming.

Clear Water said, "I've been here the entire time since they brought you in, Black Shell. If your dog came to you—"

"He was here. He licked me." I swallowed hard, another pain, unrelated to physical wounds, opening in my chest. I remembered Gnaw stopping, looking back, and whining. "Blood and thorns, that's what he was trying to tell me. Saying . . . good-bye."

I watched Pearl Hand's jaws clamp, and she looked away, blinking against something in her eyes. For a long time we sat that way.

"Want to turn," I whispered weakly. "Sore."

Pearl Hand gave me a soft-eyed and sympathetic look. "Copper Sky says you can't. He says that you've got to stay quiet for a day or two until the stitches are fixed."

I blinked and swallowed hard.

Seeing movement, I glanced at the door as my brother strode in followed by several of the clan minkos. His expression was concerned; fatigue lay behind his eyes. From the smudged war paint on his face, I could tell that whatever had been happening, he'd had no time to attend to it. His clothing—consisting of a cape, a war shirt, and high moccasins—was mud smeared and soot stained.

Seeing me awake, he beamed with genuine relief and reached for one of my hands. At the sight of the grease that smeared them, he thought better of the idea. Instead he just smiled. "I am glad to see that your souls are safely back home in your body, brother."

"What's happening?"

"We have to evacuate. The Kristianos are marching on Black Oak town. Our best guess is that with Chicaza town nothing more than smoking ruins, and half of their people naked, they'd rather sleep under these roofs than in the open."

He stood, attention shifting to Pearl Hand. "Warriors will be here with a litter to transport Black Shell. They are to follow your orders. Copper Sky will try to check with you, but he's busy with other wounded."

"We'll be fine," Pearl Hand told him.

And as quickly as that, my brother was gone.

Even as he and his entourage stepped out, the warriors were carrying the litter in. Clear Water was on her feet, calling orders to the servants. In the flurry of activity, boxes were filled, blankets appropriated, and supplies packed.

I have to admit, the warriors tried. They really did. With four of them lifting the blanket I was on, and Pearl Hand helping, it still felt like my side was being physically torn in two.

When they'd finished, the room was spinning, my stomach churning with the dizzy sensation of endless falling. Flickers of light danced behind my eyes and the edge of my vision went gray.

"Careful," Pearl Hand needlessly ordered as they maneuvered me out the door and into the cool afternoon air. She called, and to my relief, Bark and Blackie appeared from where they'd stayed by the door. And Gnaw? Where was Gnaw?

One by one, we're being whittled away.

Gray clouds hung low in the sky, threatening even more rain. In the plaza, people were milling, packs on their backs as they evacuated their most cherished posses-sions. Women were calling orders to children and the town dogs were trotting back and forth.

Using what little mobility I had, I kept craning my neck, expecting to see plumes of smoke rising from the clan houses and storerooms.

Burn the town!

But the thought came to me too late. I was already being hustled up the forest trail to the ridgetop, past the burial mound where Patches and Squirm lay.

Then it hit me. Unlike the rest, Gnaw had had no prayers said over him. He'd been given no provisions for the long journey to the edge of the world.

And the chances of finding his body in the immolated remains of Chicaza town?

A spear of anger mixed with the grief and rage in my heart. I *hated* Kristianos. Let them freeze, starve, and die in misery. Let them—

I glanced around. Surely now that the Kristianos were naked and vulnerable, my brother wouldn't leave that abomination de Soto with a perfectly good town to shel-ter in.

He *had* to order Black Oak town burned.

Something I couldn't see bumped us from behind, and I just opened my mouth, wishing I could have found the breath to scream.

Just one . . . good . . . scream . . .

FIFTY-TWO

ALL THINGS IN BREATH GIVER'S WORLD ARE CON-
nected. I might have finally killed Antonio, but with his
corpse now nothing more than a charred husk, he continued to work evil through the wound he'd cut along my
ribs. Had I not been incapacitated, I'd have ensured that
Black Oak town was burned prior to de Soto's arrival.

As it was, de Soto's cabayeros—most of them riding
bareback—swept into Black Oak town and claimed the
hastily abandoned buildings as their own. Immediately
they initiated sweeps to round up any stragglers and
marched them off into slavery.

I'd been evacuated to Wild Plum town to recuperate.
As a result I only heard secondhand accounts of the on-
going struggle against the *Adelantado*. But my brother, again
to his credit, listened to both my counsel and Pearl
Hand's.

Night after night Chicaza warriors marched in immediately upon cover of darkness and surrounded Black Oak
town. All through the night they beat drums, played

flutes, and sneaked close enough to launch arrows at the lines of sentries de Soto posted in an attempt to ensure infiltrators wouldn't burn him out again. On occasion Chicaza sorties erupted into pitched battles fought by the light of torches or Kristiano bonfires. De Soto's casualties began to add up by ones and twos. Chicaza archers concentrated on the cabayos, risking life and limb in an attempt to hit them when the cabayeros raced out into the night to break up attacks. After the night when we killed four of the beasts, de Soto grew more cautious.

Just before daylight, the squadrons would pull back and race away into the forest.

The night belonged to the Chicaza.

With morning, the roles reversed. Just after sunrise the cabayeros would sally forth, hoping to snare any fleeing Chicaza, ride them down, and either kill or capture them.

Chicaza warriors suffered their own casualties, with lagging warriors occasionally lanced during the daytime sweeps. The nightly attacks took their own toll. Leading one such attack, Minko Cut Hand, along with fifteen of his warriors, died at the head of a Crawfish Clan squadron.

With pride and respect I followed the exploits of Chicaza warriors who, with as much courage as the Apalachee, continued the slow process of destroying the invaders.

Setting my bias aside, it would be difficult to say which people were superior warriors. The Apalachee had had better ground on which to fight, country laced with thickets and swamps that allowed them freer movement, concealment, and maneuvering. At the time the Kristianos had been better supplied, armored, and mounted, negating many Apalachee advantages. Chicaza country was mostly rolling hills covered with old-growth forest, which allowed the Kristiano cabayeros to sweep like the wind beneath the high branches. Chicaza warriors had fewer places to hide or spring ambushes. Offsetting this, much of the Kristiano armor—particularly the cotton-batted shirts—had been burned; they were increasingly vulnerable to Chicaza war arrows.

In the end, however—just as was the case in Apalachee—my Chicaza were prevailing. For every Chicaza killed or wounded, five more were ready to step in and take his place. Each *soldado* or cabayero the *Adelantado* lost was irreplaceable.

Through it all his men spent every day in the forest, chopping down white ash trees to replace the handles on their spear-axes. They also began roasting *hierro* in that big metal contraption I'd once carried and pounding on it with hammers. Perhaps to call some Spirit quality into the *hierro*? Who knew? Whatever their efforts, the Kristianos were surrounded, exhausted, and living in a state of perpetual warfare.

They might have had the buildings in Black Oak town, but due to the constant raids, they weren't allowed to enjoy them. For the most part they spent their nights out under the weather, in defensive formation, struggling to catch what rest they could between attacks. Their bedding burned, half-naked and freezing in the cold spring rain and occasional snow, most of them made grass mats for cover.

I could almost admire them for the discipline they showed in spite of the misery inflicted upon them by both our warriors and the weather.

As the forest began to flower and the spring leaves burst from their buds, the Chicaza licked their lips in anticipation. Thickets that had consisted of bare stems provided excellent concealment once fully leafed out. Where a passing Kristiano would have spotted five or six crouching warriors but ten days ago, now he would only see a wall of green.

And a half moon past equinox, just as I was getting up

and around, the *Adelantado* packed up his dressed-in-grass army. Pearl Hand had told me how they'd rebuilt shields and refitted their weapons. They are, after all, a clever, if malicious, people.

Nevertheless, my first sight of the *Adelantado*'s army was a revelation: Lined up in the forest was a collection of bearded men wearing corroded *hierro* helmets and carrying green-wood shields banded with metal. Where their breastplates had always been at least partially polished, the ones worn by those who still had them were a muddy brown color.

So desperate were they for clothes, some wore tunics of grass. Others had partially tanned deer, raccoon, bear, or dog skins tied about their bodies with lengths of vine. The *soldados* marched with hide wraps on their feet. Cabayeros, many on crudely manufactured saddles lacking stirrups—they had no leather left—rode barefoot.

What had become of that once colorful, gleaming, and mighty thousand who'd marched into Ahocalaquen town? They'd had the great colorful banners fluttering from long poles; sunlight had glinted on polished armor and waving plumes; the brightly dyed, fine-cloth clothing had dazzled the eye; and their high leather boots were polished black and shiny. Everything about them had reeked of splendor and fabulous wealth, color and shine.

I remembered the elegant arrogance of the cabayeros who rode with backs straight, heads high, long lances glinting with *hierro*-tipped death. Their mounts had pranced on dancing feet, necks bowed, tails waving and bobbing. Each of the riders and mounts had been marvelously outfitted with an emblazoned shield. Bright blues, reds, yellows, and greens had decorated beast and rider.

So, too, had the *soldados* marched, weapons clacking rhythmically to the beat of their booted feet. Spear-axes had been shouldered precisely. Thunder-stick shooters had swaggered while crossbowmen paraded in precise formation.

Behind them had followed the well-dressed household servants, the cooks and tailors, and their domestic possessions, including the heavy tents, chairs and tables, great pots, endless ceramic jars, bales of cloth, casks, a wealth of beads, mirrors, and trade *hierro*. Some of it had been transported on the backs of nearly a hundred big-boned cabayos. The rest had been borne on the shoulders of a thousand slaves chained at the neck.

We brought them to this.

I smiled grimly from my forest hide as I watched the motley survivors pass, a long thread of weary men, their worldly possessions carried on their backs in packs made out of floor matting they'd ripped up from Chicaza houses and somehow laced together. But for the thirty or so riders in the vanguard, most of the cabayos had heavy packs—mostly salvaged *hierro*—strapped to their backs. Their riders, also burdened, led them by sections of poorly braided fiber rope.

In the rear came the twenty or so wounded, some limping, others with bloody bandages visible. Six of the critically injured rode in litters borne by Albaamaha or Chicaza slaves.

The women and converts followed. All but the one surviving Kristiano woman were *indios* de Soto's men had kidnapped from their people. Many of them, like Garden and the Coosa High Sun's niece Yellow Stem, were pregnant. On tired bare feet they plodded along, heads down, grass skirts on their hips, burden baskets either on their shoulders or hung from tumplines they'd constructed. Mixed in with them were the converts, looking anything but happy with their lot. Many exhibited burns slathered with grease, having barely escaped Chicaza town with their lives.

I didn't wait for the reduced herd of little *puercos* to

pass. I'd seen them when they numbered nearly a thousand and traveled like a swarm.

"Go on," I told them as I watched. "As much as Chicaza has already taken from you, we have yet one more surprise in store."

With that I slipped back into the brush where Pearl Hand, Two Packs, and my dogs were waiting.

We would have to hurry.

Redbuds and dogwoods splashed vivid color against the spring green bursting from every branch and stem. A heady perfume from honeysuckle, wild rose, catalpa, and magnolia scented the air. Mixing with the lusty odors of awakening forest, daisies, mayapple, and phlox bloomed in profusion. At our feet lush grass was growing in the open sections, while bud hulls pattered down from the high branches where oak, ash, hickory, elm, chestnut, and mulberry leaves curled out and unfolded in splashes of green.

I led the way as Pearl Hand, Two Packs, a handful of warriors, and my sister Silent Spring atop her litter descended a winding tree-lined trail into the upper Tallahatchie bottoms. My sister had insisted on accompanying us despite the danger. Not that I could blame her. Her husband waited just up ahead. He and his Alibamo had been preparing for a couple of moons now, knowing that the *Adelantado* had set Quizquiz as his next goal.

Originally Minko Fire Tail's Albaamaha intended to cut off any escape had some lucky Kristianos managed to survive the battle of Chicaza town. They hadn't anticipated that most of de Soto's army would survive intact.

Neither had the rest of us.

That de Soto's army had somehow extricated itself from total disaster was a circumstance that had become depressingly familiar.

Most Chicaza remained optimistic that de Soto's

troops would be crushed when they arrived at the Alibamo fortifications and found the northwestern trail
blocked.

Pearl Hand and I would remain skeptical until we actually saw what Fire Tail's people had built. Bitter and
bloody experience had taught us: The Kristianos always
found a way to avoid extinction. At Chicaza town we had
come closer to achieving it than anyone ever had.

With Bark and Blackie coursing back and forth ahead
of us we emerged from the forest onto the open and
grassy floodplain of the Tallahatchie.

Before us stood Fire Tail's "surprise."

The sum of his and his people's labor was a U-shaped,
triple-walled palisade sitting astride the Quizquiz trail
where it crossed the Tallahatchie River. The fortification
consisted of upright logs set in a trench, then woven together with stout vines, and finally covered with a thick
layer of clay plaster. The rear of the enclosure was open
and backed against the steep-banked Tallahatchie River.
Any attempt to flank the structure would leave the *Adelantado*'s *soldados* floundering in the water.

The first wall was a little over head height with a
shooting platform on the top and loopholes cut every
four paces for archers to shoot through. Three small gates
allowed warriors to sally out and engage the enemy in the
trampled grassy clearing before the walls.

A pace and a half behind the first wall rose the second,
slightly higher and similarly constructed of upright logs
bound and plastered. It, too, boasted loopholes and an
overhead shooting platform. Every twenty paces, a flimsy
bridge linked the first wall with the second, allowing the
defenders to retreat without having to climb down and
file through the small interior gates. Behind the second
wall rose yet a third and even higher wall, also linked by
the rickety bridge ladders.

Fire Tail, after greeting his wife and seeing to her

evacuation to the forest beyond the Tallahatchie, gave us the grand tour from atop the third wall's shooting platform.

"Our hope," he told Pearl Hand and me, "is that they will mass and attack us." He pointed at the grassy flat stretching back to the forest. For the moment it was filled with several hundred warriors lounging or inspecting their weapons. "I've had the squadrons running drills to improve how we charge out to fight, and even more important, retreat behind the walls when they finally overcome our resistance."

"At least you realize they're going to beat you out in the open," Pearl Hand told him.

Fire Tail nodded, thoughtful eyes on his warriors. "We're counting on it. The hope is that the fifty or so warriors will be bait to draw the cabayeros into archery range from the shooting platform atop the walls. Our goal is to disable as many cabayos as possible."

"And when they push you back?" I asked. "Those three gates are only big enough for one man at a time."

"We did that on purpose to slow the Kristiano advance. My warriors have been practicing how to get through those gates at a dead run. The rear guard understands the importance of covering the retreat. They are all volunteers willing to sell their lives holding off the Kristianos as long as possible."

"And once you get your people back inside?" Pearl Hand asked.

Fire Tail rubbed the back of his neck. "We fight them at the first wall, literally raining arrows on the attackers. You told us how they approached the walls of Mabila beneath overlapping shields. We expect them to do exactly that here, too. As soon as the first wall is breached, everyone evacuates to the second wall."

"Hence these bridge ladders? The warriors on the shooting platforms are supposed to scamper across?" I asked, staring skeptically at one of the fragile-looking bridges that ran to the second wall. Made as it was of three parallel poles and topped with bark, I wasn't sure I'd trust so much as a crow to walk across it.

"Don't worry. It'll hold two warriors at a time. When my squadrons aren't practicing evacuation drills through the gates, I have them running across the bridges. Only two failed during our practices. After that we promptly made improvements." He arched a knowing eyebrow. "Let's just say that the first time across was a test of courage for even the bravest among us."

"And once the Kristianos breach the first wall?" Pearl Hand frowned down at the narrow depths.

Fire Tail braced his muscular arms on the plaster, peering down where some of his warriors now milled. "This is where the fight really begins. Outside they can approach like a turtle under overlapped shields, but down there, in those tight confines, their shields can either be lifted to protect them from fire from above or held over the loopholes to keep them from being shot in the breast or face."

"But not both," I said with appreciation. "And these flimsy bridges of yours?"

"As soon as the shooting platform atop the first wall is abandoned, we pull the bridge back. That's one of the reasons they're so light. That or we can toss them down on the Kristianos trapped below. If something happens and the Kristianos capture one intact, what are the chances they're sure-footed enough to cross?"

"Not likely." Pearl Hand was smiling grimly, obviously liking what she was seeing.

Bundles of war arrows had been strategically placed at four-pace intervals. Fire Tail must have had men working overtime to produce them and conscripted every stone-pointed shaft his warriors, hunters, and clans possessed.

"Once they take the second wall, everything starts over again. They're trapped down in that small space while we rain more arrows down and the warriors drive shot after shot through the loopholes."

Pearl Hand turned her attention to the fortifications' protected interior, where a collection of camps and ramadas covered the flat. Even now, in the middle of the day, no less than a hundred warriors were tending cook fires, inspecting arrows, and making final preparations.

Behind them the Tallahatchie River flowed between its incised banks. The surface roiled and sucked, as if anxious over the coming battle. Additional rickety bridges had been built across the muddy brown waters, now swollen by spring storms. The banks had been denuded of willows and brush—materials used during the construction of the walls—but beyond the river the back-swamp beckoned. It remained a murky tangle of bald cypress, tupelo, and water oak through which no Kristiano cabayeros could pursue.

"That's the final route of escape," Fire Tail said, following my gaze. "The hope is that we'll have hurt them. That they'll be thirsting for revenge and we can entice them to chase after us into the swamp and the forest beyond, where we can ambush them again and again."

"Once, they would have obliged you without a second thought," Pearl Hand told him. "But you're right; if their blood is up, and they think they have the chance to pay you back for the misery they've endured over the last couple of moons, they might—"

A conch horn sounded from the forest.

We turned, seeing the warriors in the grassy flat rise to their feet, every eye on the forest trail. Then a party of scouts burst from the trees. Shouts of "Kristianos! They're coming," carried on the still spring air.

Immediately the warriors began filing in through the gates. As each ducked through the door, he turned in the opposite direction of the fellow before, hastily moving out of the way. I'd never seen such a thing before. It was neatly done, and in less time than I'd have believed possible, the grassy flat was empty but for the scouts and perhaps fifty painted and armed warriors who were organizing themselves into a formation.

"The Monster is coming," Fire Tail told us, his weight braced on the plaster wall. Then he glanced up at the midday sun. "Let's hope he gets here soon."

I licked my dry lips and nodded, an eerie premonition running through my bones.

Fire Tail gave us a horrified look. "You don't think he'll just take one look and ride around us? If he were smart, he'd just circle wide, refuse to offer combat, and be on his way. All of our hard work, the endless days of cutting, dragging, and plastering. All the drills and preparations . . . They could be for nothing!"

My wife placed a reassuring hand on his shoulder. "Minko, this is de Soto. When he sees your fortifications, he won't think of how many will die to take it—only that it is in *his* way. And to feed the monster that lives inside him, he *must* destroy this place at any cost."

Fire Tail gave us a sad smile. "If that is indeed the case, you must excuse me. I have some last details to see to."

I watched him hurry down the ladder and start through the gates toward the front.

Meanwhile the warriors on the walls around us were chanting and singing, calling upon the red Power of war to bless them with courage and skill. They painted themselves in bright crimson, donned their feather displays and leather forearm bands. Bows were strung and war clubs hung on belt thongs or placed ready at hand on the shooting palisades.

Pearl Hand asked me, "How's your side?"

"Sore and healing," I told her as I tested the pull on my Tula bow. After weeks of nonuse my muscles screamed at the effort needed to bend the Osage orangewood bow.

At that moment, the conch horn blew again and when

I turned my attention to the forest trail, cabayeros were emerging from the forest. The *capitán* called Juan de Añasco rode at the head of fifteen, with perhaps another forty *soldados* tramping along behind. They drew up in amazement, as if the last thing they expected to see was Fire Tail's fortification.

Jeers and shouts of defiance broke from the Albaama-ha's throats, drums began to pound, and shrill cries rent the air.

"Let's just hope this works," Pearl Hand whispered.

"When has it ever?" I asked, mouth suddenly gone dry.

FIFTY-THREE

"THIS IS NOT A GOOD IDEA," PEARL HAND SAID INSIS-
tently as she stood beside me before the walls, her crossbow cocked and loaded. I curled my toes in my war
moccasins, as if by doing so I could clutch the grass upon
which I stood and draw strength from the very soil.
Blackie and Bark sat, ears pricked, as they watched Añasco's party of Kristianos. Overhead, the spring sun had
begun to slant toward the west, highlighting columns of
insects that swarmed at the edge of the trees.

Around me, a hundred warriors did their best to
taunt the Kristianos into attack. Añasco had with-
drawn to a defensive position on a slight rise backed by
the trees. The Kristianos hid behind a line of shields;
the cabayeros dismounted and were protected from
our volleys.

"What are they waiting for?" White Plume, Fire Tail's
thlakko, asked. "Here we are. Come get us!"

"Remember the three cabayeros who went racing back
down the trail?" Pearl Hand asked him. "Those were mes-

sengers sent back to the *Adelantado*. Añasco is waiting for reinforcements."

"We could just rush them," Elk Moccasin growled. "We have them outnumbered two to one."

"And they still have twelve cabayeros . . . enough to cut your squadron into pieces before you make it halfway to their position." I pointed with my bow. "As soon as we start forward in mass attack, they'll mount up, circle around, and charge our flank. They'll crack this formation the way a hammer stone does a nut. You'll have warriors tumbled this way and that. Twenty of them at least will be lanced, lying on the ground, bleeding or with their guts ripped open."

When I took a breath, Pearl Hand finished, saying, "Before you even attempt to reorganize the survivors, the cabayeros will have wheeled around. Even as you shout orders, they'll hit you from the other side and spill your formation wide open again. Another ten or twenty will be dead or dying. Only then will those forty *soldados* up there charge down and send those of you still alive fleeing for your lives."

"If they can do all that, why do they wait?" White Plume demanded.

I pointed up at the wall behind us where red-painted warriors sang, shouted insults, and twanged their bowstrings in anticipation. "We're bait, remember? We're needed to lure them into range of the archers up there. Añasco's no fool. He's not going to risk Kristiano lives attacking a fortification he can't take. He's waiting for de Soto."

Pearl Hand narrowed an eye. "And the *Adelantado* won't be able to refuse the challenge."

"No brains before honor?" White Plume gave me an anxious smile. "Yes, we Albaamaha have heard."

The clanking of arms carried over the whirring of insects and the spring songs of robins, jays, and titmice in the trees. Several cabayeros emerged from the forest at a canter, pulled up, and rode over to their fellows waiting on the terrace. Less than a finger's time later de Soto himself emerged at the head of his remaining cabayeros. The scuffling sounds of *soldados* on the march followed, and as Añasco rode out to meet de Soto and explain the situation, the *soldados* formed ranks behind the first group.

I felt my throat go dry as Añasco finished his briefing and the *Adelantado* turned his gray cabayo and advanced beyond the protection of his *soldados*. Keeping more than a bow-shot distant, de Soto—with Moscoso, Añasco, and Guzman following—studied us and the fortification with critical eyes.

Riding up and down the length of the fortification, they continued to talk, pointing every now and then. Two war dogs coursed in zigzags behind the cabayos' fetlocks. Bark and Blackie rose to their feet, growling.

"I'd give an engraved conch-shell cup to listen in on that conversation," I muttered uneasily.

"Why? I can tell you exactly what they're saying. From the way they're pointing and arguing, they're figuring the best way to kill us all," Pearl Hand mused. "I'd say though that Añasco is arguing for caution."

I watched more closely, seeing Moscoso and Añasco periodically shaking their heads. In the end, de Soto rose in his stirrups, glared at his *capitanes,* and made a slashing motion with his hand. The others nodded acceptance and rode back to the main formation now arrayed in battle order just out from the tree line.

I turned to White Plume. "The Monster has made his decision. Prepare your men. When the cabayeros charge down upon us, you need to have every man back against the wall. Make the attackers ride close under the archers so they pass through a hail of arrows. At the same time, your men need to be on one knee, shields up, and loosing arrow after arrow at the cabayos. They may break your formation in the end, but it will cost them at least half of their precious mounts."

"Understood, Minko Black Shell." He slapped a salute and turned to issue his orders.

"Wait!" Pearl Hand cried. "What's this?"

I watched as de Soto dismounted his cabayeros, reorganizing the *soldados* and placing all of those with shields in the front.

"Just like Mabila," I realized. "He's not going to risk his precious cabayos but will assault on foot first."

"What should I do?" White Plume asked.

Pearl Hand shot a look over her shoulder at the archers atop the first wall, each now fitting an arrow. "Follow Fire Tail's plan. The one you've practiced. Try to kill as many as you can as they attack. Stay out of reach of the swords and the poleaxes. Shoot for arms or legs, faces . . . any unarmored spot on their bodies."

White Plume shouted his orders as a Kristiano trumpet rang out melodiously on the still air.

"They're coming," I noted, nocking a war arrow in the Tula bow and testing the pull. The healing wound in my side replied with pain, but it was nothing I couldn't live with.

The *Adelantado* had formed his men in three squadrons, one for each exposed wall. He was coming just the way Fire Tail had hoped.

The way my heart was hammering, my breastbone might have been a drumhead. Though my mouth had gone dry, cold sweat trickled down from my armpits. A feverish tension had settled on my muscles, every nerve in my body vibrating. Behind me, Fire Tail had his war drums thumping, the warriors shouting and stamping their feet.

The Kristianos came forward, the line of shields jostling with each step and knocking edges as the *soldados* kept pace. A prickling fence of spear-axes and lances angled up from the shields. Helmeted heads bobbed and shifted; Kristiano eyes turned grim as they peered out of bearded faces. Each Kristiano in the front line wore a breastplate and *hierro* shoulder or arm pieces. Behind them many of the spear-ax men and lancers were missing bits and pieces of armor. And behind them, the crossbowmen wore little more than helmets and cobbled-together shoulder pieces.

"Patience!" White Plume called. "Await my order to shoot."

I glanced down the line, seeing frightened and anxious Albaamaha as they clutched their hardwood shields, bows ready to draw. The faint breeze toyed with the feathers they'd poked in their hair or tied to their shoulders. Sunlight bathed the bright red, yellow, black, and blue colors of their face paint. Some sang prayers to invoke Power, mouths moving in time to the melodious songs. Others were shouting insults. One young man was laughing hysterically, cavorting and leaping into the air. I watched him spin around, pull up the flap of his breechclout, and slap his butt derisively.

"*¡Ballestas! ¡Listos!*" came Moscoso's cry.

Pearl Hand cupped her mouth, shouting, "They're shooting!"

Behind Moscoso, de Soto rode back and forth, as if to ensure the advance. He held a lance at the ready, helmet shining as he called encouragement to his men. As the front line stepped into a dip, I could just make out the two war dogs at de Soto's heel. An additional twenty cabayeros held their mounts just back from the *Adelantado*, ready to charge should the opportunity arise.

"*¡Disparad!*" Moscoso bellowed, slashing at the air with his sword.

From the third line came a fluttering, clicking sound, and perhaps a hundred crossbow arrows rose in a hissing swarm to arch high.

"Arrows!" White Plume warned, dropping to a knee and raising his own shield. Most of the Kristiano shots fell short. Some thunked into shields, others stuck in the damp silty clay. I only heard one Albaamaha cry out in surprise and pain.

"Rise!" White Plume ordered. "Nock, aim, and shoot!"

I smiled grimly as I drew the thick-shafted war arrow to my ear. Well within my range, the Kristiano line was spread all across the field. I listened to the strumming of the bowstrings, heard the whooshing whisper of the Alibamo arrows winging toward the *hierro* line. They hit with a clatter on brown *hierro* helmets, thunked into the wooden shields, and cracked on impervious breastplates.

I saw my opportunity when a *soldado* staggered, and taking aim, I released my shot. As quickly I drew another, nocked it, and chose yet another target: a tall Kristiano with a yellow beard. Shot by shot, I did my best to seek out some vulnerability in their armor.

Here and there a Kristiano screamed, dropped, and had his position filled as someone from behind grabbed the man's shield and stepped into the gap.

Their legs and feet were vulnerable but so hard to hit as they marched forward.

Around us, I could hear the yells and taunts as the Albaamaha warmed to the battle.

On the Kristianos came, hunching down, raising shields high as the hail of Alibamo arrows clattered and rattled on their armor or thunked into the green-wood shields manufactured after the burning of Chicaza town.

"*¡Ballestas! ¡Listos!*" Moscoso called.

"White Plume!" Pearl Hand shouted to the thlakko. "Shields up!"

"Shields up!" White Plume ordered.

Down the line I heard his seconds repeating the order and as warriors up and down the line released their arrows, they dropped to a knee, swinging their shields up.

This time the impacting crossbow bolts could be likened to the cracking of dry sticks as the metal points hammered into cured maple or hickory shields.

Immediately the warriors were back on their feet, launching their rain of arrows onto the closing Kristianos. Now the enemy were close enough that it was impossible to miss.

"Shoot for the legs!" Pearl Hand kept repeating. "Shoot them in the legs!"

I was so lost in the fight I almost forgot the danger of the spear-axes that thrust out ahead of the line of shields. Sunlight glinting off a freshly sharpened edge brought me back to reality.

"White Plume!" I grasped his arm as he reached for another arrow. "Fall back! They're getting too close."

"Fall back!" White Plume bellowed, and the call was repeated down the line.

As we began to back away, a shout went up from the Kristiano line. At that moment, de Soto, perhaps interpreting our move as a portent of defeat, rode close. He was just opposite me, no more than twenty paces distant.

I nocked an arrow, drew, and sighted down the hardwood shaft with its keen white-chert point. Gauging the drop, figuring in the lead, I released. The arrow leaped away, the polished shaft glistening, fletching imparting a slight spin.

Just at that moment he turned to say something to one of the Kristianos and my shot took him just above the brim of his helmet. I heard the crack as the arrow bounced high into the air, and I watched de Soto's head snap back at the impact.

The *Adelantado* reeled in the saddle but kept his seat. I was drawing a follow-up shot when he shook his head, as if to clear it, and spurred his cabayo farther on down the line.

A finger's width lower, and I'd have killed him! In the eye of my souls I would replay that shot over and over, wishing I'd released an instant before.

"Withdraw!" White Plume called again, and the Alibamo archers backed away from the fight.

Not that the Kristianos were having an easier time of it. The air overhead was whistling with the hiss of arrows as they arched down from the shooting platforms overhead. The crackling sound of it reminded me of a hailstorm on an exposed granite knob.

"First squadron!" White Plume shouted. "Through the gates!"

I took my time, waiting as the Kristianos staggered closer accompanied by the clicking and clattering of war arrows on their armored tops. They were so close, they thought they were homing in; their quarry appeared backed against the clay-plastered wall. At the same time, the deadly missiles from above kept them from breaking formation and charging in for the kill.

Some of the newly made shields had as many as fifty war arrows stuck into the wood.

Before me a *soldado* lifted his shield higher, giving me the shot I wanted. From no more than ten paces I drove my arrow under the edge of his shield and into the top of his thigh, clad as it was in a wrapping of deer hide.

The man screamed something in the name of *díos,* wobbled, and stopped short, obviously in pain. I had my opening in the line. Stepping forward, I had a clear shot into the man next to him. I drove my shaft up to the fletching in his hip just below the protection of his breastplate.

The *soldado* spun, dropping his shield as he craned his neck and stared in horror at his wound. My follow-up shot took him in the gap between his helmet and breastplate.

Now I had a real opening in the line. If I had just ten warriors, I could—

"Black Shell!"

Pearl Hand's scream pierced my euphoria, and I shot a glance over my shoulder to see her perhaps ten paces behind me, both dogs at her heel, watching me with worried eyes.

As I turned to run one of the spear-axes swished through the space I'd just occupied.

FIFTY-FOUR

Pus and blood, Black Shell, you're going to get yourself killed!

As soon as Pearl Hand saw me coming, she spun, taking her turn and ducking through the low doorway. Bark and Blackie rolled through on her heels. I charged through a gap between the remaining warriors shooting their quivers empty against the advancing *soldados*.

You should have heard the Kristianos. You'd have thought from the shouts, whistles, and cheers that they'd just whipped the Piasa himself!

With the last of the rearguard through the door, I helped muscle the heavy wooden slab over the entrance. Poles were dropped in place, wedging the thick planks against the wall. Not only would it have to be chopped through, but the stout bracing poles would have to be dislodged.

I scrambled up one of the ladders to the first wall's shooting platform. Pearl Hand was leaning out, taking careful aim. Her crossbow made its distinct *twang* and she pulled back, fishing for another of the bolts in her belt pouch.

"Where are the dogs?" I asked.

"One of the warriors took them back through the walls. They'll be waiting for us in the compound."

"Kill any yet?" I drew my bow, leaning out and shooting. The heavy arrow exploded into splinters as it hit a *hierro*-clad shield—one of the old ones that had survived the fire.

"Skewered a couple of legs," she growled out the side of her mouth.

Crossbow arrows were flashing up at us from below.

"Concentrate on their archers!" I cried. "Drive them back."

Those who heard me did as I asked, and within moments, the crossbowmen opposite us broke and fled, several with shafts stuck in their flesh. This let us concentrate on the *soldados* below. As expected, they'd made their turtle back and were chopping at the gate with axes and swords.

I had that brief moment to take in the battlefield. All across the grassy flat, little knots of Kristianos were hobbling back toward the rise, many being supported by their fellows. Dropped weapons marked the places where they'd been wounded.

I winced at the sight of the first dying Alibamo. He lay on his back, his chest sliced open to expose ribs, a still-beating heart, and bloody lungs. Even as I watched the heart beat its last.

And try as I might, I could only account for one other dead Alibamo sprawled on the field. Could this be?

I attempted a quick count, coming up with at least twelve of de Soto's wounded being borne toward the rear—two of them sporting arrows of mine.

"Don't get too excited." Pearl Hand noted my amazement. "The day's far from over, and your side's bleeding."

I glanced down where my flax-fiber war shirt was

spotted with blood. "Must have torn one of Copper Sky's stitches."

"See that that's *all* you do," Pearl Hand ordered, an eye narrowing as she leaned out and shot at a scrambling Kristiano. The short arrow clanged off the man's *hierro*-clad shoulder, leaving a silver scar.

As I leaned to shoot over the wall I could feel the vibrations as Kristiano axes chopped at the plaster and log. Another *soldado* stumbled back, a fletched shaft transfixing his arm. Just below my position over the gate, I could hear Moscoso shouting, and the Kristianos raised a triumphant cry as they finally splintered the plank gate. One of the bracing poles crashed down with a bang.

"About time to think about that bridge," I shouted at Pearl Hand as she struggled to reload her crossbow. All down the line Alibamo warriors were shouting insults, leaning over and raining arrows down onto the attackers.

One by one the Kristianos pulled the planks away and dragged out the bracing poles. I watched as the first of them darted through the gate below, then scuttled to one side, his shield held high. He screamed as an arrow from a loophole across from him transfixed his arm. Another splintered against the side of his helmet.

One after another, Kristianos sprinted through the opening, finding themselves hemmed in by the narrow space. They cowered in knots of twos and threes, trying to protect themselves.

It took longer than I thought before they figured out how to angle their shields before the loopholes to deflect shots while still providing cover from above. Working in teams of perfectly positioned shields to negate our archery, they began working their way down the passage.

I told Pearl Hand, "In a finger's time, this wall's going to be taken."

She took final shot at Nuño de Tovar where he rode his cabayo just out from the wall. Her arrow sailed so close to his cheek that he jerked backward, spooking his prancing mount. At my last glimpse he was fingering his cheek as if he expected blood.

Pearl Hand took a deep breath, narrowed a skeptical eye at the bridge, and trotted across, her long braid bouncing. Being no less brave than my wife but a great deal more terrified, I made a face and screamed as I hurried over the bucking and bouncing poles.

"How are we doing?" White Plume asked as he took our hands and helped us behind the protection of the second wall.

"But for that accursed armor of theirs"—Pearl Hand wiped beading sweat from her brow—"we'd have killed them all."

"How many of our warriors are down?" I asked him.

He frowned up and down the length of the wall as warriors minced their way across the bridges, abandoning the first wall. "That I know of, two dead, maybe twenty wounded."

I tried to get my head around that. "I saw maybe fifteen Kristianos carried away with serious wounds. De Soto might be an abomination and monster, but he's an accursedly smart one. He's only using a small part of his force for the attack, but they're the best armored."

"Let's see how they do against the second wall," White Plume said, then hurried away to shout orders at a group of warriors who'd forgotten to pull back their bridge after fleeing the first wall.

As the last warrior crossed, Pearl Hand and I grabbed hold of the wobbling pole bridge and tugged. The far end dropped into the depths, clattering with such force it was ripped from Pearl Hand's grasp and I had Piasa's own time keeping hold.

With the help of two other warriors we started pulling it up, only to have a couple of Kristianos grab it from down below. I watched one try to climb it, only to have a length of bark rip off in his grasp. The man bellowed, cursed, and angrily sailed the section of bark up at us. I took the moment to pull an arrow, nock it, and lean out.

Flinching, he jerked his head down between his armored shoulders, and my war shaft drilled the center of his *hierro* helmet with enough impact to stagger him and leave a deep dimple in the metal.

"If they want it," Pearl Hand told the struggling warriors battling to yank the bridge away, "let them have it."

Cheers rose from below as we surrendered the disintegrating bridge. I'm glad they enjoyed their success. They scuttled back and forth in the confines, trying to figure out how to make a ladder of smooth poles and squares of bark while our arrows banged and shattered on their shields.

We held the heights, and they crabbed around in the bottom, jabbing spear-axes up at us. I watched one such attempt end in humiliation when two Alibamo warriors leaned down, grasped the spear-ax by the shaft, and jerked it up out of a stunned Kristiano's grip. The man was screaming his rage right up to the moment that four warriors leaned over and one drilled an arrow through the Kristiano's left eye.

The warriors danced around with their spear-ax for a while, then, figuring it was a Kristiano weapon and finding the edge incredibly sharp, they came up with the notion it might cut through Kristiano *hierro* armor.

Jabbing it down at the Kristianos, it didn't take long before the Kristianos managed to grab it. Things do tend to fall easier than they rise. The Kristianos almost pulled two warriors over the edge as they tugged their spear-ax back.

"Fall back!" the order came, called by Fire Tail on the third wall.

"Second wall's breached," Pearl Hand noted.

That didn't make crossing that last bridge any easier. Not only had I watched the Kristianos pull our first ladder-bridge apart, I *knew* what a flimsy construction it was.

Horned Serpent, walk with me, I prayed as I fixed my gaze on the far wall and started across.

Amazed to be alive, I scrambled over the third wall and onto the shooting platform. I was in the process of reaching for arrows when I heard a triumphant cheer of *"¡En el nombre de dios, es victoria!"*

I don't know how he did it, but a Kristiano was tottering across the bridge just down from us. He had his eyes on his feet, his shield held before him, his sword waving above his head. The four Alibamo waiting for him shot in unison, their arrows shattering on the *soldado's* shield.

And at that, the warriors turned and ran.

I stared in amazement as the Kristiano leaped from the bridge, his hide-wrapped feet thumping on the shooting platform. From what I could see he was beaming, his mouth wide with a grin that split his bearded face. This one was blue eyed, his shoulder armor spotted with brown, his helmet dented. The man's breastplate had a hundred dimples and dents in it, and his hips and legs were clad in wraps of deer hide tied on with lengths of vine.

Wild laughter broke from his throat as he charged the stunned warriors on the shooting platform. He came in a half crouch, shield up, sword ripping the air as he swung it like a flail. Warriors ran in panic, many of them taking their lives in their hands, leaping for the safety of the ground below.

Pearl Hand swung her crossbow up, narrowed her aiming eye, and shot. The rim of the shield split; Pearl Hand's shaft stopped short a finger's width below. I followed her shot with one of my own. He caught it nicely on the curve of the shield, sending the shattered shaft flying off to the right.

Then no one was between him and Pearl Hand. I grabbed her by the shoulder, jerked her back, and charged the Kristiano head-on.

My eyes were fixed on his, and I saw the glee in those sky-blue depths as he prepared to kill me. Of course, he had no idea who I was. To him, I was just some Alibamo, an *indio sucio* who'd never seen a sword before. In that moment I wished I hadn't left Antonio's blade with our packs in the rear.

With the heavy Tula bow, I blocked his first cut, meant to slash across my abdomen. Then I parried the second and third, watching as his eyes narrowed into a crafty squint.

As quickly as he was catching on, I had but one hope. I was skilled compared to an ordinary Chicaza warrior, but no man with a bow stave was going to hold him off for long.

Rapping at his sword with the heavy bow, I charged forward, seeking to get inside his swing. I slammed into his shield, dropping the bow, reaching down and lifting the thing by the rim.

Off balance, he staggered and I ducked beneath the shield, grabbing his left arm, spinning, and lifting.

He screamed as I pivoted on my heel and bodily threw him back over the wall. He crashed down onto the shields of two Kristianos creeping along the base of the wall. The three of them tumbled in clattering confusion. Bellows of pain and rage rising, they struggled to untangle themselves.

Now, where was my bow? My position was perfect. I could take them out before they could get their shields up. Pick my shots and drive my arrows right through the gaps . . .

I winced at the growing sting in my side. "Piasa's balls!

Don't tell me I've torn that accursed wound open." Antonio would be the death of me yet.

The nagging wrongness . . . Antonio had slashed my ribs on the right.

Stepping back, I felt the odd tugging and looked down to see that half the length of the Kristiano's sword was sticking through my left side, wedged, as it were, in the ribs.

I swallowed hard, mouth suddenly dry, aware of the pain—competing as it was with the torn stitches. And yes, I'd undoubtedly torn them.

"*Black Shell!*" Pearl Hand's scream carried over the roar of battle. I reached down, steadying the blade, and turned. She stood a couple of steps away. Her gaze fixed on the sword, a terrified look on her face. I watched her crossbow fall from nerveless fingers. Then she lifted her smudged hands to her mouth, as if to stifle a scream.

Behind her, Two Packs—grinning from ear to ear—came striding down the platform, a bow in his hands. He stopped short, shocked as he caught sight of the sword.

Pearl Hand stared in horror at the terrible thing I held so carefully, then dropped to her knees. I caught movement, seeing another Kristiano boosted up from below and onto the second wall platform. He crouched behind his shield, anxious gaze on the remaining bridge. Then he started for it.

"Two Packs," I ordered, oddly out of breath. "Toss that bridge down."

He barely managed to get past me, crabbing wide of the hideous sword handle. The Kristiano made a tenative step onto the bridge. Then Two Packs, with a flip of his shoulders, yanked the bridge back. The Kristiano leaped for the platform at the last instant.

The *soldado* ducked down behind his shield as Two

Packs roared and raised the pole bridge high over his head. Like a giant club the bark-covered poles crashed down on the *soldado*'s shield. I saw the man's wide-eyed disbelief moments before the impact flattened him with such force the platform beneath us bucked. The flimsy bridge shattered with a bang.

Warriors were hurrying down the platform as Two Packs raised one of the remaining poles to hammer the *soldado* again. The Kristiano, no more than three paces away, sought desperately to hide his entire body behind the shield. Then, with a cry, he cast it aside and leaped for the depths, preferring to cower where blows only came from above.

"We've got to get that out," Two Packs told me as he disdainfully cast the last pole after the vanished Kristiano. "You can't walk with that in your side."

I was feeling woozy and uncomfortably dizzy. "But it's not bleeding. I need . . . I need to climb down first. To the ground."

A hot sweat began to warm my skin, the first fingers of nausea tickling the base of my throat. Slowly, carefully, the world starting to spin around me, I walked to the nearest ladder and, one rung at a time, made my way to the ground inside the third wall.

The horror in Pearl Hand's eyes was worse than the sword sticking in my side.

Once on solid ground, I stopped, swaying on my feet. The thing was stinging now—like a thousand wasps had let go in my side. Warriors were staring, horror in their eyes.

"Take it out slowly," I told Pearl Hand. *And stop looking at me like that!* "I need you to be brave."

To Two Packs I said, "Hold me still so I don't move. It didn't hurt that bad going in."

But . . . pus and blood, *it did on the way out!*

The worst thing was that I could *feel it* grating on my

rib bones, pulling through muscle and skin as she withdrew it.

I know I screamed. Then my stomach convulsed and I threw up. A trembling weakness threatened to buckle my knees. The world began to spin and my vision grew silvery, splashed with yellow flame and hundreds upon hundreds of whirling sparks . . .

FIFTY-FIVE

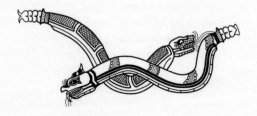

I BARELY REMEMBER BEING CARRIED FROM THE ALI-bamo fortification. My souls kept fleeing my tortured body until I lost consciousness of the blurry images of sky, forest, and the shifting bodies of the warriors who bore me through a maze of trees. I know that my souls returned to my body at least once that night. Probably because—like the rest of me—they weren't smart enough to just let me die.

I vaguely remember lying on leaves, my chest feeling as though a great stone sat on my breastbone. I kept trying to catch my breath, but gasp as I might, the sense of suffocation only increased. I remember pawing weakly at my chest, anxious to find the weight and remove it. And discovering nothing but sticky blood.

If I could fill my lungs with one wonderful breath . . .

My head lay propped on Pearl Hand's lap, her fingers stroking my face and hair. My mouth was so dry; the taste of blood lingered on my thick tongue.

Why couldn't I breathe?

"What . . . ?" I rasped, and I remember coughing. The exertion of it sent agony through my lungs, and I made a mewing sound.

"Shhh!" Pearl Hand said, trying to soothe me. "Hold still. Two Packs has gone for one of the litters."

Hold still? Gods, I had no desire to ever move again. Not if it was going to hurt like that. The weight continued to press down, increasing my desperation for air.

As my vision shimmered and warped, my souls floated free of my body. I could barely hear Pearl Hand's voice pleading, feel her desperate tears as they dripped onto my hot skin. Her soft touch faded as the dull and inflamed ache in my chest pulsed.

Just one deep breath. I'd give anything.

Someone, remove this crushing weight on my chest. Let me breathe . . .

Swallowing.

From the gray haze and illusive phantasmal images came the act of swallowing.

My body did it. Acting of its own volition.

I clung to the simple reality that I had swallowed.

Then my body did it again.

To my delight I tasted moisture.

As my souls slowly filtered back into my fevered flesh, I realized that my head was being held, my mouth open. Water was dribbling onto my tongue. Blurry voices wavered into and out of recognition.

I swallowed again.

"Not too much." The voice came to me from across a terrible distance.

Someone answered, but it was muted.

I swallowed again greedily, desperate for the liquid.

"This must be done carefully," a different voice said. "If he coughs it will break open the clotted blood."

"I understand." The first voice was Pearl Hand's. Something inside me warmed with relief.

For the time being I was happy to simply float, aware of nothing more than the slow trickle of water that wet my mouth to the point where I would swallow.

It seemed impossible to catch my breath.

What seemed like hands of time later, I thought to open my eyes. The image was blurry.

"Don't move," came Pearl Hand's order. "You're safe, Black Shell. I'm trying to get you to drink."

As weary and hot as I felt, I wasn't going to argue. Not that I was even sure I could draw the air to do so.

After a while I was able to bring her into hazy focus. She sat with my head in her lap, a wad of cloth in her hand. Every so often she would drop the cloth into a bowl of water. Then, holding it over my lips, she'd squeeze it until a trickle dribbled into my mouth.

"You're badly wounded," she told me seriously. "Copper Sky has your ribs bound, but there is infection."

I tried to find breath, seeking words from my numb souls.

"Don't try to speak," she told me firmly. "All you need to do for the moment is drink. When you can finally pee again, I can give you broth."

My vision was clearing, and I was able to determine that I lay on a sleeping bench in what appeared to be a farmstead house. Overhead I could see daylight through the square smoke hole. A shaft of light angled through the thick blue that rose to the ceiling.

I couldn't find my voice; like my poor, wounded souls, it too had fled.

Lung wound. I am dying.

The sepaya felt like ice where it lay against my skin.

All I could do was struggle for each breath and savor the miraculous water that trickled over my tongue . . .

I came awake in the dark of night, somewhere in a rain-drenched forest. Lightning flickered faintly in the distance, illuminating ghostly trunks of trees. Smells of wet leaf mat, damp bark, and rich earth filled my nostrils. Overhead drops of water pattered on a hide cover, and I could hear the irregular splatter of droplets on last year's leaves.

In the distance thunder rumbled and boomed, white flickers of lightning again ghosting through the clouds. In the flashes I could see that I was in a small camp set among thick boles of gum and shagbark hickory. Clusters of mayapple had been crushed by careless feet. At least six other shelters lay within my range of vision, though their occupants were shadowed and indistinct. A single fire smoldered no more than a pebble's toss from my bedding.

Taking me home to die. Back to Chicaza. I remembered as much, though I had no clue where I'd heard it.

Water was everywhere, falling from the sky, pooling in the leaves, and trickling down the bark in dark streaks like bleeding veins. As another rumble of thunder echoed through the hills, the rain began in earnest.

I am so thirsty.

The fire shot tentative and anxious flames from its pit. Curls of smoke and streamers of steam battled desperately with the falling rain. A shadowy form wearing a bark rain hat stepped forward from one of the shelters and tossed a couple lengths of wood onto the fire. Wet wood hissed, the Powers of fire and water angry at being forced into such proximity with each other.

Despite the faint breath frosting before my mouth, I felt hot. Desperately hot. My vision shimmered, glassy before my eyes. My souls seemed to be floating just above my body, as if in indecision about whether to stay or go.

Each shallow breath I drew was a struggle. Gods, when would I finally be able to breathe again?

Through the ripples that ran across my vision, I studied the other rain shelters, their sides glistening. Trickles of water drained in streams of silver from where it collected on the low edges.

Pus and blood, my whole body ached, but the slow-burning fire deep in my side was agonizing.

I struggled for breath and tried to shift, only to stifle a groan. Beside my leg, a dark form moved, and in the firelight I recognized Bark's scarred muzzle as he lifted his head. Firelight flickered in his eyes as he gave me a concerned look, his tail slapping wetly against my foot.

"You dead like Gnaw? Is this your soul? Come to say farewell?" I barely mouthed the words.

He gave a big yawn, exposing worn teeth, then lowered his head onto his paws before taking a deep breath and puffing one of those most canine of sighs.

Fevered, light-headed, the weight in my chest growing ever more heavy, I fought to breathe. Any attempt to really expand my lungs ended in the kind of blinding pain that made me think slow suffocation wasn't such a bad alternative.

My body felt incredibly light, as if it were made of air. Fragile and wavering, like bending patterns of light through water. At the corner of my vision, the firelight seemed to smear and streak, the patterns fading ever so slowly.

"Pus and blood," I whispered through as much of an exhale as I could manage. "Why am I doing this?"

"Why are you?"

I knew that voice.

Scrunching my face into a fierce blink to clear my glassy vision, I cocked my head, turning around as far as my neck would allow.

There *he* stood, his fur oddly dry looking for a beast from the watery Underworld. Piasa stepped forward into the firelight. Even then his cougar-colored coat appeared almost translucent, as if illuminated from within. Hard yellow eyes fixed on mine, the pupils enlarged. I could see the three-forked patterns around his eyes and watched the long bristly whiskers quiver. The water panther's wings were folded close to his back, the lines, stripes, and dark dots that decorated them muted in the night.

"Lucky for me the Kristianos finally got you on the banks of the Tallahatchie. Otherwise I might have missed this last opportunity to see just what a disappointment you are."

"What?" I whispered.

"Sorry, can't hear you." The Piasa stepped closer, head cocked to expose a round and furry ear. The beast even cupped a scaly eagle-clawed foot around it the way a human did. "Oh, but I forget. You have blood and air pooling between your lung and the wound in your side. Funny things, these rib cages. Kind of like poking a thorn through a full bladder. All the piss runs out. And no matter how much you try to pour in, you just can't fill it up again."

I struggled to say, "You've always been a hoobuk waksee."

Why hadn't Bark detected the creature's approach and leaped to rip its throat out?

"Nothing wrong with my penis, Trader. Though any future use of yours remains a matter of frivolous speculation. And don't worry about the dog. He's still in his own world, dreaming of deer haunches, marrow bones, and chasing rabbits. Canines have such immediate and simple souls. Odd, isn't it, that Breath Giver would create a creature with such limited imagination?"

He paused, the pupils enlarging in his eyes. "But then, speaking of odd creations, we have you. Dense as a cracked granite boulder. You can't recognize when you're in the Spirit World . . . or your own."

"Why are you here?" I'm not even sure whether I mouthed the words or if I just thought them.

"To collect on our debt." The round head tilted questioningly, the terrible yellow eyes enlarging in anticipation.

"Not much left to take," I whispered, that sick sensation of falling mixing with the fever's illusion that I was drifting.

Gods, yes. Anything to stop the pain.

I tried to mouth the words, "Come and get me."

"Not afraid? Oh, foolish Black Shell, when I eat your souls, it's the end of everything. There will be no journey to the west. The West Wind won't be there to smack your flawed souls into the abyss when you attempt the leap through the Seeing Hand. No eventual trial by Eagle Man where the Path of the Dead forks. And most certainly no ancestors waiting to greet you with open arms."

He paused, then added, "Fletch, Skipper, Squirm, Patches, and Gnaw? They'll be so disappointed when you never show up. Dogs never forget when they've been betrayed by a beloved friend."

I clamped my eyes shut against the hurt that truth dealt me. Despite my desperate thirst, a tear trickled down from the corner of my eye.

Come on! This is Piasa. You're smarter than this. Even dying. Think of something!

I said, "Better oblivion than something like *paraíso* with a bunch of Kristianos." I think I actually smiled in an attempt to goad him. "For a people so clever when it comes to metals and making things, they sure have an unimaginative and boring afterlife."

He leaned down, sniffing in that slow and deliberate cat manner; the bristles of his whiskers tickled my face. Puffs of breath purled over my hot and sweating skin. "You could have run from that Kristiano who killed you. Lived to fight another day."

"Couldn't run. That bridge was the key to the whole battle." I wet my dry and cracked lips. "That *soldado* had everyone in a panic. Others . . . would have followed . . ."

I paused, glancing past him at the hissing fire, wondering where the guard who'd thrown wood on the flames had gotten away to. A large panther-bird-serpent beast was standing in the center of camp. Shouldn't he at least have screamed a warning before fleeing into the forest in terror?

Disillusioned, I added, "Besides, it doesn't matter if I die. We knew it was coming, Pearl Hand and I. I lived . . . lived long enough to see the Chicaza finally beat them."

Piasa's smooth brow furrowed, the pupils shrinking to pinpoints. "Is that what you think?"

"We burned them out at Chicaza town. Everything, even their clothes. Fought them to a draw at Alibamo fortification . . . We bled them, Piasa. They'll never be the same . . ." The burst of agony as I absently tried to shift left me half-stunned and trembling. Exhausted, trying desperately to pant for air, I finished, "I can die now."

"Really?"

"Looking forward to it, actually."

"Anything's better than the suffering? The slow suffocation? You can't stand watching Pearl Hand's grief and misery as you gradually fade?"

"Stop it. I traded you my life long ago. As to what you can give me in return? I'll trade you what's left of my life for a happy and quick death."

"Even if it means your complete extinction?"

"There is an end to everything, Piasa. Even Black Shell."

He stood there, his coat unsullied by the rain, that odd internal glow bathing his fine fur in a bluish light. Those burning yellow eyes fixed on mine, penetrating, as if to inspect my very souls.

"You are afraid?"

"Of course." I struggled for the shallowest of breaths.

He stepped around Bark's body, the blocky wedge of his head extending beneath the rain tarp. Like the great cat he was, he sniffed along the length of my body, pausing where the binding of my wound pressed against the bedding.

"Exhale all you can. It will be easier for me."

It took a moment for his words to make sense. Pus and blood, I could barely breathe. How did he expect me to exhale? Easier for him? How?

Just do it, Black Shell. It won't last long.

The pain was like jagged and splintered agony that tore through my chest. I struggled to scream, to shriek my lungs out . . . and managed a rattling gasp.

Dizzying yellow streaks danced behind my eyes; every muscle in my body quivered like a thousand cactus spines stung my exposed nerves.

"No deal," Piasa told me.

What? I blinked, drained from the horrible ordeal of exhaling. I tried to raise my head, fighting against the glittering lights behind my vision.

Then, to my horror, Piasa's great mouth opened and he sank his curved feline fangs into my wounded side.

Words cannot describe the experience. Intense suffering? Fire in each nerve? How about a blast of writhing, shrieking agony? I didn't know the body could withstand that kind of shattering pain.

The Piasa's words seemed to float through my souls: "You honor your trade, and you have taught me that everything has its time. Even Spirit Beasts such as myself. But for now, if you are tough and resilient, and willing to make the fight of your life, I can give you a chance . . ."

Then the Piasa began to suck, and through the howling pain, I felt my guts being pulled sideways. If it hurt when he bit me, it was nothing to what now exploded through me. I remember jerking under the impact, eyes clamped, jaws clenched, and then nothingness . . .

FIFTY-SIX

I CAME TO IN THE DARK, FLAT ON MY BACK, LUNGS heaving. With each desperate breath, my suffering side brought tears to my eyes.

Breathing. I was breathing.

Blinking in the darkness, I let my head roll to the side. Rain continued to fall from the midnight sky, pattering and splattering on leaf mat and sheltering hides.

Piasa had just given an entirely new meaning to the phrase "sucking chest wound." Even the mere memory of it hurt. And if he ever showed up to do it again, my response would be to smack him so hard across that nose that he'd just snuff me out in wild rage. Quick and clean.

Bark slept fitfully at my side, his nose buried in his tail.

The pitiful fire had been replenished; the flames now leaped and snapped angrily at the silvered rain. The hunched figure of the guard, a bark rain hat on his head, was crouched before the fire, his brown and muscular hands extended to the warmth.

I felt life slowly stirring through my bones and muscles, a renewed clarity to my thoughts. Yes, my side hurt. But the simple joy of being able to breathe . . . to fill my lungs? How can something we take for granted from birth become so precious? Expel your breath for as long as you can, then try taking just a half breath and see how it feels.

I tell you, even the kind of pain I was feeling is a fair trade after that.

The fire flared up, and I flexed my hands, wincing.

In the mud, right there beside my shelter, I could see the great eagle-taloned prints. Water was already pooled in them.

"Back to the fight," I said to myself, delighted to have some voice back.

Bark stirred at my words, lifting his head to stare inquisitively at me.

"Power was here," I told him. "Where were you when the Piasa was trying to suck my life away? Sleeping?"

At the tone in my voice, he stood and stretched his front end, butt high, tail slashing the chilly air. Even as I raised my hand to give him the "down" sign, he was prancing, his wide paws mashing the Piasa's tracks into muddled confusion.

Pearl Hand appeared in the company of a party of Chicaza warriors. They came threading their way down through the dripping trees like gray forest wraiths. From their loose-kneed walk, I could tell they were all exhausted. Heads were bowed as they picked their way down the slope, their bows cased on their backs, war clubs hanging from thongs on their belts.

Pearl Hand made straight for my shelter, stopping only long enough to pet Bark, ruffle his neck fur, and give him a reassuring pat on his scarred head.

Then her expression tightened as she saw me. Rushing

forward, she cried, "Black Shell? You're awake? But Copper Sky said—"

I shot her a weak smile.

Desperation lay behind her frantic eyes. "I had to go last night. De Soto sent cabayeros down our trail just before dusk. Medicine Killer was short of warriors to ambush them." She closed her eyes in misery. "He begged. Said you'd want it this way. And me . . . I—"

I waved her down with an irritated hand. "It's all right." The panic in her face touched me when I said, "Piasa was here last night. He . . . well . . . helped."

She was on her knees, hands resting on her thighs, her wet braid clinging to her shoulder in a provocative curl. I could smell wood smoke and forest on her damp leather war shirt. The handle of Moscoso's *hierro* knife stuck out from her belt.

I had a hunch that by now de Soto's *capitán* was coming to the conclusion that his knife was gone for good.

"Piasa?" she said uncertainly. "Here?" The suspicious glance she shot over the top of my shelter was confirmation enough. As if I couldn't smell the Tallahatchie's musk in the morning air.

"He was his usual irritating self." Then I told her of how Piasa's nocturnal visit had played out.

"He bit you on the side?" Pearl Hand asked skeptically.

"I'd tell you about how he sucked on me, but even having lived through it, just the thought makes my stomach queasy."

She had her gaze fixed on my bloodstained bindings. Then her eyes widened. "You're talking! Breathing!"

"And it hurts like a pestle-smashed thumb."

Her eyes lost focus. "Copper Sky said you would die. That it was only a matter of time. He tried, Black Shell. He used a length of cane, inserted it into one of the wounds . . ." She made a face. "Two Packs threw up at sight of what Copper Sky removed with his sucking tube. I can't imagine what Piasa pulled out of you."

"Imagination is sometimes a highly overrated thing." I paused. "You say Copper Sky worked on me?"

"You were unconscious. He said it was better that way, that the pain would be horrible. When he'd sucked the air and blood out and pressed down on your ribs, he sewed up the holes. Said you'd live or die." She looked away. "Then yesterday afternoon when I saw the infection . . . I thought you'd die."

"Wanted to."

She swallowed hard, back stiffening, eyes clamped closed. Her throat was working as tears began to leak out from the corners of her eyes.

I waited while she fought for control. Pearl Hand might cry, but she never allowed herself to bawl. Well, but for that one time after I rescued her from the old Cofitachequi mico's slavery.

"Medicine Killer's ambush didn't work?" I asked, seeking to divert her attention.

She sniffed, wiped her nose, and blinked the tear luster from her dark eyes. "They didn't take the bait." She swallowed, trying to keep the quaver from her voice. "It's been three days since the battle of Alibamo. As of this morning, they're lining up on the Quizquiz trail. Fire Tail, meanwhile, is walking upon the clouds. We killed at least fifteen, wounded another twenty or so, most of whom will recover."

"And our losses?"

She gave me the first hint of her old self: a saucy smile. "Three."

"Three . . . *hundred*?"

"Three," she said insistently. "Two outside the walls, and one in an archery duel with a Kristiano. I meant it when I said Alibamo was euphoric. He evacuated all of his warriors from the fortification and laid his ambushes in the Tallahatchie swamps, but de Soto, for the first time ever, didn't pursue."

"Breath Giver take me," I whispered. "The Apalachee only fought him to a draw. We . . . we really and truly defeated him!"

I filled my lungs to whoop in victory . . . but it hurt way too much.

Pearl Hand, however, was giving me that horrible look, the silent and haunted one that asked, *Yes, but at what price?*

One thing was sure: Assuming I even survived my wound, I was going nowhere for the time being.

And de Soto was on his way to Quizquiz to work more misery.

The good thing about having a Spirit Beast suck pooled blood and pus out of your side?

You can breathe again.

The bad thing?

You have enough air in you to make whimpering sounds when warriors lift you onto a litter.

I was still whimpering three days later when my little party of porters—led by Pearl Hand and Two Packs—wound out of the hilly forests that divide the Tombigbee and Tallahatchie watersheds.

I was carried summarily to Red Sticks town, the new provisional capital of Chicaza until such time as the council could be reassembled to discuss the future of the Nation.

Somehow I still clung to life. Piasa hadn't lied about my chances. I most assuredly wasn't dead, but I wasn't anything like alive, either.

I was placed in the Chief Clan house—a larger and more elaborate building than the one at Black Oak town had been. Had been? Oh, yes, my brother ensured that it was burned to the ground after the Kristianos pulled out. As for myself, I wonder how things would have turned out if I'd somehow kept my wits and demanded he burn it to the ground before de Soto took it.

Perhaps the Monster wouldn't have managed to refit and re-Spirit his weapons.

Around noon on the day following my arrival, Copper Sky arrived. He entered the room wearing a panther-hide cape tanned with the fur on. The hopaye's cape didn't have a blue inner glow like the Piasa's.

After he'd soaked the cloth bindings, I made the mewling sounds as he peeled them away from my wounds.

"Hmmm." He cocked his head, inspecting the punctures in my side. "The healing has slowed. Not as much pus as I'd like to see. Your fever remains about the same. And these other red spots? Like holes? Two above and two below the wounds? Who did this to you?"

"Piasa," I told him weakly. "He came to me in the night while we were camped along the Tallahatchie. He bit me."

Copper Sky gave me a deadpan look. "That was the night after I sucked the air out of your chest?"

"As Pearl Hand explained it, yes." I paused, suddenly unsure.

He pursed his lips, the intent gaze never wavering. "Black Shell, spirit Power doesn't run in my veins like so many before me. I have sought but never found it. Never been blessed with its gifts. Instead I have studied hard, learning the roots, their tastes, uses, and secrets. I've attempted to compensate by treating people as functioning beings. With chest wounds like yours, I can occasionally save a life by removing the blood and polluted air that is drawn into the wound. If I don't, the lung collapses, the heart slides sideways, and the warrior dies."

"I see."

"Good, because even if I manage to suck the blood

and air out, then sew the wounds closed to make a seal against evil spirits and disease, it is a rare warrior who actually survives. When I open them up again in the charnel house, their lungs are full of pus and corruption. That's why I'm worried. The pus must have a place to drain."

"I don't feel like my lungs are full of pus."

"No." He frowned. "So, my problem is this: Do I open your wound and suck again or take the chance that Piasa's bite is curing you?"

I ground my teeth, wondering myself. "Let's trust in Power, Hopaye. I've made it this far. And to be honest, I'm not sure that having my chest punched open again wouldn't be just enough to drive my souls away for the final time."

He smiled at that, patted my shoulder, and rose. "You are a remarkable man, Orphan. Somehow I have the impression that our people were not whole until you walked into the tchkofa that night and announced that Power had sent you to us."

"My mother would disagree."

"Ishki Minko is allowed her opinion. But I have seen a change in your brother and your sisters. A difference in the way they act, as if by your very presence you have allowed them to be the people they wished, not the ones tradition expected them to be."

I grunted at that, feeling numb with exhaustion.

"Sleep well, Orphan. I have other wounded to attend to. Though most are not as perplexing as you."

I watched him go and continued to breathe as deeply as I dared. Was my chest slowly filling with pus? The faint pain in my heart had diminished. And while I couldn't fill my lungs the way I could before the wound, I was definitely doing better than before Piasa bit me.

Choctaw Hair darkened the doorway as he entered with Pearl Hand. A familiar split-cloud copper headpiece sat atop his tightly pinned hair. The bear-hide cloak over his shoulders was thrown back in recognition of the warm day. A long white apron dropped to a suggestive point between his knees, and he carried an ornate copper-headed ax.

"Greetings, tikba. I'm delighted to learn that you're still breathing."

"Breathing? Yes. Breathing well? Now, that's another story entirely. I'm not ready to race you around Red Stick town quite yet." I paused for breath. "Neither Piasa nor the hopaye is willing to wager on my chances. That Kristiano might have killed me after all."

"If it makes you feel any better, your Kristiano's not walking. Two Packs recognized him when he was spying on de Soto's camp. The man's legs were broken when you tossed him over the wall." Choctaw Hair gave me a mocking smile. "And you did get to keep his sword."

"Next time"—I wet my lips—"I won't be so possessive."

He lowered himself to the bed beside me. "According to the scouts, de Soto is almost to Quizquiz."

"Did you send emissaries under the White Arrow to warn them?"

"Warn the Quizquiz? Are you joking? Those people—" He stopped, realizing what he was saying. "No, Black Shell, I did not. When it comes to fighting the Kristianos, we all still have a great deal to learn, don't we?"

"It's all right." I reached up and laid a weak hand on his forearm. "Your brother-in-law Fire Tail fought a battle worthy of the finest Chicaza tishu minko."

"We counted the graves," Choctaw Hair told me. "Dug them up to be sure. Fifteen Kristianos died at Alibamo. We cut up the corpses and hung them in trees like anyone would do with evil creatures. I'm told that not even the crows will eat them. Probably Breath Giver doesn't want their taint in the Sky World."

"Fitting that you dug them up. I'm sure Piasa doesn't want them polluting the Underworld, either." Pus and blood, when this was all over, Horned Serpent wouldn't send me on a mission to dig up all of de Soto's dead and hang them from trees, would he?

My brother glanced at me. "I need you to get well. Since your arrival here, I've come to rely on you. And should you decide to stay here and take up your—"

With a chop of the hand I gestured that he cease. "My business is with de Soto."

He hesitated, finding the courage to say, "Your wounds preclude pursuing de Soto any further."

"My wounds will either kill me or they won't. Dying or not, I remain the chosen of Horned Serpent. I am too late to warn the Quizquiz. The question remains: Where will he head next?"

"Black Shell, you can't even sit up on your own. You only delude yourself with the notion that you're going to fight Kristianos. At least anytime soon."

I gave him my most menacing and dangerous glare. Then, since he didn't seem to get it, I told him, "That was my most menacing and dangerous glare."

Instead of acting appropriately cowed, he arched a skeptical eyebrow.

Pearl Hand, who had listened quietly, told him, "Argue as you like, High Minko, Black Shell is right: He's Horned Serpent's chosen. Even Piasa may have become an ally. The fight doesn't stop at Chicaza's borders. Nor will the struggle cease with Black Shell's death. He was told in the beginning that this would be a long-fought war. It didn't start with de Soto, nor will it end with his destruction."

I said, "She's right. With or without me, the battle for our world goes on. But, brother, if I survive this, and when we hear where the Monster is headed after Quizquiz, will you give me your word that you will assist me? Perhaps even transport me if I can't walk on my own?"

He was giving me that look, the one that reminded me of when he was a boy and I was being completely selfish and unreasonable.

"You have my word . . . even though it may tear the heart from my body."

FIFTY-SEVEN

I TOOK A TURN FOR THE WORSE AFTER THAT, MY
souls drifting away into delirium. Fever-hot sweats followed by a bone-deep chill tormented my wounded body.
A constant tickle of nausea threatened but never produced vomiting. Occasionally the room would spin, coupled with the sensation of an endless, tumbling fall . . .

I *really* hated that. I pleaded impotently with Power to
make it stop. That or let me die.

Several times my souls traveled to the Spirit World,
and I remember conversations with Old-Woman-Who-
Never-Dies . . . though I avoided uncomfortable, if po-
tentially ecstatic, intimacies with Corn Woman. I saw
Blood Thorn there, though I cannot remember what we
discussed. I do remember flying, carried aloft by Horned
Serpent. The image that remained was of gossamer wings
that radiated all the colors of the rainbow stretching
across the entire sky . . .

Spring lengthened into summer.

Two Packs left on a trading venture to the west—one

predicated on gathering information on the Monster's whereabouts.

I seemed to hang, neither dying nor healing, my body locked in a stasis of misery. Copper Sky and Pearl Hand managed to get me on my feet, supporting me as I shuffled to the latrine and back. Afterward I would collapse onto my bed, panting and trembling as if I'd just run all the way from Cofitachequi.

Then, just before summer solstice, on a moonless midnight, some whisper of warning blew through my souls.

I blinked awake, staring uneasily around the greased-charcoal blackness of the clan house. In the night I could hear a screech owl's mournful whinny as it sang to the Powers of the night.

Something moved in the darkness.

Pearl Hand? No, she'd been called to a council meeting. De Soto might have been fleeing west through the forest, but Chicaza had indeed been conquered. Pearl Hand had taken my people's hearts, souls, and imagination. She had made no secret of her past, but my stiff-necked and prudish Chicaza couldn't have cared less. It was a measure of their newfound respect for Minko Pearl Hand that she'd been called to determine if Chicaza town should even be rebuilt.

Something rasped on the cane-mat floor.

"Bark? Blackie?"

No dog came snuffling up to the bed or poked a cold nose in my direction. I remembered that Pearl Hand had taken them to the council session in the tchkofa.

"Who's there?"

In the eerie silence, my heart began to pound. The darkness felt heavier, oppressive, as if it sucked up even the faint glow of embers in the central hearth.

Reaching beneath the blanket, my groping fingers wrapped around the hilt of Pearl Hand's old Kristiano knife. I might not have been able to stand on my own, but I could surely jab someone.

"Piasa? Is it you, come to finish what you started beside the Tallahatchie?"

I heard a muffled exhale. Clothing hissed and a shape emerged from the shadows, stepping closer, then hesitating.

"I can see you," I said insistently. "Tell me who you are and why you are here."

"You and that swamp bitch have really done it, haven't you?" She almost spit the words. "You've made Chicaza yours. But you don't fool me. Not for one second, you worthless, dripping pustule."

"Mother? Come to Red Stick town, have you?"

She loomed over me, a blanket wrapped around her shoulders, her gray hair pinned back in a bun. She held something that might have been a wadded cloth in her hands. "Your uncle was the greatest man I ever knew . . . and your cowardice broke his heart. You gutted him, Black Shell! Gutted him just the same as if you'd reached inside him and twisted the living souls out of his body." She paused. "I know! I watched him live with the pain and disappointment until it finally killed him."

I ground my jaws, angered at the accusation in her voice. "I told you at the time how Horned Serpent warned me to run. You want to talk about disappointment? How do you think *I* felt? All of my life you and Uncle taught me to be honest, that lies were for the weak and cowardly. Then, when the greatest trial of my young life was thrust upon me, I *told the truth!*" I swallowed against the knot of anger in my throat. "And you and Uncle declared me a liar and exiled me. So much for the vaunted Chicaza honor."

"You still cling to that faded lie?"

"What faded lie?"

"Horned Serpent? Wasn't it just Piasa that you called

upon? Is that how you defy the incantations and charms? You've sold yourself to the water panther for protection?"

Incantations and charms? A cold chill ran through me. "Are you telling me that you've hired a sorcerer? You've been using *Spirit Power* against me?"

"Things make so much more sense now," she mused as if to herself. "Our charms were tailored to foreign medicines and talismans. If it's Piasa who protects you, we'll need different magics." She sniffed. "But what a fool I am. Your she-bitch of a wife is off beguiling your gullible brother. Clear Water, for whom I'd once held such high hopes, is in the Women's House preparing to deliver my next grandchild. But I can win her back after you're finally out of the way."

"Clear Water will *always* be your daughter."

"You shouldn't have returned," she told me coldly. "All you did was remind me of how much I hated you then and how much more I now despise you. I can't let the pain go unavenged. I swore on my honor that if you ever came back, I'd destroy you." She paused. "And . . . I *keep* my word!"

I eased the knife out of its sheath. Blood and pus, I was as weak as a newborn rabbit pup. Maybe it was her sorcery, or maybe Piasa's bite and Copper Sky's medicine just weren't enough, but I wouldn't have strength for more than a couple of flailing jabs in her direction.

"Murder me," I told her, "and you'll lose Choctaw Hair, Clear Water, and Silent Spring forever. You'll make yourself into a pariah."

Her laughter sounded as brittle as dry sticks. "Your lies end now, you filthy worm."

With despicable ease she batted the *hierro* blade from my grip. I heard it thump on the floor.

"You are pitiful." She leaned over the bed. "How could a creature so weak and pathetic have sprung from my womb? As soon as you slid out I should have taken the birth cord, wrapped it around your scrawny neck, and strangled you." She smacked her lips. "But better late than never."

With a flick of her shadowy wrists, she shook out what I thought might be a leather bag.

"You're condemning yourself," I told her, fear running bright through my blood and bones. "They'll blame you."

"What? Do you think I'd be foolish enough to leave a wound? Your lungs are weak enough as it is." She bent down, and I realized she was trying to fit a leather sack over my head.

I batted at her, struggling, and got my thumbs under the edge. She pressed down with all of her weight. My arms trembled, strength failing, lungs and heart laboring.

"No!" I cried weakly.

And in that instant, the old woman relented, pulling away. I heard her grunt and utter a curious gurgling noise. I ripped the bag from my head and flung it as far as my wobbling arm would permit.

Pearl Hand's voice sounded deadly and reed-thin as she asked, "Old woman, is there a single reason why I shouldn't slit your throat the way Black Shell did with that maggot Ears?"

I heard Mother whimper. Yellow sparkles of light danced behind my eyes. The dark shadows before me wavered and swayed as Mother was bent backward in Pearl Hand's grip.

"Please . . . don't." I struggled for breath. "We'll never hide the blood." I sucked all the air I could get into my wheezy chest. "And I'm too exhausted to help you dispose of the body."

"I was thinking about turning her into little pieces. Small. Easily carried." Pearl Hand sounded eminently reasonable. "But to disperse an evil like hers, we'd have to chop her into so many parts they'd be dangling from half the trees in Chicaza."

Thank Breath Giver, Pearl Hand was joking. I realized I might actually have a chance to talk her out of this. "As filled as she is with hate, I'm not even sure the crows would touch her."

Pearl Hand's voice turned deadly. "What do I do with her, husband? This is the second time she's brought pain into my life. There will *not* be a third."

I nodded, as if anyone could see me in the dark. "As much as I'd like to tell you to just cut her throat, she'd be better served by it than we would."

Mother made a strangling sound. A scuffle ensued, feet skidding on matting. I heard grunts, flesh smacking flesh, and then the shadowy figures crashed to the floor.

"Pearl Hand?" I cried, actually managing to sit up in my bed, panicked by what I could not discern in the inky blackness.

A loud smack was followed by a groan.

"Pus and blood!" Pearl Hand panted. I thought I saw her shift as she crouched over a supine shadow. "Give me a moment. I've got her choked down. Then I'm going to tie her up like a roasting turkey."

"She's alive?" I croaked.

"Only if I don't come to my senses."

I sank back, desperate for air. "Perhaps, beloved, you could disappoint me and leave her alive?"

The only thing happy in the Chief Clan house was the great roaring fire in the central hearth. It leaped, popped, and crackled, enthusiastically tossing sparks up toward the high smoke hole. Light danced in warm yellow and illuminated the honey-colored timbers that supported the roof. It shot wavering shadows over the patterns woven into the cattail-mat flooring.

It also shone on Mother where she lay trussed like some unusual cocoon. Her eyes reflected the fire like polished stones of coal, her expression one of pure rage. The angle of her head cast deep black shadows that turned the lines of her face into a midnight webbing.

My brother sat on the pole bed next to mine, his arms braced on his knees. A deep melancholy lay behind his weary brown eyes. Pearl Hand had snagged him on the way out of the tchkofa, so he was still dressed in an immaculate white apron, his hair done up in his falcon-wing headpiece. Strings of shell beads adorned his neck and a myrtle-fiber cloak hung down his back, leaving his shoulders bare.

Pearl Hand stood, arms crossed, her glowering eyes fixed on Mother. The old woman glared right back at her with the intensity of a snared bobcat.

"She admitted that she's employed a sorcerer to witch Black Shell," Pearl Hand declared hotly. "But the witch wasn't working fast enough, so she sneaked in here while we were in council, figuring to use this."

Pearl Hand tossed the leather sack onto the chevron-patterned matting between Choctaw Hair's feet. "I didn't take her down until she attempted to tie that accursed thing over Black Shell's head. If you'll look, High Minko, even the stitching has been waxed to ensure that it seals completely. As weak as Black Shell is, and with the drawstring tight, he'd have suffocated in no time. Had word not come that Clear Water had delivered her child, we might have been gone half the night. I'd have come home to find my husband a corpse. And not a mark on him."

Choctaw Hair stared woodenly at the leather hood, then asked, "Mother, is this true?"

"Wake up, High Minko." She raised her chin defiantly. "The akeohoosa and this foreign slut are just using the Kristianos as an opportunity to gain position. They've woven themselves into the very fabric of our society. I've even heard that you would step aside and allow this bit of wandering shit to sit upon the panther-hide chair. Is this so?"

"Mother, he *saved* Chicaza!"

"Bah! They've *duped* you! If your uncle were alive, we'd have marched out and crushed these Kristianos the way we've crushed our enemies for generations. All you had was this hoobuk waksee's wild stories of Kristiano superiority. He was the one who talked you into letting him play high minko. He convinced you to wait, allowing the Kristianos to take Chicaza town and make themselves at home."

Her eyes narrowed into glittering slits. "It fell to me to ensure that he didn't bring us all to eventual ruin. And I give you—my only *living* son—my word that I will not stop until the akeohoosa and his camp bitch no longer disgrace this family, this lineage, or this clan."

Even where I lay, I could hear Pearl Hand's teeth grinding. My dear woman was almost vibrating with rage. When she passed a certain point, violence always ensued, but what could I do to stop it?

Choctaw Hair raised one hand. "Mother, you are not the—"

"I am *ishki minko*! And as ishki minko, I give you my word that I will destroy the pollution that has come among us." She shot him a crafty smile. "And, son, until my body is carried cold and soulless to the charnel house, I will not stop."

Pearl Hand's anger broke. She went for her knife just as I called out, "Wait!"

All eyes turned my way.

I sucked frantically for breath, wondering if this was the way I'd live the rest of my life: half-alive, half-dead. "She is right. I no longer have a place here."

My brother gave me a panicked look. "Pay her no attention, Black Shell. She's a bitter old woman, frustrated and—"

"She's the ishki minko," I replied reasonably. "She's made up her mind to kill me and Pearl Hand, sworn it. So what are you going to do? Nothing, that's what, because any action you take will dishonor yourself and the family."

"She *dishonors* the family!" he thundered, pointing a trembling finger.

"Only if the extent of her hatred and madness become public." I continued, keeping my voice level. "And, brother, as true Chicaza, it falls to us to maintain our family's honor and act with discretion and humility."

He and Pearl Hand were both scowling at me.

I continued softly. "Pearl Hand and I are no longer needed in Chicaza. Our calling now lies to the west. Where the Monster has gone, so must we follow."

"Have your souls left? And taken all of your good sense with them?" my brother asked. "You can barely sit up! Even this old woman was able to subdue you!"

"And as long as I am here, whoever she's hired to witch me will continue to work his magic against me. Pearl Hand and I *must* leave. Our lives are pledged to the destruction of the Kristianos. We're fighting for our world."

"Fighting?" Choctaw Hair cried, hands lifted imploringly. "You can't even stand, let alone draw a bow."

"There are other ways to wage war," I told him patiently. "I remain Horned Serpent's tool, and he will use me until I am completely broken before he discards me."

Pearl Hand suggestively fingered the handle of Moscoso's knife, the narrowing of her eyes and her pinched lips expressing her opinion.

"By the Piasa's balls"—Choctaw Hair spread his arms wide—"how much more broken do you need to be? You're half-dead now."

I tapped my head. "My cunning and experience remain as keen as ever. And let's face it, no matter what nonsense the ishki minko might want to believe, we beat the Kristianos because we were smarter than they were."

"And you would go where?" Pearl Hand finally asked.

"To the Natchez," I told her. "The scouts tell us that

de Soto has passed through Quizquiz and has crossed the Mississippi. Last we heard, he's turning Pacaha and Casqui upside down. If he proceeds according to his usual plan, he will continue to head westward, in part to see if he can find this place called Mexico."

"He'll end up in the plains." Choctaw Hair gestured the futility of it. "Nothing out there but half-nomadic bison hunters who grow a little corn. If we're lucky—and he's not—he's going to run right into the Tula. I doubt he'll like the reception they'll give him."

Pearl Hand said, "To feed his army, the *Adelantado* needs a great nation."

"Exactly." I nodded, seeing it all in my head. "He's going to run out of rich nations to loot and eventually head back to winter along the Mississippi. My guess is that he will follow one of the major tributary rivers back. And when he does, what is the single largest, strongest, and most dominant nation along the Mississippi?"

"The Quigualtam alliance of the Natchez," my brother said with a nod of understanding.

"And I want to be waiting for him when he finally gets there," I said with conviction. "Is the old Quigualtam Great Sun still on the high chair?"

"He is."

I smiled. "I used to always beat his war chief, the Great Serpent, in chunkey. Even won his head once."

"You will again," Pearl Hand told me with a smile so forced it betrayed the depth of her lie.

"What?" my brother cried. "You can't travel to the Natchez! You can't even walk to the latrine without two people to hold you up!"

I glanced at Mother; her eyes, the twist of her mouth, the set of her jaw, all reflected undisguised loathing. "If you would provide the loan of a litter, I will trade you the last of my copper, brother. All but the sacred mace. And it's a solution to the problem of what to do with Mother.

Once I'm gone, I'll most likely remove the source of her current insanity."

For long moments, my brother stared at me, a thousand pleadings in his wounded brown eyes. Then he glanced long and hard at Mother.

"I will take you to Quigualtam town," he agreed. As I knew he would.

FIFTY-EIGHT

THE OLD TRADERS' TRAIL FOLLOWED THE HILLY DI-vide southeast to the headwaters of the Black River, then kept to the uplands parallel to the floodplain. We were making good time.

On the fifth night out from Chicaza, camp was made in a grassy flat where a clear stream tumbled down from the thickly forested hills. I enjoyed the sound of the water, the perfumed scent of the forest, and the twinkling of the last fireflies as the night settled around our camp.

Pearl Hand propped me up with a pillow she carried for the purpose. Bark and Blackie, panting from a vigorous rabbit pursuit, flopped down beside my litter. I could tell that both were pleased to be on the trail again.

The warriors went about making their camp, stowing weapons, building fires, and the four young women who accompanied us set about building their cook fires. Not only did they attend to camp chores, but as was tradi-tional, they would sing as we approached Natchez.

"How are you feeling?" Pearl Hand asked as she seated

herself beside me and set her crossbow on the grass. I tried to avoid her worried and knowing gaze.

"I am feeling satisfaction," I told her.

"That's not what I meant."

"The fever has subsided. I don't feel like I'm floating away half the time." I sniffed the warm air, watching the breeze waffling among the ash leaves above. The chirring of a thousand insects serenaded us from the surrounding forest. Cardinals were singing and a mockingbird warbled from the brush beside the creek. Overhead a flight of parakeets chirped.

The high minko made one last tour of the camp, ordered his scouts out for the first watch, and sauntered over to seat himself beside Pearl Hand. He gave me an overenthusiastic smile, as if doing so would change the unchangeable.

"I saw your runner arrive," I told him. "You seemed pleased with what he told you."

Choctaw Hair smiled for real this time. "The Quigualtam Great Sun has received the White Arrow and will await our arrival." He glanced at our small entourage. "I still think that your insistence that we keep the party small wasn't particularly . . ." He made a face. "Shall we say, well thought out?"

I laughed. "But for the wound in my chest, Pearl Hand and I would be doing this by ourselves. There was no need to disrupt Chicaza even more to send a large delegation. They have enough to do, rebuilding, planting, and repairing." I narrowed a skeptical eye. "It's enough that you insisted on coming."

He gave Pearl Hand a shy look and shrugged. "Considering the stakes, my presence is required."

And you don't have to admit that you know I'm dying. I reached out, taking his hand in mine. "Your secret is safe with me."

He avoided me, blinking as if something were in his eyes.

"What of the Great Sun?" Pearl Hand asked, skillfully changing the subject. "You've had dealings with him, High Minko. How will he respond?"

"The Natchez are always something of an enigma. They split themselves into just two divisions, Sun Clan and Commoner. They are less than moieties, more than clans. Currently they have fifteen towns scattered along the Mississippi's eastern uplands. The Quigualtam alliance—composed of several lineages within the Sun Clan—currently dominates most of their affairs.

"What the Natchez call the 'White Woman'—the ishki minko in our terms—is the head matron of the Quigualtam lineage. Her son has been a better-than-average ruler, and his cousin, who is also a most competent man, serves as 'Great Serpent,' or our equivalent of tishu minko. The Great Serpent handles relations with other Nations, warfare, and ensures the Great Sun's edicts are carried out.

"But there are always factions associated with other towns that are politicking, seeking influence. Overall with the harvest good and the people happy—and for the most part secure from attack—the leadership has been acting with justice and discretion. The Quigualtam alliance, as far as I can see, is stable for the foreseeable future."

Thoughtfully, I said, "They are a Mos'kogean people. While they have been Chicaza's ancient and traditional enemies, the world is changing. You could take this opportunity to broker more than just a one-time alliance."

Pearl Hand added, "Quizquiz, Pacaha, and Casqui will probably collapse after de Soto moves on. An alignment of strength between the Natchez and Chicaza would provide both of your Nations with a certain amount of security in the aftermath."

My brother chuckled dryly. "Next thing, you'll want me to ally with the Choctaw and the Yuchi, too."

"Might not hurt," I told him, wincing as I tried to resettle myself. Piss and blood in a pot! Why wasn't I getting my strength back? "Old-Woman-Who-Never-Dies told me it would be a long fight. If we crush de Soto, you have no guarantee that another fleet of Kristiano ships isn't going to land in Ochuse and drop off another army."

His expression was full of rebuke. "With all of these friendly allies you're making me, against whom will the Chicaza refine our art of war?"

"Let's see what happens with the Natchez first, shall we?" Pearl Hand suggested. "High Minko, if your messengers have found Two Packs, he should know to find us in Quigualtam town."

I closed my eyes, desperate for sleep. Truth to tell, the traveling was taking a toll. My chest hurt constantly. My litter bearers were among the best, but the ride often jolted me into excruciating pain.

Somewhere during the conversation, I drifted away into dreams. When I came to, it was the middle of the night, my bladder was aching, and I awoke desperate for a drink.

I blinked up at the night. The ash tree above was yellowed by the great fire. All around, people were wrapped in blankets, and I caught sight of bats winging through, snatching insects before vanishing into the darkness.

"Pearl Hand?" I called softly.

Bark and Blackie rose from where they slept on either side, and I petted them as Pearl Hand stood groggily from her blankets. She helped me up, and my chest felt like it was pulling apart. Together we tottered to the edge of camp, where I made water.

Helping me back to the bed, she lowered me, and I gasped for breath. Just that short trip had drained my strength to the point my muscles trembled. A burning ache filled my wounded side.

"How are you?" She crouched, arms braced on her knees.

"Standing up didn't hurt nearly as much," I lied. "I didn't get dizzy until the last."

"Among the Natchez there will be a healer who can remove the witchery. It's just a matter of finding the right—"

I placed my fingers against her lips, admiring how beautiful she was, half-silhouetted by the firelight.

"Copper Sky fixed the holes and made my lungs work. Beloved wife, you can exhaust yourself in the search, but in all the world there is no hopaye, hilishaya, or healer by any other name who can rival the medicine Power in the water panther's bite. That I have lived this long is a miracle."

She took my hand, gripping it with desperation. I watched her swallow against the knot that I knew was half choking her throat.

"Here, here," I chided. "Power has given me enough time to deliver our message to the Natchez."

"Black Shell," she said miserably, "we've known this day was coming . . ."

I used all of my strength to reach out and run my fingers through her hair. "And each day my love for you has been like a thunder between my souls. I pity all the other men alive. In their poor lifetimes they will never feel the passion I've had for you since that day when I first saw you alongside the trail."

A tear glimmered crystalline fire as it traced the smooth curve of her cheek.

"Do you . . ." She ground her teeth against the building grief. "Do you want your body to be taken back to Chicaza? Maybe placed with Squirm and Patches up in that mound?"

I considered, then shook my head. "No. When the time comes I want you to have me carried down to the river's bank. I'm Black Shell, the trader. I have to make good on a bargain."

She nodded, sniffing. In a fragile voice, she said, "I know."

"And Pearl Hand, these Natchez are peculiar. They consider it a privilege to offer their lives to accompany the dead to the afterlife. Don't let any of them sacrifice either themselves or their children to accompany me. Not only do I not want their deaths on my conscience, but the last thing I need is a bunch of fawning strangers interfering with *my* afterlife."

She nodded, that old familiar quirk of her lips warming my heart. Then she crawled into my blankets, wrapping herself around me. I closed my eyes, a feeling of warm security flowing from her body where it pressed against mine.

I reached up and pulled the wealth of her thick black hair across my cheek, thinking, *Savor this, Black Shell. In all of existence, this is true bliss.*

FIFTY-NINE

ON AN OCCASION AS IMPORTANT AS THE MEETING OF two ancient and powerful enemies—such as the Chicaza and Natchez under the White Arrow—nothing is left to chance. Even the smallest detail must be attended to to ensure that each side presents all the pomp, pageantry, and ceremony required. As we approached, runners were charging up and down the trails to ensure that everything was perfectly orchestrated. The symbolic gifts had already been delivered along with flowery speeches ensuring everyone's goodwill.

By the time we arrived at Quigualtam town, the Great Sun knew exactly how many were in our party, their ranks, ages, and honors. He had every aspect of the greeting ceremonies laid out, the feasts prepared, and appropriate lodgings established for each of us. The entirety of Quigualtam had been swept, cleaned, and repainted. The people had been ordered to prepare their finest. Everything had to perpetuate the illusion that Quigualtam was the best, finest, and most wonderful city in the world, and the Natchez the greatest of all people.

For the first time in my adult life, I was identified as Black Shell, brother to the high minko of Chicaza, and given the new title of "Messenger of Horned Serpent."

I wasn't sure how either the White Woman, the Great Sun, or the Great Serpent was receiving that. They knew me as an exiled trader. I could only imagine the curiosity that was brewing atop the high mound at Quigualtam.

On the appointed day, we waited out an inconvenient rainstorm in a trailside temple, the thatched structure perched atop a hillock less than a hand's march from Quigualtam. I stared across at the imposing city where it rose above the surrounding country. Atop a mound second only to the Great Mound at fabled Cahokia, Quigualtam town dominated the horizon. Blood Thorn—who'd been so awed by the great Nations—would have loved to have seen the place. Poking above the mound-top palisade were the high-peaked roofs of the Great Sun's palace on the west, the Great Serpent's smaller palace on the east, and shorter charnel houses and granaries interspersed among them. Above it all towered the tall red-cedar World Tree pole with red and white stripes spiraling down its length.

When the rain finally tapered off to leave a stunning double rainbow, we re-formed our procession. The local Natchez appeared from their houses and farmsteads to line the main trail. Many held flowers that they waved at us as we passed. Others shook gourd rattles and sang. All stepped into line, following behind in a throng, singing and clapping, or shaking rattles.

My brother, atop his litter, was carried behind our flute players. He looked resplendent with his face painted white around the black forked-eye design. A heavy copper falcon headpiece was pinned atop his greased black locks. He held the symbolic White Arrow before him, though a servant carried Uncle's copper-headed ax immediately behind. A panther-hide cloak hung from his shoulders, and he wore a long white apron. Gleaming copper ear spools hung in his ears.

I rode in my litter, my face painted white. I hadn't the strength to hold the ancient copper mace upright so I just rested it across my belly. Antonio's ornate sword lay on the litter beside me.

Pearl Hand walked just ahead. She'd dressed in strands of shell beads, a spotless white wrap around her hips. She carried her crossbow, Capitán Moscoso's gem-encrusted *híerro* knife in its scabbard at her hip. Bark and Blackie marched at her side. Behind me came the Chicaza warriors, their faces and bodies painted white. They had dressed in their finest, their little white arrows of merit prominently displayed in tightly coiled hair. Feather splays decorated each shoulder. They'd polished and oiled their weapons. A couple even sported Kristiano scalps tied to their bow tips.

We wound down through the gullies, across clear streams, and up the ridges—each topped with farmsteads, cornfields, and clumps of fruit and nut trees. The flutes began to play and the whole Chicaza delegation began to sing the song of ritual greeting.

Traveling thus between the swelling ranks of Natchez who'd come to watch, we made our way to the foot of the great mound where it dominated a high ridge bounded on three sides by Quigualtam Creek.

Our entourage made its way down an aisle between massed people, past granaries, a couple of shrines, and ramadas, to the western flat where the Great Serpent waited at the forefront of perhaps two hundred Natchez warriors, all decked out in feathers, paint, copper, and shining mica breast pieces.

To either side, resplendent in bright fabrics of red, yellow, blue, purple, and green, were assembled the "honored men." Behind them stood the nobles, and finally the true Sun Clan, all placed according to rank and privilege.

In the rear, lines of women were singing the Natchez song of greeting, clapping their hands, and dancing.

Marching right up to the Great Serpent, the Chicaza flute players promptly stepped aside, dropping to one knee and touching their foreheads in a sign of respect.

The crowd went silent. Or as silent as a crowd can be when people are shifting, scratching, and whispering excitedly to their neighbors.

At a signal, Choctaw Hair ordered his litter to be lowered and he stepped forward, the White Arrow in his hands, my old Kristiano sword at his hip.

Walking up to the Great Serpent, he stopped, holding out the White Arrow. Then he cried, "I am known as He Who Takes the Choctaw Hair Mankiller, high minko of the Chicaza people, of the Chief Clan, of the Hickory Moiety." He went on to recount his ancestors and his war honors, and finally ended by saying, "At the head of the mighty Chicaza I have routed the accursed Kristianos from our lands. My warriors have killed many of their *soldados* and cabayos. We burned them out of their town and incinerated their supplies. They left their dead behind them, and to their dismay we have dug them up and hung pieces to rot in the trees, removing their pollution from our soil.

"Having accomplished these great things, the Chicaza Nation now comes to the Natchez in peace, under the White Arrow, and we bind ourselves to it."

He raised his arms, as if to take in the Great Serpent and his entourage as well as the elevated magnificence of Quigualtam town behind them. "For generations the

Chicaza and Natchez have made war against each other. We each have wept at the deaths of loved ones, retaliated, and tortured our captives to death in the squares. In the process, we have built the red Power between our peoples. Chicaza now comes, our hearts full of the white Power, seeking to restore balance and to achieve harmony with the mighty Natchez Nation."

Then he turned, pointing at me and Pearl Hand. "I bring Black Shell, the Orphan, Messenger of Horned Serpent, and Minko Pearl Hand of the Chicora, who bear a message for the Great Sun, the White Woman, and the Natchez people."

The Great Serpent had aged since the last time I'd beaten him at chunkey. I could see gray at his temples. He had his hair tightly wound and pinned with a striking spoonbill-feather headdress. His face was painted white with three red stripes angling down each cheek, indicating a preference for peace, but that he'd need to be persuaded. A glistening beaver-hide cloak was thrown back over his shoulder, and the image of a fox was embroidered on the front of his apron.

He took the White Arrow and began his recitation of ancestry, war honors, and so forth.

I sighed, missing the friendly clouds as the sun now beat down, driving little fingers of mist from the damp red soil. I wished for a sunshade. Hadn't thought I'd need one. Why was I so miserable and drenched with sweat? The heat wasn't that bad. The nagging discomfort in my chest just kept getting worse.

"You all right?" Pearl Hand asked.

"It's getting very hot," I whispered.

She promptly signaled for a water jar.

"One thing about when we were racing just ahead of de Soto," I whispered. "We didn't have to endure all these hideous formalities."

"True," she agreed, winking encouragement at me.

"But this time around we don't have to wonder if we'll still be alive to watch the sunset."

I bit my lip, refusing to admit that the sun might kill me before we even passed into Quigualtam. I began to pant, wondering if I'd ever felt this hot before. The copper mace felt so hot to the touch I thought it would raise blisters on my fingers.

Fool! You survived Mabila and Chicaza town. Why is a little sunlight bothering you?

Time began to slow into eternity. I think I passed out in the end. The movement of the litter brought me awake, desperately thirsty and sweating.

I felt it thump on the ground, and Pearl Hand, my brother, the Great Serpent, and the White Woman were looking down at me.

"I'm all right," I whispered hoarsely. "Just need a drink."

After I'd been given a bottle, I weakly pulled myself up, aware that while I'd slept, my litter had been borne into the city. I was on the Great Sun's elevated veranda. I could look down onto the great plaza of Quigualtam, where people crowded the stickball grounds, reverently touched the World Tree, and thoughtfully avoided stepping on the chunkey courts. The Chicaza were walking among them, escorted by appointed nobles who ensured their comfort.

"Blessed gods," Pearl Hand said wearily. "You gave me a scare, husband."

I grinned, reaching out feebly to take the Great Serpent's hand. "Good to . . . to see you again, old friend. I come . . . under the Power of trade . . . binding myself to it. I have a . . . a message from Horned Serpent for . . ."—Gods, why couldn't I get my thoughts organized?— ". . . for the White Woman and the Great Sun."

He clasped my hand, staring down at me. "Is it really

you?" His gaze fixed on the copper mace, lying heavy as a log across my hips.

"Fit to whip you . . . at chunkey," I managed hoarsely. "Are you taking good care of my head? I wouldn't entrust it to just anyone, you know."

"Your head has suffered a little wear and tear, but I'm doing the best I can to care for it." He clasped his other hand atop mine. "I think, old friend, that in the years since you've been here, a great deal has changed." He hesitated. "It is true that you wear the sepaya?"

I took my hand back, fumbled under my shirt, and withdrew the leather pouch. In the early summer light I realized it was stained with old dried blood.

"I was being devoured by Horned Serpent when I broke it from his brow tine."

I could feel the sepaya, warm and vibrating in my hand.

"Power always did favor you, Black Shell," he said softly, frowning enough to crinkle his face paint. "Come, let us enter and approach the Great Sun." He glanced up at the White Woman, her gray hair pinned with a large conch-shell comb. "Perhaps we could dispense with the ritual given our visitor's health?"

"My son will understand," she agreed.

And summarily I was borne inside the most sacred space in the Natchez world. They carried me to the central stone, said to be the actual remains of the first Great Sun. A piece of the sun itself, he descended to earth along with his mother, the first White Woman. According to the Natchez creation story, it was he who brought fire from the sky. He who taught the Natchez the rules of proper behavior. And in the end, at his death, he turned himself to stone to preserve his body from corruption and decay.

I was placed before the stone, facing west as was customary. Knowing the rules, I kept my eyes straight ahead, not glancing at the Great Sun, who sat atop his elevated couch on the right—or north—side of the room. I raised my arms as high as I could, feeling woozy, and said the ritual *"Hau, hau, hau"* Natchez greeting.

"Bring him to me," the Great Sun ordered, and my litter, followed by Pearl Hand and Choctaw Hair, was placed before the elevated bed. About my age, the Great Sun was perched on the edge of his raised platform. Given the gravity of the occasion his intricately painted face betrayed no expression.

I glanced around at the weavings, sculptures, and ornately carved woodwork. Beautiful wooden chests, engraved and inlaid, were placed to each side.

"Who speaks for the Chicaza?" the Great Sun asked, his face painted in white with yellow rays, as if a morning sun shone over his forehead. A stunning headdress made of erect white heron and cardinal feathers topped his head. Splays of swan feather rode each shoulder.

"I am High Minko Choctaw Hair. I speak for the Chicaza Nation, Great Sun." My brother stepped forward. "This man is Black Shell, the Orphan. He, however, speaks only for Power, bearing its message to all peoples of our world. He is the chosen of Horned Serpent. This woman is Minko Pearl Hand, of the Chicora. I ask that you hear them. And as you do, know that I, ishto minko of the Chicaza Nation, am humbled to be in their presence."

At that he stepped back, the import of his words clear to all present: It wasn't just every day that a Chicaza high minko was humbled by anything.

"Tell me your story, Orphan," the Great Sun said, leaning forward.

I struggled for breath, drained even of the energy to speak. Then I felt the sepaya burning on my chest. Its heat began to flow through my breastbone and down into my clogged lungs. I ran trembling fingers over the sacred mace, and the copper seemed to impart strength to my depleted souls. The great stone in my chest shrank and grew oddly light. A sense of euphoria buoyed my souls up and I swear, a golden light filled the dim room.

I took the first full breath I'd had in days, the Power of the sepaya invigorating my flesh. "I was in the peninsula, Great Sun, in pursuit of strange stories, terrible stories, about the pale-skinned bearded men from the sea . . ."

SIXTY

I CAME OUT OF A GRAY AND CLINGING HAZE, AS IF
picking my way through tufts of cottonwood down. All I
remember from the dream was that I'd been sitting atop
Quigualtam's stunning mound, the great walls, the
buildings, and the palaces long gone. In place of the
monuments and structures the wondrous five-sided
earthwork had been covered with grass, and I had been
standing atop the high western palace mound, amazed
at the vista of rolling and broken hills that stretched off
to the west and the mighty river. It had been summer,
the surrounding forest like a lumpy carpet of somber
green that wavered in the damp heat.

"Go to the river . . . ," Horned Serpent had said, but I
couldn't remember much of the rest.

As I plucked the last of the haze apart, I blinked my
eyes awake to see my brother. He was seated beside me,
looking down. His hair was pinned up, shoulders and
chest bared, the copper ear spools dangling. He held Uncle's ax in his hands.

"Where are we?" I looked up at a pole roof covered with cane splits. I tried to sit up, only to feel faint, dizzy, and nauseous. The uncomfortable weight on my chest had grown heavier. Every breath I managed to suck in came as a struggle.

"The house belongs to one of the Sun chiefs, a younger brother to the Great Sun, I believe. Can I get you anything?"

"Water."

I drank greedily when he placed the narrow-necked jar to my lips.

"I'll have someone bring food. It's—"

"I'm not hungry."

"—been more than two days since you've eaten." He frowned. "What do you mean you're not hungry?"

"I ate this morning, just before we entered Quigualtam."

"Aren't you listening? That was *two* days ago, Black Shell. You had just finished that marvelous speech to the Great Sun. As soon as you finished, you collapsed like a cut string. You've slept ever since. Pearl Hand's worried sick."

When I blinked, my body seemed to rise into the air. Everything was spinning. I pawed for the sepaya with clumsy hands, grasped it, and felt the world stabilize around me. "Two days? Did I . . . I mean, did the Great Sun understand?"

"Understand? You were marvelous. You spoke with such passion and eloquence, we all thought you were mending. But now, looking at you . . ."

"I was only the mouthpiece of Power." I struggled to focus my eyes, most of my body numb and feverish. The discomfort deep in my chest was pulsing with each beat of my heart. "Just tell me the news."

"Two Packs arrived this afternoon. He and Pearl Hand are still sitting in council with the Great Serpent and his war chiefs. It was my turn to come and check on you.

When I'm not explaining how we beat the Kristianos, they have me off wasting time with the White Woman. She seems interested in an alliance, but the Great Sun hasn't . . . What?"

"She's the *key*, you fool," I whispered. "Do I have to teach you *everything*? Stop being a puffed-up Chicaza when it comes to women. This is Natchez. *She's the real authority*. The Great Sun will agree to anything his mother negotiates. And if you want to make a friend for life, don't leave without playing chunkey with the Great Serpent. He lives for it . . . but don't let him get carried away. Last time I was here, he bet me his head after I took all his copper and even the clothes on his back. I won, but I asked him if he'd do me a favor and keep his head on his shoulders until I might decide to claim it."

"You never cease to amaze me." He swallowed hard. "Two Packs says that you're right. De Soto has headed west across the Great Stony Ridge on the way to Coligua."

"He'll be back."

"And I've offered the Natchez every squadron the iksas can field when he comes this way again."

"The Natchez will fight?"

My brother clasped my oddly dry and shrunken hand. "I think it was the part about de Soto claiming to be descended from the sun. When you first related that, the Natchez took it like a slap to the face. But additionally, Two Packs brought a couple of Pacaha traders with him. The *Adelantado's* now claiming to *be* the sun god in person."

"Sacrilege." I swallowed hard, watching my brother's image waver and float in my vision. It was like seeing him through a silvery mirage. "It's getting hard to breathe again."

"I know."

"Don't let the Natchez get away," I whispered. "When de Soto comes back . . . you'll need them."

I blinked, trying to clear my vision. The great hot and heavy stone had grown to fill the space inside my ribs. "Tired now. Think I should rest."

I hesitated, trying to remember something important. I fished around in my souls, got it, and added, "Tell Pearl Hand . . . need to go to the river now."

"You need to go to the river?" he asked from someplace far away.

". . . The river . . ." I dreamed, floating on its roiling surface . . .

I awakened to water. I felt it dribbled on my tongue, smelled it rich and thick in my nose, and heard the musical lapping of waves. In the distance gulls were crying and squealing.

I swallowed, aware that the taste was laced with the great river's tang. Over the years I'd drunk a lot of Mississippi River water. Once tasted, you can't forget it. Pearl Hand had fulfilled my final wish.

"Black Shell?"

I smiled, thankful to hear my wife so clearly. When I blinked my eyes open, it took a moment to focus on her face as she leaned over me. The sky was so bright that it left her features in silhouette.

"You are the most beautiful woman," I told her, wondering why my voice sounded so faint. I could have been talking from ten paces away.

"I brought you to the river," she told me, taking my hands in hers. "I did as you asked."

I could hear the strain in her voice—a longing and hurt that I knew I was causing.

I'm sorry. Please don't grieve.

Something important. What?

Oh, yes. "Did the Natchez finalize peace with the Chicaza?"

"The alliance is finalized."

I tried to concentrate, wishing my thoughts weren't tumbling around like a bunch of raccoon kits atop a grub-filled log.

"... Hold my hand ... while I sleep?"

"Forever, my love ..."

When I came awake, the midnight sky overhead shimmered with a white frosting of stars. A faint glow could be seen on the western horizon. Across the dark water the tree line was barely silhouetted on the far shore. I'd just missed the setting of the moon.

I blinked, feeling oddly refreshed, delighted to have finally shrugged off the dragging weariness that had clung to my very bones since Alibamo. I could actually breathe again. I felt young.

I glanced to my right, aware that Pearl Hand slept wrapped in a blanket, her right arm extended, her long hand and slim fingers just touching mine.

On all sides I could see camps. Fires flickered in the night, and sleeping forms were scattered around. Just up from where my litter lay slept Two Packs and Choctaw Hair. To their right, the Great Serpent and some of his Sun chiefs.

I'd asked Pearl Hand to bring me here alone.

With a reverent finger I reached out and traced it ever so lightly down her smooth cheek. If only I could infuse her with the love I felt. Ensure that she knew how precious she was to me.

I eased back and sat up, thankful for the warm summer night and the faint breeze. The acrid scent of puccoon mixed with bear grease carried to my nose. Protection against mosquitoes.

At my movement, Bark and Blackie lifted their heads where they'd been curled with noses under their tails. They watched me anxiously, as if expecting some word or gesture.

"Feeling better, are we?" the familiar voice asked.

"Much." I turned to where Piasa stood ankle-deep in the lapping waves. Behind me and the collection of camps, the high Mississippi bluff rose like a blot against the eastern sky.

He inspected the camps with curious yellow eyes. "All this nobility. Natchez and Chicaza? Not even Old White was so honored."

"I only wanted Pearl Hand to be here."

His yellow gaze fixed on my wife, sleeping so peacefully. "The Monster is out there. And she still has a role to play." Piasa cocked his head. "Do you think this alliance between your prudish Chicaza men and these lusty Natchez women will seriously amount to anything?"

"I do. De Soto is claiming to be the sun god now."

"I wonder how that sits with his Kristianos?" He flicked at the water with his eagle-taloned foot.

"I need a little longer. With just a few more alliances—"

"As you told me, Trader, everything has its time. Horned Serpent would have come for you but allowed me the honor. He will bear you personally to the Sky World and your ancestors when you think it appropriate. But come, Old White would like to speak with you. And these dogs of yours! Does that Fetch *ever* tire of chasing sticks? And that Gnaw, if he chews up another cypress root, I swear, I'm going to make stew out of him."

"Gnaw's souls aren't lost?"

"Do you think Power would turn its back on a hero?"

I stood, looking down at Pearl Hand, a hole tearing in my souls. "I didn't know that leaving you would be so hard," I told her, wanting only to rush back and crush her in my arms.

Bark and Blackie stood, tails wagging slowly, ready for whatever I had in mind.

I gave them the sign to sit and stay and took a final

look at my beautiful Pearl Hand. Her delicate face seemed to glow, the midnight wealth of her thick black hair swirling behind her. Her arm was still extended, her slim fingers seeking mine.

Then I forced myself to walk nervously into the water. I hesitated and glanced back where the dogs whimpered and waited and Pearl Hand slept so peacefully. The Piasa cocked its head, giving her one last skeptical inspection.

Pearl Hand would come eventually.

And the dogs and I, we'd be waiting.

Culmination

They have carried her into the tchkofa and placed her on one of the beds. In the background, she can hear the prayers of the hopaye as he conjures yet another cure. Her souls are drifting between memories and dreams. And mixed in with them is understanding: For everything there is a culmination—the moment when forces, passions, and desires converge with finality.

She's experienced culminations before. Everything in her early life—the pain, fear, and abuse—brought her to the instant when she first saw Black Shell and the dogs on the trail outside of Irriparacoxi's town. Or the moment when she knew she had to risk her life to rescue Black Shell from de Soto's slavery. The realization that she had to return to Cofitachequi had taken longer but had been no less inevitable. The battle with the Kristianos had inexorably culminated in the sword impaling Black Shell's chest. That in turn had culminated in the hollow morning when she'd awakened beside his empty litter, the unforgiving waters of the Mississippi slapping arrogantly at the sandy shore.

Culmination. The moment when disparate threads weave themselves into the inevitable.

This night the final culmination awaits; it lurks overhead in the smoke-

filled rafters of the tchkofa. As she lies on her bed gasping for breath, she stares up at the high roof, waiting. It will be soon now. Please, let it be soon.

As if for comfort, she draws her blanket close about her age-wattled neck.

Like tendrils, images creep out of her souls. She sees herself walking through the burned wreckage of the town the Houmas people called Anilco. It was a year after Black Shell's death.

From her count, Nuño de Tovar and his cabayeros had killed more than one hundred and thirty men and boys. The Guachoya warriors who had accompanied the Kristianos on the dawn raid had murdered another two hundred or so women and children before they set fire to the town.

Black Shell would have wept.

He always wept and bled for the murdered innocents.

But what happened to me?

She'd believed herself a hard woman to begin with, but somewhere along the endless trails, she'd softened, learned to weep with him—a vulnerability once unthinkable.

Until that Kristiano sword had so keenly refocused her priorities.

Without Black Shell's patient empathy, she'd hardened into the old Pearl Hand. Tough enough that she could walk through Anilco counting the sprawled bodies. Her practiced eye could catalog the wounds despite the swarming flies and balls of tumbling maggots: Kristiano lance. Sword stroke. Arrow. War club. Each had its signature.

Butchery.

She'd stood at the edge of Anilco, staring in the direction of Guachoya town, where the Monster had curled in his lair.

Until the end, de Soto had only acted for himself. The surprise attack on the unsuspecting people at Anilco allowed him to pretend that he was still the Adelantado, el gubernator de La Florida.

I killed those three hundred and some people, *she tells herself.*

After all, she had composed the message the Great Sun's emissary delivered to de Soto.

The words still resonate between her souls: "If you are truly born of the Sun's loins, let us see you dry the Mississippi to dust. If you cannot, your claims are nothing more than the lies of a pathetic deceiver.

"You wish the Natchez to meet you in Guachoya? I am Quigualtam's Great Sun and require your obedience, tribute, and service. Whether you choose to voluntarily submit to my authority or be compelled by force is up to you. If you arrive in peace, I will welcome you. If you seek war I will destroy you before the very gates of Quigualtam."

Had some wandering trader told the Monster that Chicaza squadrons waited for him, shoulder to shoulder with Natchez warriors?

Or had his Kristiano god, seeing the end of everything, spoken to him from a dream?

The important thing was that he'd refused the challenge and taken the insult. The de Soto she'd seen at Uriutina, Napetuca, Mabila, and Chicaza would have bellowed in rage, murdered the poor messenger, and stormed straight into the ambush awaiting him across the river. Instead, as if to prove his impotence, he butchered the unsuspecting population of a peaceful town, thinking it would intimidate the Great Sun.

Anilco clarified everything. The Monster was broken. If she were ever to have peace, the final action had to be hers.

She'd carefully chosen a cloudy and moonless night. Her timing could not have been better. Having just perpetrated the massacre at Anilco, the patrolling guards were lax and careless. Any vengeful enemy should be cowering and terrified.

As if I could ever be terrified of anything again.

She smiles as she remembers the calm certainty of that long-ago night. Nothing had mattered beyond the moment. Even now, so many years later, she remembers her relaxed heartbeat as she slipped silently between the sentries and walked into Guachoya. She might have been a phantom of her own imagination, drifting among the cane-roofed dwellings. The chief's house, illuminated by a great fire, had drawn her irresistibly.

In Kristiano fashion, she'd draped a fabric shawl over her head to leave her face in shadow.

Walking up to the guard with a weary nonchalance, she'd said, "El Adelantado desea me. Él llamó para me." Her voice had been perfect, weary with acceptance.

The guards had glanced at her naked breasts, at the casual wrap around her full hips and how her muscular legs gleamed copper in the firelight.

The senior guard had glanced at his companion, stating, "Y el jefe está enfermo? Esta mujer tiene frescura, y ella podría matarlo." *The big man is sick; this saucy bitch could kill him.*

That had brought a snicker and a flip of the head indicating that she could proceed.

Passing through the doorway, she'd taken only a moment to discern that the Monster slept on the rear bed, several of his servants snoring on the mat floor before the fire. Three women were wrapped in blankets on the pole beds surrounding the room.

Pearl Hand stepped silently across the room, looking down on the shadowed face of the Monster. His sleep was troubled, his eyes flicking back and forth. Then she noticed how sunken his face was, the beak of a nose contrasting with deep hollows below his cheekbones. The stench of stale sweat, fouled bedding, and fever rose, causing her to turn away. She fought the reflexive desire to gag.

You are here to end it, she had told herself. *Do it!*

Her fingers wrapped around Moscoso's leather-handled knife; it slid soundlessly from the sheath.

At that moment he blinked his eyes open. They wavered, almost swimming in their sockets. Then he spoke, the voice barely more than a whisper. "¡Mira! ¡Hay una gran culebra . . . con alas como un arco iris! Y los ojos, como cristales illuminados. ¿Qué manera de criatura es?"

She hesitated, glancing over her shoulder, actually expecting to see Horned Serpent rising above her. De Soto's description of the Spirit Beast was perfect, the crystal eyes, the rainbow wings.

"No," he whimpered. "¡Dios mio, por favor, protege mi alma! ¡Por favor, no lo te tomas!"

What? God protect him? He thought Horned Serpent was taking his soul?

She ground her jaws and tightened her grip on the knife, Settling the point just at the V of his ribs, she angled the blade to slide under the breastbone and into his heart.

"Adelantado, I'm here for your victims. Through my knife they will *feel your heart being severed. Through my eyes, they will see your blood bubble from your chest. Dipping my hands in your blood, I will use it to wash away the grief and horror that stains their souls."*

Just a push now, and the terror would end.

"Pearl Hand? Don't." *Black Shell whispered in her ear with perfect clarity. Her knees almost buckled as his hand settled on her shoulder.* "We have other plans for the Adelantado."

"Black Shell? Is it you?" *She closed her eyes, feeling him so close, afraid to turn lest he not be there. She could feel his familiar warmth, that reassuring presence that had filled her life.* "You left me at the river," *she barely croaked, tears burning behind her clamped eyelids.*

"I'm only back for an instant, wife. I need you to sheath your knife. De Soto's terrified soul is loose in his body. Allow Horned Serpent to seize it. And then, after the Monster is buried, I need you to tell Moscoso to sink his body in the river. Do you understand?"

"I need to tell Moscoso . . . ?"

"This way the Monster will be ours. Not just for the instant that you plunge your blade into his heart . . . but for eternity."

She had swayed on her feet, swallowing hard, and slowly withdrew the blade.

He whispered, "I need you to live, wife. You have work to do. The dogs and I will be waiting when the time is right." *His breath massaged her ear and she felt his hand lift, his presence fading.*

Even then she hesitated, desperate to drive the blade into de Soto's failing heart. She took a deep breath, aware of the stench rising from the corrupt flesh, and looking up, swore that two crystalline eyes stared down at her from the smoke-shadowed ceiling.

She fought a momentary battle with fury, ground her teeth, and the knife slipped quietly into its sheath. She turned, walking silently across the floor. When she looked back, it might have been a trick of the firelight, but she thought she saw a black sinuous shadow curl and strike at the dying man.

At that moment, de Soto's body bucked in the bedding, stiffened, and the most horrible rattling sounded from his throat.

In an instant, the shadow flickered into nothingness, and the Adelantado sank back onto the bed, limp as a worn rag.

As she left she had nodded acknowledgment to the guards and walked deliberately into the night.

Black Shell came to me.

She smiles at the memory, at the familiarity of his touch and the words he'd whispered into her ear.

Nor had she failed to carry out his last request. All these many years later, she marveled at Black Shell's cunning. Only she, in all the world, could have gotten so close to Moscoso and delivered Black Shell's message.

And then, like drifting smoke, she had vanished into the night.

Years later the story came to her by way of a wandering Kristiano convert, one of the hundreds abandoned on the Mississippi's shores when the few battered Kristiano survivors fled. The reward for years of faithful service, conversion to the Kristiano god, and loyalty was to be left, kneeling in the mud, watching Moscoso's brigantines being borne south on the river's current. The men had labored like slaves, chopped wood, carried packs, and built fortifications. The women had cooked the Kristianos' meals, cleaned, packed their burdens, warmed their beds and serviced their lust, then bore their children. In payment they were abandoned to suffer murder and slavery at the hands of the embittered and vengeful Guachoya, Anilco, and Quigualtam.

"They buried him at first," the man had told her on a cold winter's night. "They told the Guachoya he had gone back to the sun. Then they grew afraid the indios would discover his grave and dig him up. Rather than see their Adelantado's body abused, they dug it up again and took it out into the river. There, they let it sink."

She remains as amazed now, tens of years later, as she was on that long-ago night. Black Shell had known. Even in the end, he'd understood how to inflict the ultimate defeat.

She reaches up, touching her shoulder where Black Shell had laid his hand the night de Soto lay dying. Was that really you, husband? Was Horned Serpent actually there? Did you come that last time to save my life?

For weeks now, she, too, has been praying to see Horned Serpent. Her old heart is failing. Like Black Shell in those last days, she can't seem to catch her breath.

Glancing around the tchkofa, through hazy vision she can see the hopaye. He continues to chant, using a blow tube to insert Power words into the latest concoction he is brewing to restore her health.

I am exhausted, tired of waiting.

She dreams of Black Shell, the long trail, and the dogs, all bearing packs brimming with trade.

Soon now, Horned Serpent. Please make it soon . . .

EPILOGUE

WITH HIS HAND BRACED ON THE MAST, LUIS DE MOS-coso de Alvarado stared back at the low green islands to the north. The wind off the gulf fluttered in his hair and flapped the collar of his deer-hide jerkin. Behind him, another six crude brigantines bobbed on the brown water.

The great river, the Rio Espíritu Santo, had expelled them, finally, into the flat and turbid waters of the gulf. Those thin spits of sand, topped by a waving fringe of salt grass, were all that remained of La Florida, with its blood, misery, and heartbreak.

Moscoso swallowed against the bile in his throat as the gulf breeze carried the pungent scent of the water and snapped the patchwork of *indio* blankets they'd sewn into a crude sail. The brigantine itself was little more than a rude wooden shell, a stepped mast, and a rudder.

I am living the end of the dream.

It was impossible. Absolutely impossible. Four years ago he had landed at the *Adelantado's* side, riding at the head of the greatest army his world had ever known.

They'd been outfitted with the finest weapons and armor money could buy. Supplies of every kind were unloaded by the ton. Talented cobblers, secretaries, carpenters, blacksmiths, tailors . . . every conceivable tradesman had accompanied them. The army's ranks had been swollen with some of the grandest nobles in Spain. Its corps of cabayeros and *soldados* was composed of hardened veterans with twenty years of experience at killing *indíos*. Many had been conquerors of Mexico, Panama, Nicaragua, and Peru.

How did it all go wrong? He tightened his grip on the mast as swells rocked the brigantine. How could the crude *indíos* of La Florida accomplish what the Aztecs, the Mayas, and the Incas could not? How could they have caused his surviving three hundred Christians to be spit out like vomit from the belly of what should have been Spain's greatest triumph?

He would have liked to blame Hernando de Soto, but who could have led them better? If there was a miracle, it was that even three hundred of them remained alive.

The impossible had occurred. He and his ragged Christians—dressed in skins and stolen Indian clothing— were witnesses of the stunning and unthinkable truth: A Spanish army had been defeated in the field and essentially destroyed.

But when had it become inevitable? Should he have known clear back at Apalachee? Seen the seeds of destruction in Cafakke's stubborn resistance? Had there been hints in the Coosa insurrection? When only the last desperate pleas of their captive chief had tempted the warriors to lay down their weapons? Or had it become inevitable at Mabila, where despite escaping Tuskaloosa's trap, and perpetrating the immolation and murder of five thousand *indíos*, the army had found itself destitute and wounded. Then, in Chicaza, they had been played, manipulated, and taken by complete surprise. From that terrible night on, their fate had been sealed. At Alibamo fort the inconceivable had happened: fifteen Christians killed outright, forty more wounded, and only three dead *indios* to show for it.

Any chance for conquest died in Chicaza. From that moment on, every move, ploy, and strategy had been defensive. Even the few offensive strikes, like the one against the accursed Tula, the Anilco massacre, and the mass maimings at Guachoya, had been to buy them time and deter an attack.

And now it has fallen on me to tell the world.

On his deathbed, Hernando de Soto had declared Luis de Moscoso governor and successor to the wealth of La Florida. Oh, and what a wealth it was.

Moscoso took one last glance at the pitiful barrier islands, the last of his domain. Behind that thin wall of salt grass, in forests and fields, remained the bodies and bones of close to a thousand Christians. With them had perished a king's ransom in armor, weapons, horses, and trappings. At Moscoso's order they'd abandoned more than five hundred *indio* converts to certain death or slavery on the shores of the great river. They'd cut the throats of the last of their loyal horses and watched those they couldn't bear to kill be shot full of arrows before the brigantines were even out of sight.

I am governor of a land of death and ruin.

And demons. He couldn't forget the demons. He remembered the warm day in May when de Soto had died. Moscoso had been called to the *Adelantado*'s side where he lay in the *cacique*'s house at Guachoya. His sunken flesh on fire with fever, de Soto had stared up at the ceiling, his eyes almost popping from his head. De Soto kept repeating the words, "A demon serpent has grasped my soul," as he sought to reach out with shaking hands. The way he clutched at the empty air, it was as if the *Adelantado* were struggling to get hold of his illusive soul.

"Your soul is fine," the priest kept assuring him. "You have been baptized in the holy faith."

But until de Soto's last breath, he weakly kept saying, "Can't you see it? With diamonds for eyes, wings of rainbows, it hovers over me. My soul is pinned in its fangs. Save me . . . Save me . . ."

Even as the priest performed extreme unction, de Soto had continued to rave. Moscoso himself couldn't help staring over his shoulder, half-afraid Satan's terrible serpent, so visible to de Soto in his delirium, might indeed be there.

A den of demons.

The night after de Soto's burial, the beguiling woman had come to Moscoso. She'd played his body as if it were a musical instrument and whispered in his ear that the Guachoya knew where de Soto's body was interred. Exhausted, he'd drifted off to sleep, and she'd simply vanished into the night.

He crossed himself at the memory, wondering to this day if she were a demon succubus that had somehow compromised his soul through her sorcery.

Nevertheless, he'd ordered de Soto's body exhumed. In the dead of night they'd rowed out and lowered Hernando's corpse into the river's dark waters. As Moscoso watched it sink, he'd have sworn he caught the briefest glimpse of a great panther down in the depths. By a trick of the waves and reflecting moonlight, the thing seemed to have a blue luminescence. Impossibly it had snatched the body, and then it was gone.

Demons. La Florida was a writhing nest of them.

He turned his face toward the south and open water, and swallowed against the knot of fear cramping his throat. It was a measure of their desperation—and the terror behind them—that they would entrust themselves to the open sea in their cobbled-together boats.

God willing, he would survive the coming voyage. In

return he would tell the story of La Florida and how its demonic and savage peoples had brutally murdered the cream of Spain's noblest, kindest, and most honorable men. The world would hear how the devil's ignorant minions, with their winged serpents and deformed animal idols, had rejected the benevolent mercy of the holy church. How they had chosen their squalid forest spirits and eternal darkness over salvation and eternal life bathed in God's glory.

"In the name of the holy saints," he prayed, "just deliver us alive. And let no true gentleman ever cast covetous eyes upon La Florida again."

When he looked back, the last of the sandy spits had vanished over the horizon.

BIBLIOGRAPHY

Adair, James
   2005 *The History of the American Indians.* University of
      Alabama Press: Tuscaloosa.
Anderson, David G.
   1994 *The Savannah River Chiefdoms: Political Change in the Late
      Prehistoric Southeast.* University of Alabama Press:
      Tuscaloosa.
Bense, Judith A.
   1994 *Archaeology of the Southeastern United States: Paleoindian
      to World War I.* Academic Press: New York.
Brown, Ian W.
   1985 *Natchez Indian Archaeology: Culture Change and Stability
      in the Lower Mississippi Valley.* Mississippi Department
      of Archives and History: Jackson, Mississippi.
Brown, James, and David H. Dye
   2007 "Severed Heads and Sacred Scalplocks: Missis-
      sippian Iconographic Trophies," in *The Taking and
      Displaying of Human Body Parts as Trophies by Amerindians.*
      Edited by Richard J. Chacon and David H. Dye.
      Springer Press: New York.
Chacon, Richard J., and David H. Dye
   2007 *The Taking and Displaying of Human Body Parts as Tro-
      phies by Amerindians.* Springer Press: New York.

Clayton, Lawrence A., Vernon James Knight, and Edward C. Moore, eds.

    1993 *The De Soto Chronicles,* vols. 1 and 2. University of Alabama Press: Tuscaloosa.

Duncan, David Ewing

    1995 *Hernando de Soto: A Savage Quest in the Americas.* Crown Publishers: New York.

Dye, David H.

    1995 "Feasting with the Enemy: Mississippian Warfare and Prestige Goods Circulation," in *Native American Interactions: Multiscalar Analyses and Interpretations in the Eastern Woodlands.* Edited by Michael S. Nassaney and Kenneth Sassaman. University of Tennessee Press: Knoxville.

Garcilaso de la Vega

    1998 *The Florida of the Inca.* Translated by John and Jeanette Varner. University of Texas Press: Austin.

Grantham, Bill

    2002 *Creation Myths and Legends of the Creek Indians.* University Press of Florida: Gainesville.

Hudson, Charles

    2003 *Conversations with a High Priest of Coosa.* University of North Carolina Press: Chapel Hill.

    1997 *Knights of Spain, Warriors of the Sun: Hernando de Soto and the South's Ancient Chiefdoms.* University of Georgia Press: Athens, Georgia, and London.

    1979 *Black Drink: A Native American Tea.* University of Georgia Press: Athens, Georgia.

    1976 *The Southeastern Indians.* University of Tennessee Press: Knoxville, Tennessee.

Humes, Jessie, and Vinnie May Humes

    1973 *A Chickasaw Dictionary.* The Chickasaw Nation: Drant, Oklahoma.

BIBLIOGRAPHY

Jacobi, Keith P.
  2007 "Disabling the Dead: Human Trophy Taking in the Prehistoric Southeast," in *The Taking and Displaying of Human Body Parts as Trophies by Amerindians.* Edited by Richard J. Chacon and David H. Dye. Springer Press: New York.

Johnson, Jay K.
  2000 "The Chickasaws," in *Indians of the Greater Southeast.* The Society for Historical Archaeology; University Press of Florida: Gainesville.

Johnson, Jay K., and Geoffrey R. Lehmann
  1996 "Sociopolitical Devolution in Northeastern Mississippi and the Timing of the de Soto Entrada," in *Bioarchaeology of Native American Adaptation in the Spanish Borderlands.* Edited by B. J. Baker and L. Kealhofer, pp. 38–55. University of Florida Press: Gainesville.

Knight, Vernon James, ed.
  2009 *The Search for Mabila.* University of Alabama Press: Tuscaloosa.

Lankford, George E.
  2008 *Looking for Lost Lore: Studies in Folklore, Ethnology, and Iconography.* University of Alabama Press: Tuscaloosa.

Larson, Clark Spencer, Christopher B. Ruff, Margaret J. Schoeninger, and Dale L. Hutchinson
  1992 "Population Decline and Extinction in La Florida," in *Disease and Demography in the Americas.* Edited by John W. Verano and Douglas H. Ubelaker. Smithsonian Institution Press: Washington, DC.

Larson, Lewis H.
  1980 *Aboriginal Subsistence Technology of the Southeastern Coastal Plain During the Late Prehistoric Period.* University Presses of Florida: Gainesville.

Laudonnier, Rene

    2001 *Three Voyages.* Translated by Charles E. Bennett. University of Alabama Press: Tuscaloosa.

Lewis, David, and Ann T. Jordan

    2002 *Creek Indian Medicine Ways: The Enduring Power of Muskoke Religion.* University of New Mexico Press: Albuquerque.

Lewis, R. Barry, and Charles Stout

    1998 *Mississippian Towns and Sacred Spaces: Searching for an Architectural Grammar.* University of Alabama Press: Tuscaloosa.

Lorenz, Karl G.

    2000 "The Natchez of Southwest Mississippi," in *Indians of the Greater Southeast.* The Society for Historical Archaeology; University Press of Florida: Gainesville.

Martin, Jack B., and Margaret Mauldin

    2000 *A Dictionary of Creek Muskogee.* University of Nebraska Press: Lincoln.

McEwan, Bonnie G.

    2000 *Indians of the Greater Southeast.* The Society for Historical Archaeology; University Press of Florida: Gainesville.

Mckivergan, David A.

    1995 "Balanced Reciprocity and Peer Polity Interaction in the Late Prehistoric Southeastern United States," in *Native American Interactions: Multiscalar Analysis and Interpretations in the Eastern Woodlands.* Edited by Michael S. Nassaney and Kenneth Sassaman. University of Tennessee Press: Knoxville.

Milanch, Jerald T., and Charles Hudson

    1993 *Hernando de Soto and the Indians of Florida.* University Press of Florida: Gainesville.

Morgan, William N.

    1999 *Precolumbian Architecture in Eastern North America.* University Press of Florida: Gainesville.

Munro, Pamela, and Catherine Willmond

    1994 *Chickasaw: An Analytical Dictionary.* University of Oklahoma Press: Norman.

Nairne, Thomas

    1988 *Nairne's Muskhogean Journals: The 1708 Expedition to the Mississippi River.* Edited by A. Moore. University Press of Mississippi: Jackson.

Neitzel, Robert S.

    1997 *Archaeology of the Fatherland Site: Grand Village of the Natchez.* Reprint of Anthropological Papers of the American Museum of Natural History, vol 51, part 1. Archaeological Report No. 28, Mississippi Department of Archives and History: Jackson.

    1983 *The Grand Village of the Natchez Revisited.* Archaeological Report No. 12, Mississippi Department of Archives and History: Jackson.

Peregrine, Peter

    1995 "Networks of Power: the Mississippian World System," in *Native American Interactions: Multiscalar Analysis and Interpretations in the Eastern Woodlands.* Edited by Michael Nassaney and Kenneth Sassaman. University of Tennessee Press: Knoxville.

Reilly, F. Kent, and James F. Garber, eds.

    2007 *Ancient Objects and Sacred Realms: Interpretations of Mississippian Iconography.* University of Texas Press: Austin.

Smith, Marvin T., and David J. Hally

    1992 "Chiefly Behavior: Evidence from Sixteenth Century Spanish Accounts," in *Lords of the Southeast: Social Inequality and the Native Elites of Southeastern North America.* Archaeological Papers of the American Anthropological Association, no. 3.

Swanton, John R.

2000 *Creek Religion and Medicine.* University of Nebraska Press: Lincoln.

1998 *Indian Tribes of the Lower Mississippi Valley and the Adjacent Coast of the Gulf of Mexico.* Dover Publications: Mineola, New York.

1928a "Aboriginal Culture of the Southeast," in *42nd Annual Report of the Bureau of American Ethnology,* pp. 673–726. United States Government Printing Office: Washington, DC.

1928b "Social and Religious Beliefs and Usages of the Chickasaw Indians," *44th Annual Report of the Bureau of American Ethnology,* pp. 169–274. United States Government Printing Office: Washington, DC.

Townsend, Richard F., ed.

2004 *Hero, Hawk, and Open Hand: American Indian Art of the Midwest and South.* Art Institute of Chicago in association with Yale University Press: New Haven and London.

Ubelaker, Douglas H.

1992 "North American Indian Population Size," in *Disease and Demography in the Americas.* Edited by John W. Verano and Douglas H. Ubelaker. Smithsonian Institution Press: Washington, DC.